SONS OF
DARKNESS

PRAISE FOR SONS OF DARKNESS

'Through humour, torture, gore, lust, magic, dangerous power games and bloodcurdling battles, *Sons of Darkness* takes us on an unforgettable wild journey set in re-imagined Vedic India'
— SAN FRANCISCO BOOK REVIEW

'A stunning debut. Gourav Mohanty is the new voice of dark fantasy'
— MICHAEL R. FLETCHER

'The sprawling scope of the epics with all the brutal and bleak nature of your favourite grimdarks... you're going to want to read this dark South Asian fantasy, infused to the brim with the *Mahabharata* and Malazan's DNA'
— R.R. VIRDI

'With bold and gut-wrenching twists, Gourav Mohanty fuses passion for gritty modern fantasy with the greatest epic ever told, delivering a fresh and page-turning spin on the *Mahabharata*. This is a series to watch!'
— PHILIP CHASE

'*Sons of Darkness* is outstanding. Brutal, lyrical and imaginative, it is an inspired mix of mythology and grimdark fantasy that I just couldn't put down'
— SHAUNA LAWLESS

'Dark, lush, and captivating, *Sons of Darkness* is an inventive reimagining of the age-old *Mahabharata*'
— APARNA VERMA

'*Sons of Darkness* contains all the trappings of a high adventure. The saga is perfect for fans of *Game of Thrones*'
— MIDWEST BOOK REVIEW

'A worldbuilding aficionado's dream come true...
don't miss this debut'
— FANTASY BOOK CRITIC

'*Mahabharata* imbued with *A Song of Ice and Fire*, *The First Law* and Malazan Book of the Fallen... nothing can stop this novel from encompassing the entire world now'
— NOVEL NOTIONS

'*Sons of Darkness* smashes open the fountain of originality, spilling insidious plot, incredible characters, and grim violence. I loved this book'
— FANFI ADDICT

'Remarkable characterization and vivid worldbuilding bolster this riveting epic fantasy'
— KIRKUS REVIEWS

'Vast and sweeping in scale, even while it is attentive to the minutia of its characters' motivations and inner lives, *Sons of Darkness* is a fresh new grimdark fantasy built on old bones and perfect for those who love their stories epic and their worlds unique!'
— REEDSY

'A wild, intriguing work of fantasy that will keep you glued from the beginning till the end'
— ONLINE BOOK CLUB

'The author's vision, and the world he has created, is breathtaking and fascinating. The Indian Fantasy Fiction genre finally comes of age with this book'
— ANAND NEELAKANTAN

Sons of Darkness

GOURAV MOHANTY

An Ad Astra Book

First published in India in 2022 by Leadstart,
a division of One Point Six Technologies Pvt Ltd
First published in the United Kingdom in 2023 by Head of Zeus,
part of Bloomsbury Publishing Plc

9 7 5 3 1 2 4 6 8

A catalogue record for this book is available from the British Library.

Cover design: Micaela Alcaino
Frontispiece: Jennifer Bruce
Map: © Gourav Mohanty

ISBN (HB): 9781035900237
ISBN (XTPB): 9781035900244
ISBN (Special Edition): 9781035900947
ISBN (E): 9781035900206

Printed and bound by CPI Group (UK) Ltd,
Croydon, CR0 4YY

Head of Zeus
First Floor East
5–8 Hardwick Street
London EC1R 4RG
www.headofzeus.com

To Mahwash
for being my wings, as well as the wind beneath them.

o

To Jejema
for introducing me to our ancient worlds.

o

To Astha
for being Satyabhama.

ABOUT THE AUTHOR

GOURAV MOHANTY was born, and currently lives, in Bhubaneswar, the City of Temples. A connoisseur of mythologies and momos, he's been certified as a nerd ever since he graduated as a gold medallist from law school. He keeps things interesting by daylighting as a lawyer, moonlighting as a stand-up comic and gaslighting as a storyteller. *Sons of Darkness* is his first novel.

gouravmohanty.com
Twitter: @MohantyGourav7
Instagram: @thekingbeyondthewall

CONTENTS

AUTHOR'S NOTE

When I took the wonderful characters of the epic *Mahabharata* and tossed them into a parallel dimension that was pervasively bleak and nihilistic, it was with the intention of making you, my reader, sit up and gasp on your couch.

The bare bones of *Sons of Darkness* saw the light after I read *A Game of Thrones*. My vision was clear. Epic grimdark fantasy was an unexplored bastion of Indian literature, and I wanted *Sons of Darkness* to be the first to conquer it. So, I started building a new world on the legacy of scores of hand-drawn maps, character sketches, raw notes, castle plans, detailed fight scenes, caste tattoos, heraldic designs... you name it. And five gruelling years later, here we are, at the threshold of an exciting adventure.

But before you fasten your seat belts, do give my bipolar invitation below a read. I was asked to draft this Author's Note because the world of *Sons of Darkness* is *completely* different from what you may know about the *Mahabharata* through books and TV shows. You will encounter strange new characters that were not part of the original epic poem. Old, loved characters take unfamiliar journeys and meet untimely ends. Am I thereby abusing my literary privilege? Who can tell? None of us were there when it happened. Then again, if you prefer the unsullied version, just read Vyasa's beautiful, original piece.

If you are, however, prepared to dive head first into a chasm of chivalry and cynicism, all I ask is that you leave your helms and shields behind. Forget what you think you know about Krishna. Forget Karna's backstory. Forget Vyasa's Bharatvarsh. Instead, enter the dark world of Aryavrat. For *Sons of Darkness* has little to do with the mytho-trope of simply *re-writing* Mahabharatan reality from a different character's perspective and more to do with *re-imagining* a brave new world that is as disillusioned and ultraviolent as our own reality.

When you enter the world of *Sons of Darkness*, you enter a vast immersive universe, a Narnia of India, if you will. It is every bit as messy and intricate as our own world. There are no good or bad characters in this book, just real people faced with impossible choices. More importantly, *Sons of Darkness* does not whittle down the sorcery offered by our lore under the guise of science or realism. Instead, it creates an enchanting magic system, premised on our *Vedas* in a way I promise you have never seen before. But the uniqueness of *Sons of Darkness*, in my humble opinion, is that it does not project ancient India yet again as a village-world stuck in the Age of the Wheel, obsessed with wooden arrows and mud dwellings. Not at all.

There are swords, morning stars, battleaxes and war hammers. There are castles, siege engines, and ports. It is a complex yet unknowable universe, with threads of its own intricate mythology. Under every sea hides the ruins of Atlantis. Behind every mountain is an Eden of history. You will not just be a reader, but an archaeologist excavating the secrets of this world, along with its characters.

And with that I invite you to leave behind the Light, and enter a world of war and riots, cruel intentions and misguided motives, of delicious Darkness, with me.

Gourav Mohanty
April 2023

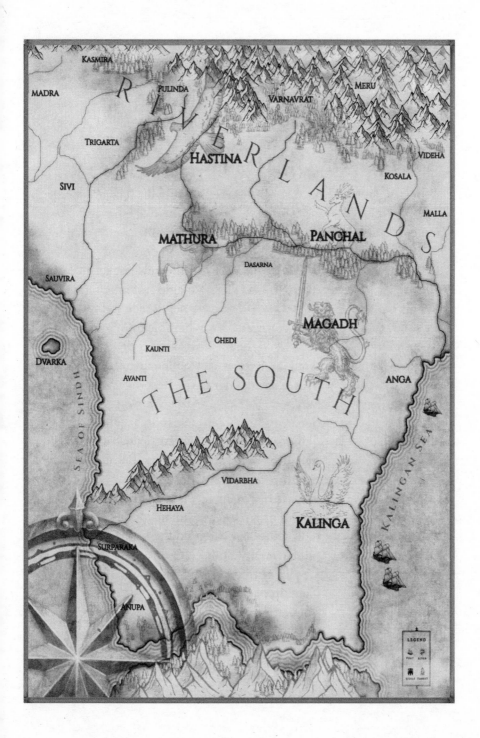

DRAMATIS PERSONAE

REPUBLIC OF MATHURA

Ugrasen	Arch-Senator
Balram	War Commander
Kritavarman	Senator
Akrur	Senator
Satyaki	Senator
Krishna	Senator
Satwadhan	Senator
Rukmini	1st wife of Krishna
Jambavan	Friend of Krishna; scientist
Jambavati	Jambavan's daughter; 2nd wife of Krishna
Kalavati	Jambavati's maid
Satyabhama	Leader of Silver Wolves; 3rd wife of Krishna
Rain	Captain of Silver Wolves
Storm	Soldier in Silver Wolves

UNION OF HASTINA

Bheeshma	Lord Commander of Union
Dhritarashtra	King of Hastinapur
Gandhari	Queen of Hastinapur

Duryodhan	Son of Dhritarashtra; Heir Apparent
Karna	Highmaster of Anga
Sudama	Nephew of Karna
Kunti	Former Queen of Hastinapur
Pandu	Former King of Hastinapur
Shakuni	Master of Spies
Yudhistir	Son of Pandu; Highmaster of Varnavrat

EMPIRE OF MAGADH

Jarasandh	Emperor of Magadh
Saham Dev	Prince of Magadh
Shishupal	Commander of Crimson Cloaks
Dantavakra	Brother of Shishupal
Eklavvya	War-Chief of the Valkas

KINGDOM OF PANCHAL

Drupad   King of Panchal
Dhrishtadyumna   Son of Drupad
Satrajit   Son of Drupad
Draupadi   Daughter of Drupad

KINGDOM OF KALINGA

Bhanumati   Princess of Kalinga
Chitragandh   King of Kalinga

CITADEL OF MERU

Varayu   Student
Varcin   Student
Ukopa   Student
Upavi   Student
Nala   Student

OTHERS

Masha   Matron in House of Oracles
Kalyavan   Archon of Yavanas
Bhagadatt   King of Pragjyotisha
Parshuram   Immortal Warrior Priest

SIGILS AND WORDS

REPUBLIC OF MATHURA
Deeds, Not Birth

EMPIRE OF MAGADH
We Do Not Bow

UNION OF HASTINA
Law Above All

KINGDOM OF PANCHAL
Death Before Dishonour

KINGDOM OF KALINGA
Voyage and Valour

YAVANAS
Arete and Kleos

PROLOGUE

I

The stench of split flesh from the carcasses of the Children of Light wafted out to mock his hunger. The wolves had come, and then left without feeding. Ravens circled overhead, yet none descended. These details remained with the rider as he drew rein at the very spot where his foes had made their last stand. With his dagger he flicked the strands of his long hair, clumped with dried blood, away from his eyes. As he took in the sights of the carnage that had taken place mere hours ago, he absent-mindedly rubbed a luminescent powder onto his blade.

For a Hero of Light, he reckoned he cast a rather grim shadow. *Hero.* The word slithered nastily in his mind. An honour bestowed upon you when you had killed all those who would have called you a mass murderer.

'Shall we, Muchuk?' Asha walked her horse amidst the sprawled bodies to where he sat astride his stallion. 'Time to deliver the good news.'

Ah yes. Trisiras is dead. He nudged his mount onto the slope of the hill, urging it into a collected canter as his sister followed suit. They made their way up the tortuous track towards the mountain fortress of Svarg – a great hulking fastness that loomed like a crystal-white orb against the dark, poisoned heavens. A faint pillar of light that rose from somewhere within the fortress served as their lodestar. *The beacon of tyranny,* Muchuk mused.

'You seem awfully quiet for someone who has won a war.' Two sharp eyes stared out from Asha's beaky, grimy face packed in a half-helm. Under her armour, her hunched muscular shoulders looked all the more ungainly without a bosom to balance her form. It was a miracle she did not slide off her horse.

Muchuk shrugged, turning to stare up at the sky. By now, the third moon was a jade monstrosity. Green light leaked out from it to the west, staining the heavens with stolen emerald hues. *Won a war...* He sighed, as if it were a great revelation. As if he had not spent years of his life severing, slashing and slitting the *Danavas*, the Children of Darkness.

But Asha was right. He should have felt victorious, elated even. And yet, despite his valiant efforts, he felt like a man who had finally opened the box of glory to find that it did not contain what was etched on the lid.

They rode past their Men who were busy cutting the heads off dead *Daevas*, the Children of Light – the few righteous ones who had aligned with the Danavas. Their luminescent white heads made for macabre lamps, if you were into that sort of a thing. It would have been beautiful had it not been for the stench. Perhaps this was why he preferred slaying the Children of Darkness. They immaterialized into the air in a puff of odourless smoke when they fell. No stink. No bodies to toss. Clean, gutter-friendly kills.

'Muchuk Und?' Asha persisted.

'Yes, yes, *victory!*' he answered dryly, half wishing he could race his stallion ahead and leave her promptings far behind. 'Tired of this place yet?' he asked in a pitiable attempt to change the topic of conversation.

Fortunately, Asha took the bait. 'I don't know... this world has been growing on me. Battles and wine aplenty. So many wonders to behold and cherish— Will you *stop* rubbing that powder on the dagger, you miser?! Now that we know how to make it, we can create it any time and drown in it.' A pleasant thought, all things considered. Muchuk Und sheathed the dagger. 'Now where was I?

Yes. Hm... I like this place. Not to forget,' her face split into a wide grin, 'the Daevas are especially ravenous in bed.'

'Just what a brother wants to hear,' Muchuk Und sighed.

She lifted her half-helm, treating the world to her scarred face and long hair. The beaky nose did no favours for her flat face. She might have got their mother's lush tresses in a cold bargain, but she looked every bit their father's daughter. Men disappeared from her path. Soldiers obeyed her commands without question. Bards shuddered to sing in her presence. Envy filled Muchuk's heart. Was there any warrior as fortunate as a truly ugly one? And Asha was as ugly as rain on a wedding day.

'On the other hand,' she continued as if Muchuk hadn't spoken, 'I do wish we could've taught those Nagas a cold lesson in manners. To usher in the Age of Man. And I'm sure you yearn for your wretched family too.'

Family. How long had it been since he saw their ungrateful faces? Now that he began to count the years, Muchuk Und could not believe he had been away from his world for a decade. *Guess time passes swiftly when most of it is spent on battlefields.*

'Hopefully less than they crave for me,' he murmured, though he had his doubts. His daughter must be what, eleven summers by now? Would she even remember she had a father? He pushed away the dark thoughts before he tumbled down into the pit of melancholy again. 'But I doubt your imperial interests will be as entertaining as we had imagined them to be, Asha. With the weapons we will carry back from here, it will be... too easy.'

'Exactly!' Her face twisted with distaste. 'Where is the joy in that? Home will just be... disappointing.'

Muchuk sighed loudly. 'But what is left to be done here?'

Asha turned to him again, her eyes quizzical as she studied him. 'Ah, I see now. You suffer the staleness a man feels when he has achieved everything, Brother. The Daevic indifference has infected you. It will pass. You are too cocky to be crabby for long.'

I hope so. Because, like a homing pigeon pining for its humble cage, Muchuk Und was homesick.

II

They swung down from their horses. Seeing Asha's clumsy dismount, Muchuk gave another deep sigh. For one who claimed to love riding, she was quite an embarrassment to the family name.

'Ready?' he asked caustically.

'Aye, aye. Stop fretting!' she said as she finally managed to disentangle herself.

Jerking their sword belts straight, they strode towards the palace. The red doors yawned open, as welcoming as a burning pyre. Inside, grim-faced Daeva guards spoiled the mood under every archway they passed under.

'I swear this palace is just *ghastly*.' Asha sniggered as they finally reached the inner sanctum.

It felt like they had crossed over into a different realm. Playful fountains threw pink spray at them. Closely scythed grass spread below their feet. Hedges, carved into wondrous monsters, stood like a guarding legion on either side of the grassy pathway that led to the Dome.

The Daevas were a strange race, Muchuk reflected. In his time here, he had realized that the Daevas had ceased to procreate; had, in fact, stopped living. Immortality was their curse. They merely continued to... exist. Passion had been extinguished from their beings, along with passion, bloodlust, gluttony and envy – all the things that made life *delicious*. If they were indeed Gods, then the Gods were really bored. And yet, they were obsessed with something as dull as gardening. Just one of the many ironies of his employers he had unravelled over time.

The other irony he had uncovered was about why the Daevas once swooped down to his world to seduce earthlings when the Daevas themselves were such exquisite creatures. Turned out, Mortals excited and enflamed them, gave them reason to *feel* again. A fact he had unfortunately come to learn from his sister's accounts of Daevic endurance.

There was also the whole thing about sacrificial worship, which the Mortals had once practised to revere the Daevas when they had not known any better. Muchuk didn't quite understand how, but these ornate rituals *fed* the Daevas. Not with food but with… vitality, a currency in which the Daevas were most impoverished.

Not that it mattered any longer for this was ancient history. All of it had happened a long time ago, much before Muchuk's time, before the Daevas had been banished from his world after being defeated in the War of Spring.

Come to think of it, no one really won that war, Muchuk reflected. The Daevas, though beaten, survived, and were gone. As for the Mortals, a hundred races became extinct overnight, and along with them the one thing that had helped them win that war. *Elementals*. To think he was going to be the one to bring it back to his world…

'Asha…'

'Yes?'

'This is my last season in this Daevic nonsense,' Muchuk declared. 'Their war is won. They can manage the measly battles that remain on their own. And they may be virile in bed, but I need the smell of mud again.'

Asha stared evenly back. 'I knew I shouldn't have brought up your wretched family.'

'It's not just about them, Asha. You were right. The staleness here has affected me. Let's go back now, while we're still young. Don't you wish to go back to awe the other races into bending the knee; to rule over all with an iron fist, and not be answerable to anyone, *anyone*, regardless of how easy defeating them now sounds?'

Asha, surprised into silence, stared at him. Muchuk stared back from beneath the rim of his helm, cold sweat prickling awake beneath his armour.

'Well, when you put it like that…' She scratched a scar on her face. 'Alright, Brother, I'm with you. The Danavas are dead. Thorin can continue holding the crown of this blasted world, and we can melt away to rule ours.'

'That's it?' Muchuk was surprised at the ease with which he had convinced her. He had been preparing a whole speech. 'You do not desire to stay?'

'I do, but someone needs to teach you how to squat on a throne. And I can see you have made up your mind.' She patted him on the back, then stopped short, looking around. '*Another* garden, seriously?'

They had entered a second garden, this one being special in its own way. The beacon, a prehistoric column of light said to come from a time before the Daevas, stood tall in the centre, the light stretching up like a pillar into the sky. The immensity of Thorin Drazeus' sanctum towered around the column on three sides, in the embrace of a scorpion. Statues dotted the cobbled path to the Sanctum. These were stony tributes to Daeva narcissism – a Daeva gifting knowledge to a Man; a Daeva giving alms to a Naga; a Daeva shielding a Danava from danger. At the end of the pathway stood a half-finished Daeva statue, chiselled only at the legs.

'I bet that'll be a Daeva massaging a unicorn's arse.'

'If it isn't the most cherished maggots of Aea!' Savitre Lios, the youngest of Thorin Drazeus' brothers, rushed towards Asha. Like the other Daevas, he was tall, with silvery skin and haunting golden eyes. Patterns were tattooed on his lean arms, which blazed with yellow light. Savitre Lios was probably the last Daeva to harbour any interest in anything materialistic. Unfortunately, the 'materialistic' here happened to be his sister.

Asha grinned as she gripped Savitre Lios' waist and leaped up, shinnying up his tall frame to kiss him full on the lips. After what felt like a lifetime, Muchuk coughed. Savitre ceased groping Muchuk's sister and turned to look at him, while Asha continued sucking on Muchuk's neck.

'Why her?' Muchuk asked with distaste. He knew the picture of this beautiful monster pecking his monstrous sister was going to visit him routinely as a nightmare.

'I am addicted to her dirty mind and pure heart.'

'Right at least on one count,' Muchuk snorted. 'Thorin here yet?'

'Yes. Faraladar is here as well. The Twins, too.'

Faraladar was the one who had signed Muchuk Und and Asha Und to this adventure in a deal forged in a *Vachan*. It bound them to the Daevas, to fight the rebellious Danavas. In return, Muchuk was taught the Way of the Elementals, or as Faraladar called it the art of the *N'yen Valren.*

It was a good deal.

For the Daevas had lost their will, their viciousness, their cruelty – all important ingredients to winning any war. They needed Muchuk, a warlord of repute back in his own world, to do their dirty work for them. And Muchuk needed their arcane knowledge to awaken the Elementals back home, to lay the foundation of his own earthly empire.

It was a good thing a ritually ordained Vachan worked the same way for both the Mortals and the Daevas. Faraladar had brayed on about how Men and Daevas had essentially the same map within their bodies: the same *nadis* through which blood, dirt and soul flowed in and out of their hearts. A Vachan had the effect of binding these nadis in chains that made the soul, or what the Daevas called *atman,* stronger. Made stronger in the manner a man wrapped in iron chains becomes when he is forced to work bearing such weight. But Vachans were a nasty business. And they were unbreakable. If one was inclined to break his Vachan, the chains would contract around the atman, and the oathbreaker would be obliterated.

Asha looked up. 'Shall we go in, Muchuk? Best not to keep the King of Daevas waiting.'

III

They passed into the Main Hall of the Sanctum, where enormous suits of armour belonging to Drazeuses long dead stared down at them. Around these dented armour-suits were weapons the Drazeuses had presumably used, rather thoroughly by the look of them. One did not need to be a sleuth to understand the Drazeuses had never shirked from a fight. It was for this reason that Muchuk thought it rather odd when he found Thorin Drazeus engaged in something as unwarlike as painting.

'My ancestors,' Thorin said, standing crabbed over a canvas and wielding a paintbrush instead of a sword. He had the mannerisms of a kindly grandfather, but Muchuk knew better. Failed artists made the worst tyrants. 'You know, not one Drazeus in the last two millennia has died in his bed. Source of pride, that.'

Of course, quite a few of them had died in other people's beds, if Savitre was to be believed, but Muchuk felt it prudent not to mention this. 'Indeed, Your Worship.'

Thorin turned from the portrait he had been working on and wiped his red-stained hands on his robe. Turned out he had drawn a lurid portrait of himself, standing atop a battlement with a sword held aloft, an army of grateful Men behind him. Muchuk gaped at it for a moment, hardly knowing whether to cry or laugh.

'Mankind, such a dashing species, I've always thought,' Thorin remarked with a fading smile. 'I mean, the Vanaras are pompous and the Nagas venomous, but one always feels there is something grotesquely gracious about the human will to survive.'

Muchuk exchanged a smirk with Asha and proceeded to bow humbly. Two blonde-haired, slender female guards took their places on either side of Thorin as he approached a basin to wash his hands with ether. *The Twins.* The long purple cloaks that trailed behind them had cowls that covered their heads, but even with half their faces hidden, they possessed an angelic beauty that was breathtaking. But then the world was full of demons with pretty faces and angels with scars. While Muchuk Und was busy gawking at the Twins, another Daeva paced over to where Muchuk, Asha and Savitre Lios stood.

'Faraladar Saan!' Asha shook his arm. 'Now this is what I call a royal welcome.'

'Lady Asha,' Faraladar smiled and bowed politely. 'Lord Muchuk Und. *May your Night be Bright.*'

'And yours,' Asha returned the traditional Daevish greeting. 'You do see the irony of calling me a *Lady*, when my breeches are coloured with the blood of your fallen kin?'

Faraladar shrugged. 'Those Daevas chose to side with the enemy. Their kinship had been severed,' he declared flatly.

'But of course. How practical of you.'

Thorin cleared his throat near the basin. 'What is the fate of Trisiras, my son?' Thorin asked, hands now white and clean.

'Well...' Muchuk Und blew out his cheeks. 'His body has been eaten by one of my Pisachas. But I ensured they saved the head for you, Your Worship.'

There was a long pause. Thorin stared at them. They stared back, like a pair of accused waiting for the judge to pass sentence. Thorin finally nodded. 'How did he die?'

'He drowned.'

'How did he drown?' asked Dewi Raith, one of the Twins.

'Well, Raith, he could not breathe when Muchuk held his face underwater in the river,' Asha stated flatly.

Muchuk Und shook his head. Tact wasn't Asha's strong suit.

Ushas, the other Twin, her dagger-whip coiled around her waist like a belt, and a spear by her side, was the kinder twin but by no means less deadly. 'But was it really necessary to exterminate Trisiras' entire army?' she asked, softly. 'Did they not surrender?'

Muchuk scowled. He had won their war for them. And while he did not hold a grudge for not being given a victory parade, he surely was not going to subject himself to an interrogation. 'In my defence, Ushas, I was left unsupervised.'

'Silence!' Dewi Raith grated. 'You had orders to let Trisiras live. He was one of us.'

Asha interjected before Muchuk could spit out another retort. Addressing the King of Light directly, she said, 'Your Worship, it is a childhood problem of his. He cannot take orders. He can barely take suggestions.'

Muchuk chuckled.

'That will be enough.' Thorin's command stopped Raith from responding but a ripple of twitches went through her cheek. 'Peace is a brittle thing, and Muchuk Und has assisted us with stretching it for a few more centuries. No one has ever achieved peace without getting their hands dirty.'

A sermon on peace from Thorin sounded like a sermon on chastity from a whoremonger but Muchuk Und nodded in solemn agreement.

Thorin turned to Faraladar. 'Let refreshments flow for our fine warriors. I am sure they would like to clean up before the next battle.'

'About that, Your Worship, I...' Muchuk glanced at Asha, who nodded, '... *we* wish to return home. Only small pockets of resistance survive, which the Men I leave behind can deal with.'

'The Pisachas, you mean,' Raith scoffed. 'Cursed cannibals!' she fumed.

'Enough, Raith.' Thorin scratched his perfect chin. 'So Faraladar was right again. He suspected you ached to return to Aea. Home is where the heart belongs after all.' He smiled amiably as he approached Muchuk. 'But don't you have everything you need here? Your race there is on the brink of extinction. Have you really thought this through?'

No. In fact, Muchuk had only thought of it a few moments ago, but now that the words were unsheathed, best to swing it all the way. 'Aye, Your Majesty,' he said. 'We have fulfilled our Vachan, and so have the Daevas. We long to return to our homes, to be with our kind again, wretched though they may be.' That fetched him no smiles. 'And,' Muchuk rallied, 'to teach Mankind the ways of civilization that we have both learned under you, Your Worship, and to protect them from the other belligerent races. As you often say, every flock of sheep needs a shepherd with a flute to entrance them, and a sword to keep away the wolves.'

'Ah, perfectly understandable then.' Thorin turned to look at Faraladar and nodded. 'Muchuk does make valid points. What was the Vachan again?' he enquired.

'I was to defeat Trisiras and the Children of Darkness for you,' Muchuk answered instead. 'You were to teach us how to use the Elementals, I mean, N'yen Valren.' He turned to wink at Asha, who smiled back. His brief spat with the Twins had resurrected the insolence in him. It felt good to be himself again. 'Naturally, not killing me and returning me home safely were part of the Vachan too,' Muchuk added.

Thorin exchanged a sad look with the Twins and then sighed with a smile. He draped an arm over Muchuk Und's shoulders as if they were old friends and guided him to the open terrace. Thorin was as silvery as the other Daevas, but the patterned tattoos on his hands shone white instead of gold. He was older than the others; that was plain to see. 'Son, your wish will be fulfilled. Truth be told, I foresaw that the moment of parting was upon us, and so I had already prepared a farewell present for you. Though I had not imagined that I would be gifting it to you so soon.' He pointed ahead. 'For services rendered, son.'

All three moons were high in the star-splattered sky as they walked outside into the night. Muchuk Und almost moaned with pleasure. Because there, right before him, resting on the terrace like a leviathan, was the most glorious Daeva ship he had ever seen. Muchuk narrowed his eyes against a rough breeze, pushing his long hair out of his face. 'Now that is what I call a gift, Your Worship.'

Thorin smiled, evidently pleased. 'It is why I built the thing, son. It is why I built Svarg. It is why I signed the Treaty to keep the Daevas out of your world. For Peace and Beauty. The old Drazeuses cared only for war, but I look towards fraternity. See there.' He pointed into the distance, to the green sky behind the enormous moons. 'There is your world, twinkling, always in sight, so I can keep an eye on it. Like the flowers of my gardens.'

'We are fortunate to have a Protector like you, Your Worship,' Muchuk lied easily.

'I do miss the Mortals' *yagnas*, you know... a sublime thing it was.' Muchuk thought he saw Thorin lick his lips. 'But hard decisions had to be taken for peace.'

'What does Faraladar say? The road to paradise is paved with pain.'

Thorin squeezed Muchuk Und's shoulder. 'Faraladar is the wisest among us, even if a little too melancholic for my taste. I wish we Daevas were half as enthused about life as you Mortals. It's a good thing you came to aid us, Muchuk Und. We had the numbers and the weapons but not the will to kill. So, tell me son, what will you do with your newfound knowledge once you get back home?'

'Do some conquering for ourselves, Your Worship.' Asha came forward, wine cup in hand. 'And you give us too much credit,' she continued. 'The Daevas were instrumental in the war effort in their own way.' She winked at Savitre Lios.

'Modesty does not suit you Mortals,' stated Thorin, apparently missing the exchange. 'Yes, our armies played a part, but it was your leadership and barbarity that brought this War to a conclusion. Your cruelty, your savagery, your love of butchery—'

'Oh stop, Your Worship, you will make me blush.' Asha laughed.

Thorin withdrew his arm from Muchuk's shoulders and walked ahead before turning to face them both. 'I can imagine the triumphant welcome that awaits you when you return. You shall ride the streets of Aea, and the Mortals will shower you with flowers to honour your victories here. You will be revered as Gods, the way we used to be. Your sons and daughters, your lovers and peers, your subjects, will all be there, waiting in jubilation.'

Muchuk wasn't really sure what awaited him back home. Ten years was perhaps not so long a period, but one never knew. But he made no demur. 'It is certainly something to look forward to, Your Worship.'

'Believe me, they would have… were they not all dead a century past.' And just like that Thorin's assuring smile fled like a gust of wind.

Metal glinted. Muchuk brought his hand up instinctively. A gurgle escaped his mouth as a wire twisted around his neck, lacerating it on either side. His thumb was the only thing between the wire and his windpipe as the wire began to choke him from the sides.

'Muchuk…' Asha tossed the cup away and started towards him, her hand on her weapon belt, mouth half open. There was another shimmer of metal as Ushas' spear pierced Asha's skull from behind.

Muchuk tried to scream in fury as his sister, his general, his companion, crumbled to the ground, dead. But all he could manage was a squeal as he felt a pair of soft hands brush against the nape of his neck. *Raith.* Her nails dug into his back as she choked him remorselessly. He could not believe that all that remained between life and death was his measly thumb. Blood trickled from his neck in vertical lines where the wire had cut into the sides of his neck. His face burned as he grasped for every breath. For a race that had become jaded and lethargic, Raith was certainly zestful about killing him.

'What have you done?' Savitre Lios dropped beside Asha, cradling her corpse but doing naught to save Muchuk.

Muchuk's free hand fished around for his dagger but someone caught his wrist and held it fast. Faraladar pressed up against him. 'I must apologize,' he whispered in his ear as he pulled the dagger from Muchuk Und's sheath. Calmly, he pushed it once, twice, and then one more time, with soft precise movements, into Muchuk Und's side. Blood shot out across the floor in long streaks.

'Have a care, Raith. He cannot die or we will break our Vachan,' Faraladar said.

Savitre Lios rose, open-mouthed, stupefied. 'Yes! What of the Vachan? Why aren't we dead?'

'The Vachan was not to kill Muchuk,' Thorin said. 'These arrogant Mortals never look beyond themselves, do they? If you are done crying over your whore, Savitre, help Faraladar drag him into the ship. Put him on ice so he doesn't die.' Thorin turned to Raith, annoyed. 'Will you take a century to knock him out, Raith? Faraladar stabbed him thrice, for crying out loud!'

'The damn wire is caught on his fucking thumb!' Raith hissed.

'Do I have to do everything myself?' Thorin walked to Muchuk. 'Give him to me! No wonder we were defeated by the Mortals.'

Raith's grasp loosened for the briefest moment. Little though he knew it, Faraladar had done Muchuk a favour by stabbing him with his own dagger. The powder he had rubbed on his blade had now mixed with his blood. Muchuk Und grabbed Raith's cloak with his free hand and focused his eyes. The purple bled from her cloak as he absorbed it. In the passing of a heartbeat, her cloak was bleached white.

'Seven hells…' Raith gasped.

Muchuk Und used the purple to ignite his Crown Chakra, the focal point of energy located between his eyes, giving him a fleeting moment of genius clarity. 'You ugly bitch!' He stomped down on Raith's foot with all his strength. Her grip slipped from the wire as she staggered back. Growling, Muchuk pushed Faraladar away, deftly snatching back his dagger and rolling away to a safe distance from them.

Raith and Faraladar prowled towards him. Muchuk began scraping the surface of his dagger vigorously with his nails. It made an ear-numbing sound. His nails tore. His fingers bled. But he did not stop. 'C'mon, goddammit!' he cried.

The zinth finally rose. And he turned to his last ally in this world, the Elemental he had barely learned to channel – Darkness. Muchuk Und raised his hand, sketching the Mandala, his finger weaving white-rimmed dark trails in the air, as if on an invisible canvas. He etched the fastest Mandala he knew how to draw.

Thorin took a step back. 'How is he channelling?' he demanded. 'I thought we had swabbed the place clean of zinth!'

'His dagger, Your Worship,' Faraladar replied in alarm. 'Get back, Sire!'

Muchuk's cloak fluttered in the power of the Mandalas as he felt some of his strength return. There wasn't enough zinth, the dagger had been too small, but maybe just enough for him to escape alive. 'Die, motherfucker!' he screamed.

He saw Thorin's eyes dart to something behind Muchuk. A coil of leather flashed. Muchuk turned, but it was too late. A leathery snake gripped his wrist and uncoiled again with the ferocity of lightning. In that instant, he realized his right palm had been severed from his wrist by Ushas's dagger-whip. The

Mandala shattered into a million tiny fragments that dissipated in the air, along with hope.

Before Muchuk could shriek, Raith's fist crunched into his skull. He felt himself fall; his head cracked sickeningly on the ground. The heel of Ushas' boot came down on one knee, sending searing pain lancing up his thigh.

This is unfair! What did we do to deserve this? Muchuk Und found his last thoughts to be pathetic. Expecting fairness in this world was to expect a viper not to poison you because you did not eat it.

'Toss him in, Savitre,' Thorin screamed.

Savitre's hand descended on Muchuk's ankle and dragged him like a rag doll, leaving a bloody trail on the white floor. Muchuk tried to grab at Savitre, but all his power had leaked out through the holes in his side, the cuts on his neck, and the flattened bones in his legs.

'Forgive me, Muchuk. I did not know,' Savitre said.

Muchuk forced his head up. 'Roll back into your hole, you piece of blood-smeared shit!' It wasn't his wittiest insult but it was straight from the heart.

Savitre did not respond as he heaved Muchuk up the ramp to the ship. But Thorin did. 'That was rude of you, Muchuk Und.' Thorin's face appeared before Muchuk's blurred vision, looking pained, as if genuinely disappointed at his lack of politeness. 'He really did not know. Do not think of us as animals, son. There is a reason, a necessity, for our actions.'

Muchuk felt himself hauled to a sarcophagus within the ship. His shoulder blades cracked against the bottom of the coffin as he was thrown in. He tried to spit at Thorin's face but the spittle flew a short distance in the air before falling back into his own eyes.

'Let me put your mind at ease,' he heard Thorin say as a cold hand wiped the blood and spit from his eyes. 'See, you learned much about us here – our weapons, our magic, our way of doing things. That Mandala you used was impressive. I am proud of you. Truly, I am. Regrettably, you were not permitted to learn everything. The thing is, time travels differently on this realm. You say you have spent ten years here… well, yes you have, but – how do I say this – you see, that is a century in your world. Do you understand what I am saying?'

A century had passed… All gone. His children. His wife. His kingdom. His life. The Daevas had cheated him. Suddenly, cold wind tugged cruelly at his hair and roared in his ears. He began to feel numb as cold water began to rise around him. He could feel ice forming over his eyes, his lips, his face, his body, each tiny crystal as pure as a star, prickling his skin like freshly cut grass. The lone tear that traced a difficult path through the grime on his face froze before it hit the rising water.

'I see wisdom dawning upon you.' Thorin smiled. 'You always were quick on the draw. So, you understand it is nothing personal. We just wanted to spare you from any vile thoughts of vengeance. Now rest, warrior. You have earned it, son.' Thorin turned to someone on the ship. 'Are the arrangements ready?'

Muchuk felt the frost settle over him like a glacier on a river. He lay sprawled and helpless, trapped in a coffin of ice, breathing in the stink of his own blood. His eyes darted around desperately, searching for some way to escape. But all that remained was the wreck of his body – the bloody stump at the end of his hand and the bone sticking through the leather of his breeches.

'You could…' Muchuk rasped, barely able to hear his own voice, 'you could still let me go. I won't come back. I wouldn't even know how to.'

'True, true. But you cannot be permitted to go back with all you have learned, to become a threat to us when we return,' Thorin said. 'You see, Mortals think they are liberated now, since they *defeated* us. But they are slowly forgetting everything that made them victors in the first place. Sorcery is gone from your world. You think yourselves to be lions, but you are merely scurrying rats upon whose tails our paws linger. The fact that the rats still live is not because of anything the rats have done.'

Thorin stroked the hair on Muchuk's head. Icy crystals snatched greedily at Muchuk's body, forming a crackling sheet over his legs, his stomach, his neck. 'A Protector is required to be harsh sometimes, son. A gardener needs to save his flowers by being cruel to the pests. We cannot have you upsetting the balance. So... sleep well, warrior. Dream of spring. *May your Night be Bright*.'

The frost spread over his heart, then his throat, and then spread to his face, capturing him in an ice sculpture of grief and agony. Thorin smiled sadly as he closed the lid of the sarcophagus. It shut with an ominous hiss, trapping Muchuk Und in cold darkness for eternity.

TEN THOUSAND YEARS LATER

MASHA'S AUGURIES

I

There was a time when young Oracles awaiting investiture were made to witness the slaughter of their families, to sear into their souls the futility of hope. This sacred tradition had, however, been abandoned by the Matrons over time, in favour of a meeker rite of passage into the House of Oracles. They reckoned the trials of initiation were lessons enough for the novices. Masha, on the other hand, thought the Matrons had grown soft. Truth be told, she considered it unfair since she herself had been made to watch her father burn alive.

But she did not have the time to brood over life's injustices. Today was a big day, an auspicious day. Today was Initiation Day in the House of Oracles, her first as a Matron.

Initiation Day was important. The route to divination was uncertain, vague, filled with mists. It was difficult to identify an Oracle from one who could perhaps read thoughts or change gender. Such people, with powers gifted to them by the Father of Viles, were considered cursed, and called Tainted. Over the centuries, many methods, less messy, less bloody, less fiery, had been tried and tested to separate genuine Oracles, the ones who could truly divine the future, from the Tainted. But they had all reached the same conclusion – there was no sieve better than pain.

And today, she would get to witness it. Soon, the initiates would be walked in silence to the Great Hall to be tested by the Sisters. If they passed, they lived. And she would be there with her scroll and quill to divine the fate of the world.

If she made it on time.

For Masha was late. Dressing as a Matron for the first time was like juggling a set of four knives with one hand. The golden-rimmed white robes had to be draped in all sorts of asymmetric angles, the gold sash around the waist had to be centrally aligned, the boots had to be iron-heeled, the lips painted, and the Chain of the Seven draped around her neck had to rest on her heart, facing the front. Not to forget, she'd completely forgotten to shave her head last night.

After dabbing the stray cuts on her pate with cotton puffs, she looked at her reflection in the bowl of water to see if any sign of hair survived on her scalp. An alabaster face webbed with a hundred scars looked back under a head that shone like a griffin's egg. Perfect. She noticed a lizard on the wall, watching her with judgemental eyes. She stuck out her tongue at it, then darting out, ran down the corridor, a smile dragging at her scarred lips.

Masha felt ridiculously happy. She still couldn't believe she had made it through six years of being an Oracle. The drugs they forced Oracles to consume put them into a dream state for months at a time, and had unavoidable side effects like death. The very few who survived became Matrons. She was one of the fortunate ones.

Now she could have real food, not just rice and lentils laced with drugs. Her mouth watered at the thought of food in its many incarnations. Of crisp purple aubergines, of milky-fleshed nuts, of fish curries, of ladyfingers flavoured with tamarind and coriander. Hunger growled inside her like a prowling animal.

Masha finally made her way to the Hall and slipped unnoticed into the line of Matrons. Being just thirteen summers old, and born with an exemplary lack of height, had its advantages. She could hear the chants of Sister Mercy. She looked around her as she stepped gingerly to the right, and then again, stepping over the bare feet of older, ruder Matrons, till she obtained a clear view of the Initiation. The Hall of Initiation reminded her of the opulent ballroom she had once seen as a child, before the Sisters had rescued her and purged her of her taint. Warm yellow light flowed from the glass globes suspended on golden chains around the Hall. Red matting streaked in perpendicular lines lay below rows of wooden long-chairs. To describe it one word would be to call it... stately. But today it smelled of sweat, fear and shit.

A black-haired boy was hanging upside down, secured to a wooden rack with metal shackles, his limbs stretched sideways to achieve maximum extension. He was screaming in agony. There were four other wooden racks, now empty, spattered with blood. The ones who had failed. *Ashes! I missed it!*

Beside the boy stood the leader of the House of Oracles, clad in the black robes of a Sister. Dark circles cupped Sister Mercy's eyes, giving her a look of profound sadness and pity. Women were not permitted to attain the honorific title of Acharya, given to the Masters of Knowledge who graduated from the Citadel of Meru. Thus, educated women resorted to having the less educated call them Sisters, even though there was nothing sisterly about these women.

'I hope you understand I do not enjoy this,' said Sister Mercy as she softly placed four glass bottles in a bag. She coiled the bag at the top and then slammed it viciously against the wall, once, twice, thrice. She then shook the bag, jingling the contents within – hundreds of broken glass shards. With one hand she turned the wooden rack on its axle so that the boy's head faced her.

Sister Mercy held the boy's face and slowly, carefully, lowered the bag over his head and cinched the drawstring tight around his neck. The boy's face was invisible; he was a bagged scarecrow, such as the peasants used in their fields.

Sister Mercy began to chant, the Matrons echoing the last few words in unison: 'But pain... pain is the great reliever, the path away from perdition, the salvation of our souls.'

As she uttered the words, Sister Mercy began to mould the bag around the boy's face gently, as if it were a clay sculpture, with all the tenderness of a mother.

'The salvation of our souls,' echoed the Matrons.

The screams of the boy were muffled in the bag but his agony was loud enough. His body thrashed under the straps like a fish out of water. Sister Mercy's pale fingers massaged his neck through the cloth, moving up to the boy's cheeks to his eyes, and finally to his temples. 'Pain will bring out the cursed demon in you; the curse gifted by the Father of Viles, to do us harm, boy,' she said. 'But we will purge you of Evil, and bring you to the side of Light.'

The bag grew redder and wetter with each movement of her hand. Stains formed where the boy's nose and ears were. The boy's wordless screams became so high-pitched that they hurt Masha's head. Her gut cramped at the memory of her own initiation. Her tears may have dried, but she could drown in that pain anytime she chose.

'To the side of Light,' the chorus echoed.

Mercifully, the screams stopped and the boy began to choke out strange sounds. There were gasps all around. The Sisters took nervous steps forward and the Matrons took out their parchments. Seeing this, Masha fumbled for her own stationery.

Sister Mercy took a step back, her hand slick with blood. Silence spread its ghostly embrace around the hall as she carefully lifted the bag from the boy's face.

Masha swallowed down the bile that rose in her throat, eager not to miss out on her first initiation as a Matron. The boy's face was a bloodied mess, the human features hidden behind a map of gashes and cuts. The nose was sliced in two. One shard stuck out of his left eye. Involuntarily, Masha touched her own scars and flinched.

Sister Mercy made the boy smell a block of moongrain. Immediately, the boy's single eye opened, like a rising yellow sun, vigour coursing through his harrowed eyeball.

'Tell us, what did you see?' Sister Mercy asked kindly.

'I saw *airavats* breaking down a high wall. Dozens of 'em,' the boy slurred every word. 'I saw men burning in a blue flame, rows of 'em.' He pressed a hand to his face. 'I felt hot. I could even smell the smoke.'

'People burn all the time. What else?'

'I saw... a battle. And olive wreaths snaking around a cow's neck...'

Beside Masha, a Matron scoffed, 'It takes no divination to see a battle coming in our realm.'

'What else?' Sister Mercy asked, patting the boy's head.

'I saw a black eagle steal the lion's head from a peacock.'

'Must have been a great eagle,' Sister Mercy remarked sadly. 'He is useless. Take him.'

'No...' he pleaded wearily, the effects of the drug wearing off, knowing he had only moments to save his life. 'The rest were just flashes. I saw jousting between living corpses behind a wall. One of the corpses held a trident in his hand, his torso spurting blood from where his head should have been. The other man stood in a golden breastplate; he had two faces – one monster, one man.'

That snatched Sister Mercy's interest. She made him sniff the moongrain again. 'Go on.' This time, the boy went rigid, his eyes unfocused, as in a trance, his mouth sagging. His eyes started to roll. He looked like he was having a seizure.

'The ashes of light drift,' he intoned in a harsh voice, quite unlike his own, 'amidst corpses of stars, and the dead storm returns, with an echo of power. And I see then... the last defiance of Asha's blood. When the sun dies, the shadows will dance in a fiery coldness, to welcome the Son of Darkness.'

The drug wore off. Slowly but steadily, the screaming resumed. Masha could not believe it. This was not a vision. It was a prophecy! It had to be. It sounded like a poem, spoke of destruction, and was completely obscure. A real prophecy on her first day! *The Light Bless Me!*

'Sister Mercy, storm, shadow? Surely, it cannot be the N'yen Valren?' one of the Sisters asked gravely over the boy's screams. 'And who is the Son of Darkness?'

'Now that is something we have to find out, is it not, Sister? Put the Matrons on double duty. And make sure the boy does not die. I see great promise.' She wrinkled her nose, looking wistfully at the wretched figure. 'And clean him up. He shat himself.'

II

The Library was lined with shelves stacked high with neatly ordered scrolls and books. A heavy round table with a stone top stood in the centre, below a sky-lit dome, where Masha sat, huddled with the other Matrons, behind voluminous tomes of divination histories. They spoke in whispers, asking questions, scribbling notes and fighting over the ladders against the shelves.

As Matrons, their main task was to make sense of the gibberish the Oracles spoke, and then weave the future as a narrative in their journals. From personal experience, Masha knew the Oracles did not always make sense. And many a time they were wrong, for the future was an ever-changing sea, with the tiniest stone setting off the largest waves. This was where the Matrons came in, taking notes of visions from the hundred or so ordained Oracles, comparing and confirming their utterances, before charting the most consistent path that lay before the realm. The Oracles divined, the Matrons deciphered, and the Sisters decided. Their conclusions were ultimately sent to the Saptarishis, the Venerable Seven. What the Seven did with this information Masha did not know.

Too bad the boy had not survived the test. More clues would have been helpful. They had been given a month to uncover what the boy spoke of, and then confirm it with the visions of other Oracles. Masha, for one, intended to impress. A few, world-saving decodes and she could be the Matron who uncovered who this Son of Darkness was. Imagine that.

'Who is the Peacock?' she asked the Matron beside her, a woman of middling years with a twisted face and a missing eye. She was called Maimed Matron. The Sisters had not come out with the glass-bag routine in those days. 'What is an olive wreath? Why can't Oracles ever speak plain?'

'Peacock is obviously Krishna,' Burned Matron interjected before Maimed Matron could answer. A mosquito landed on her darkly singed cheek and strutted about like a conqueror. She didn't notice. 'Only he wears that hideous peacock feather in his crown. I used to see him in many of my own visions.' She leaned in closer over the table. 'Most of them came true, you know.'

'Yes, the attack on the Eastern King. That was clever, Burned Matron.' Maimed Matron nodded her head sagely.

Masha listened eagerly to the older women. She barely knew what they spoke of, but if she was to get ahead in the game, she needed to acquire vast knowledge as quickly as possible. When she used to have visions, no one had ever explained who she was seeing. She certainly had not seen anyone with a peacock feather. 'Who is Krishna?' she asked, also whispering.

'Who is Krishna, she asks!' Burned Matron scoffed.

Maimed Matron was kinder. 'Krishna is quite the centrepiece to any divination you will decipher over the next few years, Little One. He was a cowherd in Mathura. Climbed to prominence through cunning, and deposed the King of Mathura in a coup to become King himself. As true a rags-to-riches story as you will ever encounter.'

'What rubbish!' Burned Matron chided. 'Krishna did not become the new King. He created a Republic. Clever lad.'

'True in theory. But he pulls all the strings from behind the curtain… much like our Saptarishis, no?'

'Who knows? It's not as if the Seven tell us what they do with what we give them. We are just cogs in a well-oiled wheel.'

'That is true,' Maimed Matron sighed. 'But this is still better than divining with sheep entrails. Just imagine the stench and the mess.'

'Why is Krishna the centrepiece?' Masha asked.

'We will not spoon-feed you what we know. Here.' Burned Matron handed Masha a leather-enfolded diary, embossed with the number 307. 'This is the journal I maintain on Krishna and Shishupal. Refer to it for your notes.'

'Erm, who is Shishupal?' Masha asked.

Burned Matron grunted in impatience. Maimed Matron placed a hand on Burned Matron's shoulder. 'She is new, Matron. We should help her out.'

Letting out a sigh, Burned Matron relented. 'Very well, child, but listen well for I will not tell you again. Krishna deposed the former King of Mathura, Kans. Now, remember that name. The coup was deadly. Some of the hoodlums went mad with bloodlust, as often happens in riots, and raped Kans' two wives, and killed his children.' She spoke flatly, without emotion. 'Krishna had nothing to do with that... but well, you know how it goes with blaming the leader. Turns out, the wives of Kans were the daughters of the Magadhan Emperor.'

Masha gasped. 'Emperor Jarasandh?'

'Good girl. Not completely ignorant I see. And there began the ten-year-long Yamuna Wars between Krishna's Mathuran Republic and Jarasandh's Magadhan Empire. The Emperor sent wave after wave of soldiers to Mathura, but the Mathuran Walls were too high, too strong, to be taken down. And... well, I am not going to tell you everything now, am I? Go read my journal. But to answer your question, Shishupal is the Lord of Chedi, a vassal state of the Empire, and currently he is a soldier in the Empire.'

'But...'

'Do not disturb me. I have shown you where to look; do not expect me to tell you what to see. Go read!'

'Yes, Matron.' Masha bowed her head and took the journal. She crossed her legs on the stool and settled down uncomfortably for a long read.

'Oi! Seven Hells! Not from the start, you silly child!' Burned Matron snatched the journal from Masha and flipped the fragile parchments over till she reached the middle of the stack. 'Start here – Twilight of the Yamuna Wars, when the untimely suicide of a Princess plunged the entire realm into hushed silence. Now

remember this, Matron, never confuse silence for peace. Auguries
have gone terribly wrong by ignoring that fine distinction.'

'Take it easy, child. You will enjoy it, you know,' Maimed Matron
added kindly. 'Krishna has stolen Princesses from sleeping Lords.
He flies a griffin. His wife Satyabhama is the War Mistress of
Mathura, who single-handedly killed the Rakshasa King of the
East. Ooh she's quite the fierce one! Then there is Karna, of course.
Oh Karna...' she uttered dreamily.

Even Burned Matron suppressed a coy smile as she returned
to her books. 'Karna... divinations of him are more like fantasies.'
She giggled like a young girl. 'He is so handsome... but absolutely
fucked.'

'Accursed, she means,' said Maimed Matron, biting back a smile.
'Yet, he is single-handedly the most dangerous man alive in the
realm. There is, of course, Mati, the Pirate Princess of Kalinga, and
even Shakuni, the poor crippled torturer. They are all fascinating.
They have talked to Gods, loved like animals, and written songs
that would make Sister Mercy cry. Though we will never leave
these hallowed walls to see them in person, yet through their tales,
we will be their companions. You can look through any of our
journals; access is not denied to any Matron. You are one of us
now. Treat them with care, for it is your gift, child. Your welcome
to the Ballad of the Fallen.'

ADHYAYA I

WINTER OF DISCORD

There is nothing more admirable than when two people who see eye to eye keep house as man and wife, confounding their enemies and delighting their friends.
—Homer, *Odyssey*

KRISHNA

I

On the terrace of the Mathuran Keep, a man rose from his divan and walked to the sideboard. Picking up the decanter, he poured for himself, then returned to his scented cushions and scrolls, subsiding into their soft embrace. He gazed at the golden wine, flecked with tints of the setting sun, then sipped, eyes closed. He raised his fingers delicately. His attendant, graceful and swift, appeared by his side with a fruit basket and softly placed an orange in the man's outstretched hand. It was easy to tell the man enjoying a good time was Krishna. Partly by the peacock feather in his crownlet, but mainly because of the cool indifference with which he peeled an orange while his city burned.

It was not as if it was Krishna's fault. He was a man of peace, yet his enemies loved to bring him war. *If only they could do it in silence,* he thought morosely. The racket of catapults in the distance made it difficult to tell the sound of drums from the pounding of rocks against the city walls. It was an act of desperation on the part of the Magadhan Empire. Huge as the catapults were, they did not have the range to throw their burdens over the Third Sister into the city. Not without coming into range of Mathura's own catapults. So, the rocks just slammed off the barbicans and defensive towers without doing any damage. And since the rocks couldn't breach the walls of the Third Sister and let the soldiers in, all the Magadhans achieved was to make the life of Mathurans miserable with migraine.

Smashing rocks against the impregnable Walls of Mathura was all very well but those musty catapults took a long time to wind up and swing. In the meantime, the Mathurans responded by slipping behind the picket lines to give the Magadhans a taste of their own medicine by burning their food tents and stealing their Imperial standards.

The siege wasn't all machines and rocks, however. To the east, where the Third Sister was the shortest, brave Mathuran soldiers on the Wall responded by feverishly shooting arrows down the throats of their equally brave but hapless enemies, who tried to climb the Wall no one could scale.

Krishna could not see all of this with his own eyes of course, but his web of informers was kept busy. What he *could* see from where he lounged was the smoke that rose high in wind-sculpted columns outside the Third Sister. The scene would certainly have impressed a newcomer, but for the Mathurans it was just another day in the ten-year-old war with the Empire.

Satyabhama, his third wife, lounged beside him. They were out here under the smoky sky merely to measure the odds of the wager between them. While Krishna read the scrolls even as he balanced his glass perilously on a cushion with the orange on top, Satyabhama was busy putting a whetstone to her sword. He turned towards her to ask a question, but stopped short. Dressed in full armour, Satyabhama looked resplendent. Krishna felt a stirring, an all too familiar sensation in her presence. He gestured for his attendant to take the glass away and leave the terrace. Krishna then set aside his scrolls, picked up his bamboo flute, and cleared his throat. 'You look exquisite today, Satya, with eyes like obsidian.' He played a melody of joy.

Satyabhama frowned. 'So, my eyes are stony?' she responded without looking up from her sword.

Krishna sighed, scratching the redacted caste mark on the side of his neck. For a man with three wives, he was rather inept at pleasing Satyabhama. Then again, for a third wife, she was rather too haughty. Deservedly so, though Krishna never told her that. He had first married Lady Rukmini, for love. Rukmini, with her impractical dresses that were best worn by heroines of tragic stage dramas, kept to herself these days. Then he had married Jambavati, out of necessity, to win her father as an ally.

But he did not marry Satyabhama. Satyabhama married him. And Krishna still thanked the Fates for his godsluck. For Satyabhama excited him. She entertained him. More importantly, she inspired him. She wasn't born into the right family as Rukmini had been. She wasn't born to a powerful creature, as Jambavati was. But Satyabhama was dark magic.

'Eyes as soft as a doe,' Krishna rallied with a teasing tune on his flute.

'Silly weak animal that is hunted on a daily basis. Save it for Rukmini.'

Krishna found himself on thin ice. Rukmini was hailed as an ethereal beauty by the small-folk. A fact Krishna knew bothered Satyabhama sometimes, though he could not fathom why. Satyabhama was radiant in her own right, even if her beauty was of an austere kind. No paint graced her cheeks. No tiara gleamed on her head. She wore her long black hair tightly braided like a commoner. Yet Satyabhama stood out like a moon in a sky of stars. She was a warrior, more comfortable in chainmail armour than sarees, and Krishna cherished her for it. *Women are not meant to be understood, just loved,* he remembered.

He swiftly changed tack. 'The ring I gifted you looks pretty on your finger.'

Satyabhama held up her left hand to admire the ring. It was an emerald, the size of a grape. It caught the light as she turned her hand, glistening like fresh dung. 'You've given me worse gifts, cowherd,' she admitted.

'It matches your viperous temper.'

Satyabhama snorted derisively.

'You are a…'

She finally turned to look at him. Her eyebrows arched dangerously, making the *bindi* between her brown eyes wrinkle as if in a challenge. Krishna knew his next words would make or break the deal, wager notwithstanding. He breathed a grave melody into the flute.

'A Goddess of War.'

That brought a smile to the side of her face she imagined he could not see. 'It'll do.' She shrugged with feigned nonchalance.

Krishna nudged her shoulder with his flute. 'I'm waiting for my share of compliments.'

'What can Lord Krishna hear from me that he has not already heard from a thousand women?' Satyabhama crept closer to him. 'Heartbreakingly handsome... with hair like raven's feathers...' She twirled a strand of his hair around her forefinger. 'Renowned philanderer with a vast network of spies, *female* spies of course. A puppeteer of kings, who has his fingers deep in every conspiracy in the realm. The world calls him the "Saviour of Mathura". Surely, if I added any more praise,' she whispered softly into his ear, 'his tiny head would fucking burst!'

'A risk worth taking, I assure you,' Krishna replied with an offended look.

'I love you too much to lose you for so trifling a cause. Alas, husband, you are eternally bound to a life without flattery with me.'

Krishna sighed. 'I guess I have no choice but to bear with vigour the curses the Gods deign to throw my way.'

Satyabhama winked. She rose and walked over to the merlon of the Keep. 'It is hard to see anything beyond the black smoke. What was the wager again?'

'The Magadhans will retreat within seven days.'

'Hah!' She turned towards him, leaning against the merlon. 'That has never happened. Even under that dolt Shishupal, they stayed a month. And that was years ago.'

Krishna joined her by the battlements, pulling out his eyeglass and extending the tubes before squinting through it. He could see the uninvited visitors battering against the Third Sister in a sea of iron and silver and polished steel, three thousand strong, a pride of paladins and knights, of cavalry and foot soldiers. Over their heads, a score of crimson banners whipped back and forth in the wind, emblazoned with the Lion of the Magadhan Empire.

'Looks like one of their rocks managed to fly over the Third Sister. There's a first time for everything.'

The Mathuran Walls, known as the Three Sisters, were a set of three concentric fortifications, forming a crescent around three sides of the city, each rising higher as they moved inward. On the fourth side, the rough currents of the Yamuna River formed a natural barrier, keeping enemies at bay. The Third Sister was the outermost wall of the city.

'Not the first time,' Satyabhama said. 'Remember last winter the wind carried one of their flaming stones into the Market Square and set afire the goldsmith's shop? Molten gold floated in our gutters. Many of the homeless became Lords that day, leaving us at the mercy of the God of Market Forces.'

Krishna would not have been surprised if there was in reality such a God worshipped by the Mathurans. Mathura was a speck of a city, humble and unassertive. For its sigil, it had a cow. It was not proud, like the Lion of the Magadhan Empire in the South, nor did it have illustrious allies like the Eagle of the Hastina Union in the North. It did not rule the sea like the Swan of Kalinga. Nor did it have vast fertile lands to graze their herds, like the Stag of Panchal. Yet the Cow was richer than them all. *A City of Ironies, my Mathura.*

'Ah, it landed in the settlement you erected in the western section last summer,' Krishna said, tracing the projectile with his eyeglass. 'I liked that idea. Do you think the Magadhans figured out it was a trick?'

'That we place straw soldiers and empty huts by the lowest points of Third Sister to fool them into concentrating their attack there? Maybe. Does not seem to deter them though.'

'Patience is our virtue. Persistence is theirs.'

Satyabhama turned away. 'Well, my patience is at an end. I think I'll retire to my chambers. I have to—'

Before she could finish, distant roars down by the Third Sister snatched back their attention. It seemed that someone more thoughtful amongst the Magadhans had decided to build ramps against the Third Sister, instead of climbing her with hooks.

It had, of course, been tried before. The Mathuran Republican Army had simply shrugged and sent barrels of oil rolling down the ramp in grisly greeting. The aftermath of the explosion of those ramps had taken the Mathurans months to mop up. Rinsing a city after a battle was a tiresome, thankless and ugly business. But the Mathurans had perfected it with practice.

For the three-walled City of Mathura had withstood many assaults in its short, crowded history as a Republic. Ramps, siege towers, munitions and hordes, fire and steel, the Magadhans had brought them all to the Three Sisters, but Mathura had never been sacked by the Empire. Not once.

And this was yet another irony of the legacy of the Republic. The Emperor who now wanted to bring the Sisters down was the very man who had built the Walls two decades ago. The Three Sisters had been a gift from the Emperor to Kans, the husband of his twin daughters, and King of the erstwhile Mathura Kingdom. Krishna had been a cowherd then.

But times change.

Now Kans was dead; Mathura was a Republic; Krishna held its reins; and the Emperor had set out to destroy his own creation, seeking vengeance on the man who had destroyed his family.

And so it was that the citizens of Mathura carried on their mundane lives as if a caravan of street magicians and cracker-makers had appeared at their gates, rather than the army of the greatest Empire in the realm. They knew this attack was not the end but a blazing, fiery interlude. The bombardment and harassment would go on for another few weeks, till the enemy ran out of supplies or the monsoon set in, whichever was earlier.

But turns out this day was to be different.

'Krishna, *look!*' Satyabhama's voice was urgent enough for him to obey without a quirky retort. He turned cautiously, following her pointing finger towards the Third Sister, where the Magadhans were climbing the ramps. But there was no fire to welcome them.

Instead, more Magadhan rocks sailed over the Third Sister to land inside the city.

'What the...' he exclaimed, nonplussed. Had they invented a new catapult? Or were there traitors in their midst? He lifted his eyeglass again. 'Why aren't the soldiers lighting up the ramps?'

As if in answer, the clouds of smoke from the hutments shifted to reveal that the rocks sailing over the Third Sister were made of flesh, not stone. The Magadhans were tossing bodies over the Third Sister in a rain of cadavers. And Krishna was sure these bodies were alive when they were loaded onto the Magadhan catapults.

Only one person had the stomach to even think of something so barbaric and dishonourable. The Yaksha of Goverdhun had come to visit.

II

Mathura's wealth, in comparison to its size, wasn't the only thing that fazed its neighbours. The realm of Aryavrat followed the traditional hierarchy of humans set out by the First Empire, classifying them into four distinct castes – the *Namins* or priestly class, the *Ksharjas* or warrior class, the *Drachmas* or coinmen, and the *Resht*, the lowborn – all struggling against each other in a murky mess of malice and might. But the struggle was especially pronounced in Mathura, for when the Republic was formed, men in pursuit of equality scratched off their caste marks. Some said it had been Krishna's masterful vision because they suspected Krishna was a lowborn himself, but such rumours had never been proven.

What was proven, however, was that nothing creates more chaos than equality. It was a useful illusion, of course, but it carried its own share of troubles, for suddenly every man began to believe the throne and power could be his for the taking. Unfortunately for them, Krishna revelled in chaos. He had managed to frustrate and infuriate the nobility across caste lines, to the extent that they had long since abandoned their attempts to assassinate him. They now contented themselves with jockeying for positions under him instead. Everyone except his elder brother.

Balram paced outside the Senate, his heavy armour clanking with every step. His hulking, seven-foot figure cast ghastly shifting shadows on Krishna, who lounged languidly on the Senate steps.

'Will you stop your frantic pacing, Balram? It is giving me a headache.' His brother was many things – a man of straight lines, clean uniform and a lack of caution that afflicted most men of his age. A military commander and warrior like none other. But he had no understanding of the virtues of moderation. He had the kind of generous nature that reckoned panic was not something you hoarded for yourself; you shared it with family.

'Why aren't *you* worried?' Balram huffed hotly. 'They are within our Walls! They threw disease-ridden bodies into the city! We could have a riot on our hands! Or worse, a plague that could kill us! That murderous Yaksha! I will smash his head to pulp with my mace!'

Krishna frowned. The name still felt sour on his tongue. The Magadhan Empire had given rise to many notable Generals in the decade-long war with Mathura, but none more vicious and vile than the mysterious Yaksha of Goverdhun. Krishna forced the name from his mind. Because there really wasn't anything to worry about. He was sure the rumours about the plague were false. No army, even one under the Yaksha, would risk carrying plague-ridden bodies so close to their own camp. It would be suicide. And even if the Magadhans managed to cross the Third Sister, the Second Sister was made of sterner stuff. Higher walls, garnished with hundreds of flamers and hot-oil ducts. The Second Sister was far more special than the other Sisters in that it descended so deep into the ground that no sappers could mine under it. The only way it could be breached was if it was broken down by an Act of God. But if Balram was finally worried, Krishna would milk the opportunity dry.

'I told you this would happen,' Krishna replied lazily. 'I have been warning you about it for more than five years. Mathura is fighting this war with both feet in quicksand.' That was true enough. The war had depleted Mathura's reserves, lost them territories outside its walls, and caused immense joy to bankers like the Sindh Guild, who were charging demonic interest rates on their loans. 'If the Magadhans truly knew the state of our treasury, they would not have bothered to climb the Sisters. They could just have waited outside, safe behind their picket lines, and by the next full moon we would have been eating each other to stave off starvation. Not you and I, of course. We would be the first to be hanged by our devoted Senators.'

'This is not an "I told you so" moment!' Balram snapped, unlimbering his mace. 'It is not as if we are spoilt for choice. Now is the time for war!'

Krishna sighed. He spent more energy containing his brother within the Walls than fighting the enemy outside them. 'Patience, Brother,' he said for the hundredth time. 'Nothing will happen.'

'You said the exact same thing in the Battle of Goverdhun! What happened then, huh?'

A chariot of memories charged through Krishna's mind. He remembered how the Yaksha had taken what was left of a newborn's body and strapped it to his shield. Krishna had not seen the Yaksha's face, but he had seen what followed. The Yaksha's men had emulated their leader, tying children and babies to their longspears and standards. It was no surprise the tide of battle had turned then like a ferocious sucking ebb tide. The Mathurans were butchered where they stood, unable to strike their swords at the shields carrying their own children.

Balram softened. 'I'm sorry. That was harsh.'

'No harm done,' Krishna said. 'But we must remember this is Mathura, not Goverdhun.'

Satyabhama walked up to Balram. 'I am ready. Shall we?'

'Will you two just *wait?*' Krishna pleaded. They were ruining the fun. 'Ah, what joy!' he remarked sarcastically, looking up. 'Another of your wolf pups is here.'

Untimely as ever, a soldier of Satyabhama's personal squad marched in, wearing old grey armour and a greyer cloak. Her dusky blue skin marked her as a Balkhan. She wore a grey robe over her chainmail, and her hair was tied to ape Satyabhama's. Two bodyguards flanked her, one short, the other grotesquely thin, both swathed in grey, hands hidden in sleeves, hoods shadowing their faces.

Silver Wolves.

The Silver Wolves carried no standard nor flew any banners. 'A military wing of social rejects,' Lord Akrur called them. 'Scavenger wolves, loyal only to silver,' he had remarked distastefully when Satyabhama had first unveiled before the Senate her plan of forming a squad picked from Mathura's destitute. And now the Silver Wolves, named and marshalled by Satyabhama herself, had turned into an effective force. The fact that they were all women only made them more dangerous.

The Balkhan in the middle saluted Satyabhama. 'War Mistress, your orders.'

Satyabhama is called War Mistress. Balram is called the Giant. Why do they not have such titles for me? Krishna thought sourly.

'Rain,' Satyabhama acknowledged the salute. *Rain. A name chosen by Satyabhama, no doubt.* Those who joined the Silver Wolves discarded their old names and roles and adopted strange alter egos. There was an *Arms*, a *Piety*, and even a *One Eye*, serving under Satyabhama. 'Rush to Commander Kain at the Walls, and rotate the defence on the Sisters. Ask the Reserve Force to send a quarter of their strength to the Dreamstone Spire to retrieve Lord Kritavarman. Send Piety to prepare the griffin.'

'You're taking Garud!' Krishna exclaimed. The half lion, half eagle was *his* pet, his alone, but Satyabhama seemed to have assumed joint custody without notice.

'Is that a problem?' she asked in the most menacing way a woman could string those four words together. Something very much like a smile tugged at the corner of Balram's mouth. He always did love to watch Krishna squirm.

'Have you forgotten how badly injured he was in the third battle? He isn't a fire-breathing lizard, you know. Just a fluffy lion with wings. No, Satya, he is too young to be flown into battle.'

'He is a hundred years old! Our line of vision is blocked by the smoke pillars. We need eyes in the sky.'

How many armies in the world could say that? he mused with pride for a moment before shaking it off. 'Griffins live eight hundred years, so by that scale of measure, he is just entering his growth spurt. Besides, he is the last surviving male of his line. Stop, Satyabhama! I will make another wager with you.' Krishna craned his neck to look at the sundial on top of the Senate House. 'Within the next hour the battle will cease. Will you take the wager?'

Satyabhama pursed her lips. 'What's the prize?'

'No holds barred tonight. Surely you can appreciate the odds are stacked against me?'

Satyabhama looked at the sundial, and then at the dust clouds rising inside the third Wall. She sighed. 'Alright, I'll stay.'

Balram ignored them both. 'Rain, remember I will have a horn and use it to relay commands. If I fall, the horn will pass to Lady Satyabhama. And if she falls…' he turned to look at Krishna with disapproving eyes, '… to Lord Krishna.'

Rain looked at Krishna, and then nodded at Balram. 'A lot seems to rest on your horn, Sir. What if it falls silent? What if Lord Krishna is cut down?'

Krishna looked at her, aghast.

'Sir!' A messenger came running, panting and heaving, his face begrimed with dust and soot. He whispered something to the tall guard standing beside Rain.

The guard pulled back her cowl to reveal an animated set of bluish-grey eyes under deep black hair that was cropped short and pointing in every direction. She was wiry and much too young to be a soldier. Pockmarks covered her pert nose and cheeks, and her armour was a jumble of foreign fetishes over a threadbare, stained uniform. A short sword hung in a cracked wooden scabbard at her hip. 'The Magadhans have withdrawn their forces! We have won!' she declared, her voice hoarse with joy.

'Easy there, Storm,' Rain warned, but she did not do a good job of suppressing her own smile.

Storm. Krishna grimaced. *Just what are these names?*

'How?' Balram asked, looking dismayed at being deprived of the opportunity to die heroically.

'Uhm, we don't know,' the messenger murmured.

A droll silence descended amidst the disbelieving men and women of war. Krishna could not help but raise his head to the sky and laugh. His hair gleamed in the sun, offsetting his dusky skin and blue eyes so deep they were violet, even in the sunlight. 'Guess we'll never find the answer to your question now, Rain, will we? *War Mistress,* time to pay up.' Krishna smiled mischievously at Satyabhama.

Balram, leaning over the merlons, swung his neck left to right like a pendulum. 'How did... why are they retreating?'

Satyabhama took off her helm. 'Well, that was anticlimactic. But a wager is a wager. Come to my chambers tonight, husband. I'll keep something special handy.'

'Something romantic this time, Satya. Remember the fine distinction between strawberries and shackles.' Rain and Balram exchanged horrified looks. Storm giggled. 'Apologies for the unrequisitioned information, ladies. My brother is, of course, used to it,' Krishna said.

'Doesn't mean you have to hammer me with it again and again,' Balram grumbled. Krishna was about to jump in at that chance when Satyabhama dragged him away. Balram gave Rain a sympathetic pat on the shoulder. 'Forgive my brother his manners, Rain.'

'It's alright, My Lord,' Rain replied stoically. 'The damage is done. All that is left for me to do now is to drink till the part of my mind that creates mental images dies a horrible death.'

III

Krishna woke, bruised, tired and sore. Through dry eyes he stared at the sky outside. It was too early even for dawn. Yet there was a racket going on in the corridor. He turned wearily on the bed to find Satyabhama seated on a stone bench, her naked back towards him. She was combing her hair before a mirror adorned with daggers and fetishes. Satyabhama would never look at a mirror adorned with roses and cherubs. *We are nothing if not our reputations.*

She dressed, but not before Krishna took full measure of the long scar running down her back. In a battle long forgotten, some fortunate sword had found its way through her armour, cutting a deep gash down her spine. *A stripe on a jungle cat.*

Mild stirrings. Krishna smiled. 'Come to bed, Satya. It's too cold for you to be so bare… and so distant.' He frowned as he heard chatter again outside the room. 'At least draw the bed curtains. I have a feeling we are about to be disturbed.'

'I've never been a champion of modesty, Krishna,' Satyabhama replied as she pulled a cotton *kurti* over a corset and draped a thick ornate *odhni* like a cloak around her neck. 'You think we look for shrubs to hide behind when we change on the frontlines?'

'I don't know why but that information isn't particularly comforting, wife,' Krishna said, imagining her stripping naked in front of her squad. *I find I prefer nightmares of famine to this.* 'Why are you dressing so early? The day has barely begun.'

He turned on his side again, propping his head on his hand. There was a certain militaristic aspect to the furniture in Satyabhama's chamber; the little there was could at best be described as conservative Magadhan in style. The functional basin for washing had no jasmine flowers floating in the water. The walls had no murals. And it was known that Satyabhama had no patience for the furs and silken mats that covered the floors of every other room in the inner district. Krishna smiled at a memory that rose suddenly in his mind.

Satyabhama's brows rose. 'A joke worthy of sharing?'

Krishna got out of bed and stretched, hoping to distract Satyabhama as she had distracted him. 'Just remembering Senator Akrur's face when your motion to ban animal fur and wall hangings was defeated.'

The Senator had, in fact, broken into a victory jig, but not for long. Satyabhama had been banished from the Senate for a year for breaking Lord Akrur's nose. But it had been worth it. 'Honestly, I felt it was an improvement on his features,' Satyabhama said flatly. 'When your soldiers, fighting in the cold, need the animal fur to stay warm, you don't hoard it to impress your mistresses.'

Krishna nodded. 'What is all that chatter outside?' he asked, frowning. *Does no one sleep anymore?*

'An envoy has come from the Magadhan camp to parley.'

'Parley! Why?'

Magadh had been at Mathura's throat for years, with intermittent moments of sobriety. The Yamuna Wars had seen so many battles that the bards had abandoned giving them names. The enmity between the Republic and the Empire ran as deep as the river for which their war was named. But a parley? It had never happened before. No one sued for peace when they were winning.

'Don't know. It might have something to do with the Emperor's daughter. But then you already knew about it.'

Uh oh. 'About *what* exactly?'

'That she jumped off the palace terrace and was found impaled on the gates. You knew there would be a call from Magadh to observe a period of mourning, didn't you?'

No point in lying. 'I did not *know* Magadh would call for a truce. I… merely guessed. And I did not want to trouble you with the news till I confirmed it.' The Emperor's twin daughters were a sensitive subject in Mathuran politics. Old history. Forbidden history, in fact. Krishna let out an exasperated sigh. *That one negligent oversight could have been handled so much better.* He shook off the thought. Regret and self-pity could easily become a favoured path if one was unwary of their seduction. Yet the long sword of that memory still felt as sharp and terrible as the knives the bastards must have used when they butchered the Emperor's grandsons.

'I wonder, had the Emperor known how close he was to victory today, would he still have sent the recall order? We were plain lucky,' Satyabhama finally said after an awkward moment of silence. 'Nonetheless, I would have expected rage rather than restraint as the Emperor's response.'

'His new religion requires strict observance of rituals. Perhaps he thought this was just another pointless battle that would end in a stalemate.' The last traces of sleep as well as stirrings had now vanished. 'So, what about this parley? When is it?'

There was a sudden knock on the door, loud and insistent. 'State your business,' Krishna called, wishing whoever it was would go away. He had enough on his mind.

'My Lord...' his personal guard called through the door, 'it is Lord Akrur, with Lord Kritavarman.'

Akrur, former-thief-now-Senator, was a powerful noble on many counts, and a pain in Krishna's arse. Kritavarman was little more than a boy, who led the Andhaka Tribes in Mathura. He had been recently elected to this post, after his father was slain in the Battle of Goverdhun.

'They are here with the Magadhan emissary,' the guard informed Krishna through the door. 'I told them you had left orders not to be disturbed but they insisted you be woken, My Lord.'

It was Satyabhama who spoke. 'It's alright, Jenal, I asked them to come. Let them in.' She turned to Krishna. 'To answer your question, the parley is right now, right here.'

'Now? In your chamber! Satya!' Krishna hurriedly searched for his clothes. But he had barely managed to find one boot when he heard Akrur's voice outside. With more haste than grace, he jumped back into bed and snatched up the covers. He glared at Satyabhama, the silver speckles in his eyes glittering accusingly.

'Well, that's what you get for cheating in a wager. Now behave, they are here.'

Akrur walked in pompously, without any salutation to the couple, but stopped short when he saw Krishna. He cut a gluttonous figure in a robe of purple silk with a ring of cows worked upon the right breast in golden thread. It fit him badly, bulging around his paunch. His hair was neatly combed, scented with oils and brushed straight back from the deceptively soft lines of his face. The scratched caste mark on his neck fooled no one. If there was ever a quintessential image of a Drachma, Akrur fitted it like clay in a mould.

'Lord Krishna, you should dress this way when you come to the Senate, to allow all your worshippers to truly admire you as Yami created you.' He chuckled.

Krishna scowled but before he could answer, Kritavarman entered next, modestly dressed in Mathuran blue. Akrur had helped him with the transition to Chief, from kindness no doubt, though there was gossip he had done it to sway the Andhaka vote in the Senate: gossip started by Krishna himself. But what grabbed Krishna's attention was the boy who followed close on Kritavarman's heels.

Clad in a brown hide shirt, his long wild hair was confined in braids adorned with feather fetishes. His roughspun breeches were ribboned with leather stitching.

'May I introduce,' Akrur started in a honeyed voice, 'Lord Eklavvya, Acting War-Chief of the Valkas? Lord Eklavvya, I must apologize for Lord Krishna's state of ah… undress. The war bears differently on each of us. Some take it *harder* than others.'

'What can one do, Lord Akrur, when I have to do all the running around for you?' Krishna jerked his chin at Akrur's ponderous belly. Half-naked or not, Krishna was not going to be thwarted in words by a charlatan. His eyes swung to the newcomer. Krishna noticed a thumb was missing from the right hand. The boy's eyes looked guileless, yet they roved ceaselessly. 'Greetings, Lord Eklavvya,' he addressed him in Valkan.

'Eklavvya is adequately gratified by your formal, nay flattering, welcome, My Lord.' Eklavvya surprised everyone by answering in High Sanskrit. 'But Eklavvya must confess he is no Lord. He is just an inquisitive inhabitant of the forests, who begged for the chance to come to cast curious eyes upon this joyous event. A simple "Eklavvya" will suffice to appease his anticipating heart. And as for Lord Krishna's state, well Eklavvya couldn't be more grateful, seeing how he has taken cognizance of Valkan culture, where we often host talks naked.'

Suddenly, silence had a sound. Everyone was staring at Eklavvya. Krishna himself narrowed his eyes at the boy. Valkas were forestfolk, just one of the tribes that haunted the woodlands of the Empire, and were rather vocal against all things urban. It had been odd to find one of them so far from home. He had initially wondered why Magadh had sent a Valka as an emissary. They were uncouth savages who barely spoke Sanskrit and took offence at the slightest provocation. Hardly the first choice for ambassador to a parley. Yet Eklavvya spoke the language of nobles flawlessly. A little too flawlessly for his understanding.

'You are welcome, Eklavvya,' Krishna finally managed to say. 'It is our honour to receive such an erudite emissary in times of such turmoil.'

The Valka bowed again. 'So, to matters at hand, Eklavvya supposes you enviable warriors are curious as to what he has to say in this momentous meeting of Magadh and Mathura?'

Akrur turned to give Krishna a queer look. *The feeling is mutual,* Krishna indicated with a shrug for he could barely keep track of what Eklavvya was saying. He turned to Satyabhama, who was smiling at the boy. *Trust Satyabhama to gravitate towards mavericks.*

'Before we begin, I must ask,' Akrur said, the fingers of his right hand tapping his left knuckles. 'You know, out of curiosity after today's events at the Third Sister. What is the Yaksha's real name? We have often wondered about the name of our... worthy adversary. We were hoping you could tell us.'

Krishna found himself leaning in despite the lack of tact on Akrur's part. The identity of the Yaksha was Magadh's best kept secret. Even Krishna's spies had returned with naught. If Akrur thought he could beguile this naïve boy into revealing the secret, well Krishna hoped Akrur was shifty enough to succeed.

'Birth names are but contrivances by enthusiastic breeders to proclaim to the world their ownership over the fate of their progeny, my dear Lord Akrur,' Eklavvya answered. 'The name preferred, Eklavvya thinks, should be the name that enemies bestow upon one. It is only fair, no, when they have striven so hard to deserve such a distinction. The name by which My Lord has addressed the Yaksha is sweet and short enough, and is the name by which the Yaksha, Eklavvya is sure, would like to be addressed for future correspondence,' Eklavvya explained with a beatific smile as he sat down at the edge of the bed.

While Krishna found himself at his wit's end merely trying to decipher his meaning, Satyabhama nodded. 'Well said.'

Akrur rubbed his temples in confusion. 'In that case, say your piece, Emissary.'

Eklavvya handed a scroll to Lord Akrur and turned his attention to the tankard of ale and dish of half-eaten strawberries at his elbow. 'Such wondrous hospitality, Krishna of Gokul,' the Valka sighed as he took a bite of the fruit and poured the ale into the glass beside the tankard. 'Eklavvya's insides groan with orgasmic pleasure. And this ale, so deliciously warm, such a relief from the vagaries of the weather. But Eklavvya wonders why the glass feels so slippery.'

Krishna draped the sheet around himself to veil his midriff, which gleamed with yoghurt residue, and went to stand behind Akrur, reading the contents of the scroll over the Senator's shoulder.

'What does it say?' Kritavarman asked impatiently.

'*Daeva take me!*' Akrur cursed. 'Princess Prapti has... left us. The Emperor has declared a mourning period of a year. A period when there shall be no war. A period of peace, it says,' Lord Akrur announced suspiciously. 'An Armistice.' Krishna exchanged a glance with Satyabhama as Akrur continued, 'It also stipulates that the conquered Mathuran territories will remain theirs. If they are not provoked, they will not attack. The unconquered regions remain ours, and the taxes and levies on them as well.'

'Sounds suspiciously fair,' Satyabhama remarked, still eyeing the Valka boy, who was busy emptying the tankard.

'But...' Akrur raised a finger. 'Magadh will establish a blockade in the East to stop Pragjyotishan tribute from coming into Mathura.'

'Ah...' Krishna turned away, the sheet trailing behind him as he went to stand by the window, half bathed in dawnlight.

Pragjyotisha was not a vassal of Mathura, but when Krishna had formed the Republic, he had got the world's attention by marching into it, and defeating the Rakshasa King of the eastern kingdom of Pragjyotisha. It had not been by means that could be termed by the book. But as victors, they could re-write that book or toss it into the fire for all Krishna cared. The Mathurans were obviously unable to hold the region and had been more than happy to receive the annual bounty of gold agreed upon by a Vachan between the two powers.

The tension in the room was palpable, the situation threatening to go south at the flash of a sword. Akrur wore an expressionless mask but his flexing belly revealed he was seething. Justifiably so, for Pragjyotishan tribute was the one thing standing between Mathura and total annihilation.

'Eklavvya.' Akrur raised his hands in protest. 'Armistice does not mean cutting off an arm. The tribute itself—'

'Why does Mathura need tribute, Lord Akrur? Lord Krishna could always use the magical *Syamantaka*, which his worshippers rave about,' Eklavvya mumbled, his mouth full, but they got the gist.

Syamantaka was Krishna's infamous magical jewel that bards sang about across the realm. It was said to produce copious amount of gold when rubbed against one's chest. It was how the world believed Mathura had survived against Magadh. Whenever men found it hard to justify success, they inevitably fell back on luck as the reason. And if the success was completely unimaginable to their feeble minds, they called it magic.

Except that in this case it was true.

'Surely, Eklavvya, you don't believe in such hogwash,' Lord Kritavarman snorted derisively.

'Eklavvya doesn't know what to believe, you know. All he sees is a tiny cow being crushed by the jaws of a lion for over a decade, yet somehow, Eklavvya sees men and women dress in silks here, deal in diamonds, and erect the finest looking wine stalls. Even their chambers,' Eklavvya sniffed the air around him, 'smell of berries and yoghurt. Strange, don't you think, for Mathura to find such an inexhaustible resource of coin, its industrious workers notwithstanding?'

'Be that as it may,' Lord Akrur said, flapping his hands as if to shoo off a fly, 'it is too harsh. The East is where most of our trade comes from.'

'On one condition,' Krishna stated, ignoring Akrur's quizzical eye. 'While we will not ask Pragjyotisha for our rightful tribute till next winter, we will be at liberty to trade in the West, from which region *you* will keep away. You take the East from us. We get the West.'

'The dance of diplomacy!' Eklavvya cried, catching them unawares with his boyish enthusiasm. 'For Krishna to so easily give away the East... the issues it opens up consist of infinite possibilities of which virtually one and all possess confounding implications. But what? What, indeed? Ah...' he glanced at Akrur's cocked eye, and then towards Krishna, 'even Lord Akrur is not aware, is he, Lord Krishna? The Mathuran Senators seem to be a skein of geese rather than the line of racing horses as the Magadhans were led to believe. Alas, it falls to the humble curious mind of yours truly, Eklavvya, to disentangle this knot of conspiracies, and pierce this veil of diplomacy. But Eklavvya must confess, even he cannot, at this juncture, see what could be Mathura's salvation from the West, assuming, of course, the extant and existing geopolitical realities and variables are taken as a constant.'

Lord Kritavarman massaged his temple. 'I do not understand a word that comes out of your mouth, Emissary.'

But Akrur had understood. A frozen moment of distrust wedged itself in the space between them.

Ignoring Akrur, Krishna appraised the Valka in admiration and irritation. *Your affectations are but a ruse, are they not?* While the boy did not know what was planned, he realized there was indeed a plan. Jarasandh had chosen well. How was it he had never heard of this boy?

Eklavvya cleared his throat. 'We agree to the terms.'

Krishna nodded, ignoring the shocked faces and staring eyes around him.

Akrur walked to Krishna and seized his arm to whisper, 'You can't agree on our behalf, Lord Krishna! There is a Senate, a process...'

'Lord Akrur.' Krishna placed a hand on Akrur's shoulder. 'I suppose you should escort Eklavvya to the lawscribe to solemnize our understanding. We can always *celebrate* later.'

Akrur looked like he would burst. But, to his credit, he held his peace and walked out without a word. Eklavvya chirped and followed. Kritavarman paused only to say, 'Akrur will have words for you, Lord Krishna,' before leaving Satyabhama and Krishna alone once more.

'So, what now?' Satyabhama asked, returning to comb her hair before the mirror. 'You've run out of funds. The Third Sister almost fell yesterday. You've no friends left in the East or,' she pointed at the retreating figures of Akrur and Kritavarman, 'the Senate. You have just a year before Magadh returns with its entire might against Mathura. What are you going to do?'

'I'm working on it,' said Krishna with a half-smile. 'For now, we're going on a much-needed vacation.'

SHISHUPAL

I

It is said that the greatest gift the Gods can give you is to *forget* about you. And Shishupal wanted nothing more than to spend his life unnoticed by the Gods. A life unnoticed by the Gods is boring and unimaginative, but a happy and long one. And he worked hard to make his life precisely thus. He had toiled in the army of the Empire, dutifully rising to the rank of Claw in the Imperial Forces, then retiring at the ripe age of thirty, on moral grounds, disgusted with reports of the Yaksha's gruesome acts of war. Now he served as the lazy Commander of the Crimson Cloaks, the Capital's Peace Enforcers, much to the Emperor's chagrin. For some unfathomable reason, the Emperor had considered him to be a promising protégé; a case of mistaken identity no doubt.

Had the dice of fate thrown a six instead of a one, Shishupal would have now been a Prince. He was the son of Lord Damogjosha, erstwhile King of Chedi, now Vassal Lord of the Empire. If the Magadhans had not marched into Chedi all those decades ago, Shishupal's fate would have been to labour on a throne, hold court, decide tariffs, and perform other such hazardous duties. But the good old Empire had marched into Chedi, razed a few kingly buildings, and would no doubt have indulged in more fanfare had Shishupal's father not bent the knee before Jarasandh.

Shishupal had thus been reared in Magadh to ensure Chedi's good behaviour. A 'ward' they called Shishupal to his face, a 'hostage' behind his back. He did not mind the japes. For Rajgrih, capital of the Magadhan Empire, was as good a place as any to grow up in.

Though the Emperor had not paid any attention to Shishupal for the last two summers. Ever since Shishupal had resigned his commission as a Claw, he had moved out of the Emperor's peripheral vision – a shadowy place Shishupal embraced. But then, the Emperor paid little attention to anything these days; not since his last surviving daughter had impaled herself on the palace gates. He had even imposed an armistice on the blasted war with Mathura. Not that it made any difference to Shishupal. His evenings were filled with quiet contemplation, and Shishupal lit a candle to the Gods every day, to keep his life just this way.

It was during the performance of one such ritual candle lighting that there came a heavy knocking on Shishupal's door. It was a public holiday and Shishupal tried to pretend he was not home. But just then the matchstick in his hand flamed into life, betraying his presence. Grudgingly, he rose and opened the door, only to be informed the Emperor required his presence urgently at Lady Rasha's mansion in Lion's Tooth. Shishupal cast a look of betrayal at the idol of Xath beside his bed, then, grabbing his cloak, rushed off like a cyclone to answer the imperial summons.

Lion's Tooth was an incredibly choice part of Rajgrih, high above the River Ganga, away from its all-encompassing stench. The residents of Lion's Tooth came from old money, which usually meant vast lands, honour and glory, but little coin. These old families all had Ksharjan blood, having earned their holdings and power through robbing, looting and such, till people stopped questioning their title deeds. It was whispered that old money was better than new, the coin now amassed by the Drachmas, though Shishupal had never possessed enough of either to appreciate the distinction.

He rubbed his half-sleeved armour in an attempt to polish it as he hurried to the rendezvous point. He needed to look proper. People in Lion's Tooth were so snobbish they did not even use the city-run garbage collection or scribe services for fear of their Resht or Drachma pedigree. Even with the onslaught of the Emperor's new faith that preached equality amongst castes, the Lion's Tooth held out in arrogant defiance.

Lady Rasha's house was not difficult to find. Shishupal had passed the ageing façade of her towering mansion many times in the course of his official duties. She was the widow of Lord Gardhon Visht. Shishupal had never met her personally for the rumours of witchcraft had kept him at bay. He reckoned he would have liked to know her, considering both of them had their lives destroyed by the same person. So, rumours of witchcraft notwithstanding, Shishupal hoped that when her door opened to his knock, he could set things right and make a new friend. He surely needed one in his corner if the Emperor was inside, waiting for him.

Taking a deep breath, clearing his throat, brushing a sleeve over the helmet he held, he knocked. He thought he heard something or someone howling at the back of the house. The door finally opened. An olive-skinned apparition loomed over him. Over legs draped in gladiator strips, the apparition wore a knee-length red-rimmed white skirt that doubled as a drape over one shoulder, leaving the other bare. The entire mess was held fast by a red cloak.

'Ah, a member of the Crimson Cloaks, no less!' Shishupal found himself grabbed by the arm and pulled inside. 'My good man,' said the foreigner in a thick accent, 'you come opportunely. Now tell me, do you know anything about *mating*?'

II

'It's about Surajmukhi Rahami, you know,' said the foreigner, as if that explained all. 'Despite what Lady Rasha says, I don't think Surajmukhi is capable of it.' The man dropped a sly wink. 'Maybe we could hold her so you can do your bit, which is obviously the trickier part. I'll keep her legs wide apart.'

Shishupal did not want to image what this odd man was talking about, or indeed what the 'tricky part' was. Nor did he know any Surajmukhi. Perhaps the man in the saree was part of a cult of sex-crazed sodomites. Shishupal knew the rich had a different way of doing things, but this was taking things too far really.

'Sir… *Madame…*' he stammered, not wishing to offend.

'Sir, your ignorance does you no credit. This is a toga. *Malaka!* You Vedans are imbeciles when it comes to fashion.'

A Greek! Light forbid. A Mlecchá. It was said that Mlecchás were unclean; something about not using water to wash the arse. Shishupal was sure it was pure fiction, jingoism. Surely the Greeks bathed regularly and had large containers of water in the privy? 'Be that as it may, Sir, I am an Officer of the Empire and I must warn you that rape breaks the most severe laws of the land.' *And probably all the rules of mankind,* he thought. 'I must advise you to release Lady Surajmukhi immediately.'

'What are you talking about, man?' The Greek was clearly nonplussed.

'What, indeed, are you talking about, Claw?' The icy voice made Shishupal tremble. Lady Rasha strode forward. 'Surajmukhi is my *bloody* griffin.'

III

Though she barely reached Shishupal's shoulder, Lady Rasha was a towering figure in her own right. Perhaps because of her differently coloured eyes, one a grassy green, the other oceanic blue, and the way her voice sounded like the cracking of ice in spring, or maybe because she cradled a half lion, half eagle, Lady Rasha was rather difficult to ignore. Her heart-shaped face with its aquiline nose sat elegantly with the blood marks on her cheekbones. Many called her beautiful. Some called her abandoned. Everyone called her dangerous.

It took some time to clear the confusion. Shishupal felt like an idiot, but in his defence, he had never heard of a 'griffin breeder'. Normal people did not think of mating an eagle with a lioness. But he could sympathize with the obsession. Ever since they had seen

Krishna ride into the air on a griffin, the Magadhans had been obsessed with obtaining griffins of their own. It was obviously unfair. The Magadhans had a goddamned lion as their sigil. The Mathurans had a cow. If Krishna had flown on a cow with wings, Shishupal was sure no one would have given it a second thought. But a half-lion, now that was difficult to swallow for any proud Magadhan. Adventurers and opportunists had scanned the known world for griffins, but come back empty-handed. They did find a few eggs, but these did not hatch. And thank the Light for that! As if a cat's hump and a tail on an eagle made it somehow a fine idea to climb on its back!

Lady Rasha seemed to be, however, in the business of using these so-called retrieved eggs to create a *creature magnificus*, but progress was slow. Surajmukhi was an adult griffin, yet she was the size of a puppy. Huddled on Lady Rasha's lap, the creature looked positively timid, rather than the roaring lion-bodied eagle customers would pay gold for.

'The Emperor is running late, I see,' Lady Rasha said, the consonants sharp enough to cut through teak wood.

'The Emperor never runs late, my dear Lady, it is we who are early,' interjected Shalya Madrin, Lord of Madra, who had been listening intently to the conversation.

Shishupal had no way to verify it as he did not get around much, but Shalya seemed to be an important Lord. Anyone whose paunch walked into the room before the rest of him was surely most important. Shalya, however, soon lost Shishupal's attention, which was now focused on a more pressing problem. Surajmukhi, who had trotted up to him, had placed her muzzle between his legs. She was a small thing. But what Surajmukhi lacked in size she made up for with her piercing glare. She looked up now at Shishupal, gently drooling something acidic over his thighs. He made vicious jerking motions to dislodge the creature.

'You know,' Lady Rasha said, 'if it's a bother, you can just pat her underside. Oh, don't worry. Unfortunately, they don't bite. As Kalyavan has informed you, her body proportions do not permit her legs to be opened for mating. It's *chop chop* for the tragic thing.' Shishupal had no interest in touching the griffin's belly, so he remained silent, getting used to the uncomfortable feeling of a malformed eagle getting comfortable against his nether regions.

'And as for you, Lord Shalya, if I had a penchant for banal quotes, I would've studied today's horoscope again.'

Shalya laughed. 'Guilty. But if the stars do capture your attention, may I interest you in a prophecy?'

The Greek, who was lounging on a divan, groaned. 'Not again, Lord Shalya,' he complained weakly. It was apparent he really wanted the story to be told. He cut quite a dashing figure, foreign blood aside. Shishupal had heard tales of this Kalyavan – a civilized warlord of the North-West, who led the Vedan-Greeks, the Yavanas, on raids across the water-starved West.

'Pray tell,' Lady Rasha replied frostily.

Shalya coughed. Assuming a voice appropriate to the recitation of prophecy, he intoned: '*No Man born in this Age can kill Kalyavan, the Last of his Kind.*'

Shishupal frowned. That was vague. He was well read enough to know they were in the Age of Dwapar, and an Age was roughly ten thousand years, and Dwapar was nowhere close to its twilight. They might as well have kept it simple and declared Kalyavan invincible. Unfortunately for all of them, prophets often thought of themselves as poets. Not that Shishupal believed in such blather.

Lady Rasha seemed to share his reservations. 'So, if I were to take the dagger from your belt right now and slowly slice your throat, you would let me?'

'My dear Lady Rasha, I would let you cut me in *any* way you desired,' Kalyavan said gallantly, rising, apparently in ignorance of the obscene yawning cavity his toga had exposed; or worse, fully aware of it.

'Lord Kalyavan…' Shishupal began.

'Call me Kalyavan,' he smiled.

Gods, he is just a boy! 'Kalyavan, speak that way to Lady Rasha again and we will discover the truth about that prophecy; whether no man born…' he fumbled.

'In this Age,' Shalya supplied.

'Yes, born in this Age, can *imprison* Kalyavan, the Last of his Kind.'

Shalya laughed. 'I like this one. But I feel there may be some credence to it, Claw.' Shishupal groaned at the title but felt it impolite to enlighten the Lord of Madra about his voluntary demotion. 'Our dear Kalyavan here has never lost a battle, a duel or even a raid for that matter. Unbeaten. He has… I don't know… killed thousands without a scratch on his perfect olive skin.'

'Why, Lord Shalya, it sounds like you are in love,' Lady Rasha said. 'Maybe you should give up your seat in the Hastina Union's Council of Eight so that you can spend more time with the lad.'

'It is envy, Lady Rasha, not love. For there was a time my belly looked like his, rather than one that might have given him birth.'

The conversation stopped dramatically as the imperial horn sounded outside. Surajmukhi hastened away from Shishupal's thighs to the safer spaces behind Lady Rasha's skirts. An appropriate response, considering the Emperor had arrived.

IV

One of Lady Rasha's attendants wheeled a silver-domed cart towards the august gathering and slid it into place beside the Emperor's chair. Shishupal saw the cart held a gleaming golden urn of wine, and sweetmeats in the form of lions, painted in the colours of Magadh.

'If you do not consider it an affront to bite into the sigil of Magadh, Your Grace, pray partake of these small confections, a mark of my cook's reverence, I assure you.'

'It seems you are trying to make a point, Lady Rasha,' the Emperor said without a trace of humour.

Shishupal remembered the Emperor from his days as a Ward of State – the fiercest warrior of the realm, a peerless lion, a giant among Kings. He was certainly bigger than most, with broad shoulders and a chest shaped like the end of a mace. The jaw beneath his wild beard was wide and sharp. But his shadowy eyes drooped in a defeated face, a dogged reminder of the man he used to be. A faint blue tinge streaked his neck as he spoke to Lady Rasha. Jarasandh brought to mind an old lion forced out of retirement only to find he now ruled over a pride of meerkats and warthogs. He had lost interest in life. He was dressed like a commoner, having dispensed with even the imperial gold crown.

A true Emperor does not need one, Shishupal reminded himself as he saw Shalya adjust his own ornate circlet, no doubt feeling overdressed and humbled.

'Just rewarding my cook for keeping his promise to impress,' replied Lady Rasha. She gestured to the attendant waiting in the shadows, to serve the mulled wine.

'You have not given me my griffin yet, have you?'

'Animal husbandry is a difficult science, Emperor. Now, if I could just lay my hands on a *live* griffin…'

The Emperor considered her. 'Do you not prefer your lavish life here? Do you really wish to smuggle yourself into danger and live a life of hardship, only to… well, I don't really know what it is you wish to achieve, my good woman, for you know I have forbidden any—'

'Aye, I know what you have forbidden,' Lady Rasha interrupted him. 'My ambitions are my own to keep. And the Emperor knows the stairs to the temple of blessing is paved with the stones of hardship. And have I not done enough—'

The Emperor raised a hand, eyes closed. He massaged his temples. 'Only because I tire of this… I permit you to be smuggled abroad if you take a Vachan that you will not indulge in anything dishonourable like poisoning.'

Shishupal had no clue what they were talking about but he was aware of Jarasandh's distaste of poison. A craven's weapon, he had called it, when he had disallowed his Council's suggestion to use it against the Usurper. Vengeance is after all a personal affair. And poison is a professional tool, not a personal one.

'If you insist on a poor widow succumbing to your wiles,' Lady Rasha said with a smile on her face, 'then so be it, Your Grace. I will comply.'

'Now show me what Shalya and you have brought for me this time.'

Shishupal spent no effort in attempting to understand what had transpired between the Emperor and Lady Rasha. Best to keep out of the games the powerful played. He was still wondering what *he* was doing here. No one had spoken to him after the ultimatum he had given Kalyavan. He preferred it that way. Invisible. He picked up the wine cup in his hands and inhaled deeply. The fragrance of orange blossom, mingled with pomegranate and lemon grass, rushed up to meet him. When he sipped the warm liquid, the steam gently rolled into his nostrils and ran warmly down his throat. Ahh... Shishupal let out a gratified sigh.

'Your Grace,' Lord Shalya said, with a flourish of hands, 'I wish to introduce a close friend of mine – Kalyavan, Warlord of the Yavanas.'

'A pleasure to finally meet you, Emperor,' Kalyavan said without standing up or even bowing. He flicked a glance sideways. 'Why Shalya, my friend, the Emperor appears almost naked beside your magnificence,' he quipped.

Shishupal almost choked on his wine. *Such insolence!* Remembering his duty, his free hand flashed to his sword. Seeing this, Jarasandh gently shook his head, commanding him to be still.

The Greek raised his hands in a gesture of mock apology. 'My apologies. We Greeks do not know our manners, and have the nasty habit of saying out loud what we think. But it is true, no? Shalya spends more on clothing than the virgins of my court.'

Shishupal noted that Kalyavan was not exaggerating. Shalya's dark blue brocade robe had a score of golden swans embroidered on it. A cloth-of-gold half-cape was casually flung open over one shoulder and fastened with a glittering sapphire brooch. 'There are far worse crimes,' Shalya retorted. 'Like heading to battle in skirts, or to dinner in a saree.'

'You Riverlanders can hardly hope to understand fashion,' Kalyavan said, his lips curled in scorn. With haughty disdain he returned his gaze to Jarasandh. 'I have wished to meet Your Grace for some time. But I confess I had hoped our meeting would be on a battlefield.'

'It is never too late for wishes to be fulfilled, Firelord,' Jarasandh replied, a chill in his deep voice. 'I do own an arena, as it happens.'

'It seems we must content ourselves with words today, Emperor,' Kalyavan replied, his eyes flicking over Jarasandh's large frame. 'But I would like to take you up on that offer sooner than you may wish.'

Shishupal chuckled softly. The Greek was tall and dashing, but Jarasandh was a veritable giant. He may have grown old, but his reputation as a bull in battle had never been questioned.

Shalya hurried into speech, ignoring Kalyavan's impertinence. 'As we all know, the noose around Mathura tightens. Their resources have dwindled significantly. The infighting within the Republic has left its leadership weak. The Usurper and his Senators continue their vigilant tyranny over the people, who cry out for deliverance by the Emperor. There are arrests and hangings every day. The people brim with fury. Vengeance is due.'

'What, no foreplay, Shalya? So unlike you to get straight down to business,' Kalyavan joked in boyish humour. He looked at Jarasandh. 'Finally, eh? Fifteen or sixteen attacks, is it not?' he audaciously questioned the most powerful man in the realm. When Jarasandh did not answer, he continued, 'But what do you need me for? I have no interest in Riverland politics. And when I enter a battle, I swing my sword to slay. From what I've heard, the Emperor withdrew his army from the Mathuran gates on the brink of victory. Too melodramatic for me.'

Shishupal decided to stop sipping his wine altogether before he choked on it again. Lady Rasha's face was unreadable. Shalya looked like he was suffering from a case of loose bowels. It could not have been that Kalyavan did not know the Emperor's daughters had been raped, and his grandchildren smashed to death by miscreants who had broken into the Palace when Mathura had been sacked by traitors. One daughter had died of shock soon after returning to Magadh. The other had killed herself a full moon ago. The Emperor's new religion, Unni Ehtral, had required him to abstain from violence for a year. Bringing the day up so casually to the old bull was an interesting way for Kalyavan to test the prophecy of his own immortality.

'There were *reasons* for that withdrawal, Kalyavan,' Shalya said in the reproving tone a mother adopts when a child misbehaves in front of important guests. 'And you already knew why I have brought you to Rajgrih. What games are you playing?'

'Times have changed, Shalya. Sakas and Tusharas trouble me to the north. I have Gandharans to steal from. And the Balkh Kingdom harass us with their tariffs. So why me? Magadh's army could give *me* sleepless nights. The Emperor does not need my Yavanas,' Kalyavan stated with an elegant shrug.

Shishupal disliked the game Kalyavan was playing. This war of words. But diplomacy demanded that every vagary and vice of its participants be entertained.

'What Sakas and Tusharas?' asked Lady Rasha with a twist of her mouth. 'Spare me such foolishness. You raid their settlements whenever you get bored. And that is often enough, sometimes even when they have paid their tribute. You do not even desire their lands. And you know very well why we need you, Firelord.'

'I am flattered by your knowledge of me, Lady Rasha. But kingdoms are nothing but lines drawn on a map,' Kalyavan remarked casually. 'Constantly realigning them gets wearisome for map-makers.'

'He's run from every chance he's had to rule,' Shalya whispered to Shishupal. *Ah, I can relate to that.* 'Time to bait him. Kalyavan only thirsts for battle, not for power.' He turned to the Greek. 'Are you aware of the Usurper's achievements?'

Kalyavan shrugged. 'The rags-to-riches story. He is an inspiration to my own herders,' he said with exaggerated nonchalance.

'This Usurper defeated Narkasur and brought Pragjyotisha to heel,' Shalya informed him.

It was well known in the taxonomy of power that Aryavrat had four sides on a map. The humid Riverlands in the South below the Ganga was ruled by the Magadhan Empire. The cold Riverlands, north of the Ganga, was divvied amongst a score of kingdoms, most of whom had pledged allegiance to the Hastina Union. Panchal was the only other powerful independent kingdom in the North. The savage Tree Cities of the East was isolated from the rest of the realm by the Remnant Monarch of the Rakshasas. Then there was the dry spice laden world of Westerlands where Kalyavan prowled. And in the center of this world lay Mathura, the buffer between civilizations.

The Greeks might prowl the lands almost five hundred leagues in the opposite direction, but there was scarcely a Vedan who was not aware of the savage East. In his prime, Narkasur had boasted of an army equal to the rest of Aryavrat combined, most of them almond-eyed slaves from the Golden Islands.

'The Usurper's brother, Balram, is unrivalled with his war-mace,' Shalya continued. 'He commanded the armies that defeated Narkasur's army at Guwhat. Lady Satyabhama is said to have slain Narkasur in single combat. Do you see the glory that awaits the slayer of these traitors?'

Despite himself, Kalyavan's face was an open box of childlike curiosity. 'I have always wondered how Mathura managed to triumph over Pragjyotisha.'

It was Jarasandh who answered. 'Narkasur was a mammoth amongst warriors. His defence plan anticipated an attack by someone as powerful as himself, an airavat. Instead, the Usurper worked like a mouse. It does not occur to an airavat the places through which a mouse can scamper.'

'You think him so low, Emperor?'

'As a human, yes. As a strategist, no. A mouse is a hardened survivor, after all.'

Shalya nodded. 'Krishna may be a coward but his mind is unparalleled,' he said carefully. Seeing Jarasandh nod, he continued,

'He sees beyond what our eyes see or our minds comprehend. You must have heard of Asrith Tali.'

'The wealthy cliff-city, whose inhabitants died in the flood,' Kalyavan nodded. 'Terrible business.'

Shishupal nodded absent-mindedly. It was the closest river-state to Mathura and had aligned with the Emperor in the Yamuna Wars. Losing Tali had been a grave strategic loss, a disadvantage that continued to plague the Empire. 'Rotten luck. But nature bends to none.'

'You prove my point,' Shalya sighed. 'We are simple beings, with our naïve world views. We look at disasters as isolated events, disconnected, unable to see the web of cause and effect. A river descends with all its might into the city, killing thousands. We see the effect: destruction. The cause: flood and landslide. Or one might feel like investigating how in the winter prior to the flood, every tree within sight was cut down, including those above the forested hill under whose shade Asrith Tali had prospered for centuries. The river used to flow a league away, beyond the forest on the hill, in greener days.'

Shalya took a sip of wine. 'So why did this happen? Did the people of Tali suddenly become gluttonous, as is the case with any prospering civilization, or did it have to do more with the sudden popularity of Tali as a river port destination, which led to more incoming ferries, and rapacious fishing in the rivers, resulting in scarcity of fish as a food source? So maybe now it stands revealed that the hunger for more grazing animals was to avoid starvation, and the thirst for wood was to support the new demands of shipbuilding, and it was perhaps this that caused the carnivorous deforestation of the cliffside forests. So, were popularity and prosperity the true culprits behind Tali's downfall or... was it the fact that a year past, Krishna had imposed an overnight embargo on the number of ships passing through the Mathuran river port, at great personal loss? An embargo that suddenly deflected dozens of ferries a week to Asrith Tali in their journey to the East.'

Kalyavan's jaw fell. Shishupal shuddered at this tale of unconstrained ambition. He had not known this. Cause and effect. *How simple. Yet how complete the devastation.*

Shalya continued, 'Krishna is the moon behind the cloud, the faceless player in the deadly tapestry of the rise and fall of every town along the Riverlands.'

'Fine, fine, Shalya, your point is taken. Krishna is a formidable foe,' Kalyavan relented, lifting one hand.

'Vanquishing the slayer of Narkasur, is that not the sort of glory you seek?' Shalya asked softly.

Shishupal could see Shalya was attempting to manipulate Kalyavan's youth, his craving for conquest, renown and glory. Kalyavan looked like he was salivating, but then he swallowed and straightened his shoulders in defiance. 'The proposal is just not lucrative enough, Shalya. I too would like to discard my plain toga for a robe studded with jewels, like Shalya. Something shiny red and mythical.'

Oh no, you don't! Shishupal realized what he was going for. He turned to see Jarasandh place his palms flat on the table. Shishupal was sure the Emperor was controlling himself from snatching one of the bottles and smashing it over Kalyavan's head.

'I will attack Mathura from the South and East with all my might once the Armistice is over,' the Emperor spoke, as calmly as he could manage. 'You will attack Mathura from the North-West. And bring your *blazebane* with you.' It sounded ominously like an order. 'When Krishna and Balram are dead, along with the rest of the Mathurans, you can take the credit for being the War General.'

Kalyavan did not utter a word. His expression was unwavering as he waited for what he actually desired. Jarasandh sighed as he leaned back, kneading his eyes with the heel of his palms. 'And once Mathura is won, you will get the Syamantaka jewel. I swear this. You can send me the parchment to seal and sanctify.'

Kalyavan did not pause for so much as a momentary breath. He immediately bent the knee to the Emperor with a flourish.

'My Assyrian sword and my army are at your disposal, Emperor Jarasandh.'

The Mlecchá had anticipated this. Shishupal glanced at Shalya, who looked dissatisfied but gathered himself. 'That... uhm, that is good. Shall we, uhm, now partake of the sumptuous dishes Lady Rasha has prepared for us?'

'Some other day,' Kalyavan said, rather too sharply. He must have realized this from the looks he received, for he added in a softer tone, 'Forgive me, Emperor. I am tired and my time here is short. I wish to take in the delights your fine capital has to offer. Let us break bread when we are well rested and do not have the stink of griffin dung to ruin our appetites. No offence, My Lady. It has been a pleasure.' He took Lady Rasha's hand without permission and softly kissed the air above her palm. Shishupal wondered what that felt like, then ferociously evicted the thought from his mind.

'Will I be seeing you at the Panchalan swayamvar, Emperor?' enquired Kalyavan casually.

'Perhaps,' Jarasandh replied, his voice hard.

Kalyavan was not daunted by this curtness. 'Lord Krishna will be there I hear,' he said nonchalantly. 'And he has this intriguing habit of winning the woman at every swayamvar he attends... by fair means or foul. Something to consider, eh? Imagine if Panchal joined the Yamuna Wars.' He let the dire words hang in the air. 'Shalya, I hope the accommodations you have arranged will be as pleasurable as always? Your servant, Emperor.' Kalyavan turned and strode out of Lady Rasha's mansion without waiting for the Emperor's permission to retire.

Did Kalyavan really not know he was a hair's breadth from being flayed in the most imaginative way possible? But Jarasandh apparently had other things to engage him and gave Shishupal no orders.

Not so Shalya. Looking deeply troubled by the bargain, he said, 'Your Grace, the Syamantaka! I apologize for the Greek. I didn't know he was going to ask for that. It is too steep a price, even for *his* support.'

'What's a Syamantaka I have never beheld, to the storm that has wreaked havoc in my life?' Jarasandh asked, his voice strangled by memories. 'No, I need Kalyavan. Krishna is the kind of fire you don't throw water on. You suck the air out of the room and watch him fade. Kalyavan's blazebane and his attack from the North-West will choke off the Mathuran supply lines.'

Ah, blazebane... that's why he is called Firelord. That was his real contribution, apart from his charming personality. Fire that could not be extinguished by water. Fire that pierced armour and spread on the slightest breeze. It was said the blue flames of blazebane had been given to Mortals by the Gods for the war against the Daevas, but it seemed only the Greeks had been wise enough to take notes.

But Shalya wasn't done. 'I still seek forgiveness on Kalyavan's behalf, for both his demeanour and his demands. I regret I must entertain him for the next week. My treasury will be half empty by the end of the ordeal.'

Jarasandh, however, was in a pensive frame of mind. 'Haughty, reckless, and full of empty chivalry. But not without honour. Not yet. I felt I was talking to myself; a younger version of me,' he admitted sadly. 'A green boy, more like to be brave than wise. But arrogance is a poison... it seeps into your soul when you've had the misfortune of winning every hand. Every man should lose a battle in youth to stay alive in wars when old, eh, Shishupal? Don't you agree?'

If this was all he was going to be asked to lend his expertise on, he was glad. 'Indeed, Your Grace.'

'Now, Shishupal, you must be wondering why I brought you here, away from the shadows of anonymity you prefer, unlike your brother. Where, by the way, is Dantavakra?'

Probably seducing the daughters of your important nobles. 'Preparing for the tournament no doubt, Your Grace.'

'Many wagers on him, I hear,' Lady Rasha added.

Not mine. 'We must hope he brings them fortune.'

'You have heard of this swayamvar of the Panchalan Princess. What's her name?'

'Draupadi, Your Grace,' Lady Rasha answered. 'I hear all sorts of Vedan heroes are going there to participate. The winner will receive a handsome dowry, no doubt. Chedi could use some dowry.'

Swayamvars were quirky ways for the powerful to bestow their daughters in marriage. There were the auction swayamvars, the pageant swayamvars, the tournament swayamvars, the heavy-bow-lifting swayamvars, the find-and-kiss-the-sleeping-princess swayamvars, the slay-the-local-monster swayamvars, the blindfold swayamvars, and even the solve-a-riddle swayamvars for the more intellectually inclined. Recent liberalism had even seen a few swayamvars where the man chose his wife from amongst a cache of willing participants. No two swayamvars were ever the same, but the basic premise was that the bride-to-be could choose her tormentor for life from amongst the assembled suitors. Over the centuries, different interpretations had been given for 'choice'. But none of these ever mistook 'choice' to mean choice of the bride herself. The Panchalan swayamvar Jarasandh spoke of was of the *winner-takes-it-all* kind.

Shishupal had no interest whatsoever in swayamvars. It was a cock-fest with a lot of chest-thumping and tail-flashing. He already knew where this was going. His idiot brother would be asked to vie for Draupadi's hand. Well, it was about time Dantavakra settled down. Shishupal leaned back in his chair and took a sip from his goblet.

'She would also bring prestige to the Chedi family.'

'Indeed, Your Grace.'

'So, I have decided that *you* will go to Panchal, and I will accompany you.'

Senses infused with the wondrous wine, he murmured, 'Yes, Your Grace.' Suddenly, he noticed Lady Rasha's eyes flash towards him, a wicked smile on her lips. Hastily, he played the Emperor's words in his mind again. The hot wine spilled onto his lap. 'Your Grace... I... I am honoured, but I am a married man!' Shishupal protested feebly. Everyone knew he and his wife were estranged, that she lived in Chedi with their son.

'So?' Lady Rasha enquired, brows uplifted in gentle malice. 'That didn't stop Krishna from having three wives. Why should it stop you at one?'

Shishupal fumbled for a legal defence but came up empty-handed. 'But... but...' he stammered. 'Surely, my brother...'

'Is best suited to prance on a stage for the best-looking horse,' remarked Lady Rasha.

Shishupal could not disagree with this assessment. If this was a pageantry-swayamvar, no doubt Dantavakra would have been the prized stallion to put your money on. *Damn.* 'But Your Grace...'

'Let me clear the confusion, Shishupal. This is not a request. You *will* go to this swayamvar, wear the finest perfumes coin can buy, and strut like a flamingo before the Princess till she drops her petticoat and begs you to give her the heir to Chedi. Remember the words of Magadh: *We Do Not Bow.* You are one of the finest swordsmen we have, an Imperial Contest winner. You will win the Panchalan girl and her army for me! I will have the smithy forge an Assyrian sword for you. We leave at first light, day after.'

Shishupal's jaw dropped. He should have felt elated, at least about the Assyrian blade, said to be the finest, most expensive sword in the world, but all he felt was lost. He looked down, defeated, his crotch burning from the spilled wine. Surajmukhi stared at him from behind Lady Rasha's skirts. *Two creatures bound for a similar fate*, he thought dismally. *Chop, chop.*

KRISHNA

I

'Are you confident about this?'

Now that was the sort of question one asked *before* a man sharpened his razor. But when he had the mad bull's scrotum tied in threads, castrating implements at the ready, and the beast's legs squirming to smash his skull, surely it was a little too late to enquire whether he was confident about it? 'About as sure as I have been about anything in my life,' Krishna replied as calmly as he could, though he rubbed his thumb nervously over the alien material of the obsidian bridge.

Satyabhama said nothing. Instead, she stared up at the time-worn towers, soaked red in the sunset, that stood on either end of the bridge. She placed a callused hand lightly over his as the day died around them. An unseasonal chill bled from the paved stones at their feet. Under his fidgeting hands, a faint blue light glowed wanly, then spread along the railing of the bridge, like the roots of an invisible carnivorous plant.

'The hour of *Roshnar* is upon us.'

Silver-blue light zig-zagged like luminous veins across the bridge, along the streets, climbing over the shrouded towers, and spreading over the primeval island like spilled mercury on black parchment. And right on cue, the animated gasps from his guests below the bridge filled the evening air. He empathized.

The obsidian found abundantly on the island had been combined with glass by its ancient builders, to construct the city. This strange material had been called numerous names by the small-folk of yore. Frozen Fire. Mithril. The primitive texts of the Saptarishis called it *vaikunshard*. A name lost to time, for no one had actually set eyes on vaikunshard for centuries. That is, until now.

Every day, as the sun was swallowed by the West, vaikunshard fought against the night for a while longer than the rest of the world. It shimmered wanly in the twilight for a few hours, with shades of blue, illuminating the island in hues of sapphire, as if in a bid to defy Nature.

He would just have to come up with a logical explanation for this eerie light. He was still not quite used to it himself. The notion that this island's former dwellers had possessed the power to capture light fascinated and terrified him in equal measure. The vaikunshard on the bridge seemed to read his mind, for it gleamed with a cerulean ferocity, reminding him that he had work to do and could not waste time in idle thought.

'Don't tell them this used to be the City of Daevas,' Satyabhama called over her shoulder as she donned her own inscrutable silver mesh mask and strolled down the bridge to meet the others on the pleasure barge below.

Well, that much was obvious. The Daevas were the haunted slave masters of legend, driven back to their world by Mortals, hundreds of millennia ago. If the Senators even suspected they were in a long-lost Daeva city, they would jump into the sea and take their chances with the sharks rather than remain here a moment longer. Ancient prejudices were hard to break. *Prejudices reminds me I still have to come up with a new name for this place.* The Daevic name *Alantris* would never do.

Krishna took in the ethereal island as he followed Satyabhama to the barge. A network of canals split Alantris into an archipelago of island-esque segments, where the Mathuran nobility were now enjoying the Armistice on their pleasure barges. Around the revellers, guards-for-hire commanded sleek brown cutters, keeping the Republic's peace. Each cutter was rowed by raw recruits from the Mathuran army, using long poles to maintain direction through the drifting chaos of boats. If Roshnar bothered them, they did not show it.

The barge Krishna stepped onto was a double-hulled wooden rectangle named *Nymph's Daughter*. It looked regal as it floated like a small villa on the clay-coloured waters of the canal. The barge could carry a hundred souls with ease, but today it held half that number – only the most powerful men and women of Mathura – its Senators. The earthy aroma from the flowing casks of Vidharbhan wine filled the air. The sound of cups being touched in toast ebbed sweetly around him. Satyabhama emerged from a throng of Senators and handed him a cup, emblazoned with the Mathuran sigil, before disappearing again. The stuff in it was silvery and viscous, showing him a wobbly reflection of his own face. He savoured the scent of anise for a brief moment before taking a sip. Warmth trickled down his throat in a tingling stream.

'Lord Krishna!' Akrur called out drunkenly, greeting him with both hands raised. He pulled off his half-mask of stylized bronze, a rising sun with carved rays spreading from the brow. 'Did the Yaksha kill us? Are we already in heaven?' He pointed up at the bridge, where the vaikunshard glimmered like a ceiling of blue fireflies.

'Lord Akrur, even if that were true, I highly doubt that any of us will end up in heaven.'

'Well said, my friend. Please accept my apologies for having opposed your plan for the Armistice. Oh…' Akrur stepped aside to allow a serving wench, clad only in body paint, to pass. 'Would you please excuse me, My Lord?' He hurried off to trail the wench.

The celebrations had begun hours ago and the Senators were now as drunk and lecherous as Kings. No one had even asked him about Roshnar. What they did ask was whether there were any private rooms below. It was a good thing the families of these Senators were being entertained on barges too swift for the *Nymph's Daughter* to keep up with. The war had clearly been rough on these old souls, and they deserved a break. No wonder the Senators had grabbed the chance of this paid retreat without second thought. *Fools.*

The milk is thick. Krishna put on his mask, designed in the pattern of peacock feathers, and stepped forward to mingle with the guests. *Time to scrape out the yogurt.*

II

The Chief of the Senate was Ugrasen, a centenarian who still retained considerable powers of speech. He had once been King of Mathura. He had doted on his son, Kans, who had rewarded his devotion by deposing and imprisoning his father for life. Royal families were complicated. So, when Krishna decided to install Ugrasen as Head of the Mathuran Republic, one could say Ugrasen was grateful to Krishna, and freely forgave him the murder of his unfilial son.

But Krishna did not stop there. To legitimize his rule, lest his idea of a Republic be cast out on some senatorial whim, adoption papers were drawn up. Through the legal ingenuity of various Acharyas of Law, Krishna was proclaimed to be the grandson of Ugrasen. It was a confounding document of legal jargon with no context for the small-folk. All they were fed was that the cowherd Krishna was somehow the rightful heir to Mathura, and that he had graciously decided that Mathura ought to be ruled by the people.

Fortunately for Krishna, the old man had grown so fond of him that he happily obeyed every instruction that fell from his new grandson's lips, as long as an adequate number of men bowed before him from time to time. Royalty was a habit difficult to outgrow after all.

So, one could rightly surmise that when Ugrasen rapped his gavel for attention on a makeshift podium on the barge, it was in fact Krishna who did so. The Senators shuffled into a crescent, all wearing glorious masks that hid their sneering faces. But not from Krishna. He could mark them out easily. His staunchest foes – Kritavarman, Satwadhan and Akrur – huddled to his left. Satyaki and Balram stood to his right. Satyabhama lounged somewhere at the back. Krishna stood close behind Ugrasen.

'I call the Mathuran Senate to order,' Ugrasen intoned.

The men drunkenly tapped their wrists with two fingers, signifying the Chief had the floor.

'My friends, my fellow republicans. I am honoured to address you all Mathurans on this night. The important ones at least, eh?' Ugrasen offered a toothless grin. His lines had been written by Krishna, but Ugrasen performed them like a thespian at the height of his career.

The Senators hooted their agreement. They smiled genially under their half-masks and nodded, confirming to each other how important they were.

'Lend me your ears, friends. We have matters of profound import to discuss tonight, for I have something grave to confide in you. I waited till you had sampled some of the joy before I plunged deep the dagger of despair.'

Krishna groaned inwardly. *Stick to the lines!*

'What is it, Lord Ugrasen?'

'Mathura is dead!' Ugrasen declared in a voice of doom. 'For the Syamantaka is, regretfully, depleted.'

III

It was as if he had started an avalanche with a soft tap on the boulder. The force of the unleashed onrush was astonishing. Ugrasen barely had to egg the Senators on for they unrolled for him like carpets.

The rumour of the Syamantaka Jewel, unlike many others, had not been spread by Krishna. Some maid must have heard the name. Thereafter, like an unseen wind, it had moved in hushed whispers, mouth to ear. Soon, the myth of this magical jewel, which was so enormous that each tiny chunk of it was worth a thousand gold coins, began doing the rounds in seedy taverns and street corners. It made sense to everyone. After all, how else had Krishna managed to keep the treasury full during the ten-year war with Magadh? How else could he afford three wives? From there, the rumour entered the homes of the merchants, and then the nobility. Balram had to dedicate special guards to protect Krishna's room, for it had been ransacked several times by opportunists in his absence.

It pleased Krishna to fan these rumours and let friends and foes alike think him richer than he was. Many a time the Senate had demanded Krishna reveal the Syamantaka Jewel to them, but he had refused, and the Senate could do nothing about it. It was the myth and magic of the Syamantaka Jewel that had kept riots in Mathura at bay. Without it, someone would surely have come up with the idea of handing over the Senators in chains to the Emperor, and being free of the wretched war forever. And who knew, fetching a reward in the process. After all, the voices that cheered a crowning were the same that brayed at a beheading. But when the ruler had an infinite gold-making jewel, why bother with such things? *Fools.*

But now, with the Syamantaka gone from their imaginations, anguish rushed in to fill the crevasses of the Senators' minds. Without Krishna's magical jewel, their own mortality crystallized before their eyes. Festivities forgotten, the Senators huddled like sheep in a pen, gabbling about the plight brought on by the Yamuna Wars, of the high taxes, of the death tolls, of the territories each Senator had lost from his taxable domain, of how the shadow of death, famine and fear had become familiar to the people, and how this had reduced profits. They rattled on about what they could do to thwart the crisis. Strategies from growing opium, taking loans from the Sindh Guild, and even dipping a finger into the slave trade, were discussed.

Ugrasen, in a show of exemplary oratorial finesse, charted the conversation towards fantasy rather than actual solutions, picturing what the future could be without the enemy at the gates. Of the luxuries they could have had if there was no war budget to fuss over. The naked serving girls and boys promptly re-filled the empty goblets. The fantasy soon drifted to the topic of a new city, a world where they could all begin anew.

Just as Krishna had planned.

'In a new city we could keep the fisher colony at a distance, you know, what with their rotten smells and all,' suggested Asmai, her face hidden behind a gold-rimmed black mask. 'Keep the good folk away from the stench.'

'It always gives my missus a headache,' agreed Gobba.

'And we could outlaw outsiders. Mathura has entertained enough refugees, I say.' The baritone voice belonged to Gamand. The others tapped their wrists in assent.

'Damn right, Senator. Clogging up the Third Sister. Driving property rates down. I haven't been able to sell a prime piece of land for all the squatters that have cropped up around it.' Akrur raised a shaky goblet. Spilled wine trickled down his arm in rivulets.

'Yes! A new city with exclusive land for us Senators, nobles too, if you will, caste notwithstanding,' Maramar chimed in. 'If they pay enough, of course.' He winked at no one in particular.

'No Mlecchás, though,' Gobba stated flatly.

'Oh yes, no Mlecchás. Hate moonskins. Namins yes, for who else will conduct the ritual sanctification of the city? And you can't protect the city without the Ksharjas, and well, you may hate the Drachmas…'

'Hey!' Hiriam, the lawscribe, presumably Drachma, objected. It was hard to tell his caste from the redacted mark on his neck.

Maramar raised his hand pacifically. 'Drachmas are important too. No to Reshts, though.'

So much for equality, thought Krishna.

Whispers hissed among the Senators like reptiles on the move. It was rumoured that Krishna himself was a Resht, though none had dared confirm it, of course. They did not maintain written records in the village Krishna had come from. It was moot anyway, now that his adoption had wiped out any potential birth defects.

'No, no, without Reshts the whole system would collapse. Who would mind the horses, clean the gutters, take the dead out of the city?' Harivansh observed practically, having imbibed less of the Vidarbhan wine than the others.

'No!' Ugrasen coughed harshly. 'New Mathura must be open to all! That is how we built the Republic.'

The Mathuran Republic, in a bid to advertise its openness to investment and prosperity, had diluted many inter-caste barriers when it came to vocations. The move had considerably helped the Senators, considering most were Namins and Drachmas, classes widely considered unsuited to govern. So, theoretically a sweeper's son could now become a farmer, and a farmer's son a soldier. Such things rarely happened in real life, of course, but it did lead to mandatory removal of the caste mark from every Mathuran's neck.

Just as Krishna had desired.

'Ah, yes, yes...' the Senators brayed in unison, perhaps remembering that their masks could only do so much to hide their avarice.

Krishna finally spoke. 'I think,' he said, nodding at the most self-serving Senators, 'that a new city should reserve the best sections for the *deserving*.'

So many said *Aye!* that it almost seemed orchestrated. There followed an intellectual pause as the assembled Senators mentally divided the people they knew into the deserving and the undeserving, placing themselves in the former. Krishna, an amused smile on his face, saw his plan unfold like a scroll as they debated the merits of moving to a new city.

'It would only be fair,' said Akrur slowly, 'but I do not see a new city manifesting just because the fish smell bothers Lord Gobba's missus. No offence.'

'I agree with Lord Akrur,' Satwadhan said. He took another loud gulp from his goblet before continuing, 'Building a new city costs money and time. And where would we even build it? Where would we find Walls like the Three Sisters? Not to forget the Emperor would hunt us down wherever we go.'

The Senators hummed noisy agreement.

'Mathura is providentially located; doubtless blessed by the Gods. Mother Yami caresses our back, the trade routes meet

at our door. It provides a good living. It's just this damn war...'
Vanisth said grandiloquently. Whoever had redacted the Namin
caste mark on his neck had clearly done a bad job.

'Agreed, Senator,' said the Chief. 'Truly, the good folk of the
Republic have fallen under the heel of a tyrant, and this war is
slowly crushing us. But where can we go? Mathura has been
ravaged. Its extended territories gone. The Yaksha has seared our
souls with his barbarity...'

'And poisoned our wells!'

'Looted our caravans!'

'Bleached our farmlands!'

'If only a magical city apparated out of nowhere...' Satyaki said,
his voice touched with the melancholic wistfulness of youth. He
was the youngest Senator from the Vrishni Sangha, nominated
thanks to Krishna's generosity when it came to bribes.

Things were going well. Surely, for all their narcissistic stupidity,
one of them would be inspired enough to make the suggestion he
was waiting for, Krishna mused. He did not have to wait for long.

'What about *this* city, *this* place?' Maramar said suddenly. From
the alien lights of the vaikunshard towers to the snake-like canals,
to the enormous obsidian breakwaters, to the floating barges, the
island shone in dazzling welcome. 'Lord Krishna told us no one
lives here. We could take it.'

'Yes!' Asmai raised her hand. 'I was wondering that too. It looks
abandoned. And so beautiful with its blue lights... Is that a new
kind of torch our Acharyas have invented, Lord Krishna?'

'Something of the sort, Lady Asmai.'

'If the sea is navigable, we could redraw the trade routes,' Gobba
chimed in. His body clumsily swayed with the effort to remain on
his feet. 'It would even connect us to the Far West, the Egyptians,
and other Mlecchá lands.'

'They do love our spices and linens, Lord Gobba,' Gauragriva
added, pawing the wench refilling his cup.

'And our munitions,' Maramar added to a chorus of cheers.
'Cursers, and of course bellowers. Nobody does munitions better
than Mathura.'

Krishna offered a silent prayer in thanks to any God who happened to be listening. He'd been right to trust their rapacity. Sooner rather than later, their malleable minds took them where Krishna wanted them to go.

'A noble idea indeed, Senators,' Ugrasen boomed.

'But it wouldn't work,' said Akrur dourly. 'We cannot just... hold my goblet, love.' He extended his cup to a serving boy, and stood holding the youth's shoulder for support. '... As I was saying, we cannot just walk onto this island and claim it. Surely there are laws against that sort of thing.'

They turned to Hiriam, but Krishna stepped in, resting his goblet on the makeshift podium. 'But what if we *could*?'

'Beg your pardon?' Akrur said. 'Refill it, fool!' he half-spat at the boy, still holding his goblet.

'I said, what if we could? What if, under the prevailing laws, Mathurans could stake a claim to this island? What if we could *buy* it? Hoist our flag, and pay enough kingdoms to recognize us? That is all the *Manusmriti* requires.'

A nervous laugh sounded from the depths of Akrur's stomach as he eyed Krishna suspiciously. 'Well, I wouldn't know much about the Book of Laws but still...'

'And what if I said the island is already bought and paid for, without any expense to the Senate? What if, Lord Gobba, you lived in that mansion over there, looking out to the sea as you woke next to your missus every morning? What if, in exchange for your cramped place in the Noble Quarter, Lady Asmai, you could live there, with your own rooftop garden?'

'That... would be wonderful!' she agreed dreamily.

'It would be marvellous!' Hiriam added, grateful Krishna had the legal answers he did not.

'It will certainly solve my... I mean, many problems.' Gobba nodded.

The other Senators quickly screeched their assent, lest they be left out of such a generous redistribution of assets. Only Balram eyed Krishna suspiciously, but thankfully he did not share his reservations aloud. For the next hour, they discussed the merits of relocation, debating the tariffs they would impose, the societal rules they would relax. By midnight, each of the Senators there had turned into a city planner, each with their own vision of a New Mathura.

'What do you say then, Senators? Do we vote on this now? Seal it on this momentous day? Seize our lives and say *No more!* to tyrants?' Ugrasen cried in a voice so thunderous that Krishna feared the old man's lungs would collapse, along with his plan.

'*No more!*' many voices cried.

'What do you mean, Chief?' Kritavarman asked, hushing the others. He was suddenly sober. The cheers faded as he pulled off his mask. 'I thought we were just discussing the *what-ifs* of life.'

The Chief stepped in with aplomb. 'My son's faults were many...' Ugrasen said, wiping a tear from his eye. 'I can never undo the damage he did to Mathura or the War he brought upon us. I... have sold all my assets, all my jewellery, everything I owned... to buy this island for Mathurans to carry on my legacy. This was the surprise Lord Krishna desired to show you, on my behalf.' He walked into the midst of the Senators, who cleared a circle around him. 'This island is *yours*, bought and paid for.'

The information dropped in front of their mousey little minds like a lump of cheese. There was no bigger trap in the world than a free gift.

'Aye!' the Senators cried and cheered. Many more bowed before Ugrasen, thanking him profusely. 'Let's vote! Let's do this now!"

Naturally there were temperate voices that cautioned against such haste, led by the now clear-headed Kritavarman. 'Sounds rather *daring* to me, you know,' he said. 'I mean... while not wishing to question this grand idea, it does mean the redrawing of maps...' His voice trailed off.

'Yes,' said Akrur. 'That is, er... the Ksharjas' domain. Changing of territory can only be brought about by conquest, and there has been an embargo on that by the Citadel of Meru for the last decade or so.'

'Demarcation, they call it,' Satwadhan informed them dryly. 'Just as warriors and rulers do not go around fiddling with currency and foreign exchange, we as traders cannot go around redrawing maps.'

'Yes, then there are the Saptarishis.' Vanisth scratched at his beard. 'They would erupt under us like a volcano if they catch us doing anything like that.'

'I really don't see why the over-indulged Namins should be our problem,' Krishna said. This was the last lap. The Saptarishis, the puppeteers behind the screen, hadn't been heard of for decades, but Krishna could see their hand in the rise and downfall of dynasties across the realm. The world still feared the Seven. And wisely, so did the Senators. He just had to prod their tiny minds a little further and he would hold Mathura in his grasp. Their astoundingly unintelligent self-obsession had not disappointed him so far. He had to trust it to move over the waves of opposition.

The Senators shuffled uneasily. Then Hiriam spoke. 'Lord Krishna is right. Ksharjas!' He spat sideways into the water, immediately creating a silvery effervescence. 'What do they know about an honest day's work? They treat the comforts of palaces as their birthright.'

Krishna breathed easy. Their mean-minded resentfulness against their former tormentors had prevailed.

'Oh yes, when we created the Republic, all they cared about was the caste of our Senators. Dumb idiots! Don't they know what Republic means?' Paras demanded. He was in charge of the Senate appointments, a man Krishna regularly bribed. The investment had finally paid off.

'Aye!' agreed Asmai. 'They won't even let us women in on their decisions. And where were they when Magadh was at our gates, killing our children? Perhaps Kingdoms are meant to be ruled by Ksharjas, but the scriptures said naught about a Republic!' Heads nodded sagely.

'The same goes for the Namins,' Hiriam added. 'If it weren't for their stupidity, we would never have lost the magic of the Chakras and Mandalas.'

'You know, I have always wondered what they really are?' Asmai said.

'Chakras are lamps of light within a body,' Vanisth explained. 'And Mandalas, oh...' he said dreamily, 'Mandalas were mystical runes, a writing system if you will, that were used in the time of the First Empire to awaken the Elementals. You will find many Mandalas painted on the walls in the ruins of Ayodhya. A dead language, I am afraid,' Vanisth added, sadly. 'But the Chakras and Mandalas are still here, Hiriam. What the realm lost were the Elementals. And the Namins had no hand in it!'

'It may be the wine but I understood none of that, Lord Vanisth,' Asmai admitted, sheepishly.

'With due respect, Lady Asmai, it is too complex a subject for civilians,' Vanisth said.

'That is what you claim,' Satwadhan added tartly. 'Forget Mandalas. They are a myth. Men and women with legendary powers of healing, weapons that could destroy cities, channelling wind and fire!' he scoffed. 'Tales to scare children. Forget the lullabies of the past. Come to the present. Even now, the Namins tell you not to go around doing sacred rituals on your own, on account of only them knowing the Vedas, the universal cosmic balance, and the like. Load of cow dung in my opinion.'

'We-ell...' Vanisth hesitated, annoyed. 'I don't know. I mean, if you get the ritual wrong, it could lead to wasting a lot of good money on pleasing the wrong God. If you are praying for rain and worshipping Varunā, God of Water, it would be a damn shame if Agni, God of Fire, turned up, wouldn't it?'

'Aye, but as Lord Hiriam said, it's you Namins who say that,' said Satyaki thoughtfully. 'Is it any wonder they do not allow us to learn to read and write High Sanskrit? And why is the Sanskrit *we* speak Low Sanskrit? It could've been called Sanskrit II. Why do the Namins deign the rest of us lower than them?'

'Aye,' Kritavarman finally joined the fray. If greed didn't work as a motivator, jealousy was a good second. 'I tell you I think they're onto a good thing and don't want the rest of us to discover their secrets. They are so rich. It's just moving the rosary and chanting gibberish when all's said and done.'

'Never could stand them myself, truth to tell,' Ugrasen opined dourly. 'It was a Namin who told my son to imprison me.'

'Aye, fuck 'em!' Gobba shouted crudely, and the others cheered. 'Fuck anyone who isn't a Mathuran! I say let's vote!'

'Vote,' Asmai seconded.

'Yes, we vote,' Kritavarman relented.

IV

'I see you are rather pleased with yourself,' Balram said the next day, seated opposite Krishna, as his brother was about to break his fast. The vote to move from Mathura to Alantris had been carried by a thunderous majority. Of course, Krishna was pleased with himself.

Nineteen thousand gold sovereigns had already been spent in the last year. The island was half-reconstructed, the city map drawn up, the houses tended to. The island looked beautiful. His *Hastina Game* was well ahead of his original plan, and his *Panchal Game* was beginning to take root. Krishna was certain he could get the Princess Draupadi to follow his advice when it came to her impending nuptials, but he wasn't as sure about the Hastinas. Five brothers, two cousins, and one mess of a family tree. Hastina was a bubbling cauldron that was going to spill over once the Yamuna Wars were done. Krishna did not want to be on the shit end of that dump. He wanted to be away from it all; away from the nonsense of his own wars, so that he could manoeuvre his pawns into warring with each other while he ruled. Ruled over all, from a distance.

'Just how on earth did you find this island?' Balram asked. His face was still strong and taut but lines extended in serried ranks from his eyes and ran down in deep grooves beside his mouth.

Krishna no longer saw the man who had crossed the countryside of land and life with him… the brother had become distant in their journey from rags to royalty, and only the ally remained.

But Krishna smiled. He was too happy for Balram to ruin it just because Balram could never find a reason to smile. The coin from the Syamantaka had kept Mathura afloat, but that ship was sinking too. That had been the truth. No, he had needed more of a magical resolution to his troubles, an out-of-the-world idea. And just like that, in that opportune moment, when he had prayed the Gods would take heed, an out-of-the-world island, belonging to the Age of Heroes, had suddenly resurfaced out of the sea. *Alantris*, the Daevas had called it. It was a city from lore, which had sunk eons ago into the sea, but now rose to aid him to pull off the mother of all manoeuvres.

This was his grand plan. The greatest cover-up in human history. To slip Mathura away, right under the eyes of the Emperor, before the Armistice was over. The Magadhan Empire had no ships in the West. It was a good thing Krishna had a close friend in his father-in-law – Jambavan, who studied blocks that made up a land. It had been Jambavan's extraordinary prediction that Alantris would rise again. And Krishna had made sure he was there with the Mathuran flag when it did. Now that he thought of it, he was reminded that he had to pay Jambavan a visit soon.

'You know me, Brother. Always at the right place at the right time.'

'You took advantage of us,' Akrur groaned from his seat, an edge to his speech. He had drunk enough last night to sustain a small village. He took another sip of the lime juice and groaned again.

'I remember you grabbing enough advantages for yourself, Lord Akrur,' Krishna remarked dryly. 'Why don't you indulge me instead with proof of your penetrating comprehension of Mathuran defences. How do they stand?'

Akrur was spewed up like a broken spider. He had clearly drifted into the arena of the unwell. 'Krita,' he groaned, 'answer him for me, I pray.'

'The Mathuran Walls are strong enough but the Yaksha's technique of using bodies seems to have undermined the Third Sister. Nothing we cannot handle. But we are short of coin. If what you say about the Syamantaka is true, we do not have enough to withstand a long siege. Not in any comfort. And if there are two sieges, not at all.'

'Where did all the coin go?' Balram asked.

'In building underground tunnels, should the Walls ever fall.'

'An absolute waste of money,' Balram grunted, disgusted. 'The Walls are called impregnable for a reason. I daresay the underground tunnels are a sign of lack of faith in the army.'

'I am sure Kans thought the same,' Krishna said.

Balram seethed but settled down. 'Setting history aside, we have doubts, Krishna. Reservations. I know the plan to shift to this island is yours and not the Chief's. It is risky. It is dangerous. It is unpatriotic. It is cowardly. It is sudden and comes from the blue. But I know my little brother has already thought of these things, yet he still promotes such a move. I for one would like to know why.'

No point wasting time. 'The Greek Warlord Kalyavan has joined hands with Jarasandh,' Krishna announced without preamble.

'Bollocks!' Akrur cried, suddenly resuscitated, chin trembling.

'But why?' Satyaki asked, eyes shut in a feeble protest against the light.

'That's absurd!' Kritavarman said nervously. 'Why would the Greeks be interested in venturing so far south? The Riverlands have never concerned them before.'

'And what about the kingdoms between?' Akrur asked. 'There is Madra... Gandhar. And the Sindh Guild... so many powers to contend with. And why didn't the Chief reveal this on the barge last night?'

It was Balram who answered. 'Not all of us have the stomach to digest bitter melons, Senator.' He studied his feet assiduously. 'There are those who would panic, run helter-skelter; some may even decide that Mathura was a lost cause and open the gates the next time the Yaksha of Goverdhun comes knocking. The grave truth is, it is our burden to bear. We, the more able.' Balram frowned as he turned to Krishna. 'I should have been told of this.'

'I am telling you now. My spies say Lord Shalya of Madra arranged the meeting between Jarasandh and Kalyavan,' said Krishna.

'Is Shalya in the fray too?' Akrur's voice sounded like a chicken being throttled. 'Surely that is nonsensical, for Madra is part of the Hastina Union. The Union and the Republic have a treaty. The Union will not take sides.'

Balram shook his head, grasping the situation with great rapidity. 'Shalya is also a war broker. He isn't joining the war but making money from it. This complicates matters.'

Kalyavan was just a boy, all things considered, but he had never lost a battle. A fearsome reputation and a brilliant strategic mind were what Krishna had gathered from his espionage reports.

'Can't we, you know, send someone to assassinate Kalyavan?' Akrur whispered ominously, as if Jarasandh were in the next room.

'A cowardly act,' Balram grunted.

'Wouldn't help,' Kritavarman said. 'Haven't you heard the prophecy?'

'That is just superstition,' Satyaki declared, waving an airy hand.

'You're a young fool, that is all,' Akrur pronounced. 'Prophecies are real. My grandmother had the Long Eye. She once had a vision that I was lifted into the air, coiled in the trunk of a large elephant. Roses surrounded me and wolf cubs played amidst them.'

'Are you sure *you* weren't the elephant?' Satyaki asked.

'Funny.'

But it was not the Greek's invincibility in battle that was causing these powerful Senators concern, it was the Greek Fire Kalyavan possessed. Blazebane. A nasty liquid that, on catching fire, seeped into wood, cloth, leather and even steel and stone. If the Greeks joined hands with the Magadhans, the Sisters would burn and the Mathurans would be caught like foxes in a shepherd's trap.

'What about our allies?' Satyaki asked.

Balram and Krishna both laughed. They had no allies. Mathura was backed into a corner. Krishna knew it was futile to expect help from any neighbouring kingdom. Most dared not affront Jarasandh. The rest would refrain, envious of Mathura's monopoly on the trade routes. Mathura, located at the junction of several important caravan routes, had earned the ire of less fortunate Vedan Kings, who would gladly watch Mathura burn.

'Alright, alright.' Akrur rubbed his arms as if he were alight with blazebane. 'I see why shifting Mathura might make sense. The sea as a protective border is as good, if not better, than the Sisters. My problem is one of manpower and psychology. Shifting the Mathurans out in small numbers could work. But that would mean a reduction of men here. Fewer guards to man the caravans, fewer field-hands, fewer foragers… Well, you get where I'm going with this.'

'Yes, but as the Chief said, the Syamantaka and his own wealth—'

'Yes, yes, we heard it, Lord Krishna, but the Syamantaka Jewel can only take care of so much with its last resources. My issue is about *people* in general. The Gods know I'm not much liked in Mathura.'

'Shocking!' Krishna commented dryly.

Akrur threw him a sour glance. 'There are people who don't like Lord Balram, who don't like Lord Krishna, who don't like the idea of the Republic in general. Only their Mathuran loyalty has united them against the Southerners. But when you ask them to leave for an unknown island, loyalties are bound to shift. And there are a large number of us now, you know, if the last census is to be believed.'

'Your point being?' Balram's voice was brusque.

'One slipped word from a single Mathuran to a Magadhan spy, and the Emperor will forget the Armistice and raze our Walls. And what is worse, we will only have a few men remaining to guard the city, a few farmers to sustain us in a siege, a few… oh hell, you know what I'm talking about.'

'A Vachan,' Satyabhama said, entering the chamber. 'They must all take a Vachan, to pledge their silence.'

The Senators all rose, bowing.

'Lady Satyabhama.' Akrur rubbed his nose absently where she had cracked it a few summers ago.

'I thought you said you were dining with the most powerful, Beloved.' Satyabhama sat down on the seat Kritavarman hastily vacated next to Krishna. 'What then is Lord Akrur doing here?'

'Well, I was just around the corner and thought to visit those who respect and value me,' Akrur responded, deflecting her offence with some skill.

'So…' Satyabhama asked quizzically, 'they weren't home, I take it?'

Akrur laughed awkwardly. 'Lady Satyabhama, you are always yanking my chain.'

'Dove, if I had the chain in my hand, yanking would be the least of your worries,' said Satyabhama with a smile.

Krishna was oddly drawn to the way she emasculated such wealthy, influential men. He shook the thought away. 'Now, about the Vachan, what do you all think?' he asked.

Kritavarman strode to the far end of the room and sat down. 'Aye, that could work.'

'No, it could not!' Akrur retorted hotly. 'Vachans are expensive, *expensive* business. And have you forgotten that they are banned? Even if we find a Black Acharya to do it, they must be well adept, or else…' His fingers flew out to denote an explosion. 'And just the fees of the Namin priests would drive the Republic to insolvency.'

All eyes turned to Krishna again. He smiled. 'Well, why do we have to *tell* the Mathurans that it isn't a proper Vachan? Who is to tell them the one who took their Vachan was not an ordained priest but a dummy?'

'Lie to the people!' Balram said, appalled, almost as if Krishna had asked him to cheat on his wife.

Sometimes Krishna could not help but wish he had been an only child. 'Not lie,' he said placatingly, 'just… not tell them.

Have a person sit in saffron robes and do the thing. Who is to know? The people's fear of burning alive will keep them loyal. We can sprinkle a few real Vachans in as well, and bait the more wretched into revealing it to our agents. They will, of course, burn for such treachery. That will get the word around, and keep tongues still.'

'Nothing like a good roasting to make one a good secret-keeper,' Satyabhama agreed.

'We don't spend any additional coin, apart from what we already pay the Namin priests. And we will, of course, proclaim New Mathura to be a place where the Vedan Pantheon will be worshipped. That'll keep the Namin priests happy.'

'*Say no to Unni Ehtral*,' Satyaki chanted.

'Exactly. The Vedan priests are rather threatened by all these new cults rising on the horizon. This should take care of that.'

Akrur frowned. 'Alright, alright. This could work.'

'It better work my friend, for you will be in charge of our exodus. We must be extremely careful about this, for you are right, one slip and it's armageddon for us all.'

'I'm in charge of this?' Akrur was at once appalled and emboldened. 'I agree that I never feel more alive than when I put my hand inside a lion's jaw, but what if it snaps shut?'

'You don't have to worry about that Senator, for I'll buy you the whistles you need to tame the lion,' Krishna soothed.

'Well, alright then I suppose. My Thieves Guild can take care of it. Guess that's that. I support the plan.'

Kritavarman let out a gusty sigh, then nodded. Krishna turned to Balram. 'Yes, for the sake of our people,' Balram said. 'But mind, no burning of innocents to pull off your Vachan trickery. We taint our souls with such games.'

'Fine,' Krishna agreed, exhausted.

'But what is this city to be called?' Akrur asked.

'Alantris,' Balram answered. Krishna had told him the name of the island last night.

'To Alantris!' said Satyaki.

Krishna shook his head, a half-smile tugging at his lips. 'Not Alantris,' he said, his eyes surveying them with a disquieting gleam. 'It is our Gate to the Future. It will be called the City of Gates: *Dvarka.*'

SHISHUPAL

I

Shishupal was having one of his epiphanies, an out-of-the-body experience, much like a fish being jerked from the placid waters of the lake that had hitherto been its universe, by some cruel god. He was to leave for the Panchalan swayamvar in two days, battle with the heroes of Aryavrat, and somehow bag a fresh new wife.

It was not that he was incapable of such a feat. He could swing a sword well enough. He was, after all, an Imperial Contest winner, the same tournament his brother Dantavakra was currently jousting and goofing around in. But Shishupal had never made wind-sounds with fast sword swipes to catch the female eye. Such posing felt like a sham to him. He had not drawn his sword even when Krishna had run away with his betrothed. Some said, with her consent. Others claimed abduction. But the truth that mattered was that Krishna had wed Rukmini a week later.

Since the incident, Shishupal had grappled equally with his doubts and his anger about what had happened. He nurtured no real desire to kill Krishna, but he would not mind if someone else did the job for him. Now here he was again, headed to yet another swayamvar, where Krishna would no doubt be present, with his ropes and climbing tools at the ready should the Panchalan Princess feel shy about using her own drapes to escape her lonely tower.

Why me? His depressing thoughts were interrupted by a flying splinter that narrowly missed his head to tear into the fabric of the Magadhan banner behind him. Being a Ksharja of royal blood, he had a seat in the upper tiers to watch the Contest. It was a prime position, but it did come with the occupational hazard of dodging stray axes and arrows flung from the arena.

The winner of the Contest received a boon from the Emperor, and could expect doors, otherwise closed, to open for him or her, especially in the Imperial Service. The melee had been going on for hours, and just four warriors remained. Splinters of wood lay scattered around like seeds in a ploughed field during planting season. Light played mysterious tricks, bouncing off dented armour.

It was only by winning the Contest a few years ago that Shishupal had managed to wangle his way out of the Yamuna Wars, disgusted with the Yaksha's gut-wrenching war tactics. He had never met the Yaksha personally, and hoped never to do so. The Emperor's disappointment at the boon Shishupal sought had been crushing, but Shishupal knew he had no other choice. He was all for shock-and-awe and could digest most war crimes, but he drew the line at crimes against humanity.

In the arena, he saw an unhorsed warrior in a blue cloak, holding a long trident in one hand, swing aside to deliver a backhanded blow with his trident to the foreleg of his pursuer's horse. The crowd oohed and aahed as if on cue. The move toppled the horse and flung its rider to the ground, the injured horse falling on top of him. The blue knight raised his trident triumphantly to the crowd, beaming, his infamous crooked teeth showing between bruised lips. *Dantavakra.* Shishupal would have recognized his brother's teeth anywhere. Clearly, the idiot had thrown caution to the wind by refusing to don a helm. The crowd seemed to appreciate this for their cheers drowned the screams of the man buried under his horse, even as his squires rushed to his aid.

Disinterested, Shishupal turned to survey the arena. He could picture how, when stripped bare of humanity, the galleries and stairs stretched over each other like the petals of a rose. Construction was still underway. He saw masons working atop high bamboo scaffolding, shouting in a foreign tongue, even as groans of pain rose from the other end of the arena, where another warrior had just vanquished his foe.

'This arena is quite something,' Shishupal observed to his squire, Mayasur, a half-breed who had come to the city to seek his fortune. Not many forestfolk ran amok in cities. Certainly not any Rakshasas. It had just been Shishupal's ill fortune to have the only one in Rajgrih assigned to him. He had strictly instructed Mayasur to never smile or take off his hood in public. His sharp canines, and the thickness of his hide in a robustly boned face, could frighten even the most liberal of the seculars. But, despite his sheer mass, big even for a Rakshasa, Mayasur was a man of scrolls. 'You look like you've something to say. Spit it out.'

'I did not wish to interrupt you, My Lord...' Mayasur gushed excitedly. 'But it's not an arena. It is technically an arena within an amphitheatre. Though there is a Contest currently in progress, it can be easily used to stage shows and dramas. The overlapping tiers you see there have been designed in a manner to empty the place in minutes without causing a stampede.' Mayasur stepped to the balustrade that guarded the front tier, pointing downwards.

He's my squire and he beckons me! Shishupal shook his head, but obliged. Sand filled the floor of the central arena, but it seemed at odds with the ground around it.

'The actual ground is wood, but it has been covered with sand to give the impression of earth, and also... to ease the pain of a fall.' Mayasur directed Shishupal's gaze to the periphery of the arena space, which seemed to slope gently on all sides. 'A maze of rooms and corridors spans the area beneath the arena, where contestants prepare for their duels above. There is another section on the right...' he leaned closer to Shishupal, 'where I've heard rumours say the Emperor plans to cage beasts of the most terrifying aspect.'

The stunted shape of Surajmukhi came to Shishupal's mind. 'I highly doubt that,' he murmured. But he had to accede that the arena was glorious with its multiple descending tiers of

benches in different colours for the various castes. A true
testament to ingenuity and skill. The last time Jarasandh had
built something so magnificent was when he had raised the Three
Sisters of Mathura.

Shishupal sighed at that memory, and returned to his seat. No
matter the present, the past always seemed like a simpler time.
Jarasandh was seated in the royal box, his face a hard bargain
between indifference and gloom. *It's true for him at least.* Shishupal
reminded himself to engage in small talk. Now that he was headed
to Panchal with the Emperor, he might as well brush up his
conversational skills. He'd learned the hard way that success in life
was inextricably linked to one's ability to make polite, pointless
conversations with anyone and everyone.

'Your Grace, this is a marvel! It is a wonderful creation, fit for
the Gods.'

'Yes indeed,' Mayasur added. 'I hear Nar Ad Muni is all set to
include it in his Wonders—' Shishupal gave him a clout on his ear.
'Ow! Apologies, My Lord.'

'Your delinquent squire isn't far from the truth, Shishupal.'
Jarasandh smiled, barely. 'Nar Ad is planning to visit. Rightly
so. A civilization without vaulting architecture is akin to a man
without a soul. Forgotten and foregone. Some day, the Magadhan
Empire will fall to dust and nothing will remain of it save for this
colossal structure, this *Virangavat.* That is how I want Magadh to
be remembered. Or at least that's what I thought when I started
construction more than a decade ago.'

Shishupal remembered sadly how the Emperor had once been
a guffawing buffoon, when Shishupal himself had been a child;
a man who drank till his liver revolted, and danced until his legs
gave way. Unlike Shishupal's father, Jarasandh had led his army,
fighting multiple but lesser foes, often breaking into booming
laughter the moment their weapons touched his shield – a sound
that struck more terror into their hearts than his mace. But that
laughter was something for the history scrolls now.

Another ancient memory rose in Shishupal's mind, as if tied
with a silver thread to the happy memories of Jarasandh. The

two Magadhan Princesses had never borne him any kindness, treating him as nothing more than a prisoner with privileges. Yet Shishupal could not forget the icy hand that had gripped his heart when he'd seen them return from Mathura after the Usurper's coup, stripped of all their finery, their heads shaved bald. Draped in widow's white, they had been but ghosts of their former arrogant selves. It was then that the Emperor's laughter had left him, replaced by something that was in equal parts sorrowful and sinister.

The cheers of the crowd brought Shishupal back from his wandering reflections. Among the High Lords on his tier, he recognized Lord Hiranyavarman, as sombre as ever since the humiliation he had suffered when his daughter had ended up wedding a Prince of Panchal who turned out to be more of a Princess. Beside him sat Lord Visharada of Kaunti. Shishupal was amused to find him here, but not surprised. *The chains are invisible but he is imprisoned alright.* The Kauntis had sided with Mathura when the war began. After his crushing defeat two winters ago, Visharada was now the biggest supplier of the Empire's soldiers. Such was the way of war.

Saham Dev, called the Young Cub, the haughty, undeserving and imbecile son of the Emperor, and Crown Prince, was seated to one side, his mud-stained sword propped against the back of his chair. The Prince, noticing Shishupal's gaze upon him, gave him a curt nod. It was no court secret that Jarasandh abhorred his son as much he had loved his daughters. Saham was no Lion, that was plain to see, with his limp eye, his fits, his hunched shoulders. Jarasandh could not believe the Crown Prince had been sired from his seed. Why else would he have chosen Shishupal, a man once wed, son of a vassal, to compete for the hand of Draupadi, when his own son sat unfettered at the age of nineteen? Shishupal might have nurtured a lamp of sympathy for the Crown Prince if he had not done everything in his power to deserve his father's scorn. Weakness was one thing, cruelty another.

On the field, yet another combatant had lost to Dantavakra. The first tier roared its approval. '*Chedi!*' the gallery cheered.

'*Dantavakra! Chedi!*' Only two men were left in the fight now, and there was no doubt who the gallery favoured. *The smallfolk love showoffs*, thought Shishupal. Dantavakra, now mounted on an abandoned white steed draped in silver mail, bearing the sigil of a lion on its saddle, spurred his mount towards the last man standing. Who was a rather petite knight in green armour, his emblem too faint for Shishupal to see.

It was bow versus trident. As they closed the distance, the petite knight, atop a black horse, raised his bow and let fly a string of arrows at Dantavakra. Dressed in chainmail, Dantavakra easily deflected the arrows with his shield. But the barrage of arrows was relentless. Quickly replacing his bow with a curved sword, his opponent struck away Dantavakra's shield. The horses, the one white, the other black, circled each other like birds during mating season, the riders exchanging blows. Sword flashed and trident whirled. The trident slipped, barely jabbing the knight's leg. The back of the sword slapped against Dantavakra's head, sending him into what Shishupal hoped was a world of headache. Dantavakra kicked his horse away before the knight could finish him off.

Dantavakra ran his fingers through his silky hair and pulled it back, winking at the crowd. Women swooned, not realizing the fool was losing. He turned his horse in a tight circle and dashed at his foe. Then suddenly, he climbed onto his horse's back and stood upright. Shishupal took a nervous step towards the railing. *Imbecile! There is a real war to fight!*

'Your brother is nothing if not a theatre artiste, Shishupal,' Prince Saham remarked with a grin.

'Duelling is, after all, a form of art, My Prince,' Shishupal retorted.

'We'll see.'

Just then Dantavakra jumped from the saddle and speared his shoulders into his foe. The crowd erupted. They had got their money's worth just to see Dantavakra perform that stunt. Though both combatants fell off their mounts, Shishupal saw how the small knight turned mid-fall, at precisely the right moment, to land on Dantavakra, who took the full impact of both men.

The small knight was quick to rise. He swung around, sat on Dantavakra's stomach and caught him in a vice-like grip between his thighs. The knight picked up Dantavakra's fallen shield and aimed its sharp end towards his chest. *Surrender, you fool!* But his younger brother continued to struggle against him till the knight aimed the shield's edge at Dantavakra's face. Dantavakra tapped the ground forthwith, his palm flailing like a fish on a hook. And that was the end of it.

There were no cheers, no shouts. Clearly, many had lost money. Dantavakra had always been the crowd favourite.

When the small knight took off his helmet Shishupal chuckled to himself, as he discovered the knight's humble height probably had something to do with his age. Shishupal could not stop grinning. Was there anything better than witnessing your obnoxious brother being taught manners? Yes, there was. When the teacher turned out to be just a boy! The young knight's face was as smooth as a baby's bottom, not a hint of a beard in sight. The knight wiped the back of his hand across his sweating forehead. Braids stained with grease and knotted with bone and feather fetishes hung down to his shoulders. He rose unsteadily to his feet and raised Dantavakra's shield in the direction of the royal enclosure – the salute of a champion to his Emperor.

Saham Dev rose, applauding heartily. 'If a boy with nine fingers can vanquish your brother, I daresay it is time Dantavakra needs to start training with steel instead of wood.'

Shishupal ignored the jibe about his brother's immoral reputation. The boy's strange grip on Dantavakra's shield had snared his attention. Blood trickled down the boy's hand, his four-fingered hand, which was awkwardly but firmly holding his shield high. Shishupal's eyes widened so much it looked like he was making room for the shock to move in permanently. It wasn't enough that a boy who should have been fighting off playground bullies had won the Imperial Contest; the boy had done so without a thumb! Shishupal joined in, clapping profusely for such a gifted warrior.

Arena attendants scampered onto the field to help victor and vanquished alike. Shishupal saw the young knight help Dantavakra up, exchanging a few words with him. Dantavakra pushed away the fall of hair from his eyes and wearily shook the victor's hand. He turned to the crowd and raised his trident. Shouts and cheers broke out again. *Idiots!* Cheering as if he had won. All the hard-earned manners will now count for naught.

A high-pitched scream made Shishupal turn. A herd of men were mumbling somewhere close by. He saw Dantavakra exchange a sombre glance with the winner as they hastily moved out of the arena. *What was happening?* White-robed priests marched into the arena with the ominous discipline of an army. *Priests.* Shishupal's mind filled with venom. *Unni Ehtral.* Fanatical worshippers of Xath and Yama. Narag Jhestal, the Head Priest, his head hooded under the sombre white cloak he wore, emerged from nowhere and stepped into the royal enclosure. The crowd quieted, as though the shadow of death had passed over them.

'The Goddess of Light and Life has been kind to these noble warriors for she knows they are her horsemen, who will deliver gifts on her behalf to her twin, Yama, when the time comes.' Jhestal paused for effect as other hooded men began to surround the arena.

'Oh, no, no…' Mayasur whimpered, cowering.

'Don't fret, Mayasur,' Shishupal said, dragging Mayasur to one side. 'You will be in trouble if you show fear.' Shishupal eyed the crowd for anyone who might have overheard. 'Though I still do not understand how the noble families of Magadh permitted the rise of a religion whose idea of faith justifies the abuse of its own devotees.'

'Because it is an ancient instinct to be enslaved, to be in servitude,' Mayasur spoke softly. 'In the past it was the Daevas. Sometimes it is Kings. And now it is the Ehtrals. No different from the Namins, in fact.'

'Namins?' Shishupal asked, surprised.

'The Namins managed to shroud their knowledge from the world, and convince ignorant smallfolk that their lives were somehow valued higher than the rest. As in love, the priests gained true power by withholding it. In this case, withholding knowledge from those whom they considered inferior. And they weren't the only ones in history to do this. The Godlings, or Nardevaks as they are known, inter-bred to keep their lines pure. The same with the ones whose blood was tainted. Uhm, they don't count. They were exterminated. My point is that exclusivity makes something valuable. I suppose once the Ehtrals became popular, they closed their doors. Made it exclusive. And anyone who wasn't quick to embrace it was thrown outside the circle.'

That made sense. Unni Ehtral was a separate faith within the Vedanic ethos. They did not make a new deity but just worshipped one, fanatically, refusing others, fervently – the Cult of Xath, Goddess of Light and Life, and her twin, Yama, God of Darkness and Death. Yama wasn't one of the Vedan Gods, he was one who ferried souls on his buffalo across the Lake of Afterlife for Judgement, an oft-used name for curses by soldiers. But the Ehtrals raised Yama to the status of a deity, a religion within a religion. And that was why the Namins never opposed it, for ultimately it was still the worship of one of their deities. Not before it was too late, anyway.

With the benefit of hindsight, Shishupal could see how the Unni Ehtral grew popular across Magadh, because it never tried to convert the ones with deep pockets, the ones who could have been obstacles on their path to domination. No, they went after the cults of the Lesser Gods. The Vedan Pantheon was formed of the Seven Gods of Fire, Earth, Water, Wind, Light, Darkness and Life. They could only be worshipped in rituals moderated by the Namins. Which was why cults worshipping other deities grew on the fringes of society. You name it, flowers, ocean, tide, winter, disease, tools, everything had a deity that could be worshipped by the poor without paying hefty costs to the Namin priests. And the Namins tolerated these lesser Gods. For these small deities were a cage for the poor, the downtrodden, a path of hope, for without them the poor would rise from their poverty and prowl into palaces, killing kings and princes alike. It had happened before.

And these fringe cults were those that the Unni Ehtral assimilated first, by giving them a chance to worship Xath, as

long as they accepted Yama as a God too. The young who were
frustrated, the ones who could not get women or coin or both, who
burned at being looked down upon condescendingly by the rich
Vedanic royals, these were the easy pickings the Ehtral targeted by
giving them a sense of higher purpose, of empirism entwined with
religion. The Ehtrals knew that resistance to a new religion was too
deeply rooted in the elders of a cult, in the disgruntled priestesses
and priests who would lose power in the face of a new God. So,
the Ehtrals had them assassinated, and worked through the young
to spread their web. By the time the rich liberals of Vedanism
knew it, their servants, their horse groomers, their chamberlains,
their guards, had all turned to the Ehtral. Even joking about the
Ehtral became fraught with dangerous consequences.

'You are right, Mayasur.' Shishupal nodded gravely. 'The
followers of the Ehtral grew not through the lure of power, but
purpose, a far more potent poison. Even when it came to coin,
the Ehtral priests grew filthy rich. They might not have had
royal patronage but only a fool could doubt the power of tiny
contributions from each devotee. And this was when reality
finally dawned on the Magadhan royals, at least the ones who had
resisted the tyranny of a God that revelled in sacrifices. We were
few. They were many.'

Meanwhile Jhestal continued, voice uplifted, certain none
would dare oppose him, 'But the good Xath should not be ignored
as she often is in our single-eyed devotion to Yama. Life needs
life. A life given, not out of necessity, as in death, war or famine.
No. No. Such events lead the soul to Yama. Xath desires not what
is rightfully her brother's.'

The other priests stepped out on either side of Jhestal in semi-
circles that simulated the stretching of wings. They stood silently,
their faces hidden behind their ghastly masks, carved into animal
faces. It was no secret that the Acolytes of Unni Ehtral often
blinded themselves in one eye, and sometimes both if they were
in a particularly compulsive religious fervour.

'A life given out of choice is a gift. To the cause of a just war,
born not of base desire for conquest and imperialism, but love.'

The screams of children, as they were raised on poles, reverberated in the arena. Shishupal gasped, his mind unwilling to comprehend. This had gone... too far. The prisoners were covered with death-flies. They crawled over their faces in aimless paths. Shishupal's gaze fell on the girl closest to where he stood. Blood still flowed from where nails had been driven through flesh and bone. She had no eyes, her breasts had been chopped off... yet her chest was heaving. Molten anger flooded Shishupal's heart. *The girl is still alive. They all are!*

'Goddess of Light and Life,' Jhestal intoned in a voice as deep as hell, 'let the sacrifices of these *Kauntiyas* usher in blessings to our good Emperor. Bless him with iron. Bless him with steel. Bless him with blood.'

The acolytes and the crowd chanted: '*Bless him with blood.*'

Bile rose in Shishupal's throat but he forced it down. Chants rose around the arena, in the name of Xath and Yama. Shishupal could barely suppress his urge to push Jhestal from the royal enclosure to his death below. The bodies of the children continued to dangle an arm's length above the ground as the stones below them became stained crimson. Shishupal turned to look at the Emperor, aghast, a foolish part of his mind still believing Jarasandh would put a stop to this. But the Emperor rose, bowed slightly to the priest, and departed.

'Oh Yama, if you truly are a God, have mercy, mercy on these children...' Shishupal whispered. 'Surely the Emperor cannot have sanctioned this! It is a period of Armistice, peace. This... is unnecessary.' Even as he said the words, he knew he was wrong.

'Was there ever a war where people have not bled unnecessarily, Lord Shishupal?' Visharada spoke beside him, shaking his head, his eyes vacant of all emotion. 'The simple truth, Commander, is that torture is unnecessary.'

'But these are your people, innocent children!'

'Aye,' Visharada agreed. 'I made a choice. I chose Mathura. Now I must make my peace with the outcome.'

Shishupal noticed the dark circles that ringed Visharada's eyes. He was under the influence of opium. Coatings of moongrain dotted his nostrils. A surge of sympathy flooded Shishupal's soul for this defeated King who had lost a lot more than a kingdom. *My Emperor, what have they done to you? What has pushed you to… this?*

A messenger came up to Shishupal and saluted. 'His Grace commands that you see him before you journey north.'

The invisible chains that bound his soul tightened, suffocating Shishupal in their angry embrace. But he merely nodded, making his peace with his fate.

'Mayasur, go home and pack.' Hearing no response, he turned towards the squire, but he had fainted, his body held upright only by the railing on which he leaned limply. Shishupal sighed. 'Have someone bring some water,' he said, but the messenger barely heard him over the collective gasp of fifteen arrows that finally sent the children to sleep.

KRISHNA

I

The wind in the tunnels shrieked to a fierce chorus. Like hungry worms in old wood, the Mathuran miners had ravaged the belly of Mathura to create its twin tunnels. Krishna and Satyaki were winding their way through the twisting path of one of these. Their footfalls sounded hollow in the gloom. Satyaki looked around at the entombing rocks in fear. Tunnels terrified him. To Krishna, this was completely irrational. Yes, tunnels did collapse and people were often buried alive. But so did bridges, walls and roofs.

Krishna shook his head, nudged his fearful companion forward. 'My spies have not reported any suspicions among our neighbours. They think Mathurans are merely enjoying the Armistice with vacations.'

'I hear Akrur is doing a splendid job with the moving operation,' Satyaki said, his voice reedy, breaking on the edge of manhood. 'Slowly and steadily, small batches of nobles are being led through multiple routes to the island.'

Krishna nodded. It was a good thing the clandestine *Operation Dvarka* was being carried on the able shoulders of trustworthy thieves.

The tunnel continued to angle upwards, the warm bedrock turning slippery first, and then wet, bleeding from fissures, perhaps from the Great Baths. *Will have to fix this,* Krishna thought as they slithered along. He was good with tunnels. 'What of essential services?' he asked.

'Yes, that too. In fact, cartloads of farmers, fishermen, and boat-makers are being sent in advance to prepare the island for the others. As instructed, a few of them have been administered the real Vachan. Still a long way to go.'

'A month before the Armistice is over, I wish to see Mathura deserted.'

'Aye.' Satyaki chuckled. 'Akrur says that will be difficult, but he performs well under deadlines. When do *we* move?'

'Two full moons before the end of the Armistice. If we move now, the vultures will immediately take note. We have to be the last ones to leave. Ah, we are here.'

A shaft of light appeared ahead. They had reached the mouth of the tunnel. Here, the tunnel narrowed, and the pair were forced to duck into a shambling crouch to get to the exit. Krishna stepped back just before the door to let Satyaki pass, then followed him outside.

They emerged into an alley of the Third District, that led to the Market Square, which had been turned into a mock battlefield. A howling mob of the City Guard rained down hell on the hundreds of scarecrows scattered in the alleys. Krishna saw a section of the Silver Wolves trying to drag the scarecrows away from harm, even as another squad gave them cover. *A rescue drill.*

Ever since the news of Kalyavan joining the Magadhan alliance had reached their ears and the prospect of the Sisters falling had become real, Mathura had been broken into pieces like a jigsaw puzzle, each piece defined by gates and low defensive walls. Though Krishna assured Balram that they would all be safely in Dvarka by the time the Armistice was over, Balram was not leaving anything to chance. He had turned the defence of the city into a multi-tiered nightmare for any advancing army. Unless the assailing force was comprised of giants, Krishna could not imagine any soldier mustering the patience required to cross even half of Mathura through these gates, corners and cul-de-sacs.

For Krishna's part, he was in charge of maintenance of the two tunnels, one leading from inside the Iron Curfew, and the other leading from the Market Square in the Third District, to safe places outside the Third Sister.

'I've heard she's completely changed the mock drills,' Satyaki said, keeping an eye out for Satyabhama, mortal dread in his eyes. If Balram was busy with the army, Satyabhama was busy with the City Guard and Silver Wolves. 'From blocking covert assassination attempts to shielding the Walls to turtle manoeuvres, she is breaking their bodies, limb by limb. Poor girls. I even heard one of them name every cul-de-sac in the city in her sleep.'

'Still strolling around the Silver Wolves' barracks, Satyaki?' Krishna winked. 'Ah... to be young and foolish again. You remind me of me,' he sighed.

'You have three wives, Krishna. I don't even have a woman to send ravens to!'

'I've already told you, you need confidence. Go to the alehouse. Tabetha will take good care of...'

'My first time is not going to be with a lady of the evening,' Satyaki said grumpily. For a seventeen-year-old unplucked flower, he sure did have his qualms about the garden. A blast of munition dragged their attention back from prostitution to politics. 'She'll break them, Krishna.'

'I wouldn't go that far.' Krishna scratched his chin. 'The Silver Wolves are the third or fourth daughters of their families, discarded in the streets or in temples that would have them. That kind of pain turns into a rather tough sense of self-preservation. It doesn't allow them to bend the knee easily.'

'I reckon that makes sense.' Satyaki nodded sagely. 'No wonder Lady Satyabhama has adopted them. But the way she is training them is fanatical! It's like she knows another battle is coming. Are we not shifting to Dvarka to *avoid* a battle?'

'Battles take place all the time, young one,' Krishna said. 'She just knows we are going to lose the next one.'

Satyaki gave another grim nod. 'Die in a mock battle today, live to become a legend tomorrow.'

'Inspiring words, Satyaki. Perhaps you can be a legend by opting not to bunk our next drill,' said a stern voice. In the rising dust they saw Satyabhama leaning down from the balcony of a house that jutted out over the narrow street leading to the Market Square.

Satyaki barely suppressed the urge to flee. 'War Mistress,' he said, bowing. 'Didn't see you there. Yes, yes, of course. Just the duties of the Senate and all this tunnel business, you know. Tiring stuff.'

Satyabhama threw him a scornful glance. 'The scarecrows are supposed to be foolish citizens, too dumb to move on their own. Perhaps you can join them, Satyaki.'

'Remind me to bring Akrur when I'm out in the streets', Satyaki whispered to Krishna. 'He is a true martyr, taking her blows for the team.'

But Krishna wasn't listening. 'A really wicked idea with the scarecrows, Satya,' he said. She nodded curtly.

'The Seven protect me! Even Krita reported for training today,' Satyaki said, pointing. 'Now I must really make myself scarce.'

Kritavarman clouted a hapless Silver Wolf recruit on the side of her head, hard enough to leave her sprawled unconscious in the dust. Quick as lightning, another Wolf appeared and threw the fallen one over her shoulder and carried her from the battle. Krishna recognized Storm. *If Storm is here, Rain is sure to be somewhere close by.* Rain and Storm had grown a reputation for being a legendary pair of sword-dancers in the Silver Wolves, famous for their in-sync fighting formations.

As Kritavarman jogged up the dusty track to the barricade where Krishna and Satyaki stood, a figure darted out, colliding sideways with Kritavarman and tossing him into the air. He crashed against the wall of a nearby house. *Rain,* Krishna mused. Satyaki grinned as he helped Kritavarman up from the dust. But Rain wasn't done yet. She charged again, this time at both Kritavarman and Satyaki's frail form.

Krishna raised his hand. 'That's enough, Rain. Take Storm to the healer.' Rain stopped short of punching Satyaki in the jaw.

'I'm fine,' said Storm, rising weakly. She scowled at Krishna, her face all bunny teeth and glowering suspicion under a pixie haircut. 'I was bait, Lord Krishna. You ruined it.'

'My apologies, Storm, for caring about Satyabhama's favourite Wolf.'

'She said that?' Storm looked up at Satyabhama on the balcony, in sudden delight. 'She really said that?'

'No.' Satyabhama's voice was flat. 'He says that to every Wolf.'

Storm scowled at Krishna, making a crude gesture with her fingers, and allowed Rain to drag her to the side to mend herself. More of the City Guard descended on the Wolves ahead, but Krishna could see the Guard was being routed by the Wolves.

'I think the Silver Wolves are winning,' Krishna observed as he climbed the stairs to where Satyabhama stood. Rain followed behind. Upon reaching the balcony, he found an injured Silver Wolf on the ground, gazing at him in sheer horror. He knew her name. *Piety*. Her long curly hair was tied in a top knot. Blood trickled down her branded right cheek. Piety looked at him and then at Satyabhama, understanding something Krishna had failed to grasp.

'Ah, you shouldn't have said that, Krishna,' Kritavarman said, resting against the barricade below, rubbing his bruised ribs.

Satyabhama whistled for her horse, and jumped off the low balcony into the saddle. 'Where are my bowmen?'

Thirty men of the City Guard emerged from the houses along the walls of the narrow street, carrying crossbows. The quarrels had been blunted with strips of cotton and leather, but the impact from such close range would have been enough to blind one. Krishna's eyes widened as he realized what Satyabhama was about to do. It was going to be a massacre.

'Fire!'

And then, Krishna saw magic. The Silver Wolves positioned themselves in front of the crossbows and, in silent symphony, turned sideways to avoid the quarrels. Half of them failed to do so, but the remainder were numerous enough to prevail over the death-addled crossbowmen. The fighting had begun in earnest. He saw two Silver Wolves fight Satyabhama, one attempting desperately to bring her horse down. Satyabhama knocked the Wolf unconscious with her cudgel as she swung to jump off the horse, and found herself facing six more Silver Wolves. And though Krishna could not see her face as her back was turned to him, he could picture the expression on her face. Grinning.

Kritavarman looked at Krishna sadly. 'If only there had been more Wolves still standing… seven is just too few… Perhaps two more and then, just maybe, the War Mistress would lose a duel for a change.'

II

After all the seven Wolves had eaten dust, Satyabhama jumped over the barricade to greet Krishna. Dust coated her face like paint. 'What brings you boys to the Third District? Is there a spy missing?'

'Espionage is as important as an army, Satya,' Krishna said gruffly, turning to Satyaki for confirmation.

'I'm not getting into this debate again,' Satyaki said, discovering something amusing between his feet.

Krishna mouthed, 'T-R-A-I-T-O-R,' at Satyaki before turning to his wife. The Silver Wolves did well today. Giving them an afternoon off?' Satyabhama's expression was one of pure bewilderment, as if Krishna spoke in a foreign tongue. Shaking his head, he added, 'They almost won against you, War Mistress. They are exhausted. They need to mend bones, you know.'

Satyabhama frowned. 'The day they actually win…'

Time suddenly came to a grinding halt. Everything seemed to slow as the air whistled behind Satyabhama. She raised her hand lightning fast to catch a quarrel mid-air, and turned towards the attacker. Yet another quarrel struck her breastplate with a loud *thwack*. The impact pushed her momentarily onto the back foot. Red dye smeared her breastplate from the cotton end of the quarrel.

It seemed that everyone had stopped breathing. The fallen City Guard and Silver Wolves no longer tended to their wounds. Satyaki looked like it had been he who had been shot with a crossbow quarrel, his mouth gaping wide. Krishna warily turned to find Storm astride the balustrade, while Rain peered between the pilasters of the balcony on which Satyabhama had been standing so short a time ago. Both their crossbows were levelled at the War Mistress. Storm had meant it when she had said she was bait.

'The day they actually win?' Krishna asked innocently.

'Shut up, husband!'

Satyaki slid slyly towards Krishna and whispered, 'Is that a smile on Satyabhama's face? I think… I saw… one.'

Satyabhama turned to Satyaki. 'Send word to the Silver Wolves and the City Guard. Tell them that once they've cleared the scarecrows from the streets, they can take to the Boar's Tavern. The rounds are on me. They have earned drinking rights.'

The Silver Wolves and the City Guard cheered. Some of the Wolves hoisted Storm and Rain onto their shoulders for a victory parade. Satyaki smiled at the celebrations till he noticed Satyabhama's eyes on him. 'Oh now? Yes, War Mistress.' Saying which, he hastily disappeared from sight.

'You are too hard on him,' Krishna said once Satyaki was gone and they were slowly walking down the street. 'You know he is afraid of you. He is little more than a boy.'

'Scare them when they are boys, then they continue to be afraid even when they become men. What brings you to the dirt of the streets, Lord Husband? Did Lady Rukmini not pat the cushions of your bed well enough?'

She is in a mood. 'I was just inspecting the tunnels before coming. I'm headed to Syamantaka. Thought of taking Satyaki with me. You know, we need a third person to act in my stead when I'm not around or the bears will forget who they answer to. I will get there by nightfall and return on the morrow. But I might not have time to see you again. Best to catch the daylight when I leave again for Panchal.'

'Yes, I know,' she rasped. Satyabhama did not bother to check her pace as she walked out of the training alleys.

As they climbed into her chariot, Krishna was filled with a familiar sense of dread. Whenever they were out together, she always insisted on driving the chariot. One could not master everything after all. A simple rule of life, really. Satyabhama, however, seemed ignorant of this limitation the Gods had placed on Mortals. No one would have dared call her a reckless driver to her face, unless they could carry off a broken nose. And since the alert Mathurans, each one a guerrilla warrior in their own right, always removed themselves from her path with their usual agility, no accident had ever besmeared Satyabhama's speckless career as a charioteer. Sighing, Krishna followed her into the chariot. But to his surprise, Satyabhama did not take up the reins. Dahanu, her loyal charioteer, was confused, but seeing Krishna nod, proceeded to handle the reins himself.

'My Lady,' Krishna flashed his dimples, 'you look tired.' His fingers slid down the back of her neck, tracing its shape, his touch feathery soft, trying to erase her unease. 'You should stop putting yourself through this war-drill ordeal every day.' He noticed a book lying on the floor of the chariot. Picking it up, he asked, 'How's the book?'

'*The Fall of Chakras*, in two volumes. They say it's one of the great Vedan classics. Load of rubbish, I say.' She snorted condescendingly. 'Full of devious Daevas, knights in shining armour, stern Acharyas with their mighty rosaries, and Queens with even mightier breasts. Magic, action and romance in equal measure. It's utter shit.'

'Surely there must be something to keep you busy other than boring books? Perhaps you could do something with your fellow wives: a team activity to boost morale.'

'And what would the great Lord Krishna suggest?'

'Rukmini can teach you embroidery. Jambavati has a vegetable garden.'

'Fuck you.'

'Love you, too.' Krishna smiled. The best method to unravel Satyabhama's knots was to get a rise out of her. It was when she was calm that it spelled trouble, for Satyabhama had a dark unforgiving side. And it seemed he was under its shadow today. 'Satya, has Jambavati troubled you again?' The cold war between his second and third wives was the favourite tavern tale of Mathurans.

She answered by unravelling her purse and handing him a parchment. Krishna looked at her, amused, as he unhooked the diamond-studded knot of the gold strings of the parchment. The broken seal showed a saffron stag. *Panchal*. He began to laugh as understanding dawned, but hastily swallowed his mirth when he saw her grim face. 'It's not like that,' Krishna said reasonably, putting an arm around her shoulders.

'Then explain!' she snapped, pushing his arms away. 'Why is that Princess of Panchal sending you ravens? Do you want a new wife to bring you yet another region, for, clearly, I brought nothing with me? Yes, I've precious little money, no royal blood, and do not deck up in jewels like an idol. But you listen to me, Krishna: if yet another wife of yours enters the Walls of Mathura, the Yaksha of Goverdhun himself will not be able to keep me from beheading her.'

'Satya, I've told you already. The swayamvar is for the Panchalan Princess to choose her husband from a throng of suitors. I merely need to ensure her choice aligns with Mathuran interests.'

Her eyes narrowed. 'If you believe that this choice must be you, you are sick with a fever of the mind. Is that why you are going to Panchal a full moon ahead of the swayamvar?'

Krishna smiled. 'I am going to the swayamvar, yes, but to prod, not to participate. I've already told you about my plan. Swayamvars are such exciting affairs, after all. And the Panchalan Princess is like my sister.'

Satyabhama snorted in derision.

Krishna changed tactics. 'In fact, why don't you come along? Just you and I.'

'Oh yes,' scoffed Satyabhama, 'I can just hear them all talk. Lord Krishna, patron of democracy! What a damn fine fellow! So handsome. Born a cowherd, then rose to King's Secretary. Then, killing the King, rescued the people, don't you know? True heir to Mathura, you see. A hero. Then he went on to conquer the Eastern Kingdom. No breeding whatsoever, never one of us, but a damn fine hero for a cowherd. Shame about that upstart wife, too clever by half, and so violent. Only the third wife though. They say she wields a sword and fights in the army, and does not wear a saree.' Satyabhama's eyes flashed as her monologue fell to an icy whisper. 'No wonder she can't get him a child. Doesn't even know how to curtsy, I'm told. Best to just keep away from that barren woman.'

Sighing, she looked away from Krishna. 'You and I both know everyone will be happier if I just stay here. If I go, the men will ignore me, and the women cut me dead with their eyes.'

Krishna took her hands in his, rubbing the palms softly with his thumbs. He waited to be sure she was done with her words. Then he asked quietly, 'Since when does the cow care about the opinion of the grass it eats?'

Satyabhama looked up at him, smiling sadly. She had never known wealth growing up. She had never flirted coquettishly at high-society parties in tight-fitting blouses, while swaying teasingly to the music. She had never sailed in the brief, tragically glorious ship of friends gossiping about lordlings, had never experienced a theatrical episode of courtship, a bit of pretend-game, to raise her above the sea of life. Come to think of it, she only had terrible hatreds in her life, irritation over the daily injustices that were so commonplace one would think they were part of a law.

But Krishna liked that about her. It had made her... realistic about things. She laughed with the knowledge that it wasn't meant to last, and cried with the self-assurance that it was futile. She was like a glacier, relentless and implacable. But eyeing the letter from Panchal, he reckoned that sometimes even a vast glacier could crack into crevasses under deer hooves.

'Fine, I'll come,' Satyabhama suddenly decided, making Krishna wonder if he had made a strategic blunder. It was a lot easier offering help when you knew the other person will certainly refuse it. But his godsluck was clearly taking a break. She threw him a measuring look. 'And you are also taking Storm with you to Syamantaka.'

Krishna was not deterred. 'My Lady, there is no need for an escort. I am sure you have other ways of punishing Storm for shooting you in the chest.'

Just then, Satyaki came back, panting. He looked worried about setting foot in the chariot since Satyabhama was in it, but he took his chances upon seeing the reins in Dahanu's hands. 'The barkeep has been given due instructions, My Lady,' he informed Satyabhama.

'See,' Krishna murmured, a twinkle in his eyes, 'Satyaki here is so efficient. He'll guard me.'

Satyabhama turned suddenly, her knife a blur in the air as it faintly scratched Krishna's right cheek, drawing blood. 'Satyaki is too slow. You are taking Storm with you.'

'I see you made your point,' Krishna said, wiping the blood from his cheek.

'About time you had a scar.' She winked as she lightly stepped over the guard to where the charioteer sat and took the reins from him.

As Satyabhama whipped the horses, Satyaki closed his eyes in silent prayer and the denizens of Mathura prepared to flee her path. Krishna leaned back, dabbing the cut, wondering who to choose as a husband for the powerful Princess of Panchal. *Decisions. Decisions.*

SHISHUPAL

I

It was late at night and a persistent rain had fallen all evening. Stars glittered like sword-points overhead. The pools of water by the road shone silver in the moonlight, as if reflecting back memories of the day that had sauntered past. In Rajgrih, unsavoury humans went about their nocturnal professions: thieves thieved, night guards whistled, whores moaned, assassins killed, and the Unni Ehtral priests danced and maimed in bizarre rituals.

'We've got to get him off the streets as soon as possible, Lady Rasha,' Shishupal said. 'I cannot believe he was so foolish as to venture into the Valka camp for a rematch! Always a sore loser, my little brother. And what if he wins, eh? Next thing you know he'll be knocking on the Emperor's door demanding his boon that very moment.'

Lady Rasha merely smiled mysteriously as the carriage lurched over the rutted road. It was she who had brought word to him that Dantavakra, having got drunk in a tavern, had stormed off to challenge the winner to a rematch. *Bloody idiot.* But Shishupal expected no better, not when Lady Rasha informed him Dantavakra had been nursing his wounds, physical and emotional, with Kalyavan of all people.

'How could Your Ladyship possibly imagine it was a good idea for those two to meet?'

'Shalya was tired, and Kalyavan needed a city guide. They are both young warriors. Kalyavan is a most gifted swordsman. Could teach Dantavakra a trick or two.'

Tricks! Tricks, she says. It must have been Kalyavan's idea. *Hyperactive hyena meets roused rat!* There was nothing worse than hot-blooded youngsters meeting in a tavern. Nothing good ever came of such ill-fated mingling. There ought to be a law against that sort of thing.

'Let's hope Dantavakra is a slow learner,' he said morosely. As if a drunk Dantavakra was not problem enough, Shishupal had learned that the winner his brother had stormed off to challenge was a Valka, a member of the fiercest forest tribe this side of the Ganga. Valkas were known for many things; hospitality towards cityfolk, however, was not one of them. His own guards had searched Dantavakra's usual haunts but had not found him. Since the Valkas were encamped in the Weeds, that was the only place left to search.

Lady Rasha had been kind to give him a lift so late at night. Shishupal frantically peered through the carriage windows for any sign of a tall fool walking arm in arm with an olive-skinned Mlecchá. Surely, they would stand out in any crowd? But Shishupal saw no one he recognized. Though it was late and wet, the streets of Rajgrih were raucous and teeming with people. Lanes of chaos wound down to more lanes, cobbled steps, and muddy passageways. Much like any other city, save for the naked corpses that hung from the trees, wooden boards pinned to their chest, with *Infidel!* written in blood. *Unni Ehtral.*

'Jhestal seems to have rattled you,' Lady Rasha quietly observed. 'I saw your face at the Contest today.'

'Uhm....'

'Speak freely. I'm a keeper of secrets.'

If Lady Rasha was indeed a witch, she would have read his mind. There was no point in resistance. 'Well, My Lady, it's just that... I'm not into crucifying children. There is no... justice in it.'

'*Tch, tch.* Justice. A child's notion. There is not going to be justice anywhere, not for a while. Justice can have the leftovers after the Emperor is done.'

'Yes... but this....'

'Is this why you left the war?'

'Uhm, I don't understand your meaning, My Lady.'

'I have heard winners of the Contest ask grand boons of the Emperor – a position in the Kingsguard, a garrison to command, a nobleman's daughter to marry... But you... you asked to be allowed *out* of the war; a war Magadh has been slowly but steadily winning.'

'With respect, My Lady, there is nothing peculiar about that. Folks get tired of war all the time. Injury, trauma, battle fatigue...'

'Indeed.' Lady Rasha turned her blue eye towards him. 'Yes, I can certainly see that happening to others, but you have, shall we say, personal motivation, to bring Krishna to heel, don't you?'

'I guess there is no one left who does not know of my humiliation.'

'Well, they might have forgotten the tale by now. After all, brides get abducted all the time in the countryside. But you, dear lad, sat at the altar for a full hour, crying rather than galloping after Krishna. Some even thought you had lost your mind.'

Shishupal felt like he was being forced underwater to drown. 'Maybe I did. Who knows?'

'I do,' she said, a rare smile on her face. 'In fact, I did you one better.'

'How so?'

'I waited an entire day for him,' Lady Rasha said. 'In the rain, if that fetches me any custard points. Families, friends, priests, you name it, all came to drag me home, to tell me Krishna had left the village for good, that he had run away, that he had got cold feet... But I waited. We were, after all, the most famous lovebirds of my village. I waited till the family of the next couple who were to marry in the temple took a stick to my head.'

Shishupal was at a loss how to respond. A variety of unappealing options presented themselves: holding her hand, looking away, foolishly delivering words of sympathy, cursing Krishna, cracking a joke. He said what his brother had said when he had come to comfort him: *Find someone who is worse off than you.* 'I guess the Emperor bests both of us in that regard. Dead grandchildren win.'

Lady Rasha laughed. 'Dark, but yes. That he does. So why do you think Rukmini left you for Krishna?'

Shishupal was not inclined to become an exchanger of confidences with Lady Rasha, but she was using that tone which made him obey. 'I barely knew her. I suppose he was better at climbing through windows than I was. What about you?'

This time the green eye twinkled. Lady Rasha straightened herself. For a flickering moment, Shishupal saw sadness in her dual-coloured irises. 'So, coming back to the question from which this conversation spiralled for the worse, why would a warrior leave the Imperial Army for a position with the Crimson Cloaks?'

Shishupal sighed. 'The Yaksha.'

'What of him?'

'I don't know who he is, My Lady, but the things that were done in Goverdhun, the babies…' Shishupal shrank from the memory. 'It wasn't the best of times. And trust me, I've been put in a cage with a skunk before.' He smiled wearily. 'I… the War had become something else, and I wanted no part in it. No hand in those…' Shishupal stumbled into silence.

Lady Rasha nodded. '… Those war crimes?'

'Crimes only if Mathura wins. If Magadh wins, they become laurels.'

'Hmm…' Lady Rasha ruminated like a Namin scientist concluding an experiment. 'Such an interesting man you're turning out to be, Shishupal, wanting away from fame and glory. Yet you are going to the swayamvar to win the Panchalan Princess' hand. A feat that will make you the envy of every Lord, Noble, Prince, King and Warlord.'

'Trust me, Lady Rasha, it is not from choice. No matter how I try to run from trouble, it always seems to catch up with me.

I must have lit candles to the wrong God. Unni Ehtral seems a popular option these days,' he added dryly.

As the pair continued talking, the carriage moved into the Weeds. The Imperial Cloaks were much in evidence here, yet no one seemed to care about them. Shishupal looked back at the city from the carriage window. From this far out, the Virangavat arena resembled some primeval creature rising into the sky on open wings to challenge the moon.

As the carriage turned away from the city walls, they heard the whistle of arrows, the clanging of swords, the cries of men, loud yet indistinct. Every great city in Aryavrat had a section like the Weeds. It was usually the oldest part, full of immigrants, located on the outskirts, with names like the Ruins, the Shades, the Crows. The Weeds was such a place in Rajgrih, an area of outright lawlessness. It was where the armies of Jarasandh's allies were currently camped, alongside brothels, smugglers and thieves – the dark underbelly of Rajgrih.

Shishupal stuck his head out of the carriage. Thousands of charcoal briquettes coloured the air with a pale smoky hue. Further ahead, the elephant lines stretched for leagues. Enormous siege engines moved at turtle pace, significantly impeding the progress of the carriage. As they waited, they saw light-haired giants from the Kauntis, who often got into brawls with the lean, dagger-wielding men from the dangerous cities of Kalinga. He could hear chatter in half a dozen languages in the Weeds. They saw all kinds of soldiers: men with axes and men with swords, men in loosely fastened armours and men in chainmail. They saw whores unabashedly trotting from one tent to another, ugly maids fussing over the washing of vessels, and squires fetching spent arrows for archers. *He certainly leaves no stone unturned,* Shishupal thought, observing the fruits of Jarasandh's call to arms. The Emperor was clearly intent on the making the next battle with Mathura the last.

They arrived at last at the army camps. Fireflies lit the tents like ornaments. The vast field was a resplendent sight, with rainbow-hued banners of the vassals snapping proudly with the emblems of their Lords. Even in the dark, Shishupal could make out the jaguar of the Hehayas and the vulture of Anupa.

But though they passed several pavilions, they saw no sign of the Valkas or of Dantavakra. A dishevelled woman raced past, giggling and clutching at her dark cloak, her drunken pursuer stumbling in pursuit. As Shishupal's gaze followed them, he spied a stream in the distance. A young archer was drawing the string of his bow, his chest bare and slick with sweat. 'Lady Rasha, see that boy? He's the Contest winner. If that Valka boy is here, surely Dantavakra must be close.' Saying this, Shishupal opened the carriage door and hastily jumped out.

Had he exercised a modicum of restraint, he would have heard Lady Rasha warn him about approaching the boy at his own peril.

KRISHNA

I

Overhead, the stars hung meek in a thundering sky but cast enough light to tinge the three hooded figures who scurried through the streets of the ghost town, a few leagues from Mathura. It was blackened and smoky, with skeletal corpses hanging from trees to welcome passers-by. The temples, schools and merchant houses had all been torched. The Yaksha did not believe in subtlety.

It was easy to miss the sign of the bear singed into the lintel over a tiny door in one of the meanest alleyways. The nightsoil of the town had once flowed through this alley to the river in happier times. It had been noisome with the stink of pigsties, mixed with the sour stench of winesinks. Even now, it smelled like a poisoned cat. Whatever the reason, the Yaksha had ignored this door in his rampage of destruction through the town, and for that Mathura was grateful.

One of the hooded figures rapped a complex code on the wood, the imprinted bear barely discernible above his head. An iron hatch opened and a suspicious eye peered out.

'The owl was snared by the rat,' uttered Krishna.

'Yet the rat remains blissfully unwise,' intoned the voice on the other side of the door.

'For the rat did not eat the owl's brain,' countered the visitor.

There was a pause, broken only by the sound of one of the visitors impatiently fiddling with her sword. 'Oi!' she called impatiently to the one within, but there was no response.

'My error, Storm,' the leader said. 'For the rat did not eat the owl's *mind*,' he corrected.

The door opened. Satyaki let out a yell and drew his sword while Storm put a palm on Krishna's chest, pushing him behind her. From the darkness behind the door emerged a massive bear, upright on two legs, draped in a long cloak. Lightning chose that opportune moment to blaze in the sky, and in that light, the hirsute face flashed horrifyingly. His eyebrows hung down like a walrus moustache, his eyes barely visible. His tufted ears poked through a shaggy, reddish-brown mane.

Storm drew her daggers. '*Yama's sweet breath*! What is that?'

The bear-man shook his head and let out a sigh that would have embarrassed a bull in heat. 'How the humans have fallen since the Lankan War. Ignorant and impolite,' he lamented with a deep, sad voice.

'*May you always have doubts*,' Krishna greeted the bear-man with a traditional greeting. 'Forgive my companions, Jambavan. They do not travel much,' said Krishna.

Jambavan's smile returned, exposing sharp pointed canines. '*May your answers be questions*,' he returned the greeting. 'Welcome, my son. It's about time! We are starving.'

This revelation did not help make things less tense for Storm and Satyaki, who stepped back warily again.

'Apologies for the delay,' Krishna said. 'The Armistice has finally allowed me to bring you your supplies without worrying about running into unfriendly Magadhans.'

'Ah yes. Such a commotion when the Magadhans were here.' Jambavan's eyes combed the mausoleum of carnage behind Krishna with indifference, although Krishna could see his good-father's tufted ears twitch angrily. 'And they call *us* barbarians.'

'Who is this fellow?' Storm pointed a finger towards Jambavan's gargantuan figure.

'Mind your manners, Storm,' said Krishna. 'Jambavan is my father-in-law.'

II

Timid though Satyaki was, he was also a reliable indicator of what was going through the mind of the average man.

The fact that Jambavan was a Riksha, a race of bear-like humans, was accepted by him after the initial shock faded. It was not as if humans did not know of the Rikshas, but the Rikshas were reclusive and rarely ever left their icy cave-towns. Most cities treated them as a myth, and even the few villages who remembered them had not seen a Riksha in centuries. But since Satyaki had seen Jambavan's daughter, Jambavati, Krishna's second wife, on countless occasions, he warmed to Jambavan soon enough. The Rikshas were not all that different from Men. The Acharyas of Meru would have even called the Rikshas human, but for the offspring any union between a Man and a Riksha yielded. Though Riksha men could indeed mate with human females, the offspring of these unions were puny and deformed, often sterile, like mules. And Riksha women, when mated with human males, brought forth only stillbirths and monstrosities.

'How is my daughter?' Jambavan asked as he led them underground through a staircase.

If being childless was not enough, Satyabhama's presence amplified Jambavati's woes manifold. Satyabhama made no secret of her disdain for Jambavati. And the fact that the Mathurans respected Satyabhama more, despite Jambavati being the more senior consort of Krishna, only added to insult to injury.

But Krishna's partnership with Jambavan rested on a child out of Jambavati, though Krishna found himself less than enthusiastic in the matter. 'Jambavati lives the life of a Queen. I have set her up in the highest room in the highest tower in Mathura. Kind winds keep the insistent heat at bay,' he now said with complete truth.

Jambavan had played a central role in Krishna's rags-to-riches-to-Republic story. The Rikshas had always been a scholarly race, and Jambavan was one of the brightest minds amongst the

Rikshas. He was, however, shunned by *gurukuls* and kings simply because he was different. And Yami bless human prejudice, their loss had been Krishna's gain. He had needed Jambavan's mind to uncover the secrets of the Syamantaka Jewel and its mystical workings. He had needed someone who was motivated to keep it a secret, for reasons beyond gold.

Such able-minded yet shunned souls made for truly dedicated partners. The alternative would have been to engage an Acharya from Meru and, well, that would have put an end to any notion of secrecy. Not unless he had cut off the tongue of the said Acharya and kidnapped his family. For if the secret of the Syamantaka had leaked then, the Saptarishis would have claimed it, and Krishna would still be toiling as a Private Secretary to a despotic King.

'By the way, Jambavan, the Senate has approved the shift of Mathura to Alantris. The name is now Dvarka.'

'Dvarka... yes,' he spoke slowly, the way Rikshas often spoke, 'City of Gates. That is well thought of.'

'It would not have been possible without you. You and your magical devices.'

'There is no such thing as magic, Krishna. Just secrets the world doesn't know about yet. You got the glass?' Jambavan cocked his shaggy head expectantly.

'A large shipment of vaikunshard is on its way to you.'

'Capital!' Jambavan beamed and sauntered forward.

'Why don't you just carry the Syamantaka Jewel to Mathuran Keep? How big can it be? I will carry it on me,' Satyaki whispered to Krishna as they followed Jambavan into yet another tunnel. Satyaki really didn't like tunnels. 'Travelling all this distance to this blasted place...'

'Patience, Satyaki. I know I have kept you in the dark but the brightest stars are always seen on the darkest nights,' Krishna said to allay his fears.

'But you know what they say about stars – look at them too closely and you will burn,' Jambavan offered unhelpfully.

'Whaa---t?' Satyaki looked at Krishna, his eyes wide.

'Ignore him. He has a funny way of looking at things.'

'What did I say?' Jambavan asked innocently. 'Three things you should never stare into – a star, your mother-in-law's eyes, and a Naga's butt. Trust me on this.'

'Nagas?' Satyaki chuckled. 'You mean, talking serpents?'

Storm suddenly spun around, blocking Satyaki's path with her tiny body. 'Something funny, noble boy?'

Satyaki was taken aback. 'I mean, we all know there's no such thing.'

'The Nagas killed my mother. The forests are swarming with fucking Nagas!' She lifted herself on her toes to stare Satyaki in the eye. 'So don't tell me there's no such thing.'

Satyaki looked to Krishna for support but received only a shake of the head. 'Come, Satyaki, time to rip that refuge of ignorance from your mind.'

III

The underground hall was extremely cold, for the Rikshas kept it that way. The Vedan sun wasn't meant for their beastly bodies so they needed a constant supply of ice blocks to keep their minds sane. The group emerged into a dark room beneath a sky faintly dotted with stars. *A cloudless sky*, Krishna thought, staring up. Satyaki momentarily forgot the insult at the hands of Storm as his jaw hung lifelessly. He was awestruck. Storm clutched her sword, lines appearing beside her mouth as she clenched her teeth. They both knew it was impossible for the sky to be visible when they were underground but the illusion still raged a pitched battle against this knowledge.

'What is this, Krishna?' Satyaki asked. He looked around. There was a circle drawn on the floor, surrounded by four concentric metallic rings. A black luminous orb hung suspended in mid-air, above a short pillar as high as his waist. Large chunks of shattered vaikunshard lay all around, with thin metal tubes protruding from the walls and corners like snakes. The tubes were clearly broken, and emitted tiny streaks of lightning.

'The Syamantaka, of course.'

'What do you mean?'

Krishna pointed to the black wall behind Satyaki. Some form of ancient writing was etched on it, the writing ruined by decay, algae and erosion. Only a few of the letters were still visible. They were in High Sanskrit. Satyaki read, *Sy-aman-taka*. He turned sharply to Krishna. 'I don't understand.'

Krishna exchanged a sly look with Jambavan, enjoying the moment. 'Syamantaka is not a jewel. It is a Daeva ship.'

IV

And once again Krishna used Satyaki as a sort of rat from an apothecary workshop to predict how normal people would react to the Syamantaka. So, when Satyaki was told the Syamantaka Jewel was actually the ruins of a Daeva ship, rather than an actual jewel, and how its enormous reserves of alchemical gold had funded all of Krishna's campaigns, his consequent collapse was a helpful indicator.

Satyaki finally regained consciousness when Jambavan threatened to give him a hairy kiss of life. There ensued a series of explanations about how they had stumbled upon the ruins of this ship; how they had kept the secret hidden from the world; how it had funded Krishna's ventures, and so on. 'Satyabhama's father, a lowly soldier then, found these halls,' Krishna said quietly. 'I was Kans' Private Secretary when he arrived with the news of a discovery. Suffice to say, the news never reached the King. I had already met Jambavan in my travels and enlisted his aid. The rest, as they say, is history. Secret history.'

Satyaki gulped. 'So...' he said nervously, after his short education in the Syamantaka was complete, 'this... this ship used gold as a candle uses wax.'

'Aye, gold and some form of lightning. The Rikshas have found a way to safely extract the gold from the Daeva oil, in return for unhampered freedom to tinker with its secrets, and a handsome salary of course,' Krishna said.

'And now,' Jambavan added sadly, the tufts of his ears drooping outward, 'since all the gold has been extracted...'

'The Syamantaka ceases to be the jewel it once was. Storm,' Krishna turned to the Silver Wolf, '...you've said nothing.'

Storm shrugged. 'Either way, I don't give a shit. I'm just here to make sure your head remains on your shoulders.'

'Charming.'

'I don't... believe it.' Satyaki was shivering. 'Daevas do exist, then. I guess I was happy not knowing.'

Krishna held Satyaki's shoulders. 'Not everyone has the privilege of choosing ignorance, Satyaki. We are the future, remember. The same goes for you, Storm. Satyabhama sent you here because she thinks you are her brightest cadet. Will you disappoint her? Where is your curiosity?'

Storm groaned. '*Fine*... But I know nothing of what you speak. Who are these Daevas? What is this place? And if this is a ship that crashed, why is it so empty? It must have been carrying something.'

'Shall I treat her to the big reveal?' Jambavan asked, a happy grin on his face.

'By all means.'

'Come, my children. Time to meet a friend of mine.'

V

The Riksha slid a key into an unseen hole in the wall behind the circle in the centre. Suddenly, there was a loud noise. Krishna saw Satyaki bend forward, hands clamped over his ears, while Storm frowned. With a sound that brought to mind a carpenter sawing wood, the world began to shake. Satyaki started fearfully. 'It's moving! It's all moving!'

The rings around the circle they had first seen on entering began to turn, revolving one about the other. By turning the key in the lock, Jambavan had set it off. The whole arrangement was tilting, turning, rotating and revolving at the same time. Only the orb in the centre remained still. The whole world seemed to hum with a strong buzzing sound as strange lights erupted from cylindrical objects fixed to the walls.

The parts of an invisible machine clicked against each other with rapid, audible sounds. Soon, light flooded in from the orb – piercing light, hurtful to look at after the muted darkness. It came in spurts at first. And gradually, the Rikshas working on the wall at the far end, and even Krishna, who stood on the other side of the orb, became first slightly out of focus to Storm and Satyaki, and then completely blurred behind the apparition.

To Krishna, looking at Satyaki through the apparition felt like gazing at a riverbed through rippling water. Satyaki stared up at the translucent figure coalescing before them, and his jaw sagged open. Jambavan's use of the word 'friend' had been as misleading as 'jewel' for the Syamantaka. It wasn't until Jambavan clicked his fingers and the workers, in tandem, blew out the torches closest to where they stood that the apparition congealed into the form of a tall man, tall enough to make Balram seem tiny. The form could, however, barely be described as a man. He did stand upright on two legs and had two hands and an ageless human face. His skin was luminous white, beyond the measure of men. His brilliant amber eyes seemed to have been snatched from a tiger. His ears pointed sharply towards the sky, and he wore robes that looked as if they were made of specks of starlight.

Krishna watched his companions stare gormlessly at the figure. 'You wanted to know what a Daeva was, Storm. Well, here he is.'

VI

'Is this a… *real* Daeva?' Satyaki stammered.

Storm approached the form as he floated in mid-air. She glanced towards Krishna; he nodded. Her hand extended, she felt the gelatinous texture of the being with the tips of her fingers. She poked and saw her finger enter his stomach. Around her intruding hand, a formless mist swirled and danced.

'What makes you think it is not a real Daeva?' Jambavan asked. The Riksha's ears had perked up happily.

'Well, it isn't chopping my head off,' Satyaki replied.

Jambavan chuckled. 'There is hope for the boy after all.'

'Why would it chop off our heads?' asked Storm.

'That's what they built their reputation on,' Jambavan told her. 'Demons made of light and fire. The ancient enemy. The only one that matters.'

Storm shrugged. 'They've done nothing to me.'

'The Daevas are long dead; as dead as the Immortals and the Children of Blood, gone twenty thousand years ago,' Krishna explained. 'Any newly graduated Acharya will tell you they never lived at all. No living man has ever seen a Daeva. But here we have proof that they did indeed exist. This…' Krishna pointed to the ship around them, 'was how they travelled, as I travel on Garud.'

'Children of Blood? Immortals? What—'

'One question at a time, Storm. One at a time,' Krishna said, holding up a hand to pause her queries.

'Then what is this?' Satyaki raised a finger at the throbbing translucent figure of the Daeva.

'It is a reflection of sorts. A memory or a letter, if you will. The Daevas knew how to send messages using this device, using secrets we don't yet understand.'

'And what does the letter say?'

Jambavan pressed the trinkets on the orb, and suddenly the figure of the Daeva spoke, its voice crackling like dry leaves in a forest fire. Though the form stood before them, the sound came from everywhere around them, through small black webbed boxes placed in different alcoves in the Syamantaka. The speech was garbled, with gaps in between. *'Sorry, Muchuk Und----the Others didn't approve of your methods-----they were afraid of you---the cannibalism, the destruction, the cruelty you left in your wake, they saw themselves----they will come now to enslave your kind again---- mortals have forgotten Astras----I left your zinth dagger------I will miss her----We all deserve the deaths you wish upon us---For your sake, I hope you never wake from your sleep. Savitre Lios, May your Night be Bright.'*

The Daeva's form then fizzled into nothingness. Krishna smiled at the horror-struck expression on Satyaki's face. The Daevas of yore, the Children of Light, the monsters of fables that made little boys squeal, riding their winged horses, hungry for sacrifice and fire; to know they had really existed filled even him with an exhilaration no conspiracy could match.

'Madness!' Satyaki finally sputtered. 'What is this?'

Krishna could see Satyaki did not feel well at all. Things he had dismissed as myth were suddenly revealed as fact before his eyes; the world was a different place from what it had been the night before, an unsettling place where a tiny jewel turned out to be an otherworldly ship, where his ancestors were owned by monsters of myth, where those monsters spoke of a future when they would come again. Satyaki closed his eyes, his lips moving in fervent prayer.

'Breathe, Satyaki. Let us take it easy on him, Jambavan. Enough for today.'

'I do not understand why I am here,' Satyaki said grumpily, opening his eyes on a world that suddenly eluded his understanding.

Krishna sympathized with Satyaki's plight. The boy knew precious little about alchemy, even less about lore. Daevas were just things in dusty scrolls and the stories of bards, heard and forgotten as a child, holding no interest for him even then.

Krishna spoke softly. 'You are here because the gold may have run out of the Syamantaka, but this is still a dangerous place and it is too risky for me to travel here. I am always watched. I need someone to be my voice here.'

'Why is this a dangerous place?' Storm asked with the first hint of interest, still unsure, still uncaring about the rest. 'It shits gold but the gold has run out. Yes, it has strange ghosts, but I see no danger in it.'

'Come with me,' Jambavan said to her, his tufts dipping down again. 'Satyaki, can you take another surprise?'

'Another *friend*?' Satyaki asked sourly.

'You've no idea.' Jambavan's eyes glinted with a malice only spied in the mien of a true scholar.

VII

'Surely this is blasphemous,' Satyaki whispered to Krishna as they walked into the inner chambers of the ship. 'You are intruding into what is not supposed to be in the human realm. The Seven should have been made aware of this.'

'On the contrary, tampering with things we don't know is the very essence of being a human,' said Krishna. 'That's how we discovered how to make babies,' he joked, hoping to put Satyaki's mind at ease.

He needed Satyaki to wrap his head around the tasks Krishna had for him in the Syamantaka, and wrap it around, fast.

'And you humans already knew about all this,' Jambavan said. 'Didn't you hear him say how *the mortals had forgotten*. He was right about that. What we are discovering now is essentially a re-discovery.'

'How does that work?' Storm asked.

'Imagine time as a river, girl.' Jambavan waved his shaggy palm horizontally to symbolize flowing water. 'Knowledge travels in tiny boats on it. Many start down the river only to be wrecked and lost, stranded on the riverbanks and shoals of memory. They have to be retrieved... using the few fragments of knowledge that have endured the ravages of time.'

'If the gold is depleted, why bother?' Storm asked.

Always the practical one. 'Gold was just the tip of the bull's horn. Alchemy, metal-binding, explosives... how do you think we Mathurans became famous for our munitions? Who do you think devised those cursers and bellowers? Ah, here we are.' Krishna pointed to a long box lying in the centre of the chamber.

Carved with reliefs and hieroglyphs, the ebony and weirwood sarcophagus rested heavily on a limestone bed. The white grains on the sides of the box swirled and twisted in strange interwoven patterns. It was mesmerizing, yet somehow frightening. There was an ice sculpture inside, a body floating in a blue transparent liquid, lying here, if the inscription was correctly translated, for thousands of years.

'We believe this ship crashed here, and this is the one the Daevas call Muchuk Und. He is a Mortal. Yes, I know he is grotesquely tall. Not a giant, but tall. But it matches your records, when your ancestors were much taller and bigger than we are now. Even Ram and his Ayodhyans were a lot taller than you all are.'

'What!' Satyaki looked shell-shocked. 'You mean the man... the godforsaken Daevas feared, the one whom they called a cannibal, he is... still alive? Fuck that, he is still here, five fucking leagues from our city?'

'Actually...' Krishna ventured.

'What?' Satyaki asked, afraid of the answer.

'We entered by the second entrance to Syamantaka in order to keep its whereabouts veiled. All this,' Krishna pointed to the ship and its occupant, 'is located right under the Senate House.'

VIII

Satyaki suffered a nervous breakdown of sorts. He was taken outside by some of the Riksha workers to inhale some fresh air.

Only Storm, Jambavan and Krishna remained in the chamber where the allegedly most dangerous man in the realm slept peacefully in ice.

'You need more gold,' Jambavan stated with certainty. 'That is why you are here.'

He is blunt. 'The Guild was difficult to deal with, and you know this Dvarka enterprise rests entirely on gold…'

Jambavan's face was stoic as he shook his head. 'You know the Syamantaka has been bled dry. If we take any more gold out of the pipes, this thing will crumble into itself.'

'About that… You will have to close the Syamantaka down, Jambavan. I will be too far to protect you, and it's too dangerous to be kept here. I was not lying to Satyaki. My movements are being tracked. Satyaki will recover, and he will liaise with you on the best way to salvage what you can from this place.'

'Hold your spear, son! There are still things to uncover here. You cannot shut it down! We had an agreement.'

Krishna forced himself to smile. 'Giving you a grandson sounds like a fair compensation. Is that not what you wanted? For your line to merge with humans so the blood of the Rikshas can go on after the Age of Ice comes to another end? So, extract every ounce of gold till this ship crumbles into itself.'

Jambavan's nostrils flared. 'And how many years has it been that she lies barren in your house? No, Krishna. It can't be done, even if I wanted to. The ship is too weak. I say give me two more winters; I will find you a solution.'

Why can't I ever get something when I play nicely? 'Skirting around the Guild is dangerous, especially considering they will be our neighbours in Dvarka.' Krishna stroked his beardless chin. 'I will have to initiate some austerity measures to fill the gold gap. Balram often chides me for my luxuries. You have yourself seen my wives and the baggage they carry, with their carvings and silk draperies. Their servants are better dressed than most kings. And then there is the issue of summer. Maintaining Jambavati's mansion, finding ostrich feathers, importing snow from Madra…'

He gave a sigh. 'This summer will be a trying one for the people of Mathura. Especially the women. I may leave for Dvarka before them, simply to escape their wrath.'

Jambavan's face had turned ashen. Using his daughter to intimidate him had been cruel, Krishna admitted, but Jambavan had brought it upon himself. The Rikshas, being hirsute, could not survive a Vedan summer. So, they either went into hibernation or took a trek to the Mai Layas when the days grew longer. With Jambavati in Mathura, however, she did not have that luxury. It was either the myriad cooling devices he had installed, or a pyre.

'You play a dangerous game, Krishna.' Jambavan's voice hid none of his fury. 'Do not forget that in our race, widows can remarry. And she has only witnessed eighty-five turns of the world. A very young girl, all things considered.' Krishna, however, did not break eye contact with Jambavan. There was the hint of a sly smile on Krishna's face as he sensed the father in Jambavan overpowering the Riksha in him. 'But I will see what I can do about the gold,' Jambavan said at last. 'It won't be much, however. I do not claim to perform miracles. Come to me in three weeks.'

Krishna smiled. 'I knew we could come to an understanding. We are family, after all. As for closing down this place, you have a few months till the Armistice ends, to pack whatever you need, to take to the ice caves, and eventually Dvarka. We burn the rest. Of course, Mathura will arrange the manpower and foot the bill.'

'With the gold I give you?'

'Mere formalities, you know.'

'You promise to take care of my daughter, Krishna? You promise! I will play your dirty games for her sake.'

'Well then, now is as good a time as any to announce that Jambavati is pregnant.'

Jambavan's eyes widened, then filled with tears. He hugged Krishna, taking him by surprise. Jambavan's embrace was gentle, but Krishna was nevertheless relieved to get out of it in one piece.

He had knowingly saved this news for last, to sweeten the wounds Krishna had inflicted on the old man. There was nothing like the prospect of being a grandfather to make one forget one had just been blackmailed into giving up on life's greatest quest.

Fathers, Krishna sighed, *can be so predictable.*

SHISHUPAL

I

The roots were thick underfoot. They spread out to bridge the gaps between the trees. Even when the trees themselves thinned out beyond the camps, the knotted roots remained thickly woven on the ground. Stepping over them carefully, Shishupal tracked the nine-fingered boy. There was still no sign of Dantavakra. Nothing else moved. The only sound was his breathing, the tread of his feet on the endless carpet of tree roots, and the soft slapping of his sword.

The boy stopped, unslung his antlered bow and strung it in one fluid motion. Shishupal watched him lay out five long, stone-tipped arrows and squint into the darkness. Shishupal traced his eyeline to the target on a distant tree. A whistle of wood later, Shishupal saw that the boy had pierced the target with his first arrow and split the embedded arrow with a second. Shishupal had seen it performed many times by great archers. But never by one without a thumb.

'The show is over.'

Just what I needed, thought Shishupal glumly, *to be caught peeping on a boy.* 'It was a good show,' he rallied. *It was art.*

The boy bowed. 'Eklavvya is glad. Allow him the opportunity to be more presentable, lest it be said the Valkas are savages.' He bent over his sack and rummaged to pull out a thin shirt of rabbit skin.

Shishupal was momentarily confused, but he could not decide by what exactly. Was it because the Valka spoke High Sanskrit in the third person, or was it because he was wearing a shirt of rabbit skin? Eklavvya looked innocent enough, however; though for a boy his age, the strain marks on his arms wound deeper than one usually saw in archers. His torso bore bruise marks. The one around his ribs, probably left from Dantavakra's daredevilry, gloomed with the purple glow of orchids.

'A stream of apologies to keep you waiting,' Eklavvya said as he pulled on a glove over his maimed hand. 'Lord Shishupal, if Eklavvya is not mistaken?'

Shishupal nodded. 'I believe I have you to thank for teaching my brother some humility.'

The boy laughed. 'Fortune smiled on Eklavvya today. The move on the horse was valorous, almost trumping Eklavvya, not with force of course, but with the dark magic that the clouds of surprise thunder with. It was most outstanding, Eklavvya confesses.'

'But you managed to turn him, right at the fall.'

'Agility has been Eklavvya's long-time mistress.'

Shishupal had a nagging feeling the lad had done time with a theatre troupe. But he had bigger concerns to contend with. 'You wouldn't have happened to cross paths with my brother now, would you?'

'Not since the Tournament. Is Dantavakra missing?'

Shishupal saw no harm in confiding in him. 'Danta hasn't been seen since he got wasted at the Old Hog.'

'Ah, inebriation. Most imprudent. Eklavvya deplores its effects.'

'Are you heading to your camp?' Shishupal asked, moving aside to let him pass.

'Eklavvya is, Lord Shishupal, but it is that way.' He pointed in precisely the opposite direction to which the other camps stood. Eklavvya seemed to read his thoughts. 'Valkas are bawdy people to be around, especially when drunk. Best left in a far corner at night. Why don't you come see for yourself? Allow Eklavvya the pleasure of your company.'

Shishupal agreed. It would be just as well to confirm that his brother had not strayed into the Valka camp. And this unusual boy was a refreshing change from the dark conversational alleys Lady Rasha had driven him through.

II

'The Valkas have their funerals when they cross their first year of life,' Eklavvya answered.

'I beg your pardon?' Shishupal took a step back. While he had little interest in things holy, he admitted to some curiosity as to why the Valkas left their dead to rot on the battlefield. But when he had asked Eklavvya the question, he had not expected this answer.

'The life of a Valka is one of peril. Most forestfolk end in the stomach of an iron jaw during mating season or on the riverbed in a flood. Souls cannot enter the afterlife without a funeral song, and there can be no funeral song without a body to hear it. So, our shoulder-men carve magic into the trunks of trees, weave nourishing baskets and bury every baby, once they have passed their first summer, by the roots of a tree, for half a day. If the baby survives, the Valkas know his soul has been blessed by the Forest Spirits to walk into the afterlife once he dies. If not, it is known that the Spirits have claimed the child's song. It is then left buried, and in this manner receives a conventional funeral. So, you see, when grown Valkas die on battlefields, their souls have already received a funeral song in infancy. The body that remains is a shell, a gift to the crows.'

Shishupal must've looked horror-struck, for Eklavvya explained, 'It must appear strange to an outsider. Eklavvya remembers how the Imperial Army took it upon itself to burn the fallen Valkas after the Battle of Goverdhun, only to be met with sniggers from the forestfolk.'

This boy fought in that cursed battle too! Shishupal felt suddenly sad, for he knew what the Battle of Goverdhun had been. A merciless massacre of innocents. Shishupal could only hope Eklavvya had not witnessed first-hand the horrors committed by the Yaksha. He

wondered if he should broach the subject of the Yaksha. Ask who
he was. His Chedi soldiers had claimed the Yaksha fought with
the Valkans, though it had never been confirmed. Eklavvya might
know who the Yaksha was. Conscience pricked his curiosity and
squeezed out a drop of pity. Perhaps not. Those scenes of horror
must have left a dagger lodged in the poor boy's memory. Best not
tap on its hilt.

'Forgive my curiosity, Eklavvya, but...' he grasped for another
topic. 'How are you so good with the sword and the bow despite...'

'Despite Eklavvya's disability, you mean.' The boy waggled his
nine-fingered gloved hand.

Yes. 'No, I meant despite the difficulty.'

'Eklavvya does not let the thing he cannot do interfere with the
thing he wants to do.'

'Admirable. So... you... lost your thumb... was it to some animal
or frostbite— If you do not mind my asking?'

Eklavvya's boyish face suddenly turned older. 'Animals are
nobler, Shishupal. It is humans one needs to worry about. Let's
just say the more sheathed the betrayal, the deeper the gash...' He
pulled off the glove to show the stump where his thumb used to
be. The scar was a jagged circle, a woad tattoo drawn on it in the
shape of a bear. The cut left no doubt that it had been sawn off
with a blade.

Someone did this to him! This was why Shishupal desired a
sheltered existence, where boys were left whole, women had
single-coloured eyes, and goats were the only creatures sacrificed
by priests.

Eklavvya nudged Shishupal. 'Do not grieve for Eklavvya,
friend. Though Eklavvya can never be as good as he used to be, he
is grateful for it. For with a full set of ten fingers, Eklavvya would
have no foes to challenge. Now the others at least have a chance.'

Shishupal laughed. 'Very humble of you.'

'Eklavvya was born with the mark of humility on his left bum.'
His hand suddenly darted out and pushed Shishupal down as a
hammer went flying over their heads.

'Assassins!' Shishupal unsheathed his dagger.

Eklavvya laughed, helping him up. 'No, no, just the usual evening entertainment in Valka camps. Best keep an eye out.'

Red-eyed, worried and hungry, Shishupal drew his cloak tighter and kept his head low as he warily surveyed the stirrings in the massive smoke-wreathed Valka encampment. Misstepping in a Valka camp was akin to pissing on an angry snake. The Valkas were considered to be exotic barbarians by cityfolk, though their civilization was far older than those who made such judgements. They were divided into numerous clans, each identified by their woad tattoos. Some said the tattoos depicted the history of their families. Duels to the death between rival clan members were common, tolerated, and even encouraged.

The Imperial briefing on the forestfolk all those years ago had been detailed and thorough, and Shishupal could pick out the various clans by the standards fluttering above the haphazard groups of tents. He saw the troublesome banner of the two-hundred-strong camp of the Arja Clan, who were distinguished by their enormous neck rings. Perhaps the wildest of the clans was the Esseram, avowed enemies of the Nora Clan. With painted faces and strange nose-rings, they were dancing to a distinctive drumbeat when Shishupal walked past. Many of the clansmen paused their dance to briefly nod at Eklavvya.

Shishupal knew Eklavvya belonged to the Nora, marked by the bone fetishes in their hair. Their camp was at the centre of the encampment. Around them, a score of minor tribes contributed to the confused mix of Valkas. To an outsider, they may be all forestfolk or Valkas, but it was indeed a wonder how the Emperor had managed to rally these mutually antagonistic tribes, with long histories of deadly rivalries, under one banner.

His historical musings were interrupted by the approach of a huge warrior. Bedecked in hair matted with human scalps and holding a platter in his hand, the giant greeted Eklavvya. On bended knee, he raised the platter above his head as an offering. 'Chief, we catch a long sambar today. First offering.'

'Excellent, Taur! Your Sanskrit is improving. May the Spirits bless you. But it is a *large* sambar, not a long one.'

The warrior, who was taller than Eklavvya by at least ten hands, blushed. Dropping his sack, Eklavvya accepted a generous helping of the meat. As he did so, Taur said something in the forest tongue. It must have been about Shishupal, for Eklavvya turned to him.

'Lord Shishupal, you must be hungry. Taur is a most legendary cook. Taste a morsel and be enchanted.'

Shishupal was handed a rather suspicious-looking sausage by the huge Valka. All this hunting for his brother had indeed made Shishupal hungry, but looking at the human scalps around Taur's neck, he realized he was never going to be *that* hungry. 'I have dined, I thank you… ehm… Also *Chief?*'

'*Acting* Chief,' Eklavvya corrected. 'Patre is the War-Chief of the Noras.'

'You are Avaya's son! My apologies, Chief Eklavvya. I did not…'

'Oh rubbish! Valkas don't believe in titles, Lord Shishupal.'

'Just Shishupal, then. I have heard reports. Your soldiers think highly of you. If only my squad was so obedient.'

'Just rumours,' Eklavvya said as he chewed the meat. 'It is probably because of Eklavvya's father. Valkas respect blood. But if Shishupal says his soldiers are disobedient, kill one or two, then the others will respect him.'

Shishupal shrank back in horror. 'I believe it is my job to keep them alive, not kill them, Chief.'

Eklavvya shrugged, munching the sausage with relish. *He was obviously joking,* Shishupal told himself. He looked around the camp, hoping Dantavakra had not wandered in by mistake. He would be chopped to pieces here. Then, even an Oracle would not find him.

'Taur,' Shishupal said. The giant cook turned to regard him with distaste. 'Any chance a Chedi walked into this camp?'

'Many Chedis.' Shishupal followed the direction of his pointing finger. He spotted Valka women leading men from other Magadhan squads into their hide tents. Men from Avanti, Kalinga, Kaunti, Hehaya, Anupa… and *Chedi.* His eyes widened at the trident sigil on some of the cloaks. 'Valka women fierce.

They, uhm, cityfolk like. They say cityfolk, uhm, lambs who need to learn.'

'And you don't stop them?' Shishupal asked Eklavvya. A man who had learnt command by disciplining his soldiers so that the enemy wouldn't have to do it later could be forgiven for being uncomfortable with this display of wanton vulgarity.

'Stop a Valka woman from mating?' Eklavvya snorted, almost choking on the meat. Taur laughed too, each chortle like rumbling thunder. 'Shishupal is funny.'

Shishupal did not know what was funny. As their Lord, he thought of marching up to the eager Chedi soldiers and giving them an earful, but decided against the notion. *The war is about to begin again after the Armistice. They might be dead in a year for all I know. And you are no longer their Claw, remember?*

'Shall we go inside, Shishupal? Maybe your brother is in one of the tents. Best to wait. Come, come.'

He followed Eklavvya and Taur as if in a trance. Observing the Valkan camp was akin to pouring a bowl of spice on a dish. Exciting at first, yes, but Shishupal was moments from running around in search of a glass of milk. He turned his eyes away from the scenes of open fornication, keeping them instead tethered to the cooking fires, of which there were many. Clansmen were gathered around the huge red carcass of the sambar, suspended over one such roaring fire, skewered on a spit. Blood and grease dripped into the flames as two Valkas turned the meat.

'You are not eating a single morsel till I ride you, Eklavvya!' The woman's hair fell down in a wild cascade to her shoulders. Like Eklavvya, she wore braids bound with crow and bone fetishes. A throwing axe was pushed into the belt that encircled her waist. A coarse robe covered her left shoulder but did nothing to hide her lithe form.

'Eklavvya despises the night and all the demonic urges it brings in women. Oh, Spirits take me...'

'The Spirits can take you after I am done with you.' The woman laughed. She turned towards Shishupal. 'You have large hands. I could ride you after I am done with him. Or together. Eklavvya cannot handle me alone.'

Eklavvya turned almost pleading eyes towards him. 'Would Shishupal like to join?'

Shishupal turned a shade of hibiscus, feeling like Surajmukhi, whose legs Kalyavan had been trying to spread apart. *What is happening?* Suddenly, the roar of warning voices turned them around. A bleary-eyed youth had tottered into the camp, only to be greeted by spears.

The boy could not have made a timelier entry, thought Shishupal, blessing his stars. 'Eklavvya, that is my squire,' he said quickly. 'I would be remiss if some harm were to befall him.'

Eklavvya gave a whistle and the guards let Mayasur through. 'You have a Rakshasa for a pet?' Eklavvya asked, crinkling his nose. 'Mind your throat when you sleep.'

Mayasur walked unsteadily towards them. Seeing Eklavvya, he swallowed whatever he had been about to say. Even Shishupal's questioning eyes did not elicit an answer from him. Eklavvya looked on, amused. Shishupal went up to him and grabbed his shoulders.

'Ap... apol... apologies, My Lord. Lord Dantavakra has been found,' Mayasur muttered. 'Lady Rasha requests you to hurry.'

'Where?'

'Uhm… lying in a ditch behind the tavern…' He cast a nervous glance around the camp. 'The tavern from where he set out to complete his task.'

'That I—' Shishupal fumed but restrained himself before strangers. Turning to Eklavvya with a grunt of frustration, he said, 'Duty calls, Eklavvya. It was an honour to make your acquaintance. Will you join me for supper on the morrow?'

'By the time this woman is done with Eklavvya, he will not have enough strength in his legs to trot anywhere.' Before Eklavvya could complain further, he was dragged away by the Nora woman.

III

As Shishupal was taken back to the carriage upon Mayasur's mule, he became aware that Lady Rasha was striding towards him, chin stuck out like an anvil.

'What were you doing with that Valka?' she demanded in what she erroneously surmised to be a whisper. 'Have you lost your wits, Commander?'

'Oh, Lady Rasha, nothing like that. That was Eklavvya, the Contest winner. A Chief, in fact. A noble soul... a kind youth. Speaks funny, though. He is just...'

'Oh *stop*, you *fool*!' Lady Rasha commanded. Her stern injunction rang out in the silence of the Weeds as her bosom fell and rose like an empire. Those in earshot turned, amused to see a woman scolding a man. 'I thought you went to attack him!'

'Attack? That poor boy? No, no, I went to enquire about my brother.' Shishupal turned a quizzical look on her. 'But... I did not expect you to disturb yourself over him. Most cityfolk are not much concerned about forestfolk. You are most...' Shishupal hunted for a word, for he could not imagine associating 'kind' with Lady Rasha. '... Considerate,' he finally managed.

'I was concerned for *you*, idiot! Can't have you killed just when Jarasandh is about to set off for Panchal. He'll take it as another of his freaking omens and my plans will be ruined.'

'Killed?' Shishupal laughed. 'Oh really, Lady Rasha, do not look at me so. You have nothing to worry about. Yes, the Valkas may be savage in their customs, but they're soft at heart, really. And that boy...'

Lady Rasha raised her hand to silence him. That hand would have silenced thunder. 'That boy, you ignorant man, is the Yaksha of Goverdhun!'

KRISHNA

I

From a distance, the Three Sisters shimmered white behind a veil of heat like a mirage. But as he came closer, the Third Sister rose, sudden and sheer as a mountain cliff. *I am going to miss Mathura when I leave.* Mathura really worked, partly because no faction was ever powerful enough to topple it. Namin priests, Drachma counters, Ksharjan Lords, Resht unions, all competed enthusiastically in a race for the top, without realizing there *was* no top. They were all running in a circle like pigs, all the while pulling the others behind in an endless loop.

Krishna did not favour the term 'dictator', for that had been his rallying cry when he had brought down Kans. Also, because he never told anyone what to do. He didn't have to. Most of Krishna's efforts had been directed towards arranging set-pieces so that the state of affairs most conducive to him continued. Of course, there were groups who wanted him brought down, who hated him, but that was a healthy thing, necessary for a well-functioning society. After all, he'd founded most of those groups himself, using his pawns. The same pawns he used to keep these groups bickering with each other over grit and weevils while he ate the rice. Humans, he mused, were beautiful things. Once one understood how to pull the strings. He hoped Dvarka would be more of the same.

Near the Third Sister, a skeletal group of soldiers were practising drills. The Republican Army was on one side, with a section of the City Guard behind them. The Silver Wolves were on the other side. There was a commotion underway and Krishna asked Dahanu to slow the chariot as they rounded the bend to the gates of the Third Sister.

Balram, who was observing the commotion with a jaundiced eye, walked up to a Silver Wolf who held her sword in one hand but did not possess another to hold the shield. 'What's your name, soldier?'

'Misery, Lord Commander!' she replied.

The Republican Army men sniggered in the background. Balram looked up at the Third Sister behind him. Krishna followed his eye-trail to see the distant figure of Satyabhama lounging on the ramparts, both legs hanging dangerously. 'I understand enlisting women, but this one is disabled, Lady Satyabhama!' Balram shouted through his horn. 'Her shield hand is missing. How will she defend herself? How will she be part of a phalanx? How will she…'

Balram was silenced as Misery's fist lashed out and caught him on the bridge of his nose. Balram's head snapped back but his feet did not budge so much as a whisker. Misery screamed and wheeled around, her one hand pressed between her legs, as if she'd just hit a stone wall. A healer immediately rushed to her. A fractured wrist.

Deathly silence fell, till the faint sound of Satyabhama's mocking laughter echoed from above. Even Storm, beside Krishna, couldn't help chuckling. The sound sent a chill down Krishna's spine. *This could get ugly.* The Republican Army, which served under Balram, raised their spears. The Silver Wolves gripped whatever weapons were handy.

Then Balram smiled. His nose wasn't even bruised. 'Very well, Misery.' He bowed. 'Accept my thanks for correcting me. You can be part of the squad, but not the phalanx. We will find you duty more suited to your punching skills. But before that… ten rounds of the Iron Curfew before the sun sets and no milk in your rations for two days.'

Painful tears rolled down Misery's cheeks, but she managed to salute Balram all the same.

'Storm, attend to me,' Captain Rain announced, patting Misery's back. 'You shouldn't have laughed.'

'Me? Not at all. I would never laugh at the *misery* of another.'

'Ten rounds.'

'Fuck!' Storm grunted and stepped out to accompany Misery on her rounds. She turned to glance at Krishna. 'The trip was… entertaining, Lord Krishna. My thanks.'

But Krishna wasn't listening. He was staring at the faint spirals of smoke rising above Satyabhama's head. *She is smoking. This can't be good.*

II

Krishna negotiated the stairs of the Third Sister – a height only Daevas were fit to climb. The food in his stomach made zealous enquiries about emerging in a torrent and his throat seemed rather inclined to grant the request. He paused, looking around warily. He saw the burnt bodies impaled on sharpened stakes at different places along the Third Sister, their elbows drawn up tight in front of their faces, as if to fight off the fire that had consumed them. Vachan-breakers. Their bodies would serve as a deterrent to all his people, for even thinking about spilling the secret of Dvarka. But it did not help his stomach.

The sky was bluer than the Mathuran sigil, fitting neatly over the overcrowded city behind which the Mother Yami sluggishly flowed. Mathura fell away behind him in a vast arc as he finally reached Satyabhama, resting as if she were in a garden, her untied hair shining brown in the sun, pipe in hand. A kohl-streaked tear, dark as death, traced a path against her fair cheek. The wrinkled toxic stick in her hand had an overpowering stench.

Many bards had attempted to describe Satyabhama, but they had all failed. Perhaps it was the sheer contradictions of her personality – the stern, unforgiving, ruthless warrior and the

Mother Patron of a hundred orphaned girls; a beautiful damsel with lips patted with crushed rose petals till they were scarlet as blood, and a scarred woman with not a shred of care for her callused palms.

Krishna had attempted a poem himself not so long ago. He had described Satyabhama as being as full of life as a nun in a field of cucumbers, as bright as a whore in a temple, as colourful as a rack of poisons, as stern as a guard in a prison of paedophiles, as loud as a curse in the House of Saptarishis, and as complicated as Eklavvya's vocabulary. So, when a person of such high calibre sat smoking alone on a high wall, Krishna knew it was something serious. He sat down beside her, still dressed in his travel-stained cloak and mail hauberk. His boots were dusty and spattered with dried mud. He kissed her on the forehead and then wiped the sweat from his lips. 'Lady Satyabhama, is it wise to sit out in the sun in this way? You are sweating like a buffalo.'

'Husband,' Satyabhama muttered, 'don't you know that men *sweat*, women just... shine?'

'Ah, allow me to correct myself then.' Krishna beamed. 'Well, Satyabhama, you are *shining* like a buffalo.'

She gave a short, sad laugh. Krishna was about to open his mouth when she said, without looking at him, 'Don't!'

'I assure you I will not comfort you,' he promised.

'I know,' she sighed. 'But you will try, will you not?'

Krishna laughed. 'You know me. I fiddle with everything. But fine...' He tried changing the topic. 'I wonder why Balram is tiring out the soldiers with drills? There is an Armistice on. Even if the Emperor breaches the peace, which he won't, the Walls will hold. And the weapons Jambavan has given us—'

Satyabhama interrupted him. 'The Sisters are strong and high, but we don't have the men to man them. Half the army is escorting our people to Dvarka. And yes, Jambavan gave us catapults, and those carpets that can stave off blazebane, but the City Guard and the Silver Wolves are too few and too green, and there are no others. A bowl of blazebane with a swift strike, and this great city will fall.'

'But we will be long gone before that, trust me. Since you didn't ask, the Syamantaka trip was a success. Storm took it well. Satyaki fainted.'

'Why do you think I sent Storm?' Satyabhama shrugged. 'The girl shows promise.'

Krishna laughed. 'All set for Panchal? We head out in a few hours.'

The pipe fumed, emitting an aroma fit to raise the dead. 'About that,' she said, 'I'm not coming.'

That is certainly good news. 'But why not?' Krishna tried to sound sincere.

'You know.'

Ah, this is it. Krishna said quizzically, 'I don't.'

'Well… I won't fit in. Those high-born women with their hand fans and face paint, they'll look at me like I am filth, ignore any attempt at conversation, and treat me as a pariah.'

'Why would you want to fit in when you were born to stand out? Why do you have to even look at those pasty-faced ladies who make you the centre of their lives through their gossip?'

'I can shut my eyes and ears, but the trouble is I cannot shut my mind. To them, I am evil. A killer. They see me merely as a third wife who has forgotten her place.'

'And since when did we start measuring our acts on the scale of good and evil? They're just words. We know that.'

'Yes…' She touched her face. 'It doesn't make sense to me, you know, why it affects me so. It's just annoying to have them prick at me.'

Krishna wished he knew the right thing to say to comfort her. He was good with words, but when it came to truly healing those close to him, he failed miserably. He could manipulate, but not mend.

'You know there are days,' Satyabhama continued, 'when Rukmini stands beside you at official gatherings, looking radiant and womanly... I build dark worlds, dark stories, a dark shell around my mind, stories about how Rukmini is a dullard, a stupid cow who cannot tell sword from a spear. They help me keep reality at bay, to wake without screaming.'

'Despite knowing I wouldn't have you any other way?'

'It's not about you, Krishna. I know you like me the way I am. It's about me: that I allow myself to feel vulnerable this way. It is moronic.' She blew out another malodorous ring of smoke. 'I wanted to learn pain and steel, but perhaps I should have learned people instead. I am meant to be left in a battlefield.'

'Maybe... but then I think of those hundred girls out there, who you saved from a life of fire.' He pointed to the distant figures of the Silver Wolves. 'I think you learned *life* instead.'

Satyabhama said nothing. Krishna knew this stuff bothered her, no matter how wrong she was. Satyabhama was a diamond, but there were times she could be glass. He knew nothing he could say would make her feel better. Only Satyabhama could do that. He remembered a young soldier who had apprenticed under Satyabhama coming up to her after visiting Goverdhun and saying, 'This shouldn't have happened.' Krishna remembered what Satyabhama had replied, and decided to use it now. 'Satya, a wise woman once said, there is no way things are *meant* to be. Things just happen, and then it comes down to what we do.'

Satyabhama smiled, and continued from where Krishna left off, 'We can only guard those who cannot protect themselves, for they are the ones who need watching.'

His voice blended with hers to say, 'And most importantly, we never ask for any reward. For it is the only thing that gives us the right to stand before Yama on Judgement Day and have the fucking right to *complain!*'

Satyabhama nodded. 'You remember?'

'I wrote it down, and memorized it over two days.'

Satya shook her head. 'Krishna, you imposter!' She looked at him sideways. 'So, you think I should come with you to the swayamvar? Even if those women get under my skin?'

Krishna was on the whole not the most truthful person. And there were times when the waters did not neatly part in the middle into 'false' and 'true', but 'truths one needed to hear at that moment' and 'truths that one did not need to hear at the moment'. He looked at her and said, 'I think you should do whatever the hell you want.'

'You know, when I first took a drag of this, I saw my life branching out before me like an apple tree. From the tip of every branch hung a magic apple. On one apple I saw a wondrous future with a happy home, children, and silken apparel instead of swords, friends instead of subordinates, admirers instead of rivals. In another apple I saw a brilliant war-leader, drenched in blood and sweat, and another led to a library of scrolls, to infinite knowledge. Yet another showed an Empress, and another a cook, churning the most delicious food. When I craned upwards, I saw an apple with a famous poet, another had the first female Acharya, and another the first female Imperial Contest winner. Above and beyond, there were many other apples I couldn't quite see.'

'What were you doing there?'

'Just starving to death at the roots of the tree, trying to make up my mind which apple to choose. I naturally wanted them all.'

'Classic. But choosing one would deprive you of the others.' She nodded.

'So, what did you do?'

'Nothing till now.' She blew out a final circle of smoke. 'Now, I burn the goddamn tree.'

Krishna smiled.

She stretched down her legs and closed her eyes, turning her face to the sun. 'My father always said: *Never whine about wishes daughter, grow a spine instead.*'

'Wise man, your father.'

'That he was. So, aye, fuck it! My life may be an assortment of anguish, but it is my life, lived my way, and it is dear to me.'

He could see it coming back to her – Satyabhama the warrior, who knew exactly who she was and how she wanted things to be. Her way. She stubbed out the malodorous weed on the wall and tossed the stub away.

'We are late if we are to leave for Panchal. Mind-washing princesses takes time, you know.'

'I will not go, Krishna, for I do not wish to.'

It was what he had hoped she would say, but it surprised him nevertheless. 'Don't you? You know you want to teach those high-nosed women a thing or two with insults their tiny minds cannot comprehend.'

She threw him an amused, knowing look. 'Sure, I do. But I have decided to stop handing them that kind of power. I don't have a fucking thing to prove. Let them do what they do best; I will do me. I will say whatever I want. People may call me rude, but I call myself the Teller of Unfortunate Truths. I may not be a woman the Vedans are used to, but you know what, that's their problem.'

'Your father would be proud.' Krishna stood up, facing Satyabhama. She was five fingers taller than him. 'The world will never control you.'

She leaned down and kissed his lips. In each heart was solemn gratitude to the Gods for giving them the courage to live as they wished to do.

'You are one hell of a woman,' Krishna said when they drew apart. 'I will miss you, Satya.'

'Liar.' Satyabhama turned to climb down the Wall steps, saying over her shoulder, 'So you're really going to mind-wash that poor Draupadi into doing your bidding? Must you always play your games?'

'You have your sword, I have my mind. And a mind can be sharper than any Assyrian blade. We play with the gifts the Gods bestow upon us. And who are they to us? Either carpets to our thrones or casualties on the way.'

'We seem to be rather clever with our words today. Have you chosen who she is to marry?'

'I have some ideas,' Krishna said with a twinkle in his eyes that belonged on an arsonist about to light a torch near a fireworks shop.

'I know that look. Trouble… trouble. Where to now?'

'The griffin stable. It's time I reclaimed *my* ride.'

III

The first thing Krishna saw on entering the enormous stable was Vial, one of Satyabhama's Silver Wolves, stretched on Garud's back, her hands slowly massaging the enormous white wings of the griffin.

'So, I see Garud has found a new friend,' Krishna remarked, startling Vial. 'A friend who is quite eager to skip the drills, perhaps.'

Vial looked positively aghast till Garud brought his blue eyes protectively in front of her and moved one of his enormous foot-long talons towards Krishna.

'But I'm not one to rat her out,' Krishna said quickly, hands upraised. Garud grunted and went back to his repast.

'Has he let you ride him yet?' Krishna asked suspiciously.

'Not yet, My Lord,' Vial replied sheepishly. 'But I do not wish to ride him,' she added nervously. 'He is just... so wonderful. Majestic...' she added dreamily as she snuggled further into the thick golden coat.

Krishna looked at Vial. She could not have been more than eleven summers. He had heard of her from Satyabhama. A lover of strays, she was singly responsible for the health of half the street dogs of Mathura.

'Vial,' Satyabhama said from behind him, startling Krishna, Vial and Garud alike. 'Ten rounds.'

Krishna turned to look at Satyabhama with affectionate eyes, hinting at a pardon for the poor girl, but saw no quarter there. Vial gloomily nodded.

'Of the First Sister,' Satyabhama added.

Garud raised his head at that and turned sharply towards her, only to cower before her steely gaze. Vial looked down sadly. 'Yes, War Mistress,' she said and grumpily headed out of the stable.

'She is just a child, you know,' Krishna said as he readied the saddle and climbed onto Garud's high back with all the grace of a dancer.

'A child barely rescued from the flesh-eating priests of Unni Ehtral. They would have mutilated her... Unlike most of the other Wolves, she has not been sanctified by the fire of pain. I want to make her strong, so that should the day come, she can face pain with a sword in her hand.'

Krishna sighed. 'I was just saying... sometimes we can let the children be.'

'Why do you think I did not stop her when I saw her sneak out of the ranks to play with Garud?'

Krishna smiled as he released the harnesses. 'Please do not burn down Mathura in my absence, wife, or kill my brother, despite how annoying he is. I have just the one.'

Satyabhama smiled primly. 'I promise nothing, Lord Husband. Also, Storm and Calm will accompany you to Panchal, as royal escorts. I daresay Garud can seat three. If I can't be there to look over you, my pups can.'

Well played. Krishna eyed her teasingly.

'Don't flatter yourself. I am training those two to be more than mere soldiers. I could use some highbrows in the Wolves. I have asked them to dress in civilian clothes. And they are under strict instructions to chop Draupadi's nose off if she so much as touches you.'

'Glad to know.' Krishna bowed. 'Well met, Calm... Storm,' he said as they emerged from behind Satyabhama. 'What the...'

'Is this what passes for civilian clothes, Wolves?' Satyabhama rasped.

Calm, who probably even went to the privy in her uniform, was looking uncomfortable and red-faced in the man-suit she wore for funeral pyres. Whereas Storm...

'Storm, civilian clothes mean clothes you wear *outside* of work,' said Krishna dryly.

'But this *is* what I wear outside work, My Lord,' replied Storm reproachfully.

'Don't little boys run after you with stones when they see you dressed like this?' Satyabhama asked.

Storm shifted uneasily. 'Why would they?' She adjusted the big feathers and plaid on her hat and pulled up her imitation gold-studded, flared pantaloons.

Krishna laughed. 'Trust me, Satya, *no one* will mistake them for guards. Come, girls, heroes and princesses await.'

Garud tossed his fierce head and flexed his powerful wings, anticipating flight. 'Away, my friend!' Krishna lightly patted the griffin, who trotted out of the stable, shook his wings, and in a torrent of air, took to the skies. It was a strange thing that Krishna hated climbing high walls, but loved flying a griffin hundreds of feet into the sky. Perhaps it was the way Garud made him feel. *Safe.*

He could not say the same for the Wolves, howling like banshees behind him. Storm's hat flew away, no doubt snatched by some offended God of Fashion. 'My hat!' she cried despairingly.

MASHA'S AUGURIES

The faded tapestries hung dead on the wall behind the ornate desk. In the narrow spaces in between, numerous scrolls were stacked on desktops, alongside pieces of obsidian and stone. In this repository of tomes, eyes the colour of a dirty pond regarded her, not appearing to approve of what they saw. Huge tusks framed the thin mouth and jutting lower lip. The greyish cast of the skin of the only Rakshasa Matron in the House made her look ghastly, even in the hearth's warm light.

'You smell like a fresher.'

'I'm a Matron,' Masha said defiantly. As if anyone else would be found in the Restricted Section of the Library. None but Matrons and caged Oracles lived in the House. And Banshees, of course. Masha drew out the papers Maimed Matron had given her. 'I seek access to the journals on the Sun. I have the approval here.' She handed over the papers.

The woman smiled at her. 'Of course, you have. A thousand restricted books here and all you girls care about is flicking off to that golden-chested boy. So be it. Your name?' She picked up her quill to write in her leather-bound register.

Masha hiccupped. She obviously could not say 'Masha'. It was her old name. She wasn't even supposed to remember it. But the official naming ceremony hadn't yet begun. After that, she would be called by something dark and ominous like Burned Matron and Maimed Matron. 'I… I am just a Matron.'

'Ah, told you I smelled a fresher. Those scars fool no one. These papers,' she pushed back the references from Maimed Matron, 'do grant you access to the Sun's journals, my girl, but you are not permitted entry to the Restricted Section till you are a named Matron.'

'Please! I need to study him to complete my Links.'

'Do you even know what Links are?'

'Certainly. Links are bridges connecting the visions of various Oracles to form a single narrative.'

'Memorised rather than understood.' The woman snorted and went back to her register, pointing her quill at the door that led outside.

Masha was crestfallen. She didn't have much time before the deadline ran out. Burned Matron had told her she needed to know about the Sun before she studied the Panchalan Wedding. 'What do I do now?' she wondered. Her naming ceremony wasn't due till the next blood moon. Tears welled in her eyes.

The woman raised her head to look at Masha. She peered at her and coughed. In the House, a cough was equivalent to a slap on the back of the head.

'Yes, yes, I'm going. There's no rule to say I cannot sit here.'

There was a pregnant silence, then the woman said, 'What if…' she stroked her left tusk, 'I help you out?'

Masha looked up. 'Why would you do that?'

'I used to have visions of him, you know. Of course, I came to know of it only after I was pulled out of Oraclehood. Uhm…' She cleared her throat. 'Matronhood didn't suit me so I chose to be an Archivist, a Keeper of the Scrolls instead. I could help you out. My memory is not what it used to be, so you'll just have to take whatever I give you.'

Masha felt her heart flutter like the wings of a bird. 'I would be very much obliged.'

'Now, foundling, what do you know of our dear Karna?'

'Not much. He was born a Resht. A bad thing in itself, no? To add to the cauldron of calamity, he was born with a rather strange condition.' Burned Matron's journal had described how Karna was born with a golden breastplate attached to his skin. Not with divine powers, not with an extra limb, not with multi-coloured eyes, but an extremely inconvenient golden breastplate that made strutting round shirtless impossible.

'All true.' The Archivist leaned back in her chair. 'But biological deformities aside, he had a malady of the mind as well, growing up. He wanted to be something more than he was. As cancerous a disease as any, for Reshts were not permitted to be something more.'

Masha nodded. It was not as if career choices for a Resht were limited. They could be sweepers, cleaners, gutter diggers, charioteers, stable boys, animal tamers and so on, but Karna wanted to be a warrior. This was blasphemy, even to the most liberal-minded Ksharja. If he liked weapons so much, Masha thought, why had he not apprenticed with a blacksmith, and made his living at a forge? No, Karna had been stupid enough to want to wield the weapons.

'Karna entered the Tournament of Heroes in Hastina, to "shake things up" as you foundlings say. The Tournament was touted as a forum for the young Princes of the Kaurava House, the ruling family of the Hastina Union, to show off their skills. But one Prince stood out even before the contest had begun.'

'Arjun,' Masha chirped.

'Are you telling the tale, or am I?' the Archivist snapped.

'My apologies.'

The old Archivist snorted. 'All Karna ever really wanted was to challenge Arjun in single combat; a duel to establish his own supremacy and so topple the structure of caste. Just how he entered as a caste-revolutionary and exited as Highmaster of Anga is something of a haze in my mind. Anga was some sort of tributary, I reckon,' she muttered vaguely.

Masha knew of Anga from the maps she had studied before she became a Matron. It was a region far flung to the South, above Kalinga. A useful trading post for the Hastina Union, but too far from it for the exercise of direct supervision.

'I remember he was denied permission to compete against Arjun. Prince Duryodhan... you know who that is?'

'Heir Apparent of the Hastina Union.'

'Yes, he is what we call a generous fool. When he saw Karna being denied an equal opportunity to compete, egalitarian notions overpowered the pragmatist in him, and he rose to crown Karna Highmaster of Anga, a territory in his gift. Naturally that made many people unhappy.'

'Did Karna fight Arjun then?'

'Oh, I wish he had, child! That would have been a fight for the Gods to witness. No… there was some commotion, arrows were shot, maces flung, and so on, but the good patriarchs of the Union put a stop to the petty squabble of the boys. But a little too late, I would say. The damage was done, and the lines drawn.'

Masha could imagine. She had never heard of a Resht being granted such a high position in the Hastina Union. It would have set a bad precedent. It would have given the Reshts hope. A thoroughly bad idea.

'His troubles did not end there. While Karna and Duryodhan became the closest of friends… two cursed souls often find solace in each other… in Anga, Prakar Mardin, the now demoted Highmaster, was not about to give up his position to a Resht without a fight. Anga was too far from Hastina for a military solution, so diplomacy it was. It was mostly Lord Shakuni's doing. He was Prince Duryodhan's uncle on his mother's side. So Duryodhan, Prakar Mardin and Karna were to meet at Chilika, the capital of the neutral kingdom of Kalinga, to discuss terms for a peaceful transition.'

Masha took a deep breath and exhaled. Kalinga. The land of dashing seafarers and bold captains…

'Karna travelled by sea with Prakar Mardin, no doubt with the intention of charming him. Duryodhan travelled overland.'

'Why?'

'Well, he never did admit it, but we Matrons know. Duryodhan was afraid of the high seas, so he left his recently promoted, clueless friend alone to deal with Prakar Mardin on a merchanter. The ripples of this single decision set loose a storm in the realm. No, no more questions. Just listen.'

ADHYAYA II

ALL THAT GLITTERS

For all the water in the ocean, can never turn
the swan's black legs to white,
although she lave them hourly in the flood.
—Shakespeare, *Titus Andronicus*

MATI

I

Some ninety *yojanas* from the House of Matrons was located Chilika, the Maze of Harbours, at the easternmost edge of what the Vedans called civilization. If one could float in lethargic circles over the city, like the army of gulls that infested Chilika's roofs, balconies and window sills, one would see how the dark islets gave the place its name.

Chilika sat on a cluster of islands, cutting each other at random angles to resemble a garden of divided plots, reshaped into amorphous confusion by an earthquake. The gulls hovering over the city-island found company in the greylag geese of Jade Harbour, the poor man's port. They could even dine on crabs with a jacana from Purple Harbour, where Kalingan ships were received. If the gulls were particularly unlucky, however, the white-bellied sea eagle, swooping in from Diamond Harbour, would make them his lunch. Diamond Harbour, as its name suggested, was reserved for royalty.

Enlightened Acharyas from the Meru had warned that Chilika was slowly sinking, due to erosion of its shores, and would become a lake in the future. No one paid any heed to such dire predictions, least of all the mass of humanity huddled in the Maze. They were concerned with the present. The future could take care of itself. The King of Kalinga too seemed to share the optimism of his brave subjects, for he had set up his capital in the very centre of the prophesized lake. He believed that a thing of beauty ought to be admired while it lasted, rather than abandoned before its time. Hence, despite half of Jade Harbour having sunk below the sea waters, Chilika remained crowded with ships of all shapes and sizes. Ferrymen poled back and forth across the Tiers, trading galleons unloaded goods from Anga, Kamrup and the Golden Islands, and river runners came and went. All the while, Chilika sank a little more every day.

Just a few *kos* from Jade Harbour, well beyond the pull of the inland current, a galleon with the green sails typical of a ship for hire, drifted aimlessly on the sea. Caught in the doldrums like a slow dream, the *Fat Mistress* had lost all power from rudder and sails alike and had been floating ponderously for a week off the coast. But now the first fluttering among her sails promised relief to her sixty oarsmen, nine crew members and five passengers.

The cleaning girl, however, was not on the deck to witness the first signs of wind. Her body, glistening with sweat, moved feverishly on her bed, her long red hair tumbling down her back. Her tan showed she was well-travelled, and she had indeed seen strange people and curious things. Cleaning jobs offered myriad opportunities after all. Outside, the moon's pale face was shrouded by clouds racing each other like galleons. The stars were fleeting points of light in the dark sky. If she had paused to listen, she could have heard the sound of the banners flapping and the keening of the lines, but she was otherwise occupied.

They rolled on the bed till she was on top of him again. She took his face in her hands. The honey hue of his eyes swirled with golden flecks. In all her years of travel, she had never met a golden-eyed person before, and now she had two orbs of fire staring back at her. She parted his tousled hair and kissed him deep. His brownish black hair felt thick and soft in her hands. Her hands scratched the side of his face till they reached the shadowy hollow under his cheekbones and rubbed his wide-set lips. He was delicious. As she was about to kiss him again, he pushed her aside violently and spat acrid bile into the bucket that stood beside the bed.

'Well,' said Mati, 'isn't that flattering now?'

'I'm sorry, Kala.' The man muttered the name she had assumed for this voyage, still bent over the bucket, heaving wretchedly. But he had already emptied his guts and all he could do now was make un-erotic retching sounds. Mati had to grudgingly admit that even puking the man was easy on the eyes.

The sufferer managed a wry smile. 'As you can see, I am thoroughly enjoying my first sojourn on a ship.'

'Can I do anything to make you feel better, Ser?'

'Just put me on land,' he moaned, turning over to lie flat on his back. 'Some place where the world does not move up and down, sway and shake.'

Mati laughed. You needed a special kind of stomach to be seasick on a ship was stuck in the doldrums. 'You pitiful land-dwellers,' she sighed, shaking her head sadly. 'You look greener than phlegm, Little Lamb.'

'Flattering...' he managed before hurriedly turning back to retch again. When he lay back once again with grunt, as if he'd spent hours working on a farm, she noticed that he was a shade thinner than he had been when she had seen him board at Tamralipta. The strong winds near Ganjam and the roughness of the Kalingan Sea had not agreed with him. Still, it had done little to mar the perfection of his muscled arms, the hard planes of his stomach, his high-ridged face. He still smelled of spice and rain. Pity mingled with lust rose in her, and she crawled back on the bed, finding her way to his chest, her hand seeking, grasping hungrily.

'Really, even now?' her Lamb asked, staring in astonishment, but eagerly wiping his mouth with a rag. His voice was warm, like honey dripping off the comb.

'I don't have to kiss your mouth.' She batted her eyelids innocently.

II

Afterwards, they lay on the floor, exhausted, having arrived there from the bed in rapid descent. She returned to her newly acquired habit of counting his scars. She found pleasure in him, but in truth the greater pleasure was after, when they lay together and he told her stories of the great peaks he had climbed, conjuring the riverlands, tree by tree.

She was a Kalingan, born of the Ocean Goddess. The old men spoke of how the first Kalingans had sprung forth from the Great Sea, riding on whales and sharks. The Salt Men, they were called. They came to the land and were made Gods by the Green Men, who offered them their daughters as offerings. In return, the Salt Men showered them with the riches of the sea and told them of the many ways to fool the Storm God. But the Green Men were not content. They trapped the Salt Men on land, killed their whales, and tortured them into revealing the secrets of conquering the Ocean Goddess. The Green Men forcibly married their daughters, and from this violent union came into being the Kalingan race. *Not the most pious history.*

With her Lamb, Mati felt like a Salt Woman who'd secretly come on land to mate with a Green Man. She taught him the magical ways of her bed, the Two Arts of the Sigh, and the secret ways to keep sea-fever at bay. In return, he spoke of the luxuries of ice. He painted scenes of meadows and glaciers. It was a world far removed from hers. He weaved a life before her eyes, of his days as a Resht in the casteist North, and she listened to him raptly.

Casteism was rare in Kalinga, for most of them did not know which caste they belonged to. The Namins had been banished years ago, when they had attempted to preach against the Sea Gods. With them gone, there was no one to etch each child with the mark that signified their caste. In Chilika, you were either a free man or a slave, a pirate or a merchant.

'You're getting a lot more candour out of me that I am wont to offer,' he said, surprised at himself.

'Pity we don't have more time. I would have flayed your soul.'

He called himself Aradh. On the crew register, he was marked as a lowborn Angan steward, bound for Chilika to trade in horses on behalf of his master. She knew it to be a lie. Men of honour made pitiful liars. His shoulder bore deep bow marks, which marked him as an archer, not a steward. His being lowborn was true enough. The two tears, mark of a Resht, were seared deep into the left side of his neck. But she let him keep his lies. It wasn't as if she was a role model of honesty.

As she ripped his linen shirt down to his waist, the glint of gold welcomed her, like fire from the sun. 'After the numerous times I've ridden you on this cursed voyage, you would think I would have got used to this...' *Imagine its worth in the market.* Her eyes sparkled with greed as she studied the armour he wore under his shirt. It was very thin, and gleamed with inner fire, as if the Gods had polished the gold themselves and wrapped it around his chest. It was the same colour as the rings in his ears. She licked her lips. *For once, stop thinking like a fucking pirate.* She had often run her hands over his chest, exploring to find what held the strange armour tightly secured to his torso, but he always held her hand still. She never made much of it. *He was probably worried she would steal it. And rightly so.* Or maybe he was hairy. Perhaps he had a third nipple. She had had her share of men with three nipples.

'Has not anyone tried to rob you of all this gold?' she had asked him.

'They have tried,' he had answered in a tone that had ended that conversation.

'Are you married?' he had asked in return.

'They have tried,' she had replied, and that had been the end of that conversation.

But the question had brought forth memories of broken promises. For the last year, Mati had been religiously abstaining from temptations of the flesh. But when the Ocean Goddess conspired, there was little one could do. First the doldrums, then the shortfall in rum rations. And finally, the Lamb's beauty. Wisely, she found the only way she could triumph over temptation was by yielding to it. It was good to have an attitude like Mati's, for circumstances eventually found a way to justify what she really wanted.

And the Lamb was quite the find. Naïve certainly, but equipped, dedicated, and best of all, unblemished in the art of love. The fact that he had resisted her initial attempts had only made her want him more. He had been a block of clay to be moulded as she deemed fit. And Mati was too charitable to let him go without turning him into a giver. It was her gift to the Reshts, for surely their women deserved at least this much happiness.

The Lamb was her last adventure, she reminded herself. Now all she looked forward to was getting off this cursed ship to meet her beloved betrothed. After all, her wedding was just a winter away.

KARNA

I

Most ballads say that Luck is a Lady, naked and shapely, reserving her blessings for the most valiant and dashing of heroes. Perhaps this was so, as the bards were usually Namins. If Karna had been asked to give his luck a shape, it would have been a female praying mantis, the creature that made love to its mate, then decapitated him and devoured his body for dinner.

He was a Resht. If he'd taught children to read or steal cutting implements or even hoarded grain, the world might have sympathized with him. But what Karna had wanted as a child had been unheard of. Treasonous, even. For his yearning to be a warrior, he'd been banished from his village. His mother was now dead and his brother had joined the rebels. Karna was left to care for his five-year-old nephew. If this did not qualify as tragic enough, Karna had, in his short life, managed what generations of men passed their lives without. He'd been cursed by *Shraps*.

One did not need to be well-read to know what a Shrap was. A Shrap burned up the atman – soul energy that flowed in the nadis of one's body, the same way blood flowed in the arteries, and dirt in the veins. So, if you had a mind to curse your landlord with gout, you were required to have a bounty of atman flowing through your body to utter a valid Shrap, and use it effectively. A bounty that came after decades of sacrifices, hard diet, severe penance, and starving meditations. Amongst Men, only the ascetics frozen up in the mountains were known to have used a Shrap and lived to tell the tale.

Though there was also the Suicidal Shrap, a Shrap invoked with so much anger and vengeance that it burned through all your atman, using up your age to fuel it. Even then there was no guarantee it would work. For all these reasons, Shraps were extremely rare. But Karna had managed to be cursed by a Shrap not once, not twice, but thrice, by three fine individuals, in three unique ways. Karna was, for all practical purposes, doomed.

On the other hand, having been shunned by every teacher of the weapon arts, he was fortunate to have apprenticed under Acharya Parshuram, the Immortal Teacher of Heroes from an Age the Namins called 'Golden'. His closest companion was Hastina Heir Apparent, Prince Duryodhan. And last month, he had become the first Resht in history to be appointed Highmaster within the Union.

A loving praying mantis.

Why had he ever entered the Tournament of Heroes? Before that, he had only lived by the code of honour which Ksharjan warriors called *Abhimaan*. It meant Pride and Honour. That fed him. That cultivated him. That enflamed him. Since the Tournament, he'd been pushed onto a confused highway without milestones. He could no longer control the momentum; he just kept going, banging his head against one tree and then another, without any sense of direction.

It was the same momentum that had brought him onto this ship. For some reason, Duryodhan trusted him to convince Lord Prakar Mardin, former Highmaster of Anga, to give up his title to him, Karna, the newly appointed Highmaster of Anga. *A fool's errand.* The Mardins had been Highmasters for so long, it was almost a hereditary title for them. He had learned that the Mardins had raised the Tamralipta Port in the days they still wore the Swan Crown and practically ruled as kings. But now, Tamralipta was a Hastina seat, its window to the Golden Islands and the ivory trade of the Kalingan Sea. So, when Duryodhan installed Karna, a Resht, as the new Highmaster, the Mardins could be forgiven for resisting with riots and strikes. And that was why, to Karna, this errand of charming Mardin had sounded much like convincing a man to give up his wife. He knew it had been done before, but he had absolutely no idea what words to use to achieve this result.

It had not made his life easier that Shakuni, Spymaster of the Hastina Union, had asked him to travel on the ship under an alias – Aradh – to protect him from the attentions of right-wing fundamentalists in Anga, who also had reservations about his appointment as Highmaster. Truth be told, Karna had plenty of reservations himself. Though he had once fended off seven bandits with a hunting knife, when it came to using the daggers of politics, he was about as skilled as a toad frying an omelette.

But the mantis moves in paths he can never understand. For when, with the aid of some liquid courage, Karna had finally walked up to Prakar Mardin, the man had not needed convincing. He was apparently satisfied with the bribe Shakuni had offered. Nothing could have surprised Karna more. His warrior instinct warned him to be wary. Nevertheless, he had been content to let the matter rest and be happy that the rest of the voyage would pass by without any awkward incident.

Or so he thought till he met Kala. He had stood no chance before her greyish blue eyes, her dark skin, her lean-muscled arms, her firm breasts, her way with words; the way she did not care about the Resht mark on his neck. She had taught him the ways of the bed, making Karna eager to please her in turn. He loved her raw smell, and the way her red hair curled behind her ears. He was fond of her long-callused hands. She let him lick her fingers, and he'd made up a funny tale about every one of them to keep her laughing. He had never made any woman laugh before. Come to think of it, the last week had been an initiation for him into manhood. Though he did wish she would stop calling him Lamb.

But the passing of the days made him sorrowful. He knew that with every lingering kiss, every touch of their flesh, they gave each other shards of their hearts they'd never see again. Kala did say women from the South had a different way of doing things, but

surely the sharing of bodies was a sacred act everywhere? He liked
being with her. Maybe, if he had not adopted his brother's son, if
he wasn't indebted to Duryodhan, if he did not have promises to
fulfil... maybe then he could have done right by Kala. Perhaps he
still could. The thought continued to nag at him.

'Kala,' he began, struggling to speak out loud the words that
were hovering on the tip of his tongue. All he had to do was ask
her to marry him. *You can do it. You can! Do it!* Kala looked at him
with an amused expression. 'I never noticed them before,' Karna
said, suddenly losing his nerve, pointing to the caricatures drawn
on the ceiling. *Coward.*

'Uhm, what about them?'

'The ceiling,' he said again. 'There are pirates drawn on it... I
think. The paint has chipped so I cannot be sure. I never noticed
them before.' Of course he had not noticed them. The way he had
focused on pleasing her, a unicorn might have peered through the
cracks and he'd never have noticed it.

'Yes, pirates,' she said disinterestedly. 'Kalingans.'

'Kalingans?' Karna was confused. His knowledge of history was
rudimentary. Reshts did not attend the community schools. They
could not even own property. The mildest transgression resulted
in banishment or worse. 'Do they not have a rather robust navy?'

'Make pirates rich enough, and they turn into a navy.'

Karna did not understand but he had learned to get around his
ignorance. 'So, what brings you to Chilika?'

'I see you've time to talk now,' she teased, tracing a finger down
his thighs. 'I'm a cleaning girl. I go where the ship goes. That's
the one perk of my profession – mobility.' That much was evident
from her tanned face, which she wore almost like a mask at a fair.
Though he could not identify the scars on her hand, he could see
how a cleaning job on a ship had its own work hazards.

'What about you?' she asked.

He had the answer prepared and memorized. 'I'm travelling to
Chilika to seek passage to the Golden Islands. My Master owns
a few stables and wishes me to find new markets. It is hoped that
the good folk of Sumatra will welcome what I sell.'

'The Golden Cities are at war, my friend,' Kala told him with a strange look on her face. 'Can it be you do not know this?'

Abyss take me! They had not told him that. 'Well, wars are fought on horses,' he rallied. 'The Islanders will pay a good price for my fine breeds.' She flashed him that curious smile again, as if she knew he was lying. No, it was not possible. She was a cleaning girl, not a mastermind tactician, he thought.

Kala rose from the bed to collect her strewn robes. 'You must leave now. I must get to my chores. The ship isn't going to clean herself. And we don't want the Captain wondering why I am missing.' She winked.

He too rose, naked but for the gleaming armour on his chest. 'I'm sorry, Kala.'

'Sorry?' Her smile faded from her sharp face, replaced by a confused scowl. 'For what?'

'I wish I could have done right by you, Kala.' He mentally traced the bond that had formed between them but decided he could not plunge her life into darkness along with his. 'But I have a debt to repay back home, and this,' he pointed to her dishevelled bed, 'I cannot...'

Kala stared at him in bewildered surprise. Then she stepped forward and gave him a long kiss. It felt good. 'I understand.' She sniffled. 'I... will try to live with just the memory of you. I hope you remember me too.'

'Always.' Karna held her hand. 'Forgive me, Kala.'

She buried her face in his bare shoulder. For a moment, he thought she was laughing, but then realized she must be shaking so because she was crying. He felt like a fish out of water. He thought again of proposing marriage. But before he could ponder this, she stepped away, wiping her eyes. *It had to be done.* 'You will always be my first,' Karna said with a smile to take some of the sting from his rejection. 'Maybe someday, when I have paid my debts—' Kala pressed a finger to his lips, perhaps to stop him from giving her false hope.

They heard the muted call of the cox. Twenty-six sweeps slid out, blades settling in the water. The *Fat Mistress* groaned as it lurched forward. The doldrums had finally given way to winds. *Shit*. It was time to meet Prakar Mardin and get him to hand over the signet and sign the transfer deed. It was now or never.

Hastily, Karna got dressed. 'Would you happen to know where Prakar Mardin is?' he asked.

Her face darkened. 'You aren't going to tattle on me to that prick of a Highmaster, are you?'

'I heard he is no longer a… Highmaster. And no, of course not, My Lady. Your honour is mine to guard. I merely have urgent business to settle with him.'

'Best be on your way then lest he become *unavailable* later,' she said with a sly smile. 'He must be on the deck. But Aradh, before you leave… you said something about a debt. I gather you meant it metaphorically?'

That was a strange word for a cleaning girl to know. An educated cleaning girl! Hastina obviously had much to learn from Kalinga. 'Aye.' He nodded, trying to understand the meaning of the word from context. 'I am oath-bound to my benefactor. But now I find myself lost, and I don't know the way back. Have you ever found yourself in a situation you just wanted to be out of, no matter how blessed your life seemed to be?'

'Counting *this one*,' she pointed at him, 'maybe a few times. You are not a child, Aradh. Do what you want. Forget promises and debts. You have just one life to live.'

'A man is not known by the promises he makes but by those he keeps.'

She gave a shrug. 'You Greens are funny men, Lamb, with your honour and codes. I have found, at great cost, that the best way to keep your word is by never giving it.'

'I'll remember that the next time,' Karna said, smiling. '*May the waves carry you.*'

'Ah, I always said you're a quick learner. *May the current bring you back*,' she returned the traditional Kalingan greeting.

Karna hastened out. He thought he could feel her unwavering gaze on his back. He imagined her standing by the door of the cabin, watching him go. *I'm not going to look back*, he decided resolutely. It was for the best. He knew that sometimes one had to be stern to be generous. So, when he heard the cabin door shut amidst peals of laughter before he had barely stepped away, Karna had a sudden, fierce suspicion that he had got something wrong.

MATI

I

A thing of beauty is said to last forever, unless it begins to speak. Mati thanked the Storm God that her Lamb had not proposed marriage. Nothing ruins an affair more than an effort to make it last. It was all she could do not to laugh in his face. Silly Northern virgins, the fantasies of those lovesick puppies could outrun a galleon. Her first had been so uncomplicated. He'd been a muscled sailor from Madurai, with a gorgeous mustachio. He only knew three words of Sanskrit but 'cunt' was luckily one of them. That reminded her that once she got off at Diamond Harbour, she would have to seek out a *devadasi* who could brew the moon-tea to keep her belly flat.

As she looked up, a flight of sea crows sailed over her in the direction of the ship. Sign of land. She could see the Sassan, Kalinga's fortified shipyard, to the far west, against the rich blue-green sea – the heraldic colours of Kalinga. Yet now the banners that fluttered from its battlements were red, not blue, and where the Kalingan Swan had once flown proudly, there now roared the crowned lion of the Magadhan Empire. She knew Kalinga wasn't truly conquered by Magadh; it was too free to be contained by a conqueror. Jarasandh, however, managed to rule Kalinga through indifference. Magadh didn't care about the everyday administration of Kalinga as long as the seal of the lion was stamped on official documents, and Kalinga provided a ship or two in times of need.

So, Kalinga remained Kalinga, and these days, even less regulated than it had been in the past. For the poor, their life of unhappy comfort and adventure continued. For the rich, they had to bow their heads from time to time. The Kalingan royalty, however, was a miserable breed. Bending the knee did not come easily to the Swans. Frowning, she turned to look straight ahead to where the lighthouse on Diamond Harbour loomed, beckoning the ship, carrying the diplomats, home.

High time. She grabbed the rope that went down from the upper deck. She had strong arms from a lifetime of sailing. It was traditional for children of the Swan to be given a taste of seafaring from the time they were young enough to keep their balance on a rolling vessel, but no one had taken to shipboard life as eagerly as Mati. She first crossed the Strait of Malacca at the age of seven, sailing to Bali with an aunt. And thereon, she made such voyages every year. And it was not as if she travelled as a passenger, in comfort. No, she tied knots, raised and lowered sails, manned the crow's nest, climbed masts, scrubbed desks, tended to the horses, caulked leaks, and learned to navigate by the ancient stars. Her captains said they had never seen such a natural sailor. She had sailed the Kalingan Sea for a decade as an oarsman, a quartermaster, and finally Captain of her own galleon, before retiring to a desk. *Good times.*

She had travelled north on a business matter, to broker a deal for fishing canoes, when she had first met him. He'd come, a representative of the Council of Hundred of the Union, to complain about the high prices the Kalingans charged for their products. *Nothing more insufferable than a man of duty,* she remembered thinking. He was stiff and disciplined, with a jaw as unmovable as a mountain. Worst of all, he had some sort of immunity to winking and bribery. Mati had loathed him.

She had never thought much about love till then. One could thirst for coin, glory, or love, but could only possess two of them. And for her lovers were like servants: plentiful and easily forgotten. But just when she was surest of her imperviousness, love crept on her like an assassin, lurking under the table of documents, tariff sheets and contracts over which she and the Northerner discussed freight, levies and bribes. Just when it emerged to stab both of them in the heart Mati could not tell, but the job had been clean and effective. The moths of trade had been replaced in a night with the butterflies of attraction. She knew land and sea did not mix. Sooner or later, she would have to leave him. She decided it had best be done on the morrow.

But the morrow never came.

It was an affair like none before. Neither was of a poetic bent. Mati knew nothing of flowers, which was just as well, for he would never have thought of comparing her to one. It dawned on her that the dalliance did not fade, no matter how long she waited. And astonishingly, she didn't want it to. She had heard bards drawl that love made you weak in the knees, and upset the stomach, but she hadn't realized it could make you selfless as well. What else could explain her adventure on this ship? She was only here, risking her life, to prepare his wedding gift and clear the thorns in his path, once and for all. After all, love without self-sacrifice was just lust.

It hit Mati again that she should not have lain with the Lamb. *Ugh*. Regret and guilt were those aunts who always came after a disaster to say 'I told you so'. Unhelpful, uninvited, utterly annoying. *Well, do not men host pillow-house celebrations before marriage?* But she knew her Northerner was not that sort, no matter how much she wanted him to be. It amused her to feel this sense of… guilt, a new emotion she had ached to sample for a while. She had always envied the ability of others to impose moral cages on themselves. The cages that allowed them to suffer pain and share happiness, rather than remain outside, forever acting. Sometimes she felt she had dovetailed into her future with the Northerner for the sheer pleasure of experiencing the ordinary, but here she was again, repeating the same mistakes. Wild and wildly unpossessed. *Never again.*

II

She felt the galleon slow. It was amusingly named *Fat Mistress*. Amusing for the unlikelihood of what the name connoted. It wasn't much of a ship for a second look, unless it was to wonder how she managed to stay afloat. Her hull figurehead showed a laughing woman with a fat paunch, pocked by worm holes. Drab brown paint covered the hull. There was just one Royal cabin, inhabited currently by the former Angan Highmaster, Prakar Mardin, a stateroom for the Captain and three sub-par cabins for other passengers. The crew was housed with the horses the *Fat Mistress* was ferrying. She would need to soak in perfumed rose water when she disembarked at the Diamond Harbour to rid herself of the stench of manure, Mati thought. *Just an hour more.*

In the distance, a loud hollow thud came from the water, like a large stone dropping to the ground. A disquieting sound followed – a rude discord of trumpets blown for noise rather than music. Ninety yards ahead, to starboard, a vessel was approaching. Mati's first thought was that it was a pirate ship, but then she heard the man in the crow's nest shout fearfully, 'Customs Guard!'

Storms! She felt light-headed rather than afraid. Adjusting her maid's turban, she scurried across the deck to the port rail. A pair of delicate customs skiffs had scudded out to meet the *Fat Mistress*, red and orange lanterns bobbing in their bows to the rhythm of six heaving oarsmen. 'What vessel?' the duty officer shouted through a speaking trumpet as the customs stoop came up.

'*Fat Mistress*, Anga,' came the return shout from the waist of the ship.

'Are you bound for Jade?'

'No, Diamond Harbour. Got me a dignitary; can't land him at Jade.'

'Goods?'

'Horses.'

'We've heard news of a plague ship in these seas. We are coming up to check. Get all your passengers out. After our healer gives you a clean chit, you can be on your way.'

'Aye! We'll throw you a rope.'

'For fuck's sake!' Mati grunted. Even with the turban covering her red hair, the customs guards would recognize her immediately. She remembered the Kalingan adage: *If there is a whirlpool to port and a kraken to starboard, a Captain steers a third course.* She rushed to the stern of the ship, where a few small dinghies were strapped to the railing near the craplines. She would have to escape in one of these, all the way to Diamond Harbour. It could be done.

A sailor was leaning over the rail, watching the customs guards approach, when Mati came up behind him. He looked around, surprised to see her. 'Best find your way to the line, lass. The Customs Guards mean nasty business. They'll take you for an unlicensed whore and put you behind bars or worse if you try 'n hide.'

'I suppose the fact that I'm not a whore doesn't count?'

'You got teats, don't you? That's whorish enough for them likes.'

'I was wondering if I could escape off the ship on one of those dinghies?'

The sailor gave a sharp cracking laugh. 'Won't that be fascinating to watch, eh?'

An official's high-pitched voice came up from the main deck behind him, complaining to the Captain, who responded in an indistinct rumble. She was out of time. Mati handed the sailor a gold sovereign. 'Maybe I can change your mind?'

The sailor's mirth faded. He took the coin and bit it to check. He was sorely tempted, telling himself it was not cowardice if he was saving the woman's honour. But instincts of self-preservation were stronger. 'Can't do it, lass. Not with the Customs Guards here. The Captain will have my head if he finds the dinghy missing. I'm no turncloak.' Reluctantly, he handed back the coin, his saliva glistening on its surface.

'I thought you'd say that.' Mati carefully wrapped the poisoned coin in her handkerchief and tossed the lot into the sea. It had done its work.

The sailor watched the handkerchief plop into the water then turned to look at her, his eyes wide with horror. His hand went to his throat, but no sound came. He fell to the deck. Dead men tell no tales.

Mati pulled hard at the pulley, the ivory rings straining against her scarred, muscled arms. The dinghy made a quiet splash as it hit the waves and she quickly took the oars. She craned her neck to spot Diamond Harbour, but there was no sign of the lighthouse. Dread crawled up her back as she realized her folly. *Storms! I got down on the wrong side of the ship.*

KARNA

I

The deck resounded with screaming voices. Crewmen and stevedores busy hiding contraband made it difficult for Karna to find his way to Prakar Mardin without bumping into them. Officers in the blue uniform of Kalinga scrambled around him. *Customs Guards.* They were all staring at a disappearing dinghy on the western horizon while the *Fat Mistress* turned violently in the rough waters. It was all Karna could do not to retch again. Past the stern, he could see the shrinking shape of the lighthouse of Diamond Harbour. As he moved towards the stern, he heard the Captain shouting commands: 'Tack and sheets, you slothful dogs! Smartly now!'

He spotted Prakar Mardin by the railing, dressed in his blue jacket decorated with silver buttons, probably worth the entire crew's annual wages. His cheeks were powdered pink in some court fashion. He was flanked by a pair of guards, their dark faces buried in snarled beards. They stared at him, or more particularly at the Resht tattoo on his neck. Karna stared back, and they returned to ignoring him. Karna himself was dressed in passably aristocratic style in a caramel-brown knee-length coat that he was sweating in. A mark of a fraud, for the truly rich never sweat.

'Ah, welcome, Lord Karna, or should I say Aradh?' Mardin chuckled, dismissing his guards and beckoning Karna closer. 'About time you came to speak to me.'

I have been chasing you for a week!

A stevedore ran behind them, hands flailing. Mardin frowned. 'I daresay we should tell the Captain to shift our belongings onto the patrol boat. With the ship turning to Jade, it will take a lifetime to reach the Diamond.' Karna frowned. 'Ah, you don't know. Seems that someone stole a boat and escaped just as the customs guards came alongside. An absconding criminal. Imagine, we've spent all this time on the ship with a murderer in our midst!' Karna flinched momentarily. 'And just when I was beginning to think this journey so very tedious. At least you have had that maid to entertain you.' He grinned at Karna's horrified expression. 'Privacy on a ship at sea is about as real as a Daeva. She was with me before, did you know? Like Anga, you have inherited her from me. A fan of leftovers, are you?'

Karna knew Mardin was trying to get a rise out of him by lying. He kept quiet.

Mardin laughed. 'To be honest, I don't remember much about it. I vaguely remember her entering my room, all seductive in her steps... you know what I'm talking about... and then it's all a haze. Too much wine. What's her name again, boy?'

'I do not recall asking,' Karna said shortly, not wishing to get Kala into trouble.

'Admirable policy.' Mardin nodded approvingly.

'I wanted to talk to you about the signet and the transition documents. I...' Karna hated this part, 'I assure you that as a former Highmaster, you will continue to enjoy the luxuries you and your family are used to. The Prince's vision is...'

'I don't give a rat's arse about the Prince's vision, Karna,' Mardin said, smiling affably. Karna's hands stiffened on the rail, itching for the dagger hidden in his coat. 'Shakuni told me you stink at this, but I had no idea how much.' Mardin put a hand on Karna's shoulder. Despite himself, Karna was taken aback. Ksharjas did not touch Reshts. From the corner of his eye, he could see his guards flinch. 'I like you, Karna. A classic brooding Northern specimen.'

They heard the Captain blow his whistle. 'Haul off all, you maggots! Lines on! Braces on! She is getting away!'

'Come inside. It is too noisy out here. Have a drink. But before that, I want to know: how did you manage it?'

'How did I manage what?'

'Don't be coy with me, boy. You managed to befriend the Prince of the Union, and somehow convince him to crown a Resht as Highmaster of Anga. Clearly, your diplomatic skills are as fresh as yesterday's cheese, so how did you do it? It's all such a mystery to us, so far as we are from the capital.'

Just how he had managed to enter the Tournament of Heroes as a revolutionary for the Reshts, and left it as an ally of the Ksharjas, was a mystery to Karna too. All he'd wanted was to shake things up by defeating the finest Ksharja archer, Prince Arjun, and bring about the awakening that even lowborn Reshts could be warriors, could be heroes. But what Karna was ignorant of was that an essential qualification to be a hero, in addition to secondary attributes such as skill, was the art of brandishing. Arjun flourished his well-oiled bow in just the right way to catch the light and dazzle the audience. After all, hitting the target was mere ritual. Arjun's quiver was ornate and unique, created by Hastina's best craftsmen. Just touching it practically conferred heroship. Even his arrows were studded with magnificent gems that twinkled all the way to the target, leaving no doubt that he was the Chosen One. Chosen for what precisely, no one bothered to ask.

Karna, on the other hand, with his worn-torn tunic and second-hand bow, had found no takers. No sponsors. He did not have the coin to compete, no lands to mortgage, no gold to pawn... When he'd stormed into the field and taken down the target from a distance, he had expected gasps of shock. Instead, he was booed. No Resht dared cheer for him. He would have been imprisoned had not the kindness of a stranger saved him. Duryodhan, cousin to Arjun, had risen to vouch for Karna.

That had not stopped some of the other contestants from leaving the lists to show Karna his place. There had been six against the two of them. There had been anger in those men, a hardness, the need to defend tradition. It had not been about winning the Tournament. The Tournament had been contrived as a display, an entertainment for the city, an opportunity to show off Prince Arjun's skill, not as a to-the-death contest. Even so, those eyes beneath their helms had brimmed with cold fury, and none had come forward to stop them. They had not even cared that they were coming at the Heir of Hastina.

But in the end rage and numbers had not mattered. The fight had been over so swiftly, it still felt like a dream. Karna had fought those six men back to back, and then side by side with Duryodhan, a man he had never seen before. It had been an unsettling experience. Karna fought with a bow. Duryodhan used a mace. But it felt strangely akin to having doubled himself. They had not spoken during the fight. No tactics. No warnings. But they had fought with one controlled mind. In no time, their foes had fallen. Usually, Karna remembered a duel as a play, every thrust and parry and feint etched into his mind for him to study later in solitude. His mind worked that way. But that evening was a blur.

Karna had spent his life alone, whether at home or at war. Even in his darkest years he had never sought a company to command, or even a friend. Who would want to befriend a Resht with a death wish anyway? Over the years, having been cursed thrice, he had come to see the world as a place where he walked on a bed of burning coals by himself. He had never married. His brother had a child. He knew his line would continue. He had been young then, wealthy, with notions of his invincibility, possessed of an awed realization of all the shimmering possibilities that revolution held. But all that had changed that day, when Duryodhan had said simply, *Come, Brother!* as six men walked forward to encircle the two of them. *Shall we teach them how this is done?* They had taught them alright.

He had looked at Duryodhan after it was done, and seen him smiling at him with the same strangeness Karna felt. As if they both realized something, and knew what the other was thinking. Karna had been wrong. For Duryodhan, in a bid to silence the enraged crowd which was on its feet with raised fists, appointed the glazed Karna Highmaster of Anga. He said something about Highmaster being an administrative post, and not one of royalty, which was reserved to Ksharjas. But Karna didn't remember much. He had been too unfocused. It was only when he had seen a small part of the crowd, all Reshts, throw their turbans and scarves into the air in excitement, that he had finally... bowed.

'I was lucky, I suppose,' Karna answered.

'Oh, don't be so humble. Humility is nothing but artfully disguised arrogance. But you should have politely refused Duryodhan's offer. The highborns hate you for your guts and the Reshts think you sold them out. Even my guards don't know who you are. You, my friend, are in a strange and lonely place called *no man's land*. Not a comfortable place to be.'

'You'll forgive me if I don't yell in shock and run.' Karna shrugged.

Mardin smiled as he led his guest to his cabin while the ship's bow titled past the wind to stare straight at Jade Harbour. *No man's land. How about that?* There was even a name for the mess he found himself in. But he owed Duryodhan. *He saved me once with his word, and once with his mace,* Karna thought. *And then he destroyed me with his offer of friendship.* The world stopped making sense when a Ksharja Prince shielded a Resht upstart. But it is always that kind of truth, the truth that is stranger than fiction, that brings about real change in the world. Maybe Duryodhan and Karna were destined to turn this no man's land into a place where no man's caste could ever be an obstacle to what he could truly achieve.

Or so Karna hoped.

II

A lavish meal was laid out. There was a great joint of mutton, roasted with spices, fish chops sauced in honey, peppered chicken, and cold fruit soup. Mardin chewed a succulent chunk of goat meat and took a noisy gulp of the fruit soup. 'Anga is smaller and meaner than Hastinapur because it is a place of eternal strife.' He paused to finish chewing. 'See, Anga is not composed of soft greens like Hastina, or filled with tardy fish like Kalinga; it's a cauldron of conflicting civilizations and cultures. Even Kalinga with its massive naval force cannot boast a port like Tamralipta.'

Karna had been taught this by Duryodhan. Anga was Hastina's door to the rich markets of the Golden Islands, and with such a mix of cultures, Duryodhan believed Karna's caste would not be the issue it was in Hastinapur.

'But Anga lies *well* beyond the reach of the Eagle's talons. Hastina's method of ruling through treaties rather than outright subjugation, as Magadh does, is fraught with flaws. With your Blind King having lost the regions conquered by Pandu, Anga might indeed start clawing for freedom.'

Karna recalled what he had heard. 'Anga might be an ally of Hastinapur in theory, but Hastina's conquest of Anga is indeed complete. Hastina laws are Anga laws now, as is its culture. And our laws allow no secession.'

'Yes, yes, I am well aware of Hastina's obsession with the Rule of Law, but to *continue* ruling, Hastina must *keep* Anga. However, the intervening Riverlands are full of bandits, and worse, forestfolk,' Mardin said. Karna saw beads of moisture sparkling on Mardin's forehead.

'The Emperor might be breaking his back in Mathura,' Mardin continued, 'but even the remnants of his host are enough to take down three Angas. The Yamuna Wars are at an end now. The next battle will be the last battle Mathura will face. But it won't be the Emperor's last battle. A thousand Valka savages prowl the lands fringing the tracts that connect Hastinapur to Anga. To Anga's south lies Kalinga, the Emperor's vassal.' Mardin coughed. 'It is only a matter of time before Anga slips away from Hastina, for mark my words, Jarasandh *will* turn his eyes on Anga next. You see, that's the thing with conquerors, they cannot stop conquering, for then they would have to start ruling, and my guess is Jarasandh isn't as good a ruler as he is a conqueror.'

'We can strengthen our defences, build walls…'

'No doubt the Swan Kings thought the same thing when Hastina conquered Anga all those decades ago. My advice, boy, is to make friends on both sides.' He coughed again. 'And I don't mean diplomatic relations.'

'Make friends with the Emperor?'

'No, no… Jarasandh would gladly hang you and the Prince from the same tree. He has become most religious with that mad cult of his. I mean, make friends in the merchant guilds. Take some, lend some. It is the way of life.'

'A fancy way of saying *bribe them*.'

'Hah, that's what I admire about you, Karna. Straight to the pith. I see you are sceptical, but this is the East, the Land of the Crafty. Have you heard of the Black Swan Uprising?'

Karna nodded. 'Seven or eight years ago, wasn't it? But it was put down.'

'The Kalingan King put it down,' said Prakar Mardin, coughing again. 'Pardon my coughing, Karna.'

'Are you alright, Lord Mardin?'

'Oh absolutely. Just this change in climes, you know. First doldrums, then storm. Where was I? Yes. Decades ago, when Magadh came with its horses and elephants to conquer Kalinga, there wasn't much of a fight the Pirate Islands could put up, unless you count hiding as fighting. But Magadh knew it could not tame Kalinga, and Kalinga knew it could not defeat Magadh. A situation fraught with possibilities, you perceive.

'So, a treaty was entered into on the Isle of Rose, whereby Magadh agreed to withdraw, in return for Kalinga's fealty and adherence to the Imperial Code. Magadh did not know the way of the Storm God: that amongst Kalingans, every man and woman is King of their own ship, and each ship a kingdom unto itself. But pirates are nothing if not an adjusting race. Chitragandh, a feared ship captain, rose to the occasion and donned a crown. Naturally some folks were unhappy. Pirates are nothing if not a jealous race.'

Mardin helped himself to some more wine. 'So, eight years ago, these squabbling seagulls got it into their heads to make a bid for power. They asserted their "right" to levy taxes on ships in the Bay of Kalinga. By taxes they meant plundering and looting.'

'Black Swan...' murmured Karna.

'Aye. She was the Captain they all followed. Black Swan was a legendary pirate of Kalinga, its pride. It was rumoured that she had been one of King Chitragandh's navy captains before she turned cloak.'

'A traitor?'

'It is a matter of perception, boy. One man's traitor is another man's rebel. All depends on where the play is being performed. So, as I was saying, the pirates hit Ganjam and Soro, and just about every port and landing on the northern Kalingan coast. It was the greatest aggravation Kalinga had faced since the Magadhan invasion. They raided merchant ships in full view of King Chitragandh, and hauled sail for sea when the Kalingan galleons darkened the horizon. But they were trapped by their own status as rebels.'

'What do you mean?'

'Pirates and mercenaries, they can run, hide, surrender and melt away indefinitely, but when you become rebels, you usually end up in a battle to hold on to your status. They were all strong pirates, every one of them, but they were no match for the war galleons when it was line against line on the open sea. No doubt the coin lent by Magadh helped. Still, people expected a contest. Bets were laid.'

'People bet on a battle?'

Mardin smiled. 'There is little men will not wager on. It keeps life interesting. You will come to realize that Easterners are most industrious when it comes to commerce, but many lost their money that day. Mysteriously, the navy knew each move of the rebels before it was made. The navy sank half their fleet, assassinated the hardy pirate lords, and sent the rest pissing their breeches to prison. Black Swan wound up on a podium with a noose around her neck, the end of the rope in King Chitragandh's hand. In a twist that would make a playwright weep in envy, the King kissed the Black Swan's forehead.'

'What!' Karna's eyes widened in proportion with the twist in the plot.

'She was his daughter. She had knowingly led the rebellion to bring all the errant pirates into one basket for the King to set fire to.' Karna's jaw hung open. 'With that, piracy became a fairly unpopular choice of profession in Kalinga. Good times ensued for wily merchants, dishonest counters and crafty insurance men. There are still pirates, of course, but they don't come within seven yojanas of Chilika, nor anywhere near Ganjam or the coast. The peace on the seas has meant that Hastina's navy in Anga has had nothing more serious than plague ships to deal with for the last five years. A quiet time.

'But quiet isn't happy, Karna. Peace meant less piracy and fewer pirate ships on the seas. The merchants used to pay baskets of sovereigns to the Hastina navy to escort their ships across the sea to the Golden Islands. All that income.' He blew away an imaginary puff of powder. 'Anga has ceased to be profitable because of this peace. So you see, when Lord Shakuni offered me his inducement to vacate the position of Highmaster, I was more than happy to accept. All this is your headache to deal with now.'

So that's why he caused the riots in Anga. Not to retain his seat as Highmaster, but to leverage his position. Karna frowned, shifting in his seat. Every man must face waters in which he feels out of his depth, but Karna felt he was drowning, chained to the goddamn seabed.

'But, to ensure Duryodhan's charity continues, you have to be aware of what I have come to know of certain plans. Devious...' The former Highmaster sopped some of the gravy with a chunk of bread. And coughed again. It was loud and thick, the pain almost audible. Prakar Mardin looked queerly at the bread, and broke into a violent fit of coughing. His face turned red.

'Sip some wine, My Lord,' Karna suggested, pleased to see the scheming rat suffer. The riots he had caused had made Duryodhan very unpopular in Hastina. Nobles had left his side. Merchants had screamed murder. In times of a succession crisis in Hastina,

Mardin had proved to be the greatest thorn in Duryodhan's side. It was all Karna could do not to strangle Mardin himself.

'Yes...' *cough* '... excellent notion...' The Highmaster raised the chalice to his mouth, but before it could touch his lips, he broke into another outburst of coughing, so savage that he fell back in his chair.

'My Lord!' Karna rose, alarmed now. He hurried to Mardin's side and propped up the shivering body. Dark wine had stained his robes and was running in little rivulets on the table, rushing forward then rolling back with the swaying of the ship. Karna spun the old man around and thumped him on the back with the heel of his left hand. Prakar Mardin spat out flakes of the food he had just eaten. He clutched at Karna's hand with desperate strength.

There was a loud knock, and the Highmaster's guards filed in, weapons in hand. 'Get away from him, you cretin!' the leader shouted.

So much for being Highmaster. 'He is not choking but his throat has swelled up as hard as a stone. Get the ship healer here,' Karna ordered, eyeing the food on the table with dread. Mardin's struggles in his arms grew alarmingly faint. But the guards did not budge. They lowered their spears, their faces etched in horror as they stared at Prakar Mardin. Frowning, Karna turned Mardin towards him. His pupils had all but disappeared, replaced by ghastly whiteness. His neck was bleeding from the cuts left by his own fingernails frantically gouging at his own neck. *He has been poisoned,* Karna realized.

Suddenly, one of the guards bellowed, 'Spears!' and Karna found a score of sharp points aimed at him. 'You low-life! Time to die, Resht!'

III

He was aware that his left hand, unbidden, had unsheathed his dagger, and two fingers of his right hand, acting on sealed orders from his mind, had raised themselves in a threatening gesture. Reason told him he should first try to resolve disputes without a fight. It was just that he could not remember the last time Reason had dished out practical advice to him.

Madness erupted as the news of Mardin's poisoning spread. Karna was such a convenient scapegoat that he himself was half inclined to believe it. Naturally, no one believed him when he declared that he was the new Highmaster of Anga.

'May I remind you of the consequences of apprehending a Highmaster, my friends?' Karna said.

'If you are the Highmaster,' said one of the fat customs guards, chewing tobacco with the vigour of a cow, 'then I am the Queen of Panchal.'

Karna could hear the rasping voice of his teacher: *The finest victory is one that is won without violence.* Taking a deep breath he said, 'There is really no need for all this unpleasantness. Land is but a short distance away. Let justice take its due course.' He eyed the Angans, still gripping their weapons, then turned towards the customs guards. 'I am a guest of the Kalingan Overlord, Chitragandh. Is this how you treat his guest? I am entitled to the privileges of a diplomat.'

'Leave him to us!' Mardin's guard growled to the customs guards. 'We will take care of him and no blame will come upon you.'

'Aye! We will blame it all on that bitch that left Ago for dead!' a sailor echoed. Catcalls greeted this suggestion.

'He is a cur... a Resht dog!'

Karna frowned. He was used to such attitudes in Hastina, but he had not expected it in Kalinga. Caste prejudices had an international appeal, it would seem.

'No wonder we were stranded at sea for so long. Let's gut him before we reach Kalinga.'

'Our wheat stock all spoiled 'cause of him!'

'Kill him!'

'I saw that wench go to his room! She was the Lord's keep before,' said one of Mardin's guards. 'Him and that wench are in this together. The wench got away, but we'll get him.'

Karna froze. *So, it was Kala who fled in the lifeboat. Surely, she could not have...*

'Aye! Let's toss him overboard with his legs tied!'

Karna instinctively dodged a half-eaten apple which arced past his neck. *Fuck it. Diplomacy be damned.* He head-butted the nearest man, shoved past a second, elbowed one of Mardin's guards in the eye, then rushed towards the storage area below.

Below deck, he saw an Angan ship-boy struggling to calm a mare. The other horses were neighing and rearing in fear at the footfalls above. The Angan never saw Karna coming. He simply went down with a soft sigh when Karna hit him on the head. As the boy fell, the mare bolted. Karna grabbed the bridle of the barebacked animal. *Easy... easy...* He leaped onto the frightened mare and gave her free rein. The mare, eyes rolling white, thundered up the ramp onto the deck, neighing and snorting.

This is a mad idea, but I've done worse. An arrow flew past Karna's ear. *If the mare hesitates, I will have to end them all.* He felt the blood surge through his body and it took all his will to curb the savage fire within. *No. No more murder.* 'I'm right here, Lady,' Karna whispered to the mare, running his hands over her chestnut skin. '*Hiyah!*' The mare rushed forward. Lightning streaked the dark sky, portent of the coming storm. Karna glanced down ruefully at his new caramel jacket, even as the guards and sailors scattered to get out of the mare's way. *I just bought this,* he sulked as the mare cleared the rail of the ship and leaped into the foaming sea.

MATI

I

*C*omedy of Errors was a callous name for a play. The audience watched the scenes with glee, without realizing that their laughter came at great cost to the characters. Such profound epiphanies ran through Mati's mind as her dinghy was carried by burgeoning waves towards Jade Harbour, the *Fat Mistress* hot on her tail.

Had things gone according to plan, she would have disembarked at Diamond Harbour, changed out of her disguise and slipped away with the trusted men she had planted at the dock. Instead, she was stuck rowing to a harbour where there were no known Kalingans, with no coin to her name, and arms that felt like lead from all the rowing. Fortunately for her, the *Fat Mistress* was no acrobat. The time it took her to turn her bow gave Mati a fine headstart. As the salt waves propelled her boat onwards, she passed the stone-throwing engines of the watchtowers. They could reach across the sea with forty loads of fire-oil or rock, and burn or sink anything in no time. These towers stood on the outermost island, their base white from a millennium of salt spray. Outbuildings clung to it like cockles on the rocks, where on-duty soldiers of the Kalingan Harbour Guard lounged, bored. In the last years of peace after the Magadhan conquest, the most action they had seen was the occasional plague ship.

Mati approached the quays where she could see the masts of a myriad of foreign vessels – carracks out of Anga, trading galleons from Pragjyotisha, wine cogs from Madurai, and pot-bellied whalers from faraway Lanka. Being on a dinghy allowed her to squeeze and zig-zag past the queue waiting to drop anchor in the harbour. She soon saw the checking post ahead, where all incoming vessels were required to show their documents and declare their cargo to the port officials.

Must get off before the checkpoint. Mati turned away from her study of the quays, where the sinking moonlight turned the sea into a purling sheet of beaten pearls, and frowned at the sudden odour. The acrid stench of burning seaweed, used by wenches to bream the bottom of a vessel, filled the air. She turned to see workers scurrying over cogs, like ants on a sack of sugar, to mend the ships on the sea lane to the left of the watchtowers. The ferry berths and little piers on the side were made for shrimpers to moor, but for now they lay empty, save for the cleaning folk, who worked on the ships that looked like injured elephants, lying on their side. Mati grunted, and oared her dinghy into the shadow of one of these. She jumped onto a nearby plank without even anchoring her ride. With the workers in a rush to wind up work for the day, no one noticed an unmanned dinghy crash into the side of a cog, or the red wig on its bow, till it was too late.

II

The murky water showed her a vivid but wobbly reflection of her face. She was glad to feel the cool breeze on her neck. She had never understood how women kept their hair long. The ends of her own hair tickled the nape of her neck as she placed a crescent-shaped bindi on her forehead to relieve her fatigue. *Time to escape.*

Jade Harbour was the noisiest of all the harbours she had been to. It smelled of salt water, smoke, piss and sweat. And wherever there were sailors of such noxious variety, there were also whores galore. She passed many along the wharf, as well as sailmenders, ropemakers, porters, and even brewers, serving and preying on the traders who crowded the alleys. The south side had grown busier as the north side of Jade Harbour was weathered to ruin by the encroaching sea and residual silt. The summer before, the north side had been abandoned by royal edict, even though the shortcut to the Palace lay through those ruins.

Mati pushed past boisterous Javans with their almond eyes and dark faces, and yellow Cinas who were deliberately making high-pitched foreign sounds to frustrate merchants into selling cheap. She brushed against fair-haired Yavanas, who were quick to cop a feel. Mati did not shy away either, and left one Yavana clutching his balls in pain. She turned, smiling wistfully. And then her smile dropped when she saw the *Fat Mistress* sail past the checkpost, escorted by a patrol boat.

Turning towards a commotion ahead, she saw a pair of Kalingan guards barricade the alleys leading to the town. 'Oh, c'mon!' she heard shouts from disgruntled sailors. 'What do we care if you must search for a murderer! This is Kalinga! Everyone is a murderer!' Other sailors hooted and cheered but the Kalingan guards did not budge. No one in their right mind would mess with the guards.

Storms! She had counted on more time because of the long queue at the checkpost. *News has travelled fast.* She considered her options. She had three copper marks and a half-filled dart of poison. It was not enough to rent clothes or a pony. Diamond Harbour had been minutes away from the Palace, but Jade Harbour was over an hour's ride away, and she would have to go through the drowned northern ruins to avoid the Watch. If they were barricading alleys, they would be conducting searches. She did not even have the coin to bribe a skinseller to rent her a room. And no, it was too dangerous. These ladies of enterprise would gladly part with information on anyone if it meant a week free of harassment. And Mati wasn't an easy face to forget, even without her red wig. Her swaying hips and luscious lips left a lasting impression. *Why did I have to be so enchanting?* If not anyone else, the Lamb would surely identify her.

She needed time. She had to stop those on the *Fat Mistress* from disembarking. She needed a horse. It was imperative to avoid the Kalingan Guards. She had to take care of all these problems with one stone or else she would find a crossbow quarrel in her gut before she could even say *sorry*. She looked up at the tower where the banner with the Magadhan Lion hung limp. *The Lion may rule the land, but on the ocean the Swan flies above all,* she thought, smiling.

An idea began to form in her head. *Storm God, forgive me.* She wondered if her guardian deity shuddered every time she apologized, for it was a clear sign of something diabolical about to take place.

III

Mati rushed through the overcrowded bazaar where petty merchants were hawking everything from cold rum to plump parrots. Behind her, the *Fat Mistress* was already queuing up for the dock formalities. Ignoring the touts, she rushed to the next lane, where beggars sat, calling out improbable reasons for their disabilities and malnourished state. Mati chose the ones cursed to sit at the end of the line, by which time any philanthropist's purse and guilt usually lightened. And there she found three worthy men. One of them was missing an arm, another limped, and the third was remarkable for his nasty boil-filled face. *Perfect.*

She shook the empty coin pouch in front of them as she drew them to a dark corner. When she explained her plan, the beggars cheered as if they were part of a revolution. They were all eager to do their part. Perhaps it was the excitement of crying out something else instead of the old sorry tales about the same sorry wounds. Or maybe it was the promise of gold that bought their tongues. Mati didn't care, for her game was afoot.

IV

They were ready in their places when the *Fat Mistress* came up to be tied at the moorings, the patrol boat right behind her. In the crowded confusion due to the barricade, Mati softly pricked a Yavana, and then a dock agent, hoping two should suffice. She carefully placed the emptied poison dart back into her belt and gave the signal.

The beggar with the boils nodded to Mati and ran to the wharf's edge, screaming. She had promised him a feel of her tits if he burst all his boils and he had been more than eager to oblige. Bloody pus flowed from a dozen sores on his face. The beggar with the limp screamed at the top of his voice in alarm, pointing to the pus-faced beggar. The word 'PLAGUE!' shrilled across the harbour like a chant. The crowd around him turned as one, as if on cue, and saw the man drowning in pus. Then their eyes went to the watchful one who had spotted the health hazard, and saw his outstretched hand pointing to the *Fat Mistress*. 'PLAGUE SHIP!' he cried with the flair of a damsel in distress as he gave the performance of his life.

People began to move back instinctively, the place echoing with fearful whispers and strange shouts. Mati emerged from the crowd, her timing faultless. 'Look! There's another!' The Yavana she had pricked doubled over as if he'd been kicked in the gut. He coughed hard, forceful coughs. He took a faltering step, clutching at the nearest figure, who rudely pushed him away. The Yavana fell to the ground.

'Stand back!'

'It is the plague! Ocean Goddess save us!'

'Turn him over. Give him space to breathe!'

Mati looked on as the veins began to bulge in the man's neck and his eyes turned bloodshot. He clawed at his throat, coughing blood. His face became rigid while his body jerked madly on the cobbles like a landed fish. The whole dock teetered on the brink of chaos.

'This is the plague! I saw this man jump from that ship over there! Look!' Mati cried. It was sheer luck that the crew of the *Fat Mistress* chose that moment to carry Prakar Mardin's wrapped corpse onto the deck. 'There is a dead body they're trying to disembark! It's a plagued body! They have raised the barricade to quarantine us!'

A woman gave a scream as the dock agent beside her fell to his knees, coughing, hands at his throat, face turning red. He crashed down, white foam dripping from his lips. Mati gave the sign. The third beggar climbed onto an empty crate. Strangely, his arm seemed to have grown back and he had on a clean cloak. *Resourceful.* 'It's a plague ship!' he shouted. He paused for effect, then yelled, 'Run!'

And, as if the Emperor himself had roared for the army to charge, the wharfside plunged into hysteria. Mati was nearly trampled as the crowd turned and ran. The pair of Kalingan guards were no match for the mob. The men and women of Jade did not represent the best sailors, and now they did not even represent the best of humanity as they rushed away from the water, crying and screaming. Panic was far more potent than plague. Those that fell were trampled. Those in the way, tossed aside.

Mati felt someone shove her and lashed out with her hand, slapping the man away. Nevertheless, she was caught in the tide of fleeing humanity, like a leaf in a current, shoved, pushed, jostled and tangled. Her feet scarcely touched the ground as she was swept along with the crowd. A few guards ran out of harm's way, up the stairs to the watchtower, no doubt to relay important instructions.

She felt one of the beggars grab her by the elbow and pull her to safety. He was the same one who had been pretending to be armless. They made their way to a warehouse that afforded them a vantage point. The clamour faded behind them. Mati was wheezing like a whale. She felt dizzy, her mouth dry as a desert. She saw the sea of men and women spread into rivulets beyond the alley as they rushed to the town, overturning the barricades.

Those that stumbled were left behind, lying where they fell, crushed in the stampede.

'You were right. We're going to be rich,' the beggar said, eyeing a box of coins that had been left behind, its contents spilled over the floor, forgotten. He looked at Mati sheepishly.

'It's all yours.'

'You're too kind, Mistress.'

There was the sudden sound of drums beating and bells sounding the alarm in the harbour.

'What… what is that?' the beggar stammered.

'End game.'

'Holy Teats of the Goddess!' cried the beggar, blinking to clear his vision, but what he saw wasn't an illusion.

Within moments, the *Fat Mistress* was afire. From atop the tower, arcs of orange fire crashed down onto the ship's deck, spreading fiery tendrils in every direction. Those on the deck ran screaming, trying to escape the inferno, many already alight. Stones crashed against the side of the merchant ship, shattering its rails and sending splinters flying. The more agile of the crew jumped into the water, but arrows from the guards stationed in the tower took care of them.

'It's almost like they're dancing.' The beggar chuckled, watching in fascination the frantic figures on the ship trying to douse the fire with sand. 'Poor bastard,' he muttered as they saw a horse, his mane on fire, gallop across the deck, killing many under his thundering hooves, before crashing still against the mast-pole. Fingers of red capered into a sky wreathed in smoke of variegated shades of grey. The *Fat Mistress* was a pyre. The green waters around it now rippled like a scarlet mirror.

Through the smoke, Mati saw the flying arrow that took the life of her new colleague, the first 'plague victim'. The other already lay dead, his face crushed under the sea of feet. 'Sorry about your friends,' she said to the third man.

He waved a hand. 'We didn't like each other. But do I get the same deal now that he isn't here to collect?' The lascivious eyes glinted, leering at Mati's chest. She smiled and unsheathed her poison dart. He did not know it was empty. The grin vanished from the man's face and he shut his mouth.

'What will you do now?' Mati asked, wondering if she ought to let him live.

'Find another place to beg. Something tells me this harbour is going to be unpopular for a while.'

She decided against taking another life on her ledger, and let him scramble after the coins on the floor. Too many lives had been sacrificed to the Storm God today. She could still hear the frightened neighing of horses left behind by their fleeing masters. She followed the sounds to a barn behind the row of warehouses. A score of abandoned horses stood in a horse-keeper's stable. One did not find many horses in Kalinga.

The Storm God looked down upon these creatures of the Greens, which turned men weak and lazy. But necessity was stronger than divine precept. Mati shoved a bare foot into a stirrup and swung herself into the saddle. But a lone woman on horseback was certain to attract attention.

She looked around and saw a cart. She had no sword, no dagger, the dart was empty. 'Oi!' she called to the beggar, who turned from his frantic collection drive. 'Help me load hay onto that cart, and that barrel.' One of the fire-oil barrels from the tower had missed the ship and landed on the ground, but failed to explode. 'Scavenge me the other horse, then scamper before the men from the tower descend.'

'Aye, lady.'

Behind him, the *Fat Mistress* was a mountain of red and orange flames, reaching from water to sky. *Prakar Mardin received a funeral after all.* Mati would have liked to believe she felt a twinge of guilt for the Lamb, but who was she fooling? Conscience was but a front for cowardice.

KARNA

I

The dying light of the sun shimmered across the sea beneath the first stars of the evening. A rhythmic whisper under the black water grew into a cascading hiss near the filth-infested ruins of the harbour. The bank seethed in the egg-laying frenzy of strange eels that nipped at the strange creatures emerging from the blue darkness of the sea. Warm blood seeped from the nostrils of the four-legged beast as she trotted a few steps and collapsed in a heap. Her sides heaved in exhaustion as her rider patted her gently, then sprawled in the mud himself, drawing fitful gulps of air into his lungs.

'You will live, Lady,' Karna whispered. 'And what is more, you will be free.' The mare snorted in response. Karna smiled as he squirmed and then rose to his feet. He bent beside the mare, pulling off the eels that clung to her skin like leeches and flinging them out to the sides where he could hear the skittering of harbour-rats. The mare finally rose. Karna patted her rump and set her trotting into the wild.

Karna looked around, wondering why the harbour was so deserted. By his calculations, he had swum to Jade Harbour, but what he saw did not quite match its reputation. He walked up a flagstone path to find an agonizingly silent street. *How long have I been swimming?* He was exhausted to the bone, wanting nothing more than a straw bed to collapse on.

As he walked amidst the dilapidated ruins of the supposed harbour, he realized he was utterly exposed, like a deer strolling through a levelled forest. He should not have let go of the mare. *She had done enough.* He reminded himself how close the creature had been to death. Faint sounds thrummed in his ears, coming from far in the distance. So, civilization was somewhere around. *This must be the abandoned portion of Jade Harbour,* he realized, looking around at the damage done by the high tides. This was what Duryodhan had meant when he'd called Chilika the Sinking City.

It was then that he heard them. Figures moving in stealth, taking positions. The realization that his pursuers were professional assassins and not a ravenous mob did little to lift his spirits. *How could anyone have possibly known I would land here?* But there was no time for idle thoughts; not when Mardin had died in his arms, and certainly not now. He could curse his stupidity later. Karna suspected a sinister plot underway, of which the murder of Prakar Mardin was only the first step. He looked at his hands. He had no weapons. He was cold. And thirst plagued him like a swamp fever.

Karna scraped up some mud and rubbed it over his golden breastplate. Tonight, the moon was his enemy, and he was grateful to the stormy clouds for keeping her well cloaked. Heartbeats drummed their warning message as he treaded softly on the slippery cobblestones, keeping to the shadows of the sinking ruins. The eerie silence was broken only by the lapping water. He slipped past drowning buildings and tilted wagons till he came across a door that did not have a padlock. *A trap.*

He took a step back till he stood against the shuttered window. Then he threw himself against the window, breaking through the wooden shutters and rolling onto the floor inside the house. Karna's attack had been so sudden that the two figures hiding by the door had no time to draw their weapons. He crunched his left fingers into a claw, and smashed brutally into one man's throat. He slapped the palm of his right hand over the other's mouth as he drove his skull back to crunch against the wall. Both men collapsed in a heap.

A moment later, Karna was searching their bodies for weapons. Unarmed a few moments ago, he now had a wealth of copper-headed fighting axes, knives and a bundle of throwing stars. The assassins appeared to be Northern, though he could not place them exactly. In the faint light, Karna saw the tattoo of the double-headed scorpion on the side of their necks, etched over their caste mark. *Can't say I disapprove.*

Karna slipped out of the house through a back door. He heard the muted snap of a crossbow but there was not enough space for him to evade the quarrel. It hit his collar bone but was deflected by his breastplate. The force of the hit from such close range knocked him to the ground. Karna used the momentum to roll backwards on the wet mud. But instead of retreating, he charged at his attacker, who was fumbling to let loose another quarrel.

Karna ducked and twisted, swinging the throwing stars even as the assassin fired low. The quarrel lodged deep in Karna's thigh. He knew his first star had missed the assassin. It had been a deliberate ploy to throw him off. His second throw took the assassin low in the belly. The man staggered back and fell. Karna withdrew the assassin's quarrel from his thigh. Dark blood crept out of the wound and dripped into the wet soil. He dabbed the wound and raised his fingers to smell his own blood. It was as he had suspected. *Poisoned arrow.* His breastplate afforded no protection against poisons, but the knowledge taught to him by Acharya Parshuram still held power. He took a deep breath to still the flow of blood in his body, to slow the work of the poison.

A pair of knives interrupted his efforts. They would have stabbed his neck had he not dodged with what seemed inhuman alacrity. At a crouching run Karna dashed back into the house, and stormed out of the front door, smashing it. A familiar monster surged inside him, straining to be let out. *Never again.* He willed the monster back into its cage. Karna stumbled out into the alleyway, crashing against a wall. He could see a faint pillar of red on the horizon. Black smoke rose into the sky. *It is going to be a night of blood.* He unsheathed the dagger he had borrowed from the assassin. *Time to rattle the stars.*

II

The watery streets made it easy to hear the sound of footfalls. Not that it was needed. Angry whispers echoed in these ruins.

'They never told us he was *this* trained,' an assassin hissed. 'He has hunted down five of us.'

'They were novices,' the cold voice of a woman answered. 'Good they were culled out.'

'But he is—'

'Just a man. And Men fall. Knife into that alley mouth and climb to the roof. I will check here. Eyes on the sides and back.'

A shadow edged into view and stopped no more than an arms-length away. The woman twisted even as Karna let loose the quarrel. He missed. The woman did not. The dagger struck him just beneath his left arm. Another dagger embedded itself in the wall beside Karna's head. But Karna still had the second quarrel lodged. He pressed the release, and the woman tumbled back with the quarrel lodged in her chest, screaming her final defiance even as she fell dead.

It was the last of his weapons, and his fifth wound of the night. A sword had found his thigh in the last skirmish. Fortunately, swords were never poisoned. Too risky for the swordsman. Not that it mattered. His internal exercise at slowing down his blood was in shambles. He was weakening with each heartbeat.

Suddenly, Karna saw more shadows take shape around him. The woman's scream had alerted his hunters to his position and Karna had been too distracted by his wounds to move. The killers converged. A refined voice reached him from the balcony of one of the abandoned houses. 'Settle down, Highmaster. It's over.'

Karna surveyed the assassins. Ten. Their gait reflected their training. In his poisoned, exhausted state, he could probably take down more than half of them before he went down himself. That was assuming there weren't more lurking in the darkness. His thoughts drifted to his nephew, Sudama. No. He could not go down. He had vowed to look after the boy. It was a vow he was not going to break. But poisons cared not for the promises of men.

Buy time. Karna sank against the wall behind him, close to where the voice, perhaps belonging to the leader of the assassins, had come from.

'You fight rather well for a boy,' the voice said again. It was soft, cultured. 'You cost me five stringers and a lover. Pity. We could've used you. We have an affinity towards skilled social rejects.'

'I left three alive,' Karna panted.

'Rest assured we won't make the same mistake.'

Karna looked up. The underside of the wooden balcony from where the voice emerged was now directly overhead, the height of two men above the ground. A good jump would have allowed him to reach a strut, but even if he managed to grab hold of it, it would leave him wide open to the approaching assassins. *Impractical.* 'Who sent you?' he asked, taking deep breaths.

'Some men who were angered by the rapid strides you have been making in royal circles. Haven't you heard? Best to keep a low profile in life lest the Gods take note of you.'

Karna's eyes scanned the shadows. There were three by the cart on the left, two on the right, four coming straight at him, one above him, all of them closing in. His right leg was sticky with blood from his thigh wound. His armpit hurt. His crossbow was empty. He was running out of options.

'You sent the woman to kill Mardin. And now you want to make it look like I was murdered by a mob for killing the Highmaster?'

There was a laugh. 'You give us more credit than we deserve, Resht,' the voice said. 'While that would have been a brilliant move, we were waiting for you at Diamond Harbour till we heard news you had taken a detour. Fortunately, horses run faster than they swim. We set up a grand welcome for you here instead. But we had nothing to do with the murder of Prakar Mardin. We never take life for free. It is the one rule we have. And rules are important, don't you think? Now that I have answered your question, answer mine. Head or throat?'

Karna heard the thundering sound of wheels, and spied a small barrel rolling into the midst of the approaching assassins. 'Fire-oil!' the woman cried. 'Positions!'

Time slowed as the barrel collided with an abandoned cart. The impact of the detonation threw the approaching assassins into the air. Karna dived for cover, not knowing who had rolled the barrel and come to his aid. He was thrown against the wall again and heard a snap. *My arm.* Unheeding, he stumbled to his feet and scurried, half-bent, along the side of the shadowed street, gripping his broken arm.

'Oi, Lamb!'

He turned, stopping short. A horse-driven cart was turning in the street behind. Then it charged towards him. Crouched low behind the reins was a woman he knew. Karna stepped aside, a breath away from being ridden over, grasped one side of the cart and let the momentum swing him up behind the woman. Wind buffeted him as the cart rattled on. Twisting back, he saw shapes in pursuit, on horseback.

Kala handed him a crossbow with two quarrels affixed. 'Borrowed it from your friends. Can you use it?'

Fortunately, he was ambidextrous. 'I can manage.' He took his time and shot an arrow that knocked a rider onto the cobbled stones behind his horse. He shot the second arrow at the assassin on the roof, who ducked, dropping his own crossbow in the process.

The street ahead was waterlogged. Kala wheeled right into an alley. The horses skidded before righting themselves and taking the slope ahead. Karna could finally see a town adjoining the harbour, a tangle of serpentine alleys and streets, lit like a forest of fireflies from a hundred alchemical lamps. The sound of galloping horses, hot in pursuit, did not allow them the luxury of considering their options.

'Where are we going?' Karna asked.

'Chilika Fort.'

'But we cannot ride at full speed through *that!*'

'I know, damn you!'

The next few minutes marked the wildest ride Karna had ever taken. Kala's skill was exhilarating. The cart glided through the tangles, knocking over stalls, barely managing to avoid innocent bystanders… but it was enough. A while later, Karna turned to look behind, then leaned close to say, 'I think we've lost them, Kala.'

'I'm glad you are still alive, my Lamb.'

'Not for long. You… your hair is different.'

'What do you mean, not for long?'

'Erm…' He felt dizzy. Words were tangling themselves in knots on his tongue. 'I have… have… been poisoned.'

'Did you dine with Prakar Mardin?' Kala's voice was alarmed.

So, it was her. Karna groaned. 'No. It was… an arrow.' Karna held onto the rocking cart. 'I know what you did, Kala. You…' He groaned, feeling obnoxiously weak. 'You… killed Prakar Mardin.'

'An incident I'm sure you can forget… as repayment for breaking my heart. Savvy?'

'You… you…' He fell against Kala's shoulder.

'Let me rephrase it,' she said, '… in repayment for saving your life. Admit it, I'm a guardian spirit, Lamb, sent here by the Storm God to save you.'

'You… are a killer,' he managed to say before slipping down into the back of the cart, poisoned, wounded, and drained of strength.

III

When Karna opened his eyes, he found he was lying on his back, looking up at a fiery mural on a stone ceiling. The mural depicted the Kalingan Ocean Goddess devouring mortal men. Karna glanced around the chamber. He lay on a pallet, wearing nothing but a breechclout. For once he was glad of the breastplate stitched to his skin. His left arm was in a cast. His thigh was on fire. His stomach felt twisted. Karna groaned and closed his eyes again.

'About time you woke up,' said a familiar voice.

Karna winked one eye open. He saw deep-set eyes peering at him over a stubborn jaw. It was as handsome a face as any, sporting a beard groomed with fastidious care, above a red, enamelled breastplate and maroon cloak. Prince Duryodhan, Heir

Apparent of the Hastina Union, stood by Karna's bed. A man of fierce emotions, his face was currently creased in furrowed lines of worry. He rested a hand on Karna's shoulder and his lips curved in a smile. 'I am not your wet nurse, you know.'

Karna grinned at the sight of his friend. Duryodhan had been his benefactor, friend, philosopher and guide; all one could have wished for in a Prince. Respect for him came with ease. People called him gruff and brittle, but he was a fair man, and to Karna that mattered most. 'How long have I been out?'

'Three nights.'

'Three!' Karna jerked up, realizing immediately it was the wrong call.

'Aye, I wouldn't do that if I were you.'

Karna sighed, unable to appreciate the humour in his state. 'Where… where am I?'

'You're safe, though I daresay not very comfortable. Karna, I know you said you should not go on that ship, but I'm not sure I quite grasped the gravity of your meaning.'

'What happened?'

'I thought I would ask *you* that,' Duryodhan responded wryly. 'It appears your body was dehydrated before your adventures even began.'

'Aye… I…' Karna remembered Kala's red hair between his legs, her heaving body on his, his grunting body on hers, sweat-laden, bite-ridden hours… He shook the image off. 'I forgot to drink water.'

'I was told you jumped off a ship on a mare, into a raging sea.'

'Did I now?' Karna smiled weakly.

'And that you swam the beast for leagues to reach the shore, bitten by leeches and other creatures the healer doesn't know the names of.'

'Tough waters here.'

'That you were then set upon by assassins, severely beaten, stabbed, poisoned, and nearly slain, as you ran through the streets wounded and exhausted.'

'Sounds vaguely familiar.'

'You have my sympathies. You simply collapsed, my friend. The body has a way of revoking permission to continue if you abuse it,' Duryodhan said with a trace of smile. 'As you are wont to do.'

'You're enjoying this, aren't you, My Prince?'

'It has its moments.'

'I don't suppose the people believe I am innocent of the murder of Prakar Mardin?'

'Afraid not. But that is the least of their concerns. Seems that your ship was carrying a plague. Or so the dock guards claim. They burned it.'

'Burned it? Plague! That's impossible. I wouldn't be…'

'I know. There is something fishy here.'

Murder. Kala. It all came back in a sickening rush. 'There was a wench, Prince.' Karna attempted to sit up, without marked success. 'She… she is the key to it all. She…'

'He should rest, love,' said a voice from the darkness. The sound of it singed his veins. A woman half sauntered, half swayed boldly into the light. Karna's eyes were drawn to the handsome stripes of red on her breeches, the gold lace lining the lapels of her jacket, criss-crossed by brass buckles. She wore knee-length boots, crafted from creamy soft leather, the broad tops clipped down with azure buttons embossed with brass swans. He would have recognized her full lips, high cheekbones and shadowy wind-chafed skin anywhere, though her long red hair was gone. She wore her black hair cut short, the ends resting softly on her neck. This was clearly a woman of high birth, not the cleaning woman who had seduced him.

'Look at his poor bruised body.' She came to stand beside Duryodhan, a hand possessively on his arm. She touched two fingers to her forehead. *'May the waves carry you.'*

Duryodhan smiled. *'May the current bring you back.'*

The colour drained from Karna's face. His world grew dark as icy confusion flooded his mind. He did not know what was more shocking, the cleaning wench's hand on Duryodhan or Duryodhan blushing like a schoolboy. 'I… I don't understand.'

'So…' Duryodhan began, clearing his throat.

'Let *me* explain, my sweet.' The woman placed a finger on his lips, the same finger Karna had sucked so avidly a few days before. 'I told the Prince how I was out with my girls for an outing near the Jade Harbour ruins, to get my Prince his wedding gift, when the Ocean Goddess conspired to bring you to my camp, bloodied and poisoned. Though you were a stranger, it was clearly my duty to fetch a healer to you. I rode you back to the Palace to do so.'

'It's a good thing Mati found you, Karna. Not the ideal way I would have wanted my betrothed and my closest friend to meet, of course.'

Betrothed. The other two did not hear Karna's indrawn gulp. *Kala is Mati! Princess of Kalinga! Duryodhan's bride.* The revelation sliced through him like a knife, the pain more intense than the poisoned quarrel had been.

Mati nudged Duryodhan lovingly. 'At least it's a story I won't have to shy away from telling over dinner. The mighty, valiant Karna saved from certain death by a puny damsel! Let me find a bard to believe it first.' She eyed Karna, her eyes full of glowering hate. 'Too bad you didn't give your real name when we met, Lord Karna. Could have saved you a lot of embarrassment. Now the whole world will be privy to your shame if you tell the tale.'

Karna said nothing. He could not.

'Don't let her get under your skin, my friend. No one in their right mind would call the Black Swan a puny damsel,' Duryodhan scoffed.

Karna felt like a punch-drunk fighter who'd long given up but whom Fate insisted on tossing back again and again into the ring till the water clock was empty. 'You're the Black Swan?' he finally managed to utter. *The one Prakar Mardin had spoken of.*

Mati bowed. 'In person. But now you must rest. The Prince and I have much to catch up on. He has not left your side since you were brought in.' She narrowed her eyes again. 'If I had known you were *the* Karna, I would have left you where I found you.' She laughed, but there was no humour in her eyes.

'Rest now, Karna. Father has summoned us back to Hastina. We leave on the morrow. We will handle things here when you are better. For now,' Duryodhan pressed his shoulder, 'I'm glad you are safe.'

'Let us not count our ships before they are in harbour,' Mati advised. 'Allow him to regain his strength and spirits. Wisdom will no doubt follow.' Mati dragged the Prince out of the room.

'By Vayu's beard, Mati! The arrow did not puncture his skull. He just needs rest...' Duryodhan's voice faded away.

The chamber spun around Karna. He crashed back onto the palette. With an ache in his heart to match the pain in his body, he turned to look at the words inked on his wrist. *Abhimaan*. Pride and honour. Two things he had just lost.

MASHA'S AUGURIES

Masha lay content and comfortable on a bed of grass. A large butterfly with wings of deepest blue traced with black alighted on the bare shoulders of her lover. The wings shimmered in the soft sunlight. She watched as the delicate creature unfurled a coiled black tongue to taste the blood oozing from his shoulder. She lifted a lazy hand to shoo off the butterfly, wanting nothing to mar his perfection. The butterfly softly raised itself and landed in Masha's thick hair, a glistening ornament.

She looked into the eyes of her lover. Obsidian mingled with soft brown, in a hard face. He smiled at her, running a cold finger over the scars on her face. 'I'm sorry I had to kill you,' she said.

'I know.' His eyes were sad but still kind. There was no bitterness in his voice. 'I would have brought magic back to the world, you know. But I understand. You did what you had to.'

Masha pulled her body back from his. His entrails had spilled from a hundred gashes and rested on the moss between them. Worms slithered out from him and began to crawl up Masha's thighs towards her insides. She tried to scream but could not. She struggled to push him away, but he just kept looking at her.

'Masha!'

She woke with a shiver and sat up in her bunk, brushing her thighs. She was breathing hard. A wraith stood over her. She gave a yelp before she recognized Matron Limp.

'You were screaming in your sleep,' she said icily.

'Apologies,' Masha whimpered. 'I had a nightmare.'

The skeletal face of Matron Limp did not look amused. Her eyes were gleaming stones in dark holes. 'You think you are the only one who has nightmares?' She pointed to the sleeping figures around the dormitory. Someone shuddered. Another yelped like a puppy. Someone was muttering pleas while another was making choking sounds, as if she was being strangled. Limp was right. No one really slept well in the House of Oracles.

'Now what is this?' Matron Limp pointed to the books lying on Masha's bed, half hidden under the blanket. 'You are not allowed to bring back books from the Library.'

Still half-trapped in her nightmare, Masha murmured, 'Matron, I... I was trying to...'

'Be the first to uncover the future? Yes, we are all doing that, but not by bringing books back to the dorm.' She smiled like a cat-killer. 'I was searching for someone to pass on this duty to, and now I have found you. Despite Sister Mercy's best efforts, some young brute from Meru has signed up for a month's internship with our House. You will be assigned to him; teach him our ways.'

'Ugh...'

Matron Limp raised her eyebrows. Masha tried staring. She too, was a Matron now, albeit unnamed. But who was she kidding? Matron Limp could outstare a statue and make it cry.

'Certainly, Matron.'

'Very good. I trust the books will find their way back to the shelves by dawn.'

'Yes, Matron.'

Someone coughed and wheezed. Masha thought of the man in her dreams and shuddered again. She pushed the image out of her mind, picking up the journals from under the bedsheet. She dared not sleep again. Now that she was awake, she might as well go on reading. She splashed a little water on her eyes from the pitcher beside her bed, and lit her candle, of which only a short stub remained.

Hmm, so where were we? She took a deep, steadying breath. Ah yes, the Journals on Shakuni and Nala. She turned to the volumes she had stolen and began to read: 'Shakuni had lived through a year of torture and survived to return to stand before the bosses of his tormentors. Or rather, lean before them, like the twisted string of a kite losing altitude. He was a pitiful shadow of the man he used to be. It wasn't well known but he often lost control of his leg, and sometimes his face, if you could call what remained a face. His bowels didn't listen to him either. He was in constant pain. And the memories of the time he was a Prince, naturally, nagged at him with a wily persistence. Was it any wonder then that he wasn't a man of warm disposition, given to mercy?'

Masha sighed. She needed something light to read. The life of Shakuni, former Prince of Gandhar, and now uncle to Prince Duryodhan, was as light as acid. She flipped the pages and came to Nala's life instead. This was... fun. Nala seemed to be her age, a student in a Brother Order of the Saptarishis, in Meru, a college where young boys studied to be Acharyas. It seemed almost magical to Masha that only a few leagues away, someone like her was cribbing about things as mundane as exams and teachers. Her mood brightened. Matron Limp might think it was a punishment to assign her to take care of the Meru trainee, but Masha eagerly looked forward to meeting someone who was Nala's friend. After all, she knew Nala was going to die.

ADHYAYA III

BEST SERVED COLD

How did I escape? With difficulty.
How did I plan this moment? With pleasure.
—Dumas, *The Count of Monte Cristo*

NALA

I

Many nefarious activities went on at the Citadel of Meru, the university for upcoming Acharyas, and regrettably, field trips were one of them.

'The woods are dangerous places,' Nala explained. 'There are muscular lizards, poisonous frogs, and bears. And let me tell you, if a bear is running your way, play dead. If it thinks you are dead, it will pass. If it does not, well... you're dead anyway.'

His words had the desired effect on his peers. This was how one became a gang leader. You created an environment where the others depended on your knowledge and talents. In a monastery, it was the monk who smuggled in pocket-sized paintings of princesses; in a museum it was the curator who turned a discarded drum into an antique. Here, in the woods, where vines clutched at one's feet endearingly like snakes, and roots lay in carefully hidden traps, Nala felt like a prince. He was a Valka, after all. At least by blood. His peers thought he was too comely, too slender to be Valka, with his soft, albeit marred, face and close-cropped curls. He smiled at the thought. *Comely*. He was always smiling, as if he was the only one in on some secret.

'Why would they give first years such a dangerous task this early in the semester?' Akopa asked fearfully, shivering in the cold mountain air, keeping an ear out for the sound of any animal that could eat him. Turned out, he included monkeys in the list. 'It's ridiculous!' he scoffed.

Nala was unconcerned by such fears. He knew there were no dangerous beasts in the area for he could not hear them, and his sense of hearing had been better than even his brothers' back home.

'Not really,' Varcin said. 'I mean, if we do perish in the jaws of a tiger in the first year itself, it would not be a waste of education from the Acharyas' perspective, now, would it? 'Cause for the Meru, it's a matter of plain investment.' Varcin was a Drachma. Like Nala, he too was part of Meru's affirmative action drive.

'Goddamn Drachmas,' Akopa grunted. 'It's not as if Meru has not lost its prestige already. Diluting it with coin-counters and forestfolk is a damn shame.'

Nala turned, not offended at all. 'Would you then like to lead the way, O High and Mighty Namin? Perhaps you can *worship* your way out of this?' The others laughed.

Akopa scowled. 'Bite me, Scarface.'

'Interesting choice of words,' Nala said thoughtfully, avoiding the tree roots over which Akopa stumbled. 'In a forest, I mean, for there are cobras around, of course.'

'Liar!' Nonetheless, Akopa huddled somewhat closer to Nala.

Nala winked at the other boys. They chortled awkwardly, however, too occupied with the image of a cobra nipping their heels.

These bright students of Meru, the *shishyas*, were hunting in the woods for a certain type of seed which helped in lighting alchemical lanterns. Meru had been founded by the Saptarishis, the Holy Seven, thousands of years ago, to train tomorrow's promising Acharyas. The Seven had wanted a safe haven where they could secretly teach bright Namin children the ways of knowledge and world dominion. And what better place for such education than a fortress nestled between two icy peaks of the Mai Layas, high above and far away from the rest of the realm? A graduate of Meru, much like a graduate of any other Meru-certified gurukul, became an Acharya. If you were a good Acharya, with top scores, you were sent to Emperors and Kings as advisors, to help with matters of law, polity, and the occasional childbirth of underage Queens. If you were the kind who hung from the cliff of passing marks, you were assigned to lower Lords and Guilds, though most of these graduates preferred the world of academia. They either continued in Meru as absentee Acharyas, or opened private gurukuls in their hometowns.

Meru had not always been an idyllic place. In days of yore, Meru had turned for a brief period into a training camp for would-be terrorists, who joined the ranks of the army of the Bane of Ksharjas, Acharya Parshuram, for the chance to kill tyrannical Ksharjas in the Century of Blood. And like any great romance, the fire fizzled out after the first few waves of genocide. After the Great Peace Accord between the Ksharjas and the Namins, Meru had been demoted, or promoted, depending on your perspective, to a mere citadel of learning.

Of late, the Saptarishis too were no longer heard of. Rumours abounded that the Seven had discontinued their business of king-making. No one had seen a Saptarishi for almost a hundred years. The faculty at Meru had long ago confronted this and had, in fact, perfected various devices to ensure it. After all, running terror training camps was tiring work. Hard work wasn't what one had in mind when one chose to be a teacher. With the Saptarishis disappearing behind the metaphorical curtain, the more liberal teachers of Meru had begun opening the doors of the citadel to outsiders. Talk of minority representation and the rise of new rulers in places like Mathura and the Sindh Guild, in what academicians called 'fringe society', required Meru to change with the times or let go of a significant supply of fees in the form of *gurudakshina*.

Thus, it was that Nala became the first Valka to enter the doors of Meru. The Arch-Acharya of Meru had planned to use the inspiring tale of how Nala had persevered through racism and bullying, to attract more students from other fringe tribes. So, it was rather disappointing to him when Nala got along so well with his classmates. What he didn't know was that Nala had been a big embarrassment to his family, to his mother and five brothers, for he had about the same talent for tree-swinging and boar-hunting that you would find in a dead iguana. For this short, black-haired Valka with a face criss-crossed by marks of vitiligo had a mind that wanted to think. And he had the sort of body that was only marginally under Nala's control; a fatal handicap in the dangerous world of forests. His being selected by Meru, therefore, was the answer to his mother's fervent prayers to save him from certain death. Luckily for Nala, his friends in Meru did not know this. To them, he might as well be the Chieftain of the Nora.

'Found it!' Upavi plucked the fire-berry twig and flourished it like a sword, creating a large halo of orange over his head. 'Now, let's go back!'

'What?' Nala was shocked. For cityfolk, his friends could be really naïve. 'Why go back? We'll find a meadow to lounge in, and go back when it is time for dinner. That way we won't get any more assignments, and the Acharya will think we really worked hard. Effectiveness reaps only more work in real life, Upavi.'

They all murmured agreement. They loved the way Nala thought, and Nala loved his friends. Their motley group shared tales, giddy with freedom, of this and that. They spoke without a care in the world. Nala did not have to fear any longer that he spoke too much, or worry that he was too slow or too slender. Varcin taught them how to spin stones on the lake, and Nala taught them how to carve wood. Upavi plucked fruits from the tallest branches, while Akopa chanted the proper prayers before they were allowed to eat.

It was the best of times.

As for the task at hand, they did not find a meadow but stumbled upon a hot spring. The water was warm and soothing. Most of the boys stripped down to their loincloths and leaped into the pool. Nala sat grumpily under a tree, looking wistfully at his friends. He would have loved to join them.

'Nala, jump in!' Varcin called to him. 'The water is so soothing!'

'It may be soothing now but it won't be so when you step out and the water in your hair turns to icicles.'

'Coward!' Varcin shouted, and they all laughed.

'What if he thinks we are dumb to take so much time?' Akopa suddenly asked, resurfacing from the water.

'Even better,' Nala said. 'He'll think we aren't cut out for this and reduce our forest assignments.'

It was a known fact that the Saptarishis took inspiration for their devious plans by aping Meru's first years.

II

Somehow, the shishyas ambled on to their second semester at Meru. If they thought the classes would be lighter, they were sorely mistaken.

'Deeper, you fleas!' Acharya Irum's voice thundered. 'I said *turn!* Did I say *scrape?*'

'I think my spade is laughing at me,' Akopa said softly, his voice so serious that one might have actually thrown his spade a second glance.

'I know I am,' Varcin said. 'Are you massaging the land or turning it?'

Nala chuckled. 'Why does an Acharya need to learn to farm?'

'I think they are running out of subjects to teach.' Varcin winked.

'They're already teaching us Smithy this year. Then there is Alchemy, Sanskrit-II, Chakrascience, History-II and Herblore. With Farming, that makes it a sinister seven-subject list. As you grow older, things are supposed to get easier, aren't they?'

'The more we persevere now, the more we'll prosper later,' Varcin enunciated unctuously.

'You sound like Acharya Irum,' Nala said.

'That's good then.' Varcin beamed. 'Voice of Irum, Knowledge of Parshuram, and Skill of Failknot... I will be the greatest Acharya the realm has ever seen.'

'Knowledge of *Parshuram?*' Upavi asked. 'I do not know of any Saptarishi by that name.'

'He isn't one,' Akopa said.

'Then why seek the wisdom of one who isn't even a Saptarishi?'

'Have you been living under a rock, Upavi?' Akopa snorted. 'Acharya Parshuram, the Axe-Warrior, is the greatest teacher blessed on Vrat. He has taught the White Eagle and the Gospel. He has taught Failknot, who could have used one arrow to slay all seven of you while taking a piss. He has taught Nardevaks and Men, good men every one. The Vedans speak of him in the same breath as the Ayodhyan King Ram and Kirtavirya the Thousand-Armed. He is the only living *Chiranjeevi*. Even Scarface knows of him.'

'Don't call him that,' Varcin chided.

'Actually, I don't know much about him.' Nala shrugged.

'How have you not heard of him? He is said to be the reason your ancestors were driven to the forests!'

'Because he had river nymphs to seduce back there,' Varcin came to Nala's defence. The boys laughed. However, Acharya Irum suddenly apparated behind Varcin and slapped him smartly across the head.

Once the Acharya turned away again, Upavi asked, 'Didn't Parshuram slay Kirtavirya?'

'We don't speak of it in Meru,' whispered Varcin, one eye tracking Acharya Irum's movements. Varcin was as learned as Akopa, but not half as haughty.

'Why?'

'Ordinarily, a Namin ordained in the Order of Higher Knowledge takes an oath of non-violence. The second years told me Acharya Parshuram has broken that oath seventeen times and more. But Meru makes an exception for him.'

'Why?' Nala asked. It was strange. The Namins were rather mercurial about oath, honour and peace.

'Acharya Parshuram is a display of strength for Meru,' Akopa answered. 'One that is important to preserve. The influence of the Saptarishis, hell even Namins, has waned over the decades. Parshuram is the sheathed sword Meru carries. Kingmakers that cannot threaten the rule of kings wouldn't be good at their jobs now, would they?'

A hush fell over the sun-hardened field. Varcin sighed and shook his head sadly. 'But the Saptarishis haven't made kings in a long time. Sounds like plain hypocrisy if you ask me. Parshuram himself never made any exception for Failknot.'

'One moment he was the most decorated student of Meru, the next nobody knew where he had disappeared to. What really happened here?' Upavi asked Akopa, a little too loudly.

'Upavi and Akopa!' Acharya Irum screamed from the other end of the plot. 'You are to sing all the morning prayers together for the rest of the month! That should quench your thirst for working your mouth more than your hands.'

'Damn you, Upavi.'

III

Nala privately suspected that the Acharyas of Meru were sadist criminals hiding from the law under the guise of teachers. It made sense to him and helped him limp through the nineteenth round. The days of the third semester began with rounds of the field. They started at dawn and were expected to cover twenty rounds before the sun was a finger's length above the horizon. Why an Acharya of Knowledge needed to have high stamina was beyond Nala.

The respite of breakfast did not last long. It was followed by classes with Acharya Craw. He taught them the art of kick and punch. As per Craw, one had to learn physical injury to be able to treat it more effectively. Varcin called it a conspiracy. Nala had not expected much from Craw, given his broken nose and toothless jaw. But come afternoon, Nala's bruised and exhausted body shattered any illusions he may have harboured. He learned the secrets of the fist, the twists needed to block, the kicks needed to defend. He learned how to trip enemies, shoulder them; he learned how to block and execute a roundhouse kick. They were, however, not taught anything lethal, lest they use it amongst themselves to solve inter-dormitory disputes.

'Just look at my skin!' Akopa gasped one day. 'I am more blue than dark. I'm certain my body has forgotten how to heal.'

'I think I am never going to be able to squat again.' Nala hated his time with Acharya Craw. He could barely appreciate the evening meal with his battered jaw.

'But you were good, Nala,' Varcin said. 'You are exceptionally good at dodging an attack from behind.'

'I hear them coming.' Nala dabbed salve on his slit lip. 'Fat lot of good it does me.'

Yet, with time and practice, Nala was able to dodge Craw's punches even from the front. Strangely, he heard the vibrations in the air before the punch landed on his head, and instinctively swayed behind to dodge it. He could not kick back. He was not big or strong enough to land an effective blow. But he was quick. *Little victories.*

Classes of healing were spent in company of soil and worms in Acharya Gautam's dispensary and Acharya Lujanne's gardens. Acharya Lujanne was a short man, disinterested in speech; he used his hands instead for communication. The varying pitches of his grunts were the only indicators of whether they were doing something right or not. The gardens were vast, comprising long orderly families of medicinal plants. Ukopa was a master of the subject, creating concoctions and poultices in no time. Even Varcin could soon bandage an arm and set a displaced bone. Nala was mostly assigned to pruning, a barber of trees in short. He was said to have indelicate hands. A compliment for a Valka.

History was a class the shishyas looked forward to, for Acharya Vyas spent most of his time at the blackboard, allowing the shishyas adequate time to sleep and recover from their ordeals. Nonetheless, they read about the histories of empires, the biology of the Daevas and Danavas, the laws of *Manusmriti*, the great migration and the effects of *samudra manthan* on the glacial age.

'The knowledge of our ancestors helps prevent the mistakes they made. We can learn a lot from them,' Varcin said, defending the subject.

'What's the use?' Nala replied, turning over a chapter on another war. 'We make new ones, or rather,' he read the cause of the seventeenth Lankan War, 'make the same ones again and again.'

'I still think knowledge of history is crucial. Without it, we are like tomatoes who don't know we are a fruit, not a vegetable.'

'Tomato is a fruit?' Nala was shocked.

'Nala?' Acharya Vyas rotated slowly on his axis.

'Yes, Acharya,' Nala responded, flustered by the sudden attention.

'How do Nardevaks recognize each other when they look completely like Mortals?'

'Uhm…' Nala scratched his chin, jogging his memory. Nardevaks were half-Daeva, half-Man. And that's about all he could remember. 'By their smell?' he hazarded a guess. Varcin suppressed a laugh.

'Indeed,' Vyas said, stroking his cane like a lover. 'If the Nardevaks was to smell like you, Nala, I am sure the entire world would recognize them. Too bad they practised hygiene.'

Nala looked down sheepishly as Upavi suppressed his giggles. He could have tried a comeback but Vyas was said to be related to Hastina royalty, and it was an unwritten rule that you didn't mess with teachers who were members of the Assignment Committee of Meru.

'Varcin?' Vyas commanded, brows raised.

'Their blood, Acharya. Not visible to the untrained Mortal eye, for the Nardevaks bled a shade of green that cannot be commonly seen in our spectrum, except with special optics. The colour is instantly recognizable to another Nardevak or Daeva.'

'Perhaps not all of you are lost.'

Nala scowled at Varcin. 'What? Should I have answered incorrectly?' Varcin hissed in self-defence.

'No, but you didn't have to answer *this* correctly.'

IV

The Library of Meru was the greatest assortment of texts anywhere in the realm, on every subject imaginable. Thousands of scrolls, parchments, books, diary entries and occult lore weighted its mighty shelves. There were rare books like *Saptarishis: The Age of Surveillance Naminism, Why Slavery is Important: A Kalingan Pirate's Perspective,* and even a signed copy of *Nagas: Wounded Spirits in the Promised Land.* As with any other place of learning, the Library was eerily empty. The only light in the great arched chamber was from an alchemical lantern. It swayed above the heads of two keen-edged minds engaged in some light night reading.

One was flipping over the pages of *Kings and Queens I Wanted to Punch in the Throat* by famous traveller Nar Ad Muni, which despite its sour touch was a good reference book on the lineage of the Kings of the Union. The other was probing the private secrets of the world in *The Story of Mandalas in Twenty-Five Discoveries,* regardless of whether the world gave its consent or not. The glyphs here were complicated, the language a draconic version of Sanskrit, hard to understand. But it was fascinating, even though the dust from the never-turned-before pages made his eyes itch and water.

'No one has heard of a *Mandalyen,* I mean a Mandala conjurer, since the Siege of Tyrants. Why do you keep trying?' Varcin asked.

'It is so fascinating,' Nala replied, rubbing his eyes vigorously and pushing back the lock of dark hair that fell over his forehead. 'It is the only thing I like about history. Think about it. Creating magical signs out of thin air by using the Elementals. Such power! The Mandalyens must have been Gods.'

'Hardly,' Varcin said. 'There were thousands of Mandalyens before the Siege of Tyrants, who were able to use one Elemental or the other: Earth, Fire, Water, Wind, Life, Light and Darkness. But a Mandalyen who could combine two or more Elementals, now that would have been special.'

'You could also use an Astra for the same effect, no?'

'Slightly different. Astras are easier to use because they do not use your soul energy. Nor do they require a knowledge of the glyph structures of the Chakras. Combine a *kir* with any of the Elementals, and you have an Astra.'

'What is a kir?'

'No one knows for sure… but I hear it is the remains of an old God.'

'What does that mean?'

'I've only heard rumours. They say the true God is dead, and his body splintered into many parts called kirs. They were used to make Astras to fight against the Daevas. Extremely arduous process. They can be summoned by an *Astradhari*, Bearer of an Astra, at will, if he knows the proper way to do it. But that is just what I have heard. The study of Astras is reserved only for the most senior of shishyas at Meru, which we are not. The truth may be entirely different.' Saying which, Varcin tossed an apple to Nala, who caught it with his knife.

'What is an Astradhari?' Nala wanted to know.

'Umm, so you know the standard ranks in most armies in Aryavrat? The ones approved by Meru, not the ones kingdoms are conjuring on their own. So, above knight, you have a paladin. That is the hero class. The rarest of rare heroes enjoys such a title, and they are entitled to chariots. But in the times of the Elder Men, there was another class above the paladins – the paragons or Astradharis – the bearers of Astras. Paragons almost single-handedly decided wars between themselves in those days, and could topple kingdoms at a whim.'

'Sounds horrible. Good riddance. But what did you mean, "use your soul energy"?' Nala asked, flipping the pages of the book with renewed passion. Back in the forest, knowledge was passed by word of mouth. They looked on written records with disdain, treating writing as something foul that could be twisted to make a lie permanent. Fortunately for Nala, when he had first learned the letters before he entered Meru, he found he was a fast learner.

'Soul energy, or atman or eyons, is the power of blood that flows through us. And before you scowl at me, I do not mean the blood defined by caste. Hmm, let me see how I can explain this better.' Saying which, Varcin descended on a stool nearby. 'Come to think of it, I really can't.'

'You are spectacularly useless, Varcin.' Nala went back to the book. He was beginning to increasingly compare Chakras with God in his mind, which was to say they were extinct, impractical and beyond all understanding but still exciting.

'All I know is that one can increase soul energy by certain well-defined acts that pressurize your soul; either in a good way or bad. Mostly bad. Penance, strenuous meditation, sacrifices, abstinence from pleasure, hardship; they all do their part in furthering one's soul energy,' revealed Varcin.

'Ah, so that is the source of the phrase *pain is pleasure*.' Nala nodded in newfound wisdom. For some reason, Varcin blushed. 'What?' Nala asked, mystified.

'That phrase... isn't applicable here, Nala,' Varcin said, not meeting his eye.

'What do you mean?'

'It's the birds and bees, you know. I'm sure your father spoke to you about this.'

'My Matre told me my father was eaten by a crocodile.'

'You forestfolk have strange stories.'

'Studying Mandalas, are we?' Acharya Vyas walked in, his voluminous saffron robes ballooning about him.

Nala and Varcin scrambled off their stools and fell to their knees, each striving to out-bow the other.

'Sit. It's good, though curious of course, to see young pupils in the Library.' Vyas craned his neck as he stretched himself out on a chair opposite Nala. 'So, is there anything I can help you with?'

The boys quickly unlimbered themselves to stand before him. They looked at each other in much the same way two thieves would have had the Captain of the Guard invited them in for supper.

'I may just know something that can answer your doubts,' Vyas added softly.

Varcin nodded at Nala, who took a deep breath. 'Your Worship, we were just wondering...' Varcin shot him a sharp look. 'I mean *I* was just wondering about Chakras. Brother Varcin told me Chakras use soul energy, eyons to conjure Mandalas. But I thought eyons were used for Shraps and Vachans.'

'Hmm, a study forbidden to your year,' Vyas remarked. 'Why is that when any teacher closes the curtains to a room, you shishyas immediately need to know what's on the other side? Pass me that apple, boy. And use the word atman instead of eyons. You are a student of Meru now.'

There was a pause as he sat munching the apple. 'Shraps are used by drawing on atman, the same way Mandalas are created, but Shraps deplete the atman. Mandalas merely borrow it, and then return it. Think of atman as the apple you ate, Nala. Each curse requires the reddest, juiciest, tastiest and largest apple for it to work. If the apple isn't big or juicy enough, you will not be able to use the Shrap.'

He beckoned them to take stools opposite. 'The intensity of Shraps depends on the atman one has accumulated, or the size of the apple. Especially because, unlike Mandalas that used to be channelled through Chakras, a Shrap uses no such channels. It is what makes them so unsafe and explosive. That's why a learned Namin, who performs the necessary rituals to direct the energy generated from sacrifices towards himself, has a high atman, erm... high soul energy, which, of course, comes with a propensity for quick, effective Shraps.'

'So that's the reason they are feared across Aryavrat,' Nala mused.

Vyas smiled, then suddenly stopped and peered into Nala's face. 'Nala, you....' His eyes twinkled as if he had uncovered something mischievous. Nala felt as naked as a newborn. *Does he know?* He looked away from that searching gaze. 'You are different from the other boys, aren't you?' Vyas remarked with a wry smile.

'Aye, Acharya. He is a Valka, if you believe it.'

'Quite so.' There was an unsurprised look on Vyas' face. 'But Vachans are different.' His eyes never left Nala as he continued,

'They are ritualistically invoked, and difficult to ordain, even by a trained Namin. A Vachan wraps a chain around your soul. Imagine having to do all of Acharya Irum's drills with a huge boulder on your back.'

Nala could only hope Acharya Irum was not eavesdropping on this conversation. *Wouldn't want him getting any ideas.*

'You will be tired for a few days, yes, but it will make you stronger over time. However, if the chain holding the boulder breaks, the boulder will crush your back. Likewise, break a Vachan and it will burn you to cinders. It is notoriously difficult to ordain a Vachan, and many well-meaning Namins have burned to death while administering one. That is why Vachans have been banned across the realm, except with the approval of the Saptarishis.'

An ominous silence followed Vyas' words.

'Mandalas, on the other hand, well, they… hmmm,' Vyas scratched his beard, 'they require atman in the way a lock requires a key. The more complex Mandalas don't use atman in any destructive way, like Vachans or Shraps, but connect with the atman of the world. Now tell me, what is the atman of the world?'

'The Elementals,' the boys chorused, happy to have the answer.

'I see that you have been reading attentively. Good. Yes, it connects us to the Elementals, or *N'yen Valren*, as the Daevas called it in the Old Tongue. It allowed us to use and mould them as we see fit. Show me the book you are reading, Nala.' Nala handed over the hefty volume with two hands. Vyas was instantly distracted by the book. 'Ah, I thought we had lost this one to the Rose Coterie.'

'Beg your pardon, Acharya? Rose Coterie?'

'A vigilante group, book thieves, criminals of the highest order! Ignore them. I see you are studying the basic Mandalas. Yes, I remember when I too studied them with relish. I still remember a few by heart. The design is crucial, Nala.'

Acharya Vyas raised his rosary-wrapped wrist and stabbed the air with one finger. The air suddenly bled white light, leaving a fiery trail as he moved his arm in a circle. Varcin sprang back and bounced off his stool, crashing into a bookshelf. Nala gasped as he shielded his face with his hands, peeping at the beaming circle between his palms. Vyas' fingers moved as if he were painting a mural.

'Each Mandala has a unique effect, which is determined by its shape,' he said, smiling at the boys through the glowing glyph that hovered in the air between them. 'Activation of Chakras within the body allows its wielder to channel the Elementals in desired frequencies and lengths to produce specific effects through Mandalas. This Mandala should have immediately lit up the glow-lanterns behind you by using Light, but… well, Elementals don't work any longer.'

'That was awesome!' Nala felt dazed after the Mandala pulsed for a few heartbeats before fading to dimness, and then to nothingness.

'Acharya,' Varcin asked fearfully, 'do you know why it all stopped? The Mandalas? The Astras?'

Acharya Vyas shrugged. 'No one knows. Maybe mortals don't deserve magic, child.'

SHAKUNI

I

If Hastinapur, capital of the Hastina Union, was the Eye of the World, the Eagle's Crest was its pupil. The Crest, home of the reigning King of the Union, was a vast and imposing acropolis in the centre of the pink city. It crowned a rise like a feast for famished eyes. Five graceful spires rose from the Crest's corners, their brilliant white stone marbled with some kind of shining sapphire that only glistened when the sun set. Slender arches swooped from one spire to another, soaring through the sky between them. Crafted by the Elder Men, these were wide and strong enough to hold an army. The shimmering arches were the Crest's only boundaries.

The oldest city in the known world, obsessed with law and justice, opened its arms lovingly to its citizens, provided your pockets were deep enough. At the centre of the Crest was a huge dome with great towers of marble, lined with burnished gold. The golden tips of the towers threw sunlight back in sparkling patterns that seemed to give the dome an ethereal aura. It wasn't unknown for men and women to cover their faces in awe, to kneel in prayer, to close their eyes and weep, at this marvel created by Man.

Shakuni, on the other hand, felt like barfing.

The streets to the Crest were shelves cut into the arid hillside. Sweat leaked out of every pore of his body as he trudged up to the acropolis. He clung to every trace of shade he could find, but the sun seemed intent on waging a personal vendetta against him. The handle of his cane cut into his palm with every step as he shuffled doggedly on under the Crest's arches towards the Dome.

Bees swarmed over the elongated gardens stretching on both sides of the pathway in sun-struck explosions of black and yellow. It was just dawn, but the air was already hot. A crude scattering of rock lay on the pathway like pox on a damsel's face, conspiring to topple him at every step. This cobbled path through the rose gardens was the only way to the King's chambers. Unfortunately for Shakuni, it was a hazardous one. He chose to limp through the garden instead, the soft soil absorbing the force of his cane. It hurt less. As he went, Shakuni slashed the rosebuds out of existence with his cane. *Useless fucking flowers.* He winced with every step, but destroying the roses gave him the satisfaction and strength to make it through. He saw a few Resht gardeners, keeping well in the shadows, eyes on the ground. Shakuni chuckled. *The privileged few blessed with the opportunity to serve. It is a good thing Aryavrat has banned slavery,* he thought sardonically.

His right palm felt sore on the cane as he craned his neck upwards at the archway at the end of the garden. It was cast in bronze, topped with the great red eagle of the Hastina Union, its feathers delicate flakes of black opals and fiery rubies. *All the gems looted from Gandhar seem to have found their way into this one ugly structure.* Shakuni spat at the foot of the arch as he walked through. *Creating an arch of colours for a blind man is akin to me participating in a race.*

A rising stairway cruelly interrupted his thoughts on fiscal prudence. Shakuni stared at his old nemesis with familiar spite. *One step at a time.* The stairs were an oft-fought enemy and his campaign was well planned. First came the easy stretching of the left foot, aided by a hobble of the waist. Second came the wooden cane tapping musically on the ground. And then the eternity of pain that stabbed through his right toe, right ankle and right rump as he dragged the right leg forward.

After conquering twenty steps through a litany of curses, he stumbled at the twenty-first step. His cane trembled in his hand.

Shakuni stiffened. *Here it comes, my companion, my shadow, my wife. Here it comes.* The pain descended upon him like an avalanche. His spine hurt with the jolt. His teeth grated on each other as he half collapsed against the wall. He stared up at the last few steps of the stairway with watering eyes. *Great! Now I must suffer this agony twice,* he groaned as he wiped the snot from his nose with the back of his free hand.

Beside him, a window taller than the tallest palace guard was carved along the curve of the tower. Shakuni shaded his eyes with his hand as he looked out. Hastinapur spread before him in neat grids of houses divided into sectors for Namins, Ksharjas and Drachmas, a place for everyone amidst a map of straight roads speckled with wide squares. This part of the city, around the Crest, was called the Crowns. The Crowns was carved from rose-coloured quartz, the beautiful pink lanes vaulting downwards around quartz-lined avenues, turning Hastinapur into a palette of red, pink and lilac pastels. Even the gardens were perfect, for the Hastinas were obsessed with order. There was not a vine, flower or tree in the Crowns that wasn't sculpted as it grew. From this point of vantage, it seemed a place of supreme beauty and peace.

But Shakuni knew better.

By the time he reached the King's floor, he looked so victorious it was as if he'd just scaled a peak. *Pathetic.* When he arrived, only the King's old guardsman, Ahira, was present. The eunuch always cut an intimidating figure, no matter how exalted her surroundings. She'd guarded three Hastina Kings in her lifetime. Fair skinned and white haired, she turned to face Shakuni as he approached. He always wondered whether Ahira and the White Eagle had ever got round to talking about their snubbed desires. Then again, who was he to speak of desires? The House of Kauravas had taken care of that long ago.

'Lord Shakuni, you are late,' Ahira said.

Shakuni glanced down at his crippled leg, then at the stairs, and shrugged.

'The King is now… *busy* in his chambers.'

Shakuni was well versed in the language of nuance, so he narrowed his eyes as if to ask: *Do you want me to spell out what I can do to your adopted son?*

She must have understood, for she bowed slightly, saying, 'But you may enter.'

That's more like it. 'You are too kind,' Shakuni grated. 'The Union thanks you for your dedicated service.' Saying which, the most feared man in the Union walked into the King's chamber.

II

Shakuni stood silently between two torch sconces, touched by the light of neither. It was a strange feeling to watch other people fuck; a touch of nostalgia maybe. How long it had been since a woman had touched him softly. *Decades.* Still… He had expected Kings to fuck in a kingly manner, all royal gravitas and symphony of sounds. But here he was, the Hastina King, grunting like a pig in a gutter. Shakuni waited patiently while the blind fool grasped the courtesan's left breast and sucked on it like a starved bear on a honeycomb. Shakuni had long since learned to sever his mind from what poets called the heart. He thought of himself as a surface devoid of ripples. It made it easier to watch Dhritarashtra devour a woman within earshot of the Queen's chamber. He should have felt anger, even rage, but in truth he felt only gladness for the Queen. *Better the whore suffers than you, Sister.*

'Do your best, girl. I will give you many bastards, I promise.' Dhritarashtra put a hand on her head and pushed her down. The King's pillow talk could definitely use improvement, but then again, it didn't matter. Sex, in its most unconditional form, was the most wholesome thing gold could buy. 'Children,' he gasped, 'who will grow to good ranks in our army.'

As Shakuni watched the courtesan engulf the blind King in ecstatic waves, her deadpan eyes met Shakuni's. While her moans whistled musically out of her throat… nothing reached her face. She nodded grimly towards Shakuni, who returned the gesture.

Not much difference between sex and statecraft, he mused. It would have taken naught to kill the King right then. The courtesan was in his employ, her son studying to be a map-maker in Takshashila. It was almost too easy to find female spies. Just educate their children. It was charity and conspiracy rolled into one. But Dhritarashtra was just a tool to be used to dismantle the Union, his true foe. He heard Dhritarashtra's grunts reach their crescendo as he clung to the woman's hair. Noiseless as a shadow, Shakuni slipped out of the chamber.

As he waited in the antechamber, a glimmer of light caught his eye. Even the chandelier overhead paled by comparison to the jewels that adorned Dhritarashtra's crown. Sitting atop an ornately chiselled granite slab, the rubies of the crown glistened with an unearthly charm. *Ah, I remember this.* After Dhritarashtra had been told by his Vedan priest that the sun in his horoscope was *angry,* the King had all the emeralds, topaz and diamonds that had decorated the Kaurava crown for centuries cast away and replaced with rubies. Shakuni compared it to the crown of the Emperor of the South, whom he had seen at a tourney three summers past. That had been a simple band of iron, embossed all around with carvings of creepers, its only adornment. The Greeks were even more modest. *The only redeeming quality of those godforsaken Mlecchás.* Their Archon, Kalyavan, wore a wreath of olive leaves. It was only the Riverlands that revelled in ostentation. *Fools. It's not what is on the crown that makes a King but what is under it.*

He walked to the balcony, his limping leg twitching uncomfortably under him. The ancient city of Hastina spread out below him, stretching to the horizon. A rose-coloured wall cut through the city to encircle the Crowns. If only the eyes could be stopped by the wall. For no matter how beautiful a maiden, she still shat the same ugly thing as a leper. Hastinapur was no different. In the shadow of the rose walls of the Crowns festered the squalid, stinking houses of the Crows – the Resht District. It was a giant boiling cauldron of maggots and disease, where the

Reshts nurtured false hopes of a better life in their one-storeyed shacks.

Ever since the Prince had crowned that upstart Karna as Highmaster of Anga, there'd been reports of mass gatherings of the lowborns in the Crows; more than he would have liked. Just last week, two Reshts had dared to enter the nature ceremony in the Temple of Prakioni, in defiance of the law. It had been blasphemous, of course; nevertheless, their treatment by the Namins and the Ksharjas had been... *excessive.* Shakuni could have tortured the Reshts to reveal their plans, their organization, and whether the rumours of the resurrection of the Red Blades was true. For Shakuni was not just the Queen's only surviving brother but also the Master of Peace of the Union. A step down from the Prince of Gandhar certainly, but definitely a promotion from tortured prisoner of war. *It's all about the right perspective.*

But no, why make my job easier? The culprits had been lynched and now the curfews were back. And Shakuni had a bunch of frightened Drachma merchants in the Crows on his hands, where ghettos of Reshts squatted around the modest factories of the nobles like mushrooms around lotuses. *Pathetic.*

All this divine ordainment of caste was pure nonsense, of course. While the Namins called it the burden of sins from a past life, Shakuni knew their design was more ingenious. Everything had a purpose, a grand construct drawn from the simplest phenomenon of the forest – the Food Chain. If there were no Reshts, carcasses would pile up and the stench would consume the kingdom. Without them, who would till the land, clean the stables, and run errands for their betters? If there were no Namin priests to conduct sacrifices, the soul would be entangled in another birth and earn the ire of Yama, the Gatekeeper of the Afterlife. The Ksharjas served to protect, administer and rule... and, of course, own lands. The Drachmas ensured free flow of trade. They all were part of a wheel, with each of the four spokes fixed to their respective anchors in the wheel's rim. If any spoke broke... *What am I now, a fucking philosopher?*

III

The blind King shambled out. Whorls of gold decorated the sleeves of the robe he wore over his wide pantaloons. A diamond-studded sash wrapped its length round his waist. *For a blind man, you shine like the sun, Your Grace.* Tall, hard and bronzed, Dhritarashtra Kaurava would have been every maiden's fantasy had it not been for his dark, lifeless eyes.

'Ah, Lord Shakuni.' Dhritarashtra sniffed. 'Is that a new fragrance I smell on you?'

'A new poultice, Your Grace, for the… pain.'

'Of course, of course…' Dhritarashtra laughed awkwardly. He sat down languidly on a sofa, as familiar with the chamber and its placements as with the feel of his hands. He rested his feet on the low ottoman he knew would be there, just as it was every day. For a whimsical moment Shakuni thought how amusing it would be to rearrange the furniture. *Let's see you strut around then.*

'I wish to discuss the Angan situation, Shakuni.'

'Ah yes… the poisoning of Prakar Mardin was most unfortunate. Naturally, it didn't help to have Lord Karna on the same ship.' *That damn Resht!* Shakuni had no idea how his careful plans had gone so awry, and in so dramatic a fashion.

'And what about the assassination attempt on Karna? Do you believe it?'

'It appears Lord Karna was indeed found in an injured state by Princess Bhanumati, but… there were no witnesses to what Lord Karna endured at the dock.'

'Of course there aren't. I told you, Shakuni, I don't trust that Resht. He must be in cohorts with the Kalingans to wrangle Anga from my grasp.'

'Surely Lord Karna is a citizen of the Union too, Your Grace? And a most gifted warrior, an ally of the Prince.'

'Don't call him Lord! He isn't anointed yet. Skilled warrior, maybe. You can use a spear as a walking stick, but that does not change its nature. You know the Reshts cannot be trusted. They do not like us.' *I wonder why.* 'Best not get between Duryodhan and his pups, however. I am sure the fascination will fade. But keep an eye on Karna. Use your Mists well.'

'I will do so, Your Grace.'

'Excellent…' Dhritarashtra said as he rose from the sofa, his eyes seeking the face he could not see, only hear. 'So Anga will be fine?'

'In a manner of speaking, Your Grace. Naturally, placing Karna on Anga's high seat was as unwise then as it is now. For now, we have appointed a cousin of Prakar, another Mardin, as interim Highmaster. We can revise our options once peace returns to the port.'

'Yes, yes, that is wise. Anga is too important to Hastina. I will not have the Meru record that the Union lost a port in my reign. Pandu conquered territory after territory without installing able governors, and now that those territories have gone, the world blames me for losing them.'

'It's a throne of thorns, Your Grace.' Shakuni said.

'It is indeed. I am glad I have you on my side, Shakuni. Uhm… is there anything else?'

'There was one other matter,' Shakuni said, dropping his voice to an ominous whisper. 'It is as I suspected, Your Grace. There is talk amongst the Council of Hundred about summoning a *Mahasabha*.'

The Hastina Union was different from the Magadhan Empire. Magadh assimilated its conquered kingdoms into itself. Magadh's territories did not fly their own flags; they did not own armies. The Lords and Ladies of the various regions of Magadh served at the pleasure of the Emperor. The Union, on the other hand, was a Federated Realm, formed of the founding Kingdom of Hastina, the Kingdom of Madra, the Kingdom of Gandhar, the Kingdom of Trigarta, and the Protectorate Cities of Sivi, Matysa, Varnavrat and Anga.

While the Codes of Hastina set out vast powers for the King, the Union was governed largely by a Council of Eight – the Heir Apparent, the Master of Ships, the Master of Peace, the Lord Commander of the Army, the Master of Laws, two Masters of

Revenue and Taxes, and the Head Acharya nominated from Meru. Usually, half these posts were filled by representatives from the vassal states. The Eight's duty was to keep the power of the King in check, for while the King could issue any order in the form of a *diktat*, using his executive powers, it could be reversed by a majority in the Council of Eight, provided all were present and voting.

But, during the Period of Blight, it was seen that the Eight could also become tyrannical, so the Good King Yayati formed the Council of Hundred, made up of important Lords and Ladies of the Union aristocracy, who were empowered to collect taxes from the common folk who tenanted their lands, on behalf of the Union. They also represented the common folk and could bring their grievances before the King, but almost never did. This was not because the Union was a paradise to live in, but because the Hundred were, for all intents and purposes, lazy lizards. They dispensed their own brands of justice in the lands they governed, and the King and the Union turned a blind eye as long as the revenues flowed in.

'A Mahasabha! Why in Vayu's name?' Dhritarashtra blazed. He was perhaps justified in invoking the name of the God of Wind, the guardian-deity of Hastina. Being a member of Hastina's Hundred was like being a voter in the Mathuran Senate. If voting made a difference, Krishna would never have let them do it. The counter of votes counted, not the caster. And the Hundred had not been asked to vote in the last hundred years. But these were interesting times in Hastina politics.

The Codes gave the Hundred power to summon a Mahasabha, a Great Meeting, whenever there was a formal dispute about succession to the throne. Once the formal dispute was lodged, the pauper Lords suddenly became pirates, with each vote their personal ship of war. When Dhritarashtra had resisted being superseded by his younger brother, Pandu, to the throne of the Hastina Union, it was the threat of a Mahasabha that had resolved the succession crisis. A Mahasabha meant an endless circle of bribes, assassinations, poisonings, promises, and betrayals, none of which Dhritarashtra had an eye for.

'They wish to resolve the succession dispute by calling on Lady Kunti to tell her tale so that all men may know that Prince Yudhistir, the eldest of your brother's sons, is elder to your son, and thus the rightful heir to the throne of the Union.'

'That's... that's impossible! There is no succession dispute! Duryodhan is the Heir Apparent. Vayu's beard! This is not good. We both know how the Hundred would rule in such a vote after Duryodhan's blasphemies. But I am still alive. And while the King lives, a Mahasabha can only be called by him.'

'Indeed, Your Grace. I am merely trying to think what your enemies might plan.' *Or what I have told the King's enemies to plan.* 'Would they, perhaps, brand you a mere *Regent*?' Shakuni said slowly, to let his words match the rising colour in Dhritarashtra's face. 'The laws can be twisted to mean one thing and then another, as Your Grace is well aware. And before you confound me with your sound exposition of the Codes, Your Grace, as I know you will, pray tell me one more time, who should have sat on the Hastina throne... your brother, King Pandu, or you?'

'Shakuni,' Dhritarashtra said, his voice ominous, 'tread softly. Pandu, may his soul be liberated, was dear to me. He did not wish to be King. My blindness... my brother...'

'Your Grace, I would never suggest anything to the contrary. Your brother was a saint, I know.' Shakuni was surprised at the ease with which the lie rose to his lips. 'But respectfully, Your Grace, I have heard reports of secret meetings of nobles and priests with Lady Kunti. It appears there have been feasts hosted by your dead brother's wife. The timing of Lady Kunti's feasts, coinciding as they do with Prince Duryodhan's peace mission to Anga, seems odd.'

'That's enough!' Dhritarashtra rose suddenly, kicking the footstool away. Waving a hand, he said, 'There is no conspiracy afoot! It is the time of the Festival of Prakioni, and feasts are common. If it were anything else, Sister Kunti would have approached me directly. When Pandu abdicated the throne and went to live in the forest, did I not send him and his two wives supplies to help them bear their ordeal? After his death, when Kunti returned with his sons, did I not take care of them as my own? Yudhistir is Duryodhan's cousin. *Younger* cousin. The boy was born in the forest, where there are no records; there is no way to prove otherwise.'

Shakuni bowed his head. 'Very well, Your Grace.' He toyed with the idea of letting Dhritarashtra know more. 'May I address something to you as a friend, a brother, and not as your Master of Peace?'

'You know you always have my ear and my trust, Shakuni.'

'At the Tournament of Heroes, before the Resht showed up, when the sons of your brother, dressed in red, carried their bastard sigil, and your sons in black fought under the Hastina sigil, you think it went unnoticed?' The Hastina sigil was a red eagle on the backdrop of a black sky. 'The sons of Pandu either hired a, forgive me… colour-blind designer or they deliberately appeared under the sigil of a black eagle on a red sky. And now the Hundred have split into blacks and reds.'

'All this is talk of civil war, Shakuni! This is one family we speak of. The blood of Kuru flows in all our veins! They are cousins. Black or red. I do not see colours, as you do. To me they are but names, as they should be.'

'And then, Your Grace,' Shakuni continued as if he had not been interrupted at all, 'Acharya Kripa lent me an interesting book on the customs of the savage East. The custom of widows jumping into their husband's pyres is an honourable practice there. Barbaric to us, yes, but it makes me ponder. King Pandu had two wives: the Ladies Kunti and Madri. But Lady Madri, Vayu bless her soul, hailed from the West, yet she was the one who died willingly on his pyre… What kind of mother willingly kills herself, leaving behind her twin sons to be cared for by a rival wife who has despised her throughout? These questions torment me, Your Grace. If anyone had to sacrifice their life, not that anyone should, it should have been the eldest wife. Lady Madri was the younger, a maid of sixteen. Yet she is dead, and Lady Kunti is here.'

'You insinuate grave allegations, my friend. Can you prove any word of this fable? No? Good. She has already told her tale in open court, and it is not for us to question her veracity.'

'But on a Vachan, Your Grace?'

'Vachans are banned, Shakuni. And Hastinapur has never so shamed a woman, and that too of the royal family! That will be enough, Shakuni! I do not wish to indulge this further. My two sons, Duryodhan and Dushashan, and Pandu's five sons, Yudhistir, Bheem, Arjun, Nakul and Sahadev, are the future of the Union. If you wish to question a Royal Matriarch, do so at your own peril. But do remember the punishment for failure. You will receive no special treatment, for the laws of Hastina are written in stone and apply to all equally. You know what is written under the Eagle: *Law Above All*. Even if you scrub some commoner to question a Royal, you know the seven-year-long procedure. And,' he puffed out a deep sigh, 'Mahasabhas are expensive affairs, not to mention tiresome. The war between Mathura and Magadh has wrecked the realm. So, I would not worry about a few petty Lords sitting to discuss my heir any time soon.'

'So, we do nothing?' Shakuni asked, eyes glinting.

Dhritarashtra paused, scratching his beard. 'Alright, I will entertain you. What do you suggest?'

'Why not crown Yudhistir Highmaster of Varnavrat?' He let the thought bubble in Dhritarashtra's mind.

The King nodded, suddenly smiling. 'It will offset the damage done by Karna's appointment, and keep Yudhistir away from Hastina. Varnavrat is hardly important. Two birds with one stone. Splendid idea, Shakuni! Yudhistir will also like it. He has been after me to grant him more responsibility. I will ask your friend Purochana to rebuild a mansion there to house my nephew comfortably.'

Yudhistir is not you, fool! He knows he would be more a hostage there than a Highmaster.

'Put it into motion today, lest Yudhistir hear of it and block it somehow. Lady Madri's son, that boy Sahadev, is quite a serpent when it comes to the law, I hear.'

'What of the brothers?' Shakuni asked quietly.

The King waved him off. 'They'll follow Yudhistir to Varnavrat. I wouldn't worry about the other sons, Shakuni; they are inconsequential.'

Why would you indeed? Arjun is the finest archer in the realm; Bheem the strongest; Sahadev is a learned lawscribe, and Nakul, the most beautiful boy ever seen, an instant swayamvar winner. Why worry indeed? 'As Your Grace wishes,' said Shakuni.

'Good. How are the preparations coming along for Prince Duryodhan's marriage to Princess Bhanumati? In these uncertain times, this alliance between Kalinga and Hastinapur is important. The quicker Duryodhan sires a son, the better.'

'All is well, Your Grace. Prince Duryodhan and the Resht are back within Hastina borders, and should be here soon. But again, I must object—'

'Yes, yes, I know Kalinga will not bring any strength to the Union, for it is tied to the Magadhan Empire. But my son loves this girl. Something must be allowed for the desires of young blood. And she has wrought a change in him. I give thanks at the altar of Prakioni that the girl is not a Resht but a Ksharjan Princess. Now, off you go, Shakuni. I have a long day ahead of me and I must rest.'

'I am yours to command, Your Grace.'

The King returned to his chamber, where the courtesan awaited his pleasure. Shakuni smiled as he limped out. *Win some, lose some.* Marrying into Kalinga was folly, but for now he must contend with it. He could have never imagined Duryodhan falling in love. *I suppose love is like a rain that falls on cactuses and lilies alike.* Anyway, Kalinga was too distant to be part of his schemes. All his other dice had rolled sixes. After all, it was he who had bribed the more vulnerable among the Hundred to broach the subject of Yudhistir's ascension. Half the nobles too, who had approached Yudhistir, urging him to stake his claim, had also been sent by him. Shakuni knew something drastic was needed to force Yudhistir onto the offensive. Exiling him to Varnavrat would be just the thing. He considered the blind

King as he exited the antechamber. *What a dolt! You should have crippled my mind too when you had the chance. You should've— Oh these fucking stairs!*

NALA

I

'The food must only go in,' Acharya Irum said as he dragged his long cane along the floor on his way to the teacher's dais. 'If I find even a single morsel in the air, climbing an altitude I don't approve of, you will find I was a rather generous man this morning.' Nala absently rubbed the stripes left on his thigh by Irum's cane even as the cold voice instructed, 'You may talk freely. And if you fight, no bone breaking.'

'Generous?' Upavi whispered, once Irum was out of earshot. 'If he is generous, then the Yaksha is the Goddess of Well-Being.'

'I just want food,' Varcin said, immersed in a bowl of rice-starch. Hunger heeded no etiquette. They were bone-tired, and the platters of roasted pigeon, hard cheese, fruit and flat-cakes, were the panaceas their weary bodies craved. 'If I had waited any longer, I would've eaten Nala.'

'Let's go to the rooftop,' Varcin suggested after he was done with a third serving of cake. 'The seniors told me they left a bottle of wine under the butt of the gargoyle.'

'I'm in,' Nala agreed without hesitation.

'Of course you are. You love cheap wine. Me, I prefer ale and cider any day,' Akopa stated loftily.

'Beggars can't be choosers, Akopa,' Varcin retorted.

'Wait, what?' Upavi looked aghast. 'Now? Today is the last day in the *Week of Sharing*.'

Everyone at the table groaned. The Week of Sharing was a tradition in Meru, carried out with the other Orders of Saptarishi. Second-year students of Meru were given an easy choice – a month's paid apprenticeship with any other Order, or a month's holiday. The Week of Sharing was when Acharyas from other Orders came to Meru to advertise their own faculties. They had already been through the guest lectures of five Orders, and each one had been as tiresome as the next.

'Sister Mercy is coming as a guest lecturer! It's the first time a woman is coming to Meru to lecture in the time we've been here. What sort of people would we be if we bunk such events?' asked Upavi.

'Students…' Nala answered wearily.

'*Ha. Ha.* But seriously, this is important. They never teach Divination in Meru, or at least have not for a while. This will be really interesting.'

'She'll have us dipping our noses in tea leaves and ask us to draw patterns in the clouds. The Valkas already have shamans for that,' Nala said.

'No, Sister Mercy isn't a shaman. Haven't you heard of her Oracle House?' They all shrugged. 'Please,' Upavi begged. 'I don't want to attend alone.'

They looked at each other, considered abandoning Upavi to his fate, but suddenly remembering the tenets of friendship. 'Fine,' Nala grunted. 'But you'll fetch the wine.'

II

Nala lay, head down on the open book of Divinations, drooling onto the chapter 'Methods to Torture and Reveal an Oracle', apparently attempting to learn its contents through osmosis. Acharya Vyas yawned in the last row. They had been waiting for an hour for Sister Mercy to arrive. Upavi guessed she was picking which shoes to wear. Varcin suspected she was lost in the future.

It was precisely at that moment that Sister Mercy walked in with the gait of an Empress, her feet bare. She wore a black-hooded robe with golden trim. She leaned on a weirwood staff topped with a crystal orb, which no doubt doubled as a cane. If teachers could be likened to weapons, Sister Mercy would have been classified as a weapon of mass destruction. She had sad eyes rimmed with dark circles, but that was clearly false advertisement. She rummaged in the folds of the golden sash around her waist and took out a pin that glinted in the afternoon light. With startling abruptness, she stabbed the pin with all her might into Nala's drool-smeared palm.

'*Ow!*' Nala came to life with a painful start.

Mercy grimaced. 'Didn't know we were allowing pathetic girls into the Meru now.'

Nala froze. Needless to say, Sister Mercy instantly had the class' full attention. The shishyas stared at her in the manner of those who had heard of the species 'woman' but had been disappointed with what they had learned.

'Who can tell me the best way to prepare the Truth Potion?' Sister Mercy asked.

Not even Varcin raised his hand. Whether it was because he did not know or did not wish to face Sister Mercy was anyone's guess.

'Pitiful. Which of Acharya Salas' methods for Oracle identification was discarded five years ago?'

Nala knew this! He had just read it. For the first time he knew something the others did not. In his excitement, he had raised his hand before survival instinct could warn him not to. 'Drowning!' he blurted.

Sister Mercy was the kind of person you never wanted any attention from, let alone her full attention. It had taken better men than Nala to stand before her gaze and not perish. 'Pitiful!' she almost hissed, so full of spite was the single word. 'The answer is asphyxiation by immersion.'

That's what I said! Unsure but relieved at escaping unburnt, Nala sank low in his seat.

'Can anyone quote the *Gospel of Radiance* to me?'

There was nothing but silence.

'Can anyone tell me what the *Gospel of Radiance* is?'

The silence was so intense it almost roared.

'Is this the level of teaching here?' Sister Mercy thundered like a storm. 'No wonder the quality of education has dropped at the Meru. You boys are being taught to draw scenery with a sun, a straight river and a palm tree, while my girls are learning to narrate a story in a work of art.' She turned her ferocious gaze towards Vyas. 'I doubt your students would be able to keep up in the Oracle House, Acharya Vyas.'

'Now, now Sister Mercy... that is a hasty and impolite judgement.' Under her gaze, even Acharya Vyas faltered.

'Is it now?' Her brows rose, fleeing to her temples. 'It would have been *impolite* to say the teachers who have let the pillars of education fall should be buried under them. But I did not say so.'

'That is enough, Sister Mercy,' Acharya Vyas said with the might of a leaf pitted against the current of a river.

'What is going on?' Varcin whispered.

'Something about paintings and our education. Who knows?' Nala shrugged.

Sister Mercy frowned at Vyas, but then tuned her gaze on the hapless shishyas. 'Has anyone ever divined something?' she asked in a monotone. 'No? I can show you then. Any volunteers, children?'

The *children* were busy staring at their knees. She thudded the cane so hard on the floor that all the shishyas looked up, despite themselves. 'No volunteers then? I've seen corpses with more energy than this lot.' She threw Vyas another look of derision. 'I will take your leave, shishyas. I cannot understand why I was forced to come here for this. For my classes, you need spines of steel. Till you have developed those, I suggest you do not even think of coming to my House,' Sister Mercy ended with a smile. 'Meanwhile, if you have any doubts, I have been put up on the third floor. My door is always open.' Her ghastly smile appeared again. Then she was gone.

'What a class, eh!' Varcin whispered to Nala. 'How's the hand?'

'I just hope that pin wasn't poisoned. And why can they never clarify when they mean things metaphorically?' Nala complained. 'First the paintings, then this…'

'What do you mean?'

'Surely her door cannot always be open? She wouldn't want to be changing her underpants and have a shishya walk in with a doubt on Asphyxiation by Immersion, would she?'

Varcin and Akopa chuckled at the image. 'You do pick your moments to be right, Nala.'

Nala turned to Upavi. 'Are you happy now? So much for women lecturers.'

Upavi had turned so white the biology students could have been pardoned for mistaking him for a cadaver.

'What happened?' Varcin asked. 'You okay?'

Upavi turned stiffly, as if made of planks of wood rather than bones and sinew. 'I have already signed up for the Oracle House, to apprentice under Sister Mercy. I… I didn't know.'

That night, the boys, in Valka fashion, held a pre-death funeral for their cherished friend, with the wine Upavi retrieved from the rooftop.

III

'You can choose your apprenticeship of your own volition,' Acharya Irum said. 'Remember, this is purely optional. Many wise men advise taking a vacation instead of these apprenticeships, for once you graduate, moments of quiet and peace will be rare. Understood? Upavi…' Acharya Irum read from his list, and for the first time in two years, Nala could have sworn Irum gulped. 'Seventh Order: House of Oracles. May the Light be with you, lad.'

Upavi marched to take his scroll with the determination of a death-row convict.

'Akopa, come forward. What do you choose?'

'The Second Order, Acharya.'

'Acupuncture,' Acharya Irum said. 'Those hands are not meant for caressing, Akopa. But a useful course, nonetheless.' He shook his head and turned to Varcin, who chose his order. 'The Fourth Order,' Irum repeated, tonelessly. 'You want to spend a week learning the Discipline of... Cooking?'

'I feel, to be an Acharya of holistic understanding, I would benefit from a period of learning the culinary arts,' Varcin replied, showing his crooked teeth in an earnest smile. Nala could barely suppress his laughter.

'You mean you want a week of just sitting and eating,' Irum said.

'One does indeed sit to eat, Acharya,' Varcin agreed humbly. Nala gulped down his laughter, disguised as a fit of coughing.

'That class is filled with Sisters who didn't make it to the Second Order, Varcin!' Irum roared.

'Acharya, I am convinced about joining the Fourth,' Varcin said earnestly. 'You don't have to make the proposal more attractive with the prospect of girls.'

Nala lost his struggle and gave a snort of laughter. Two hours later, as he completed his twenty-third lap, along with Varcin, he was still laughing. 'Thanks, Varcin.'

'Piss off, forest-boy,' Varcin panted, as they staggered back to the dorm. 'You're really going on a vacation?'

'I would have joined you, but Matre and my brothers have come to Varnavrat for the Festival of Prakioni. Don't ask. The Valkas, rather the Nora, think Prakioni or Prthvī, I am not sure what they call her in your world, is nothing but the forest spirit they worship. It's just a three-day ride from Meru. I'd better meet them at a neutral location rather than back in the forest.'

'Makes sense, Brother. It will be a relief to have three weeks without you.'

'Oh, you'll miss me, never fear,' said Nala, sweating from the jog. 'Once I'm back, we are going to delve into the Chakras again. I really feel there is something to be discovered there.'

Varcin groaned. 'Fine.'

The next day, as the sun was rising, Nala gathered his things, donned his boots, said his farewells, hugged Upavi, and hurried to the stables to saddle the mule Meru had graciously lent him. The clatter of hooves sounded on the cobbles as he rode towards the entrance where the local guide waited to escort him to the caravan bound for Varnavrat. Once they had climbed down the hill and reached the woods, he turned back to look up at the Citadel. The fires from the lanterns burned low as the mass of Meru emerged like a dream of stone against the lightening East. Wisps of mist raced across the Citadel, fleeing from the sun on feathers of wind.

Little did he know then that it was to be the last time he would ever lay eyes upon it.

SHAKUNI

I

Pain is a demanding mistress. She doesn't let you forget her. *Thirteen steps of pure agony,* Shakuni thought as he gazed at the steps that led to Bheeshma's office. Sometimes, he felt Bheeshma had deliberately removed the banister so Shakuni would have nothing to hold on to. Without it, he had to climb the stairs sideways, like a crab. *Look at you Shakuni, as graceful and lithe as a dancer!* he thought as he panted through the effort.

Yudhistir and his brothers had been safely packed off to Varnavrat the week before. Duryodhan had returned to the city safely the previous night. In the meanwhile, Shakuni had also sorted out the Angan mess. But nothing good lasted forever in Shakuni's life, and he had just sighed when he received the summons from Bheeshma.

Bheeshma was the finest paladin Shakuni had ever seen. He fought with a bow called Purity, said to be forged from the heart of a fallen star. They called him the White Eagle, and he would have killed Shakuni all those decades ago but for the timely marriage of his sister to Dhritarashtra, the White Eagle's nephew. Shakuni suspected the White Eagle still felt the need to complete his half-finished task before he departed to wherever heroes go after they die.

To his surprise, Karna was sitting outside Bheeshma's work chamber, looking gallant and gorgeous, quite unlike his own panting self. Karna rose and bowed, but Shakuni passed him without a glance, unsmiling, spine straight, chin up, nose haughtily in the air. The guards' crossed spears parted to let him in. He was glad to find the White Eagle not there, for it gave him time to pause, pant, gasp and curse in friendly solitude.

Having caught his breath, Shakuni looked around. The White Eagle's office was richly appointed. An ornate teak table stood in the centre of an enormous silk *dhurrie*, woven with the Hastina arms. Tall pointed casements on two sides offered ample light and an expansive view of the Halls of Justice.

A breeze wafted in as Bheeshma walked in from the ante-chamber. *The old patriarch took his title of White Eagle rather too seriously*, thought Shakuni, for the bright sky beyond the windows looked almost dirty in comparison to Bheeshma's spotless white cloak, the shock of his white hair, and the white eagle sculpted on the tip of his walking stick. To call Bheeshma old was akin to calling the mountains tall. In his long life he had played the role of son to a King, brother to a King, uncle to a King, and was now poised to play grandsire to future generations of Kings of the Union. He ought to have died ten times over, yet here he was, apparently immortal. *Though not ageless.*

'My Lord,' Shakuni said, with a creaking bow that sent flashes of pain up his side and brought tears to his eyes.

Bheeshma said nothing as he took a seat behind the table. In the natural scheme of things, he would have been King of the Hastina Union, had he not taken a Vachan of Celibacy. No wonder the White Eagle was still alive; a life without wives and children was no doubt conducive to longevity and peace.

'You know, in my time, it was customary for the young to touch their elders' feet.'

'A good thing then that I appear older than you, Grandsire.'

The White Eagle gave a thin smile and beckoned him to sit.

'I prefer to stand, My Lord. I have a swelling in my knee.'

Bheeshma smiled. 'No, you don't. The only swelling on your foot is you.'

If only I could yank those perfect teeth out with my dagger! Shakuni leaned his cane carefully against the table, stretched out his limp leg and, bending awkwardly, allowed himself to slump into a chair, his crippled leg extending all the way to Bheeshma's feet under the table. Pain shot through his thigh. He sighed. *For most people, sitting down is an ordinary affair. For me, it is positively orgasmic.*

'Prince Duryodhan is on his way here now. I wish to discuss this Angan trouble. He says he has something to tell me. I hear the murder of Prakar Mardin, thanks to your timely interference, is being treated as a case of plague.'

'Just a matter of knowing who to pay, My Lord. The fact that his ship was later burned for carrying plague was fortuitous.'

'Good. But I would like to know who was behind the assassination. If what the Resht says is true, it may not be the last attack. All this is rather troubling, Lord Shakuni.' Bheeshma rose and strode across to a window, his large hands clasped behind his back. 'It's a new world out there. Abstracts like order, system, pride and honour have fallen out of fashion. The old Ksharjan order has crumbled, to be replaced with…' He glanced over his shoulder and his colourless lips curled. He moved to the table and handed Shakuni a large round cup of spiced tea. 'Replaced with avarice. It's a pity, really.'

The spiced brew disgusted Shakuni, but he accepted the cup with courtesy. 'You are most gracious, My Lord.'

'Where was I? Ah yes, while the Namins were busy fighting the Ksharjas for supremacy, the Drachmas became the new power in the land. Goldsmiths, bankers, lawscribes, tax-collectors; wretched money-counters with their limited vision; men and women whose loyalty is only to their purses; whose only achievement lies in swindling their betters; whose honour is quantifiable in coins.'

Bheeshma scowled out at the view, then turned back into the room. 'It seems anyone's son, or even *daughter*, can get an education and be anything they want! We are behaving like those savage Southerners. And now we have a jumped-up lowborn dictating terms to his betters, thanks to Duryodhan.' Bheeshma gave a shudder as he paced the floor. 'And now I even hear that the Meru has taken in Drachmas and Valkas!'

'My Lord, it was indeed unfortunate that Duryodhan crowned that Resht. But it did not altogether surprise me, if I am to be honest. Duryodhan has always had a kind heart towards strays. But just where did the Resht learn such archery? And... forgive me for saying this, My Lord, but Karna is a master with weapons. His teacher is the one who should be flogged.'

'He learned from Acharya Parshuram.'

If Shakuni had not been a cripple, he would have jumped to his feet, toppling the chair with a crash loud enough to match what he felt. *Acharya Parshuram!* That disturbing figure in history was unfortunately a certified Immortal. He was also a Namin psychopath. Bards sang how he went mad when a Ksharjan King slew his father. That was a hundred years ago. Parshuram had banded the Namins together. Commanding armies a hundred thousand strong, he had spread the fire of his wrath against the Ksharjas in a war that decimated ancient families to the last infant. And then, as suddenly as he had started, he abandoned the genocide when he grew bored. But he had by then turned the fear of Namins into a trait inherited by the descendants of any Ksharjan survivors. If titles were anything to go by, *White Eagle* was dazzling enough, but *Bane of Ksharjas* was truly demonic. 'But didn't he...?'

'Yes, he taught me too. His teachings were what helped me keep Hastina united. I'll be honest with you, Lord Shakuni,' the White Eagle smiled, as if being honest was a great act of charity, 'Hastina is powerful, very powerful, with lands and armies, but beneath the skin of such power maggots crawl, eating away its insides. It is no secret that there is a succession dispute on the horizon between Yudhistir and Duryodhan. That is when our enemies will use the fruits of civil strife till Hastina is torn asunder. Prince Yudhistir is malleable and law-abiding, but too fond of gambling. Prince Duryodhan may be better suited to rule, but he wants to change too many things. Imagine permitting Reshts to have surnames! The Council of Eight, whose task it should be to steer the Union to prosperity, is filled to the brim with schemers, traitors and fools, each inclined to carve a piece of the Union for himself.'

How frustrating it must be, when the Union ought to be left whole to be ruled by you alone, thought Shakuni derisively.

'Meanwhile, beyond our borders, strange dangers are rising. I'm sure your spies have told you about the Madran King, Lord Shalya, incidentally a part of our corrupt Council of Eight, meeting with the Magadhan Emperor in Rajgrih. To what end, who knows? Jarasandh has a vigorous new religion that has fitted him for another war. Once Mathura falls, who is to stop him from advancing north? The forest tribes find themselves united under some Yaksha. They skulk on our borders in the South. Closer to home, in the Council of Hundred, bluebloods clamour for long-forgotten rights, while in the countryside the farmers clamour for new ones.'

Shakuni wondered if this was why he had been summoned. If Bheeshma had known that it was Shakuni who had asked Shalya to involve himself in the Magadhan mess, he would already be in chains. Or did the White Eagle perhaps suspect he was behind the peasant revolts in the countryside?

'Things were different in my time. No whining nobles, no thieving Drachmas, no conniving Namins. If men forgot their place in the order, they were reminded with boiling water. The Council of Eight was a noble institution then, filled with the brightest and best. And now we have corrupt fools like Lord Jaimini as Master of Taxes.'

Bheeshma sat down in his great, high-backed chair with an ease that made Shakuni envious. The old patriarch then leaned forward across the table that separated them. 'So, you see why, when I decided to take matters into my own hands to clear the maggots, I thought of calling on you?'

'For my cleansing abilities, My Lord?' Shakuni enquired, unsure where this was going.

'Oh no, no. For you are the biggest maggot of them all.'

Shakuni wondered if the tea he had drunk had been poisoned. Even if it had, there was not much he could do about it. If death was coming, he would rather be sitting down anyway. Yet he was curious. Which of his crimes had the White Eagle uncovered?

'I know of your *friend* in the Narak.' Bheeshma's eyes narrowed to blue slits. Shakuni froze. *How did he know?* His fingers trembled. 'You will bring him here on the morrow. How could you keep this from the King, Lord Shakuni? This threatens not just the Union, but the entire realm!' He rapped a knuckle loudly on the table and a guard entered, though Shakuni heard no door open. *Had I left the door ajar?* And then his thoughts shifted to a more pressing subject. *I wonder if they will dispense with the show of dressing a cripple in chains?*

'Ask the Resht to come in.' The guard left. Bheeshma looked exasperated, but then suddenly sighed. 'I am astonished by your action, but glad as well. You and your Mists have wreaked havoc in the city, with your secret raids, inquisitions and investigations. I have wanted to catch you in the act for too long, and now I have you by your worthless leg.'

'My Lord, I was just trying to protect the King; to get to the bottom of things. This is unfair...' Shakuni raised his forefinger but stopped when he saw the look on Bheeshma's face. *A silly mistake.* No one raised a finger at the White Eagle unless they wished to part with it. And Shakuni was already missing body parts. Slowly, he lowered the finger, curling it into a fist.

'You will present your *friend*, along with the keys to your office, to me in the morning. You are no longer the Master of Peace. Your Mists will be disbanded. There will be an enquiry. If you have any childish notions that you can limp off crying to the King, discard them now.'

There was a soft knock. The guard appeared again, but this time he was sweating. 'My Lord, Karna is not here.'

'What do you mean he isn't here? I asked him to be here. Has he not been waiting for the last two hours? Go fetch him this instant!'

The guard nodded miserably and hurried away.

'My Lord...' Shakuni said, knowing it was useless.

'No, Shakuni. You're done.'

II

Narak had only one set of ironbound doors, ten feet tall, guarded and locked from the inside. A square block in the door slid open as Shakuni approached, and a face silhouetted by the lantern behind appeared. 'State your business.'

'A roll of seven,' said Shakuni formally.

He heard a clatter and the heavy doors swung outward. A man stepped out to meet him, hand raised in salute. He wore a dark leather vest, bracers and boots over red doublet and breeches. A black hood was drawn around the back of his head, and his face was covered with an enamelled mask that had only two holes in front of the eyes. Three marks were drawn between the eye-slits of the mask, denoting his status as Captain. The expressionless mask-face was worn by every officer who worked under Shakuni to ensure peace within the city. *The Mists.*

Merciless hunters, the Mists were responsible for weeding out conspiracy and corruption in the city. The Secret Police. They were the faceless heroes of Hastinapur, for while soldiers earned glory on the battlefield, the Mists only earned fear for the things they did for the Union. It was due to the dark nature of their tasks that they were also considered the best gaolers for a place like Narak.

Shakuni followed the Mist into the entrance hall, which was divided into two sections by a wall of black iron bars, running from ceiling to floor across its breath. On one side, the hall led to the Office of the Mists, where the Union's dirty work was done. But Narak's true purpose was served by the two ancient stone vaults that went far beneath the ground, into the bowels of the earth. That was where Shakuni was headed now.

They reached the end of the hall where another Mist, this one with two marks between his eyes, saluted Shakuni and opened the door to a spiralling staircase, using the key strung around his neck on a leather thong. Narak was a prison built to imprison Gods. Nobody really knew who built the two levels of this gloomy pit in the bowels of Hastinapur, for the pit predated the city itself by centuries. But what was known was that Narak was cursed with dark magic. Spending more than half a day here without drugs could swallow the songs in one's head. The two levels of Narak, however, affected their inhabitants differently. The air of the first level, where Shakuni was hobbling through, was known to stunt intelligence over time, making escape impossible to plan. In some prisoners, it erased the concept of escape entirely by destroying memories, so prisoners had no reason to leave. Amusingly, the first level of Narak was the only dungeon in the realm that posted no guards. It was reserved for those prisoners who had somehow earned the King's Clemency.

He continued down the staircase till he found himself at the second level. The Mist slid a key in and opened the door, letting light into the vault of blackness. It was divided into eight vast cells, four on each side, with a twenty-foot corridor down the middle. Only two of these cells were currently occupied. The second level of Narak was reserved for the vilest criminals of the Union, a place unknown to most Hastinas living over it, above ground. The speciality of this level lay in how time did not move here. It came to a grinding halt in this vault. The prisoners here aged very slowly. And what was better, they healed. The few Acharyas Shakuni had employed to uncover its secrets had long given up. But Shakuni did not really care for its origins, as long as it got his work done.

So, instead of restraining prisoners, their limbs were amputated. The prisoners would regrow their limbs slowly, excruciatingly, but surely; only to have them amputated again. An eternity of healing… and torture, till the mind itself abandoned the body. In here, death was not a granted release. Only madness was.

One of the cells had a boy of barely ten summers, clutching filthy, bloodstained rags to himself. The Resht had dared drink water from a well in the Crowns. Even Karna knew better. The boy's face was hollow with hunger. His heels scraped the stones as he tried to push himself further back into the corner, blabbering something in broken Sanskrit, one hand raised to shield his face from the light.

In places like this, the only thing worse than darkness is light. For light only means more torture. *I remember…*

A pair of feline eyes tracked Shakuni as he stepped up to the other cell door. No torches burned in this cell. There was no need for them. His *friend* provided light of his own. The eyes moved towards Shakuni. Myriad colours swirled in those depths. Shakuni limped into the dank space, careful not to let any of the sticky fluorescent blood of the prisoner smear his robe. 'Any success?' he asked.

'None, My Lord,' the Mist replied. 'Our usual methods do not seem to be working. He doesn't seem to need to eat food or drink water. We tried the Rack on him but it didn't work. We were working to raise…'

'No time!' Shakuni snapped. He looked at the prisoner, their eyes meeting like a clash of arms. Chill clutched at Shakuni's stomach and he dragged his gaze away. 'Any reports of spies trying to get out what we have here?'

'No, My Lord,' the Mist answered confidently. 'Only one way out of this place, and I have barred any other Mist from descending to the second level.'

'Well, someone leaked it to the White Eagle.' There was no point looking at the Mist to gauge his reaction: his face was hidden behind the inscrutable mask. 'I don't like leaks.'

'I can trust my colleagues with my life,' the man answered.

'And you will surely forfeit it if you do not find who was responsible.'

The Mist nodded. Shakuni turned to look at the prisoner again. 'We have to take him to Lord Bheeshma's office in a few hours. Before that, I want my answers. Water.'

The Mist went to the corner, picked up a bucket and flung the contents into the prisoner's face. The prisoner coughed, shook his head, flicking droplets from his sun-gold hair. He tried to stand but the chains around him rattled, snatching him back down to his chair.

'Torture is a subtle art, Daeva,' said Shakuni to his guest. 'Its purpose is never to kill. Murder is anathema to the science of torture, and Vayu knows I am no murderer.'

The Mist brought forth a wooden chair and Shakuni wearily sat down upon it, moaning as pain once again spread through his body. He looked up. 'I do apologize for the untimely death of your friends but, well, they did resist arrest and killed fifteen of my guards. I assure you that I will do everything in my power to let you live the remainder of your immortal life. But perhaps not in the way you imagined.' The Daeva continued to stare lifelessly at him. 'Unless, of course, we become friends.'

The Daeva said not a word.

'I know you understand our language. So why do you not tell me why the fuck have you come back?'

Silence. The strange eyes of the Daeva glowed.

Shakuni let out a weary sigh. *What an exotic creature!* He felt an unfamiliar surge of shame rise within him that the Daeva had to be treated this way. *The beauty of a tiger vanishes when his paws are dug into your neck. Better chained than clawed.* 'I'll let you in on a secret, Daeva. I thought as you do now when they captured *me*. I was determined not to speak, even when they began slicing my leg. My determination faltered a little when they broke my teeth. And by the time they tore off my nails, I told them whatever I knew. I made up lies to tell them more! I gave up every secret of my army, every tunnel, every stratagem, everything... Still, it did not work.'

Shakuni made a humming sound as the Mist laid out his tools. 'But they did prove to be excellent teachers, for their emphasis...' Shakuni opened his mouth to reveal his broken teeth 'lay in practical lessons. So, if you think you will not talk when I start with you, I assure you, my friend, by the time I am done, you will sing.'

A guttural sound came from the Davea's throat, like the low incipient growl of a lion.

'Well, that's a start.'

III

The Daevas were said to be beings born out of Light, gone eons ago. Acharya Kripa, however, believed they never existed at all. So

Shakuni could safely claim no living man had ever seen a Daeva. And yet here he was, torturing one.

The Daeva's nails had already been ripped out; green blood flowed sluggishly, coating his hands. Shakuni picked up a hammer and felt his arm twitch with pain as he closed his gloved hand around it. The Mist brought the Daeva's left arm down and held it against a slab of rock, clawing fingers spread out pale on its rough surface. The Daeva said nothing, but amber veins stood out in his neck as he struggled. But for all the Daeva's bulk, the Mist held him fast.

The head of the hammer came down on the Daeva's knuckles with a distinct crunch. The blow jarred Shakuni's own hand, pain shooting through his arm, but he did not stop. Two... three... four times he brought down the hammer. The Daeva hissed, howled and heaved, emitting strange sounds. He jerked back his hand from the slab, his palm momentarily turning sideways. Shakuni smiled as the hammer came down again and crushed the wrist, leaving it a blackened mess. 'Will you talk now?'

The Daeva screamed, the sound making the blood surge in Shakuni's ears. 'No? Very well.' He traced his finger across the smashed knuckles, then tapped the thumb and ran his finger in a circle on the palm, finally touching the smashed wrist. 'As I told you, it's an art. A precise art.' He grinned as the hammer hissed in the air. 'So, Daeva, what is your name?' he asked even as the hammer smashed methodically into the Daeva's ribs.

'Savitre! Savitre Lios! Savitre Lios!' the Daeva screamed, again and again. 'Stop now! Just stop!'

Savitre Lios. Shakuni smiled. 'See, that was not so difficult. So, what business brings you here to our world?'

There was the creaking and clicking sound of bones adjusting. Shakuni saw the Daeva's smashed wrist turn and snap back into place. The palm that had swollen to twice its size began to heal, colour returning to his hand. The blackness of his wrist disappeared in a heartbeat.

Shakuni peered at the figure, his eyes travelling to the Daeva's face. 'This isn't the effect of this place, is it? Healing here takes weeks. Well, that's one secret revealed. Strange that your friends had no such power when we killed them. Why?' He pressed Savitre's wrist with his thumb.

'They're different,' the Daeva rasped. 'Younger.'

'You creatures are twisted, aren't you? The older you get, the stronger you become, is that it? Still, how did the hammer feel?'

Shakuni knew exactly how it felt, having been through it himself. The Daeva's feline eyes bulged, his cheeks trembled.

'That's right. You may heal bones right back, but I'm sure you cannot mend your memory of pain, can you?'

'No.'

'Wonderful. This level's purpose is then served. You will remember the pain. Your fast healing powers are a gift to those like us.' Shakuni rose from his chair and leaned down, ignoring the pain crawling up his back, his lips curling away to display his rotten-teeth smile again. 'You see, after a while we run out of parts to burn, hit, hammer, twist and so on. Hardy prisoners, not unlike you, get used to the pain. But your healing power gives us a chance to begin anew.' He raised the hammer again.

Savitre Lios screamed. 'I answer! I answer!'

'Oh, I know you do, but this will serve as adequate motivation for you not to waste my fucking time. Actually,' he looked up at the hammer and tossed it aside, '… let's try something different.' His lips snarled as he unsheathed his dagger and dug it deep into the Daeva's other hand, crucifying it to the chair's left armrest.

The Daeva screamed.

'Give me the other!' The Mist swiftly pulled out his own knife from its sheath and handed it to Shakuni. 'My apologies for the interruption,' Shakuni said to the screaming Daeva as he crucified the other hand to the armrest. 'I hope we understand each other now.'

The Daeva's face was as white and limp as a banner of surrender. Shakuni really could not understand how these creatures had ever enslaved humanity. Yes, they healed. Yes, they were Immortals. They were rather tall. But they whimpered in pain like any Mortal.

'You are a monster!' the Daeva screamed at him.

'Look at the crow calling the raven black,' Shakuni cackled. He cracked his knuckles, hurting from holding the dagger handle so tight.

'What happened to honour in Men?' the Daeva rasped

'Don't know. I didn't inherit it. Enough idle chatter. Why are you here?' Shakuni twisted the dagger into the Daeva's right arm, almost gently.

'Muchuk Und! We're here for Muchuk Und!' the Daeva blabbered through a song of screams. 'Danger. Still a danger.'

'*Muchuk Und?* Who in seven hells is he? Or is it a thing or a place?'

The Daeva probably answered diligently but Shakuni never got to hear it. Someone whistled behind him. The Mist's sword was out. Shakuni turned but the Mist came in protectively between Shakuni and the unknown assailant. The next instant the man fell limply backwards against Shakuni, who barely had the time to register the slash behind the Mist's left ear, across the skin between his leather neck guard and cropped hair.

For fuck's sake! He managed to toss the Mist's body aside but was tackled and pinned face to the ground by the assailant. His body erupted in a volcano of pain from which death would have been sweet release, but he knew better than to expect that at this level of Narak. He felt a stabbing pain behind his right ear. Before he could ask any questions, he too collapsed, limper than a wet robe in a storm. A wave of darkness crashed across his eyes but not before he heard the Daeva say, 'Thorin was right. You all deserve what is coming for you.'

NALA

I

'Caste?'
    'We are forestfolk.'
'Caste?'
'Ksharja,' he sighed. Valkas did not practise the caste system of the Vedan religion, but considering that all Valkas were supposed to be warriors, the realm considered them Ksharjas.

There was a hustle of steps behind the door but it remained closed. Nala tapped his toes impatiently. While he waited, he turned to see the Protectorate City of Varnavrat behind him. Compared to Hastinapur, Varnavrat was little more than a village, but it was the nearest thing to a true town the hillsfolk had. This ancient stronghold of the Hastina Union stood at the northernmost end of the Riverlands; a little outcrop of ice and stone, surrounded on three sides by enormous peaks. Just five leagues of hill road separated Hastinapur from Varnavrat, yet they were two different worlds. Nala had heard of how music played in pink-tiled courtyards, and how the air was always sharp with the smell of citrus in Hastinapur. The air of Varnavrat, on the other hand, smelled of smoke and dust. While Hastinapur was built of marble, all its streets cobbled, down to every turn and roundabout, Varnavrat was a sprawl of wooden hovels with thatched roofs and mud streets, albeit against a backdrop of white peaks.

The wooden door finally opened and the innkeeper peered out. Nala was neatly dressed in his shishya tunic, his hair cropped short, with just the right smearing of sandalwood paste on his neck. The innkeeper allowed him in but then stopped short as a motley group straggled in after him. 'Who are they?' he shrieked.

'My family,' Nala clarified. He could understand the man's confusion. His mother and five brothers were dressed in traditional forest attire, with an assortment of bone jewellery, and feather fetishes in the hair. Their ash-painted cheeks and hawked noses could scare the toughest townies. The innkeeper scowled. But having opened his door, there was no going back. Northerners took the guest rite of *atithi* seriously. He hesitantly gestured them in but gave them the farthest room of the inn.

'I don't know why we have to sleep here when the woods outside are perfectly comfortable,' Matre complained in the forest tongue.

'Oh Matre,' Nala said with a condescending sigh. 'It's time you all experience the wonders of a quilt, and a place we can sleep without one of us having to stand guard.'

'Rubbish!' Caani scoffed. 'I'll take first watch. Townsfolk are more dangerous than the animals.'

'They're rude,' Iweeth complained. 'That innkeeper's wife kept staring at my nose stud and earrings as if she wanted to steal them. I wasn't staring at her flower necklace now, was I?'

'Maybe she *did* want to steal them,' Caani offered.

'I will have her know the shaman invested it with spirits to guide only *me.*'

'I thought the innkeeper rather muscled for a town man,' Matre said slyly.

Her children groaned. Valka women never repressed their needs. They rode men in the open and there was little anyone could do about it. Sometimes, Nala could see why the townsfolk were so regressive in their ways. It was to keep their mothers in check.

Come night, the seven of them crumpled into napping positions without a word, weariness crawling inside their skins. But they remained awake till Matre fell asleep, for she could not bear their snoring while sensate. But it took some time for her to fall asleep, and eventually she crawled out from under the soft quilt to sleep under the bed.

'So...' Nala looked at his brothers, feeling strangely like an outsider, 'how are things at home?'

'Good,' Skruath, the youngest, said. 'Last winter we were able to goad a hundred *bursons* to fall to their deaths from the cliffsides. The Spirits were kind to us, and not a single Nora went hungry.'

'Yes, Skruath did good. He got the honour of being first to butcher their carcasses.'

Nala smiled, wondering if he should point out that they were driving the bursons to extinction, but decided against it. 'None of you are joining the Yamuna Wars?'

Caani spat. 'We were kept back to defend the peace between tribes.' The others murmured assent. 'I must admit grudgingly that the Nora Chief is doing wonders for the reputation of the Valkas. What does Yaksha mean in your High Sanskrit, Nala?'

'Demon.'

'Yes, demon. No wonder the innkeeper grew pale when he saw us, for now everyone fears and respects us.'

'Tell us, how is it to learn among those weaklings in the North? Anything useful?' Caani asked, doubt clear in his tone.

Nala did not think his brothers would find the story of the Three Glacial Ages intriguing. 'It is going well. Naturally, the townsfolk are fools with their parchments and quills, but I am making the best of what I can.'

'That's good, Nala. Nora children are survivors.'

'Ssh... if Matre wakes up, you will put that to the test,' Skruath warned.

'*Survivors*,' Caani whispered.

'Caani, I was wondering what shamans say about... Mandalas,' Nala said.

Caani raised an eyebrow. 'Do you mean a *Warren*?'

'Does Warren mean bright white circles in the air?'

Caani nodded. 'Warrens are long gone, Nala. It is known. Why are you interested?'

'So I can show those highnoses how wrong they are.'

'I wish I could help you, Nala. Shamans say the Warrens have decayed by the loss of memories. Our ancestors used Warrens to communicate with the forest spirits, who gifted them jewels of fire, ice, stone and rivers wrapped in obsidian skins. It is forbidden to speak of it for its loss is our shame. You could have been a shaman, you know, Nala. It is allowed to you, but not to us.'

Nala barely listened to Caani. He wondered what Caani meant by obsidian skins.

Skruath interrupted his thoughts. 'How is this Varnavrat place? I heard the Hastina Princes are there. I want to see a Northern Prince. See what he looks like.'

'Yes, yes…' Iweeth agreed. 'I was talking to the other Valka with us on the boat. He said the Prince is the future King of the Hastina Union – Prince Yudhistir.'

'King! Would he refuse me if I challenged him to a duel?' Caani asked, flexing his muscles.

Nala was horrified. 'Please, Brother. It doesn't work like that here. And Yudhistir is not the future King. It's Prince Duryodhan.'

'Who is that now? Will he be there?'

'Caani, *please*,' Nala hissed, worried, wondering if it had been a good idea to bring his lovable but brutish siblings here. 'The people here decide Kings on the basis of blood. They do not respect strength as we do. If you go to challenge him, he won't even look at you; his guards will arrest you and you will rot in iron chains in their underground prisons.'

'*Er Fedur!* He wouldn't do that. It would shame him before his people,' Caani said, confidence wavering.

'Think about it, Caani. The Hastina has had one ruling bloodline for the last six hundred years. You think it is because of their wrestling abilities?'

Caani grunted and turned away without a word.

'City people are twisted,' Skruath said, shaking his head in dismay. 'They wouldn't last a day in the forest.'

And you wouldn't last a day in the city. And the world is better for it.

II

There was a sad truth about family. When far from them, you longed for them; with them, you remembered the reasons you went away in the first place. Put simply, Nala thought his brothers impossible. Caani's ambitious challenges aside, Skruath wanted to go hunt peacocks in Kingswood, Iweeth wanted to claim the innkeeper's wife, and the rest of his brothers wanted to visit pillow houses without a single coin in their purses.

Let them get arrested on their own, Nala thought, slinking off to sulk. He skirted the crowded Trader Track and took a detour into the woods. He preferred the silent company of the forest. The trees in the North had a different kind of wood than what he was used to in the South. Untouched for thousands of years, this was the wood of stubborn dispassionate trees. Nala decided to sit against one of these old sentinels, in silent contemplation, away from his brothers, who refused to be awed by his knowledge of alchemy or history. He missed Varcin.

There came a faint sobbing. Nala ignored it at first but the sound grew persistent. Now this was a conundrum. A scream would have been clear, concise and commanding. You did not approach a scream; you ran away from it. But a sob was altogether different. You never knew if you would run into a rich old man in need of heroic assistance to cross a bridge. 'Erm... hello?' Nala called out.

'Who's there?' The voice sounded like rocks breaking.

'A passer-by.' Nala chose his words carefully even as he followed the voice to its source.

It was the oddest scene. A man was brooding over a feast. Seated, he was the height of a full-grown warrior, his arms the size of Nala's waist. His dark, thick hair was tied to hang down the left side of his chest, covered with knotted strips of gold-threaded silk. He wore a cloak of fox fur. A two-handed mace with a stone pommel and wooden grip rested next to him. The man cast a suspicious glance at Nala, asking sharply, 'What? Have you never seen a giant weep before?'

Nala wondered how many had. 'Uhm... my apologies, Sir. Is there anything I can do for you?'

The giant sniffled and looked him up and down. Finally, he beckoned Nala over to share his feast. Nala approached cautiously, taking his place a little removed from the great creature before him. The giant continued munching amidst tears and sobs, but waved a hand towards the grapes. Whatever tragedy grieved him, food remained his priority.

'What is wrong with your face?'

'Erm... it is *kilas*, Sir. Discoloration of the skin.'

'Looks like the rays of the sun are etched on your face! So, what brings you here, scar-boy? You don't seem to be a local.'

'I come from the Iktov Forest, Sir.'

The giant's eyebrows arched, though he continued to eat. 'A Valka? You look too comely to be a Valka. I encountered a Valka long ago. Bloody thief and upstart! Got his deserved punishment though.'

Nala was too fascinated with the food to be offended. *My brothers will burn with envy when I tell them this story. If they believe me, that is. Maybe I should pocket a grape or two. Better yet, let Caani wrestle this man!*

'Why did you leave your forests?' the giant asked. 'From what I hear, you people serve your Gods in the bark of trees and the shit of birds.'

'For a vacation, Sir. The Festival of Prakioni in Varnavrat is also the celebration of our forest deities. If we did not take my mother out at this time, it would be the death of us.'

'Mothers, eh?' the giant grunted. 'Can't drop them from a cliff and can't stop loving them. Would you like some rabbit?'

Nala did not refuse. They ate the soft white meat and then bit into fat plums, chewing the sweet flesh while red juice ran down their chins. They savoured the food and shared stories of their mothers for a while.

'Of the seven, only Caani listens to our mother. We—'

'Seven of you!' the giant interjected, cocking a brow in surprise. Nala nodded. 'What about your father?' he asked, his eyes burning frantically.

'Dead. Bandit raid killed him and a sister. Only my mother and the six of us now.'

'What's your name, Valka?'

'Nala.'

The giant grunted and joined his palms in greeting. The length of his palms joined together was longer than Nala's face, head to neck. 'I am Bheem of the House of Kaurava, the first of my name, and brother to Prince Yudhistir, rightful heir to the Hastina Union. May I invite your family to dinner?'

III

The Kaurava Mansion was a humble house tucked between two towering spires of wind-sculpted rock carved into a high peak. At the door of the Mansion, they were rudely pushed around by the guards, who sneered at them with contempt till a word from their sergeant had them escorted inside. Nala felt embarrassed. For some reason he had thought Prince Bheem's invitation to dinner was to be private, not a mass charity feeding of the indigent. Matre was just happy the Prince had invited Nala personally, while his brothers were excited to see royalty. It had taken an hour of persuasion, but Caani had promised to behave, which meant not challenging anyone to a death-duel.

Amidst the jostling crowd, Nala found himself pushed away from his family. A glance at the queue behind him and he abandoned the idea of leaving his spot to find them. The queue wound through many turns of the stairs before a hall could be discerned. Nala observed that, most unusually, there were no demarcations between the castes. They all stood clogged together, their bodies pushed against each other as they waited their turn to sit in the dining area. Here they were all defined in a single common category: *Poor.*

Nala spotted one or two odd Namins who had dared to be present in the same queue as members of other castes. *Must have been really hungry.* There was a Namin right in front of him, completely draped in ragged saffron robes. Judging by the colour of his matted hair, he was ancient enough for Nala to take a step back to avoid stumbling into him and risking a Shrap.

After what seemed an eternity of moving glacially up the stairs, they reached the eating halls. Banners of black eagles in a sky of red hung on the walls. *Hmm... this isn't the Kaurava sigil. Has it changed?* Nala shrugged. What did it matter to him? In the dining area he could see rows of men and women gorging on what smelled like heavenly food. Over the throng, chandeliers swayed in the mountain breeze that wafted in through the long windows. The aroma of rice and fish permeated the air.

But above all, the musky smell of lac pervaded the Mansion. Nala looked up to see where it was coming from, just as a beam in the ceiling gave way, threatening to drop like a sword on the neck of the condemned. Acharya Craw's training pulsed through his mind as he yelled a warning and crashed against the Namin, barely able to take him down with him. There were shrieks and cries as the beam fell behind them. Nala felt a sharp pain and raised his hand to his collarbone. He had hurt it crashing down with the Namin.

'My apologies for touching you, Revered One. I am a Valka,' he quickly confessed.

'Quite so.' The Namin rose, a queer look on his face. 'It seems you saved my life.'

Nala had the look of a runner who had panted all the way to the finishing line without realizing he had won the race. 'Did I?' he mumbled, still jolted, his collarbone aching as he turned to see the beam that had fallen.

'Everyone back into line!' the guards shouted as servants bustled about to remove the debris.

A man in an expensive robe, with a well-oiled moustache, shambled over to where they stood. 'What in the name of—How can this happen in something I designed?' he cried.

'You can ask the coin you embezzled instead of creating sturdy roofs!' a man in the queue called out.

The robed one had turned red. 'I am Purochana, Architect to Kings. This… this does not happen to my buildings!' he fumed. 'Guards! Take that man out of the line and out of the Mansion! And find out where that godawful smell of lac is coming from!' Saying which, he huffed and puffed out of the room.

It was after two more hours of slow shuffling that Nala found himself seated in the dining space, next to the Namin he had saved. The serving women put a leaf plate before his crossed legs and tossed a spatula of rice onto it. Nala's stomach growled in anticipation. He carefully tilted a few drops from the small earthen pot of drinking water into his right palm and rubbed his hands in three circular motions. He then shifted the water pot to his left.

Another group of serving women arrived, with an assortment of food in large copper buckets and straw baskets piled high with crispy treats and breads. It was a meal like no other. Onion fritters and succulent goat kebabs, followed by a healthy mound of curd rice topped with aubergine curry. Spicy roasted potato and stir-fried okra were placed on the side. Sweet of tooth, Nala helped himself to the *ghee*-laden saffron balls filled with rich dry fruits and cardamom.

The serving women continued serving, but Nala politely refused second serves of the same dish, despite violent protests by his stomach and soul. Instead, Nala was served with dessert, even as the rest of his fellow diners had barely satiated themselves with the second course. The last dish before him was milk; except it was not milk. The cream colour was that of a dusty old robe. Nala could smell saffron but was suspicious of the concoction.

'Do not concern yourself with the colour, boy,' the Namin said, as if reading his mind. His face was hidden under the cowl of his robe but he looked rather well built for a Namin. 'It is condensed milk... stirred over a low flame for so long that it has changed colour.'

'I did not mean to offend, Revered One.'

'One should never apologize for careful paranoia. It's the least that can be expected of a student of the Meru.'

Nala gaped. 'How did you know?'

'It's fairly obvious.' He peered down his long nose. 'The water bowl on the left, the clean palm even while eating rice, the slight self-deprivation. Yes, I noticed how you did not ask for another helping despite wanting to. Of all the people gathered here, you are the only who deserves to sleep on a bed rather than in a sty. Those around us are already on their third or fourth servings, clearly having abdicated being men in favour of being pigs. And the way you covered your face when you burped. Amongst savages, burping is more of a competition than a social offence.'

'You figured I was from Meru by the way I ate?'

'There were other signs too. The faint cane marks on your wrists. Why do the Acharyas think they need to beat rules into you?'

Nala laughed, annoyed that he had given himself away so easily. He couldn't help but notice that even the Namin had been eating with the precision of a surgeon, his lips unsmeared with food, the plate tidy, and the passageway between thumb and index finger clean. 'Erm... good table decorum makes up for lack of good food up there.'

The Namin chuckled. 'Meruvians, in essence, are diplomats, and table manners constitute the cradle of diplomacy. You see, when we were still barbarians, eating wasn't a mundane affair. The tools used to eat a boar were the same ones used to cleave an enemy. One could never be sure whether one was walking into a peace-dinner or a sword-fight. That is why a system of rules was devised to keep the animal spirit within us in check while we ate.'

'I did not know that. Are you from the Meru too, Revered One?'

'No. What's your name, lad?'

'Nala. What may I call you, Revered One?'

'Ah, let's keep that a mystery. No good ever comes from anyone knowing my name.'

IV

Nala could not sleep, though he wanted to. So, he rose quietly and went out to the balcony that encircled the first storey. The night was eerily warm. The air still stank of resin. He arched over the railing, breathing deeply. Below, at the bottom of a rather dizzy descent, the river wound through dense woods. He knew trees dotted the slope of the high hill on which the Mansion stood, but he could barely see them under the moonless sky.

Nala felt content. He thought of the day that had been. He had got along well with the unnamed Namin. Then there was the gracious Prince Bheem. As the day had come to an end, Nala and his brothers had resigned themselves to carrying the drunk Caani and Matre home. That was when Bheem had come forward, inviting them to stay in the Mansion's guest quarters. Courtesy demanded they refuse respectfully, but exhaustion had already claimed their pride. If this was how noble the nobles were, Nala swore to study harder to pass with good marks from Meru. Maybe Bheem could put in a good word for him, so he was sent to Hastina as an Acharya when he graduated. Nala sighed with pleasure at the thought.

Yellow shadows fell on the railing on which he was leaning. Confused, he turned. *Spirits!* He saw the monstrous shapes of twisting, dancing flames in the rooms of the towers. In the darkness, they looked like the fire-wraiths the shamans conjured in tales to scare young Valkas. Smoke slowly squeezed through the gaps in the curtains. *Move your feet, Nala!* He heard Varcin's voice in his head. He willed life into his legs and ran to wake the others. But he was barely inside when he collided against something. He did not remember falling to the floor, but there he was, his ears ringing. He felt as if he had run into an iron wall. He tried to get to his knees. Looking frantically around, he saw a giant shadow approach him. *Thank the Spirits.* 'Sir! Pray help me!' he cried urgently. 'My family is still inside. Your family too! We must get help!'

Bheem did not seem to hear him. 'You were supposed to be inside,' he said.

Nala did not understand what he meant. Bheem was dressed in filthy brown clothing and stank of mud and dirt. 'Sir, my brothers! My Matre! They are in danger! We have to get them out!'

But Bheem remained unmoved, his brow furrowed in thought, as if making a complex calculation. His eyes looked pale in the flaming torch he held. Nala thought Bheem must be in shock. He tried to move past, but a giant hand stopped him, grabbing his arm. 'It was mercy, you know,' Bheem said. 'That is why I mixed henbane in the wine.' Nala had not had the wine. 'They won't feel the flames and will die almost painless deaths. I'm glad you are here, though. You were the extra one, and you look too womanly to pass for one of us. Maybe, Nakul.' He snickered. 'But we needed only five and one woman. You were extra,' he repeated.

'What?' Nala stared, not comprehending a word Bheem said. And then it hit him like a hammer blow. The torch in Bheem's other hand, the traces of fire behind him, the smell of lac in the mansion. 'You!' Nala tried to wrest free, but Bheem held him like an insect pinned to a wall. Nala struggled desperately. He felt Bheem's nails dig into his shoulder bone. He tried to scream, but Bheem clamped a hand over his mouth. Nala wondered whether he was fated to die of strangulation, or if Bheem would crush his bones to oblivion. *Why?* he wanted to ask, but could not.

'You must be confused,' Bheem said softly. 'This game is beyond the comprehension of people like you, Nala. It's the curse of royal blood. Duryodhan,' he spat the name, 'my cousin exiled us here to deprive my brother of his rightful throne. No doubt he planned to send assassins to take care of us. Every morsel of food we ate is first tasted, every walk in the garden done fully armed, every letter we write is in ciphers. Can you imagine living like that, Valka? No, you cannot. Every passing day it felt like assassins were closing in on us and we were a locked target, like parrots in a cage.' Suddenly, the bitter lines of his face gave way to a smile. 'Until you and your family came along. Six brothers and a mother,' Bheem mused. 'Five of us, and Mother. Your Caani is tall like me too, though after the fire it will matter naught. It was a perfect swap. War always has collateral damage, Nala. And mind you, we are in a war. A war fought not on the battlefield, but within these walls. You were a godsend. The perfect decoy for us to go undercover and gain allies for the war Duryodhan is planning. The bonus is they will find lac and resin caused the fire, and blame Duryodhan for an act he anyway meant to commit.' Bheem seemed pleased. 'It was all my handiwork. Now my brothers will never again doubt my intelligence. I'm sure you can relate to that.'

Nala could hear shouts of '*Fire!*' coming from the yard below, where tents had been pitched. There were screams for water buckets, the whinnying of petrified horses, the frantic barking of dogs.

'You are trying to say something, aren't you? What is it?' Bheem moved his hand from Nala's mouth.

In that moment Nala recalled all that he had learned about combat and self-defence at Meru. He bit into the hand that had so recently muzzled him. He sank his teeth into it with all the strength of his jaw.

'*Vayu's teats!*' Bheem yelled. 'You're dead, boy! I was going to give you an easy death, but now you pay, forest scum!' Bheem grunted and took a step back. Nala kicked him, missing his balls but catching him above the knee. *Fuck!* It felt like his ankle had snapped in two but Bheem had barely budged.

Growling, Bheem came at Nala. There was a crunch as Nala's skull hit the ground. He spat out blood. 'Fucking forest scum!' Bheem's enormous boot came down on Nala's ribs, tearing a sick gasp from him. A barrage of kicks thudded into him, over and over again. He curled up like a worm, unable to breathe. He felt himself being dragged. The dark sky whirled. He was dragged back to the balcony and lifted over the balustrade. Nala kicked and struggled, trying in vain to stay alive.

'Go back to the mud where you belong,' Bheem hissed in his ear.

And Nala flew, his tunic flapping and billowing against his burning skin. He fell, tumbling over and over, the sky whirling around him. The Kaurava Mansion, the black moonless sky, the grey rocks, all rushed past as he tumbled past the trees he had been trying to trace moments before. Icy wind roared in his ears and ripped at his hair. He could see each tree now from various angles as he spun. Stony outcrops cut into him. Needle-sharp branches snatched at him. But nothing slowed his fall as he plunged down the mountainside.

But, instead of having his skull smashed out on the rocks below, as would have happened in the natural course of things, he fell against a donkey that had made half the descent without incident. Like a thunderbolt from the sky, Nala's body crashed into the creature's behind. The startled creature recoiled in fear, lost its footing, and slid braying in fright into the ravine below, taking Nala's place in the fate Bheem had planned for him.

And so it was that a poor donkey saved Nala's life.

KARNA

I

Windowless hovels clung to the walls of the Crows like old mistresses. Awnings sagged precariously above shanty shops. Water ran in ankle-deep torrents down the slopes leading away from the Crows. The downpour had stripped the flowers from the dwarf trees lining the streets, turning the walkway red and white. In the damp shadows of the winesinks, whorehouses and inns that lined the roads that led out of Hastinapur into the woods, dour-faced owners watched two figures, in mortal fear, as they passed. Fortunately for the two, apart from a few miserable mules, the street was mostly empty at this time of night. And the score of black-jacketed city guards atop the watchtowers were only too glad of the distance the towers provided them.

Both figures were wrapped in bandages, hastily gathered from torn sheets and clothing. Boiled tomato mash, still warm, blotted the bandages around their faces and arms. A coating of the stuff was plastered liberally over their groins. Limping around wearing a layer of tomato extract and wrapped in ragged strips was disgusting, but there was no better way to disguise a Daeva and a Resht born with a golden breastplate as they escaped the city.

Ravana's Curse was an incurable, painful disease, and those infected with it were treated with less hospitality than lepers. Had the pair been trying to enter the city, they would have been greeted with arrows. As it was, the guards had no interest in engaging in any conversation with two diseased figures exiting the city.

'I feel sympathy for those who truly suffer from this ailment. It is terrible the way people are shunning us,' Savitre Lios said. 'Would death be preferable, I wonder?'

Karna did not answer, but he did ponder his own death. *What if Yama was to come for me now?* Had he proved to the Ksharjas that he was a better warrior than they? No. Had he managed to uplift the Resht from the shackles of caste? No. Would people even remember him after he was gone? Not for any good reason. He wished he had performed some glorious act to leave his footprints on the sands of time, to survive the holocaust of memory as a hero. He would have liked to teach that arrogant Arjun a lesson, rescue a village from marauding bandits, save a damsel from a predator, or even conquer a kingdom for his friend. *Anything worthy of a bard's song.* Instead, he was accursed. He was accused of murdering a Highmaster; he had slept with the bride-to-be of his closest, nay, only friend. Neither would earn him a place in the annals of history. At least not in the way he wished. Yet here he was again, aiding an Enemy of Mankind.

Karna wondered whether Savitre Lios was here to seduce an earthly woman again. Savitre had told him that immortality for tens of thousands of years had turned the Daevas apathetic to each other, their physical urges lost. Perhaps lost was not the right word... extinguished. Yes. At the pinnacle of evolution, the Daevas had given away pleasure in exchange for power, innervation in exchange for indifference, diversity in exchange for perfection. They had stopped breeding, not resuming even after the Siege of Tyrants, which saw their numbers dwindle to ghastly meagreness. It was why the Daevas lusted for Mortals. They envied Mortals the thrill of the realization that any moment could be their last. The very fact that they were doomed made Mortals irresistible to the Children of Light.

Karna had often wondered about the offspring of such forbidden relationships. During his half-finished education at the Meru, he had learned much about the malformed, often diseased, Nardevaks, the half-breeds. In days of yore, such abominations were ritually drowned in a tub of milk. There was no evidence of such half-breeds in the recent past. But if they did exist, did they feel as out of place in the world as he did? Though no written record existed of the Siege of Tyrants, it was often whispered about in the corridors of Meru; that it was the Nardevaks who had forced the Daevas into retreat. It remained a mystery of fable and legend whether the Daevas had been defeated or whether they had turned back for the love they bore their children. But the Nardevaks were gone now, exterminated by humans once peace had been established. Probably from fear of the Daevas and their blood. *So typical of humans to destroy what saves them.*

Savitre spoke again. 'It has been ten years in your world since I saw you last. You look well. Fallen on fortunate times?'

Karna could not help but laugh. 'Fortunate is one way of looking at it,' he said, remembering his last conversation with Princess Mati and how she had convinced him to bury their secret for the sake of Duryodhan's happiness. How easily he had consented to sheathing his betrayal. An uneasy compromise born of convenience and lack of conscience. Karna hated Mati now, as fiercely as he had once desired her, for what she had done to Duryodhan, and what she had made him do. She was an adultress, a murderer, a cheat, a spiteful creature who could not be trusted. If Karna had his way, Duryodhan would never wed that snake.

'Karna, stop.' Savitre Lios held his shoulder. Through the bandages only one of his feline eyes was visible, but it did the work of two, and damned unsettling it was. 'You haven't spoken a friendly word to me all day. It appears you have found some reason to hate me. If that is so, then why save me?'

'To clear my debt to you once and for all.'

'What debt?'

As if on cue, the memory of the last time he had met Savitre Lios rose to Karna's mind.

II

For a boy in the ninth summer of his life, everything is dramatic. Infatuation is mistaken for passion, boredom feels like strangulation, advice sounds like a life sentence without hope of parole, while rejection feels like your heart is being crushed in a mailed fist.

Karna had just been rejected by Acharya Dron, the Master-in-Arms of Hastina Royalty, for being a Resht. It was not anything new. He had been rejected, thrown out, cast away, attacked, ridiculed, humiliated and abused at a score of archery training grounds before. But Acharya Dron had been his last hope. The Acharya himself was a Namin, not a Ksharja, meant to take up scriptures, not swords. Karna had thought he would be the one person who would understand that creed and not caste determined if one was to rise as a warrior.

He had been a callow boy then. Disgruntled in the face of despair, he had turned away from what he wanted. His bow was tucked away under his cot, his arrows dismantled, the arrow-heads forgotten in a box. His father, Adirath, had been the White Eagle's charioteer, and on retirement had been appointed Marshal of Horse. His reference had earned Karna a permit to enter the Crowns and work as a stablehand.

From then on, he had woken early every day, but no longer to tie a blindfold over his eyes and listen for the sounds made by unsuspecting squirrels. Now he woke to shovel horse dung in the stables. He no longer ran with pails of water from the well farthest from his house. Instead, he groomed the tails of the highbred destriers and brushed the dirt from their coats. He no longer sat at the end of the day to oil his longbow, striving to keep the hornwood from drying out. Instead, prior to falling into mindless slumber, he picked out any stones and grass that lingered in the horse's hooves. Everyone said Karna was blessed to have a steady job in the Crowns, when the Crows was choked with Mathuran refugees willing to slave for half pay.

One winter morning, Karna had taken a few horses to the lake to bathe them. It was early, for he wished to avoid the inquisitive, giggling washer-wives, who threw lewd suggestions at him. That day the cold had been harsh and the horses quenched their thirst cautiously. They looked ready for an uprising if Karna dared bathe them. It was then that he had seen *him*... on the other side of the lake, wrapped in the veils of morning mist. He had on a ragged hooded cloak, but Karna had recognized him immediately. He did not have many friends with feline eyes and silver skin.

'Your cheeks are sunken, Karna,' Savitre Lios had said. 'You have not been eating well.'

Back then, the only thing Karna had known about him was that Savitre Lios was not human, which was a good thing in his mind. Karna's interaction with humans had done little good for his view of mankind. It was for this reason, when most Mortals would have fled screaming, that Karna had stepped towards Savitre. Savitre didn't do much but he listened to Karna, and sometimes that was all one needed – a person to reveal your demons to. Savitre was the one who had taught Karna how to use the bow, how to track the stars, how to speak High Sanskrit, the language of the upper castes – knowledge otherwise forbidden to the Reshts. But, in the midst of all this knowledge-sharing, he had forgotten to tell Karna what Savitre really was.

Beside the chilly wind-swept lake, Karna had lifted a hand. 'It's good to see you again, Savitre. It is you behind all those robes, is it not? It's been what, three years?'

'That long? Feels like I was here but hours ago. I still find it strange that I do not frighten you.'

'Nothing frightens me,' Karna had replied boldly.

'That is cause of concern then, my friend. Fright is conducive to health.' Savitre Lios' voice had been full of mystery. 'You look unhappy. What ails you? I thought the bow made you happy.'

Karna had asked Savitre many times why he cared what happened to a charioteer's son. Without exception, he had received the same answer – silence. This time, he had pointed to the Resht tattoo on his neck and sighed. 'I lost. Will try again in my next birth.' Picking up the round brush he had resumed grooming the horses, hiding his tears in the horses' manes.

'That again,' Savitre had said. 'You do not need a teacher to be happy, Karna.'

'I need a teacher to be the best. To be the Champion. Only by attaining that can I be happy.'

'Trust me, there is nothing worse in the world than achieving what you want.'

'Why won't you teach me?'

'You know I do not know much about weapons. The little I knew about a bow, I have taught you. And I would never teach you how to be better at violence.'

'Not at violence, but defence. Better at achieving peace, better at demanding equality.'

Savitre had seemed lost in thought for a moment, then murmured, 'The things that have been done in the name of peace...' He drifted away. Karna never interrupted him when Savitre was alone with his thoughts. Finally, he had said, 'I know what you want, my friend. But Karna, it is not what you truly need.'

'You have no idea what I need!' Karna's nostrils had flared as he turned away from Savitre.

'I do... and it's no different from what *we* want in *our* world. Even there, everyone does not have what they need because they are too busy chasing what they want.'

'Take me with you then, wherever you go to,' Karna had said in a sudden rush. 'Take me there.'

'If experience has taught me anything, it is that my home is no place for a Mortal.'

'And this world is no place for a dreamer. Not a Resht dreamer in any case.' Karna had felt hot tears swoop down his cheeks and he'd furiously rubbed them away. He'd felt angry; he had wanted to attack his hooded friend. A boy's anger. He had wanted to storm out of the forest, but dared not walk out on the one opportunity fate had thrown his way – as a stablehand. 'Don't know why I thought you understood,' he had said miserably.

Savitre had sighed, defeated. 'That's not to say you can't get your heart's desire here on Aea. If you truly know yourself, then I will help you. So, tell me, what's your heart's desire?'

'To be a warrior.'

'Spoken like a child.'

'To be a hero.'

'Spoken like a boy.' He turned to leave. 'You'll get over it.'

'No, wait! What do I do?'

'Be true to yourself. What do you really want? Look within.'

Karna had paused, deep in thought, summoning *Dhyāna*. It was something Savitre had taught him on his previous visit. Profoundly meditate on the spot to concentrate on a deep, black ocean, and drown all thoughts into it to empty the mind. Become one with the black ocean, Savitre said, and one could do anything, find anything, be anything. He drew in deep breaths and found the Dhyāna that had eluded him so often of late. 'I want to be remembered...' Suddenly, it was as if someone had unchained the fetters binding him, and his wings stretched up proudly on either side. It felt liberating to say the words out loud. For all the dishonour he had suffered in his life, he had wanted the world to know he was a valiant warrior. He wanted none to spurn his name, none to think him a blot, or speak his name with distaste. He had wanted to bring pride and glory to himself, to his family, to his caste, to make them all proud. He had wanted to earn the ancient cred of *Abhimaan*. And for the Future to know that it was he, Karna, the greatest Paladin to ever walk the earth, who had changed the world.

'I want to be remembered for all the good I am on the inside. I want my name to survive for all ages to come. I want to be remembered.'

'Fame? Is that what you seek?'

Karna had pondered this, then shaken his head. 'Immortality... not of the flesh but the soul. The kind where my name lives on long after I am gone.'

Savitre Lios had not replied, but stared at Karna as if searching his soul. Karna had felt like cringing before that luminous gaze, so he had kept his eyes focused on the ridge of Savitre's aquiline nose.

After what seemed an eternity, Savitre Lios had said, 'Do you know of a man who goes by the name Parshuram?'

No one knew a 'man' by that name. Everyone knew of a 'legend' called Parshuram. Even uneducated Reshts like Karna. Many myths surrounded him. Immortal. Centaur. Teacher of Heroes. Bandit. Shrap of Ksharjas. Karna had only heard stories. 'Is he the same who is said to have taught the White Eagle and Acharya Dron?'

'The same.'

'I thought he was a myth.'

'As mythical as us.' Savitre Lios smiled.

'And what *are* you?'

'You will come to know in time.'

Karna had nodded. 'And he will teach me?' In his excitement, the rein of the horse he held had slipped softly from his hand; he did not care. 'Will he?' he had repeated, his mind desperately fighting the rising tide of happiness that threatened to pour in and flood him into oblivion.

'I cannot say. You will have to go to Meru, where they will prepare you. If worthy, you will be chosen.'

Karna had looked up sharply. 'They teach Acharyas there, not warriors.'

'Indeed, but every other year, Acharya Parshuram handpicks a student to teach the Art of the Sun. You will have to be deserving for him to choose you. Parshuram is a hard man... a very hard man. In the last few hundred years, he has taken few students. He will take many tests... tests that will show how deep inside yourself you can truly sink. You will sweat, bleed, burn... But if you get through, there will be nothing to stop him from teaching you all that you want to know.' He had pulled a scroll from an insert in his trousers and handed it to Karna. 'A map to Meru. When you reach there, say these words to the gatekeeper: *Tat Savitur Varenyam*. Repeat after me.'

'Tat Savitur Varenyam.' Karna had taken the map with unsure hands and looked up at Savitre to ask, 'What do the words mean?'

Savitre had quieted suddenly, as if regretting what he was doing. Finally, he had said, 'I cannot tell you now, but know this: what you learn in Meru will make you hate me.' Savitre had hugged Karna, surprising him.

'I could never hate you.' Karna had pointed to the map. 'If this works, you have saved me, Savitre. I owe you a debt of life.'

Savitre had smiled sadly. 'Karna, I say this with the deepest affection, concern and wisdom: Your path towards glory is intertwined with your path towards destruction. They are one and the same. For your well-being, you should desist from the path I am showing you.'

'What would you have me do? Stay in Hastinapur?'

'Yes. Stay here. Tend to the horses. And I promise you will find peace and harmony… in time… a wonderful wife who will beget you beautiful sons and strong daughters, who will themselves have children as fine as the Gods you worship. They will all remember your name…'

'And after them?' Karna had asked, knowing the answer.

Savitre Lios had sighed. 'But after your grand-children, your name will be lost. You would have made no ripples in the history of time. Yet you will have lived a full life.'

'And if I go to Meru?'

'Immortality, as you wished. Glory and your name will be mentioned in the same breath. Bards will sing of your prowess for thousands of years after your bones have turned to dust. Sons of every man in Aryavrat will know your name for generations to come, but you will have no sons.' Savitre Lios' throat had tightened briefly. 'If you go to Meru, you will die. And you will live an accursed life. Peace will elude you. You will be betrayed. You will be scorned in love. Your kingdom will never be yours. You will pay the price of friendship with the blood of your brothers. You will die a gruesome death. For your doom walks hand in hand with your bow…'

Karna had not paused to consider why Savitre Lios had said brothers instead of brother. He had but one. 'I will go to Meru!' he had cried. 'This is not peace. I will never fall in love. No one wants to be my friend anyway. The life I live now is hell. Nothing could be worse than this.'

'You are just a boy to think this way. You don't know what you will be giving up.'

'I am nine summers of age. Almost a man grown,' Karna had said sternly. 'I want to be a warrior, and not just a warrior, but the finest the world has seen!'

The thought had consumed him ever since he had been rejected by Acharya Dron. He thought of it lying abed at night, cleaning the stables, grooming the horses, bathing in the river, teaching young Lordlings to ride. And now, by speaking it aloud, he had broken the seal on his pain. 'I don't want a wife. I don't want a mistress. And I don't want sons. All I want is glory. I don't want to be defined by my birth... as I have been from childhood: "Karna, you cannot drink from that well"; "Karna, you cannot pick up a weapon"; "Karna, you cannot fight back". I refuse to be defined. The only reasons these Namins define us is to limit us. And I don't care about peace in life. Peace is only for the privileged.'

'You say you do not want a wife for you have not known a woman yet. You wish to fight for you have not seen death. You do not know the meaning of peace for you have never seen war. What do you think you will do once you have mastered the knowledge you seek?'

Karna had felt anger bubble within him. 'I will challenge the Princes, the ones tutored by Acharya Dron. I will show the world the error of its ways, bring about a revolution. When I vanquish their toughest warrior, they will know me for a Resht Champion. They *will* say the Resht out-bowed every warrior of Hastina Royalty and left them fuming. It will spark the forest fire of revolution.'

'What if the Ksharjas convince you to join them?'

'There is nothing in the world that can make me kneel to a Ksharja once I have trained to be a warrior. Neither force nor threats.'

Savitre Lios had looked at him sadly. 'There are other things in the world, Karna, far more dangerous and powerful than force or threats...'

III

'How did you find me?' Savitre asked, pulling Karna out of a vivid thicket of thoughts.

'I overheard Lord Bheeshma talking to Lord Shakuni about a prisoner who was a threat to the realm, who hadn't been seen in centuries... It wasn't hard to surmise you were visiting.'

'But I heard those masked guards talk about how unassailable the cells were.'

Unassailable! Karna gave a bitter laugh. Ksharjas and Namins thought the beauty of Hastinapur was eternal and unchanged, but Hastinapur was ancient, and beneath its rose-coloured streets lay the ruins of countless older cities, going back to the First Empire itself. The rich who lived in the Crowns had all forgotten about it, if they ever knew. But not the Reshts. For what was underground to the citizens of the Crowns was a doorway to Hastina's catacombs for a Resht from the Crows. All the Reshts knew that present-day Hastinapur was the fifth reincarnation of the city. Like the ones before it, Hastinapur too had risen on the back of civilizations buried atop one another, like layers of crushed bone with thin gaps in between. Beneath the Crowns there existed leagues of caverns and tunnels, home to the city's rats and snakes, ghosts and skeletons. The Reshts used these catacombs to steal into the Crowns from time to time, and then disappeared through unmarked grates. That was also how the Reshts secured food and water for their families imprisoned in the Narak, to help them survive that cursed place without the Mists' knowledge. After all, one wasn't a true Resht if one had not had at least one loved one imprisoned in the Narak.

'We have our ways,' Karna said. He only hoped he had not jeopardized Resht lives by using the catacombs to save Savitre. If the secret exit was found, he would have compromised the lives of all future Resht inmates.

'So, you're a Daeva. The ancient enemy of Man.'

Savitre stopped. His bandage had loosened and unfurled. revealing his face, white as snow. Tomato pulp dripped from his cheeks. He nodded. 'I told you your time in Meru would make you hate me.'

'Why would you not tell me? I thought of you as a messenger of the Gods, sent to answer my prayers. I did not know you and your kin came down to our world to rape women and enslave us.'

Savitre sighed. 'Nothing is that simple, Karna, not in your world and certainly not in mine. You cannot understand.'

'Understand what? That the Daevas are lechers who can't keep it in their breeches? You are worse than Namins, worse than Ksharjans. At least they think us dirty enough to not touch us. Your kind raped our women. Duped them to bear their children. Oh, I understand perfectly. But what I do not understand is why you are here. Clearly, you did not come to take me. Was it another poor woman who caught your fancy? And what did you mean when you told Lord Shakuni we have it coming?'

Savitre fancied himself subtle, but Karna had learned to read his face like one of his favourite books on archery, and what he read now was fear and despair. What changed? As if in answer, the air became suddenly colder. Birds burst from the branches as he walked under the shadows of the green giants. A strange haunting smell tracked them. He knew that smell. He had smelled it on Savitre Lios. And now he smelled it ahead. *We are not alone.*

Cold fear slithered along the nape of his neck as the eyes of other Daevas emerged. But even the rising horror did little to numb the aggravation that felt instinctive, akin to what a hare feels when spotted by a leopard. The air around him turned fetid and dank. Karna could see the Daevas clearly now. Beings of Light emerged from the darkness of the woods, their blood shining within their silvery-white skin.

One of them sprang into sight about forty yards away, leaping onto a branch and balancing there on the balls of her bare feet. Her straight blonde hair shone. Her amber eyes glinted as she spied Karna, and her full lips stretched to reveal a pair of canines. *Ethereal.*

'*May your Night be Bright*, Raith,' Savitre Lios greeted the Daeva woman in Sanskrit.

Crouching on the branch, she touched it with her fingertips and her body coiled. She launched herself into the air. Her figure became a ball of light and then it landed gracefully on the ground, suddenly slowing, as if held back by invisible strings.

'He is harmless, Raith,' Savitre Lios said, nudging Karna to bow. 'He saved me from a rather unpleasant experience.' Savitre raised his fingers, the nails of which had grown back but the dried blood was evidence of the treatment it had received. 'Did you find Faraladar's ship?'

Karna tried to rise but the freezing fingers of Savitre Lios tugged at his bandaged shoulder, informing him to stay low. Despite his pride, Karna complied.

'No,' Raith responded in the Old Tongue. It was a good thing she did not know Karna had become well acquainted with the language during his time at Meru. Or perhaps she simply did not care. Did the lion care about the experiences of the gazelle? 'But the search continues. Did you find what you were looking for?'

'No.'

Raith shrugged nonchalantly. 'It's disappointing really, to see what Muchuk Und's blood has come to.' Her voice was not loud but it overwhelmed every other sound. 'Men have become little creatures squabbling for the privilege of hiding like rats. The Blood of Bharata no longer sings in their veins. They have forgotten who they are. I had hoped some part of their ancestry remained in their blood and bone, something left to steel them for the long night coming, but there is nothing.' Raith's amber eyes rested on Karna's kneeling figure. 'Time to leave.' She turned in one nimble move and ghosted across the soil so quickly that her feet had no time to sink in. She left no prints.

None of them did. The mist lightened but the Daevas had all disappeared into the thicket. Karna lost sight of their retreating figures. Savitre Lios left with them, never turning to look back. Karna's mouth twisted into a bitter smile as he stood there, a gatherer of dust, wishing the one named Raith had hurt him, just to let *that* pain take over; allowing it to numb the torment of being abandoned yet again, like a forgotten thought. He began to walk back. *Some poisons have no antidotes.*

IV

Karna sat bolt upright, gasping for breath, shivering in the cold. He'd had a dream of Daevas dancing around a bonfire in which Duryodhan was being roasted alive. Karna rubbed his eyes and looked around. Half-devoured logs blazed in the fireplace over a hot bed of coals. Someone had been there to tend to it while he slept. Sudama was asleep on the bed beside him. Consciously, deliberately, Karna slowed his panting. He wiped the cold sweat from his face with a hand that was unsteady. Outside, the sun was well up in the sky. His belly rumbled, and he got up stiffly, making his way to the basket lying on the table. He moved aside the cloth and found a loaf of crusty bread. It was still warm. Karna smiled. Sudama's hand in this was plain to see.

Taking large bites, Karna approached the bed again. All of his clothes were clean and neatly folded on a low stool. *Oh Sudama, what did I do to deserve you?* He bent and pulled the blanket up to Sudama's chin. It was enough to waken him.

'Uncle,' he said dreamily, opening his eyes. 'You were so exhausted I let you sleep through the day.'

'You did well. If I ever folded my clothes half as well as you, my mother would have knighted me. And to think you have just seen six summers! Good boy.'

Sudama laughed, pleased. 'Where were you?'

'Running some errands. Sudama, how would you like to go on a long holiday?'

'Holiday?' Sudama was up in a flash. 'Yes! Let's go! What is a holiday?'

Karna scratched his head. 'Holiday is time spent away from work with a lake or hill to keep worries at bay.'

'So no chores? Yes! Yes! When do we leave?'

'Easy there, panther,' Karna said, nudging him back to bed. 'I have a plan. You get ready to pack, okay? Not now. Sleep first. I'll leave some broth for you. Sudama, *not now!* You are going to be a pain in my arse today, aren't you?' Sudama's eyes gleamed with mischief. Karna shook his head. 'I am going to meet Prince Duryodhan, to have a word with him. When I return, we will talk.'

Karna could not help but marvel at the innocence of the boy as he nodded giddily and pretended to go back to sleep. Resht children never stayed guileless for long, but his nephew was different. He was not plagued with the sewage that clogged the rest of them. He carried his arrows in the open. And he deserved a better life. Karna got ready and left the house, determined. The moment he closed the door, he heard Sudama rise to pack their clothes. Smiling, he departed for the Crest, determined and resolute to quit.

He crossed the murky puddles filling the wagon ruts on the track, then ascended the slope leading to the Crowns. An old man with one leg nodded at him as he hobbled past on bent crutches. A skeleton of a woman peered out at him from a doorway, offering him a smile. The owner behind the poorly stocked stall threw a fresh fruit for him. Noting the half-rotten, flyblow fruit on offer at the stall, Karna politely returned it to the generous fruitseller. He narrowly dodged the ragged children playing on the dusty streets. Karna was pleased with himself. It was only half a summer ago when one had to zig-zag between piles of refuse on the street. Most of the Resht District had no sewers at all. And the ones that did had the stink of rot where the only wealthy creatures were fat rats and angry flies. But a word to Duryodhan had seen covers installed on every gutter in his neighbourhood. His people were happy with him.

Duryodhan's grand festival in the Crows for his nineteenth Name-day had also earned him admirers. The whole of Hastinapur had been taken up with dancing and singing and feasting, with contests in almost everything, open to all castes. There had been contests not only in archery, as was usual, but prizes were also given for the best with the sling and quarterstaff. Unfortunately, no one save the Ksharjas had participated, but it was a start. There had also been contests for the best fiddler, for the quickest at herding sheep into the barn, for the best dart-thrower, and for the best dancer, as well as one for solving riddles.

The celebration had been another one of Duryodhan's innovations with which he hoped to make Hastina more inclusive. It had certainly made him popular in the Crows. Karna was sure Duryodhan would carry on his developmental work even after Karna left. Or so he hoped.

He soon reached the narrow bridge that led to the rose-coloured walls of the Crowns. He could not help but frown at the sight of a wall inside a city.

'No more petitions for work today, Resht,' one of the soldiers guarding the bridge said. 'Try tomorrow.'

Karna unclasped his cloak to reveal the Union diadem pinned to his tunic. This was his permit. Since the time of the Red Blades, the Reshts had only been allowed within the Crowns with a permit. Mostly it was given to those who worked in the Crowns and the Crest as servants for the upper castes. Some exceptional stablemen and craftsmen were also permitted in from time to time.

The soldiers grudgingly stepped back. Karna entered the Crowns and frowned at the different world on the other side of the wall. In the Crowns, houses were beautifully sculpted, but by law rose only four storeys in the Namin sector, three storeys in the Ksharjan sector, and two storeys in the Drachma sector. But each house had a green plot of land in front for gardens of red and violet. There was no ceiling on the height of official buildings, and so the Crowns boasted beautiful priestly enclaves and Guild Halls, on streets lined with trees on either side, trees that bowed and twined with each other like the braids of a bride's hair. Beyond, the Crest rose high above them all.

By the time Karna reached the Crest, he was lost in his dreams. He wondered how his life would be, now that he had decided to sell his house and leave Hastinapur. He could lend his sword to a merchant, or sign onto a ship and sail to Egypt with Sudama, to see the great sphinxes for himself. *As long as it is away from the people I have betrayed.* It was plain Duryodhan did not need him anymore, for Yudhistir had been exiled to Varnavrat and was no longer a threat to the throne. The Prince had an over-achieving wife on her way into his life. Karna could just see how splendidly Shakuni and Mati would get along. They were cut from the same cloth. No, Duryodhan did not need another false friend, a friend who despoiled his bed and stole his prisoners.

Suddenly he heard morning bells pealing from the Law House to the Temple of Vayu. The bells rang all the way across the Crowns to the Crows. He could see archers moving behind the merlons on the Crest's ramparts.

'Lord Karna!' A shout from a page swung his head around. He saw the tattoo of a scale etched beneath the boy's left eye. 'Lord Karna, we were looking for you! Prince Duryodhan requests your presence.'

'What has happened?' Karna asked gravely, knowing the answer. The news of Savitre's escape must have spread like blazebane. 'Is the Prince safe?'

'Prince Duryodhan is safe, Vayu be praised.' Hesitantly, the page added, 'My Lord, Old Ragha sent a boy to deliver a message he swears cannot be entrusted to a raven…' Karna could see fear in the page's eyes. 'The sons of King Pandu, with Mother Kunti, are no longer of this world. Their mansion in Varnavrat caught fire; they were all burned to death.'

Karna was speechless.

'A mob has gathered outside the Crest! They believe Prince Duryodhan to be responsible. He has commanded me to fetch you with all haste. He told me to tell you that he needs you beside him.'

SHAKUNI

I

Shakuni's teeth grated against each other as he locked his jaws to trap the scream. It still managed to screech out of him. His nose sprouted mucus into his hands as he breathed in heaving gasps, his crippled body shivering with the effort to stay upright. *Am I laughing or crying?*

The bandages on his shoulder stank worse than shit. Dung would probably be more aromatic than the poultice the healers had applied on his wounds. He had been advised to rest for a month while his shoulder healed, but there was no time for such nonsense. As if the Daeva's escape did not squat on his horoscope already like a pimp with loose motion, the sons of Pandu had managed to get themselves burned alive in a fire in Varnavrat! *I am poisoned for a moment and all hell breaks loose!* He almost wished the assailant had killed him rather than merely scratch him with a blade dipped in visyroot. But then again, the poison had made him sleep through the better part of a week as his body recovered from the tribulations of being tackled to the ground. He was glad he hadn't been awake for that. Shakuni sighed as he staggered through the narrow corridors of the official side of Narak, where he did some of his best work. *The Hall of Findings.*

Shakuni gave a blackened smile as he heard the screams from behind the doors on either side. His Mists were keeping busy. Good. After the messy affair of the Daeva, Shakuni had been confident that if he survived his wound, Bheeshma would surely kill him. But the death of the White Eagle's grand-nephews had given Shakuni one more chance.

For warriors did not run the Union. Highmasters and Nobles did. Highmasters and Nobles who manipulated and misled the King at every step. With the brutal deaths of the sons of Pandu, Hastinapur threatened to plunge into riots. The border bandits, the Resht's Resistance, and the Hundred would see it as an opportunity to sow chaos, and even Bheeshma knew it. Without Shakuni and his Mists, there would be no force to keep them in check. An army can shut down a riot, but only police can prevent it.

In ordinary circumstances, Shakuni would have himself orchestrated anarchy in the city to destabilize the Union. Unfortunately, he had to now prove himself indispensable again after his gaffe. *Just my rotten luck.* Duryodhan was indisputably Heir to the Hastina Union now, and the loud whispers of kinslayer would do no charity to his reputation. Duryodhan wasn't helping matters either. He had been avoiding him, avoiding everyone, really; holding secret meetings in his tower. Apart from Karna, Duryodhan had shut his doors to everyone, even family. He seemed to think the murder of Prakar Mardin, the assassination attempt on Karna, and the arson at Varnavrat were all related, and was hell bent on finding the culprit and clearing his name. *One would think the death of his political rivals would make him happy, but Princes can be greedy.*

Shakuni knew there was only one way to clear the Prince's name in the murder of his cousins, and that was by obtaining a confession from someone else. He finally reached the door he sought and shuffled his way in. The only source of light came from the one torch burning at the far end of the damp room. Atop the table in the centre sat his ornate tool box. Shakuni sank into his chair, his shoulder sending brutal stings down to meet the fire rising from his crippled leg. He nodded at the Mist standing in the shadows. The man stepped forward and pulled off the sack from the head of the prisoner seated opposite.

Corpses of rats fell from the sack as it was lifted, hitting the ground with soft thuds. The man's face was smeared with bile; it lolled listlessly to the left. *Puked inside the sack, did we? Oh, Purochana, you have fallen on such hard times.* Shakuni nodded and the Mist slapped Purochana, jolting him awake. His eyes scrabbled about frantically, trying to make sense of where he was, hoping it was a bad dream from which he had awakened. His eyes fell upon Shakuni.

'Evening.' Shakuni smiled.

Purochana yelped, trying to rise, the manacles on his hands rattling with the wasted effort. He screamed for help and violently shook his chair, to no avail.

Shakuni heaved a sigh. 'Seriously, Purochana? I am offended. Do you really think screaming in Narak is going to get you any help? If anything, it will look like I am doing my job right. And you should be thankful since I have not even started my work on you. You do realize those rats could have as easily been live ones.'

'Lord Shakuni!' Purochana goggled at him with beseeching eyes. 'What is the meaning of this? You know me! I am the Chief of the Architects' Guild. Why am I being accosted like a common criminal?'

'Now, now, Master Purochana.' Shakuni smiled again. 'Who said you were a "common" criminal?' He straightened his back and lifted his chin, his bones hurting with the effort. 'You think common criminals deserve the hospitality of Narak? Don't be a fool. You have managed to single-handedly solve the succession problem of Hastinapur royalty, avoided an impending civil war, and probably saved thousands of lives. If anything, you are a national hero, Purochana.'

Purochana looked at Shakuni, confused and bewildered.

'But you see the problem, there is no ongoing war. Hence the murder of Royal Princes, however noble your motives, is still a treasonous crime… a capital offence.'

Purochana's eyes widened, and he tried to rise again. 'Murder! The Princes! I did nothing of the sort! Yes, I was tasked with redesigning the Varnavrat Mansion into a suitable residence for

Prince Yudhistir. I executed the project in the same way as every other I have undertaken, including my own home. I have told you, I smelled lac on the day of the accident…'

Shakuni nodded earnestly. 'Yes, yes, I have read your report. What is this tunnel you speak of?'

'Like every Hastina royal house, there is an underground tunnel that leads from the Mansion to the forest. The latest hand-drawn plans do not show it for it fell into disuse decades ago. But, but…' he panicked, 'I am sure that is where the arsonists must have come in from.'

'Does anyone else know of this tunnel? Did the sons of Pandu know?'

'No, only I knew of it. Maybe the White Eagle. It was built before his time, but he may have known of it.'

Shakuni smiled. 'Then you do see my problem, don't you? Even so, let's say an arsonist sauntered into the abode of five Princes of Hastina and set fire to the place. How do you explain the entire mansion burning down, with nothing left standing? Would an arsonist really have coated every surface with lac without even one of the sons of Pandu catching them in the act? Trust me, I have seen burnt palaces in my time. They are blackened ruins, yes, but they are still standing. The sketches of Varnavrat brought back by our men look like a cremation ground.'

'I… I don't know…'

'Now that's a problem for one who claims to be an architect.' Shakuni nodded at the Mist, who turned Purochana's chair and slapped him hard.

Dazed, Purochana took a while to regain his bearings. Whimpering, he spoke again. 'Lord Shakuni, I swear…there is something sinister at play here.'

'On that we agree. Why don't you just confess it was you who designed a lac palace, and we can put all this in the past?'

'Never!'

'Do you not have two daughters of prime age?' *Sometimes I truly hate myself.* 'Stunningly beautiful…'

Purochana's face paled. 'Lord Shakuni, please... I am a citizen of Hastina. Its laws are the same for all. I deserve a trial. I have my rights.'

'What would one call the daughters of a traitor? Where would they be sent? To a whorehouse, perhaps. I hear new establishments have come up in the Crows.'

'Lord Shakuni... have you no compassion?'

'Look at me, Purochana. You have heard my story, have you not? You think that being in constant pain leaves any room for kindness?' Bitterness was sharp in Shakuni's voice. 'I am going to leave you in the company of my colleague, and a potential client of your daughters, for say... half an hour. He's the best in the business. Nothing but the finest for our favourite architect. Perhaps that might aid you in cooperating with me.'

The Mist slowly pulled on his leather gloves, one finger at a time, with a flair that made Purochana whimper. The Mist was eager to prove himself after the White Eagle had let him live, upon Shakuni's recommendation. He had, after all, taken the blame for the escape of the Daeva. Bheeshma had decided against revealing the news of the Daeva to the King, and the people. He had settled for the Mist being blinded in one eye. In all honesty, it did not make any visible difference. Shakuni groaned as he rose from his chair and made for the door. Purochana wailed after him until the door clanged shut.

A woman stood in the corridor, one leg propped on the wall behind her, whistling softly behind her mask and running a hand through her long straight hair. The mask covered most of her face, revealing only her lynx-like brown eyes. She wore a long black coat. When she saw Shakuni come through the door, she straightened and gave a little bow.

Startled, Shakuni stopped short, wincing at the sudden jerk. '*Vayu forfend!*' It was plain from her eyes that she was smiling. It was unnerving. 'What are you doing here, Panna?' he asked, peering around to make sure no one could see them conversing. 'Brave of you to show your face after the Kalinga debacle.'

'I am called Anayasa now. I have discarded my Wolf name. And brave?' She stepped closer to Shakuni, raising a booted foot over Shakuni's crippled foot. 'I wonder what I am braving?' Her eyes smiled again.

But Shakuni was an old card hand. His face remained impassive, even as he tried not to contemplate the world of pain her heel would bring.

'That being said, yes, Kalinga did not go as planned. No one could have accounted for a plague ship showing up in Jade Harbour, and then Princess Mati appearing out of the blue to save the wretched target. On behalf of the Cult, I apologize, Lord Shakuni.'

'Well,' Shakuni's voice was cold, 'your goof up turned out to be fortuitous. The plan was to implicate the sons of Pandu for the murder of Karna, and rile Duryodhan. Two birds with one stone. But it appears the need no longer exists, with the damn Pandu sons having died in a fire.'

'So… no need to kill Karna? Pity. He would have made a good trophy. He killed a few of mine.'

'Don't fool yourself, Anayasa. If he had not spent an hour swimming through those choppy Chilika waters, you would have lost them all.'

'We'll never know now, will we? Here,' she handed him a pouch, 'we don't take gold for kills we do not make.'

Shakuni had an idea. 'Anayasa, are you not an assassin?'

A derisory snort sounded from behind the mask. 'Astute observation, My Lord.'

Ignoring this, Shakuni pulled at his beard contemplatively. 'Will you look at a report and share your expert opinion after thorough investigation? Especially your views on the use of a tunnel under the site?'

'Are you confusing me with a spy, Lord Shakuni? We don't do dirty grovelling work.' An eyebrow shot up over the mask as she saw the map Shakuni held out. 'Ah, the lac palace. I like kingly affairs. So why not? My way of making up for the botched job at Kalinga.'

'Excellent.' Shakuni smiled thinly as he pointed with his cane to one of the doors further down. 'Let's find a room where we can converse comfortably.'

II

Shakuni limped back to the chamber he had left Purochana in. Leaning his cane against the table, he sat down painfully. But once seated, comfort approached him with eager arms. *Sitting is the closest thing I have to a proper fuck these days,* he thought morosely.

Purochana was covered in bluish-black bruises, his face swollen beyond recognition. One of his eyes was sealed shut while the other stared lifelessly. His lips were split and bloody, his nose twisted out of shape. In short, he looked ready to confess.

'You could say, perhaps, that you were an agent of the Namins of Anga, who wished to seek vengeance for Prakar Mardin's murder,' Shakuni suggested. 'You cannot be seen to do nothing, after all. It'll make the big temples nervous. Or that you lost a relative in some duel with Arjun. Vayu alone knows the sheer numbers of Lordlings that one killed on a whim.'

Purochana looked at him blankly. Shakuni leaned forward, a touch away from the bloodied face. 'I assure you, the Mist here is a doe compared to me,' he whispered. 'Once I start with you, Purochana, you will look back at your time with him with nostalgia.' He leaned back in his chair and opened the carved box on the table with a theatrical flourish. 'You remember this box, don't you, Purochana? You gifted it to me yourself. Such beautiful craftsmanship. None better than you in all Hastina. You should have stuck to crafting boxes, Purochana. Architectural design seems to ill suit you.'

As the lid opened, Shakuni's tools of trade appeared in all their morbid glory. There were tiny bottles of acid, neatly sitting in sleeves. On a hinged tray that pulled out were needles and blades of varying shapes and curvatures. Below this was another tray, occupied by a hammer and wrench. Screws abounded. There were instruments, the uses of which were easily discernible.

'You are going to confess, Purochana. The only question is the time it will take and the state you will be in when you do.'

Purochana smiled weakly as he lifted a hand in surrender. He struggled to lift the quill but managed to scratch his signature on the blank parchment. 'Fill... what... you want.'

Shakuni felt a twinge of remorse lance through his chest for his old acquaintance. 'Good judgement, Purochana,' he said, rolling up the parchment. 'You have shown me consideration by not wasting my time.' He turned to the Mist. 'Have my scribe write out a confession. Blame Prakar Mardin's living relatives and issue a summons to them. They will refuse to come, of course. It gives us an excuse to hang them on sight. With this ugly business done, we can get on with our lives.'

Shakuni turned once more to Purochana. 'I thank you again for your cooperation. Rest assured that if you reveal to a living soul what you told me of the hidden tunnel under the lac palace, you will find the mining colony you are going to a heaven compared to what will befall your daughters.'

Shakuni struggled to his feet and limped towards the door.

'Shakuni, what will happen to them?' Purochana called out.

'I will hire a swift ship to take them to safety. They will not want for comfort. That is the least I can do for you.'

'Shakuni!' Purochana's voice was a broken whisper.

Shakuni turned at the door. 'Yes?'

'Does it matter to you that I am innocent?'

Shakuni flashed a smile, revealing the yawning toothless gap between his upper molars, the bruised, battered and blackened gums. He tapped his cane lightly, then rested his weight on it. His beard was shaggy, unkempt, deliberately so to hide the scars on his cheeks. He remembered asking the same question of his tormentors, and then coming to the realization that the phrase *the innocent have nothing to fear* was nothing but a gruesome lie. 'No, Purochana, it does not,' he said.

NALA

I

When Nala opened his eyes, he could not see the ceiling. It was too far away. He could scarcely lift his neck. His head rolled sideways and he saw a table. On it lay a business-like arrangement of knives, saw, pliers, needles and scissors, their edges clean and cruel in the firelight. This was either a healer's hut or a torturer's chamber, depending on whether he had made it to heaven or hell. Nala tried to sit up, but his spine protested so swiftly that he nearly retched. He suddenly realized he was held fast by restraints. *Definitely a torture chamber.*

'Matre?' His voice was a miserable bleat. His throat, his nose, his gums, all felt sorely abused. Every intake of breath was a shudder. Every turn of the neck sent sharp thorns through his shoulder, down his right arm. He could hear water bubbling and the soft crackle of fire in a hearth. He bit through his lip in pain as he turned his head to the other side. The first thing he saw was an enormous double-handed axe, carelessly resting against the wall. The blade was etched with ornate, golden glyphs, which Nala could not make out from where he lay. Nearby, a muscular Namin hovered over a pot, scraping the scum off the surface of the bubbling brew within. The muscles that glistened on his shoulders and arms belonged to a woodcutter, but the sacred thread across his back was unmistakable. Then again, not all Namins were priests. This one could have been anything: a herbalist, a healer, a teacher, a scientist… a closet torturer.

The Namin carried the pot to the table beside the bed. His beard was long and thick, falling over his chest. His saffron garments looked ancient and disreputable, out of date, and spattered with either dried blood or dried tomato pulp. The coils of grey hair were pulled to the top of his head, into a bun, set with a worn-out rosary. The bowl smelled of something acrid. Nala could see a thick suspension had formed. The Namin strained the thick liquid through a cloth and then added charred *babul* leaves to it. Humming to himself, he rolled the congealing mixture into a ball.

Certainly a torturer. Nala jolted up, trying to rise, but the restraints snatched him back with equal severity. He clenched his teeth to stop himself from screaming.

The Namin looked up from the bowl, watching Nala's antics with mild amusement. 'Are you done?' he asked.

'How did…' Nala wrestled to get out the words. 'How am I here? Why have you chained me?'

'The straps protect you from rolling off the bed in your sleep. I don't have the patience to mend you again.'

'Wha… what do you mean, *mend*? Wait. What do you mean *again*?'

The Namin whipped away the blanket with the flourish of a street magician. Gaunt, withered and skinny as a ragpicker, Nala's body was stained with bruises of all colours. He had apparently been sewn back to life, for his ribs were stippled with stitches. The stitches also decorated his legs all the way to the ankle.

'Your bones were broken by the beating you got,' the Namin said. 'And then there was the long fall, of course. I wonder if it didn't occur to you to extend a hand and grab onto something?' Nala merely looked at the Namin, too weak to even glare. 'Of course, these things are difficult to think of when you are tumbling down a hillside. But you see, the rocks severed your tendons here, and here.' He pointed to Nala's right thigh and then his fingers. 'You hit your head many times. You must be experiencing a painful headache. What do you remember?'

'I… I can't remember. But my head is fine.' He attempted to raise his head but the pain was so intense he fell back with a groan.

Suddenly, his eyes widened as he saw his clothes were different. 'You... you *changed* me?'

'Aye, I did...'

Nala lay back, head throbbing. 'So, you know...'

'That you are a girl? Aye, I do.'

II

Valkan life was one of violence, but it had not always been so. In their worship of the flesh of the earth, the hair of the forest, the breath of the wind and the bones of rocks, they had long abandoned their worship of wonder, of knowledge. The Valkas had been holders of arcane secrets, passed on from one generation to the next through word of mouth; knowledge that had helped them tame nature. Now, they just lived with the answers their ancestors had unravelled, having entirely forgotten their questions.

All they cared about now was gazing beyond the borders of their tribes with dark hunger. Nala still remembered the blessing Matre sent Nala's brothers off with every day: *May the cries of your foes feed your dreams.* There was no caste system within their tribes, nor any distinction between man and woman, for everyone was born for war and bred for battle. They were driven only by the thirst to claim enemy scalps. A life lived in two dimensions, not three. And that worked well for a caterpillar, but not for a butterfly.

For Nala had not been born for this life. She had wanted to learn the distinctions that made the world. Not the way the Valkas made distinction – those who were kin, and those who were not. She wanted to know the reason behind everything. This was odd for a Valka, but manageable. But what made it worse was Nala's aversion to killing. She had been cat-called and treated as a pariah ever since she had failed to wring the neck of the deer she had found snared in one of the tribe's traps. Not that Nala wanted their attention or their company. She had been pushed to the brink of loneliness long before by the emptiness of the conversations she heard around her.

Meat and blood. That was all they could talk about. Years of identity crisis had driven her mad. Matre had always said the true objective of a woman was to have power over men, but Nala only wanted power over herself. She would have taken her life had she not heard a chance remark from a passing ascetic about how the Meru had opened its doors to the Valkas. A Citadel where they taught one to be a Master of Knowledge. A place filled with books. Nala could not believe the place of her fantasy existed in reality. She couldn't think of anything else but going to this magical place. The fact that the Meru did not permit girls within its ranks didn't faze her.

And when she had said as much to her family, they hadn't laughed or mocked her. Maybe they wanted her gone too, for she was an embarrassment. Nala didn't care. Neither did she fret that all the Valkan tribes had treated this invitation to Meru as an insult and had declined it flatly. Matre had taken her to the tribe's shaman who, fortunately for her, had found it amusing to send Meru a girl disguised as a boy. 'A fitting insult to the old vultures,' she had muttered.

And so, Nala had disguised herself as a boy, to escape the insensate, bloody life of the Valkas. Being flat-chested with a distaste for long hair made it easy. Her brothers had asked her in Varnavrat how she had managed to have a conversation like a boy with the others. She had told them she had just talked like an ordinary human being, leaving her brothers to grapple with the thought that women and men, when left to converse without the curtain of gender, talk very much like each other. She could still see them clearly. Their expressions of hilarity suddenly changed, their cheeks burned and blackened, their eyes hollow and accusing. *Avenge us.*

Nala woke to find a greasy pillow propping up her head.

'Ah, it appears you have navigated your way back to the shores of the living.' Her saviour's face flickered back into focus, stern and taut like a hangman's rope. 'I was beginning to worry you had been a waste of good healing herbs.'

'Are you a black alchemist?' Nala muttered drowsily.

'If you mean have I had formal training in any collegium, then no. There weren't any when I was growing up. King Ram established the first one long after.'

Nala frowned. Well, it was not that she was spoilt for choice. While black alchemists could work on you without questions being asked in the underworld, one had to take a chance with their credentials and skill. While some were trained healers fallen on hard times, others had been banished for crimes such as experimenting on the living.

'King Ram? Of Ayodhya?' murmured Nala.

'Who else, child? I expected a Meruvian to get it,' the Namin grumbled. Ungently, he pushed Nala's head firmly down on the pillow. 'Do not rise. You shattered your thigh bone, and your shin was fractured beyond repair. I had to spare a lot of screws, you know. It will make your one leg shorter than the other. Your lungs,' he shook his head, sighing, '... a lot of work. Someone really went at you. Had to make the necessary incisions but I've done my best to keep the scars to a minimum. Granted, my healing hand is not what it used to be. I'm good at killing people, not sewing them up. But I seem to have done a passable job.'

Nala's breath hissed through crushed teeth as she tried to move her fingers. They barely moved but her hand burned as if she held hot coals.

'Careful now. The tendons of your thumb were severed. And small bones take longer to heal. So do me a favour and not undo my work.'

How did he know I'm from Meru? Nala looked at the healer, confused, and then recognized him as the Namin who had been sitting beside her during the charity meal at the Kaurava Mansion.

'Why did you work so hard to save me?'

'Well, I owed you, you know, for saving me from that falling beam. Not that it would have hurt me, but I give credit where it is due. You killed my donkey in your fall, however, so I reckon that made us even. But I thought it a shame to leave you to die like that. So, I hauled you back to my hut, and well, once I got started, it didn't make sense to leave things half-finished.'

'How long was I out?'

'A few hours.'

'Before that?'

'Through the winter, into the summer.'

Nala stared at him in horror. She thought of her family, their killers; then she thought of Meru. Varcin and Upavi. Would they think her a deserter? Had she lost everything? And was she really thinking of Meru when her family had been burned alive? Her face crushed into a hopeless grimace. She realized her hair had grown out of its shishya crop and now hung over her neck.

'Winter will start soon, a time of new beginnings for you. You should be happy you recovered. Even with my skills it was nothing short of miraculous.' Raising her head, he brought the water pouch close to her mouth. 'Just palm candy water for you now.'

She took a sip. The sweet liquid scratched down her throat like claws.

The Namin threw her a glance. 'Do you want to talk about why you were pretending to be a boy?'

'No.'

'That's that then.' He turned away.

III

She had been trying to walk with the Namin's help, with limited success, falling backwards like a felled tree more times than she could count. Taking a deep breath, she rose again with a groan. Turning, she tried to put pressure on her left foot. The grinding ache brought nightmarish memories.

'I have seen ducklings recover faster. I have seen Kirtavirya continue to fight without both hands, and you have all your limbs. Surely you understand I have other things to do apart from fussing over you? Stretch it!'

She wanted to throttle him, shriek curses at him. But she knew she needed him, so she held her tongue. 'It won't budge!'

she hissed, her knee joints making ominous sounds. 'They won't budge!' she cried, defeated.

'You've just been lying around for weeks. I did not stitch you up for you to become furniture. Try fucking harder! Here…' The Namin's palm closed mercilessly around her leg and forced the bent leg into a straight line. Nala's neck split in five distinct muscle threads as a loud breath hissed through her, too fast for even a scream. Bile rose to her throat. She turned her head and vomited.

'Pain is the great forger, Nala. It drives us to our true potential.' The Namin patted her back.

Nala struggled to push him away but she might as well have nudged a wall. 'You sound like Sister Mercy,' she sobbed.

'You know her? She's a friend. Now turn the ankle.'

'I cannot. Please… stop!'

'Use that hate to beat the bone into shape, Nala. Think of your mother, think of your brothers, burned alive. Hate will give you strength.'

'Fuck!' She turned her ankle in a half-circle. 'FUCK! FUCKING-MOTHER-ARGH!'

'Excellent. See?'

She screamed and stumbled in a bid to claw at the Namin, and would have fallen if he had not caught her. Nala sagged back onto the bed, clutching her purple leg, whimpering like a kitten in a storm. Hate. Why not use Hate to her benefit? She had heard of Shraps. She tried to use every bit of pain to summon a Shrap on Bheem, but could not. She did not know how. She fell back, defeated. One needed tons of eyons to summon one, and she had done nothing in her life to earn even one.

'Good try. Still hurts, eh? Where precisely?'

'EVERYWHERE!'

'That attitude will not help you recover your humour. Another round now. Push yourself. Pain is…'

'Do not say "the great forger" again!' she screamed. Shutting her mouth, she rose and gently touched the floor with her feet. She growled through the effort as pain slowly became an ally. The Namin was right. She pictured the charred bodies of her family, and she walked. It did not matter that she did not have the strength to do it; she used her rage to walk. Taking long breaths, she waddled towards the door, her arms held out for balance. She made it to the hearth, her whole arm and side throbbing.

She gathered herself and turned. She was going to grow strong every day. Every day. She began to walk back to her bed, clenching her teeth through the pain lancing through her knees and ribs, into her back. Sobbing, cursing, groaning, whimpering, spitting, but she did not stop. Turning made her head ache. She massaged her scalp. She remembered the way Matre would plead with her to keep her hair long. Pain shot through her fragile ankles as she took another step. She remembered how Caani had applied balm to the same ankle when a wild Nora girl had pushed her off a branch. Her bloodshot eyes hurt with the effort of keeping them open.

She remembered how she had felt when she saw Meru for the first time. She remembered complaining about Craw's lessons with Varcin. She thought of the life she had fought so hard to earn. Bheem had taken it all from her in a night.

Pain is a great forger. To and fro. To and fro.

IV

'You said you owed me for saving your life,' Nala said. She was able to walk with a limp now, able to eat solid food, and was working towards using her arms for something useful.

'If that beam had fallen on me, it would have broken in two. But I do appreciate the gesture. It would have been inconvenient otherwise.'

'You *said* you *owe* me.'

The Namin hesitated. 'I guess I do. Wouldn't you say that killing my donkey and using up so much of my time, along with the supply of my precious herbs, clears my debt? What do you want?'

'I want you to teach me.'

'Healing? Go to a collegium and get…'

'I want you to teach me vengeance, Acharya. I pushed you out of the way of that beam, not caring about my own life! You owe me, and I am claiming it. Teach me!'

'*Acharya*? Does your head still hurt?' the Namin asked, concerned, turning her skull to examine it. 'How can I possibly teach you vengeance?'

Nala pushed away his hands. 'You of all people should understand, Acharya. I beg you.'

The Namin looked at her curiously. 'And why is that?'

'Because you swore vengeance when a Ksharja slew your father. You destroyed entire lineages of Ksharjas across the realm in retaliation. You led an army and set fire to the world to quench your thirst for revenge. Who else would understand better?'

The Namin stared at her, his eyes as black as night. 'How did you know? he asked gravely.

Nala gave a painful laugh. 'Muscles on a priest, a two-handed axe in the corner, a non-certified physicker who smokes *golis* directly instead of in a chillum, talks nonchalantly of kings gone hundreds of years ago, is better at causing wounds than sewing them. It was not too hard to guess who you are, Acharya Parshuram.'

A long silence followed.

'I know what I said of hate.' Parshuram turned his back and quietly wrapped his tools in a silken cloth. 'But vengeance is a sword with a hilt made of jagged glass. You will bleed when you swing this sword. All those kings and their families that I butchered brought me no peace. No happiness. No satisfaction. Take it from one who has suffered, girl: do not walk that path. The Ksharjas have forgotten about you. Go back to Meru. Or some other gurukul. Or marry someone rich. Life with me is a life of exile.'

'Perfect for one who has lost everything, Acharya.' Nala rose and slowly, painfully, fell to her knees. 'Look at my face, my body. I am scarred. Do you think anyone would take a hideous, disfigured girl as an Acharya? I am now the stuff nightmares are made of. I do not wish to kill an entire line of Ksharjas. I will be happy with just one. Bheem. Take me as your pupil, Acharya Parshuram.'

He said nothing.

The pain in her knee was unbearable. Her eyes were rimmed in raw sockets of pain. Her knee burned, but she did not budge. Her entire body trembled with the effort. Her mouth filled with sour spit. Her toes arched and ached. Her mouth ran dry, parched, her lips cracking as she waited. Her back was on fire, as if someone was rubbing a hot coal along her spine in a sadistic massage ritual. Blood trickled from Nala's nose. She coughed, spattering blood on the floor. But she did not budge.

'I do not take just anyone, girl,' Parshuram said, his tone altogether different. The carefree healer was gone, replaced by the true visage of a maniac. 'It will be a hard life, and you will not be up for it.'

'A chance. That is all I ask, Acharya.'

'No more pretending then. If you are a girl, so be it. If you are a boy, or both, or neither, choose now.'

Nala, feeling oddly free for the first time in years, said, although with a little hesitation, 'I am a girl.'

Parshuram nodded. He muttered a few choice curses at the sky before looking down at Nala. 'Rise, Nala. I make no promises. I will see what you can do. *Ashes! Can't believe I am doing this again,*' he cursed to himself. 'I reckon it is time for your apprenticeship to begin.' Parshuram frowned when Nala did not answer. 'You can rise now. I granted your request.'

But Nala did not rise. She could not. She tried, but her legs flew out from under her and she landed on her arse, senses blotted out by the pain that shot up her spine. She bit her tongue as her head cracked down on the floor. Then there was only merciful blackness.

'Hardly an auspicious start.' Parshuram shook his head ominously over Nala's sprawled body.

KARNA

I

Karna had never been in this chamber before. The maps of the palace, for the protection of the Royal family, included only the hallways and routes through the kitchens and servant quarters. The far wall had a door leading out to the balcony, but there were no other exits. It had been six moons since the arson at Varnavrat. Purochana's confession had calmed the riots and protests but there were still parts of the Union where effigies of Duryodhan were being burned. Two assassination attempts on the Prince, one on the King, and even one on Shakuni, had the Palace in lockdown. Karna had dedicated all his wits to keeping Duryodhan safe. He had insisted on taking over command of Duryodhan's personal guard, which the Prince had grudgingly acceded to even though the King had been aghast at the arrangement. Dhritarashtra heard the rattle of the guillotine in anything remotely revolutionary.

The King was pacing back and forth beside a large teak wood desk. His blind eyes were much darker in truth than the paintings of him showed. He was speaking to Queen Gandhari, an elegant woman showing the first strands of grey in her hair. A silken blindfold bound her eyes. Karna could only imagine the scandal that must have been the talk of the town when the Queen adopted a blindfold upon marrying Dhritarashtra, to mirror her husband's world. Karna had always imagined it to be a noble sacrifice, till Duryodhan told him she had done it because she did not wish to look upon a husband she had not desired to wed.

'Parakrama,' Karna said to one of his men, pointing, 'see where that door leads. Virya and Dharam, stand watch outside. None but a member of the Council of Eight comes in until you have checked with us in here.'

'I do not recognize the voices of these guards.' Annoyance sounded in Dhritarashtra's voice.

'They are new,' Duryodhan told him. 'Karna's men. And Karna, can you stop fussing? There is no other way onto the balcony. It is three floors up. Anyone trying to climb up will fall to his death!'

'Good to know,' Karna said implacably. 'Kalpa, join Parakrama on the balcony. Close the door behind you. Be alert for any movement.'

'I just said there's no way to reach the balcony from outside.'

'Then that's the way I'd try to get in if I wanted to,' Karna said calmly.

Duryodhan smiled in amusement, but Bheeshma nodded. 'That's good, very good. You can see how a Resht might know places to crawl out from.'

'I will take that as a compliment,' Karna said.

Bheeshma frowned. 'I must have said it wrong then.'

The door swung open as Shakuni limped in, carrying a scroll in his hand. It shut noiselessly behind him.

'Reports?' Duryodhan asked.

'I suspect you know what you will hear, My Prince,' said Shakuni. 'The outskirts of the city are still on fire. Riots, protests, you name it. Everyone is irate. They still think the celebration you held for your Name-day, in the Crows, was in anticipation of the unfortunate demise of your cousins. The confession from Purochana has done much to alleviate the concerns of the Hundred, but they seek to use the unrest to raise the issue of the Prince's nuptials with, I quote, "pirates from a swampland at the end of the world".'

The King sighed, settling into his seat. The White Eagle said nothing, nor did the Queen. Shakuni found a seat reluctantly. Duryodhan remained standing, looking out of the window.

'Then there is Shalya, Lord of Madra,' continued Shakuni. 'Two of the sons of Pandu, who died in the fire, were his grandsons. He is threatening to move out of the Union unless we remove Anga's Protectorate status, seize its assets, and make it a part of the Union's dominion. Naturally, such a move, echoed by other members of the Hundred, will upset Kalinga, and the wedding on the horizon. And by extension, the Magadhan Empire.'

'This isn't good,' said the Queen.

'That's one way of summarizing it, Sister,' Shakuni said. 'It's actually a disaster. The threads inter-connecting the Union have suddenly become exposed and fragile. We know Shalya met Jarasandh in Magadh. It can be safely assumed that if Magadh decides to head north towards us, after Mathura, Madra will not be rushing in to aid us.'

Bheeshma spoke for the first time. 'By itself, the Union can hold the Empire, but with Madra gone, it will raise tough questions. Shakuni tells me Kalyavan, whose Yavana tribes border us in the North-West, has joined Jarasandh as well. It appears that the Emperor means to create a belt of influence around the Union, which he will use to choke us. We cannot afford to lose Madra.'

'Can we not march into Anga?' the King asked. 'That will keep Shalya happy. I'm sure Duryodhan could placate the Kalingans and explain to them our troubles here.'

'We have lost the territories along the route directly connecting Hastina to Anga,' Bheeshma reminded them. 'The Valkas prowl those forestlands and will not take kindly to intrusion by our armies. We could route through Panchal, but I believe the King has his hands full with the wedding of his daughter.'

The swayamvar of the Panchalan Princess was all anyone could talk about these days. For some reason, Shakuni had made it a point to discuss it every time he met Karna: how the groom would be fortunate to win the daughter of the Panchalan King; how large the dowry would be. If Karna had not known better, he would have thought Shakuni secretly wished to participate in the swayamvar. Even now, Shakuni looked towards Karna in a way that made him as nervous as a maiden.

'What the Union needs is a distraction,' said the King.

Shakuni shook his head. 'Respectfully, Your Grace, I believe we need more coin to bribe the leaders of the dissenting groups in the Union.'

'If we give coin from the treasury, it would amount to giving into blackmail,' Bheeshma said. 'A bad precedent, especially after our last experiment with peasant rights.'

The Queen rose and turned in Shakuni's direction. 'This Magadh threat scares me. Have you heard what the Unni Ehtral does to women? It's barbaric. Shouldn't we be building up our armies?'

'If we summon the Union allies, and even one of them refuses to send its legions, it would weaken the Throne. Many of the allies were friends of Pandu, and his son Yudhistir. The death of Pandu's sons has alienated them. We need to be able to summon them from a position of strength,' Bheeshma stated, his voice harsh.

'These are all fair concerns but none of these keeps me up at night as much as the nightmare of who will win the Panchalan Princess' hand at her swayamvar,' Shakuni said, eyeing Karna from the corner of his eye. 'I hear the Emperor himself is attending, and so are a host of other Lords, Kings and even Drachma nobles. If a rival of the Union wins her hand, the Union will be encircled by enemies.'

Grave silence spread its misty presence around the room.

'Jarasandh is going?' Gandhari said. 'Didn't think the old lion could still growl.'

'This is ridiculous!' Dhritarashtra fumed. 'Who are we sending from Hastina?'

'Lord Arama, Your Grace. Son of Lord Aparshakti of Kaithal. If you remember, it was he who came to us with the proposal for the network of canals.'

'That upstart inventor! A blot on the Ksharja name. Will he *invent* his way to winning at the swayamvar?' asked Dhritarashtra.

'This is troubling indeed,' Bheeshma agreed, one eye on Duryodhan's silhouette against the window. 'If only Panchal stood beside Hastina, we could keep the South away from us.'

Karna saw Shakuni idly playing with the small clay boat that sat on the table. Unbidden, the *Fat Mistress* flashed into his mind, and with it, the heaving form of Mati. 'What if Prince Duryodhan won the hand of the Panchalan Princess?' Karna said into the silence.

All eyes turned on him. The White Eagle frowned, as if speaking amidst Ksharjas was not a right Karna enjoyed. It probably was not. But it seemed to Karna to be the only way out. Duryodhan turned to him, his eyes wide with disbelief.

But Shakuni nodded, egging Karna on. 'I want to hear what Lord Karna has to say. As they say, *all hands on deck.*'

'I beg your pardon, Your Graces, My Lords,' Karna replied, 'but it appears the problem is one of creating a distraction, military strength, and gold. What if...' Karna looked at Duryodhan, whose face had turned to stone. But if this was the only way to remove Mati from Duryodhan's life, while also saving the Union, Karna was willing to put their friendship in jeopardy. And from what Shakuni had said of Draupadi, she seemed obedient, dutiful, the perfect person to be Duryodhan's Queen. A proper lady. 'What if the Prince was to participate in the swayamvar and win the hand of the Princess? I hear it's a competition. Prince Duryodhan is best with the mace.'

Shakuni nodded, as if deep in thought. 'If he wins, we will secure the Panchal forces, which will help us forge a path to Anga. And the gold from her dowry...'

'And there is no bigger distraction in Aryavrat than a wedding,' the Queen mused, pondering the suggestion. 'Marriages have often lifted the Union out of trouble. It could work.'

'Magadh would think twice about marching north if Panchal was added to the Union's might,' the King agreed.

Duryodhan looked at each of them before turning back to Karna. 'It would appear that all of you are forgetting that I am promised to Mati.'

'A Pirate Princess for the heir of Hastina!' the Queen scoffed. 'I even heard that she is slim and snake-hipped. Hardly a good choice to bear the heirs of the Union.'

'Mother...' Duryodhan's voice sounded a cold warning.

'Prince, you can always wed the Kalingan. No one is asking you to break your betrothal,' Bheeshma said patronizingly. 'The pirate can be your second wife. Your uncle Pandu married two princesses. Your grandfather married the twin Princesses of Kosala. I see no issue.' He rose. 'So, it is decided. Duryodhan will go to Panchal and bring it into the fold. Before that, he will be anointed as Crown Prince.'

'You cannot seriously be considering this,' Duryodhan uttered in disbelief. 'And anointed as Crown Prince? My cousins have just passed away in tragic circumstances—'

Bheeshma interrupted him. 'The steps to the throne are not carpeted with rose petals, boy. We cannot send just any Prince to Panchal. It has to be the Crown Prince.'

'But... I love Mati.'

'How the Kurus have fallen,' Bheeshma lamented with a weary sigh. 'In my day, a Prince was incapable of feeling attraction until instructed to do so by the King.'

The Queen approached Duryodhan and laid a hand on his shoulder. 'There were no Vachans made, Duryodhan. You are the future of the Union, my son. You have been from the day of your birth. Love is all very well in its own place, but it is up to you whether it will warm your hearth or burn down your throne.'

'Love does not buy allies, son,' Dhritarashtra said.

'I am not trying to *buy* Mati!' Duryodhan fumed.

'But you will pay heavily if you do not consider this course,' Shakuni interjected.

'Ask Dushashan. He can go to Panchal.'

'A younger brother to wed before the elder and bring forth the heir to the throne? No, I will not have the Union plunge itself into confusion again! And Dushashan has settled in Balkh, far away,' the Queen said. 'You know he doesn't want anything to do with us. Do not compel the King to pass a diktat!'

'Do as you will,' Duryodhan replied, walking towards the door. 'But I refuse.'

Karna quickly stepped in front of him. He saw a broken man. He could see Duryodhan's iron will falter within him for he knew that what they suggested was indeed the wise, the practical thing to do. It was what was expected of him. It was the price of his royal birth. 'I know this is a heavy price to pay for the future of the Union,' Karna said quietly. 'But the very fact that it must be paid is proof enough that it is worth paying. I know you hesitate to wrong a woman, but courage lies in doing what you must for the greater good.'

'You are my friend, Karna,' Duryodhan said, shaking his head in disbelief. 'Why would *you*...?'

If only he knew. 'I am your friend, but first I am a Highmaster of the Union.' Karna leaned closer to whisper, 'Remember what you said when you appointed me: "*Other people may see a crown on my head, but only I will know that I carry a mountain.*" You are a Prince of the Union first. Love does not last forever, Prince; land does.'

'There has to be another way.'

'I know no other way, friend. If there was, I am sure you would have found it by now. Your cousins are dead. A civil war has been averted. But you heard the others. Lions circle the wounded Eagle. Your decision can avert a war and save thousands of lives. Do not let what happened to Mathura happen to the Union.'

Slowly, Duryodhan turned to regard the others, all of whom waited in silence. In that moment of despair, Karna saw in Duryodhan a man who had constantly toiled in the fields of others' expectations. Many had been buried alive in such fields.

The King finally spoke. 'I know you are distressed, but you are not an ordinary man on the street, Duryodhan. Your mother and I too married from duty, not love. You are a Prince of the Union. You have no will of your own, no choice that is not bound up in the Hastina banner. It's about time you learned that. There is always a price to be paid for the throne, my son.'

'Mati will never agree to be a second wife,' Duryodhan said, his voice heavy with certainty.

'Perhaps not,' Shakuni said reflectively. 'But we only need to get her *father* to agree. Surely, he could never find a better match for his daughter than the future King of the Hastina Union? Pragmatism always wins over passion, Prince.'

'Why can I not wed Mati first?'

'You know that does not solve the problem,' the Queen said. 'Mati is betrothed to you. Draupadi has a swayamvar. You need to win her, and it would be best if you were untethered when you present yourself to her.'

'You speak as if it is a given I would win.'

'Don't be a defeatist, Duryodhan,' Bheeshma said. 'It is unbecoming of a Prince.'

Duryodhan looked away, his face pale. He left without a word.

Shakuni smiled as he limped towards Karna, and slowly patted his back. 'You did the right thing, Lord Karna.'

'But will he agree?'

'Aye, he will. It will take a little nudging from us, but there is nothing Duryodhan places above his duty to the Union.'

Karna nodded slowly, having not the faintest notion that he had just been used as bait by Duryodhan's family to ambush him.

NALA

I

'Are you ready, Nala?' Parshuram asked for what seemed the hundredth time. The air whistled with fearsome swipes as he stalked towards her, wooden sword in hand, though it felt like Assyrian steel every time he inflicted it on her.

Clearly not but do I have a choice? The girl who wanted vengeance against Bheem had perforce to be an ardent student of the world of pain, however ill-suited she might be to it. She had to learn to fight with intent to kill, though that was the life she had escaped from. Thus far she had failed miserably. Every time she fell, fainted, or retched, she thought it was the final straw and Parshuram would give up on her. But he didn't, and she forced herself to rise on her feeble feet, swear a curse and hang on for dear life. Fortunately for her, Parshuram seemed to enjoy beating the shit out of a crippled girl and bending her into submission. Unfortunately for him, there was something fierce in Nala that would break before it bent.

It was not that Nala expected herself to become a master of the sword in a month. In her time at Meru, she had scarcely touched a weapon, spending most of her hours studying Chakras, the uses of alchemy, and the systems of government in far-off places. Yes, she had learned the basic art of self-defence from Craw but none of that had prepared her for a swinging sword wielded by a Master. Though in all fairness, going up against someone called the Bane of Ksharjas did not make for an accurate assessment of her skills.

'Strike me, Nala! And controlled breaths. You are panting like a dying airavat! Remember, this time I have made it easy. It is not the first to be bloodied or the first to fall. This time, the first to get wet loses.'

Nala surveyed the two small puddles in the ring he had etched on the muddy ground. *I can do this.* But the first blow from his sword slapped Nala's right cheek, turning her round with such force that her shield slipped from her right hand. By some stroke of luck, she managed to parry the next blow away from her face with her sword, but it landed on her right shoulder instead, sending her stumbling to the ground. 'Fuck you!' She pictured the face of the bastard she had to kill. Bheem. She quickly recovered, took a step back to dodge a lazy swing, and then surprised Parshuram by darting her sword at his face. He sidestepped it easily.

She remembered his third blow only in hindsight. Blinking, she spat out dirt and saw she was lying on the ground. Her body felt numb. She could not rise. Parshuram's legs came into view, and she looked up.

He held out a hand. 'Well, you parried one.'

Fight with your mind, not your fists. She grasped a handful of dirt and tossed it upwards at Parshuram's face.

He did not move. 'You are full of cheap stunts today, aren't you? You really thought that would work?' He rubbed the dirt from his eyes.

'No, I thought *this* would.' Pushing herself up using her arms, Nala jumped into the air, brought her knees to her chest and then kicked at Parshuram's legs. She landed painfully on her haunches while he took a step back.

'That was just pathetic, Nala.'

'Master,' Nala smiled as she pointed to where Parshuram had stepped, 'you are wet.'

II

'The Art of the Sun,' Parshuram said as they walked back to the hermitage, Nala following behind, struggling to drag the sack of weapons. 'I have trained many in the Art of the Sun – the mastery of any weapon that shines in the sun – swords, arrows, axes and the like. Master it and you can hold your own in a battle. Rest for a while.'

Nala sank down on the ground, relieved to give her aching muscles a moment of rest.

'But I have never seen anyone as pathetic at holding a sun weapon as you, girl.' Parshuram sat down near her. 'I thought Valkas were warriors. Are they not?'

Nala stared at her feet. 'I am a Valka who was sent to Meru to *study*.'

'Ah...' he scratched his scraggly beard, 'fair enough. But it remains that you are not fit for the Art of the Sun.'

'Master, I beg of you...' Nala panicked. If Parshuram gave up on her, all would be lost. How would she avenge her family? 'I will try again. I will be a warrior.'

'No, Nala, you will not.'

'But...'

'But... just maybe...' Parshuram looked at Nala's slight frame, assessing her with a healer's eye before dropping his gaze to his muddy feet, 'you may have what it takes to be a *killer*.'

III

Nala was happy. *Murder* was exactly what she had in mind.

'What I propose to teach you is murder, plain and simple; the fine art of assassination, with the accompanying skills of maiming, blinding, poisoning, you get the gist, eh? You won't know what to do if ten soldiers headed towards you on a battlefield, but you *will* know how to cause impotency in a man. You *will* know how to force locks and break into houses, and bring about a plague in a city. No one will cheer you on. None will sing tales of you. If you are caught, there will be no trial. They will hang you in a cage or toss you to the sharks, depending on where you are caught. Considering you will grow into a woman, they will do other things. Do you understand what I am telling you, Nala?'

Nala nodded. This was the moment she had been waiting for. This sounded like something she could do, and even excel at. It seemed to use more mind, and less body. She was not in this to be a hero anyway. From whatever she had read, heroes would rather die than besmirch their honour. *Fuck honour.* She wanted to roast Bheem on a slow pit and kill his dog, if he had one. Adrenaline surged through her arteries like horses at a chariot race, but her tongue seemed paralyzed. Ultimately, she managed to mutter three coherent words, 'I am ready,' and then added, 'Master.'

Parshuram looked at her for a long time. 'We will see. I have learned a few lessons in my torturous career as a teacher, and I have little patience for the dullard, in mind or body. You must already know I teach no Ksharja. I hate those cursed sword-wielding wretches. You are a Valka, forestfolk. Warriors yes, but not strictly Ksharjas. So, you pass. But there is something else you must do first. You will have to take a Vachan.'

IV

The Vachan had been simple enough though it took till noon to ordain: *She would never disobey Parshuram.* That was it. Crisp and concise. Not that Nala had any thought of disobeying the Bane of Ksharjas. She suspected there was some other reason he wished her to take the Vachan.

The ritual left Nala hardened; a sudden vigour flowed through her nadis when Parshuram invoked the first mantras. By the next hour, the mantras had invigorated her and sharpened her senses. She felt cleaner for some reason. She had read enough about Vachans at Meru to know the physiology. The ritualistic Vachan had increased the muscle mass of her nadis, strengthening and stretching them, as in yoga. The Vachan helped her somehow ascend a level. She knew she needed it to face the trials to come.

Now, Nala looked at Parshuram marching ahead, his newly acquired donkey by his side, burdened with books and bottles of wine. Around them, the sun was shrinking behind the peaks, letting in ghostly fingers of dusk.

'Master?'

'Hm...'

'If what you are going to teach me is not the Art of the Sun, what is it called?'

'The Dance of Shadows.'

V

Nala began her journey by slaving away at the hearth every other night. Not in the forge to craft splendid weapons, but in the kitchen, cooking Parshuram's recipes for dinner. 'Mathurans and Gandharans are the finest connoisseurs of food,' he told her. 'The others wouldn't know fine food from camel piss.' So, for the next few weeks, Nala smashed and ground, pounded and sliced, chopped and cut delicate mixes of cumin, quail, fennel, lichen, colocassia leaves, khas root, fenugreek greens, lamb meat and so on. It was not as if Parshuram procured the ingredients himself to make her life easier. Nala was sent on these errands. But truth be told, she did not mind this part of her training. Ever since Varnavrat, her hearing had developed immensely. She trapped partridges with ease. She uncovered the hiding places of rabbits with panache. She could close her eyes and pinch a fish from a lake, using just her ears and hands. She enjoyed wading out into the shallows to collect lotus stems, shake fruit from trees, dig for roots and raid bird nests to find the ingredients her Master demanded. It reminded her of the treks at Meru. By the time Nala returned to the hermitage, she would be covered with bark and pollen, but wearing a smile on her scarred face.

But that was as far as smiles went. Parshuram had her cooking meals so complex they sometimes required precariously balancing a hundred ingredients. At other times, Parshuram wanted something simple, like rice steamed with flowers, or lake fish baked in green coconuts. If a single grain was misplaced or the sauce did not have the right undercurrent of flavour, the food was thrown to the dogs and Nala had to toil at the hearth all over again.

Months passed and the breadth of Parshuram's instruction expanded into new useless areas, and so did Nala's frustration. But she never showed it. One such area was languages. Nala had been told she had to grasp both the Old Tongue and Greek. She already knew Magahi Prakrit from her days in the forest, and High Sanskrit from her time at Meru. But those languages were nothing compared to what she had to learn now. She was asked to master the bastard Sanskrit accent of the Reshts. Parshuram made her do two hours of scribing and reading each day, in each language, until he finally announced she no longer spoke the Old Tongue 'like a pig giving birth to triplets' or wrote Greek 'like a blind man with a maimed hand'. Nala still did not know how knowing Greek would help her avenge her family, but she had vowed to obey, and obey she did.

Once Nala grew familiar with the languages, Parshuram forbade her to speak anything else for hours at a time. 'You will not hear these languages amongst the Vedans,' he told her, 'but you will hear them on ships, and among merchants. And when you hear the tongue, do not let them know you understand, unless you absolutely must. You will be surprised how much you will come to know when people think you do not understand the language.'

Parshuram also had a penchant for playing games. One time, he asked her to poison the wine barrels of a visiting troupe of theatre performers so they would be unable to rise in time to perform their controversial play, *Battle of Goverdhun*. Later that month, Nala switched the report on Kasmira's apple production in an auditor's caravan with the forged one Parshuram had prepared.

At the Summer Festival, she added a certain herb to the daily fodder at a farm so that the enormous goat was stricken with loose bowels. The goat could not be sacrificed at the new house ceremony of the Overseer later that night, a sign considered so ominous that the Overseer decided against moving to Kasmira.

'You might be terrible at everything else, but you seem to have a penchant for instigating trouble, Nala. A good thing, considering you are not pretty enough to be stupid.' Parshuram had chuckled and tousled the hair that had once again grown into annoying curls.

Nala never knew the reasons for the tasks Parshuram set out but she did not let this bother her. The man had committed genocide. She knew she could trust him. She simply set her mind on how to achieve a task rather than why achieve it. Maybe if she impressed Parshuram enough, he would finally teach her the Dance of Shadows. But that day never came.

Instead, he taught her about cosmetics. For a week, Nala was made to sit as one of the initiates of Agni, the God of Fire, clad in orange, trying to look suitably poor and pathetic. Parshuram taught her how to use pastes and dyes to mask her vitiligo and change her disguise. Passers-by dropped coins into her worn sack and prayers poured from them like a waterfall: one asked to be rich, another prayed for forgiveness for burning his neighbour's crops; yet another for fucking her neighbour's husband; many women wished for sons, but one asked for her son to die.

Still, the moment of redemption did not come. Sometimes, Nala felt Parshuram kept her for his own entertainment, especially when he ensured she got into trouble during her tasks. She always needed to have a worthy tale at hand to explain why she was stealing the undergarments of the boatsman's son or why she had released a host of mice into the local granaries. Needless to say, no lies were ever worthy enough. Once she was caught by the villagers and whipped till her back was lacerated. But Parshuram had just stood and watched.

Pranks were not the only games Parshuram liked to play. He had Nala talk to people. He would sometimes send her to the blacksmith to ask whether the steel imports that year were leaner than last year, or to the port to discover the tariff on mountain fish. Or to the temple to discover which God had received the highest donations that quarter. She was asked to head to the lakes when the thaw came and the houseboats resumed commerce, to chat up tourists and boatmen alike.

But she was growing tired of all this. The Art of the Sun began to look extremely attractive from where she stood now, but what could she do? Disobey Parshuram and break her Vachan? Unthinkable. At least all this talking to people allowed her to make a few friends, from the leathery-skinned boatman to the old corn-seller. She gossiped often with the lady who sold lotus roots at one of the floating gardens on the lake. The woman's children liked to play with Nala as well, and confided their secrets to her. She began to notice how she was apparently considered trustworthy because she was maimed, invisible and non-existent. She was never considered an intrusion when she cleaned the tables where traders gathered to gossip over hookah or warm kasmira tea. Even in the local whorehouse, no client batted an eyelid in her direction when she entered through the doors with wares to sell, not unless they were curious about the white stripes on her face.

It was as if she had turned invisible for the world.

VI

'Stop crying.'

It was only then that Nala realized her eyes were swimming. She wiped them, ashamed. Sniffing, she turned to make the evening tea.

'What is it, Nala? Onions?'

Nala hunched over the pot and did not answer. She heard Parshuram grunt behind her. Swallowing, she slowly turned. 'Master, today is my Matre's Day of Morning, when the shaman unearthed her from the soil after our ritual; the day we Valkas celebrate as our Name-day. I cannot stop thinking about them,

Master. Their burnt bodies must have been gorged upon by vultures.' She sniffed again. 'And here I am, learning how to cook, how to speak in languages no one gives a shit about, talking to people with whom I want to have nothing to do; pathetic vermin who complain about trivialities of life when they have no inkling what true sorrow feels like!'

'Are you done?' Parshuram wrestled the pot out of her hand. 'Would you like some tea?'

Suddenly, the dam within her broke, and her thoughts flooded her tongue. 'No! I have taken a Vachan to never disobey you, for I know I will burn if I do,' Nala sobbed. 'But sometimes I feel like breaking it just to be released from the countless hours of learning things that will get me nowhere close to achieving vengeance!' Nala was panting, her chest heaving with effort. She was afraid to even look up into her Master's eyes.

'I need to harm someone! I want release from my pain. I sometimes feel my anger fade away, and that makes me angrier. My brothers were burned alive and here I am, playing with children! I desperately clasp the memories of the wrong done to me with an iron will, but I cannot hold onto them when I am fixated on how much cinnamon to add to your lunch! I don't want to stop being angry. I have held back grief with the walls of anger, Master. So fucking well tell me whether you intend to help me wreak vengeance or help my spirits, else I will slit my own throat and curse you with my dying breath!'

'Well, I don't have any sweet vengeance to offer you today, so it is either tea or nothing.'

Aghast, Nala stormed out of the hermitage. A lifeless wasteland of weathered rock stretched out beneath her. Stars gleamed sadly overhead, their light wavering, as if brimming with tears themselves. She sank to her knees. After what felt like an aeon of despair, she heard Parshuram walk to the door and step out of the hermitage.

'The languages you learned were so that you could decipher any letters you grab. They can lead you to the location of your enemy, or confuse your foe into going where you want him to go.'

Nala turned, staring up into his iron-grey eyes, speechless.

'The food you learned to cook… Did you ever think you could kill Bheem by smuggling yourself into the Palace as a cook and poisoning his food? Do you think they allow just anyone to be a Palace cook?'

Nala rose and walked towards the Acharya.

'And the people you spoke to, conversations overheard with your donkey ears… do you not know their secrets now? Could you not blackmail them into doing your bidding if you chose? You are not so naïve that you do not know that *knowledge is power*. And while pulling all the pranks you did, did you not learn how to slip into a house, a farm, a mansion, even a temple, without anyone noticing? Or to conjure a lie at will? How do you think that skill could help you?'

Nala stood ashen-faced, hands clasped before the Acharya.

'I am disappointed that you could not see beyond your tasks. The goat whose sacrifice you interrupted: *that* prevented an infamous tyrannical overseer from shifting to this village. The *Battle of Goverdhun* play that you stopped from being performed was because an Unni Ehtral delegation was in town. What would have happened if they saw a grisly depiction of the Emperor in a village play? They would have voided their contracts to fund the village schools, or worse, they would have sent men to punish the village. As a Shadow Dancer, you are expected to identify every source of light, even invisible ones, that can potentially magnify into something big. Should I give more examples or are you satisfied?'

Nala rushed into Parshuram's arms, face pressed against his hairy shoulders as shudders ran through her fragile, small frame. Stunned, the Acharya remained still. Nala wept for a long time, but Parshuram stood unmoving, as solid as a rock in a storm. He let the child in his arms, for child she was, cry in the throes of hope.

'Tomorrow,' he finally said as Nala let him go, 'we learn the *asanas*, the postures you will need to master to learn the Dance of Shadows. Now, will you have tea? Yes? Go make it then.'

VII

'I see you are well versed in yoga.'

'I completed Yoga III in the third semester. We were done with the basics of Ashtanga Yoga and Bhakti Yoga.'

'Asanas?'

Nala nodded. 'We were made to wake early and practise them every day.'

'Headstand pose.'

Nala complied.

'Cobra.'

Nala complied.

'Half Spinal Twist.'

Nala complied, grunting.

'Warrior Sequence.'

Panting and struggling, Nala complied.

'The Triangle.'

Nala fell.

'Useless! You are a girl; yoga should flow from you like a river. Is this how you plan to become a Shadow Dancer?'

The dreaded Shadow Dance. The days when she had pined for Parshuram to teach her the Shadow Dance now seemed a distant, alien memory. He had said that she would have learned everything he had to teach her when she could do a complete routine of the Shadow Dance before a cult of priests who worshipped Ratih, the Goddess of Darkness, and her lesser sister, Usha, the Bringer of Dawn, and *they* deigned her worthy of a black rose.

Nala had been taken to watch this secret ritual on the last new moon. It was a secret form of worship of the supposed illegitimate brother of the deities, where devotees saw not the dance but the dancer's shadow, cast on walls, on the floor, and on the ceiling. Nala had gasped when a dancer had formed eight shadows, and all eight forms – tall, slender, large, thin – had danced together in perfect unity. If Parshuram thought she, Nala, capable of performing such a dance, he was more deranged than his reputation made him out to be.

'Nala!' Parshuram's voice boomed. 'A word of advice. Do not let your mind wander. It is too small to be let out all by itself. Understand? Now, do the pose again.'

Nala hated the standing poses. Her sense of balance was atrocious. The number of times she had fallen in the Tree Pose would have been downright comical had it not been so pitiable.

'Do you know what the *Dwi Pada Sira Asana* is?'

Any asana with such long a name could only spell trouble. In that moment Nala wanted nothing so much as to give up her plans of vengeance and retire to the forest. 'No, Master.'

'I wonder who pissed in the soup of Meru's yoga teacher? It is the Sleeping Tortoise.' Saying which, the Acharya sat, drew his legs behind his neck to cross each other. It did look like a tortoise withdrawing its head into its shell. But all Nala could see was a world of pain.

'This will draw your limbs closer, aiding you to see the breath you inhale move towards every part of your body.'

I can definitely see my life move out of every part of my body. 'How long, Acharya?'

'Long? Did I not say it is a Sleeping Tortoise pose? You will sleep in this pose. Simple.'

Sleep in an asana? Nala could see why they called him the Mad Priest. She almost suspected he had gained the title 'Bane of Ksharjas' not for killing them, but for torturing them with yoga.

Seeing misery writ large on Nala's face, Parshuram stopped. 'See, Nala, I could say your body is as stiff as that of a pig, but that would be offensive to pigs. So let me try this way. Tell me, what do you think is the singular goal of all the yoga disciplines you have learned?'

'To be flexible?' Nala ventured.

Parshuram took a deep breath and then exhaled softly to stop himself from beheading his pupil. 'To learn the magic of the *Chakras.*'

'Chakras?'

'You think you will become a proficient apprentice on the strength of your looks? Activation of the Chakras is essential to what we do, and for that you need to open your body and your mind. To be able to summon Dhyāna at will. Body, through the asanas I teach you. Mind, by solving the Mandalas I give you.'

'But Chakras have no power now. They are useless.'

Parshuram threw her a glance of disdain. 'The use of Chakras for Elemental Binding was just a side effect of their activation.'

It seemed rather high-handed to Nala that he termed the magic Mortals had used to defeat the Daevas a side effect.

'Chakras are more a tool of self-discovery, to unlock the doors of our true potential. An average Mortal uses only a portion of his soul power in his entire lifetime. Chakras are the keys to unlocking the doors to higher levels of power. No Chakra, no Shadow Dancer.'

Nala nodded. She had studied Chakras as a history lesson, never as biology, though she had a faint idea of what the Acharya spoke of.

Parshuram's cane touched the crown of her head. 'The Thousand-Petalled Chakra: The Crown,' he said. 'Violet invokes it. Your goal has to be to wangle the snake out of your spine against the force of gravity, to reach your crown. It stands for...'

'*I understand.*'

The cane slid to the space between her eyes. 'The Third Eye. Powerful. Indigo helps in its accentuation. Stands for: *I see.*' He pressed the cane to Nala's throat. 'Which is this?'

'The Space Chakra.'

'Invoked by?'

'Blue.'

'Hm. It is the purest Chakra of the lot. *I speak.* Which Chakra is invoked with green?'

'The Heart Chakra: *I love.*'

'Which is the Jewel City?'

'The Yellow Chakra. I mean, the Solar Plexus Chakra. Invoked with yellow. *I do.*'

'Which Chakra activated in you when you saw the woodcutter chopping firewood?'

A hint of vermillion stained Nala's cheeks. 'The Sacral Chakra. Orange. Located above the *sisnas*, erm... genitals. *I feel.*'

'And which is the last one?'

'The Dormant One. The Root Chakra, where the Spinal Snake resides. *I am.*'

'Apparently all is not yet lost. But rote learning isn't enough. Remember, Nala, women are inherently far, far stronger than men can ever hope to be. So, you are lucky. Men must learn to strengthen their feminine energy, *Shakti*. But you can use your inherent Shakti to draw the spinal snake through your body, ignite the Chakras, and unite with the masculine energy, *Shaiva*, in your Crown Chakra. Find the true balance between male and female energies and you will find your answer to *who you are.* The answer is key to the Seventh Chakra and true, limitless power. No one has unlocked all the Chakras in centuries, but you *will* unlock it. Do you understand?'

'I understand, Master. I had a question.'

Parshuram nodded.

'Was Chakra unification the way you... you attained immortality?'

Parshuram's face lost its harsh lines. 'Unify your Chakras and you will find out.'

VIII

That was that. From then on, if Nala wasn't practising the asanas, she was spending hours unscrambling the Mandalas, the mazes Parshuram prepared for her. Turned out the Mandala Vyas had conjured in Meru had been a simple one. The ones used by their ancestors to drive out the Daevas were truly complex, and the way to understanding a Mandala was to unlock its maze. And for that, she had to practise them on parchment. No matter how complex, they always contained a seed at the centre – the seed which Parshuram said symbolized the sacred snake in Nala's spine.

When she was not working on these, she was meditating to summon Dhyāna but it felt like stumbling after smoke. More often than not, she ended up napping while seated in one of these 'meditative' trances. Mostly, she used her meditation time to conjure alternative universes. During one of these ventures, she was imagining Varcin and herself ruling over a world where Acharyas were slaves, when she heard the sound of urgent footsteps. She immediately straightened and began chanting a meditative mantra.

'You aren't fooling anyone, Nala.'

She opened her eyes guiltily.

'I was hoping to have more time here, but I have been called back to work. Your training will now have to be on the road.'

'*You* work for someone!' Nala was shocked. Who would be pinecone enough to employ him?

Parshuram smirked. '*Everyone* works for *someone*. And we are going to meet those *I* work for.'

Nala swallowed, her throat suddenly dry. '*We?*'

'Yes. It is time for you to meet the founders of Meru. It is time to meet the Saptarishis.'

MASHA'S AUGURIES

I

Masha made her way up the ice-sheathed stairs with morbid enthusiasm. She was on Oracle duty today. She suspected it was her supervisor's way of telling her to come up with results or be sent to the Banshee quarters. She had not managed to unravel a single link. Even Maimed Matron had ceased to aid her.

She reached the high-ceilinged chamber with an overwhelming sense of familiarity. The Oracle, no older than six summers, lay spread-eagled inside a ring of vials and candles. The air in the chamber was a mix of suspended frost intertwined with steam. A large stone, from which heat rose in waves, rested on the Oracle's breasts. It had not been so long ago when Masha herself had been tied up in the same way.

Burned Matron had told her that almost all of Masha's visions had been useless. Incoherent gibberish about a man called Muchuk. It was difficult to separate dreams from visions, but that was the Matron's duty. Masha had apparently sent all the Matrons on a wild goose chase when she had 'seen' Muchuk, the man of her visions, slay a monster made of smoke. False leads were common in the House of Oracles.

Not every oracle dreamed of important people. Perhaps that was why Masha had survived. She dreamed of no one important, so they left her alone. For when an Oracle turned out to be good, they pumped so much smoke into her that she never again woke with the same mind she had gone to sleep with.

There was a loud cough. The other Matron sharing duties with Masha today was a tall woman in her fifties, who looked almost ill in her gauntness; a lacerated wound circled her neck like a choker. There was a steady coldness to her gaze.

'You are late.'

'Thousand pardons, Rope Matron.'

'Kids these days!' Rope Matron shook her head in dismay. 'No sense of propriety.'

Ashen-faced, Masha gazed down at her feet as she sat on the stool reserved for her. The oracle on the floor was still mumbling incoherently. 'She say anything interesting yet?' Masha queried tentatively.

Matron Rope frowned. 'Nah. Same gibberish about Prince Ram. Yes, we know he jumps into the river... move on!' she screamed at the oracle as if the girl could hear her.

'Who is Prince Ram?' Masha asked. Almost every King, Prince, Noble and Lordling of the realm was going to attend the Panchalan swayamvar, and Masha had memorized the list. This name did not ring a bell.

'Prince Ram, she asks!' Rope scoffed. 'The King of Ayodhya, when Ayodhya mattered! Seriously, girl? So ignorant?'

'Oh, oh.' Masha shook her head, confused. 'But then why would the oracle be dreaming of him? That is long in the past.'

'You daft girl. Oracles dream all kinds of nonsense... some of it immediate, some decades in the future, and some ten thousand years ago.'

Masha froze, her eyes gleaming like a lantern. Realization seeped through her mind, and goosebumps erupted across her nape. She was so excited she felt a growing wetness between her legs. 'Holy fuck! Oracles also divine the past. Of course!' Masha jumped up and hugged Rope Matron tightly. 'The cage of ice! It all makes sense!'

'Have you run mad, girl?'

Before Rope Matron could admonish the clearly unhinged girl before her, Masha said, panting, 'Matron, the Archives of Yester Centuries? How far back do they go?'

'Uh, I don't know. Fifteen thousand years, I suppose. Why? Those are silly old parchments, crumbling to dust no doubt.'

'I've got it, Matron! It is I. I am the key! That is why no one understood my visions. I was divining the past.'

She turned so urgently that the stool she had been sitting on fell over with a crash as Masha dashed for the door. She could hear Rope Matron uttering the choicest of curses behind her, but Masha was on fire. The stars had finally answered her prayers.

II

Masha spent two days combing through the vast corridors of Yester Centuries. The scrolls were covered in the poop of spiders dead decades ago. The writing of the old ones had been abysmal to say the least. Masha had stopped at every junction to make notes, staring till her eyes watered, waiting for some spark of inspiration. Libraries were full of dangerous ideas lurking in the corners, after all. But nothing. Nothing, that is, till she found her answer in a tiny footnote. A footnote on the list of deceased members of the Royal Ayodhyan family, stretching back thousands of years, long before Ayodhya rose and fell as an empire. But the name was clear. Muchuk Und, son of Mandhata, reported missing along with his sister, Asha Und. 'The blood of Asha'... that was what the boy's prophecy had foretold.

A footnote can change destinies, Masha thought. For the name on which the entire prophecy hinged, she had used to divine her brother when she was an Oracle. With that boy dead, she was the key. Unfortunately, the Matrons had ceased to journal Masha's visions when she had divined them years ago, believing them to be useless. Only one entry in Burned Matron's diary made any sense: '*When the last battle of the never-ending war is over, the snow will thaw, gold and ice will melt, and the world will wake into itself, and along with it will rise the Son of Darkness.*'

III

The courtyard reeked of excrement and piss; streams of the ugly mess seeped through the flagstones. Hundreds of drugged Oracles had settled in the courtyard for the annual health check-up. Mumbled entreaties and hacking coughs followed her as Masha made her way past them to the chambers of Sister Mercy. She could not believe that she, Masha, had divined the Son of Darkness before that boy. And the Matrons had skipped past her visions. She could not wait to reveal this to Mercy.

Steep stone stairs led down from the entrance to her door. The sun had dipped deep on the horizon and the door was shrouded in darkness. Masha halted at the top of the steps and peered down at a white-robed figure waiting for her in the gloom.

'Ah, a young one, aren't you?' The man smiled. 'So good to see young talent around these geriatric halls.'

Ignoring him, Masha descended boldly. She rapped twice on the door and waited. A hint of movement made her flicker a glance sideways. The man wore a simple black wool tunic that reached to his ankles. He had a kind smile that Masha knew to be false.

'Now, now,' the man said, suddenly grabbing her from behind. His wrinkled hands stroked her, plucking, pawing and pinching as Masha struggled silently in his arms. It was known that the Oracles and Matrons who did not show promise were sent to the Rooms, where they catered to the desires of sick minds. Rich sick minds. They were called Banshees.

'Let me go, Sir! I am not a Banshee!' She rattled the key at her waist.

'A Matron?' The man jolted upright. 'My apologies. You are indeed young for...'

The door cracked open. Masha could not believe how pleased she was to see Sister Mercy's haunting face, even though she had the look of a fox staring at a pair of sheep.

'Narag Jhestal,' Sister Mercy said coldly, 'what brings the Priest of Light to our dark abode?'

'Darkness cannot exist without Light, Sister Mercy. A collaboration is often needed.'

'And how did your Master spare you? I hear you rub the Lion's balls on a daily basis.'

'Your crudeness is an aphrodisiac, Sister Mercy. Emperor Jarasandh has left for the swayamvar of the Panchalan Princess. Do tell me, am I going to have to cater to a new young Queen soon? They are quite tiring. What do your Oracles say?'

'You know I cannot answer you without payment, Jhestal, but yes, you will be serving a new young Queen, and she will indeed come from Panchal. Just not the one you think.'

'What does that mean?'

'You know every answer has a price. Now why don't you proceed in and wait.' She opened the door wider. Jhestal walked in, but not before leering lecherously at Masha.

'I don't like him, Sister Mercy.'

'I will remember that if I decide to wed you to him. Now why are you here? Shouldn't you be—'

'I solved it.'

'Is that supposed to mean something to me?'

'I know when the Son of Darkness is going to rise.'

THE SWAYAMVAR

PART I

... madness is merry, and merriment's might,
when the jester comes calling with his knife in the night...
—Cicero

 KARNA knew that the swayamvar of Panchal was, and who would dream of denying it, the most marvellous event he would ever attend. Kings, nobles and fabled heroes had come from all over the realm to compete in the swayamvar, and the whole kingdom of Panchal had turned out to watch. Karna was stupefied by the splendour of it. The week had been filled with feasts and songs to mark the count-down to the big day. Karna himself had been to King Drupad's palace with Duryodhan, and several times with Shakuni and Sudama to the sumptuous luncheons hosted in honour of the illustrious suitors.

Princess Draupadi, however, had not graced any of the feasts. Many of the suitors had grumbled at such insolence but Karna scarcely cared. Sudama and Karna had reclined on the couches in ancient fashion as half-naked servants served them. Sudama had used the elaborate long spoons to taste the sherbets, kept frozen in the cellars by snow brought down from the Mai Layas, while Karna had sipped cool sweet wines.

Karna was not invited to take part in the discussions between the royal suitors that followed every meal, but he did not mind. It gave him time to explore Kampilya with Sudama. It was the least he could do for his nephew, having promised him a holiday, and, in pursuit of the endeavour, he had closed the curtains on the horrors of his past. If not for himself, then for Sudama.

Kampilya, capital of Panchal, was a very different place from Hastinapur. A world of gardens with flowerbeds and splashing fountains. At every corner some musician played otherworldly music under tall, haphazard trees that rustled in the breeze, offering shelter from the sun. They had passed through a bazaar where the stalls were separated by cages that were home to a thousand gaily coloured birds. Flowers and trees even grew and bloomed on the terraced walls above the stalls. And in the bazaar, it seemed that everything the Gods had so generously endowed on the Riverlands was for sale.

The air smelled of almonds and lemons. The streets were filled with faces that smiled at the foreigners streaming through their city; one of whom would wed their beloved Princess. Beyond the city, pavilions dotted the riverside, with the shield of one kingdom or the other hanging before each. Sunlight gleamed on gilded spurs and bright steel. Low rows of silken pennants waved in the wind.

Perhaps this is what living in the Crowns feels like, Karna mused. Even the tent allocated to him was enormous, big enough to house an entire Resht family. It was adorned with many-coloured cushions, colourful rugs, and silk hangings that depicted the Panchalan Stag. He had dispatched a raven to his father mentioning all the wonders they had enjoyed, but Karna knew Adirath wouldn't believe him.

Karna did wish, however, that he could have shared his awe with Duryodhan. But the Prince had not spared him a friendly word since the day he had taken the decision to vie for Draupadi's hand. Duryodhan had written to Mati, promising her his love, but explaining what his duty required of him. Mati had not bothered to respond, and her silence had wounded Duryodhan more deeply than any arrow Karna could shoot. To Karna's mind, this only proved that she had never genuinely cared for Duryodhan. Man was, for Mati, a means, a plaything; just another ship for the common shore between her legs. One left, another came. If only he could tell Duryodhan that.

He worried about Duryodhan, but Shakuni had told him with a shrug that the Prince would recover. 'Some diseases can only be cured by time,' he had said. Karna could only hope that he was right. He had nurtured a flicker of hope when he had seen Duryodhan conduct himself with the charm and grace of a future King at the feasts.

But as the Hastina retinue walked to the last of the grand banquets before the day of the swayamvar, with Duryodhan walking alone, five paces ahead, shoulders hunched and defeated, the flicker of hope turned hostile. Had he made an error of judgement? He made to walk towards Duryodhan, but wrinkled hands grabbed his arm.

'Leave him be,' Shakuni said, utterly unconcerned someone might overhear. 'Asking him about his well-being will only reopen his wounds. Many and wondrous are the things this night holds. For a Resht to be invited to such an event...' he frowned as the high harper's song of chivalry filled the night, 'is an honour as rare as summer snow. Try not to fret, and stay away from the Prince.'

Karna nodded weakly and allowed himself to be ushered by Sudama to the banquet tables. Today's event was hosted on a grand terrace, the size of a Resht colony. But it still looked packed with dignitaries. It might have had something to do with the whispers that the Princess would finally make an appearance tonight. Clearly none of the suitors wished to miss that, and so the rich and the powerful of the realm were all here, dressed in their finest, on their best behaviour. Attendants in orange and green livery, with rows of golden buttons valued at Karna's annual wage, held the curtains of different sections of the terrace open.

'Uncle, look!' Sudama squealed in delight.

The banquet tables with their gold-trimmed linen cloths were forty feet end to end. Acharyas and women from the Fourth Order, learned in the Seven Gourmet Sighs, stood to attention in their ceremonial robes, holding multi-coloured rosaries, each grain a symbol of their mastery of the one of the Seven Sighs.

Karna's stomach growled in anticipation. The smell of chicken marinated in yoghurt and spices, being baked in the searing heat of a clay oven, tickled his nose. Sudama followed the trail like a hound, to a seating section where the Royals sat on low golden chairs. Some had already begun partaking of the sumptuous feast: stews simmering in spices and butter, rice scattered with dried fruits and *vark*-covered nuts, freshly baked flatbreads, including corn and millet rotis cooked with buttermilk. There were also roasted pheasants adorned with their own gilded tail feathers, and partridges stuffed with nuts and raisins, which simmered in copper pots of saffron-spiced butter. Nearby, there was a whole lamb, slow-roasted over applewood for three nights and flavoured with cardamom, ginger, saffron and cinnamon, complete with a pomegranate in its mouth. Attendants passed with bowls of finely ground gram flour for guests to dip their fingers into, to cleanse them of grease, and brass bowls of scented water to rinse their hands when they were done.

'There are no separate food stalls for Reshts, Namins and Ksharjas,' Karna observed.

'More food for us then.' Sudama smiled, nodding in understanding beyond his years.

Karna ruffled his nephew's hair and looked about awkwardly. All around him men and women of note were spearing delicious morsels with dainty prongs and chewing with elegant precision. While there may have been a common banquet table for all castes, Karna had never before thought that there was a *higher-caste way* of eating food. He now realized his mistake. There were no separate stalls because no one anticipated a Resht amidst the guests.

Karna saw an old man with a thin mane of silver-white hobbling along doggedly with the aid of a son and a cane to meet Duryodhan, who had been talking to Lord Dharmeyu of Sivi and Lord Niarkatt of Mathura. The son had curious blue skin.

'Bahlika the Ancient,' Shakuni explained as he joined Karna. 'Said to be the oldest King in the realm. Believe it or not, he is Uncle to the White Eagle.'

Karna gasped. 'That would make him...'

'*Ancient*, aye. He was in line to the Hastina throne but love took him to the exotic West. Don't be fooled by the colour of his hair. He may be half blind but has the sharpest foresight. Sometimes I suspect he is an Oracle. He has won wars, more wars than Hastina has seen, without shedding a single drop of blood.'

'How?

'Economic warfare, they call it: bankrupts kingdoms instead of bombarding them, and spits in the name of all Ksharjas. The blue-skinned one beside Bahlika is his grandson, Bhurishravas. I think you have met Bahlika's granddaughter, Vahura.'

'Only in passing. She's a scholar, I hear.' Vahura had been more interested in the alchemical properties of the breastplate on his chest than the mark of Resht on his neck, so that had been refreshing. 'I remember Arjun made an open wager that he could bed her.'

'That boy does like to sow his seed around,' Shakuni said. 'If you must know, she wasn't interested in him. On the contrary, she was more interested in the female spy I had planted in her household.'

Karna gave Shakuni a shocked look, praying Sudama had been too busy looking at the food to pay attention.

Shakuni shrugged. 'Don't be a prude. Ah, I see Lord Shalya Madrin. A member of the Eight. I envy him. He has made a glorious and rich career from war without once stepping onto a battlefield.'

Karna had met Lord Shalya in one of the feasts earlier. Grandfather of King Pandu's two youngest sons, Sahadev and Nakul, he always looked like he had been forced into his clothes, his pink jowls bulging over the gilded collar of his lilac robes. 'Let me guess... economic warfare too?'

'Not at all. He... erm, exports it. A war broker if you will. They say he brought in the Greek Warlord, that one in the strange saree beside Shalya, to the Emperor's cause. He is Kalyavan, Archon of the Yavanas.'

Karna had heard of Kalyavan. The Greek was a sleek, smiling boy whose fame with the sword, along with his flamboyance, was a byword on both sides of the Saraswathi river. He had been kind to Karna and Sudama at the feasts last week. But no matter how kind, the other suitors always called him Mleccha the moment he left the room. Karna reckoned he had it better, for people never had to speak behind his back. Reshts didn't deserve such decencies.

'I don't see the Emperor anywhere,' Sudama said, standing on tiptoe and craning his neck to look around.

'You will not miss him when he does arrive,' Shakuni assured him wryly.

Shakuni pointed to other delegates from the different glittering kingdoms of Aryavrat: Shishupal, Claw of the Imperial Army, dressed defiantly in Magadhan fatigues. The young Princess

Chitrangada from the Tree City of Manipur, a foxy lady whose deep-red saree trailed behind her like a river of blood. But it was the necklace of rat skulls around her neck that caught the eye of even the most jaded onlooker. Karna had heard of the fierce women warriors of Manipur, where daughters and not sons carried on the family name. The grey-skinned Bhagadatt, the last Rakshasa of the East, stood still as a frozen shadow. Karna knew of this Eastern King, whose father had been slain by Lady Satyabhama, but this was the first time he had seen him. His hair was sharply combed over his grey skin, and his red eyes glittered like rubies in the night. He seemed uninterested in whatever Kalyavan was saying to him.

Karna still could not believe he was seeing a Rakshasa in the flesh. It was often said that Man had conquered this realm by fighting against the Nagas, the Vanaras and the Rakshasas – the stronger, larger and faster races – by virtue of being blessed with sharper minds. *Nothing could have been further from the truth*. Man had achieved the feat by his sheer appetite for brutality. But having conquered the New World in order to rule over all the other races, he forgot to leave any space for them.

'I can see a man churning *kulfi*!' Sudama cried gleefully, pulling at Karna's hand and dragging him relentlessly through the throng of Kings and Queens.

As they threaded their way through the tables, they came upon the crowning glory of the Fourth Order – an edible sculpture of the realm of Aryavrat. The rivers ran deep with some blue liquid that was being poured in by an Acharya standing beside the sculpture. Each major kingdom was represented by a crystallized *gulab jamun* with a sigil on its soft brown surface. The deserts to the West were adorned with brown *jalebis*, while the forestlands were packed with green sweetmeats made of pistachios and clarified butter. Yellow *ladoos* decorated the plains of the South, while dark green *kalakand* made up the forested Eastern Kingdom.

'Uncle,' Sudama said cautiously, 'I think we should find another sweet table. There is no way we can eat from there without...'

'Destroying the whole thing? Yes, I agree,' Karna responded without hesitation. 'I fear it is not for eating.'

But they were not disappointed for long. Next to the Aryavrat sculpture was a more proletarian sweets section with a board that read: *Sixth Gourmet Sigh*. There were gulab jamuns topped with dried nuts encased in shells of gold leaf that could be eaten, jalebis painstakingly assembled with honey paste into the shape of stags, a whole herd of them, with raisins for hooves. There were ripe watermelons, their green heads cracked open to reveal the coral flesh inside, every black seed having been meticulously extracted. Every exposed surface bore the Panchal sigil – the Stag.

Sudama took a saffron-flavoured pot of cold kulfi while Karna helped himself to *halwa*, the carrot-based pudding which was a recent invention of the Fourth Order. 'Get me a kulfi too,' Karna called after Sudama, grinning, as the boy hurried off to try another flavour. Karma had forgotten all about his queasiness, as well as the fact that he was supposed to be royalty attending a stately dinner.

From the corner of his eye, he spied a handsome man walking towards him with an intent stare. His angular features and the erased caste sign on his neck bespoke his Mathuran blood. Curiously, he wore a long peacock feather in an ornate silver band around his forehead. Karna did not trust this man one bit. The last King who had, had died by his hand.

 KRISHNA approached Karna, a bowl of grapes in his hand. A faint smile hovered on his lips; the sort of smile one might see on a crocodile that has spied a particularly bold swimmer. Storm was right beside him, almost unrecognizable in a Balkhan dress coupled with a short jacket. It was form-fitting from bust to waist, with a flowing skirt below. A sash was draped over her right shoulder, held fast with an army of pins. To a stranger, Storm might have looked elegant. To anyone who knew her, it was downright comical.

'Lady Storm, may I introduce you to Lord Karna of Hastinapur, Highmaster of Anga? His reputation with a bow precedes him.'

'My Lord honours me.' Karna blushed at Krishna's compliment, but turned to Storm and bowed awkwardly.

Storm scowled till she remembered Krishna's instructions. 'A pleasure to make your acquaintance, Lord Karna.' She did not bow. She probably could not. Calm's heavings on the strings of her corset gave her little choice. She could, however, have blushed as Krishna had taught her, or enquired about Karna's well-being. She did not. All those classes tossed aside, she dragged Krishna by the elbow to one side. 'Can you please dismiss me? My lungs have emptied out! I cannot breathe in this damn fucking corset!'

'Unless it is cutting you in half, it isn't doing the job.'

'But I am not able to eat what I want!'

'Eat? Storm, do you see any other woman eating anything here? You are moving in royal circles, and royal women do not eat in public. It makes them look human, and mystique is in fashion right now.'

'Ugh!' Storm grunted, looking like a mulish child. 'All this heavenly food and I can't even eat?'

'I told you to go for a Vedan saree, but you wanted a dress. Well, this is classic Balkhan wear. Sarees are easier...'

'And messier. I would surely trip.'

Krishna sighed. 'Leave then. Just see to it that Lord Niarkatt reaches his accommodations without incident. He seems to like the wine a little too much.'

'Oh, thank you!' Storm said with real gratitude. 'And good luck with Karna.' Storm waddled off like a duck in Niarkatt's direction. Krishna shook his head and returned to Karna.

'Suda, that's the last sweet for you. We still have to eat the main course.' The soft-haired boy sulked but handed over the ladoo to Karna, who ate it in one bite. The embargo on sweets clearly did not extend to adults. 'All well, My Lord? Lady Storm looked... uncomfortable.'

'Just the clime,' Krishna replied, looking at the boy. 'What my mother would have given to buy a bit of that obedience when I was his age.'

'He's a good boy.' Karna's voice had a fatherly ring.

'Where did you adopt him, Lord Karna?' Krishna asked, knowing perfectly well who Sudama was. But his plan to embarrass Karna required some foreplay.

There was a moment's hesitation, then Karna said, 'He is my brother Shon's son.'

'I hope you do not mind my asking,' Krishna dropped his voice to a whisper, 'is Shon no longer alive?'

'He just... became occupied with his goals. And sometimes what you want in life interferes with what you already have.'

When Krishna, claiming ignorance, begged explanation, Karna exchanged a look with Sudama and said tersely, 'My brother Shon is a member of the... Red Blades.'

Krishna had not expected such candour. *You don't lie, do you?* 'The militant group? A rebel, then?' he remarked nonchalantly, all the while eating his grapes, dribbling the seeds onto his lip, and then flicking them off with a finger.

'A revolutionary cuts closer, Lord Krishna,' Karna said flatly, putting an arm around Sudama's shoulders.

Krishna silently mulled over an idea. The Red Blades were a bygone, almost mythical, rebellious group. They had spread their fire across the Riverlands years ago, aimed at establishing equality amongst all castes. Ksharjan knights who renounced their titles and lands, low-caste soldiers, destitute women, abandoned daughters, fanatics, ascetics... there were many tales of these defenders of equality. But all agreed that they had committed unspeakable atrocities in furtherance of their goal. They had pissed on sacrificial fires, left dead cows in the verandas of temples, inducted untouchables into their ranks, and hanged many Namin priests in their wake.

'I understand why the Red Blades were formed a millennium ago,' Krishna said, 'but why now? We have given the lowborns much. Food, clothing, coin. It's a time of peace between the castes. Why disrupt the harmony?'

'For *freedom*, Lord Krishna,' Karna said. His awkwardness had all but dissipated. *As expected.* 'The freedom to choose their vocation, the freedom to pursue their dreams... You gave us food, clothing and coin. That's the very question they are concerned with. Why is it that Reshts do not already possess all these things? Why must they be bestowed as munificence by you? You are mistaking *quiet* for *peace*, My Lord.'

'Poverty... it's as simple as that.' Krishna shrugged. 'Don't make it a caste thing. It's not just the Reshts. There are poor Namins as well. Ask your own Acharya Dron how he managed to make ends meet before the Ksharjas of Hastinapur took him under their shade. Likewise, there are poor Ksharjas. The Valkas live in forests, with only fruits and their own hunting skills to feed them. And similarly, there are rich Reshts. The revered author of the *Ramayana* was a Resht. In fact, Prince Duryodhan's own great-grandmother was a fisherwoman; as lowborn as they come. Equality is just a myth, Lord Karna, like the Daevas. It all boils down to ability. If the Reshts aren't permitted to pick up arms, neither are the Drachmas or the Namins. Similarly, the Ksharjas aren't permitted to read sacred texts or till the fields. Every caste has its own chains.'

'If only it was that simple.' Karna shook his head sadly. 'The Resht shall never live in the mansions made of the wood they tear from the trees. The Resht shall never taste the wheat they grow in your fields. The Resht shall never learn the letters on the scrolls they cure from animal skin. And the Resht cannot even think to protest, for the Resht is forbidden to have a voice. If the Reshts were only meant to toil for you like cattle in the field, then why did the Gods give them desires? Why give them the ability to grieve? Chains?' Karna scoffed. 'The Reshts die in bondage while the riches of the world, be it knowledge, land or coin, are carved up between the Namins, the Ksharjas and the Drachmas. To be honest, I find it ironic that you are arguing this with the caste mark erased on your neck. Not everyone is offered such a chance.'

'But does it justify what comes with violence?' Krishna asked. 'The Red Blades are a militant group. That means there will be many lives lost. Is it worth it?'

'The end justifies the means,' Karna said, his voice suddenly harsh.

'Any end achieved through violence ends in a pit of despair. It is not a destination to aspire to, my friend.'

'Then you should never have usurped the Mathuran throne,' Karna retorted hotly.

Krishna saw Sudama clutch Karna's hand, as if to calm him.

'They are not the same, Lord Karna,' Krishna said, a smile playing on his lips.

A serving man, who had come to offer Karna another plate of kulfis, hurried away seeing Karna's face. Experience had taught him to identify moments when a man had no interest in putting anything icy into his mouth.

'And that's what the Red Blades fight for. To make people understand that they are the same!' Karna's words fell like heavy stones into a quiet pond. People were beginning to turn in their direction.

'That may be,' Krishna pressed where it hurt, 'but as humans we are encumbered with prejudice: the more privileged against the less privileged, the stout against the skinny, the comely against the gaunt, the dark against the fair. It is an intrinsic human trait to *judge*.'

'I disagree, Lord Krishna.' Karna eyes were blazing now. 'Prejudices are man-made creations... chains forged by men... for men... to keep men apart.'

'Everyone is prejudiced and a subject of prejudice, Lord Karna,' Krishna said condescendingly as if he were talking to a child. 'There are cultures in the East where men and women of light eyes are considered inferior to others. Look at Princess Chitrangada there. In Manipur, men are treated as inferior to women. Or look at Lord Putakatu, puffing out his chest and strutting around like a turkey. Everyone judges him for his pretensions though there is no one kinder. Prejudice can never be rooted out in the human mind. What I don't understand though...' Krishna raised his hands in gentle query. 'You are now Highmaster, of Anga, no less. Shouldn't you be happy?'

'No matter how expensive the crown, it cannot cure a headache, Lord Krishna,' Karna said. 'As a matter of fact, that's my point. So what if I am a Highmaster? I am so by the generosity of Prince Duryodhan. But not everyone is so favoured. All those people who are stopped at the gates, unable to prove themselves...'

'*So what if I am a Highmaster?*' Krishna mocked, having successfully wormed under Karna's skin. 'It is always easy to preach from atop a hill. Peace is achieved by coin and compromise, not murder and riots. You are now permitted by law to ride a horse in the Union army. You really think there is no difference between a king and a knight?'

'Do they all not go back into the same box after the game of chess is over?' Karna's hand clasped Sudama's shoulder tightly, as if he was restraining himself from a violent outburst. 'It should not require a compromise to give people their rights... or coin to respect merit.'

He could feel the rage seep from the Resht. Karna was precisely where Krishna wanted him, at the edge of the precipice. In a matter of moments, Karna would snap and turn beserk and probably find himself imprisoned – or better, slain. He had not expected working the poor boy into a senseless fury to be this easy. But it was precisely in moments like these that Fate sometimes sneaked up on him to push him off the precipice instead. Krishna froze. A large grizzled man with heavily muscled shoulders, wearing a slender crown on his head, entered, followed by another in a blue coat. The large man's heavy crimson cloak was clasped with gold miniature lions.

Krishna's gaze met Jarasandh's, like two swords clashing in battle. His heart beat like that of a trapeze artist. The Emperor halted, red rage blazing a trail across his face, the veins stretched taut on his neck. King Drupad quickly came up to Jarasandh, signalling his guards to be ready.

'Your Grace.' Krishna bowed. He could feel the eyes of everyone on the terrace stabbing into his back. He usually enjoyed the attention, but now, not so much.

'Evening, Usurper,' Jarasandh ground out, releasing a hot gust of air. 'How strange to find you here, walking in the open, without a climbing rope. The Princess isn't to your taste?' Only the Emperor could have made such a statement about their host's daughter in front of him.

'I have retired from that profession, Your Grace,' Krishna said, unoffended. 'Seems that one needs a strong back to abduct Princesses, and frankly I have grown old.'

'I do enjoy your japes, Krishna. I hope you will still have that smile on your face when I roast you alive and sell your wives as harlots to the three corners of the world.' Jarasandh walked away without another glance.

It seemed the entire terrace let out a collective sigh. Krishna knew it would have taken little for the Emperor to wring his neck right then and there. But Jarasandh was too much of a traditionalist fool to break custom. As Jarasandh walked over to join the motley group of Kalyavan, Shalya, Bhagadatt and Shishupal, all in clashing colours, Krishna felt unease crawling up his back. *I still have a lot time before the Armistice ends,* he reminded himself. *We will be gone to Dvarka in six moons. It will all happen as planned.*

'So, the rumours were true. The Emperor is vying for the Princess' hand,' Karna said, rather bemused, breaking into Krishna's reverie.

'No, no...' Krishna replied absently, not looking at Karna. What Jarasandh had said had unnerved him more than he cared to admit. 'Magadh is represented by Lord Shishupal. He is the one in blue, following the Emperor like a lost dog. I have to go now, Lord Karna. Plenty of things to enjoy and so little time. I am too big on weddings to miss its delights.'

SHISHUPAL was not big on weddings, having been left at the altar at one and married a monster at another. But seeing the festivities and the feast lifted his spirits. That was the charm of opulence. He had not counted on it, having been forced to watch Bhagadatt's fighting airavats at the bidding on this year's Chorus but an hour ago. Gentle beasts, resembling elephants, only much larger, with four tusks instead of two, pitted against one another within high earthen barricades, fighting until their grey hides were lacerated, their tusks dripping with blood. It had ruined Shishupal's appetite.

Or so he had thought. The terrace where the feast was being held was as big as a battlefield, but made to look even larger by the great mirrors which enclosed three sides of the space. A multitude of candles flickered and waved on the tables; their soft light falling on the golden-ware, glittering on the jewels of the guests, men and women alike, was reflected back from the mirrors, as if the stars themselves had fallen down.

It was absurdly magnificent, of course. A score of the Riverlands' finest musicians played soulful tunes, and the music mingled seamlessly with the swell of satisfied chatter. Both of which had stopped abruptly when Jarasandh had come face to face with Krishna. Shishupal had been behind Jarasandh, so he had seen the way his hands had curled into fists. They might have been asked to leave their weapons at the entrance, but Jarasandh had never needed weapons to do his killing. Come to think of it, Jarasandh had actually smiled for the first time that day when he had threatened to burn Krishna alive, for he had viewed the revels all week with the cheer of a mortician.

Jarasandh had not planned to attend the pre-wedding festivities, but it turned out that even here, in the midst of a swayamvar, the war did not stop, for Shalya had found another ally for the Emperor. 'Shishupal, I am tired and Lord Shalya is taking his time,' the Emperor declared. 'Go and see what they are up to. Make sure I have the beasts in my army by dawn.'

Shishupal frowned as if he had been asked to solve an unsolvable paradox. But what choice did he have? 'Aye, Your Grace,' he said, looking across at the familiar figures of Shalya and that brat Kalyavan, standing beside Bhagadatt, who was clad in black robes that did nothing to mute the shine of his grey skin. Shishupal had seen Rakshasas before. He had a squire who had Rakshasa blood, but it appeared the Eastern Rakshasas were born in a different barn. The red pupils of Bhagadatt's eyes made Lady Rasha look meek. Shishupal took a deep breath and went to join the conversation.

'I know the crimes he has committed against my father...'
Bhagadatt stopped to briefly acknowledge Shishupal, who
returned the nod. '... But we all know my father was not the sanest
of men. Anger and folly often walk arm in arm. My duty lies in
serving the people. And I swore in the peace agreement not to
retaliate against Mathura on the battlefield. I do not mean to be
forsworn. I sympathize with the Emperor, but all I can give, Lord
Shalya, is my sympathy.' His voice was cold, without emotion.

Shishupal had heard of Bhagadatt from Jarasandh. He was Tusk
of the Tree Cities of the East. A poor nation by all counts; their
only claim to fame were the airavats they bred. But Bhagadatt
was a cautious man, subtle, reasoned, deliberate; even lazy to a
degree. Shishupal saw for himself how the Rakshasa weighed the
consequence of every word he spoke.

'You were a minor under duress when you were made to sign
the treaty with Mathura, Bhagadatt,' Kalyavan reminded him,
patting Bhagadatt's back. It looked like a squirrel cosying up to a
crocodile. 'It doesn't hold true.'

'The Laws of Men,' Bhagadatt allowed himself the briefest
of smirks, 'are so malleable, ever twisted to suit themselves. I
understand you want my airavats for your war effort, but I simply
cannot acquiesce. I gave my word to the Mathurans when I signed
the Treaty, and words are like arrows. They cannot be returned
to the quiver, no matter the magic your lawscribes wield. We
should return to the feast. The East can certainly learn from these
Riverlanders how to liven a celebration.'

Kalyavan was unfazed by Bhagadatt's cold demeanour. He was
only a boy, made to play the games of men, oblivious of the rules.
'Then you should learn not to spoil a party. Can you imagine me
riding one of your airavats, entering conquered Mathura? Now
wouldn't that do wonders for your reputation, Bhagadatt?'

'Your frankness is refreshing, Archon.' *As refreshing as a dissected
corpse.*

'The lads and I are going hunting tomorrow,' Kalyavan rallied,
not hearing the subtle insult in Bhagadatt's words. 'Now that is
refreshing. Care to join us?'

'During the day?' Bhagadatt asked, sceptical.

'Where is the fun in that? Tonight. We are having a wager on who bags the most shadowcat hides,' Kalyavan responded with a laugh.

The boy was cursed with all the arrogance of youth, unleavened by the survival instinct of self-doubt, wed to the narcissism that came so naturally to those born strong and skilled. *It will be the death of him*, thought Shishupal.

'Yes, I will come,' Bhagadatt said, surprising Shishupal. Bhagadatt did not look to be the social sort.

'Splendid,' Kalyavan chirped. 'And you, Shishupal?'

'Not I,' Shishupal said immediately. 'There is a tournament on the morrow, is there not?'

'Well, the three of us are not participating. Bhagadatt for his race, Shalya for his age, and I for my colour. But my coin is on you, Shishupal. Shalya?' Kalyavan asked again, seemingly unoffended by the fact that, though invited to the swayamvar, he had been subtly informed not to participate in the tournament. It was hardly surprising. No man would willingly give his daughter to a Mlecchá.

Shalya laughed, pointing to his girth. 'I fear I would become the hunted rather than the hunter.'

'Rubbish!' Kalyavan scoffed. 'I never allow my bait to get hurt.'

'My dear Kalyavan, do remind me to hit myself on the foot if I ever call you my friend,' Shalya said.

'Your Grace.' Shalya turned to Bhagadatt, pulling at his scanty beard. 'I do understand your reservations about Men. I would be cautious too, if I were tricked into bidding the highest for the damn Chorus.'

Bhagadatt smiled faintly at the jest, even if it was at his expense. 'You are not wrong. Treaties are honour-bound. My own hands are tied by the treaty with the Union I serve. Or do you think me so cold-hearted to continue to work for those who murdered my two grandsons, burning them alive? We all have our burdens to bear. Do correct me if I err, but you do wish to see the Usurper's life shortened, do you not?'

'Yes,' Bhagadatt answered, his red pupils softening at Shalya's candid confession.

'Then what if I were to tell you that you could assist without joining the Yamuna Wars at all? That would take care of your moral dilemma, I suppose.'

'What do you have in mind, Lord Shalya?'

'Nothing but the welfare of your kingdom, Your Grace. An economic venture. What if you were to *loan* your war-airavats to us, you know, at a discounted rate, without interest? We could draw up an agreement, and you would just be signing another lend-lease contract. We can do as we please with the airavats. Whether we use them for ceremonies or battles would not concern you.'

Bhagadatt did not smile, but Shishupal did. Shalya was rather impressive. He had softly moulded what Kalyavan had asked and been refused, to suit Bhagadatt's wants. Kalyavan was not meant for this game of words between men. Then again, neither was Shishupal.

The music changed. Shishupal turned towards the archway through which Princess Draupadi now emerged. *So, the rumours were true.* They called her the Princess of Fire for the beautiful dark colour of her skin. Shishupal had feared the alias meant she was as fierce as Lady Rasha, but all he saw was a sparrow who blushed prettily. *But she is just as comely as Rukmini,* Shishupal thought. He could not help but admire her lissom figure. Her hair was a rich reddish-black, her eyes the colour of midnight. Her saree of gold clung to her impossibly slender form and spread out behind her, gleaming. She wore a gold band with a stone so big it seemed to weigh down her head. An air of sadness clung to her that made her at once vulnerable and appealing. She walked beside her twin, Dhrishtadyumna. A magnificent pair without doubt. They were arrayed in matching gold and white. Behind them came King Drupad's son and heir, Prince Satrajit, looking like a commoner beside the dazzling beauty of the pair.

'I can almost smell Her Highness,' Kalyavan sneered, no doubt referring to the white garlands of jasmine and tuberose that bound her hair and flowed down her back.

A score of ladies-in-waiting, each dripping with jewels, followed the Princess. The crowd of suitors, weighty under their brocades, rubbed shoulders and craned necks to get a better look at tomorrow's auction prize. Krishna walked out of the throng to the Princess and gracefully bent before her. Taking her hand gently, he led her forward. As they passed Bhagadatt, Krishna gave him a wink.

'I hear they are calling Krishna a God these days, Lord Shalya,' Bhagadatt remarked when the bridal party had gone safely past.

'That they are, Your Grace.' Shalya came to stand beside Bhagadatt. 'Quite a growing cult.'

'Good,' Bhagadatt said. 'I've always wanted to see a God bleed. Draw up the papers.'

Shishupal found his appetite returning as he looked at the retreating figure of Krishna. Just a few months of Armistice left. When Spring came, the Empire from the South, the Pragjyotishans from the East, and the Yavanas from the West, the largest host ever assembled in Aryavrat, would march towards Mathura with blazebane and upon airavats. The Usurper stood no chance.

 SHAKUNI spied the figures of Shishupal, Bhagadatt, Kalyavan and Shalya behind Krishna, and wondered what the chances were that Krishna would end up outsmarting them all. The way he was gallivanting around the place like a flamingo amidst alligators made one almost wonder whether he was even bothered by the war the Mathuran Republic was embroiled in. But then again, one cannot refuse to eat just because there is a chance of being choked.

Mayhaps Krishna could teach Mati of Kalinga this lesson. The girl was as dramatic as a Balkhan play. Of this fundamental flaw in her character she had afforded yet another ghastly proof. Unbeknownst to Duryodhan and his dimwit lackey, she had in fact responded to his letter. He reckoned a necklace strung with strange black feathers and severed fingers of the messenger still counted as a 'response'. Tattooing words with a hot pin on the bare skin from where his fingernails had been ripped off was a little too-too thespian for Shakuni's taste. *'For the love I still bear you, I hope you die before I see you.'* What pests the gentler sex turned when denied a husband. Even in the days when Duryodhan had courted Mati, Shakuni had never warmed up to the girl, and her latest correspondence had done nothing to inaugurate a cosy relationship. He would have liked to know how Duryodhan would have answered upon learning of the hospitality his innocent messenger had received at the hands of his lady love but he strangled his curiosity in the cradle. He could not save his nephew from the wooing but he would be dashed if he did not spare him from the repenting. And so he had burned the feathers and the fingers and the former owner of those fingers for good measure. If only Duryodhan knew of the favours his uncle was doing him, but the dullard was too busy playing the forlorn lover. Meh. *Time will soon help calm succeed turmoil, and his madness shall pass.*

Shakuni's musings were interrupted by the sound of flutes and harps. The attendants ushered the guests away to create an empty circle in the central space. No one cared about cripples in a crowd, and he had no plans to steal the limelight from the Princess with a sudden performance of pain. He saw Karna and his nephew at the furthest corner of the terrace and limped over to where they stood. It also gave him a good view of the show about to unfold. While he made a show of disgust at having to share space with the Resht, privately he was not entirely averse to his company. No one liked to be alone in a place filled with people. How long ago it seemed since *he* had been the centre of attention at such parties…

As the assembled crowd moved away like an ebbing tide, attendants lumbered in with an enormous weighing scale. Two large plates, their rims set with lozenges of smooth-polished rose quartz, swayed drunkenly from thick chains. The chains were fitted into a large oaken frame. A yellow canopy was soon erected over it.

Ah, the weighing of the lamb before the slaughter.

In her saree of gold that accentuated her burnt skin and still girlish figure, Draupadi, Princess of Panchal, advanced to the weighing scales to the strains of a *veena*.

'What's going on?' Sudama asked.

'Grocery purchase,' Shakuni commented dryly.

Draupadi approached the scale and awkwardly seated herself on one of the plates, sitting cross-legged. The scale dipped to the ground and remained there. Servants staggered in carrying heavy iron bars and placed them around Draupadi. The guests looked on in surprise for this was not the usual form. More servants marched in and put down several heavy chests. The lids were thrown open. Predictable gasps were heard. A ripple of appreciation made its way round the throng of spectators. The chests were filled with treasures, though none quite matched the shimmer of the chains around Draupadi's neck.

Drupad rose to the beating of the royal drums as the veena faded away. He cleared his throat and spat into a golden spittoon. 'As has been the tradition over centuries, an amount equivalent to the weight of my beloved daughter will be given as dowry to the valiant champion who wins her tomorrow.'

There were loud cheers of approval.

Drupad held up a hand and silence fell. 'But I wish to give the mighty champion more than the gold equivalent to my daughter's weight, for as we know the weight of a Princess is a state secret.'

And it surely has nothing do with how weak she looks! thought Shakuni sourly.

'Hence the iron bars which surround her, and weigh far more than the Princess herself.' He allowed his words to sink in.

As comprehension dawned, a loud chorus of cheers greeted such generosity. The one to win the Princess would be fortunate indeed. Needless to say, every one of the fools gathered thought himself to be the one so blessed.

'Let the Weighing Ceremony commence!' announced Drupad, raising his hands.

Silver and gold chains were the first to be placed on the opposite plate of the scale. The plate holding Draupadi did not lift by so much as a hair. Coins in wide-necked, deliberately overstuffed brocade sacks were put on the scale next. Then came jewelled flasks containing ambergris, frankincense and aloewood. Finely woven pashminas, goat's wool and bales of embroidered silk were added to the scale.

Draupadi continued to sit meekly on the plate within the circle of iron. Shakuni felt an unusual stab of pity for the young Princess who sat on the scale like a prize exhibit at a fair. It reminded him suddenly of his own sister, Gandhari, when she had been sold off to Dhritarashtra as a token of peace. But when he looked at Draupadi again, through the eyes of Shakuni, and not a brother, he realized the White Eagle had been right. The people of the Union longed for something higher than themselves, Royalty worth worshipping. For a long time, they had bowed before all manner of Kings, but none of them truly royal: Dhritarashtra's brother Pandu had suffered from a sexual disease, Dhritarashtra himself was blind, and Duryodhan... well, he had too grim a jaw, that seemed crafted only to issue commands. But no one could deny that Draupadi was all that a Queen should be, and more. The mere idea of a pirate sitting alongside Duryodhan on the throne of Hastina seemed absurd now.

Nine chests were emptied before the plate bearing Draupadi finally began to rise from the ground and then slowly levelled. The show was over. As the plate was lowered again, Draupadi rose, picking up the shreds of her self-respect even as servants began to empty the opposite plate of the dowry. Suddenly, men were hovering before her, sucking in their stomachs, puffing out their chests, flexing their muscles. They stood side by side, shoulder to shoulder as the Princess walked by them, escorted by her mother, Queen Prishita, like a general inspecting his troops.

Not this again. Shakuni looked away.

'What's happening?' Sudama asked, bewildered.

'I was going to ask you, little one,' Karna said.

'It's the Princess Dance. The first and last dance a Princess performs in public, before she is wed,' Shakuni answered stiffly. 'It's a strange Panchalan custom. She will choose one amongst her suitors to dance with. It's a strong indication for the betting guilds, however, about who her choice will be at the swayamvar.'

'Is this why Duryodhan forced me through those dance lessons?' Karna asked, looking betrayed. For half a moon, a skilled eunuch had called upon Duryodhan to train him in the required dance forms, but the Prince had refused to learn unless Karna underwent the ordeal with him. 'He told me it's a Kaurava tradition, undertaken to restore a relationship that is fractured! He used that to blackmail me.' Karna was aghast.

'Seems that our Prince nurtures a hidden sense of humour, Lord Karna. I do hope the Princess chooses him. I got Acharya Kripa to find the finest perfume to dab on his neck to make up for what he lacks in looks. Do not look at me like that. We all know Duryodhan's skills lie… elsewhere. And we still don't know what the competition in the swayamvar is to be, so we cannot even gauge his chances on merit. Not to forget the Prince has not smiled once since we got here.'

Karna sighed. 'That is true. Just where is he, though?'

'Probably sulking in some corner. Do not concern yourself. He will come when he is needed. Family, duty and honour are precious to him.'

'Aye, that it is. Come, Sudama.' Karna effortlessly hoisted Sudama onto his shoulders.

'Put him down!' Shakuni muttered, outraged. 'This isn't a circus!'

Sudama chuckled gleefully, looking around bright-eyed. 'But no one is looking at us!'

 DRAUPADI felt conscious as everyone looked at her, following her every move. She moved listlessly past her suitors, turning her head gracefully to look at them without any movement of her shoulders. Everywhere she looked, Draupadi saw the lustful eyes of her suitors, the envious smirks of the women, the expectant eyes of her family. If the pony show on the scales had not been mortifying enough, she

now had to undergo the ordeal of choosing from amongst these *bidders* a dance partner. Her sadness felt unassailable as she looked at these strangers, one of whom would ravage her the following night.

She had always dreamed of this moment: how her chivalrous and dashing champion would swing her into the air to perfectly synchronized movements as they fell in love. She would giggle at the jealousy of her handmaidens as she glittered in the choicest of necklaces and prettiest waist-chains. But, much like the rest of her life till this point, this too had just been the empty imaginings of a foolish girl.

'Don't think!' Queen Prishita whispered, casually placing an arm under Draupadi's elbow as she inclined her head right and left. 'I can feel the shivers in your shoulders. If you cry, your kohl will streak your face and ruin the entire event. So, drink up those tears now!'

Draupadi had a wild urge to flee; to shock all these pompous men who wanted her body and her father's wealth. But Draupadi was first of all the daughter of a King, a Princess of Panchal, trained since she could walk to be always soft-spoken, gracious, and sweet-smelling; to cook, sing, dance, swoon, moan, sigh, embroider, and even clutch at a man's arm in feigned fear. And she had loved every bit of it, taking pride when her tutors said she was as graceful and womanly as Goddess Prakioni herself.

But that was before the man chosen by her father to wed her had been burned alive by his cousin.

Draupadi lifted her head, mastering her shivering. She continued to walk, smile and bow, just as she had been taught. Her handmaidens gushed and chirped like birds behind her. *They are silly girls. They know nothing. They think this is a dream of love fulfilled.* How foolish she too had been, for it was what she herself had thought before her twin had shown her the true place of a woman. Draupadi pitied her girls, yet envied them their happy ignorance.

'Are you planning to walk all the way to Meru, child?' How the Queen managed to hiss the words without breaking her clay-encrusted smile was an enigma. 'Choose someone quickly. Your father grows impatient.'

Once, this very ritual had fascinated Draupadi; now she dreaded it. *Courage.* She took a deep breath. *I am the Princess of Fire. I can be courageous.* She laughed silently at that. If not for Krishna, she would have trespassed over death's door. She had been told since she was eight that she would wed Arjun, the younger brother of Yudhistir, rightful heir to the Hastina throne. The fact that Arjun was probably fourth or fifth in the line of succession had not deterred her father, for like most men in the Riverlands, he had a soft corner for archers. Arjun was said to be the most skilled archer of them all. His likeness in clay sculptures and wall paintings filled her room, all sent by Krishna in the three years they had been quill-companions. Draupadi had given herself, mind, body and soul, but mostly body, to Arjun without ever having met him. So when the news of his untimely demise came to Panchal, Draupadi had been heartbroken. But not more so than her father, who might as well have been the bereaved damsel, so great was his distress. He had wished to cancel the swayamvar, which was to be an archery competition, but Krishna had turned up in the nick of time to avert such a turn of events.

Draupadi had secretly hoped Krishna had come to take her as his wife himself. He was, after all, handsome, gently spoken, and had the charm of a conman, or so the bards said. She had never met a man who was not related to her, till Krishna came. His skin was as dark as her own; a pair of perfectly matched dark doves. But all her hopes had been dashed when he had walked into her chamber with a pair of women soldiers in tow and addressed her as 'Sister'. That had hurt more than Arjun's death.

Krishna had managed to convince King Drupad to hold the swayamvar as planned. For the most part, Draupadi was happy Krishna was there with her, guiding her, educating her about the suitors who would be coming to Panchal to win her hand. Despite her insistence that her *hand* was already cut off and placed on a platter for the winner of the archery competition, Krishna had persistently told her she always had the choice to say no.

This clearly went against all royal instructions. She still remembered the way her brother had slapped her when she had suggested choosing her own husband. The idea of standing up to refuse the winner of a swayamvar was laughable; it would be the scandal of the century, and utterly pointless, for Father would definitely burn her alive if the spurned winner did not kill her first. And it was safe to assume his aim with an arrow would be true.

So here she was, standing solely on the strength of the liquid courage she had taken from Krishna's silver flask, before walking to the terrace in much the way she would have gone to the gallows. Turned out liquid courage was best taken in small doses, or it swiftly slipped into recklessness. It was at this point, poised on the precipice of pain, that she first saw them. They stood in a corner, as far from where she was as possible. They did not look at her with lusty eyes or gawk at her like the other suitors, so she felt safe in walking towards them.

Of the three men she crossed first, one was muscled like a weightlifter, with a greying mane of a beard, and hair that hung to his shoulders. Draupadi was nonplussed; the man was old enough to be her father. Then she noticed he was wearing a doublet covered with golden studs in the shape of lions' heads. *Prakioni, give me strength!* It was the Magadhan Emperor!

'Your Majesty,' Draupadi bowed, her palms joined in a namaste. 'It is a great honour for Panchal that the Emperor has graced this event with his august presence. I wish you good fortune tomorrow.'

'No, you don't,' Jarasandh scoffed. 'You are like one of those parrots from Pragjyotisha, aren't you? A pretty, dark parrot, repeating all the pretty words they taught you.'

Draupadi blushed furiously. 'Your Majesty?' she murmured, unsure how to respond. She looked meekly at her mother, who nudged her to maintain eye contact.

'Do not concern yourself, Princess. I am not here to vie for your hand. I am here merely to bless you: *May you be the mother of many children.*' The Emperor turned his face slightly in the direction of the man beside him.

The man was certainly unattractive, lean to the point of gauntness. Yet sinewy muscles corded his arms and neck. His hair was dark and his gaze respectful. Draupadi bowed before her suitor. 'Princess Draupadi,' the man said, bowing in turn. 'I am Shishupal of Chedi. I admire the Princess' ability to carry all those jewels in this weather with such grace.'

A true compliment, unrehearsed and sweet. He looked like he had a kind soul. *Should I dance with him?* Before Draupadi could decide, her mother nudged her and she took a step forward, towards a Mlecchá, whose olive skin shimmered in the moonlight. He was comely, but more boyish than anyone else present on the terrace, with a mass of brown curls and strange eyes that dared her like a flashing sword.

'Archon Kalyavan, Your Radiance,' the Mlecchá said, bowing and taking Draupadi's hand. Much to her shocked surprise, he kissed the air above her palm. 'I hear the stars are annoyed at having to look upon beauty far beyond their own and have thus retreated behind the moon.'

Draupadi thought she heard Shishupal snort. Ignoring him, Kalyavan handed her a red rose. Draupadi took the bloom, charmed by his gallantry. She inhaled the sweet fragrance and wondered if she should dance with the Greek. He was quite dashing, certainly bold, but foreigners were known to be unclean. Who knew the diseases they carried on them? 'You honour me, My Lord,' she said, with all the demureness learned over long years of training. 'I have heard much about your victories.'

'Victories over sheep-stealers and farmers, you mean, Princess,' someone from the crowd jeered.

Kalyavan's face darkened with anger. 'Would you care to draw a sword then, Lord Niarkatt? See how long you last against my blade?'

'Who invited this savage to the feast?' The man named Niarkatt snickered. 'Yavanas, the only tribe that went from barbarism to silk clothes without bothering to create a civilized culture in between. Now, now, Storm.' He pushed away the hand of Krishna's guard. 'Don't hurry me. You can't have a proper feast without a fool prattling on about his prophecy. Pray tell us again, Lord Invincible.'

Kalyavan made a move to step in Niarkatt's direction but Shalya held his shoulder and shook his head. 'You will regret your words, Lord Niarkatt,' Kalyavan finally said in a voice as cold and sharp as steel. He took a step back, visibly fuming.

Flushed by all this excitement, Draupadi moved on to the next suitor. But she held on to the rose as she did. Draupadi looked up at a man staring at her with liquid ruby eyes. His skin was... grey, so polished that it shone in the moonlight. His jaw may well have been crafted by an artisan, but Draupadi could not call him handsome. He looked dangerous, feral. Some deep-buried instinct told her to stay away from him.

'Congratulations, Princess, on your nuptials,' he said, his breath an icy cold whisper that buffeted her face. 'I see the name *Fire Princess* is well deserved.'

'You are too kind, My Lord,' Draupadi said, ill at ease. The man wore a cloak with a thick fur collar, fastened with a silver airavat brooch, and appeared unaffected by the heat. He had the effortless manner of a Royal, but she did not know who he was. 'I have not had the honour, My Lord,' she murmured.

The Queen quickly took her hand. 'Sweetling, this is His Grace Bhagadatt, Remnant Monarch of Kamrup and Tusk of the Tree Cities.'

The Rakshasa! Draupadi's eyes widened in fear but she quickly remembered her courtesies. *Father has invited a Rakshasa as a suitor?* There were all kinds of vile rumours and tales about their kind, but clearly her Father had cared only about the suitors' treasury reports rather than their skin tones. 'An Honour, Your Grace. I trust the Panchal weather suits you?' Draupadi rallied.

'A few hailstorms and it will suit perfectly,' he reposited effortlessly in a honeyed voice.

Draupadi bit down a gasp, bowed, and hurried along. She tried to remember why Rakshasas were not actually dangerous, but she could not breach the fog that filled her mind. She realized with dread that the end of the line was in sight and she had not yet chosen a dance partner. *Father will hurt me.* In that moment of torment, she looked beyond the queue, and the sight of a man eating sweets like a child hit her like a flash flood in summer.

He stood with a boy astride his shoulders, looking statuesque and utterly out of place. Beside him stood a bent man with a cane. The man with the boy was well dressed in an open-buttoned *achkan* and cream *kurta*, both of which garments failed to conceal the imposing figure beneath, one that must have dealt a blow to the self-esteem of every other man present. His chest was puffed, as if he wore armour, but his lean and lithe figure was that of an athlete. He was almost pale, with dark shadows under his eyes that bespoke sleepless nights. One thing she was sure of, the man was devastatingly, inhumanly beautiful. He did not seem interested in the ceremony, and seemed annoyingly fascinated with his kulfi. But if he was here, he was at least a Lord. Draupadi made her choice and passed on without greeting the man with the grim jaw at the end of the queue.

The melting stream of kulfi misbehaved playfully, trickling down his chiselled jaw and sharp collarbones into the deep secrets of his achkan. Draupadi thought how it must be streaming down the contours of his hardened body till it merged with his white trousers, in a manner to answer the prayers of every woman, and render to their eyes the secrets hidden behind that obnoxious white garment. *By the Seven! What has happened to me? Prakioni, purge your servant of these impure thoughts!* Draupadi felt her cheeks flame into hot life as his face came into focus.

Yet she could not resist. His face was a haunting love affair between beauty and hardness. There was a certain grimness in those bright eyes. His cream-smeared lips were full at the bottom, with a delectable curve on top. She would dance with him. *He seems safe. What's the worst that can happen?* She set off in his direction, barely feeling her mother's warning pinch on her arm.

KARNA winced as Sudama pinched his neck to get his attention. His eyes cast around until a movement in the crowd opened up a channel to reveal the glittering figure walking towards him. She wasn't quite a woman yet, still growing into her saree, but the sight of her caused a shock that pulverized Karna's mind, sending lightning bolts to the pit of his stomach. The last Karna had seen of the Princess was from a distance, when she was headed in a completely different direction. So, when she suddenly appeared, her hands clasped nervously before her, a rose between them, Karna was understandably at a loss for words. He had the briefest notion of something cold and wet slithering down his chest. It grew difficult to think clearly.

When the Princess indicated he was her choice for the dance, Karna did not even hear her. Her fragrance hit him like a chariot. There was no painting violent enough to capture the force of what happened to Karna in that moment. In that instant he was no longer the wretched human he had once been. All that remained was bliss. She stared at him, waiting for an answer. The last of the kulfi slid from the stick in his hand and splattered on the ground between them.

Behind Karna, Shakuni groaned. Angrily, he whispered, 'She is asking you to dance, buffoon!'

The terrace grew strangely quiet. Karna dragged his eyes from the face before him to see Duryodhan appear in the distance. And for the first time in a moon, Duryodhan smiled. He nodded to Karna, who gulped and said, 'It… would be an honour, Princess.'

Draupadi offered her hand, and Karna took it, suddenly realizing that Sudama was still sitting on his shoulders. He withdrew his hand gently and turned to put Sudama down. He saw the grimace on Shakuni's face and hastily turned back to Draupadi, who handed her rose to a girl behind her. Her hand guided him to the centre of the terrace. As they faced each other, Karna suddenly became aware of the silent ring of spectators. It felt ominously similar to what he'd experienced when he had stepped into the duelling circle with a bow against Arjun, only worse. Karna stood still as a statue. Taking a deep breath, he extended his hand, palm upwards, to receive the light touch of her fingers. A shiver went down his spine. She lifted her chin, and Karna followed suit.

Karna remembered Duryodhan instructing him, in the unlikely event of Karna having to actually dance in his life, to compliment his partner. 'You… look very bright,' Karna managed. As opening remarks went, this was surely the worst, but Draupadi tossed her head back and laughed. A laugh that fell gentle and wild like rain. He waited in unease for the music he had been assured would flow.

But there was no music. Karna dared to glance towards the musicians. They seemed to be waiting for a signal from King Drupad. Clearly this was a scandal in the making. Finally, Drupad grunted and nodded, none too pleased, and the first tones sobbed out from the strings.

And then they were off. The flowing gold of Draupadi's saree swished across the floor, her feet out of sight. She glided effortlessly, while Karna… he knew not what he did for he could not even feel his feet. It was as if Draupadi was orchestrating the musicians with her fingers. They moved one way, and then another, the mirrors creating mesmerizing reflections. It was as if ten different Karnas and Draupadis danced, though in none of these reflections did Karna manage to keep up with her.

He knew past all knowing that he was an utterly incompetent dancer. Draupadi moved with such poise that she could have danced with an arrow resting on her head. The sitar grew bolder, and Draupadi's tempo hastened with it. Karna was taught by the tutors that the man was supposed to be the *lead* in a dance but he soon realized that his style of dancing was that of a lead that was led. To his credit he did try to guide the dance at the start. Draupadi, however, stepped effortlessly around his attempts, feinting one way, and then the other, leaving Karna bewildered. It was all he could do not to look an utter fool. It did not help that Draupadi was slightly drunk, if her breath was any indication. Yet she moved in rhythms of perfect balance against him, the finest archer of his age. At one point she almost tripped him with her foot, but held him up gently as she twisted away in a graceful arc, returning the same way into his arms.

Karna noticed a faint crease on her brow and the slight hint of a tear at the corner of her eye. 'Are you alright, Princess? You look… sad.'

Draupadi looked taken aback. Her dark cheeks flushed as she swirled around him. Karna wanted to slap himself for asking so impolite a question. 'It is the first time this week that someone has asked *me* how I am feeling,' she answered morosely. 'I apologize. I hope I am not embarrassing you, Lord…'

'Karna,' he managed to say, swallowing past the rock lodged in his throat. 'The embarrassment is all mine, Princess. It is all I can do not to fall flat on my arse. Ah, I beg your pardon for my coarse language.'

Draupadi smiled, but the little V between her eyes, a residue of her sorrow, bothered him. He wanted to smooth it away with a fingertip. But he could not, of course, touch her more than the dance allowed. It was unsafe in a hundred ways. Draupadi looked up into his eyes and made as if to end the dance, but Karna, perhaps emboldened by the kulfis he had eaten, clasped her hand and bade her stay. He was not ready to let this end.

'Why are you so sad?' he asked again.

She blinked rapidly, looking up at him, confused. It was impertinent of him to ask such a question, but he had abandoned caution and courtesy to the wind. He knew now that to die without knowing her secrets would be an empty life. He felt a sudden reckless desire that made him want to try all, dare all and feel all.

'Well, My Lord, would not you be miffed to be weighed on a scale before everyone?'

The music that had been slowing to mark the end of the dance, awkwardly resumed its cadence.

'No, tell me,' Karna insisted, not prepared to settle for her rehearsed answer. 'Why are you so sad?'

Draupadi did not stop dancing but looked up into his eyes, her own swirling in a cloud of suspicion and trust. 'Because, by tomorrow night, I will be the prisoner of anyone strong enough to win the competition. A complete stranger. He might be old, cruel, ugly, or smell foul, but none of that will matter if he wins. Oh,' she blushed, 'I... I didn't mean that, My Lord. Of course, it would be Prakioni's honour for me to...'

Karna clasped her palm tighter. 'It's alright. I understand. It can't be easy... being a trophy.'

Draupadi took a deep breath as she swayed softy. 'It isn't.'

'Do you perhaps have feelings for someone?' Karna asked, hoping she would answer no.

Draupadi looked up at him again, frowning at such a direct question. The Ksharjas never spoke in straight lines. But Karna could not assuage his relentless need to know everything behind that beautiful mask she wore. He did not break his gaze, oblivious of how awkwardly everyone was now looking at them. The sitar played plaintively on.

'How could I do so? Apart from Lord Krishna, I have never met any man outside my family till today,' the Princess said with a wan smile. 'So here I am. This is what my family wants. It is my duty, the only ideal I have been taught to live by. Love is not a word permitted to me.'

'I know that feeling,' Karna replied, almost consumed by an overwhelming desire to shield her from the world. 'For some reason our duty always lies in making others happy, by bowing our own heads.'

Draupadi looked up at that, meeting his eyes. 'Yes, it does. It feels...'

'Unfair.'

She smiled wide. The smell of the flowers she wore in cascades down her back saturated the air around them. Karna's throat burned but it was all he could do not to lean in closer.

'The music is slowing again. Father must really want our dance to end.'

'Or someone has sympathy for me, for they know I am utterly outclassed,' he said, making Draupadi smile again.

'My gratitude for lifting my spirits, Lord Karna. You have a kind heart.'

Some instinct, perhaps to self-destruct, made Karna spin her around and then pull her back into the circle of his arms, closer than before. He caught her by the hip, then leaned in, twisted into a dip, almost lifting her off her feet, even as the music whined to an astonished stop. She sighed in pleasure as the ends of her hair brushed the floor but he barely heard her over the gasps of the onlookers. Her smell, spicy and flowery, made him want to lean closer to inhale. He raised her back slowly. The gold threadwork covering her breasts brushed his face, a charming sheen of sweat shimmering in her cleavage. Then came her delicate collarbones cradling the sweep of her neck, then the parted lips, the patrician nose, the haunting eyes, deep as a lake at midnight. They gazed at each other, breathing rapidly. Karna felt his breeches suddenly shrink. *Must be sweat*, he thought but a growing self-awareness soon acquainted him with the subject of involuntary jolts in the human body.

 DRAUPADI was jolted from her dreams by a growing lump that suddenly moved a little against her navel. She did not understand it but thought the heat from Karna's body would physically burn her. She suddenly felt foolish for being so wishful. Was this man really interested in her? He could not help being chivalrous, or having gorgeous eyes. He could not control how his collarbones glinted as he spoke. He had, after all, been more interested in the kulfi, she reminded herself.

'That was… quite a swing, My Lord.'

At that moment, there was nothing more endearing than Karna's embarrassed, sheepish look. Tiny coils of tension formed in her stomach when Karna stepped back, only slightly, to let space invade the distance between them. Draupadi frowned at that, but she felt happy. The dance could not fix the world. The anger and pain were still there. But Karna was so warm, and his eyes were... Gods, it did feel like hope, like a promise that she wouldn't always have to feel this way. His earnest questions had touched the deepest part of her, and somehow awakened her. A smile exploded out of her like a song.

But Karna's smile deserted him as he looked around and saw the staring eyes, as if for the first time. A hard look crept into his eyes. 'A thousand pardons, My Princess. I do not know what came over me. Are you alright?'

'I am, My Lord,' she said quickly. *A lie!* 'I believe our dance will long be remembered, My Lord. I am in your debt for being such a splendid partner.' *That was better.* 'You were most gracious and kind.' There was a flare in her eyes, a hint of indecision, as she murmured, 'Are you good with a bow, My Lord?'

'I can... manage.' Karna flashed a grin tinged with wickedness, and Draupadi found herself smiling in return.

Her heart was beating so loud that she was sure he could hear it. 'I must take your leave now,' she said quickly as she saw the Queen prowling towards her. She couldn't even look to see what her father's reaction was, though she was sure it was nothing short of volcanic. But there was something she had to tell Karna. It had taken her a while to realize that he, whether he was aware of it or not, had kept her from shattering completely. If he won...

Karna placed a hand over his heart and bowed slightly, his gaze never leaving hers. 'I wish you true happiness, Princess.'

That decided it for her. 'I will let you in on a secret, Lord Karna. The swayamvar tomorrow is an *archery competition*.' She looked at him, letting her words sink in.

But Karna's face darkened as if she had disclosed a mortal illness. 'I... am not participating, Princess,' he said in a low voice as he drew himself up, taut as a bowstring. 'I came only to support Prince Duryodhan of the Hastina Union.'

Shame and sadness twisted Draupadi's features. She had been right. He was not interested in her. She had been fooling herself. But she could not help asking, 'Why not?'

'I'm just a vassal, Princess. A Highmaster. Moreover, I am a Resht. I must have broken a hundred rules just by talking to you tonight.'

Resht. Suddenly her senses were overcome with the memory of a foul smell, so thick it almost choked her. She knew it wasn't real but the echo of it in her mind was overwhelming. She tried to ignore it, but failed miserably. Then hands icier than glacial water grabbed her heart and crushed it. *Karna...* she remembered the name now. *No...* Krishna had spoken at length about him: a lowborn upstart who had made his way to power using deceit and sycophancy; Duryodhan's crony; how he had poisoned the Highmaster of Anga; how he had conspired to kill Arjun. A dangerous, vile man, born amidst filth and rot, destined to bring ruin to anyone he touched. *Why does Prakioni play such cruel japes on me?*

The pungent odour seized her nose again. It was strangely familiar. She had smelled it every time Krishna had spoken of Karna in the last two months. No one else seemed to be disturbed by it, but the smell made her gag. Nodding curtly to Karna, she abruptly turned to where her mother waited to escort her back to her chamber.

Meanwhile, bewitched, Karna forced his eyes away from Draupadi, angrily aware of how he had lost control. *She is for Duryodhan,* he reminded himself. *First Mati, now Draupadi. What is wrong with me?* Moodily, he walked away, trying to distract himself with other thoughts. The sight of Krishna was just what he needed. His smile cooled Karna's passions as surely as a block of ice.

 KRISHNA smiled at Karna even as he gestured to Prince Satrajit to usher King Drupad away before his wrath set the floor ablaze.

He joined them soon after. The King's private audience chamber was not as large as his throne room, but Krishna was fond of its Mathuran rugs and wall hangings. It reminded him of what Dvarka might look like in the future. As he entered, the King's steward announced, 'Lord Krishna, Overseer of Mathura.' He liked that too. The gaggle of sons Drupad had spawned were on their knees before the King. Krishna's smile turned to ash when he saw Drupad slap Draupadi, sending her staggering to the floor.

'Could you not see the fucking mark on his neck?' Drupad screamed at her. 'What are our words, girl?'

'*Death before Dishonour,*' Draupadi sobbed.

'Yes, *Death before Dishonour*! Remember that!' Drupad boomed. 'Take Princess Draupadi back to her chamber, and see she remains there,' the King instructed the eunuch guards brusquely.

Krishna flinched but stood stone-faced, waiting for the King's ire to cool. For a moment he considered helping Draupadi to her feet and sending the Silver Wolves in to assassinate Drupad. *Why such a hypocrite, Krishna?* he asked himself, for surely the slaps were nothing to the pain he had planned for her.

Drupad turned to Krishna. 'First Shikhandi, then Draupadi... sooner or later my children embarrass me. Lord Krishna, that lowborn means business when it comes to archery. And the way he shamelessly danced with my daughter... MY DAUGHTER!' he repeated as if Krishna hadn't heard him the first time. 'It is all her mother's fault. Too much freedom can only raise a whore!'

Drupad rose to his feet, shaking his head. 'The competition at the swayamvar must be changed. He is a Highmaster of Hastina. The rules do not permit me to deny him a chance if he throws in his lot. But I will kill Draupadi before I permit her to run off with a Resht!'

'A sound suggestion, Father,' Prince Satrajit said, eager to impress. 'May I suggest a chariot race instead?'

'The lowborn is a charioteer's son,' Krishna said dryly.

'A mace melee, then?'

Drupad grunted and fingered his beard. 'I have seen the kinslayer swing his mace. Nothing can stand in Duryodhan's way. Why has this happened? I designed the competition for Arjun to win! Why did the damn fool have to die?'

'Karna will never wed Draupadi,' Krishna said calmly. 'He isn't participating. We saw the names. Duryodhan is representing Hastina. And even if Karna does, he will never be allowed to win. Everything will turn out the way it should. Just trust me.'

Drupad stared at Krishna for a while, calculating. 'Very well,' he said finally. 'Work your tricks, Lord Krishna. I am counting on you.'

'You may do so, Your Grace. You have, after all, generously agreed to a loan to Mathura in her time of need. It is my turn to repay the debt.'

Drupad frowned. He had paid Krishna for his allegiance in the same way a goldsmith hires a master thief to guard his treasures.

'If you will permit me, Your Grace, I have work to do.' Krishna walked unhurriedly out of the chamber towards the courtyard with its lily pond.

The royal women's chambers rose in two graceful floors on three sides of a courtyard with a lotus pond. There, young girls sat sewing tapestries and braiding each other's hair with beads and ribbons, flowers and feathers. Krishna glimpsed Shikhandi, sitting with three girls, getting his hair braided. Krishna smiled at them and took the serpentine steps to the upper floor. By the time he reached Draupadi's chamber, Calm was already there, stretched out in a chair outside the door, one leg over the other.

'Why are you outside?'

'The Queen asked me to advise the Princess of her duties, but sent me off after she heard what I had to say.'

Krishna froze. 'And… what did you say?'

'Lord Krishna, I am not a fool. I asked her to marry whoever her father decides she should wed.'

Krishna looked at her suspiciously. 'That's not bad…'

'And I told her to keep a wad of cotton handy for her first night lest she bite her tongue. Tongueless princesses don't make good queens. Told her not to scream unless he wanted her to. To become his slave. Do as she was told till he began to trust her, and then get him hooked on moongrain. That she should light the hookah for him herself. A little moongrain at first. A little more with each passing day, especially after he emptied his seed into her. That way, he would associate the drug with pleasure and power. And then he would stop wanting her body and be content with the powder. I said she should ply him with more and more until his mind was destroyed by dependence on the drug. Then she could truly live as a Queen. A Queen married to a walking corpse, yes, but at least she would have his gold to—'

'Stop talking!' Krishna's ears hummed. 'Where is Storm? Why is she taking so long?'

'Getting that drunk Niarkatt home was no easy task. He did wound the poor Greek boy's pride rather badly.'

'I wouldn't worry about it. Boys get over insults. It is the ego of elders that worries me. Storm should be here by now. We will be in need of the rot soon.'

'She will be here. How's the mind-washing going?' Calm glanced behind her at Draupadi's door.

'Clearly not well, considering what happened today.'

'Wouldn't have happened had you managed to embarrass Karna as planned. Maybe you should have given Niarkatt the task. He seems to have the knack.'

'Thank you for that succinct summary, Calm. But the day is not yet lost.'

'It can hardly be that difficult. You have entered both her bedchamber and the King's council chamber with ease ever since we arrived. Trust they have in you aplenty. And the Princess isn't needle-witted. Each night I hear her pray for a *true hero* to champion her... Such a soft head rarely requires intricate manipulation. You can actually fool her with a glimpse of the truth, without the dung-smell business. It takes two trips to the baths for us to get rid of the stink.'

Krishna had already considered that. 'Naïve minds are the most dangerous to twist, Calm. For you never know who may undo your work and twist it right back. Now, make sure the concoction is ready. When I click my fingers, release it slowly into the chamber. Why am I explaining this again? You have already done it a number of times.'

'Yes, release it whenever you utter words like *lowborn, poverty* or *Karna*. Noted.'

Krishna nodded and was about to knock on the door when Calm said, narrowing her eyes, 'Lord Krishna, I have excellent hearing. I do hope you call to mind Lady Satyabhama's orders if I hear anything untoward?'

Krishna smiled at the unsubtle threat and knocked on the door. He entered Draupadi's chamber to find her crumpled at her mother's feet, choking back her tears.

 SHAKUNI thought he would choke if he did not stop laughing. He clung to the railing of the terrace, gasping. A spasm finally grew in his toeless leg that set shivers up his twisted spine. *The Gods love a buffoon!* The chances of Draupadi picking Karna to dance had been a million to one, but it appeared that in this particular year, the million to one chance happened eight times out of ten.

I love weddings, Shakuni mused. *Such scandals.* If there was anything more amusing than Karna's fumbling dance steps, it had been King Drupad's face upon seeing his daughter gyrate her hips against a Resht. Drupad had stormed off before the night was over, Krishna in tow. But even Drupad would have to admit Draupadi and Karna had looked like a divine couple out of some falsified tale of legend, though Shakuni in his better days could have out-danced them both. The throbbing of his leg reminded him his good old days were far behind him.

A few hours later, the moon was well up, and the suitors had been well fed. While most of the noblewomen ambled back to their accommodations, talking of the swayamvar to be held on the morrow, the suitors moved to the riverside to commence the night's drinking in earnest. There were many who were not present, however. Karna had retreated to his tent, with Sudama. Jarasandh, Kalyavan and Bhagadatt were nowhere to be seen either. Drupad did not appear, but his son and Heir Apparent,

Prince Satrajit, and Draupadi's brother, Prince Dhrishtadyumna, were present to play host. Shakuni rocked back and forth, hissing between his teeth, trying to get the cramps out of his legs. He was glad of the opportunity to walk again, painful though it was. Too much sitting around was as deadly as too much walking.

The air smelled of some exotic spice. Six monstrous barrels of ale were rolled in. Tables and benches had been raised, piled with bowls of strawberries, freshly baked bread and sweet-grass. An old woman played a cheerful air on the pipes. Dancers swayed seductively around a bonfire, swatting at the hands that groped them as they passed. There were sturdy broad-cheekboned, almond-eyed women from Pragjyotisha, slight green-eyed Balkhan girls with skin the colour of sapphires, and voluptuous women from the South, eyes rimmed with kohl. They dressed in flowing silks cinched at the waist with beaded belts.

Shakuni felt an old stirring in his groin that he could do little about. On his left, Duryodhan stood stiff like a stone, as if he were watching a funeral procession. If only he knew what he was passing up on. Duryodhan could have learned something from his uncles. On a cushioned divan, a drunken Bhurishravas dandled a buxom dancer on his knee. He had unlaced her bodice to lap the thin trickle of wine he had poured over her breasts.

Shakuni's expression must have been one of longing, for one of the dancers, a woman in black flowing silks, found her way to him. She wore a chain of pink flowers in her honeyed hair. A half-mask covered the left side of her face, though in the darkness of night the rest was barely visible. Shakuni had to force himself to look away from her toned breasts, the shadow between them drawing his eye like a bee to a sunflower's mound. 'Er... you are slithering up the wrong tree, love,' he said, pointing to his cane.

'Well, you can always sit, can't you, while I do the rest?' Her voice was flowing honey, liquid with the accent of the distant Golden Islands. Her painted lips twisted up at one corner, part smile, part sneer.

Beside them, Duryodhan turned sharply to look at the woman. He looked at her as if there was something familiar about her which he could not quite put his finger on. Finally, he let out a deep sigh, smiled, and then walked ahead, perhaps to allow his uncle some privacy as he explained to the woman why he could not be seduced.

'I'm afraid I am damaged all the way,' Shakuni said with assumed nonchalance, looking regretfully at the gleam of her thigh muscles, showing through the long slit in her skirts. The woman grimaced and sashayed away.

Shakuni joined Duryodhan, whose spirits seemed to have somehow revived. When the King's Fool sang a song about the Matron of Meru, he laughed so hard he spilled wine on himself. He turned to Shakuni, grinning for the first time in weeks. Shakuni's pleasant mood evaporated. 'What is it, My Prince?'

'There comes a time in every Prince's life when he wonders if a throne is worth all the sacrifice.'

'The mood will pass, Prince.'

'Always ready with an answer, are you not, Uncle? Alright, answer me this. I am here so Panchal can be added to Hastina's power. Is it not so?'

Shakuni was almost afraid to answer. 'Yes.'

'Karna told me the Princess revealed to him that the swayamvar is an archery contest.'

Vayu's beard! 'So?'

'Karna is Hastina too, isn't he? You saw the way those two danced together. And there is no restriction on a Resht participating in the swayamvar. I checked the rules.'

'My Prince! I must advise against...'

Duryodhan did not let him finish. 'No, Uncle. Her words have sealed my fate. Karna will take part in the swayamvar. I have decided. He will win Draupadi's hand and bring power to Hastina, while I wed Mati and forge an alliance with Kalinga. Surely two is better than one?'

Damn arithmetic. Shakuni turned towards a juggler who kept a cascade of burning balls spinning through the air. He thought of Karna and Draupadi together, standing high on a pedestal like monarchs of myth, dressed in shining gold. *So young, so beautiful, with their rich, powerful and happy lives ahead of them. Hurrah! My shrivelled heart thumps with joy.* But maybe he could work with that, turn friend against friend. He would have to think over it.

'Let's take our leave, Uncle,' said Duryodhan. 'I want to inform Karna myself! Not a second to waste!'

 KRISHNA had already wasted the better part of an hour inside Draupadi's chamber. The Queen had left long before. Through the door, Calm heard the soft sound of Krishna's flute, mingled with the occasional carolling of a song. Krishna's voice was muffled by the thick walls but the verse was known to all: *When you need shelter from the rain, I will be there for you time and again.* Inside the room, Draupadi lay reclining on a pile of cushions. Her black hair was tousled, her robe of orange-gold samite caught the light of the lanterns and shimmered as she shook with laughter at Krishna's farm jokes.

'I have another one,' Krishna said. 'What do you call an angry sheep and an angry cow?'

Draupadi laughed, shaking her head. 'I don't know.'

'Baaa...aaad moooo...ooood.'

Draupadi giggled in amusement and poked Krishna. 'Stop it, you! That was terrible!' She rose and went over to the table to admire herself in the mirror. As she turned and twisted, considering her reflection, the candlelight bounced strangely around her, throwing Krishna's face alternatively into light and shadow.

'Farm life was tough. Jokes were all we had growing up. By the way, your face has seen better days, my child,' he said dryly, knowing that sometimes the best medicine for pain was indifference.

'I didn't know he was...'

'I know you did not, but I bet you enjoyed it. He is quite handsome, the Resht. But life is not a fairy tale, my sweet friend. Some day you will learn that to your tragedy.'

'Why is it always a tragedy with me, Krishna?'

'You are a grown woman now, as beautiful as a song. In our realm there is nothing but sorrow for such curses.'

'I can never tell whether you are complimenting me or insulting me.'

'Be a glass half-full person.' Krishna winked, putting the flute aside to pick up the pot of salve near the mirror. He gently dabbed some of it onto her cheek where the imprint of a palm remained clear, even in the shadowy light. He blew softly on the cheek and saw Draupadi flush. *I still got it*, he thought, mischievously pleased.

'How go the preparations for my auction?' Draupadi asked distractedly.

'Now, now... auction means someone has to pay to get you. Here, your father is paying someone to take you away. Surely you must be quite the troublemaker, Draupadi.'

She nudged him playfully again. 'Krishna, I have a query.' He could see she was trying to find the words, or perhaps the courage. 'Why are Reshts considered inferior?'

Krishna's eyes suddenly focused intently on Draupadi, and his lips moved sideways in a smile. 'Before I answer, what has fuelled this... query?'

'Intellectual curiosity.'

'That's very good.' Krishna sat down and began fiddling absently with a peacock feather. Without looking at her, he said, 'And here I presumed it was a consequence of your steamy performance.'

'Do not distract me. Pray answer!' she pleaded.

He had foreseen this the moment he himself had set eyes on Karna. He had, of course, heard tall tales of his skill with the bow. He knew Karna's weakness lay in Resht politics and his obsession with becoming the best archer. But nothing had prepared Krishna for how handsome he was, even though he had been fair-skinned.

'Well,' he began, 'it is so that men who call them inferior can feel superior.' Krishna rose from his seat, suddenly restless. 'Reshts are as pious as Namins; as hard-working as Ksharjas. They have their own important role in the system we have in place, and are supposed to be accorded the respect due their station. But Reshts suffer from a curse for which there is no reprieve: they are poor;

made deliberately so by the oppression of Ksharjas and Namins over the centuries.'

Draupadi was listening raptly. 'Unfortunate souls,' she uttered sadly, quite unable to imagine the gallant Karna as poor or unfortunate.

'That is where men like Karna come in. He is a crusader, fighting for the rights of the Reshts; fighting the world, all alone.'

Krishna was sure by now that Draupadi was thoroughly enamoured with the Resht; a vigilante fighting against the oppression of the ages. Karna sounded like a hero. But that was the thing about heroes. They died.

As if on cue, a putrid smell filled the room, making Draupadi gag. She hastened to the basin filled with jasmine water and sprinkled some on her face.

Storm is finally here. 'I see Lord Karna has thoroughly charmed you,' he said. 'I do see in you the resilience you would need if you were to wed him. I think you should choose him if it comes to it.'

'I should?' Draupadi asked, confused. 'Choose a Resht? Is that even possible?'

'Why does the Princess of Panchal need to spare a care about hardships? Imagine your life as the spouse of a revolutionary, Draupadi,' Krishna offered. 'It will be the stuff of legends.'

'Like Ram and Sita?'

'Better, I daresay. Like Sita, you will spend most of your life in thatched huts, cooking on dung fires. But true love can turn anything fragrant. You will, of course, have to wait to draw water from the well, for the higher caste women draw water first, but what of it? His good mother and you could take turns. After all, you will be sharing the same space and she will be your new mother, considering the Queen would never be allowed to visit you. But that is the charm of young love – it conquers all.'

'Surely it will be different if the Resht is a Highmaster?'

'Indeed, if the Highmaster in question lived in his Protectorate,' Krishna replied. 'From what I know, Karna still lives in Hastinapur, in his old house, in a ghetto reserved for Reshts. Revolutionaries have to keep up such pretences. I do not blame him. A lifetime of habits does not change in a moment, even if fate does. He is, after all, the confidante of Prince Duryodhan, the rumoured murderer of Prince Arjun. Some say the Resht too had a hand in it. And then there is his nephew, whom he looks after as his own son. You will have the blessings of being a mother before ever carrying your own child. And the adventure of living in squalor, cooking meals on open fires, bathing in rivers and waterfalls, oh the countryside is full of romance.' Krishna sighed. 'I almost feel envious.'

'It will not be that difficult.' But Draupadi's face had by now lost its colour. True love was a nasty business.

'Oh no. Like a vacation for the most part. You would have to be careful of the Namins and Ksharjas, though. A revolutionary's life is a short one. Assassins, poisoning and lynching... These days Reshts are tied up to chariots and dragged through villages on the slightest provocation.'

Before she could respond, her nose wrinkled. 'Oh, that rotten smell!' she cried. 'Aila!' Her maid came running in, head bowed. 'Get the entire lavender oil crucible from the stillroom. Now!' Aila left to comply without a word.

Soon, oil lamps carrying myrrh, frankincense and cypress were hanging from different places in the chamber. Yet the smell never left. Krishna could see Draupadi struggle with it. *Good.*

'What about love, Krishna?' she asked plaintively, leaving all pretensions behind. She was just a young girl inside, scarred and scared. 'You said it can conquer all.'

Krishna wanted to laugh but kept his expression grim. 'Love is a fire,' he answered, 'which may warm your soul but might also burn down your house. Love feels overwhelming for a moment, but once wed, the excesses dissipate in the air, and what is left behind is torment. Women have to make peace with the insufficiencies in their husbands all the time, but having to contend with insufficiencies in his house, his coffers, his rank, is no ordinary task.' Krishna smiled patronizingly. 'But you are no ordinary woman, Draupadi. You are the Fire Princess of Panchal. You will not let the idea of a lifetime of poverty dissuade you. Just remember how handsome Karna is.'

Krishna could almost feel the sobs rising in her chest. She tried to suppress them, but he knew. Time to change tack.

'Draupadi, do you know anything about this Aila whom you order about in so sharp a fashion?'

She looked up. 'I did not mean to be rude. It is just this smell…'

Krishna interrupted her. 'I am not questioning the way you handle your household staff. *Dominion of women*, I say. I am asking, do you know her?'

'Of course, I do. She is…' Draupadi stopped short. She thought of the treatment she had meted out to Aila. The way her ladies mocked the woman's dress. Of the mark of two tears on her neck… the same that Karna had.

Draupadi burst into tears. She ran to Krishna and hugged him in a tight embrace. He did not flinch, merely stroking her hair in a brotherly manner, one eye on the door, lest Calm stride in and carry out Satyabhama's threat.

'I don't want that life!' she sobbed. 'But he is so…'

'… gorgeous,' Krishna completed. 'I know, little one, but even beauty tarnishes with time, exposing the suffering beneath. Princess,' Krishna patted her back, 'it's alright. Release the darkness before tomorrow. Renew. Rejuvenate. Tomorrow is a new day, the start of another chapter; when you can be who you really are. Use the wisdom learned from past mistakes. I am not going to lie to you that it will not be hard. But I know you are ready. Let the girl go and the woman be born.'

Draupadi did not answer, barely understanding the words he spoke. But somehow, they comforted her. 'I know I have been childish,' she finally said. 'All this debate for what? He isn't even participating.'

'The one thing I have learned about swayamvars is that they never go according to plan. Nothing is certain. But we have to be prepared for the eventuality that Karna vies for your hand.'

Draupadi's eyes brightened momentarily, and right on cue the noxious smell in the room intensified. It was all Krishna could do not to gag himself. The ointment he had applied to his nostrils to deaden his sense of smell helped, but only to an extent.

'There is no way a Resht can compete with the great nobles who have sought my hand, let alone win,' said Draupadi. 'It's not as if I have a choice. My feelings for the Resht are irrelevant. Let him compete and lose. Destiny will take me where I am bound.' Krishna stiffened, visibly. 'Did I say something wrong?' she asked.

'Karna cannot be allowed to compete, Draupadi,' he said. 'Under any circumstances. Not if you do not wish to wed him.'

'But he is just a Resht,' Draupadi said. 'How can he possibly win?'

'A Resht he is, but with exceeding great fortune,' Krishna told her. 'He got to dance with you, after all. Luck can cause strange mishaps. If he wins, no one can deny him your hand.' Krishna could see this still sounded like music to her ears. She knew she could not have him, but she wanted to see him fight for her.

'But what can I do?' she asked, half-heartedly.

'It is your swayamvar.'

'Only in name,' Draupadi scoffed.

'You *always* have a choice, regardless of what King Drupad tells you, Draupadi. Even if you do not stand up and make a choice tomorrow, that in itself is a choice. And remember, your decision will determine your destiny. Once you are out there before the Kings and Princes of Aryavrat, you can say anything as the Princess of Panchal, and His Grace will be unable to deny you your wishes in public, the same way he could not stop you from dancing with Karna. One of the many disadvantages of having to keep up appearances. Know that I am behind you, whatever you choose. If you wish to wed the Resht…'

Draupadi shot to her feet and rushed to the basin with jasmine water, retching deeply from her gut. Krishna smiled. *It actually worked.*

'I must take your leave, Draupadi,' he said, rising, pleased with himself. 'Rest now. You have a big day ahead.'

Draupadi nodded weakly, her face buried deep in the basin. Krishna silently summoned Aila, who helped him place Draupadi on the bed. This done, he beckoned Alia outside.

'I crave your pardon, My Lord,' Aila hurried into speech once the chamber door had softly closed behind them. 'Reshts are not allowed to accompany her out of the women's courtyard. I could not prevent her dancing…'

Krishna hushed her, not unkindly. 'Aila, you did well. She might have been too captivated by Karna's beauty had she seen him directly tomorrow. No, this was best. Now remember, every time she speaks or anyone around her speaks of Karna or mentions Resht…'

'I will crush the dung pellets Storm gave me, My Lord. I know the Resht is too skilled to be allowed to compete.'

'Aren't you a smart spy?'

'Obliged, my Lord. I think we can trust the Princess to do the right thing tomorrow should the need arise.'

Krishna nodded. Everything was going well. Yet he could not rid himself of the nagging feeling that something bad was about to happen.

 SHAKUNI could not believe something so wonderful was about to happen to Karna. He was after all a Resht, cursed to have a wretched life. Shakuni, on the other hand, had been born Prince of Gandhar. But Fate is ever a fucking fiddler, sticking out her leg to trip you at each turn. No point in crying foul.

They found Karna in his luxurious tent at the far end of the city, part of the large encampment provided for the entourages of the noble guests attending the swayamvar. The smell of oysters as they entered made Shakuni leave the tent flap open, allowing the overwhelming fragrance to depart. He could see Sudama had never eaten oysters before, and Karna was showing his nephew how to get the meat out of the shells, feeding him the succulent morsels himself. It was annoying to see him like this – so vulnerable and soft. It made plotting his downfall difficult.

Duryodhan went forward, smiling mischievously. 'Suda! What did you think of your uncle's performance?'

Light from the alchemical lanterns caught the sudden flush on Karna's face. 'Do you come to mock a wounded man? It was all I could do not to fall.'

'Fall for her, do you mean?'

Karna had a wary look in his eyes, as if he had been caught stealing. *Ah, he does like her. And that too, over the course of one dance! Boys... always thinking with their cocks*, Shakuni sighed.

'I do not understand, Prince,' Karna rallied.

'It's quite simple. I love Mati, and I do not wish to wed this Fire Princess. You seem much enamoured with Draupadi, and you are sworn to me. So, it is decided. You will be taking part in the swayamvar tomorrow. You will win Draupadi with your bow, and add Panchal to the strength of the Union.'

The shells fell from Karna's hand. What followed was a melodrama between friends, all rather distasteful to Shakuni. He limped out of the room into the grounds. The sky was dark now. A chill wind was blowing. Shakuni felt cold as he contemplated the cruelties of Fate yet again. How long he stayed there he could not have said, but after a time he heard a bell ringing in the distance, across the city, to signal the midnight hour.

Duryodhan stepped out of the tent wearing a wide grin. *So, Karna has agreed. My sister is going to kill me.* Crestfallen, Shakuni walked back with the elated Duryodhan to their own chambers in the palace. The streets that had thronged with merchants in the day, selling their wares, was near deserted now as the pair crossed them. A swirling wind gusted, drawing a shivery scream from the cracks in the buildings that pressed close on either side. Now that Kampilya was empty, sound did queer things here.

The woman had been waiting for them in the shadows to Duryodhan's right. Somehow the stones of the street seemed to drink up the noise of her steps, shrouding her movement in a blanket of silence. But Shakuni instantly knew she was the same dancer who had approached him in the afterfeast. He would have recognized those thighs anywhere. One of Duryodhan's sleeve knives dropped into his palm, but the woman stayed some distance away.

'Prince Duryodhan,' the woman said in an even voice, deserting her Golden Islands accent. 'I know you are carrying arms, but let us not be uncivil. I hope you are aware we have you at a disadvantage.'

Duryodhan's hand moved to his sword but Shakuni's left arm shot out and stayed his hand. Slowly, he shook his head. They were not alone. Seemingly drunken revellers wandered about, throwing them curious glances. Each wore an unseasonably heavy coat, concealing all kinds of weapons no doubt. Figures darted above. Duryodhan mouthed, 'Rooftop,' jerking his chin to where the silhouettes moved, carrying thin, curved bows.

Shit. Where is Karna when you need him? Shakuni grunted and limped forward. 'You appear to have us at a disadvantage, My Lady. You must really like me to follow me all this way.'

'That ship sailed long ago, Cripple.'

'To what do we owe the pleasure of your company?'

'I just want to have a conversation with you.'

Shakuni spread out his arms, his cane dangling from one hand. 'Splendid. Over a midnight repast, perhaps?'

'Somewhere slightly more uncomfortable and private.' She gestured ahead. 'At the next corner, turn right. You will see an open door, second building. Go in. Follow directions.'

Sure enough, the door stood ajar when they got to the indicated spot. Duryodhan hesitated.

'Do not act the fool, Prince,' the woman's voice said. 'If I wanted you dead, you would already be on the floor, less a head. Hand over your weapons or your uncle will forfeit his life, or whatever remains of it.'

Duryodhan handed over his weapons to the ruffians who appeared behind him. Then they began to hit him with batons and sticks, nothing sharp, and not on the head. *She is right,* Shakuni thought, *they don't mean to kill him.*

'Unfortunately, there is just room for one on our boat,' the woman said, turning to Shakuni as the ruffians began to drag Duryodhan's battered figure away.

Shakuni felt sweat trickle down his face. Urgent footsteps sounded, then strong hands seized him. *Murdered in the shadows like a rat. Perfect ending, I suppose.*

Apparently, he was not at the end of his line, for the woman said, 'They will escort you safely to your quarters.'

Shakuni raised an eyebrow. 'Surely, abducting a Prince instead of the Princess at a swayamvar, being unorthodox, will attract the unwanted attention of a host of unsavoury people with arms? If you could mayhaps give me a time and place where we could meet to discuss terms?'

'He will return to you soon,' the woman said.

'Presumably with all his limbs?'

That elicited a muted chuckle. 'That depends on *your* good behaviour, Cripple. Keep this quiet and he will live. Needless to say, my men will be all around you at the ceremony tomorrow. You can make whatever excuse you think fit for him. Perhaps that he is too cowardly to show his face among real men.'

Shakuni wondered whether it would be apt to reveal that Duryodhan was not participating, but decided against it. 'I don't suppose "Why are you doing this?" would fetch a response?'

The woman said nothing as she pulled the mask from her face, the wig from her head.

You've got to be fucking joking!

THE SWAYAMVAR

PART II

Stronger than lover's love is lover's hate.
Incurable, in each, the wounds they make.
—**Euripides,** *Medea*

 SHAKUNI frowned as he surveyed the swayamvar arrangements. *So much colour! Is this a competition or a rainbow's arse?* When he'd first heard that Drupad had rented the ground that stretched beyond the back wall of the Sindh Banking Guildhouse, he had thought Panchal had fallen on hard times. It was a bad sign if the Ksharjan King and his daughter were to emerge into the arena of the swayamvar from the back doors of a Drachma house.

But Panchal was as far from poverty as Shakuni was from comfort. The staging area of the swayamvar was as mystical as a fevered dream, rising in shades of rose, lily and umber. Multi-storey wooden galleries surrounded the central arena. Each gallery was said to be operated by an important family or merchant combine of Panchal and was decked in the colour of the caste allowed to sit in them. Even before the contest began, the arena was its own spectacle – a great swarm of rich and poor, Namin to Resht, seated and standing, jostling for vantage positions to watch a ceremony much loved for its competitive spirit. The Panchalan Guards were out in force amongst the galleries, but more to prevent murder than hard words or minor scuffles, for inter-gallery brawls between caste members were a common feature, and were in fact encouraged for the entertainment they provided.

Tall cages hung suspended in the air over the makeshift arena, sliding over wires from one end of the arena to the other. Within these cages, silk dancers, knife-throwers and other curiosities regaled the crowds below. In one of the cages, four jugglers entertained spectators with a cascade of throwing knives. In another, three acrobats spun around a pole, wearing tight-fitting chequered motley skins. In one of the cages, there was a pyromancer spitting fire into the air through its bars, which seemed rather unwise considering the arena had consumed two small forests in its pillars, galleries and ceilings.

There was something familiar about their faces, Shakuni thought, as were the faces of some of the guards in armour, who shielded the two royal platforms. Perhaps it was his paranoia, but he distinctly felt he had seen these faces last night. *Surely, she has not sent so many just to keep an eye on me? Not to mention they are too far to even see me.* Shakuni shook his head and went back to his drink, trying to drown his uneasiness in his goblet.

If the feasts were all about food, the swayamvar seemed to be all about the liquor brewed in the kingdom's famed stills. There was no discrimination in this matter between the green rows of the Reshts or the blue galleries of the Drachmas. The same refreshments were served in the grey corridors of the Ksharjas and under the orange canopies of the Namins. In short, everyone was equally drunk. It also seemed to be doing the job of waking the suitors up, considering the swayamvar was being hosted at the auspicious hour before daybreak.

King Drupad himself was seated on a wooden platform that jutted out seven man-heights from the wall at the end of the arena, where there were no galleries. On either side of the King were the chairs occupied by the Panchal Princes, Satrajit and Dhrishtadyumna. Behind them was a lute-player, playing soft notes into the air. The King's platform was connected to the door in the wall that led to the Sindh Banking Guildhouse.

A flight of steps, carpeted in flowers, led from the arena floor to the Princess's makeshift platform, which had been constructed right below the King's platform. Two female guards flanked the Princess on either side, while Krishna sat on a chair behind her, shrouded in the deep shadow cast by the King's platform above – though Shakuni doubted anyone would be looking at them. The Princess looked regal, draped in a lehenga that shimmered like stars in the sky. Its skirt was a deep midnight blue with delicate gold embroidery that depicted scenes from ancient history of Panchal, and its blouse was a rich, warm gold, with intricate beading and long, flowing sleeves. Over the lehenga she wore a dupatta, also crafted from midnight silk, whose centre was decorated with a stunning stag motif – in gold work, of course. Shakuni was sure her subjects would be mesmerized by the beauty of the Princess's attire that would never be worn again, and that cost more than their life's wages. Shakuni scoffed. It was as if Draupadi had a sacred duty to remind everyone that she was royalty; though even he had to admit he was awed by the way the fabric flowed in sumptuous waves around the Princess's legs.

At the centre of the arena stood a bronze archway. It was high enough for a small galleon to pass through, shaped in the likeness of two stags facing each other, their antlers delicate flakes of spinels and obsidian. Lapis lazuli served as the eyes for one stag, and citrine for the other. The archway itself was studded with rough-cut gems. The stags appeared to be holding up a large wheel between their antlers. A fish was tied to the inner rim of the flat wheel. A rope connected the wheel to a camel. The humped creature slowly plodded round the circumference of the arena, rotating the wheel held between the antlers.

'Trust humans to complicate things.' Bhagadatt's voice startled Shakuni. 'What should be a simple archery contest has turned into...'

'A circus?' Shakuni offered.

The Rakshasa smiled faintly. 'I'm afraid we have not been properly introduced. I am...'

'I know who you are,' Shakuni said. *The grey monster of the East.* 'The Great Tusk of the Tree Cities. I am—'

'Lord Shakuni. I understand you are the Rumoursmith of the Riverlands.'

Shakuni gave a resigned shrug. 'One has to make up for lost legs and teeth. But I am honoured Your Grace knows of me. Pardon me, but would you not rather sit there?' Shakuni pointed to the gallery beside theirs, where Shalya and Shishupal were seated.

'Ah no. I believe Archon Kalyavan harbours the suspicion that I used unsavoury means to win a hunting contest last night. He is...'

'A child,' Shakuni said.

'I was going to say *expressive*. Though I admit he was rather upset by the words of Lord Niarkatt. He has invited me today to another hunt. A rematch, he calls it.' Bhagadatt gave a small smile. 'I do not spy Prince Duryodhan.'

Not again. Shakuni had answered the question a hundred times already, and the sun had yet to rise.

'He's taken ill, Your Grace. I'm afraid what melted like snow on the tongue last evening has descended like iron into the guts.' Shakuni could only hope Duryodhan would be returned alive. It would be a great travesty of justice if all his efforts to sow poisonous seeds in the Prince's mind yielded no harvest.

'My sympathies. Will he not be vying for the Princess' hand then?'

'Lord Karna will be participating instead.'

Shakuni had barely recognized Karna when he strode in. The shy man of the evening before, clad in unostentatious raiment, was gone, replaced by a warrior with a golden half-sleeved plate over lean-muscled arms that made one yearn for some talent with a paintbrush. Shakuni had also noticed the puppy glances Karna had cast at the Princess. His face revealed his state of mind as clear as an autobiography. The lad was hopelessly in love. Draupadi, on the other hand, was a different story. Shakuni could not quite gauge her feelings, for her inscrutable face was clearly a work of fiction.

'Ah, the day breaks,' Shakuni said, noticing the first glimmers of dawn through the coloured glass of the semi-circular windows.

For some reason, Bhagadatt visibly tensed. 'I fear I may be suffering from the same ailment as Duryodhan,' he lamented. 'I wish Hastina good fortune, and hope there will be future economic ventures between our kingdoms.' Bhagadatt bowed and hurried off without waiting for Shakuni to answer.

Shakuni frowned at this sudden departure and the feigned ailment. Shaking his head, he made his way to where Karna sat with Sudama.

'You look tired, Uncle Shakuni,' Sudama said.

'Lord Shakuni will do, boy,' Shakuni mumbled without malice. Despite his misgivings about Karna, he liked Sudama. He was a good-hearted lad. His unruly hair curled over his forehead, constantly annoying his bright eyes. For some reason he reminded Shakuni of himself as a boy – naïve, foolish, and utterly clueless.

He softened. 'Just jitters before the tournament,' Shakuni lied. 'Have you seen the other stalwarts present here? Every one a mighty knight in their own right.'

'They are nothing. I know my uncle will win!' Sudama's eyes shone with pride.

Before Karna could respond, another voice boomed behind them, 'I sure hope so, for I have put my wager on him.' The ancient King Bahlika limped in, with his grandson Bhurishravas in tow.

Karna immediately rose and bowed. 'It is an honour to meet the grandest of all Kauravas, Your Grace.'

Shakuni half rose and bowed too, with difficulty.

'He means the oldest when he says grandest, Grandfather,' Bhurishravas said. The Balkhan had waxed his greying moustache into great curves. 'My nephew did speak at great length about your skill with the bow, Karna. Lucky for you it is an archery contest. Were it a melee,' he laughed condescendingly, 'none could have stood against a Balkhan.'

'And here I thought none could stand against a Balkhan where ledgers and stock certificates are concerned,' Shakuni remarked dryly.

'They are indeed our more subtle weapons,' Bhurishravas conceded cheekily. 'Why destroy the enemy when you can use him? Do you not agree, Lord Shakuni?'

'I see your sister, Vahura, has been training you in the art of quick retort, Prince.' Shakuni smirked at the Balkhan. Of all the Kauravas in the extended family, he disliked Bhurishravas the least. 'I wish she was here to liven things up. This swayamvar is much too dull for my taste. The last time I saw Vahura, she had just made an Acharya weep.'

Bhurishravas laughed. 'I have been waiting to see it happen again, but Grandfather discourages her.'

'It isn't nice to insult Namins, no matter how much they deserve it,' the old King said, suddenly turning his head. Lord Ketu of Malla had approached to sit beside them, but on encountering Bahlika's stern gaze, he turned tail and went to the next row of seats, sulking.

Bhurishravas laughed and turned to Karna. 'As I was saying, Duryodhan and his mace, you with your bow, Grandfather with his *ledger statement*, and I with my morning star... we will make sure the Kauravas win every Princess in Aryavrat, so they can do away with swayamvars altogether.'

Just then, Shishupal climbed the steps to join their ranks. He cast an eye towards Lord Ketu, unsure whether he himself ought to be there. Probably not. 'Prince Bhurishravas, my thanks for inviting me to your gallery,' Shishupal said, bowing.

'Of course, lad. It doesn't make sense for you to have that old grump for company any longer than you need. Withdrew your name, did you?'

Shishupal nodded, red-faced. 'My skill is with the sword, Prince. With a bow, I might end up shooting the Princess.'

'Why are the Emperor's sons not here?' Bahlika asked.

'Erm...' Shishupal glanced at Shakuni before turning to the old man. 'Your Grace, Prince Saham Dev isn't as interested in athletic endeavours as the Emperor. So, the Emperor desired the Prince to remain in Magadh to look after affairs of the Empire in his absence. I believe the Emperor seeks a more traditional betrothal for him.'

'No need to sugarcoat it, lad,' said Bahlika. 'We are all aware of the rotten egg. Prudent of the Emperor to bring you here in his stead.'

'Much good that did! I'm just glad Princess Vahura isn't here. She would have left no opportunity unsought to embarrass me. There was this time...'

'When she made an Acharya weep!' Sudama chirped.

'I see the tyke here knows everything.' Shishupal tickled Sudama in the ribs and the boy's innocent laughter filled the gallery, doing more good for Shakuni's spirits than the goblet in his hand.

A hundred conch shells sounded, and the entertainers stopped performing in their suspended cages. A blanket of silence fell over the arena. Drupad rose.

'And so it begins,' Shishupal whispered morosely.

'Kings and Lords, Paladins and Princes,' Drupad spread his arms wide, 'I welcome you all to the noble city of Kampilya. I thank you for honouring us with your gracious presence this week. The moment of reckoning, however, is now upon us. I therefore declare the swayamvar of Draupadi, Princess of Panchal, open to all. May the best man win!'

A hundred tiny mirrors installed on the ceiling turned together to reflect the light of the rising sun onto Draupadi. It was apparent none had thought to inform her of the arrangement. She blinked her eyes, trying to focus through the blinding brightness. The loud cheers from the stands were drowned in the beating of the big drums, their wide rims covered with hide, stretched taut.

Prince Satrajit rose and lifted a hand. The arena shuddered as if an earthquake had struck. The tremors sloshed some of the wine from Shakuni's goblet onto his thighs. *Perfect.* Unseen hands pulled a dozen ropes and the centre of the arena split apart to reveal a small lower level under the bronze archway. There stood a large brass container, filled with water, on the surface of which could be seen the reflection of the rotating wheel and fish above.

'What in the name of Vayu is that?' Bhurishravas asked.

All those assembled had the same question on their lips as they craned their necks to see, brows furrowed in surprise.

'He means for the contestant's arrow to hit the fish on the revolving wheel,' said Bahlika, who had been an archer of renown in his younger days, though seeing him now it was impossible to imagine he had ever been young. He had more wrinkles than a sack of prunes, and looked like he had been born that way.

'It's a modification of the Isle of Mirrors,' Karna said, thinking aloud. 'The archer has to look at the reflection of an object and hit the target. Only here, the target involves a fish on a revolving wheel at a height of more than two hundred hands, where the air current, more than the arrow itself, will determine the hit. And the fish is not reflected in clear glass but in the murky waters below.'

Bahlika nodded. 'Made trickier as the archer must stand on the artificial surface, and not next to the water.'

'Why would that be an issue?' Shishupal asked.

'Because the archer will have three relative heights of the fish to consider – the actual height, the height as ascertainable from the water, and the relative height of the archer from the bowl and the wheel. Quite ingenuous,' Karna admitted in evident admiration.

Soon enough, the announcer confirmed the rules of the contest, exactly as Karna had described. The challenge was onerous enough. King Drupad apparently did not think so, for the bow to be used had to be carried into the arena by five strong men and carefully placed on a table. It was unstrung. A bowstring lay coiled beside it. The bow was reflex, curving away from the archer when unstrung. It had to be inverted to string it into the classic shape, and hence required great strength.

'There is something nefarious going on with the bow, is there not, Karna?' Bahlika asked, squinting at the table on which it lay.

'Aye.' Karna eyed the bow like a jeweller investigating for impurities in a gem. 'It is a composite bow made of different constituents, but quite unlike any I have seen. Bows are usually made from a combination of horn, sinew, softened bone and wood. But this one has significant chunks of iron in it, making it terrifyingly heavy to lift, let alone string and shoot. And I do not think the arrow is any simpler. It is significantly disproportionate to the length of the bow, and made of weak wood, which is prone to warping over distances.'

Shishupal sighed happily. 'I am so glad I withdrew.'

Bhurishravas nodded. 'You and me both, my friend.'

Bahlika turned to Karna, a gleam in his eyes. 'Well, Highmaster, what do you think? Is it possible?'

Karna smiled. 'Too easy, Your Grace.'

 KARNA found it difficult, however, not to stare at Draupadi. She looked ethereal. Her hair was a mane of wine-red ringlets that fell all the way to her hips. Her blouse was an airy confection of Mathuran lace, sheer crimson silk, and seed pearls. A complimenting embroidered *dupatta*

covered her head. Her burgundy tiered skirt was long, with resham flowers at the waist and a contrasting gold frill at the hem. Her gold bangles were embedded with red coral roses, as was the *maang tika* that accentuated her lovely forehead.

'What now, Uncle?' Sudama asked.

'I must ride around the arena in a chariot. For a change, I will be sitting instead of driving it.'

Sudama gawped. His grandfather Adirath came from a long line of charioteers but never had one of his family been bestowed the honour of being driven in a chariot. He kissed Karna proudly on the cheeks, tears in his eyes.

'I know...' Karna clasped the back of his nephew's head as he touched his forehead to the boy's. None in the arena, save the two of them, could in that moment fathom the dream of the countless Reshts that Karna was about to fulfil by simply stepping into the back of a chariot.

And so it was that the suitors rode in chariots drawn by matched horses, sitting in haughty silence, brandishing their weapons of choice. The scene was rather heroic, and the musicians outdid themselves playing different tunes for each suitor. Karna found himself behind Vrihatkshatra, the Kekeya Chieftain from the West.

Once the Kekeya had proudly circled the arena, unsheathed sword in hand, the announcer finally called: '*Karna, Lord Highmaster of Anga!*' Karna rose. He had decided not to wear a shirt for he certainly could not afford anything as expensive-looking as his own breastplate. The best part was that none suspected it was part of his skin, for it passed off as a thin gold-coated chainmail shirt. He saw his chariot being led into the enclosure, the snow-white steeds boasting tasteful saddlecloths glittering with topaz. *Where are the horses I rented?*

The stableboy leading in the horses handed him a tightly rolled scroll, the wax seal embossed with the red eagle of the Hastina Union. Karna broke the seal and unrolled the parchment: '*Your time has come, my friend. The arena is all yours. I know you will win. And by winning, you will achieve what you have wanted all your life – a place amongst heroes that is rightfully yours. Show them!*

Karna felt the salty taste of tears on his lips. With one fluid movement, he climbed into the chariot. *I really wish you were here, My Prince.* But Sudama more than made up for the lack of his closest companion. Karna glanced up at the young face: no malice. No ambition. Guileless. Sudama was on his feet, cheering from the stands as if his life depended on it.

The Panchalan crowd cheered as well when the horses took off. *The cheers are not for you, Resht,* a voice in his head reminded him. *They are cheering everyone who passes.* But as he looked at the Resht tiers, and then the Drachma ones, he saw the fervour in their eyes. They were looking at him, shouting with elation and joy. The women in a few tiers gasped as he passed, and one even parted her robe to expose a breast. Karna looked away, blushing. And there he saw the bald heads in the orange tiers, complaining bitterly amongst themselves, their disgruntled faces betraying their anger that a Resht was riding in the chariot instead of driving it. *The Namins are cursing me,* Karna realized in sudden amusement.

And that was all the motivation he needed. He raised his bow hand, triumphant, his muscles taut, his golden armour shining like the sun. The crowd cheered mightily. The women sighed, looking after him with dewy eyes. Karna brought his arm down, parallel to the ground, his bow aimed straight at the Namins in their tiers, to the shock of many onlookers. The other tiers erupted. There was no need for any music. The chants of his brethren and sympathizers filled the arena with one resounding voice: *Karna! Karna! Karna!* It felt good.

The chariot had traversed half the arena when he passed Draupadi's platform. Their eyes locked for a moment, at once fleeting yet lasting an eternity. In her eyes he saw something more beautiful than the stars. Karna's stomach coiled in knots when the colour rushed to her cheeks upon seeing him. Hard as he had tried, the melody of their dance had plagued his mind like a sweet endless lullaby. She had danced with him despite the mark on his neck. Duryodhan was right. The fact that she had conveyed to him the secret of the tournament meant she burned in the same fire he did. Sometimes, all the answers of the universe lay in someone else's hand.

The charioteer's whistle brought the steeds to a prancing halt where they had started. Karna leaped nimbly from the chariot, smiling mindlessly at the prosect of kissing Draupadi's red lips and caressing her fiery hair, even as the world chanted his name. Duryodhan was right. Karna would show them all.

 SHAKUNI guffawed as no one showed up to volunteer first. *Cravens all.* Not Karna, though. The lad could hardly wait to jump the barrier, shoot the fish and claim his love, but Shakuni kept him on a tight leash. *No need to show off your strength unless it actually embarrasses someone.*

The announcer finally took matters into his own hands, and reading from a list, called: 'Patcharanihanta, Lord of Karusha!' The Karushan stepped forward warily. He wore a blue cloak and, beneath it, a shining suit of green.

'I'll wager he won't even be able to lift the bow,' Shakuni said. He unabashedly enjoyed the prospect of the Royals failing. For a change, *he* was not the laughing stock.

'I will take your wager, Lord of Gandhar,' Bhurishravas said, raising his goblet. 'A gold sovereign that he at least displaces the bow from its place.'

Shakuni nodded his acceptance. Lord Patcharanihanta's spotted hand looked like a chicken claw as he extended it to raise the bow. His brow furrowed in waves of tension, and a throbbing blood vessel leaped out on his forehead. The bow moved four fingers before he gave up, heaving and panting.

'Well earned, Shakuni,' Bhurishravas laughed. 'One more?'

'I won against a Balkhan,' Shakuni said cheerfully. 'I am going to savour it.'

'If only we were in Balkh. You would have to pay tax on your winnings… and I would have got the money back.'

Shakuni laughed. They watched the heroes of Aryavrat march forth, each more fabulous-looking than the last, each failing more miserably than the one before. The crowd booed each suitor who failed as he made the long walk back to his seat, dejected and forlorn. Shakuni had not had so much fun since Dhritarashtra had slipped in the mud and fallen face first in his garden.

But the whistling and laughing of the drunken revellers set like the moon before dawn as the Magadhan Emperor rose. *The Emperor was participating himself!* In the gallery, all eyes turned to Shishupal, who cringed in embarrassment. 'He insisted...' was all he said.

Jarasandh had the build of a wrestler. Shakuni saw how Karna shifted uncomfortably in his seat. *Ah... a threat, I see.* But when Jarasandh did not run his hands over the bow, Karna heaved a sigh of relief.

'He won't be able to lift it,' Bahlika said. 'The iron makes it too heavy.'

Jarasandh grabbed the bow. Veins bulged along his arm as the bow moved, then shook, and in a flash was high in the air. The crowd was on its feet, caste and clan forgotten. Cheers erupted from all corners. Karna's mouth hung open, his eyes gleaming in admiration.

Shakuni wasn't sure what to think. 'Did he...?'

'He picked up the bow using brute force, didn't he?' Bhurishravas said.

'It would seem so,' Karna found his voice. 'But the sheer strength required...'

Shakuni's eyes fell on Krishna, seated in the shadows behind Draupadi, and he laughed aloud at the deep frown that suddenly appeared on his face, as if trying to shatter Jarasandh's focus with his will. But Jarasandh curved the bow, the veins on his arms popping out with the strain, a blue tint to his sweat. After the bowstring had been tied to the notch, Jarasandh dropped the bow, breathing heavily. It was perfectly curved now.

'Can he do it?' Bahlika asked.

'I don't know...' Karna murmured. 'The strain on the back from such exertion will make it very difficult to align the bow for any length of time. He would have to shoot immediately.'

Jarasandh stretched his arms and picked up the bow again, using his gargantuan strength. As Karna had foretold, he did not hold the bow high for long. One look at the reflection below and the long wooden arrow whistled and screeched through the air, piercing the wheel with a resounding thud. All eyes were on the reflection of the fish in the mirrors. The arrow had lodged cleanly on one of the spokes of the wheel. Jaws dropped, but none more than Krishna's.

The crowd rose to their feet to applaud Jarasandh. Even Karna clapped with genuine admiration, though Shakuni could see sweat trickle down his face. Jarasandh merely eyed the target with devastating menace, threw the bow down where he had picked it up, without unstringing it, and walked back to leave the arena.

Public acclaim, however, is a fickle mistress and the crowd was already cheering the next suitor, Uttara, a handsome youth from Virata. The contest went on, even as the sun rose into the noon sky. Servants kept cups filled. Wagers flew. The King's Fool, dancing about on stilts, made mock of every suitor with such deft cruelty that even Shakuni ended up spilling wine on himself, laughing hysterically.

If the suitors who followed thought Jarasandh had made their task easier by stringing the bow, they could not have been further from the truth. The bow was still heavy to lift. Most failed. Two did pick up the bow, but missed the target. One focused so hard on the bowl of water he fell over, dragged down by the weight of the great bow. Another's arrow bounced off one of the cages holding a juggler, much to the delight of the crowd.

It was early evening before Karna's turn came. Shakuni suspected he had been placed last in the list in the hope that one of the others would pip him. The first to complete the task always won, unless another successful candidate challenged him to a duel that was accepted by the first. But that would not be required today. No one had won so far. The crowd was restless now. The fate of their Princess hung in the balance. If no one won, it would not only be considered an ill omen, the suitors would also raise a hue and cry at being insulted with an unachievable task. Shakuni could already see the Panchalan Guards sweating nervously under their helmets.

The announcer hesitated briefly, then called for the second time that day: *'Karna, Highmaster of Anga, representing the Hastina Union.'*

Shakuni sighed. *Ah, so it is going to be Karna who wins Draupadi. What a predictable tournament this has turned out to be.* Suddenly, some instinct made him scan the crowd, then the royal dais, then the throne. The suspended cages of the entertainers were unlatched and open. One of the knife-throwers was looking intently at Shakuni. He felt the wine burn in his throat. *Ah… I have a bad feeling about this.*

KARNA had a good feeling about his chances as he heard his name called. If there was anything more nerve-wracking than throwing away an opportunity, it was the exhilaration of grabbing it. His breath quickened as he walked into the arena. The noise of the crowd faded into the background. He saw only the bow. His instrument. His one true God. It had stayed with him throughout his cursed life. He could not fail it.

His eyes fell on the shades of colour on the bow, and the patterns of wood floated before his eyes. He picked it up with an easy swipe of his left hand. The collective gasp of the crowd sounded like the cracking of dry leaves in the forest. His breastplate shimmered like bridal jewellery in the sunlight now pouring into the arena.

All my life… this is what I have wanted. It is here. The arrow will not only strike the eye of the fish, but at the very foundations of the prison of caste, shattering the illusions that cloud the eyes of every Ksharja present. They will know that I, Karna, am the best. And that we will not be left behind anymore.

As he walked to peer at the water in the bowl below, he thought of Draupadi. Today, a lowborn would marry the Princess of Panchal. Together, they would usher Aryavrat into a new age. They would go back to Anga. With Panchal's help, he would establish peace and learn to rule. Sudama would have a loving aunt. Duryodhan would gain Panchal as an ally for the Union. And he, Karna, would finally get his due, despite his wretched beginnings. *It all works out in the end,* he heard his mother saying.

His eyes searched for Draupadi. She was perched at the edge of her chair, as if posed for flight. She seemed unwell. Her cheeks were red, and she had a hand on her throat, as if trying not to retch. Karna paused. He saw Krishna appear and stand beside her, patting her gently. But Karna could not long ponder on what he saw. He knew she was praying for him. *Maybe it's true what they say about love,* he thought. *It is a sickness of mind and heart...*

He bent down one knee and looked down at the reflection of the fish revolving on the wheel above. Time slowed. Everything receded from his mind. The wheel began to move slower and slower... till it stopped moving. He saw the body of the fish in great detail. The gold had faded from its skin and what remained was a silvery mass. He could see the rotting scales... And then he saw nothing but the eye of the fish. He waited for his moment. Haste was, after all, the invisible pothole before the gates of glory. He stretched the bowstring back, hearing its familiar music in his ears. *For you, Mother....*

'*Stop!* He is a Resht! I will not marry his kind.'

Pain pierced Karna's heart with searing intensity. He knew her voice. He had heard it a thousand times in a thousand dreams in the course of one night. But the words she spoke were impossible. The voice was the same, but the woman who spoke was cruel. It was not the Draupadi he knew, not the woman he had come to, as ridiculous as it sounded now to him, fall in love with. Invisible hands grabbed Karna by the throat, threatening to choke the life out of him. A stunned silence fell on the arena. Then the crowd began to whisper and snicker, rant and rage.

'Blasphemy! How can she insult a suitor this way?'

'The Princess is right! He is a cur!'

'Oi! You don't get to choose!'

'This is most improper!'

'He is the Highmaster of Anga, Princess!' Karna heard a voice roar from the tiers. *Bhurishravas.* 'And you will give him the respect he deserves, or I will destroy your Royal family and burn down your palace for this insult!'

Several Panchalan nobles responded with the choicest of slurs on Bhurishravas' parentage. These were returned in kind by the Ksharjas on Karna's side.

A silvery voice called out, 'Friends... let not the flame of our hearts rule the judgement of our minds. No one has to burn anything.' Krishna emerged into the light and turned towards Bhurishravas. 'Indeed, he is a Highmaster, Prince. But this is the swayamvar of Princess Draupadi, and as such, *her* choice is paramount, don't you think?' he asked the rhetorical question gently.

'Since when do we listen to the clucking of women?' Shakuni asked, and someone sniggered.

Draupadi was weeping hysterically, repeating '*He is a Resht!*' again and again like a mad woman. The Resht tiers bellowed their disapproval, thumped their chests and raised threatening fists, as did many Ksharjas.

'Let the King settle it!' cried one voice.

'What do the scriptures say about this?' called another.

Karna was no longer listening. He remembered his time in Acharya Parshuram's hermitage. The pain of wounds endured, the Shrap of his teacher, the violence he had seen, had done... nothing hurt more than the six poisonous words from Draupadi's mouth: *I will not marry his kind!* The woman he thought he would love to the end of his days, the woman he would have done anything for. She was repulsed by the very idea of their being together.

Karna lifted his chin and scanned the faces in the crowd. And he came face to face with his worst nightmare. There was no rage in their eyes, not even the Namins'. They looked at him with the emotion he feared most – pity. It was the most brutal gesture of all. Karna could handle their hate. He had learned how. But as their faces tried to extend him comfort, as they made *tch tch* sounds of sympathy, he felt the glass palace of his pride shatter in his head.

Let me out! the dreaded voice of the animal he had caged in the black ocean of his mind growled.

The animal rumbled in his stomach, raging to be released. The voice screamed at him to turn the bow towards the Panchalan throne. He could have easily broken the arrow into two and taken down Krishna and the wretched Princess before they even realized what was happening. But Karna continued to hold the bow that most of the noble-blooded suitors had not even been able to lift, his bow arm outstretched. *Let me out!* The voice sounded like two men screaming at him together. How badly he wanted to oblige. He realized that the longer he stayed, the more the fumes of rejection would choke him and release the other within. It had already filled his lungs and deadened his senses.

The humiliation Karna felt soon turned to grief and regret, and the voice inside faded away. Grief that he had thought she would come to him. Regret that he had ever danced with her. All energy seemed to seep out of his body. He forced himself to rise and place the bow gently back on the table. Proud as the sun at noon, head held high, beautiful to behold, Karna walked slowly back to the gallery.

Bahlika saw him come and quieted. But Shakuni and Bhurishravas continued to exchange insults with Krishna.

'Let it go,' Karna said in a tone that left no room for argument.

The dangerous streak within him must have left a large imprint on his face, for Shakuni nodded and sat down without a word of protest. Karna went to his seat and sat with his head down, his jaw clenched in fury. Even Sudama knew better than to approach him. Silently, they all resumed their seats. But there was no more cheering, no more laughter, no more jeering.

A fraught silence fell on the arena.

Unable to contain himself, Bhurishravas said, his voice loud and harsh, 'The Princess will no doubt get what she desires, to remain unwed and barren all her life!'

Murmurs of approval greeted his words. A babble broke out, as if a dam had released its flood waters. Many complained about the level of difficulty of the competition. Others were livid about the humiliation suffered by Karna. Clamour filled the stands. The drunken crowd was growing agitated, feeling cheated of the fierce competition they had expected. There was to be no winner.

The Panchalan Royals were worried about repercussions from the Ksharjan Lords, especially Hastina, who would take this as a slight. Satrajit nodded to Dhrishtadyumna, who purposefully walked to the Captain of the Guards and gave instructions. The crowd in the galleries was visibly drunk and boisterous. The Panchalan Guards filled the space between the common folk and the King, preparing for violence.

'May I try?' a voice spoke in dulcet tones from amongst the poorer ranks of Namins in the lower gallery on the left.

Despite himself, Karna's eyes shot up at the voice. Bun wrapped in a rosary, crematory ash from post-mortem rituals on his face, the man was a living testament to the fact that high caste did not necessarily mean high living. Even the other Namins in his tier had given him a wide berth. From the unwashed matted hair to the skull cup in his hand, it was easily discerned that he was an *Aghori*.

Bhairava or the Snake Ascetic might now be an Old God in the North, but the Aghoris tenaciously held to his faith. And in their zeal, they exhibited unparalleled severity in their eremitic penances and macabre rituals. With the soul-power they possessed by virtue of such practices, Aghoris were known to sprout Shraps easily, without blinking. But it had been long since any Aghori had been known to have uttered an effective Shrap. Avarice and contempt for the rest of humanity had dampened their soul-energy, and hence their ability to utter a Shrap. But that did not dampen the reverence and fear the Aghoris commanded among their fellow Namins.

'Why, Aghori, dead bodies aren't exciting you enough these days?' one of the suitors jeered. Many of the Ksharjas and Drachmas burst into raucous laughter.

'Go back to your prayers, Namin! No place for you here!'

'Maybe he will smear ash on the bow and make it light.'

More catcalls and taunts followed, met with ghastly stares from the Namin faction, though they dared not respond with words. If the Aghori failed, their entire community would be shamed. Some Namins whispered to the aspiring suitor to back down, but the Aghori remained standing, flashing a winning smile with ash-smeared lips. These were not the only whispers, however. In hushed tones, the older and more conservative Ksharjas warned the younger ones of the certainty of curses and hellfire for taunting the Namins.

But the Aghori simply walked to the archway in the centre of the arena and dropped the tiger-skin cloak from his shoulders. His body put Ksharja warriors to shame. Tall and lean, he stalked like a leopard and bowed with folded hands before Drupad, his bone cup hanging from the corded belt that tied the deerhide skirt he wore.

Drupad's face contorted with the dilemma he now faced. Refusing the savage would invite the wrath of the Namin community, but to allow him to participate would disrespect the Kings and Princes in attendance. Caught in a bad place, he looked unsure and wretched. His face turned to Krishna, who nodded, more than pleased to save the day, again.

'Considering there is no suitor left,' Krishna said calmly, 'surely there can be no harm in letting a poor Namin try his luck? After the events that have transpired, it would at least be entertaining. It might even remind certain classes not to impinge on the domain of the Ksharjas.' This was met with murmurs of assent from the crowd.

'I don't like it when Krishna speaks,' Shakuni said. 'Everything he says feels like a move on a chess board.'

'This is my daughter's swayamvar,' Drupad said finally. 'As Goddess Prakioni is my witness, I have permitted anyone who wished to participate to do so in a fair manner.'

'Fair he says…' someone snorted loudly

Drupad ignored him. 'Aghori! I permit you.'

Some of the suitors objected to this with loud roars, but there were many who were satisfied as there was nothing more gratifying than a Namin being shown his place. The Aghori bowed to Drupad and casually strolled to the great bow. He folded his hands in reverence. Then, with one swift move, he raised it high, as if it was a child's toy.

'Karna!' Shakuni's voice was urgent.

'I saw.'

The Aghori stared down at the bowl of water, the bow not moving a hair in his grip.

'He is going to do it,' Karna said, observing his posture. Others around Karna heard his words with shock.

'I hope he does,' Bhurishravas spat. 'It is what she deserves.'

The Aghori drew the bowstring and let the arrow whistle upwards. All eyes were on the reflection of the fish on the mirrors in the corners of the arena. Karna saw the strike before he heard the cheers. Like approaching thunder, hundreds of Namins shouted and hurrahed in ecstasy, waving their orange scarves in the air, throwing their marigold flowers, reserved for the wedding ceremony, at the Aghori archer. Many of them descended to the ground, raising the Aghori onto their shoulders. No elephants, however, trumpeted the triumph. The drum-beaters stood dumbfounded, awaiting instructions. But there was no need for music. The jubilant chants of the Namins filled the arena and rose into the heavens. The fish remained on the wheel, its eye pierced by the arrow.

'Well, that was unprecedented,' remarked Shakuni. 'And quite the scandal!' Suddenly, he grinned. 'I should never have doubted a swayamvar.'

Bhurishravas laughed weakly. Karna too momentarily forgot his woe, mesmerized by the feat. If there was anything more important to him than honour, it was pride in his skill with the bow. And nothing was more thrilling to a man like him than to face an equally skilled foe.

As they watched, other ash-smeared Aghoris emerged from the crowd, members of the cult. Prince Satrajit looked on uneasily, unsure what to do. Dhrishtadyumna seemed to have swallowed a slug. As for Draupadi, her face was a mask of horror. She stood trembling, ready to flee. Karna saw Krishna holding her arm firmly. Draupadi looked up towards the royal platform where her father sat, hoping for a command that would reverse the outcome; something that would rescue her from a life with an Aghori. But Drupad sat stone-faced. Dhrishtadyumna too looked to his father for guidance, but receiving none, merely stood like a stuffed effigy.

Next to Karna, Shakuni snorted. 'I hope the irony of this is not lost on the Princess. She refused a life in a stable to settle for a cremation ground.'

 SHISHUPAL felt unsettled by the furore around him, which was suited more to a swarm of stablehands than a gathering of champions. Some of the Namins had jumped over the barricades and raised the Aghori onto their shoulders for a victory parade. It was rather unbecoming of the Northern Namins, otherwise reputed for their austere conduct.

Draupadi rose, muttered something to Krishna. Shishupal saw Krishna urgently whisper into her ear, but Draupadi pulled away from his grasp. The cheering paused. The music screeched to a halt. Eyes turned towards her. Black eyes glinting with malice and hate. Apart from the vague creaking of the revolving wheel, the arena grew silent. All wanted to hear what the Princess had to say.

'I will not marry an Aghori!'

Shakuni chuckled. Guards marched. Namins roared. After that it was a blur. The Aghori, who had been carried on high, was forgotten. Someone shouted from the Resht gallery: 'If it is her choice not to marry a Resht, then it is her choice not to marry a Namin!'

'How dare you compare a Resht to a Namin? Blasphemy! We will not stand for this!' a Namin shouted.

'What do you mean, you bald fucker? Do you think we Reshts are lower than you?'

'You are a cur, Resht! How dare you even speak to me!'

'I do not wish to speak to you, sod, but I will spit on you!' Saying which, the Resht spat in the Namin's face.

The Namins reacted as if a temple had been desecrated. They jumped on the offending Resht, kicking him. Another section of Namins shouted, 'We'll see how the Princess does not marry this Aghori!' Climbing down from their galleries and rows, they rushed towards the dais, the tufts on their bald shiny heads bobbling in excitement.

'The Namins seek to attack a Ksharjan Princess!' Lord Dharmeyu of Sivi exclaimed, rising to his feet and calling on his fellow Ksharjas to defend the Princess against being forcibly married to a Namin. 'Create a ring of Ksharjas around her!'

Many Ksharjas rushed into the fray, creating a guard below the platform where Draupadi still stood, her face pale, her eyes dilated in fear. But suitors and attendees had not been permitted to bring weapons to the swayamvar, and without their swords, the Ksharjas were powerless against a mob that outnumbered them three to one.

One of the Ksharjas noted this and cried out, 'Why are we defending her? Abduct the Princess! That will teach her father a lesson for humiliating Ksharjas with an impossible task! This contest was clearly rigged!'

Suddenly, a bottle flew through the air, end over end, its surface gleaming in the sunlight, till it crashed into the Ksharja's head and shattered into a hundred shards.

'What are you pissants doing there, squabbling and gossiping like fishwives?' Lord Harivansh of Kasmira bellowed from the eastern gallery. 'Forget the Princess, you lustful ingrates. These uncouth barbarians have shamed us. Shamed our honour. Shamed our caste. If we cannot touch their scriptures, they cannot touch our weapons!' His face was crimson with rage.

Many Ksharjas nodded in assent.

'But Lord Harivansh,' Ketu spoke from beside Karna, 'what can we do? We are oath-bound not to harm the winner of the swayamvar.'

'My Lords,' Visoka said, 'we are oath-bound not to harm any suitor who wins at the swayamvar. But that heathen necromancer is not on the official list! He is not covered by the oath. And Lord Harivansh has the right of it. If we allow the Aghori to walk out, another Parshuram will be born! Let's teach him a lesson!'

A woman in the crowd gave a long, shrill scream. Shishupal turned towards the sound. In the centre of the arena, one of the Aghoris, a large man by any reckoning, was shielding the Aghori who had won against another pack of rabid Ksharjas. The giant had grabbed a bamboo shaft from the railing and was holding it up for protection. *Why up?* And then he saw the acrobats jump from their cages onto the large man and the winner, wielding artificially sharpened claws. Many Namins jumped in to save their champion, but the acrobats pranced like silken drapes, slashing and stabbing the Namins with their long nails. *Why have they meddled in this mess,* wondered Shishupal, *unless...*

'The acrobats are assassins,' Bahlika said gravely. 'Ravas!'

'We leave now, Grandfather,' agreed Bhurishravas.

'Sudama, we must go!' Taking his nephew's hand, Karna turned towards the exit.

'But Uncle, look!' Sudama pointed, and everyone's gaze followed his outstretched finger. On the platform, Dhrishtadyumna was on his feet, shouting orders to the guards, while Satrajit sat in his chair, stunned. One of the musicians behind them smashed his lute and pulled out a dagger, with which he proceeded to slit Satrajit's throat. And just like that, the Heir of Panchal was dead. Before the musician could attack Drupad, the Panchalan Guards stabbed him in the chest, and sent him crashing to the ground.

By now everyone was wailing, bawling or shouting. Women and men cried; a cacophony fit to deafen the dead. The arena was suddenly full of stumbling bodies, running to nowhere. Madness had spread like fire in a dry field.

Guards rushed to Dhrishtadyumna's aid. In the scuffle, the ladder used to reach the King's platform, fell to the ground. Shishupal saw one of the dancers slit a Panchalan guard's belly with a curved knife as he raced towards Draupadi's platform. Lord Dharmeyu, who was leading the Ksharjas guarding the flower-strewn stairs to the Princess, grabbed the dancer and pulled him down to the ground. He was about to choke him to death when a burst of orange shot out from one of the cages. It was the pyromancer.

'Vayu's balls!' Bahlika cried as they all stood transfixed by the madness unfolding around them. 'How many assassins are there?'

The pyromancer reached stealthily into his bag again and put something into his mouth. A spray of embers shot from his lips. Lord Dharmeyu would have dived if he'd had the time, instead, he was instantly alight, burning and shrieking as his silken garb caught fire. On the wires above, the pyromancer's cage slid towards the Aghoris, who were fending off the acrobats. He emptied another cup into his mouth and spat liquid fire through his rod. Fire slithered like a serpent around the Aghoris, who leaped away to escape its wrath, but the three acrobats were incinerated on the spot.

The Aghori who had won the swayamvar knocked off one of the gems in the bronze archway. Using a sling, he shot it at the pyromancer's face. The pyromancer was about to sprout another burst of flame when the gem hit him squarely between the eyes and he fell backwards, showering globs of liquid fire upon himself. Fire descended on him like a fiery cloud, and his screams flew on anguished wings from between the bars of his cage as it burned and fell from the wire with a resounding crash into the arena.

The flames spread from the cage, up the vine-encircled rope that tied the camel that had rotated the wheel with the fish. At first, it was just a crackle, then a roar as the greedy flames leaped to the camel's regalia. The poor creature shrieked and began a maddened, fear-crazed run, but was unable to escape the burning rope that bound it. Inadvertently, the camel carried the fire to the wooden galleries, turning the arena into a wild flickering inferno. A confusion of shouts and shrieks filled the air.

'Guards, to me!'

'Water!'

'Fire!'

'Assassins!'

'Arson!'

'Out of my way!'

'Help! Help!'

'Protect the King!'

Some commoners had overpowered the Panchalan Guards and wrested their weapons from them. Angry, drunk, weapons in hand, they looked ready for carnage.

'We must leave!' Lord Ketu yelled from below.

Shishupal couldn't have agreed more. They hurried towards the exit nearest the gallery. A pair of servants picked up King Bahlika bodily and carried him out. Shakuni limped, visibly wincing with the effort of hurrying along. Karna was about to lift his nephew onto his shoulders when Shishupal saw him turn and cast a look back at the platform, to where Draupadi stood shrieking while Krishna and the two female guards fended off the assailants trying to climb up. Without the ladder to the King's platform, they were trapped.

Below Draupadi's platform, the Panchalan Guards and the flimsy Ksharjan Circle were doing their best to keep the drunken, crazed mob away. The rising flames cast a murderous glare across the faces of people rushing in where no sane man would have dared to tread. One of the Panchalan guards raised his sword to chop down a man trying to climb up, but caught Lord Markendaya on the backswing, taking off part of his head. Markendaya circled round, squealing like a gutted sheep, hands clapped to his shattered skull, blood streaking down what remained of his face. Seeing this, a Ksharja stabbed his rigid fingers into the guard's eyes till he crumpled in blinded agony. The Ksharja snatched up the fallen man's sword, shrieking in joy as he swung it around him in a drunken frenzy, slashing friend and foe alike.

But the mob on the ground was not the only threat. One of the cages in the air was slowly sliding towards Draupadi, the juggler inside poised to hurl his knives at her. Shishupal saw the look in Karna's eyes, and realized Draupadi was to Karna what Rukmini had been to him. It did not matter if these women had spurned their affections in favour of other men. Love had the strength to walk the boulevard of smoke and flame alone. Taking Karna's arm, Shishupal stared into the fiery amber eyes. 'Go, save her! I will take care of Sudama.'

Karna nodded. He bent down to kiss Sudama's forehead, and then shoved unceremoniously past Shakuni, rushing to rescue Draupadi. Shishupal closed his eyes, whispering a prayer. When he opened them, he found Shakuni staring at him, his hand on Sudama's shoulder for support. He was panting, but a wild glee lit his eyes as he said, 'Now this is what one might call an entertainment to die for.'

KARNA was not about to let Draupadi die. He tracked the knife-juggler and saw the cage inching closer to the platform. There was no way he could reach her in time through the throng of madmen. Without hesitation, he leaped down from the gallery into the pit, where the enormous bow and arrow of the contest lay discarded. Sprinting across, he picked up the bow and arrow in one fluid motion. Sand whispered into his hair as he pulled the bowstring past the eye that glinted in the flames. The arrow whistled past, warping in the air and striking with impeccable precision the wire that held the cage of the juggler. The cage fell on the embroiled crowd of Ksharjas, Namins and Reshts below, by the staircase to the Princess' platform, injuring half of them under its weight. Caught in the cage, with no space to move in that claustrophobic mass, the assassin was soon swallowed by the mob.

But there was no time to spare. Karna climbed the bronze archway, using the embedded gems as handholds, till he reached the stag-heads on top. He crawled to the rim of the wheel attached to the antlers. Standing upright, he jumped towards the door of the cage from where the acrobats had attacked the Aghoris. Hanging on to the edge of the cage with both hands, he used his weight and momentum to slide the cage along the wire that connected it to the wall behind the King's platform. The cage floated over the skirmishing men below, and before it could slide back, Karna flung himself forward and landed on the King's platform. He crawled to the edge of the platform and lay spread-eagled, peering down to the platform below where Draupadi's doe eyes were staring up at him.

'Need help?' he asked.

 DRAUPADI gazed up into Karna's amber eyes, which had turned almost luminous, as if filled with fire. She held out her hand, bloodied from a knife thrown by the juggler. Karna hoisted her up effortlessly, then turned to help the others.

Draupadi saw flames leaping all around the arena. She could hardly breathe from fear, barely move. She shrank down trembling behind her father's throne, clinging to one leg. Could it have been only an hour ago that she had complained about the weight of her lehenga to Satrajit as he had blessed her? Now Satrajit lay dead, and she was probably going to meet the same fate too. Had this all been because of her treatment of Karna? She had not wanted to! It was the smell... the things Krishna had said. If Prakioni would only let her live! She realized she was muttering it like a prayer: 'Let me live... Let me live...' She would right her wrongs if she was allowed to live. She would marry Karna, marry the Aghori, whoever Prakioni wanted. She would wed them all. 'Let me live...'

Suddenly, Draupadi let out a shriek. Her pursuers had placed the ladder against the King's platform, and five of them had climbed up, breathing hard, torches and broken bottles in their clenched fists.

'That's far enough,' growled Karna, his voice deadly calm.

How can he be so calm? she wondered. *How could anyone be calm ever again?*

'You've got something that belongs to us,' the man with a Namin mark of flames on his neck said.

'Give her up, dog!' barked another, the voice so sharp that Draupadi flinched. Their faces looked so deranged they were hardly human. Devils. They were devils.

Karna's fist sank into the Namin's jaw. Draupadi heard the crunch of bones, felt the force of it. Karna grabbed the man's robe and jerked him off his feet. Lifting him like a sack of rags, he flung him at the others so hard that they fell off the platform to the ground below. Storm was quick to throw off the ladder, which fell back into the crowd below. Turning with a smile, Storm stumbled over Satrajit's corpse, but Karna grabbed her before she fell.

'Oh, is that a sword in your sheath or are you really happy to see me?' Storm gave Karna a flirtatious nod.

Calm groaned. 'She meant to say you have our thanks for saving the day!'

 KRISHNA's day was ruined. *Who sends assassins to a wedding?* he fumed. What was worse, he could not see who could possibly profit from such anarchy. Nobody hated the Panchalans. Who would want the Princess dead? And why would they wait till the winner had been announced? Had one of the suitors, arming himself against rejection, hired assassins in case he did not win? Krishna had met and surveyed every suitor invited to the swayamvar. None had presented such a threat. Could it be Bhagadatt, then, who had left before the swayamvar began? Or Duryodhan perhaps? Had he discovered... But that did not explain the crowd turning into a bloodthirsty mob. There was no time to make sense of any of it now. All that mattered was who

survived, and who did not, and he had no mind to join the latter. He coughed. 'If Lord Karna and Lady Storm are done, shall we depart? Draupadi, can you run?'

Without a word, Karna scooped up the shaking Draupadi and began to run, the others at his heels. Krishna shook his head but followed. They rushed towards the door connecting the platforms to the Drachma House. Karna flung open the door and entered the gut of the building. A corridor with doors on either side led to a stairwell. A man in Drachma robes came barrelling along the corridor just as Karna appeared. They stared at each other for a moment, both uncertain what to do.

Storm stepped forward and punched the man in the face. He fell back rigidly, like a statue. 'What are you waiting for?' she demanded, rudely brushing past Karna.

'He could have been one of the Drachma coinmen.'

'Well, he can get medical benefits then,' Krishna said as he closed the door behind them. 'Now where? Someone has jammed the staircase ahead!'

Shouts sounded behind them, jagged laughter and lecherous catcalls. Slapping knocks on the door echoed off the white walls of the corridor. They were out of time. They flung themselves desperately at every door they passed – locked, locked, locked. Finally, one flew open. They rushed in. A hand with a flaming tattoo snaked between the panels, clawing at his hand, just as Krishna tried to close the door shut. Storm slashed at it, severing the Namin's hand at the wrist; the bloody limb slithered back trembling through the gap. Krishna wrestled the door closed and dropped the latch.

He turned to survey the room. It must have been a meeting room, for an enormous oak table stood in the centre, with padded wooden stools around it. Shelves of books, scrolls and red-sealed parchment records lined the room.

'What now?' Storm asked, panting.

Krishna stared at her, eyes wild. 'You reckon I have all the fucking answers? This wasn't supposed to happen!'

Karna put Draupadi, dumbstruck and wild-eyed, on a stool and turned. 'What about the innocents out there?'

'I believe they have a term for such extreme circumstances,' Krishna remarked laconically.

'It's called *every man for himself*,' Calm said as she dragged a chest of drawers to block the door that was already shuddering from blows outside. 'Storm, are you alright?'

'I need a pay raise,' Storm said, clutching at her elbow.

The door shuddered and creaked, as if trying to hold out against a battering ram.

'The door won't hold for long,' Krishna observed. 'I have an idea. Draupadi, we will need to borrow your lehenga.' *Yami knows it is long enough.*

Karna nodded and turned to Draupadi. 'Princess, there is no other way. With your permission...' Draupadi shook a nod out of her shivering body. Karna closed his eyes as he carefully lifted the hem of her lehenga, exposing the rich blue silk, and began to rip the fabric apart from below her knee, creating a long strip of cloth. He knotted the strip of silk into a makeshift rope and secured it to the leg of the mahogany table.

Storm smashed the glass of the sealed casement and, grabbing the free end of the rope, tossed it out. The ground was four floors down and the rope dangled woefully short.

'Will it work?' Draupadi asked, glancing at Krishna.

'Trust me,' Krishna said, a grin on his face.

Storm nodded. 'Yes, trust him. He has enough experience climbing walls using women's clothing. Draupadi, go.'

Karna gave Krishna a level look. 'I don't!' he said shortly. Then he quickly bent and threw Draupadi over his shoulder, as easily as if she had been a child. Climbing onto the window ledge, he grabbed the makeshift rope with one hand. Then he was gone.

'Ugh.' Storm frowned. 'Heroes disgust me.'

KARNA landed on the street to find himself deluged with glares as if he were a villain. He could not blame the crowd that had gathered outside the arena. A Resht landing in their midst with a Princess over his shoulder, through a window, by means of a rope torn from a woman's lehenga, did not send the right message. But Karna had other things to worry about.

'Are you alright?' He put gentle fingertips on Draupadi's cheek as he helped her to her feet. 'You are safe now.'

'I... I am sorry for what I said, Karna.' Tears streamed down Draupadi's face as she struggled to swallow her sobs. She opened her mouth, probably to blurt some excuse. Puke some lie.

He did not need the pity. 'I do not blame you,' Karna said. 'I wouldn't want to wed me either. It's just…' He could not find the words. He sighed, turning his face away from her.

Beyond the immediate throng of people, a horde had gathered around the main exit of the arena, gazing at the black smoke rising from within. The Panchalan Guards were attempting to get in, but the stream of people rushing out was like the waters of a flash flood. The guards, intent on beating their way in, were entirely oblivious of the fact that the Panchalan Princess stood a mere hundred steps behind them. Karna saw no reason to alert them to the fact.

'I did not mean what I said.' Draupadi's voice shook.

'What do you mean?' Karna was confused. Her words had been clear enough.

'Step away from my wife!' a viperous voice warned.

DRAUPADI perked up at the rich, decadent voice that reminded her of desserts. She turned to see the Aghori who had won her hand emerge from the throng. He was smiling, but not deferentially. The ash had been washed off from his face, revealing a clean-shaven jaw and eyes as clear and blue as a river in sunlight. His matted dreadlocks were gone. Now, a thick mop of hair fell to his collar like a black glacier, parted in the middle by a signature streak of silver.

Draupadi gasped. It was him! She had seen him on so many paintings! If there was a handsomer man, she did not know of him. But he was looking beyond her, at the man who had saved her from the mob.

And so Karna, Highmaster of Anga, and Prince Arjun of the House of Kaurava, came face to face outside the burning arena under the noonday sun. Draupadi, caught in a tempest of her own emotions upon seeing Arjun alive, saw the look they exchanged. It was like a clash of steel. She turned from Karna to Arjun, then back to Karna. She shuddered, without knowing why.

 SHISHUPAL knew from the commotion behind the arena that it must involve Draupadi and Karna. He pushed through the small crowd, Sudama in tow. Narrowing his eyes against the harsh sun, Shishupal looked around for Draupadi. Her eyes were swinging back and forth between two men, unnaturally calm, facing each other. One of them was Karna, and though Shishupal had not the least idea who the orange-robed man with the silver-streaked hair was, he could see the man was no Aghori. And then he himself felt the weight of the stares the two warred with. He did not know why but even though it wasn't cold, he shivered.

Back home, the Unni Ehtral priests often chanted that an unseasonal shiver meant only one thing: death was around the corner. Disturbed, Shishupal held Sudama's hand as he pushed to the front of the crowd in silence. Karna and the Aghori still had not taken their eyes from each other. Others around them began to take notice of the exchange as well, and involuntarily stepped back. There was something unnerving in the quality of stillness that possessed these two.

From the corner of his eye, Shishupal saw Krishna climb down a strange-looking rope from a window in the Drachma House. Krishna turned to look at Karna, and then at the Aghori. A look of horror spread over Krishna's face. Clearly, the Usurper knew the history between these two. Shishupal searched for respect, anger, or even admiration in the two faces, but he saw none of these things, though the elements of all were present. Shishupal, a former Head of the Claws, suddenly felt fear; the way he had felt as a child at night, hearing his mother's tales about the valkyries of death.

The Aghori turned to Draupadi. 'Princess, come! I am here as your father desired.'

Karna instinctively closed his fingers round Draupadi's arm as he pulled her gently behind him. 'And what if she does not wish to go?'

Strangely, the Aghori smiled. A condescending smile that could have curdled a man's blood. 'Now that you have touched my wife inappropriately, the Codes allow me to slay you, Resht,' he said softly, taking a bow from an orange-robed giant Aghori behind him. 'About time.'

Despite himself, Shishupal shouted, 'Fighting an unarmed man with a bow? Where is the justice in that?'

'Justice is dead,' the Aghori said coldly, as he tossed the bow and a quiver of arrows at Karna's feet. 'But these were for *him*.'

 SHAKUNI realized bitterly that the only time he thought of injustice was when it happened to him. But it was unjust! The men he had tortured, the plans he had had to revise, the sleepless nights he had endured, all for naught. For it was Arjun who had won Draupadi's hand. If that showdancer and his giant brute of a brother were here, alive, no doubt the other brothers were also prowling nearby. Shakuni had suspected from Anayasa's reports that Pandu's sons had escaped the fire at Varnavrat,

escaping through the long-forgotten tunnel, but he had no inkling that they planned to use the Panchalan swayamvar as their staging arena to announce their resurrection. How in the world had those dimwits planned such an elaborate ruse?

Realization hit him with an iron fist when he saw Krishna exchange an urgent word with Bheem. *Oh, you monster!* Nevertheless, Shakuni's mouth curled down in admiration as he understood how Krishna had used the briars into which Shakuni had thrown the sons of Pandu, to fashion invisible strings around their wrists, to pull on at his will. *You are the grand puppeteer behind this.*

The harsh sun overhead forced Shakuni to shield his eyes. He saw Karna striding towards Arjun, the sun shining on his golden armour and striking sparks from the golden rings in his ears.

'You always draw quite a crowd,' Karna observed.

'If they came for a display of mercy, they will be disappointed.' Arjun's hand darted out like a cobra, nocking and releasing an arrow faster than any eye could follow. Karna moved a leg to the left, leaned his neck only slightly to dodge its flight, before turning in a half-circle and shooting his own arrow. Arjun deflected it with an easy swipe of his bow before sending another arrow Karna's way.

Shakuni hobbled for cover, huddling beside Shishupal and Sudama. *The idiots are duelling with arrows in the middle of a crowd!* But if Shakuni thought the two archers foolhardy, he was nonplussed by the audience. The simple-minded crowd had come to sudden life, as if released from some spell. Tongues uttered pointless advice, spoke prayers and loud encouragement. Next to Shakuni, men shoved and shouted themselves hoarse, some hiding behind carts lest a stray arrow take them. Many climbed into nearby trees and sat like monkeys in the branches, screaming and shaking their fists. These two were about to quench Kampilya's thirst for the blood of heroes, so unfairly denied to the city in the swayamvar.

Shakuni's mind began to devise throws of his dice for when either one of the two died. The sheer gamut of possibilities made him gush like a girl on her wedding night. Karna and Arjun wielded their bows at each other like swords, shooting lethal arrows aimed to maim each other's legs, but careful about range so as not to hurt anyone in the crowd. They ducked, clashed, pushed, shot and even head-butted each other, neither giving a step. The circle around the two flexed with their movements, never still. Despite having no affinity for such drama, the thrill of battle surged in Shakuni's blood. His skin tingled with horror and hope. *Vayu forfend!* Shakuni thought as any notion of scheming was destroyed by this fire of hate between Arjun and Karna. He knew how fierce their enmity was. They could burn the world to ashes with it. And now, Karna had laid a hand on Arjun's prize, and Arjun had shot the first arrow. *And what was staved off years ago in the Tournament of Heroes in Hastina finally comes to a conclusion in Kampilya.* Somewhere within, Shakuni had always known this day would come. Karna was Arjun's destiny, and Arjun was Karna's. They had finally found each other with a justification to kill.

Karna and Arjun had begun fighting in close combat. Karna locked his bow into Arjun's. Arjun twisted, and turned backward, forcing Karna to turn his back as well. Karna bent forward, forcing Arjun to backflip over him. But Arjun twisted his bow in the bow-lock as he landed in front. His bow now faced Karna's chest. Arjun stepped back nimbly, drawing the bowstring and letting loose the arrow. Karna slammed his wrist down in time to deflect it to the ground, unlocking his bow from Arjun's as both men darted away from each other.

Few arrows remained in their quivers. Karna aimed one at Arjun's neck. But Arjun, who had been running towards Karna, dodged it by sliding along the ground on his knees. From his position on the ground, he shot an arrow at Karna, who caught it in his free hand.

Did he just catch an arrow in his fucking fist? gawped Shakuni. It surprised Arjun too, and he took a fraction longer to rise. Wielding Arjun's arrow like a spear, Karna stabbed at Arjun's body as it slid by him, leaving a bloody trail along the side of his bare chest.

Arjun managed to dodge the back jab of Karna's arrow-spear, rolling front to spring to his feet. He had barely flinched from the grazing of the arrow, but he felt incensed. Karna had drawn first blood. Arjun's blue eyes turned wild like an approaching storm. 'You will pay for this, Resht!' Saying which, Arjun sprinted into the distance, emptying his quiver behind him.

'Arjun is nocking three arrows!' someone shouted.

This is too dangerous, Shakuni grimaced, *the space too narrow.*

'Arjun,' Bheem growled in warning.

'What is happening?' Sudama asked. 'I cannot see!'

Shishupal must have remembered Karna carrying his nephew in the Weighing Ceremony, for he lifted Sudama onto his shoulders to watch his uncle duel. 'Your uncle is fighting the Aghori. Can you see now?'

'Yes! Thank you, Sir! C'mon, Uncle!'

'Put him down, Shishupal—' Shakuni began but his words were cut off abruptly. There was a soft whistle of air, and time slowed down. Shakuni saw the tiny details of the arrow shaft, the sharp arrowhead, the warped wood, the shredding of air in its wake as it whizzed towards them. Then Shishupal felt a weight fall off his shoulders as Sudama's body slumped backwards.

When Shakuni felt the boy's blood splatter his face, he shuddered. Sudama's head had not touched the ground. His face still flashed a confused smile as his head hovered a finger's width above the ground, with the shaft lodged in his forehead, the arrowhead propping his skull like a cushion. But as the arrowhead dug deeper into the ground, Sudama's head slid bloodily down the shaft till it came to rest, almost gently, on the ground. The arrow shaft jutted out from the centre of his forehead like a flagpole.

'No!' Shishupal yelled in horror.

KRISHNA whispered hoarsely, 'No...' Arjun's three arrows had missed Karna, but one had claimed his nephew's life. There was no way Krishna could now have Yudhistir announce his campaign for the Hastina Empire here. *Fuck! No matter how well you sow, someone comes along to trample your seeds.* Turning to Storm, he said, 'It's going to turn ugly soon. We should go.' But Storm jerked her chin towards Karna.

Karna had turned strange. His amber pupils had widened and the whites had disappeared, as if his eyes were filled with golden fire. *Yami protect me,* thought Krishna. A vicious smile spread across Karna's mouth as he moved in a dizzy trance towards Sudama's corpse. There was a cold fury about Karna that made everyone back away hastily. Even Arjun frowned and took an involuntary step back.

Krishna knew what happened to Karna when he was beset with rage. He had even planned to exploit it at the Weighing Ceremony. But he could not let Arjun die at Karna's hands. He could not afford to have Karna go berserk here. Not now. He whistled a short-pitched sound, barely audible over the screams and shouts of the people crowding around, but he knew it had been heard.

'Storm, Calm, make your way to the Palace. I will meet you there.'

'Will both of you be safe? He looks... demonic.'

Krishna gulping, looked towards the crumpled form of Karna. 'This is no time to be afraid.'

DRAUPADI was afraid. Krishna stood before her, shielding her from prying eyes. But she could not help but look past his shoulder at Karna. Her beautiful, innocent hero had turned into a stranger. Catatonic. He knelt crumpled beside the boy's lifeless body, cradling the head in his arms, the arrow still lodged in the skull. A crippled man was hunched over beside him, gazing with unseeing eyes, and Shishupal was shedding tears. *I didn't want anyone to die. Is this because of me?* People were shouting all around them. She didn't know whether they were bystanders, rioters or assassins from the swayamvar. She didn't care. *That poor boy.*

Krishna whistled again, louder than before. A shadow rippled overhead. The shouting died. A hundred voices stilled. Every eye turned skyward. A warm wind brushed Draupadi's cheeks as she heard the sound of flapping wings. Many of the onlookers dashed for cover, gabbling prayers. The rest stood frozen, staring up in amazement. Above them, a griffin turned, dark against the sun, his plumage dusty white, his talons sharp as knives. His wings, stretching the length of two grown men, tip to tip, were as brown as the hills before the rains came. Garud flapped his wings as he swept over them, the sound like waves crashing against a rocky shore.

'We must go now!' Krishna's voice was stern.

'But… what about…' Draupadi stood transfixed, looking at Karna's white face. 'He saved me.'

Just then Karna looked up at the sky and unleashed a cry that set the world trembling. His voice was as terrible as thunder, sounding as if two voices were screaming at the same time. Draupadi gasped.

'Just look at him, Draupadi. Karna has lost his mind,' Krishna said. 'We must go! Arjun was always the man you were destined to marry, and I made it happen. You know I have always looked out for you. And now I am telling you it is time to go!'

Meekly, she nodded, allowing him to pull her away. Krishna called to Bheem, who caught hold of Arjun's arm and dragged him away from the scene, pushing him towards the impatient Garud, who was snapping his beak at any who came too close.

'Pity we never found out who was the best,' Arjun said, looking genuinely regretful as he vaulted onto Garud, having apparently forgotten that his arrow had claimed an innocent, or that it behoved him to help Draupadi into the high saddle.

She struggled up with Krishna's help, trying to protect her modesty even as her torn lehenga climbed up her calves to her thighs. There was no way to do this gracefully. She fell onto Garud's back, panting and trembling, pulling herself up to sit behind Arjun. Krishna climbed up behind her.

Some of the spectators, gathering courage, began throwing whatever objects they could find at them. Rocks, sticks, drinking pouches, all flew their way, mostly hitting and falling off the sides of the giant bird.

'Garud, away!' Krishna ordered.

The griffin's wings beat once, twice, and spread wide. The smoking ruins of her swayamvar fell away beneath Draupadi. She could feel the heat of the griffin between her legs. Her heart felt like it would fly simply out of her throat. Dizzy, Draupadi closed her eyes. When she opened them again, she glimpsed Panchal beneath her through a mist of tears, soot and dust. Only a faint glimmer of Karna's golden armour remained visible. She heard Krishna urge Garud higher and clutched Arjun in fear, her fingers scrabbling for a grip.

Forget Karna. This is a new beginning. Leave it all behind. She had got what she wanted, hadn't she? She would start a new life with Arjun. But with everything having gone so wrong, she could not help but pray to Prakioni to ward off the bad omens.

MATI was to be married, and with everything having gone wonderfully well so far, she could not but thank the Ocean Goddess for her good fortune. But all that could wait. She grunted in his ear, her lips curled back into something between a snarl and a smile as she nipped at him with her teeth. He returned the gesture, softly nibbling her neck and arching his way to the lobes of her ears. His hand slid under her right breast, thumb rubbing back and forth over her nipple. He was slightly clumsy, mostly pleasant. Mati's own hand rubbed against his cock, up down, up down, as he pushed her against the wall.

Around them everything was cheap and gaudy. The bed was narrow, obviously not intended for two, suffocating under swags of second-hand silk. The only other piece of furniture was a cabinet beside the bed, on which stood coloured bottles, supposedly liquor, but Mati was taking no chances. The ceiling was crusted with fungus, moulding, and a broken chandelier that hung too low for comfort. Behind the bed was a crude mural of a woman with an unlikely pair of breasts, eating an apple.

'*Ow, ow!*' he yelped as she fumbled with his belt, dragging it open, feeling his pants sag down. 'Easy near the waist. Your men bruised me.'

'Not *hard* enough,' she said as she planted hungry, mouth-crushing kisses on him.

'Rest assured if it gets any harder, I will turn into a stone gargoyle.'

'Then suppose you shut up and fuck me?'

'Aye.' He slid his hand over the knobble of her hip bone as he swung her about so that it was now he whose back was against the wall. They stood heaving beside the open window, ignoring the world outside. He had on nothing but the blindfold that lay limp around his neck.

Mati was naked but for her thigh-high boots. They had been a nuisance to put on in the weather but experience had taught her that, for unfathomable reasons, they always elevated a man's game. Wrapping her legs around him, she lifted her legs, the heels of her boots scraping loose plaster from the wall. She spread her legs wide around him, wedged against the windowsill. She ran her nails through his short-cropped hair, pulling at whatever she could tug hard, forcing him to open his mouth in pain as she pushed her tongue into it. He tasted of morning breath and dried blood, but she probably stank too, she thought. Who gave a shit?

He fumbled with his cock, about to enter her. 'Um, where...'

Mati grimaced. 'You Northerners couldn't find your butt cheeks with both hands. Here!' She quickly spat on her hand, clutched him and guided him in. He grinned in a lopsided way for half his mouth was badly bruised. 'Ah...' Mati moaned, 'that's it.' She drew him close, pressing up against him, sliding her hands along his back, scratching with her long nails. Her mind was blank now.

Nothing about the murders she had commissioned. Nothing of the ale she had spiked. Nothing of her humiliation. Nothing about what she had to do. Just his cock and her cunt.

He made no sound but his eyes did all the moaning. He moved his hips vigorously, easing deep with each thrust. 'Aye...' He ran his fingers down her navel into her short hair, and began rubbing vigorously with his thumb, slowing to match the pace of thumb and cock.

'*Oi!*' Mati screamed. 'Savage! You aren't trying to rub a wine stain from a shirt, fool! I will take care of it.' Saying which, she arched back further, and rubbed herself with her thumb. Her head fell back in ecstasy. They finally found their rhythm: his cock, her cunt, his thumb on her nipple, her thumb between her thighs, their tongues in each other's mouths; all moved in perfect symphony. She kept her eyes open, catching a glimpse of her work unfold outside the window with every thrust. The scenery outside only drove her crazier. The burning of *Fat Mistress* was an ember compared to this. *Ah.* She was close now.

Suddenly, he spun with her so that her arse rested on the windowsill. She slid her left hand onto his buttock, squeezing it as it tensed, slowly moving towards his crack with a bold finger. He jerked back as if she were about to poison him. 'No!' he gasped.

'I wasn't going to do it,' Mati said, laughing. 'Though I assure you you'd like it, you have my word.'

'Not that. What is happening out *there?*'

The fucking scenery, Mati swore silently. Just then, she heard the soft scuffing of feet below, as if someone was trying not to make any sound. Natural selection had established over generations that the Captains who survived longest were those who could distinguish a mutinous First Mate by the sound he tried not to make. In pirate circles there was always someone trying to promote himself by slitting the throat of the Captain.

Mati pushed him off and began to pick up her clothes. She pulled her breeches on over her boots and donned her shirt. Pulling on her gloves, she cast a glance at the mask she had worn last night to the afterfeast. She had been hoping for one last fuck, but what the hell. *My plan worked. Guess that's all the climax I need today.*

'What…' Duryodhan turned to her, 'what is happening?' He stood naked by the window, the window framing him like a tragic painting. An orange hue highlighted his figure, turning to red, then black as the smoke billowed from the burning arena in the distance. Finally, Duryodhan turned to face Mati, his expression that of one who has just realized he has been betrayed. Mati knew that look. She had seen it in her mirror when she had received his raven.

'What have you done, Mati?' he croaked.

'A wedding gift.' Mati smiled. 'You really didn't think we were back together, did you?' She went to stand beside him, her left hand on her hip, the other lying casually on the pommel of her sword. Black strands of hair blew across her scowling face. 'Admiring my handiwork?'

Raising two fingers to her mouth, Mati gave a short sharp whistle. The door opened and a score of men rushed in. There was a loud thud as Duryodhan went down hard on the floor. He groaned, trying to push himself up, blood trickling from his forehead.

The door creaked open again, ever so slowly. Another man, dressed in a scarlet coat with embroidered sleeves and golden cuffs, entered, a sneer on his face. His beard was impeccably trimmed but failed to disguise the second chin. He strode to Duryodhan and swung a boot viciously into his ribs. Duryodhan barely reacted. The man turned away, clicking his tongue. A bigger man came forward and kicked Duryodhan in the ribs, this time making him curl up in a naked ball on the floor.

'I suppose your interrogation is complete, My Princess?' the man in scarlet asked. 'I apologize for breaking in earlier than our agreed time, but I hear some unfortunate developments have taken place at the arena. We should be off now.'

'Aye, love.'

'What did you do?' Duryodhan rasped.

'Sent a few people to make sure the Panchalan Princess and her husband-to-be do not find their way to their wedding night,' the man said. 'They were hired to kill the Panchalan royal family as well. Ah, I only wish I was there to admire my handiwork.'

Duryodhan laughed through bloodied lips. 'Karna was to win Draupadi's hand. There is no way your assassins could hurt him with their bows.'

Mati shrugged. 'If that fire is any indication, I have done a swell job. And who do you think they will suspect? The only Prince who absented himself. The only Prince who is known to have murdered his cousins using fire,' she mocked.

'*We* did a swell job, my beloved.' The richly dressed man took Mati by the waist and tried to kiss her.

'Not so hasty, My Prince...' Mati pulled away, cringing at the storm of perfume that accosted her. He may have been younger than her by years but he repelled her. She realized she preferred the morning taste of Duryodhan, but evicted the thought as quickly as it came. 'It would not be conventional.'

'Of course, of course.' The man backed away as if stung. He looked down at Duryodhan, a sneer on his face. 'I suppose you are confused, Prince? Well, when Princess Mati came to me with a proposal, I simply could not refuse. We are kindred spirits, you see. Rejects of this swayamvar, if you can call it that. So, we joined hands.' He clasped Mati's hand, his palm strangely cold. Grudgingly, she allowed it to linger, knowing how the sight would stab Duryodhan deeper than any spear.

'Panchal falling into any other kingdom's sphere of influence would have disrupted the power balance in Aryavrat. We couldn't have that now, could we? Princess Mati came up with an elegant solution, and I came up with the resources to fund her venture. Assassins dressed as entertainers, spies amidst the royal guards, and not to forget,' he winked at Mati who now stood behind Duryodhan, 'the spiked wine... those were my humble contributions. The wine was a kind donation by the Unni Ehtral. They use it to aggravate horses before sacrificing them. They say the blood is thus purified.'

'You killed innocent people for what, Mati?' Duryodhan asked without turning to look at her. 'I was going to make you my wife.'

Duryodhan's chin was jerked back as steel appeared under his bruised chin – a dagger, polished to an icy shine. Mati's face, jaw clenched, appeared beside his. She leaned closer and murmured in his ear, 'You make me nothing, Duryodhan,' as she twisted the blade until a thin line of blood ran down his neck. 'I am not defined by you. After spurning me publicly, did you think I would crawl back to your bed, swooning with gratitude? Did you think me so pathetically predictable?' She turned him around and spat in his face. 'You planned to make me your *second wife*. And you expected I would leave you in peace?'

'But I rejected the swayamvar. Appointed Karna in my stead. I was never going to participate! You were going to be Queen of Hastinapur.'

'And why would she want a dustbowl when she can have an Empire?' the well-dressed man said from where he stood near the door.

Duryodhan looked uncomprehendingly at Mati through rapidly swelling black eyes.

'When I said wedding gift, I meant for me.' Mati rose and went to stand beside the man, grudgingly landing a soft kiss on his cheek. 'May I present His Highness, Prince Saham Dev, son of His Grace Jarasandh, Heir to the Magadhan Empire – my husband.'

'But... you are *mine*...' Duryodhan snarled as he clambered up, wiping blood from his mouth. 'I am going to marry you,' he promised her. 'I swear it by the blood of Kuru that flows in my veins. Even if it is a decade from now, one day you will be mine. You are my Mati.'

The hilt of her dagger caught Duryodhan above the eye with a hollow ping and knocked him half senseless. She frowned as she stepped forward. Planting her boot on his hand, she ground it under her heel. 'No, I am the Black Swan.' Light from the flames in the distance flickered across Mati's dark face, yellow, orange and red, the colours of fire and vengeance. She touched two fingers to her forehead. '*May the waves carry you.*'

She turned to Saham Dev's men. 'Make sure he is alive when you toss him into the river.'

INTERLUDE

NALA

I

As they trudged up the mountain, beyond which the House of Saptarishis supposedly existed, they passed over and around trees that looked like moss-slung giants, maimed and misshapen, with tentacles for roots, under which little orchids blossomed. Parshuram walked ahead of Nala, climbing the slope against a backdrop of a misty sky, where the Kasmira peaks, whittled out of ice, were briefly visible above the vapour. Mist enveloped her, flowing down the great flanks of the slopes to attack her like some mystical water creatures.

'The tragedy at the swayamvar was lamentable,' Parshuram droned on, still discussing gossip from faraway lands, as he had been doing ever since they had left the hermitage. 'But for the Princess to have married *all* five brothers...' He shook his head in deep dismay. 'It hardly bodes well for the future Queen of the Union to be a harlot. But then again, their mother, Kunti, is no saint. If only you knew the things I did.' Parshuram laughed. 'I definitely see her hand in this.'

Nala was barely listening. She was still trying to desperately come to terms with the fact that Parshuram was employed by the Saptarishis! She thought the kingmakers had long fallen from their pedestals. Meru's teachers knew nothing, then. But could she really begrudge them their ignorance? She herself had spent almost a year with Acharya Parshuram, yet she realized she barely knew anything about him.

They reached the top of the slope they had been climbing, from where they could see the City of Lakes spread below them. But it was what was above them that suddenly changed Nala's mood. Prakioni and Vayu had drawn a rainbow in a perfection of colours in the dreary sky. She adored rainbows. They were fireworks without smoke, order born out of the chaos of rain. Nala smiled.

'I'm glad to see you remember how to smile, lass,' Parshuram said, turning towards the rainbow. 'Which can only mean you have not understood a word I have said.'

'I heard everything you said, Master. Uhm, polyandry isn't unheard of, even among the Namins. Sadharani married all the Maruts,' Nala quickly rallied with an opinion of her own. 'Uhm, Jatila had seven husbands. But times are conservative in this Age—'

'Quiet. There is a difference between hearing and listening.' Parshuram sat down on the wet grass, stretching out his legs. He took the ale skin from the bag he carried, for his second drink of the day. '*Think* and *reflect* upon my words, imbecile.'

Nala scratched her chin as she pondered. Some Panchalan Princess' swayamvar had been a disaster. Many had died. What else did he say? Yes, an Aghori had won the Princess' hand, only he was not an Aghori at all. And that the Princess had ended up not only marrying the not-an-Aghori, but also his four brothers. There was something about a promiscuous woman being Queen of the Union— Nala's eyes widened. *By the Dead! The Hastina Union. Five brothers.* She turned sharply to Parshuram, realization spreading frigid fingers through her veins. Bheem and his brothers had finally resurfaced!

'Master!' Nala could barely contain the urgency in her soul. 'When do we leave for Panchal?'

'Took you long enough,' grunted Parshuram. 'They have already left for Mathura, from what I hear. And we will leave when you are ready. Bitter patience yields the sweetest fruits. Now, sit and watch me drink, in silence. You do not want to go meeting the Saptarishis sober.'

'Master, then should I…?' She nodded towards the ale.

'Shut up, Nala.'

Nala turned back to the rainbow, gritting her teeth, having forgotten all the beauty nature had spread before her eyes. But for all her thirst for revenge, she had to admit she wasn't ready yet. No matter. Days, weeks, or even years did not matter. What did was that she would sit on Bheem's helpless body as she slowly carved his throat. After she slew his family, of course. His four brothers, his mother, and now, his whore of a wife.

The mass of mist slowly dissolved in the valley beyond the mountain. And there, rimmed by the teeth of white peaks, stood a great grey structure, shimmering with an eerie bluish light. To a bird flying above, it doubtless resembled a glowing orb in the open mouth of a white bear. But Nala knew what it was.

The House of Saptarishis.

II

The House of Saptarishis appeared to be a monstrous hallucination – a swirl of warped metallic forms that glinted like fish scales, giving it a strange, otherworldly presence. The House was surrounded by an artificial water body, lending to the structure the appearance of a misshapen silver griffin that had crawled out of a lake to rest on land.

At the end of the walkway stood guards in silver chainmail. Their eyes nervously darted around the man Nala followed. Truth be told, Acharya Parshuram was nothing to look at. Somewhat unusual, considering he was a Namin carrying a weapon, but

Nala had often seen travelling mendicants and ascetics carrying a blade or two while crossing treacherous routes through the forests. Some of the godless goons who lived there did not share the same reverence for their sanctity as cityfolk did. But Parshuram might have had three serpent heads for the way the armed guards shrank back from him.

'Acharya Parshuram,' the leader of the guards murmured.

Spears rattled to the ground as they all bent the knee. *Acharya Parshuram…* the name travelled through the ranks of guards in waves. Nala saw terror in their eyes. Parshuram, in a drunken haze, seemed not to see or hear. He continued walking. The guards scattered before him as if he might kill them all on a whim.

Nala saw her Master anew from the perspective of others. Dangerous, confident, fearless and powerful. A God. Or better, a Demon. But if the guards had run helter-skelter in the face of Parshuram, the soldiers by the door stood unfazed.

Standing motionless on either side of the main door were the Iron Order, the Seven Guards of the Saptarishi, visored and in full glittering armour. Parshuram had told her of them last night. They were said to be the finest swords in all the realm. They took no spouses, had no children, and lived only to serve the Saptarishis.

'Acharya Balthazar,' Parshuram said in muted acknowledgement, removing his battleaxe, twin daggers, the darts strapped to his rosaries, and a number of vials from his jute sack.

Acharya Balthazar said nothing but began patting down Parshuram rather vigorously. A female guard of the Iron Order did the same to Nala.

'Is this really necessary? You know that if I wanted to kill anyone in there, I could do it with or without weapons.'

Balthazar flushed. 'Why don't you shove…'

'What Acharya Balthazar means is…' another soldier, presumably the Chief of the Iron Order, hastily pitched in, 'why don't you pretend not to be a danger to us, and we'll pretend that we were the reason.'

'What about the whelp?' Balthazar asked. 'An ugly little thing. What are these white streaks on your face?'

'It is *kilas!*' Nala said, incensed. She had been teased all her life because of the vitiligo that spread on her face like streets on a map, but the way Balthazar said it made her feel like a filthy thing.

'She is my apprentice,' said Parshuram.

Everyone's attention swung sharply to Nala. Balthazar approached and raised her chin.

'You haven't taken one since...'

'Failknot, yes.'

'Quite an end for that one,' Balthazar said with a sneer. 'Really tragic what you did to him. But then, he knew what he was getting into.'

'May we proceed?' Parshuram asked wearily.

'Yes, of course,' the other man said. 'Right through the tunnel. You know the way. Your apprentice isn't allowed, of course.'

'She comes with me.'

The Chief let out a sigh. 'Acharya, I don't wish to make a fuss about this but I am the Guardsman of the Saptarishis, yet even I have not seen their faces for two summers. Kindly bear with me.'

'Let them come.' A loud sonorous voice reverberated through the space behind the Iron Order.

Balthazar smiled but it did not reach his eyes. He moved aside to let them pass.

III

Inside, a colossal set of white pillars ascended more than two storeys to a vaulted ceiling, where torches blazed pure white light. A criss-cross of walkways and balconies traversed the space above them, dotted with orange-clad figures who looked down ominously upon the pair walking across the hall.

In the middle of the vaulted chamber, more than fifty sheep were sculpted in wood, sprinting in a long line across the central space. The sheep in front were in different stages of leaping high in the air, sculpted to give the appearance that they were colliding violently with a glass wall that was beautifully designed to look as if it was in the moment of shattering. The glass itself shimmered in a blue haze, as if from the inside. As Nala crossed the shattering wall, she gasped at the high pile of sculpted sheep heads on the other side of the glass.

Parshuram gave a dry chuckle. 'I can see why it would impress you. Art of the Daevas. I believe the sheep were meant to represent us, humans, symbolizing our lack of courage in diverging from the norm, even when running towards our own oblivion.'

Nala shuddered. She could never have guessed that was what the sculpture meant. She kept her eyes to herself as they were ushered through a door and down a long narrow stairway, curving downwards. Hand on wall, she began to descend gingerly. The steps curled on, winding ever deeper.

'Do you think I'm dangerous?' Parshuram asked.

The question brought Nala back. Was it a trick question? If the man singularly infamous for the annihilation of Ksharjas wasn't dangerous, then who was? 'Uhm, Master…' she mumbled, then remembered what the Acharya had told her about lying. 'Yes, extremely.'

'The Saptarishis are far more dangerous than I,' Parshuram said. 'So, head low and shoulder slouched.' Just then the stairs ended abruptly and they found themselves in a large open space. 'We are here.'

Nala stepped into the Saptarishis' Council Chamber without once raising her eyes. The hall was in a cave, yet it was white, like she had walked into the mouth of the moon. Half the furniture seemed made of ice. The floor was uneven, rocky white, the ceiling crystalline white. It disappeared into a white sky, which seemed impossible considering they were underground. Yet, despite all the whiteness, Nala sensed a darkness in the room. One thing was clear: if the place was designed to inspire fear, it did a bloody good job.

Seven chairs were placed in a semi-circle on a raised platform. The Saptarishis sat on the chairs, sombre in their white robes, silent behind their carved, aspected masks. At Meru, Nala had been taught that each New God represented one aspect of the

One God. The Saptarishis considered themselves the vehicles, the prophets, through whom the Gods gave guidance. So they were aspected as *vahanas* of each God, represented by an animal. Though varied, the masks were singularly horrific. The Saptarishis' true expressions lay hidden behind the caricatured, unmalleable expressions of the fearsome masks: Fish, Tortoise, Boar, Lion, Dwarf, Peacock and Human.

This is straight out of Caani's horror stories. Nala had the nagging feeling she had entered the interrogation chamber of hell. The fact that the white walls, and even the chairs, were carved with reliefs of manticores, drakons and screaming people, did little to calm her mind. A cold sweat ran down her back as she saw glittering eyes peering at her from behind the frozen masks. Even worse was the shadowcat, a black beast with golden stripes, who sat baring its teeth beside Sapth Human's chair. Its eyes were pinpoints of gold set in black, and there was something wrong with its distended and oddly long claws.

One of the ancient priests, Sapth Fish, spoke in a drone through the snout of his fish mask, 'Is the list done, Acharya?'

There was a moment of silence, then Parshuram said, 'Three names more. Why have I been asked to come?'

Sapth Lion laughed without mirth. 'You have been summoned, not asked.'

Strangely, the second voice sounded exactly like the first to Nala's ear.

'Just another mystery of our language,' a calmer voice, although identical again, called out. It was Sapth Boar who spoke. 'But why the delay, Acharya?'

'Ran out of coin.'

A laugh. 'You would have us believe the richest man in the realm ran out of coin?' Sapth Dwarf asked.

Richest? Nala cast a sideways glance at the old tigerskins her Master wore, and seriously doubted if the Saptarishis meant 'richest' in the conventional sense.

'No matter,' Sapth Boar said. 'I am confident the Acharya will see to it that the list is completed with alacrity. He knows a moment's delay, and the future takes an inevitable turn.' He coughed delicately behind his mask. 'But the reason your presence was requested today is because one of our Oracles has divined the coming of the Son of Darkness.'

Nala heard her Master's breath hiss sharply from between parted lips. Parshuram was suddenly sober. His eyes sparked fire. 'I thought you had not told the Matrons of the prophecy about the Son of Darkness.'

'We hadn't. A promising Oracle, alas lost to the tyranny of mortality, divined him in his test. The Son is prophesized to rise when the snow thaws this year.'

'End of winter,' Parshuram said gravely. 'Barely three full moons away.'

'The moment of reckoning is upon us, you see. A bright girl in the House of Oracles unravelled the answer. Come forward, child,' called Sapth Boar.

A girl, clad in gold-trimmed white robes, stepped out of the mist. Nala gasped. The girl was about Nala's own age but her face was covered with scars. She had soft eyes under a bald head. She resembled an egg that had fallen on the ground but refused to burst. Nala's own stitches were nothing compared to the map of abuse on the girl's face. Yet she smiled serenely. 'I am honoured to meet you, Nala. My name is Masha.'

Nala looked at Parshuram, confused. How did the girl know her name? Who was she?

'She will accompany you, Parshuram.'

'I don't travel with drug addicts,' said Parshuram, 'least of all, damaged drug addicts.'

'Don't diss the Sisters,' Sapth Lion warned. 'They have helped us steer the great civilization for millennia and will continue to do so for millennia to come.'

'This girl is a Sister? That's great,' said Parshuram dryly. 'But my tasks require discretion and stealth. I can't walk around with a girl who wears an ornament of scars on her face. And what will she even do there?'

'Sister Masha is quite possibly the Oracle connected to the divinations related to the Son. So, we have the *when*, and now you have to find the *where*, and the *who*. Which you can only find in the City of Manusruti. The Sister's days of oraclry are behind her, but we think Manusruti may awaken her powers and help you find him. Do not worry about her marks of sacrifice. We will take care of it.'

'And what then? You want me to defeat the Son?'

'Regrettably,' Sapth Board sighed, 'even with your strength, you will be no match for him, Acharya Parshuram. We must stop him *before* he is released.'

'That would certainly be less complicated,' Parshuram agreed. 'But I will need some advance...' Parshuram's eye glanced towards Nala 'for cosmetic purposes.'

Sapth Lion's mask turned in Nala's direction. 'Still finding a nest for broken souls, Parshuram?'

'If not breaking them himself,' Sapth Human added. The eyes behind his mask stared Nala straight in the eye.

'Did your Master give you the scars on your face, and maim your wrist?' Sapth Lion asked. 'Poor sod. But it's nothing compared to what he is truly capable of. Has your Master told you what he did to his last student?'

Nala said not a word, but kept looking at her feet.

'Did your Master cut out your tongue, girl? What are you staring at?' The shadowcat beside Sapth Human stared at Nala as though Nala was a pigeon waiting to be chewed. Sapth Human casually stroked its head. 'If she plants her teeth on your neck, you will be dead in a heartbeat.'

Nala remembered Parshuram's warning about the Saptarishis being even more dangerous than he. She remembered how she was to slouch, her knees ever ready to scrape the floor. And to always mind her manners. The best thing was doubtless to bend the knee and whimper. She didn't know whether it was the news of Bheem or the way these men talked to Parshuram, but a sudden madness possessed her. With cold disdain, she uttered a single word in response: '*If.*'

IV

Sapth Human stared coldly at Nala, nonplussed. The shadowcat growled, straightened itself, its tail snapping like a salute. There were audible gasps, hissing like a tea kettle, from between gritted teeth behind masks. Masha almost giggled. Parshuram himself turned to stare at Nala, a bemused look on his face.

Did that really come out of me? Who was unhinged enough to insult a goddamn Saptarishi? She could imagine Akopa fainting and Varcin falling to the ground, laughing, at this tale. Presuming the wretched shadowcat left her alive to return with one.

Sapth Human finally spoke. 'My pet does not appreciate your tone, girl.'

'As my Acharya's pet, I share a similar sentiment about your tone with my Master.' *I certainly know how to pick my moments to be brave.* But now that it was done, there was nothing to do but own it. And thus, the two pets, one of the Bane of Ksharjas, and one of a Saptarishi, glared at each other.

Later, Nala would always be grateful to Sapth Boar. He hooted as if it was the funniest thing he had ever heard, but there was no laughter in his eyes when he turned them on Parshuram. 'The girl has mettle, Parshuram. A fiery streak. Hone it well.'

'Yes, yes,' Sapth Horse said huffily. 'Let's get on with it. We are the Saptarishis, and it would be nice if we behaved like it for a change. Parshuram, we will have Balthazar deliver a goblet to you by tomorrow, along with Sister Masha.'

Parshuram grunted in acquiescence, looking at Nala from the corner of his eye. She was sure she would be murdered by him the moment they left the House. The Saptarishis rose from their seats but the shadowcat never took its eyes from Nala. *Until next time, pussycat,* Nala wanted to say, but the sudden flush of recklessness had faded in her. Masha raised her hand as if to wave in farewell.

'And Parshuram, be gentle with this one. The Blood within her is strong,' said Sapth Lion.

In an instant the Saptarishis were gone, as if they had never been there. Parshuram turned to leave.

'Did they mean me?' Nala whispered as they walked out. 'What do they mean by my Blood is strong?'

'I think you've spoken enough for a lifetime,' Parshuram hissed, but Nala saw the faintest trace of a smile on his face.

V

'I can find you a job in Kasmira, Nala.'

Nala's shoulders slumped. 'But I did everything you asked.'

Their return journey from the House of Saptarishis had been marked by silence. No words. No grunts. Nothing. As they neared the town, Nala had expected reprimand, but not rejection.

'You can't...' Nala's voice sounded defeated. 'I cooked, I foraged, I spoke, I did everything you asked. I'm sorry, alright! I know I shouldn't have spoken that way.'

Parshuram was silent as they entered the town, taking a zig-zag through the throng of people going about their daily business. Once past the main market, he said, 'No, Nala, the Saptarishis are right. I have destroyed the lives of my students before. I had decided never to take another student, but...' He stopped short as a beggar girl clutched at his hand, asking for food. Rudely, Parshuram snatched his hand away and continued to walk on. Nala quickly dropped a coin in the girl's hand and hurried after him.

'You may have noticed that for the last year or so I have been teaching you everything except how to kill. Pretty odd for an assassin's apprentice, right?'

Really? I hadn't noticed, Nala thought sardonically.

'I had hoped that somehow the labours would dissuade you from your path. That it would prove daunting, and you would turn away. But you did not. Time for basic training is done. We are on the precipice of a new beginning, Nala, a new journey. This is real life, and real stakes. Time for foolishness is behind us.'

'The Son of Darkness?'

Parshuram nodded, handing her a scroll. She blew off the dust. A corner flaked off between her fingers as she unrolled it. 'Careful, you animal. It is ancient!'

She mumbled apologies, and read out loud the faded script: '*The black sun will rise behind a mountain of mortar, through the timeless void, to poison the heaven. Amidst plague and plight, with a forgotten dance, he will break open the seal of the seven.*' Nala looked up. 'A catchy tune, Master.'

Parshuram gave her a clout on the ear but smiled. 'Yes, Manu was rather colourful with his words. This isn't the complete prophecy. I will have to find the complete one in Manusruti. Know this, the coming of the Son of Darkness is the single most calamitous thing that could happen to the realm. He is the Evil that was Promised. The one prophesized a millennium ago, to dig open the evils our ancient heroes buried in the past. If he is released, he will make the stars bleed, the world kneel, and children everywhere will weep tears of blood as Aryavrat is pushed into the Age of Darkness.

'The Saptarishis may be fools but they are right. I'll not sit meekly by and wait for the world to end. I will ride to Manusruti, against the Vanaras, the Nagas and whatever else is out there in the buried city. And I will find the prophecy and kill the Son of Darkness, with or without your help. So, I'll ask you only once, Nala: are you really willing to risk your life for a world that will never know of it, or are you a girl who wants to play at vengeance?'

Nala did not know what to say. She had never heard Parshuram wax eloquent about anything. A shiver crept up her spine.

'You have done everything I asked,' Parshuram's voice softened a little, 'in the manner I asked. But be warned, this is not a life you will want. For a bag of silver, I can still apprentice you to an alchemist. I can sign you up with the royal cook and you will be called to feasts and ceremonies across the realm. You can live a peaceful, quiet life earning the ire of your neighbours. But if you come with me, you will trade everything you once valued. Once you take that step, you'll never be moral again, never be good again. You'll never love again. You'll never meet your friends again. You will earn the ire of the Gods themselves.'

'Why are you telling me this?'

'Because I did not warn my last student, and destroyed him in the process.'

'What about Bheem?'

'You're fourteen, fifteen years old? You really think you can take him on?'

'No.'

'I told you I would help you in your plan for revenge, but if you come with me, you will never follow Bheem again till I decide you are ready. Listen to me carefully, Nala. I am giving you an out from your Vachan. Take my offer. If you are intent on revenge, go be a cook in Hastina. You know enough to poison his food. In time, you will rise through the ranks of chefs and get what you seek. Take it. This might be your chance at happiness. The journey ahead with me is fraught with nothing but pain.'

Nala wondered for a moment whether she wanted happiness. The word had long lost its meaning. There had been some moments she had enjoyed with her mother and brothers, when she had been with the others in Meru, but her old life had been burned down by Bheem. No. The pages of memory only served as edges to cut her. And poison, that did not feel personal enough. Not to forget there was no guarantee that poisons worked on giants. No, she needed Bheem to know it was her. She had to slit his throat. There was no other way.

She was maimed and ruined. There lay no respectable future ahead of her even if Parshuram did as he promised. And what exactly would she be leaving behind? A few paltry friends who would go on to become Acharyas of Kings and Lords, and soon forget the girl they had shared a bunk with, without knowing her secret? It really wasn't much of a choice.

'I will come with you, Master.'

'Don't decide now. It is easy to decide to choose the night when you are in darkness. I have a gift for you, Nala, before I leave for my quest.'

VI

Hours later, he took her to the main town in Kasmira, which was bustling with people and commerce as far as she could see; granaries and brick houses, timbered inns, cremation grounds, taverns, stalls and brothels, all piled on one another, jostling for space and coin. The alleys were so narrow Nala and Parshuram could not walk abreast.

'Head into that tavern,' Parshuram instructed as they reached a crookback street. 'I will meet you at the hermitage in an hour, and I hope not to.'

And that was when Nala saw a group of young men, for they no longer looked like boys, approaching the tavern. As if in a trance, Nala followed them inside. A serving wench walked past her with an earthen carafe of sour-smelling wine to the table where Varcin, Upavi, Varayu, Akopa and the other boys from her Meru class sat. They were all drunk, laughing and jostling each other. *The third-year trip*, she remembered. The third years were permitted to go on a paid trip to any city in the Mai Layas. How Nala and Varcin had planned for this trip! The firelight fell on them, dazzling her eyes with their happiness.

Tears filled Nala's eyes as she took a table in a gloomy corner within earshot of the other table. She heard their complaints about Irum, their questions about which kingdoms they were destined to go to as apprentices, their amazement at the new comet streaking across the sky. And she heard them wonder where Nala was.

They remember me, Nala realized as she heard each of their wild theories about her whereabouts. Strangely, in each of their imaginings, Nala was safe and happy.

Through her tears she saw one of the boys rise to mimic an Acharya. It was Varcin. She saw him glance at her, his teeth white against his dark skin. Their eyes met. For a moment Varcin's eyes widened, and his mouth dropped. He almost half-stumbled in her direction. Swiftly, she turned her face away. Varcin stopped when his eyes fell on her long hair, her battered face and withered hand.

He looked away, confused. Shaking his head in sad disbelief, he went back to his friends.

Go! she told herself. *Go and tell them who you are!* But she could only watch silently, the firelight dancing in her dark eyes, as the wench brought goblets with flaming tops to their table. 'Drink up, lads!' The boys grabbed the goblets and, in one go, consumed the fire-laden drink. They screamed, hissed and laughed in inebriated joy. The world beckoned them with its tantalizing charm.

Theirs was a perfect world from which Nala had been evicted. She had no place amongst them. She brushed away unshed tears with the back of her hand. She turned away from Varcin, the boy she had probably loved, and the others, friends she had cherished, and left the tavern to follow the path to Parshuram's hermitage, into the enfolding comfort of the shadows.

ADHYAYA IV

A FIGHTING CHANCE

All hope abandon, ye who enter here.
—Dante, *The Divine Comedy*

SHISHUPAL

I

Shishupal looked down at his bare feet, callused and cracked, then at his ragged clothes, the dirt under his nails, his scratched hands, and the scars on his elbows, wondering how he had ever got to this state. Dantavakra wouldn't have recognized him. He looked at the letters in his hand. Two copies, the words exactly alike. The last missive had borne no good tidings either. He climbed down, disappointed, from the roof to the murky alley, and squeezed his boots back on.

He heard chatter in Vadeh of how the Mathurans did not care about the impending battle at the end of the Armistice, as if they had some sinister trick up their sleeve. What trick? No one knew. Worse, *he* did not know, despite working shifts as a stablehand, a woodcutter, and once, even a man of letters. It was not that he did not learn any secrets at all. While he could not sneak inside Mathura, he did hear all manner of inconsequential news coming out of it. The wife of Lord Hiriam was with child but the real father was either Satyaki, or the lawscribe Atuyla Chand. Lady Asmai made mock of superstitions at the table but had all the black cats of the town slain. The cooks despised Lord Balram when he came to the village to sup and would spit in his food. Once he even overheard a serving boy confide to a girl that he saw Prince Yudhistir in Mathura.

Mostly, he heard gossip about the damn swayamvar. All the world seemed to care about was how Krishna had managed to wed the Panchalan Princess to *all* the five sons of Kunti. It was the scandal of the century.

And again, wispy as a blown cloud across the moon, the face of the boy he had undertaken to protect, drifted into his mind. Shishupal shook his head violently to purge the flashes, desperately clutching for another train of thought. *Krishna... Draupadi... anyone else but Sudama.* It worked.

Loath as Shishupal was to admit it, Krishna's machinations made sense. If Arjun was to sire a son with Draupadi, before Yudhistir, it would sow the seeds of a succession dispute yet again. Five brothers, five wives. It was a recipe for disaster. Anyone could then pull that thread to sow discord between the brothers. And with Yudhistir clamouring for the throne, he could not afford Panchal's allegiance lying with his younger brother, rather than with him. Somewhere within, Shishupal felt sad for Draupadi; a pawn in the hand of forces beyond her control. Did she deserve it for the way she had treated Karna? Perhaps. Who was he to judge anyone? Then there was Arjun to consider, who suddenly found his new wife a common property to be shared with his brothers. He did not even have first rights over her. Shishupal did not know whether he had consented to this arrangement, but it did not require an Oracle to guess he was not happy about it. He had no doubt, however, about who the real victim of the debacle was. The face of Karna, comatose, eyes livid with rage, beside his nephew's corpse, made his head hurt again. *The Saptarishis should just ban swayamvars, and the world would be the better for it.*

Calling it a day, Shishupal strolled back towards the inn where he had rented a room. Vadeh was a river port, and it smelled of rot, shit and piss. It was far enough from Mathura to escape Jarasandh's attention, but close enough to trade with once the war clouds receded. But for all the trading the port did, its people got no richer. Filled with refugees from the years of war, the line of beggars at the temples was cruelly long. Not that he could see them. It was winter, and the lantern in his hand scarcely lit a dozen cobbles in front of his boots, slippery in the damp mist. *Xath fend, how I hate the North!*

Shishupal had never liked ports, rivers or fogs, and the three together were like a nightmare come true. Fog was known to be a spy's friend, shielding him from the eyes of men. No one had ever told him that it shielded the world from the spy as well. Men and women emerged from the mist like ghosts, and giants turned out to be buildings. Twice, he lost his footing and landed ankle-deep in puddles of icy water.

Suddenly, instinct made him dash into the shadows of a tavern's back door. He had suspected for a while that he was being stalked, but actually holding the culprit in his hands had a way of reaffirming it. The stalker struggled for a brief moment in Shishupal's grip, then began to laugh.

'You!' Shishupal thrust the boy against the tavern wall.

"Tis true, Eklavvya is the Princess Draupadi, cleverly disguised. Save me from my husbands, Sire!'

'Arggh…' Shishupal squeezed tighter. 'You think spying on your colleague is the finest of ideas?'

'Spying on a spy, you mean. Such a novel notion. Eklavvya was merely walking behind you, attempting to catch up, for despite his many gifts, long strides were cruelly left out by the Spirits to make him appear more human to ageing eyes. Shishupal looked bored. Eklavvya thought to spice things up.'

'I still do not understand why you wasted your Contest boon to come on this cursed punishment with me.'

'Friend, one man's punishment is another man's pleasure,' Eklavvya said, pulling at one of the fetishes with which his braids were amply supplied.

'I still don't understand how I ever agreed to come on this cursed mission,' Shishupal grumbled.

'Requesting exile as self-punishment for what happened in Panchal may have been a noble sentiment, but asking it of the Emperor who lost out on Panchal support due to Krishna's schemes may not have been a wise idea.'

Shishupal nodded glumly.

'Also, asking it of an Emperor who was livid with his son for marrying without his consent, murdering innocents, and causing a riot in Panchal, was perhaps not wise either.'

Shishupal sighed.

'Asking *anything* from the Emperor was perhaps the worst idea of all...'

'Yes, yes, I get it! It was a rhetorical question. Come to think of it, I got away easy. I have no fondness for the Prince, but he should not have been slapped by the Emperor in public. It was not... kingly.'

'Aye, but then Eklavvya used to be hung upside down from a tree and whipped on a daily basis. It gets the blood running, you know.'

Shishupal shook his head, his thoughts drifting once again to the Panchalan swayamvar. *My own wedding pales into insignificance before this one.* Yudhistir, Arjun, all of them... mysteriously back from the dead, along with their mother. Duryodhan's battered body found by some fishermen in Kampilya, washed ashore. *The House of Kauravas has too much drama for my taste.*

'Did Shishupal see the pamphlets?' Eklavvya asked. 'Duryodhan is leading the charge in Hastina to try Arjun for murder.' Shishupal nodded, uncomfortably. Eklavvya scratched his chin. 'Don't know why he bothers. The wine is spilled, the wench is pregnant, the piss out of the cock, no point in digging up the grave for bones. No one cares about the murder of a Resht boy. But the woes of our troubled realm shall keep.

Eklavvya is tired and hungry.'

'Did you find out where the Mathurans have been travelling to?' Shishupal asked, changing the topic. 'It sounds highly unlikely that the entire city is on holy trips at the same time, but I cannot sniff the trail. All my leads have run cold.'

Eklavvya shrugged, massaging his stomach.

Shishupal sighed. 'Fine, let's go and eat. We'll find nothing here anyway. Clearly, I am no spy. When I asked to be sent away, I did not mean as a sleuth!' *And certainly not with you!* 'I am tired of tracking Mathurans to dead ends.'

If the Mathurans were trying to hide their trail, they might as well have been using magic, for they were everywhere, and then they weren't anywhere. Mathura was somehow still surviving, even thriving, on the limited resources allowed during the Armistice. The Emperor had declared it imperative that Shishupal discover what Mathura was up to. How could he do what the most veteran spies could not? Shishupal had thought that when Eklavvya joined him, things would move faster, but the boy's verbosity only aggravated his headache. But he knew he could not leave; not before finding the source of the stink emanating from Mathura.

'Eklavvya sympathizes with Shishupal's pathosis,' the Valka babbled as he strolled onto the street again.

'Why are we not heading to the tavern? I thought you were hungry?'

Eklavvya did not answer. *Fuck.* Shishupal followed him into the foggy street. Ghostly laughter fluttered past them from the tavern left behind. Lambs bobbed through the gloom as Shishupal struggled to keep Eklavvya in sight. Folks reeled past in a flurry, mist swirling behind their flapping cloaks. It made Shishupal edgy; his hand remained on the knife hilt inside the left pocket of his jacket. The thought that Karna would appear out of nowhere to punish him for what he did made Shishupal's head throb. Felt like it had hurt for weeks. Since Panchal.

Eklavvya stopped so abruptly Shishupal nearly bumped into him. Eklavvya squinted at a door in the mist-enshrouded wall of crumbling brickwork, then rapped on it. It wobbled open. A woman stared out, long and lean as a giraffe. She held a knife in one hand, a mallet in the other. Standing recklessly, hip loose, hair to one side; green eyes in a sharp face spattered with freckles stared at the two men.

'What did you mean by hunger, Eklavvya?' Shishupal asked, incensed. 'We do not have the time for pleasure.'

Eklavvya shook his head as if Shishupal were a pervert. 'Hunger for answers, Shishupal. Hello, Anayasa,' he said by way of greeting.

'About time you showed up. You know you could just pay me and I could finish the war with one swipe of my knife. Krishna's head will be yours.'

'Why, thank you for your kind offer, overestimation of your abilities though it may be, but our Emperor seems to harbour some notions of honour.'

'Childish nonsense.'

'Couldn't agree more.'

Shishupal grabbed Eklavvya's elbow and whispered in his ear, 'Who is she? Why does she know who we are?'

'Our tour guide. Of a sort,' Eklavvya added. 'Eklavvya got her reference from a friend. She will point us to the goat trail that will help us get to our destination swiftly; where we will find our man, Gajraj.'

'Where? Who? What are you talking about?'

'Shishupal was right. We will not find anything here. So, we're taking a trip into the lion's den, or rather to the cowshed…'

'Where?' snarled Shishupal, losing patience.

'Why… to Mathura, of course.'

DRAUPADI

I

'Make way!' a Mathuran guard shouted as he rode before the litter. 'Make way for the Princess of Hastinapur!'

She peered out of the palanquin at the column of mounted guards trotting beside her in a cloud of red dust. The Mathuran sigil of the cow stood out clearly on their blue cloaks, worn over embroidered tunics of linen. One of them glanced sharply at her, requesting her to stay shielded behind the curtains of the palanquin. Groaning in mild frustration, Draupadi fell back against the cushions.

Mathura was a strange city, Draupadi reflected. It was not as populous as she had thought it would be, for all the rumours of bustling trade she had heard. Even so, Mathura's physicality, personality and psyche were singularly unique in the Riverlands. Despite its tiny size, one felt safe inside it. To say the city was walled was an understatement. Concentric rings of city walls, called the Three Sisters, encircled Mathura, dividing it into three main districts. In her education of the place by Yudhistir, who liked to talk of cities and governance, she had come to learn more about Mathura than she knew of Kampilya. The First District that lay inside the First Sister, or Iron Curfew, had the Mathuran Keep, the Senate House, and houses of Senators and their staff. The Second District lay between the Iron Curfew and the Second Sister, and had places of commerce, the houses of the nobility, wealthy merchants, and landowners, as well as gambling houses and the like. The Third District lay next to the City Wall, or the Third Sister, where the poor lived.

This was the first time she had stepped beyond the Iron Curfew without one of her consorts or good-mother Kunti, and it had all been thanks to the request for an audience by Lady Satyabhama. Draupadi had been surprised to receive her message, for ever since her arrival, Lady Satyabhama had looked daggers at her. Nevertheless, Draupadi was still excited.

Heading out had been difficult. In the house they had been graciously gifted by Krishna in the First District, everything was noise and confusion. Horses were being saddled and led from the stables, wagons were being loaded, and everyone was in an uproar to be off to Hastinapur for Arjun's trial. Arjun himself was to travel with Yudhistir and Sahadev on the griffin Krishna had lent them. Bheem, Kunti, the Twins and Draupadi were to travel by road, with a mighty escort. Leaving in the midst of all the preparations felt irresponsible, but a Princess must always uphold the courtesies, and Draupadi resolved to behave like one, present circumstances notwithstanding.

The Iron Curfew looked daunting as her carriage crossed it. Yudhistir had told her that it was built of stone, thick enough to withstand the most withering fire and munition attack. A moat encircled the Curfew like a snug necklace. It would have looked beautiful had it not been for the clouds of dust rising from the work going on in the underground tunnels inside the First District. Draupadi had been forced to veil her face even inside the palanquin as she had crossed the digging sites, the tunnel dust stinging her eyes worse than sand.

She stretched out her legs on the soft padding of the palanquin. The Merchant Street in the Second District was less likely to offer a bumpy ride, tempting her to lie down, but she could not forget the etiquette demanded of her. Consort to a Rebel Prince, after all. *Princes*, she corrected herself.

Draupadi swiped a treacherous tear as she closed her eyes, overwhelmed at the thought. Thoughts that should have been long forgotten carried her back to the silent screams of the day Arjun had brought her to her new home. Sometimes, certain episodes lie so far outside the boundaries of the imagination that when they occur, one does not even realize they are taking place. So, one does nothing to prevent them. And by the time they have occurred, one is forced to make room for a new, restructured reality. A reality where there is little distinction between a princess and a prostitute, a wife and a thrall. Perhaps that was why she had not protested, or even run away, when Kunti had declared that it would be proper for Draupadi to wed the eldest brother, Yudhistir, and not Arjun. She had stayed, even permitting herself the glimmer of hope that her champion, Arjun, would rise to defend her. So, when Sahadev, the youngest of Kunti's sons, had told Kunti the next day that, by law, Arjun, the winner of the swayamvar, *had* to marry her, she had suspected it was Arjun who had sent him. But Kunti would have none of it.

Draupadi had viewed the whole incident as some evil enchantment she had heard of in songs, but she soon realized that if it were so, the spell was one that could never be broken.

Seven days had passed since she had been brought to her marital home, and for seven days she had remained unmarried, as the men around her debated her fate with their mother. At the end of the week, when Kunti had proposed Draupadi be married to all five brothers, to reconcile law with propriety, Draupadi had laughed aloud. Surely it was a bad joke? As if such a preposterous thing would ever be allowed. One woman marrying five brothers! Whoever had heard of such a thing? The old matriarch had clearly lost her marbles. But Kunti's cold, piercing gaze had put all hope to flight.

When her father, King Drupad, and her brother, Dhrishtadyumna, had arrived to meet Kunti, and then returned without sparing her a word, she had imagined them chastising and threatening Kunti for her scandalous proposal. Never in her wildest dreams had she considered that their visit had been to discuss the best way to execute Kunti's abominable idea.

It was only when Krishna had paid her a visit that the seriousness of the situation had dawned on her. She was informed that Mother Kunti had threatened to return Draupadi to Panchal, and that her father, who now thought of her as a curse, a curse that led to the murder of his heir, had wanted nothing to do with her. She had packed her things in teary haste to escape with Krishna. So, when Krishna had held her hand and sat her down to tell her there was no other way but for her to wed all five of them, Draupadi had finally shattered. It had hurt all the more as the one who had shown her a world where she could fly had been the person who had installed the bars to her cage.

And so, in a wedding ritual that required the newlyweds to walk seven times round the holy fire, she had walked around it thirty-five times. With each round, she had felt herself sink deeper into a quicksand. She had not exchanged a word with any of her husbands, then or after. What did one say to creatures from one's nightmares?

Even at the dining table, when her husbands had agreed to share Draupadi by the weeks of a month, she had kept her head low. As if she were away from all this, away in another world, from where she could see the drama of someone else's life unfold, but where it could not hurt her.

But hurt her it did, when Yudhistir walked into her bedchambers to claim her maidenhood on the first night of the rest of her life. He had been gentle, not loving. He had done his duty by her...for a few moments before rolling over to pick up a book. He had then lain beside her, reading to her things that had never interested her.

The next week it had been Bheem. She had been scared of him, of his cruel face and hairy shoulders. A half-wild, mean-tempered elephant at the dinner table, he had surprised her when he had gently taken her hands in his and told her that he loved her. Told her he would do anything for her, that he was blessed to have her. And then he had turned her around and entered her without warning. Draupadi had been trained to be a good wife, but they had not taught her to imprison her screams.

He had wept after, snuggling up against her bosom like a child against his nursing mother.

But the hurt her body suffered from Bheem had been no match for what Arjun did to her soul. He had rejected her. He had not even shared her bed, choosing to sleep in the taverns he frequented. Till then she had dreamed love could salve her deepest unseen wounds. That Arjun would heal her, that he would console her, strengthen her, bewitch her. But when he finally graced her room on the last night of his allotted week, he had walked past her bed to sleep on a pallet on the floor as if she were a diseased creature. In that moment she realized she had made him up inside her head. She had prayed to the Gods then, but had found the sky empty.

By such small things, her life had now come to be measured and marred. She had tried to kill herself the next day. If not for Sahadev's news that Duryodhan had instituted a trial against Arjun for the murder of Karna's nephew, she would have swallowed that poison. Karna… And then it all made sense to her. This was her karma. Karma for what she had done to Karna at the swayamvar. She had heard how pain could open the doors to power that could turn even the wheel of time, and what was more painful than seeing a boy you considered your son die so brutally? Or perhaps she really had been cursed for the sins of a past life. Karma was the only thing that could make sense of her misery. If it was so then she could not kill herself. She would have to suffer for redemption now, else she would be trapped in an unending cycle of rebirths, each worse than the one before. This was what she had told herself when she threw away the poisoned milk and turned to do her duty by Sahadev.

Sahadev had asked her consent before touching her. Draupadi had found that strange, but had nodded. He was different, kinder. Which made sense considering Kunti was not his birth mother. He had only soft kisses to share with her in the first few days, talking to her gently about his life, his family, their trials. She had learned much about her husbands from him. He had claimed her on the third night, but had softened inside her, leaving the chamber in disgust, and not returning again.

Next, it had been Nakul's turn. Though he was Sahadev's twin, he was nothing like him. He was far more beautiful than Draupadi herself. His face was soft, innocent, feminine even. But he did not claim her though the two of them never left the room throughout the week. Nakul had trays brought, with figs and pomegranates. They had eaten by candlelight, cross-legged upon the bed, in silence. Then he had removed the trays, blown out the candles, and lain down beside her, though not in a dance of desire. And for that Draupadi had been grateful.

And so, the weeks turned, and husbands came and went, leaving wounds in the ashes between her legs that soon became scabs. Scabs faded into memory, and even memory was forgotten, when the week that had given it birth came again.

'Were you present at the Battle of Thunder, Storm?' Draupadi asked, eyelids half closed in a desperate bid to forget the dagger lodged in her soul. The Silver Wolf had been given the honour of riding in the palanquin with her, though Draupadi feared the soldier did not consider it much of an honour. She had been Krishna's escort at Panchal, but Draupadi had not had a chance to speak with her then.

'No, I was but two summers, My Lady.'

Draupadi's eyes opened wide in surprise. Two summers... that made Storm nineteen... just three summers older than she was herself. A scar ran down Storm's arm to her elbow, and the mottled pink flesh still looked unhealed. Her face was coated with dust, and even at this young age, lines ornamented the corners of her eyes. Her hair was cut short, like most of the women soldiers Draupadi had seen. 'A soldier at nineteen?' she asked curiously.

'The Silver Wolves is a gang of misfits, My Lady.'

'I thought it was a squad of women fighters.'

'Same thing.' Storm hesitated. 'I'm comfortable with silence, My Lady. You do not have to converse with me.'

'Oh, but it is not a formality. I am genuinely curious. So, tell me, does Lady Satyabhama recruit the Wolves herself?'

'I don't mean to offend, My Lady, but I am not here inside this palanquin of my own free will. I prefer the saddle to all this silk.

But I have been tasked with protecting you. I ain't going to be able to do that if a damned dirk comes flying in while I am busy prattling with you now, am I?'

Draupadi hugged her knees, feeling suddenly cold. 'You do not have to be so hateful, soldier. I just wanted to know about the Wolves.'

Storm's fierce eyes glared at her. 'What for? So, you can feel sorry for us? Girls forced to wield swords at an early age... oh the tragedy! My hands should have been used to stitch robes and rub men? You think women are all about finding their handsome princes and looking fine in sarees, and birthing crying monsters?' She laid the point of her longsword under Draupadi's ear. Draupadi could feel the sharpness of the steel.

'Women can also kill, My Lady. I killed my first man at seven. He was my own father. He would pay me nightly visits, if you catch my meaning. I've lost count of how many I've killed since then. Fat merchants dressed in velvet, magisters sitting behind their desks, knights on horses, trampling the poor. Oh no, do not for a moment think we practise some kind of vigilante justice. We have killed innocent virgins, married women and children too. Because people die. It is the truth. And I am proud I am the one doing the killing.'

Storm cast Draupadi a look of scorn. 'I see you enjoying five husbands, all lusting for you. The power you have! And yet I see you weeping every day. And you a Princess!' Storm spat at her feet to show what she thought of Draupadi. 'You wanted to know about the Silver Wolves,' she said, lifting the sword from Draupadi's throat, 'and now you know it!'

Draupadi felt like she had been slapped. Tears shone in her eyes. She wanted to scream at Storm the torture of being passed around like goods, from one man to another, with no thought for what she wanted. To be driven to the point when she prayed to Prakioni and Ratih for the turn of the moon so that her moon-blood would keep her husbands away from her.

Draupadi wanted to scream all this to Storm, but all she said was, 'I would like to accompany you on one of your patrols, Storm, if that is alright.' Draupadi had not been permitted to bring any handmaidens from Panchal. Storm, gruff as she was, was the only girl here she knew from Panchal. A Princess wins over her subjects with love and care, she had been taught. She would do just that.

Storm had not expected such a response. Disarmed, she managed to stutter, 'As you command, My Lady.' Looking away, she said, 'Seven pardons for my unwise words. The swaying palanquin gives me the aches. I am dizzy, and I feel sick. But that is no excuse. I should not have misspoken so.'

Draupadi smiled. *Love and care.* 'There is nothing to pardon,' she said kindly. 'I am merely anxious to meet Lady Satyabhama, and wanted to know more before meeting her in person.'

'Nothing to worry on that front, My Lady,' Storm said. 'She is as soft as a petal.'

II

From the goat trail that ran beyond Mathura into the dry hills, the Three Sisters looked daunting. Or rather, the Iron Curfew, for Draupadi could not see the other two Walls from where she was. Above her, the wind was a living thing, howling around them like a hound. Around her, serving girls stood in well-trained silence, holding a fluttering silk awning over her head. Beside her, Storm helped herself to a small withered brown apple. In the distance, Satyabhama, in leather shirt and breeches, sewn with bronze scales, and a two-handed greatsword slung across her back in a leather sheath, stood frowning down at the pass.

The sun had not set but the stars were already in the sky. They seemed brighter here. 'The stars and the sky look so beautiful,' Draupadi said with a sigh.

'I hate the sun, the stars and the sky, all of it.' Storm spat out a seed. She had grown chatty ever since they had stepped out of the palanquin. 'Stars remind me I have to camp out tonight… sleep on the cold, hard ground. The sky reminds me of the only window I had in the well where my father left me when I disobeyed him.'

Draupadi looked at her. Storm's hair was beautiful in a wild rugged way. Trinkets decorated a lone braid at the back. Dirt smeared her face but failed to hide the powdering of freckles across the bridge of her nose. She had suffered so much pain, abused by her own father. *Women are cursed to suffer,* thought Draupadi. *None can change that... not with complaints, or prayers, or revolution. But one can spit at life and dare it to hurt you more.* Draupadi pondered over the likes of Satyabhama, Storm and the other Silver Wolves. Women who had taken charge of their destinies, women fighting their fate. A losing battle perhaps, but a fight nonetheless. Why couldn't she be more like them? *Because I am a coward.*

'They are chosen young, not for size or strength, but cause,' Storm told Draupadi with a bashful look. She had warmed somewhat to the Princess, perhaps feeling guilty over her harsh words in the palanquin. 'Erm, you had asked how the Silver Wolves are recruited... Well, we all have a past we are not proud of. Most of us are the third or fourth girl-child in the family. I don't need to tell you that the North does not treat its women right. Not like the South, anyway. Burdens, they call us. Girls are given away to temples as *devadasis,* you know – temple dancers – or sold off to visiting traders. Or simply left in the streets to die. Some are fugitives fleeing charges of witchcraft. Some are considered murderers for slaying husbands who raped them. But in the Silver Wolves we are trained to destroy our pasts. The day we receive the Silver Wolves badge, past pains are extinguished.' She smiled, and then winked. 'More so because nothing can leave as many bruises on the body than the training Lady Satyabhama puts us through.'

'Ignore her words, My Lady,' Rain said, rising from amidst the rocks. She stood a good two handspans taller than Storm, and had the look of a High Priestess rather than a soldier. Her hair was tied in a tight horsetail behind her head. A scar ran from her right brow to her left cheek. A longsword and dirk hung from her studded leather belt.

'Yama take you! How do you sneak up on me every damn time?' spat Storm.

'You just have stubby ears, Storm. So, Princess, does Panchal have no women soldiers?'

'Nay, it does not,' Draupadi confessed. 'I was amazed to see women carrying arms in Mathura. Women in the army is something I could have never imagined, though I have heard tales that they do not make such distinctions beyond the Riverlands.'

'Calling us soldiers is a stretch, Princess. The Wolves are part of the army, but we aren't soldiers, not in the fight-on-the-battlefield sense. Search-and-rescue and patrolling, that is our job. Aye, we carry weapons, but we use them mostly to frighten civilians and prise open suspicious crates. The Senate doesn't pay us enough to stand around while an armed foe tries to hurt us. Ah, talking about suspicious, we seem to have our first smugglers of the day.'

The trio watched a pair of traders undertake the laborious march up the pass where it shrank to a narrow defile, scarce wide enough for three men to ride abreast. Piety and Bleed were right behind them, though the traders did not seem to know of their proximity. When they were but a dozen paces away from the city walls, Storm straightened and discarded the maize stick she had been chewing. Her cloak flapped behind her as she raised her crossbow. 'Close enough!' she growled.

One of the men turned towards her. The other, a leather sack on his back, was so startled he slipped and fell in his hurry to run, crying out as he did so.

'He don't look very dangerous to me. Seems like some trader!' Bleed snorted derisively.

'Keep six bows trained on him!' Rain shouted back. 'Any unauthorized movement, cut the bastard down. Storm, go!'

Storm strode easily through the narrow rock formations down the hill and arrived beside the fallen man. 'Rain! Get the Princess here. She should have some fun!'

'Mm...eee?' Draupadi stuttered, but regained her composure as she was escorted by Rain down the tricky slope. She took a while to descend, the thorny plants scratching her feet and clinging to her muslin skirt. She marvelled at how Storm had negotiated the slope like a fleet-footed ram. As they approached the soldiers, Draupadi saw the apprehended man on his knees. He had strange grey-black skin and slanting eyes. She could barely see his caste tattoo above his neck scarf.

'Bleed is right, you don't look dangerous,' said Storm. 'But why don't you enlighten us about how you found out about this goat trail, and what are you doing sneaking into Mathura?'

'The name is Olof, Madame,' he said. His hair glistened with oil. He had a big mouth, sharp nose, and dense curling hair that swam in a wave over his forehead. His faded green attire meandered here and there and was mended with leather patches. 'Bones of centaurs, bygone Vanaras, makaras, name you the creature and I have the bones. They do wonders for your sacrifices. As for how we know this goat path, it is known to every true trader who considers the inexorable taxes Mathura imposes as a mark of tyranny.'

'You're a smuggler then?' Bleed drawled. Unlike the other Silver Wolves, she wore no cloak. Instead, over her mail, she had on a soiled blue surcoat with the grey wolf embroidered in pale white threadwork.

'Olof is an artist and a trader, who believes in free trade and enterprise, the vagaries of market movements, and the blessings of the God of Fate.'

'Why do you talk so funny?' Bleed asked, levelling her crossbow in front of his face.

'Esteemed Ladies, being a man of modest means, Olof had to learn the ways of the thesaurus to appeal to the genteel and the distinguished. You see, it is not quality that impresses the rich, but vocabulary of the salesman.'

Storm exchanged a look with the others. They shrugged. 'Who is this other one?' she asked, spitting to one side.

The man beside him was as straight as a spear, lean-muscled, with a heavy beard. For some reason, Draupadi thought his face looked familiar though she could not quite place him.

A tense moment passed before the trader answered, 'His name is Pal. He isn't as loquacious as this charming one before you.' He pointed to himself. 'Just a guard to safeguard this one's humble life, Madams,' he said. 'Highway robbers are a real menace. One needs a couple of swords if one is to—'

'Aye, a sellsword,' Bleed cut him off. 'A ruffian through and through.' She licked her lips. 'I like ruffians.'

'Bleed, ain't no time for chatter,' Storm growled. She turned towards the trader. 'Where are you from?'

'Born in Kauntiyas. But a trader belongs to no kingdom in my humble opinion. From the God-Kings of Egypt to the savages of the Pragjyotisha, he belongs to all.'

'That's obvious enough,' Storm snapped. 'Thing is, Kauntiyas is now in Magadhan hands, and these hills are Mathuran lands.'

'Olof is aware Kauntiyas has been welcomed into the Magadhan Empire.'

'You hear that, Rain?' Storm grinned.

Draupadi knew Kauntiyas had been sacked by the Magadhans in Jarasandh's early days of conquest.

'That's a good one. A fiery welcome it was indeed,' snorted Storm. 'Now to business. You were using the goat path to enter our city, avoiding the gate fees. That's all fair and well, but the goat path carries its own charge.'

'Of course, of course... we shall pay whatever you levy in your wise and just discretion.'

'Hundred marks!'

'Oh my!' the trader shrieked. His eyes shifted nervously. 'We intend to contest such corruption, my ladies... this tyranny of tolls. Perhaps, you can consider five marks as a fairer sum? The times of war have been hard on us, and an honest trader needs to conserve his coin to live.'

Storm stared at the man for a long moment, a faint frown wrinkling her dusty brow. 'Fifty, and I do not cut off your head.'

'How about twenty-five, and Olof parts with a finger? For if you take fifty, you might as well take Olof's heart.'

Storm eyed the man, the dark face with its deep-set eyes. 'Thirty,' she said with finality.

'Very well,' agreed Olof, 'if only to not acquaint you fair ladies with the vagaries of protracted negotiation and bartering. A dirty business that—'

'Stop yammering and pay up.' Storm held out a hand.

Before the trader could set off on another monologue, Pal stepped up and handed the coins to Storm.

'Now, off with you. And keep our trade to yourself if you get caught by the City Guard, or I'll have your head.'

'Of course, of course. We bid thee farewell. We will perhaps meet again.'

Once the two had left, Rain accosted Storm. 'Should you have let them go? They could be spies for all you know. Or assassins.'

'No assassin speaks as much as that fool. It is a good thing Lady Satyabhama was not here to hear him talk. She would have slain him.'

Rain looked like she was contemplating giving Storm a good hard cuff, but it appeared that it was a thought she entertained a dozen times a day. 'Well, if you turn out to be wrong, it'll give you something to talk about with Lady Satyabhama.'

'Lady Satyabhama approves of all my actions.'

'I think I would have remembered such a conversation, Storm.'

Just then Satyabhama walked towards them and sat down beside Draupadi, stretching out her feet, her back against the rockface which protected them from the wind. Draupadi perked up in anticipation.

Storm jolted to attention. 'Traders attempting to smuggle bone jewellery, War Mistress.' Rain and Bleed sniggered behind Storm. 'Harmless sods. We took the cut, though. Thirty marks. A good bargain.' Saying which, she showed Satyabhama the loot which clinked momentarily against each other over a profusely sweating palm.

Satyabhama waved her off. 'Restrain entries, Storm. Mathura has too many mouths to feed as it is, and scarcely any farmers left.'

She regarded Draupadi for a while. 'Leave us,' she commanded the others, who promptly disappeared. 'You're afraid of me,' Satyabhama stated. 'Why?'

Draupadi clutched the edge of her shawl and began to nervously pleat it. *Remember to be queenly.* 'Not of you... so much... as your judgement of me, My Lady.'

'Hm...' Satyabhama stretched out further against the cliffside as if it were a feather mattress, while Draupadi struggled to maintain her virtue against the wind ruffling her skirts. 'You are right. I find you pathetic. But you should not care what I think.'

Draupadi looked at her, ashen-faced. She did not respond for a while. Finally, she asked, 'And why should I not? I respect you, Lady Satyabhama.'

Satyabhama gave a bitter laugh. 'Because you are wed to possibly a future King. You have a tough life ahead of you, and if you vie for everyone's respect, it will be a short life too.'

'Do you think me...' the word grew cold in her throat, 'pathetic... for the same reasons as Storm? That I complain when I have five...' she looked at Satyabhama with red, swollen eyes, 'strong husbands to... use and abuse?'

Satyabhama laughed. 'Sounds like Storm. She was in the wrong to speak to you in that manner. But no. I think you are...' she turned towards Draupadi, her features softening, 'I think you pathetic because you have not killed Arjun in his sleep yet. Worse, you fawn over the fool.'

Draupadi's back shot up like a spear. 'Arjun?' she almost shouted. 'He won my hand! Amongst all the five, it is only he I have any affection for.'

Satyabhama shook her head. 'Precisely the reason that smug bastard should have stood up for you and refused to share you with his brothers, fought for you. I am called the War Mistress, and I admit I am handy with a sword, but I've seen him use a bow. He is a weapon of precise destruction. But that damn old bitch Kunti, she secured the fate of the brothers by tying you up as the sacrificial lamb, and your gallant champion just *let* her.'

'I do not understand. She said it was a tradition of the Union. That it was not proper for the younger brother to wed before the eldest, and that meant my marrying Prince Yudhistir. I am sure Arjun must have fought for me,' she said, disbelieving her own words. 'Krishna said as much. He said it must have been Arjun's idea, for this arrangement was the only way for him to wed me without breaking custom and law.'

Satyabhama gave a weary shake of her head, as if cursing inwardly. 'A war dawns on the horizon, child.'

'The Yamuna Wars?' Draupadi asked.

'No. *The* war. A civil war in Hastinapur. Know this Draupadi… you think your life is terrible now, and the Gods have been unjust. Little bird, this is just the beginning of the slippery slope to the fire pits you will soon find yourself on. Hastinapur is complex. Aryavrat is a land of a hundred petty city states who fan their egos by calling themselves kingdoms, just so those Ksharjas can call themselves kings, even if it is king of nothing more than a rock. And brothers have fought for centuries over rocks. Nothing new in that. But there is something sinister brewing in Hastinapur. Ask any Acharya of Meru what the prediction about a civil war in Hastinapur is. He will say the war should have taken place fifty summers ago.'

Draupadi was shocked. 'Fifty?'

Satyabhama nodded gravely. 'It is a simmering pot… the pressure built by dark forces. I wish I knew more, child. The children of Kunti, Prince Duryodhan, and his Resht friend Karna…'

The name caught Draupadi off guard and she prayed Satyabhama had not noticed. When she closed her eyes, she could still see him gliding across the arena to save her.

Satyabhama continued, 'And you… you are all to play a great part in the destiny of this godforsaken realm. And for that Kunti needs all her five sons as a solid force together. A woman can be a harbinger of chaos. You brought Panchal with you, but you also brought lust. It was all the brothers could do not to tear into each other to be first with you. If you had married just Arjun, jealousy, resentment and envy would have replaced loyalty and brotherhood. Have to hand it to the old coot. She plays dirty but she plays smart.' Satyabhama dropped a wink, but Draupadi did not see, too aghast by the revelation.

'Breathe, child,' Satyabhama said. 'Trust me, I know you think you have it bad now. Surely some may consider being wife to five husbands better than being third wife to one husband. Needs the right perspective. So, my advice – forget the husbands, focus on the bitch.'

'What do I do then?'

'Fight Kunti on her own turf. Don't be a lamb. Be a...' she smiled, 'a wolf.'

Draupadi nodded, feeling cold. They sat for a while in silence, watching the shadows deepen. As the last rays of the sun disappeared over the horizon, a page arrived for Draupadi.

'My Ladies,' he said, bowing, 'the sons of Pandu leave for Hastinapur tonight. Lord Shakuni has moved up the trial date. Mother Kunti has requested Princess Draupadi to swiftly pack everyone's belongings, and be ready to leave at first light tomorrow. Since the river is swollen and in spate, we will have to travel by road to Hastinapur.'

Draupadi was silent for a while, then said, 'Tell her I will stay in Mathura a while longer. Tell them to go forth without me. I will join them later.'

The colour faded from the page's face at the mere thought of conveying this message to Kunti. Helplessly, he turned to Satyabhama for support.

She sighed. 'It will be messy, child. The boys will not agree to go without their prized win.'

Draupadi pondered this. *Be a wolf.* She turned to the page. 'Tell Prince Bheem I have requested him stay back with me in Mathura. I am sure he has no role to play in the games Sahadev has planned in Hastina. Tell Bheem I wish to spend some time alone with him.'

Satyabhama allowed herself the faintest of smiles as she turned to the page. 'You heard the Princess.'

SHISHUPAL

I

'We were almost caught by the Silver Wolves! Have you heard the tales? They don't kill you. They string you up and use you for shooting practice with blunt arrows.'

Eklavvya shrugged. 'Do not preoccupy yourself with such concerns, Shishupal,' he said, handing his companion a skin of water. 'Water calms frayed nerves, friend. The Wolves howl only when the moon is high. During the day, foxes rule.'

'I don't know which forest you come from,' Shishupal said, taking a deep swig from the flask before returning it. 'But wolves eat whenever they're hungry. Now where are you taking me?'

'To get a room and change into a new disguise. It was pure luck that Lady Satyabhama was not present herself to interrogate us. Eklavvya thinks he left a lasting impression the last time he met her, and she would have definitely recognized Eklavvya.'

And so, they had spent a day under covers in the lodgings of a lousy inn. Alone with his thoughts on the bed, Shishupal wondered at the apathy the Emperor displayed towards the unsavoury methods in use to breach the city. Eklavvya could have got into Mathura and killed Krishna in his sleep thirty times over using the goat-trail path Anayasa had guided them to. *Honour, the best disguised plague of the world.*

Anayasa had surprised him with the wealth of secrets she hoarded. She had surprised him more with how easily she had parted with her wealth. And not for money. But from fear. Fear of

Eklavvya. Whatever her motivations, she had proven useful. They learned many grave tidings. One of which was that Krishna had sided with Yudhistir in the Hastina succession crisis. If Yudhistir became the Hastina King before the Armistice ended, it could pose a real thorn in the Emperor's side. Curiously, they also learned how Anayasa had been sent to inspect the burned ruins of the Kaurava Mansion in Varnavrat. Despite informing Shakuni, who was famously on the side of Duryodhan, that the sons of Kunti had escaped the blaze, he had chosen to say nothing. It appeared the Hastina Union was embroiled in a war of its own, a war without bloodshed.

But Anayasa's final flourish had been her information that the Senate was inflicting Vachans on its citizens to bind them to secrecy. That was why Shishupal had not heard a word about the mysterious journeys the Mathurans had been going on in herds. The calculation of the sheer amount of coin it would have taken to carry out such a mass execution of Vachans made Shishupal's head hurt. Unfortunately, Anayasa could not tell them where the people were heading to. Was Krishna scouting for new allies? Or was he assembling a secret weapon for which he needed parts? Whatever it was, Shishupal knew he had to unravel the secret before the Armistice ended.

'We aren't going to meet Gajraj, are we?' Shishupal remarked when they set out from the inn on the second day. 'Didn't you hear Anayasa? He runs the smuggling scam around Mathura with a gang of thugs in the city. He lost both his sons to Jarasandh. Why would he help us? I think we should target a crony of his.'

'Pain is a great motivator, friend. Does Shishupal notice anything different about this city?'

'Huh?' Shishupal frowned, looking around. No traffic. Disciplined streets. Not too many people on the road. He had always heard Mathura was choking with people. This barely seemed a hiccup. 'Must be some feast day. I wager the Third District is a lot more crowded. Why?'

Eklavvya hummed to himself, ignoring Shishupal's question as they crossed the street to the door of a tavern in Noble Avenue.

The sign *Ahalya's Retreat* was etched on it in red. Two guards frowned at them sourly.

'Good day to you, my friends. We are here to speak to Gajraj,' intoned Eklavvya pleasantly.

'If you carry any weapons, stow them here,' one of the guards said in a flat monotone. 'If we find anything when we check, we will shove it up your arse.'

'Look, it's just a boy, Mashru.' The other guard ruffled Eklavvya's waving hair and then grimaced. As he drew his fingers away, Shishupal saw they were smeared with something yellow and sticky. 'What the...'

'Pigeon eggs,' Eklavvya said cheerfully. 'Warmed in the hair for good luck.'

'Forest freak!' muttered the defiled guard, hastily wiping his hand on his coat.

'Serves you right for touching his hair,' the one called Mashru said. 'What've you got to say to Lord Gajraj?' he asked the visitors.

'Olof would start with "How goes it with you, Gajraj?"'

'You think you're funny?' The guard put one hand on the dagger hanging from his belt.

'We made money here in our trades,' Shishupal butted in. 'We felt like spending it.'

'Maybe start with that when you speak to Lord Gajraj.' The guard patted Eklavvya and Shishupal down thoroughly. 'Follow me. Not carrying any other sharp thing, are you?'

'Nothing apart from Olof's wit,' Eklavvya said.

Shishupal groaned. The guard did not smile, but opened the door. Leaving his still-muttering companion on guard at the door, he led the pair to a dim chamber, heavy with shadows, sweat and smoke. The place was filled with sprawled opium smokers, their dark faces hanging slack and empty, as if dreaming. Some were laughing hysterically, while others had their face twisted into unsettling smiles.

A stained curtain was pushed aside to reveal a large space that reeked of ale, half-eaten meat, roadside perfumes and vomit. A man, shirtless, his back covered in a tattoo of a hawk, sat on a long table in the centre of the room. Two others, and a woman, sat around him, counting coins and cards, amidst an assortment of pipes, opium blocks, dripping candles and half-empty bottles. One of them, a fat man, was struggling to cut a strip of meat with a butcher's knife.

Besides the four at the table, there were two others. One, with a bald head, stood bored on the other side of the room, his head resting against a wall mural of a naked woman. A hammer leaned against the wall beside him. A woman with a black patch over one eye sat near the curtained doorway through which they had entered. Her hands were knuckle-deep in a mound of rice, a loaded crossbow beside her plate. Next to her stood a clock the height of a man, its sides chipped and discoloured, its workings hanging out like gutted entrails. Strangely enough, the pendulum still moved in mindless swings.

The guard walked up to the tattooed man and leaned down to whisper into his ear and then left the chamber. The man rose slowly, putting down his tankard of ale and rolling the knobs of his shoulder blades, making it seem that the hawk etched on his back was unfurling its wings.

'You are Lord Gajraj?' asked Shishupal.

'Does he owe you money, man?'

'Uhm, no.'

'Then I am Gajraj.' He bowed as a couple of the players around the table sniggered. 'What can Gajraj do for you?'

'What is Dvarka?' Eklavvya asked.

Like a newly formed hot sword quenched in cold water, the room hissed into silence; the pregnant pause before a dam bursts. Shishupal was as bewildered by Eklavvya's question as the rest of them. *What is Dvarka?* Anayasa hadn't mentioned the word. But surely there was a more diplomatic way to extract the information. They could have taken Gajraj into confidence, bribed him, coaxed the truth out of him, in return for immunity or other benefits he desired. Anything but asking him in front of his henchmen. And... henchwoman.

'Is that a forestword for shit?' asked Gajraj, eyes narrowing.

Croaky, tight laughs to hide the tension erupted around the table. Shishupal saw the woman with the patch straighten from her rice bowl. The bored man on the other side stopped picking his nose and rubbed the long handle of his hammer.

'Eklavvya knows you know what Dvarka is. Eklavvya is aware you cannot talk about it or your head will burst.' He made a booming sound, sending a spray of spit into Gajraj's face. 'The Vachan, right?'

What is he talking about? Shishupal kept his face immobile.

'Eklavvya knows the Senators have not even told their own people where they are bound. Where the place they are bound for is located... or how they will reach there. Twists, turns and deception. But Gajraj is Akrur's favourite smuggler, having been entrusted with the routes. Have you not? Surely, you have not taken a Vachan, else how would you carry out the smuggling of people? Mathura doesn't have the money for the Vachans, does it? A sleight of hand, is it not? You do not have to say a word. Eklavvya will speak and you can nod if Eklavvya is right, yes?'

'Who the fuck do you think you are?' Gajraj glared.

'Oh, don't be silly, please.' Eklavvya raised his hands. 'Eklavvya does not desire such a pleasant evening to turn uncivil. All Eklavvya wants to know is *where* is Dvarka?' He looked at each man, and then the woman, in the eyes, as if giving them a last chance to redeem themselves. None of them took it. They just laughed at him.

'Eklavvya,' Shishupal whispered urgently, 'we have no weapons! We are surrounded. What is your plan? Talk them to death?'

Gajraj smiled, putting a hand into his pocket and pulling out a silver coin. 'I'll tell you what we'll do,' he said, holding up the coin, which shone in the lamplight. 'Heads we kill you. Butts I tell you where Dvarka is...' He smiled widely. 'And *then* we kill you.'

There was a metallic *ting* as Gajraj flicked the coin high. Shishupal drew in a hissing breath. The coin spun into the air, turning and turning. Time came to a standstill. The pendulum seemed to slow down, its swinging now loud, like the echoes of some distant war drum.

Tick.

Eklavvya seized the man sitting nearest Gajraj and rammed his head through the table to the floor beneath, with skull-crushing force. Broken bottles, swirls of ale, opium blocks, wood fragments and cards, all rose into the air. Eklavvya snatched the knife from the fat man seated at the table carving meat, and flung it at the bored man against the wall. The knife flashed in the dim light before piercing his skull, all the way to the hilt. Eklavvya's fist then sank into the belly of the fat man, sinking almost to his elbow. He moved his fingers within that great gut, one – tap, two – turn, three – pinch. The man did not even scream.

Tick.

The woman was able to reach for her knife before Eklavvya reached her, but her hand had barely begun to rise when he grabbed her under her breasts and flung her to the ceiling. She crashed into the beams.

Tick.

A crossbow buzzed. A string twanged. A bolt swam through the haze as if through murky water, splitting the dusty air. Shishupal did not know it, but it was headed towards his neck. Eklavvya leaped forward and snatched it from its path and drove it through the black eyepatch of the woman with the crossbow.

Tick.

Then Eklavvya casually stepped forward and grabbed the still-spinning coin Gajraj had flicked into the air. Shishupal exhaled, his eyes barely comprehending what happened. But suddenly, the table broke and fell. The fat man's body crumpled like a dismantled statue, and the woman fell from the ceiling like a rag doll. Startled, Shishupal took a step back, and noticed the bored man's head crucified between the legs of the naked woman on the mural. He turned and saw the quarrel sticking out of the woman's eyepatch. He looked at the bodies lying on the floor, the plaster still falling from the splintered beams of the ceiling, the crumbled bodies. Cards littered the floor. Unbroken bottles rolled about.

'Heads *and* butts it is.' Eklavvya smiled.

How? Shishupal blinked, rubbing his eyes. In the span of three heartbeats, Eklavvya had somehow killed everyone but Gajraj. How could anyone move that fast? Gajraj still stood beside the broken table, eyes dilated with fear. Shishupal stood still as well, realizing he had finally become acquainted with the Yaksha of Goverdhun.

'Eklavvya supposes he can rely on your complete and unflinching loyalty now? Will you answer his questions?'

Gajraj nodded vigorously.

Eklavvya turned to Shishupal. 'Told you, pain is a great motivator.'

SHAKUNI

I

Sunlight poured in through the stained-glass windows, throwing colourful patterns across the tiled floor of the Halls of Justice. The great space usually felt airy and warm, even in winter. But not for Shakuni. He tugged at the collar of his ceremonial garb, trying to let in some whisper of air, without much success. The last time he had stood on this spot, facing the wall in front of which the Imperial Tribunal presided, had been the day the Kingdom of Gandhar had been conquered and declared a vassal state of the Union. His kingdom. He had been brought in chains, held up by three men, for his leg had been crippled by torturers. *Feels like it was just yesterday.*

The curved rows of benches that took up the majority of the Hall were crammed to bursting with Hastina's most powerful noblemen – the Council of Hundred. The air was redolent with their anxious whispering. This was surprising, considering the short notice Shakuni had given them. When last fortnight, Duryodhan, having recovered from his broken ribs, had taken off to meet Karna, who was on a self-imposed exile in a backwater region of the Union, and head on to the Chorus in the East, Shakuni had moved mountains to schedule Arjun's trial in his absence.

Only the week before, a cloud of ravens had burst from his towers to carry word of the trial to all the members of the Hundred, as was required under law. They had all rushed to attend, each wearing the glittering chain bearing the coat of arms that marked him as the Head of an important family. It was only to Duryodhan that Shakuni sent news of the trial by messenger on horseback instead of on wings, ensuring the scroll reached him only when it would be too late for Duryodhan to intercede and complicate matters. For a moment Shakuni felt something akin to pity for Duryodhan, for destroying all the hard work he had put in to secure justice for his friend.

The members of the House of Kaurava were all dressed in ceremonial black, with red threadwork on the sleeves of their robes, signifying royalty. Yet there were three who wore red instead. Prince Yudhistir had at last returned to court, with Arjun and Sahadev in tow. The fact that they had appeared in the skies above the Crowns on a griffin, emphatically just part eagle, circling thrice above the Halls of Justice, was not lost on Shakuni. Yudhistir clearly knew that, to lead, it is important to *look* like you know how to lead. When at last they had come to earth, they had knelt before the blind King, and Yudhistir had offered his spear as a token of his fealty and love. Dhritarashtra had been caught in a quandary. He had longed to slap the face of the pretender to the throne, perhaps even stab him, for the harm he had caused his son with his games. Instead, Dhritarashtra had blessed him with a smile as empty as his eyes, welcoming him home to Hastinapur. The smallfolk had sent up a thunderous cheer as the sons of Pandu had stepped into the Halls of Justice.

Even now, beyond the walls of the Halls of Justice, in the squares and streets of the Crowns, people eagerly awaited the outcome. They waited to cheer their handsome Prince, or perhaps stone him, depending on the verdict. Wagers were drawn on the result. If Arjun was convicted, it would mean the end of Yudhistir's claim to the throne. Everyone wanted to be there to see the future decided, but only a lucky few had been permitted into the galleries. Inside, high above the assembly of nobles below, people were crushed together. Shakuni wondered how amusing it would be if some of the people shoving each other were to plunge to their deaths on the marble floor below in the middle of the hearing.

Idiots! Shakuni thought. As if a Ksharjan Prince would ever be convicted of a crime against a lowborn. Especially when it was their own dashing Arjun against the most reviled figure in Hastina – Karna, the Resht who had dared to dream.

The swayamvar had witnessed more excitement than Shakuni had wished to participate in. Duels, conspiracies, assassins, abduction, fire, escape, heroic stunts, murder; it had all the makings of a fine drama. But Karna's murderous rage, that was something Shakuni had not expected. He had felt something in the air then. Like the weight of the sky before a great storm. He still remembered Karna's eyes – a ghastly shade of fire that had made Shakuni shiver. Shakuni wondered what Karna would have done if he had not shouted that Duryodhan's life was in peril.

Mati's gamble, however, had failed. Not only was Draupadi still alive, but her plan to pin the blame on Duryodhan had sunk without a trace. With the caste riots, the resurrection of Yudhistir and his brothers, and the polyandrous wedding, the aftermath of the swayamvar had been too scandalous for anyone to ponder who had orchestrated the carnage. Most had simply accepted it as a series of unfortunate events; nothing unusual for a swayamvar in the Riverlands.

The carved doors opposite opened. Shakuni's view was blocked as the nobles half rose in a rustling throng, craning their necks to look. *Fools!* One would think they had never seen the King! Shakuni heard the clatter of boots as the Imperial Tribunal walked steadily down the aisle between the benches. A flock of clerks and secretaries hurried after, ledgers and papers in their eager hands. King Dhritarashtra strode at their head, his face wearing a grisly frown. The White Eagle and Lord Vidur walked behind him. Vidur was the Master of Laws in Hastina and, some whispered, the King's half-brother. He had been on a holy tour of the temples around Aryavrat for the year past but seemed to have made a timely return to Hastinapur. Coincidence? Shakuni didn't think so.

Of the rest of the Council of Eight, Duryodhan, Heir Apparent, and Lord Shalya of Madra, Master of Revenue, were both in the

East attending the Chorus, thanks to Shakuni's efforts. Lord Mahamati, Master of Ships, Lord Jaimini, Master of Taxes, and Acharya Kripa were all present. And of course, Shakuni himself had a place on the Council as Master of Peace. Fortunately, for trials, the Imperial Tribunal was formed by the King and the two senior-most members of the Eight – Bheeshma and Vidur.

To a rising chorus of whispers, the venerable took their high chairs behind the long curved table on the podium, facing the Council of Hundred on their banked benches and the common folk in the balcony above. The secretaries laid out their papers and ink pots at the lower table, and then took their seats on the stools provided, looking up in anticipation.

In one corner sat the three sons of Pandu: Yudhistir, Arjun and Sahadev. Nakul and Kunti were reported to have left for the East to attend the Chorus, but Shakuni was surprised to learn that Yudhistir had left his bodyguard, Bheem, behind. Or for that matter, Draupadi. Truth be told, most of the crowd in the gallery had come to see the Harlot Princess, but had made their peace with the sight of Krishna's griffin instead. While he leaned forward in tense anticipation, Arjun himself, dressed in deep crimson, sat in his tall chair, smiling and running his hand through his raven locks. Now there was a boy any maiden would be proud to claim as her lover. He seemed to revel in the chin-dropping tension as much as his brothers were perturbed by it, his smile out of place amongst the sombre frowns.

Shakuni's eyes flickered over the faces of the Hundred. He saw the Blacks and the Reds amongst them, as market murmurs were wont to call them. The Blacks stood for Duryodhan, the Reds backed Yudhistir. When the time did come to choose the Heir Apparent, there was sure to be a dispute between the two factions. Then, every vote would matter. Though that was still in the future, Shakuni liked to know his hand. He saw some whose support for Duryodhan he had ensured. He spied Lord Kakustha's pink face a few rows back. Shakuni caught his eye and Kakustha quickly looked away. *As long as you support Duryodhan, you can look anywhere you want, my friend.*

In the centre of the front row, among the richest nobles, sat Lord Prithu, arms folded, a hard look in his eyes. He hated Arjun for having got his youngest daughter with child. The girl had mysteriously fallen down a flight of steps. Shakuni had ensured the case remained mysterious in exchange for Lord Prithu's vote. Not far away sat Lord Vishvagashva, regal, grandiose and old. Shakuni had no clue how he would vote if it came to it. Vishvagashva liked the blind King, but also the stately Yudhistir. Duryodhan was rather too revolutionary for him. Lord Puranjaya and Lord Ardra sat wedged uncomfortably, looking sideways at each other with distaste. Lord Ardra had been King Pandu's closest friend, a staunch Red. Lord Puranjaya owed his lands to the blind King, a Black.

Over on the far left, sat twelve bankers of the Sindh Guild, marked as outsiders by the pass imprinted on their hands, and by the cut of their clothes. Yet they counted as votes for the men they had bankrupted with interest. *Hastina has strange laws.* So, twelve crucial votes. Shakuni still had to speak to those arrogant Drachmas and join cause, find their weaknesses and utilize their greed. It had to be gold, of course. The Drachmas' only fealty was to gold. But just how much would tilt the balance was the question.

Apart from the Hundred, the Council of Eight would also be expected to address the matter should a clear verdict not result from the Imperial Tribunal. Under Hastina law, all of the Eight had to be present and voting on any matter that came before them. With the short notice, neither Lord Shalya nor Duryodhan were present. But Shakuni knew such an event would not arise. The White Eagle would always vote with the King, as was his custom; that meant that if Vidur went another way, it would not matter.

The Royal Announcer stepped forward into the centre of the circular hall, below the King. Lifting his staff high above his head, he brought it down with a series of mighty thuds. A pregnant silence fell. 'I call this day's session, to be chaired by the Imperial Tribunal, to order!' thundered the Announcer. 'As is the law of the land, since one of the matters this day involves a Royal, the Lord Magistrate will be relieved of his duty for the day and the Imperial Tribunal will hear the three matters on the board today – one criminal, and two civil. The criminal matter pertains to the case filed by Karna, caste Resht, for the alleged murder of his nephew Sudama, aged nine summers, caste Resht. The two civil matters are property disputes, one brought by Ajwan Kundir, caste Drachma, and the other by Saha Madrin, caste Ksharja. The criminal case is called out first.'

The mummer's farce was now in session.

II

There really wasn't much for the Union-appointed pleader to argue. He tried earnestly to evoke passions and emotions, but the Reshts who would have bought into these arguments had not been permitted to enter the Halls of Justice. Shakuni had to admit the grisly drawing of Sudama's gored face received sympathetic gasps, and the exposition of law on the illegal use of the three-arrows manoeuvre in a public place received serious nods from those in attendance. But he was no match for Arjun's pleader, Sahadev, who captivated the Hall with his description of the trials of the sons of Pandu. Be it the assassination attempt at Varnavrat, or their time escaping the Rakshasas of the Kuru forests in the North, or living in disguise, in constant fear of assassins, Sahadev addressed everything but the crime Arjun stood accused of.

He has the tongue of a poet, thought Shakuni admiringly.

Finally, Sahadev came to the subject of Sudama. Prince Arjun had no acquaintance or knowledge of the deceased hence there could have been no ill will or motivation, he argued. Cleverly veiled hints against a Resht using a bow were also resorted to, as Shakuni had predicted. *Predictability is good.* Sahadev went on to hint at the prospect of another trial, when Hastinapur would no doubt track down the arsonists of Varnavrat, and deliver justice.

He was clearly warming the cobbles on the road to take down Duryodhan.

It was time. Shakuni caught the eye of the King's aide, standing behind Dhritarashtra's chair. Inconspicuously, the man murmured to the King. Shakuni had already explained to Dhritarashtra how Sahadev's arguments would keep falling back on fratricide, and that he had to be stopped before he challenged Duryodhan in open court, as there would be no way out of that quagmire.

Dhritarashtra raised a hand. 'The Council has heard enough.' His words evoked murmurs of confusion from the crowd. It was not usual to interrupt a pleader in the middle of his submissions. 'I have heard your petition. I have heard your arguments.'

Sahadev's face flushed, more chagrined than composed.

'Your Grace,' Vidur rose to object, 'the arguments have not been conc—'

'And I am moved by your pleadings,' the King continued, silencing Vidur with his eyeless stare. 'I am confident the Council of Hundred gathered here,' Dhritarashtra said, knowing well the Hundred had no choice in the matter, 'will agree we have all been moved by the arguments made on behalf of the deceased. The essence of an offence, however, is wrongful intent, without which it cannot exist. Unfortunate as the death of a young soul is, absence of motive on the part of Prince Arjun is reason enough to quash any allegations of foul intent.' He parroted the words Shakuni had taught him. 'Continuing with this vexatious proceeding can only be considered dishonourable to a valiant Ksharja, who acted merely in self-defence.'

Shakuni sighed, wondering if the King even realized that Sahadev had not used the self-defence argument yet.

'I, King of Hastina Union, Holder of Scales, propose that Prince Arjun Kaurava be declared innocent of all allegations levelled against him.'

Before the public prosecutor could object or Vidur insist on due process, the crowd had roared out its approval. Word spread at lightning speed, and the sounds of jubilant firecrackers crackled outside the Halls of Justice.

'Seconded,' Bheeshma said without second thought. Vidur nodded grudgingly.

'In measure of compensation, however,' the King added, once the clamour had died down, 'but not from any complicity or guilt, rather as a gesture of compassion, a casket of silver shall be delivered in Prince Arjun's name to the family of...' He suddenly looked away, the name slipping his mind.

Quickly, his secretary whispered, '*Sudama.*'

'... to the family of Sudama.'

'Sahadev is trembling,' Lord Purukutsa whispered in Shakuni's ear. 'He might just start crying.'

Shakuni smiled. It had indeed proved to be a masterstroke. Petitions took a long time to be heard, and matters pertaining to the Royal Family could only be brought before the Imperial Tribunal, which sat once in two years. This was the one chance Sahadev had to smear Duryodhan in a public forum without inviting charges of treason; the chance the King had snatched from him. Or rather, Shakuni had.

'We are obliged by the King's Grace and the Imperial Tribunal's decree,' said Sahadev, bowing.

Shakuni saw him recede into the crowd as he himself went to lean against a pillar to restore blood flow to his aching leg.

'Most High King,' the Announcer said, 'there remain the two civil petitions to be heard.'

'Yes, yes...' Dhritarashtra sat back in his high chair, evidently pleased with himself. 'Call them.'

'The first is a matter of ancestral property between Ajwan Kundir and Bhilu Kundir, both caste Drachma. The local officers have judged in favour of Bhilu Kundir, but the Appellate Commissioner has reversed the decision. The final appeal is now listed here before the Imperial Tribunal, following fourteen years of dispute.'

The case was quickly dispatched. The King had little interest in such matters. Vidur had already written the judgement. It was a resolution that benefitted only the heirs, as both the Kundir brothers were long dead.

'Next,' the King ordered impatiently.

'Indeed, Your Grace.' The Announcer bowed and went back to his papers.

Shakuni made a move to exit the Halls. The last hearing was a civil matter regarding some Madrin. There was nothing worth waiting for. Once the drama was over, Shakuni would surely find himself in the midst of a stampede, or worse, under it. Best to make a quiet exit.

He was about to hobble away when he heard the Announcer say: 'Your Grace, the second civil suit has been brought by Saha, son of Queen Madri, caste Ksharja.'

Shakuni's head jerked round, his neck bones cracking with the sudden movement, sending shivers of pain down his side. He ignored it. *What now? What civil case?* Answers refused to emerge in his mind. And then he remembered with dread that Sahadev and Nakul were Pandu's sons by his second wife, Madri. In Madra custom, it was usual to be identified by the maternal family name. Unbidden, the words of Acharya Dron, uttered in introduction to Sahadev at the Tournament of Heroes, echoed in his ears: *A knight of the mind, the stylus is his sword, the wax tablet his shield.*

Shakuni stood frozen, every nerve stretched taut as Sahadev reappeared and made his obeisance to the Tribunal. He went back to his low table and shuffled together a sheaf of thin wax sheets, carefully and ornately inscribed in his own hand, before passing them to the Announcer, who, bowing, handed a sheet to each member of the Tribunal.

'Most High Members of the Imperial Tribunal,' Sahadev began, 'I call upon your indulgence in a matter of utmost import and relevance to the well-being of the people, prosperity of the kingdom, and peace of the realm.'

A silence of bated breaths was punctuated by the incongruous sound of a flute playing a lively tune that floated in from the street, the barking of a dog, and muffled city sounds. Shakuni had only been half interested in the case against Arjun as it had unfolded like the roll of a mat, in a precise and known direction, but now he felt himself walking blindly on a rocky shore.

'I place the demand that the Union, under the aegis of Vayu and its sacred law, written under his shade and blessing, confer the status of Heir Apparent upon the eldest living Kaurava Prince in the son-generation of the Great King Dhritarashtra...' Sahadev paused for effect. Shakuni cursed under his breath. 'On Prince Yudhistir of the House of Kaurava.' The echo of Sahadev's last words susurrated round the suddenly silent hall.

You must be fucking joking!

DRAUPADI

I

This isn't going to be a good night.

Over the past few weeks, Draupadi's prescient anticipation of what was to come had improved, and she knew he was going to raise his hand to her before the impulse even arose in Bheem's mind. Draupadi grabbed his pyjamas and hoisted herself towards him, leaving little room for the blow. But that did not help. He still hit her; not to injure, but to prove a point. Bheem coiled his muscles again, as if to impress there was more where that came from. Draupadi would have spat at him, but her frail body, that did not enjoy pain, betrayed her mind, and without thinking, she blurted, 'I'm sorry. I am ready. Just… do it.'

Satisfied, his shoulders dropped. The offer of a fortnight alone with Draupadi was something Bheem could never have passed up. Of all the brothers, she detested him the most. Yet, of all the brothers, it was Bheem who loved her the most. And Bheem never asked for anything from anyone. Probably because no one ever gave him a chance. So, when he had put his foot down about staying back in Mathura, there was little Kunti could have done. *Little victories.*

But Draupadi had clearly not thought her plan through. With his family absent from the house, Bheem grew unrestrained… almost unhinged. Draupadi became an object on which he could expend his rage. He berated her as he would a harlot, for the other brothers who had touched her. He abused her like a slave, to remind her that he could do with her as he pleased. He shook her like a rag doll, to punish her for her resistance. It was not that she did not know she would have to lie with him, but she had been planning to fulfil her duty on her own terms, as she imagined Satyabhama would do. She had refused him, told him to wait. This unexpected declaration of her power was what had caused him to hit her. *Little defeats.*

He did not even wait to get to the bed after she surrendered. He grabbed her breast with one hand and pulled up the folds of her saree with the other. Draupadi realized with dread what was about to unfold and shut her eyes. She clenched her fists as Bheem ripped her small clothes and shoved into her like an animal in heat. Draupadi wanted to shriek in horror as she felt herself tear. Involuntarily, she bit down on her tongue. Copper trickled into the cracks between her teeth but she tried not to move. Like a statue before its sculptor, who had the power to destroy her in a moment's frenzy. *No noise,* Draupadi decided, though all she wanted was to beg for him to stop.

She tried to think pleasant thoughts to help moisten the torture. She imagined Karna on her. She imagined Arjun. Even Krishna. But the pain coursed through her body again and again, defeating every effort of her mind. Just when she thought she could take no more, a part of her mind surprisingly slipped away somewhere distant from her treacherous body, to calculate her advantage. Already she could see how she could play this out. She'd make him feel guilty, finger her bruises as grim reminders of battle, as she chipped away at his image of a loving husband. But, before that, she had to endure the battle.

Agonizing moments later came his loud grunt of satisfaction. Draupadi clutched at her silks, holding the bunched folds to her chest as his calloused hand slithered to her navel. She felt him plant slobbering kisses on her neck. *No...* She pushed him away, and this time he let her. 'You are done. So am I. No need for more.'

Bheem looked like he had been slapped. He rolled away. Having wounded each other mortally, they lay on the bed, haemorrhaging in different ways.

II

The hour of the fox found her awake. It was hardly a time to sleep, considering the sounds of life coursing in through the shut windows. As Bheem snored beside her, Draupadi's mind drifted to her memories. Karna's grip on her hand as he had saved her felt like the ache of an amputated limb. *It's your choice.* Krishna's ominous words echoed once more. Draupadi knew she had chosen wrong.

A soft knock startled her from her musings. The night air was cold as the grave on her bare flesh as she padded silently across the room to the door. A hooded woman stood under the awning, her head bowed, her palms joined in a pose of request. At her feet stood a glowing lantern. She was dressed in the loose robes of a servant. Her hair peeked from under the hood, streaked grey and white amidst a flurry of black, like a river in spate. Her right hand was bandaged. Her eyes were striking for their mismatched colours. *She is so pretty...*

'My Lady,' the woman addressed Draupadi in a hushed voice, 'pardon me for disturbing your rest. Lady Jambavati asked me to hand over the ingredients Prince Yudhistir spoke to her of.'

Jambavati was Krishna's second wife. Her bear-like skin no longer scared Draupadi as it used to, not after the words of kindness she had received each time Draupadi had met Jambavati. *Takes one accursed to know another.* Jambavati, not being from the race of men, must have her own demons to contend with, though from the looks of it, the growing life in her stomach gave her little else to fret over. By all accounts, she was an erudite person. She had dazzled even Yudhistir with her knowledge of herblore. Yudhistir had said she took after her scholarly father, Jambavan, whose name she carried.

Now, Jambavati's serving woman brought out a small cloth bundle from under her cloak. 'You must grind the nuts, then mix with the herbs in some milk. It will aid conception.'

'My thanks to the High Lady,' Draupadi said, without emotion. Yudhistir was obsessed with getting her with child. 'What is your name?'

'Kalavati, My Lady.'

Draupadi took the cloth bundle in, and returned with a copper mark for the woman. But Kalavati shook her head and stepped back, turning away. 'I cannot accept, My Lady. I wish you kind dreams.'

'Tarry a moment,' Draupadi said, looking up at the stars in the sky. She felt a desperate urge to be reckless. 'Would you know where I can find Storm of the Silver Wolves?'

'At the barracks most likely, Princess. But if you will pardon my saying so, she is as likely to be drunk in a tavern from what I know of her. Is there anything I can help with?'

Draupadi considered her thoughtfully. 'Can you keep a secret, Kalavati?'

III

Even at that hour of night, people thronged the streets outside the Iron Curfew. The two women had walked all the way to the famous Hakkus, the dams that had tamed the Yamuna River behind Mathura. Draupadi knew Mathura was a great river port, but she hadn't been prepared for the riot of colour and clangour that greeted her eyes and ears. The cowl of her hood shrouded her face. *This is how assassins must feel*, she thought as she cut a line through the crowd, feeling exhilarated, feeling adventurous.

She had only read of these places, but to actually see the gaming dens, warehouses, cheap brothels, and the temples of numerous Gods lining the streets made her want to clap her hands in excitement. She wondered at the shoulders that rudely brushed past hers. Were they merciless cut-throats or seedy spellsellers? Was the man sitting at the waterfront a greedy moneychanger, or the woman eyeing her from an alley a lady of the night?

'Is this the city market of Mathura?' she asked Kalavati. 'How wonderful! All the time I have spent here seems to have disappeared in stacks of needlework. I can see what I have been missing.'

Kalavati coughed politely. 'The city market is further on, in the Market Square by the Public Baths. This is the port bazaar, where you find things at a fraction of the price.'

'Then why would anyone go to the city market?'

'Well, you won't find any flies in the city market. The scheming Drachmas there charge even insects rent. Also, you need a certain kind of courage to shop here in the bazaar. Here, you will find absolutely anything that can be sold hurriedly from a jute sack in a busy lane; wares guaranteed to be reported "missing" at the City Guard office. You see that woman there?' She pointed at a bent woman selling something in a glazed ceramic jug. 'She calls it elephant's milk, but at best it is flavoured water. "Buyers beware" takes a different meaning here.'

'And…' Draupadi hesitated. 'Is this the best place to buy what I seek?'

'Without registering your name, aye.' Kalavati nodded. 'No Namin hands out Widow's Boon without a healer's scroll, save here in the bazaar. We are at the right place.'

Draupadi nodded and breathed in deeply. A little later, as she waited for Kalavati to emerge from a shady hovel, she saw that Kalavati had been right about the bazaar. She could see that there were all kinds of illicit goods on sale in the streets: hides of striped horse from Balkh, carved tusks from the elusive airavats of Pragjyotisha, even basilisk eggs, which looked suspiciously like painted rocks. Despite the hour of the fox, the bazaar was suffocatingly crowded, not only with merchants and buyers, but beggars as well. She even gave one a copper mark, but realized her folly when a swarm of others began to surround her like bees around a honeypot.

Kalavati, emerging from the hovel, rescued her with just a stern look of her strange eyes, and then led her to the long stone quays reserved for the ships flying the Mathuran flag, though they saw none.

'You want to try something a shade more fun than needlework?'

Draupadi nodded eagerly. So, Kalavati escorted her through winding alleys to a ladder which engineers used to climb to the top of the Hakkus. Mathura spread out below like an army of fireflies against a black river. Cords of moonlight speared down from above, bathing its surface in a soft pearly sheen. Behind her, Draupadi could only see the enormous Iron Curfew, though she knew the Mathuran Keep was right behind it, connected to the Walls on its eastern side. The Senate House was deep inside the First District, but she had never seen it up close. She turned to admire where she was, for the Hakkus were ingenious structures that diverted the river's natural course. The only structure of its kind, it had been built by the Emperor, decades ago. If not for the Hakkus, Draupadi assumed Mathura would drown in repeated floods, considering how the river frothed as it sprang angrily over the rocks in its way.

'There are reports that it has rained heavily in the mountains,' Kalavati said, as if reading her mind. 'Can expect a flood any time now. Floods are bad for business. That is why the bazaar is so crowded. There was a festival tonight for all visiting merchants to sell their wares before the storm sets in for good. Lady Jambavati herself hosted a stall in her name, to sell good quality shields.'

Draupadi nodded, impressed.

Kalavati paused, and then asked curiously, 'With your permission, My Lady, why did you not ask one of your handmaidens to fetch you the Widow's Boon?'

'They were all assigned to me by Mother Kunti,' Draupadi said, wondering why she was being so candid with Jambavati's servant. But there was something about the woman's voice that made you feel like divulging your secrets. 'I apologize, I didn't mean to insinuate anything.' Draupadi knew she would be Queen one day, and Queens did not confide in servants.

Kalavati was silent for some time. 'Would you a care for a *real* drink, My Lady?' she finally asked.

Draupadi was surprised at first, but then nodded. Kalavati rummaged under her cloak for the second time that night and brought forth a skin. Draupadi noticed how her hand was bandaged all the way to her wrist, but thought better of enquiring about it. She wasn't ready to exchange stories of violence just yet. Popping out the cork that sealed the pointed ear of the skin, Kalavati offered it to Draupadi, who brought it to her lips, then winced at the pungent aroma. Holding her nose, she poured a trickle of the ruby-red wine down her throat, and broke into a fit of coughing.

'I always find it curious how Riverlanders are spoiled by the soft drinks of the South,' scoffed Kalavati. 'This is from Herat. Goes down as easy as water. Just swallow.'

And swallow Draupadi did. The bitter-sweet liquid turned into lightning inside her body, convulsing her throat in a spasm. 'Charming,' she croaked.

'You don't have to pretend to like it. It's disgusting. But you'll warm to it.' Kalavati laughed. 'In my world, we clang goblets to show our happiness in sharing wine with a friend. But today we have only this skin.' She lifted the skin in salute to Draupadi and drank.

Friend. Had she ever really had one? She had grown up with overbearing brothers. Perhaps Shikhandi. Though she hadn't seen him since his exile. Draupadi smiled at Kalavati, feeling light-headed. 'How is Lady Jambavati to serve?' she asked.

'Most kind. A delight to work for.'

'That's nice... oh!' Draupadi squealed as she spilled wine on herself, the stain spreading on her skirt like blood.

'I see the wine is working its magic.' Both women began to laugh.

'I am faring as bad as a Rakshasa, ain't I?' Draupadi asked.

'You fared very well till you abused another race by considering them inferior.'

Draupadi knew Kalavati meant no disrespect, but the implication was impeachment enough for her to turn instinctively defensive. 'But that's how it has been,' she said defiantly. Stupidly.

'Heed the first lesson there, Princess,' Kalavati said. 'As far as my knowledge goes, Prince Duryodhan is the rightful heir of King

Dhritarashtra. Yet one of your husbands seeks to be King. Merely because a thing has long existed does not necessarily justify its existence.'

She knew if it was her mother in her place, she would have exiled Kalavati for such insubordination. But Draupadi had vowed to be different. Ever since the day Krishna had pointed out her behaviour towards her servant Aila, back in Panchal, Draupadi had sworn to be kinder to the less fortunate. *Win them with love and care,* she reminded herself.

'Then why do things that cannot be justified continue?'

'Because the men standing in the light of continuity are more powerful than those cowering in its shadow.'

'You say clever things for a handmaiden, Kalavati.'

The woman's face darkened momentarily. 'My friend was a scribe. He taught me the letters when I was young. And I read books, and discovered curiosity. A curse, I say.'

'And what did you read about?'

And so, they spoke of things Kalavati had read – of toads and toadstools, pelicans and pirates, flowers and art, murder and madness; about the vulgar and the processional, the sacred and the profane, and... sex. They talked of everything under the stars but their own lives. And, without realizing it, Draupadi felt the blackness within her recede as the night grew long. By the time they were on their way back, Draupadi no longer remembered feeling like a trail in the woods, the unmarked kind that was made by horses trampling tall grass.

When they reached the Iron Curfew, the portcullis was down and the great gates sealed for the night, even though, beyond it, Draupadi could see the Keep's windows alive with flickering lights. Kalavati bribed a guard, who escorted them through a narrow postern door.

When they emerged into the torchlit alley of the First District, a shadow fell across her face. She turned to find Balram looming overhead like a cliff on his horse. He wore intricate armour of enamelled scales, with sapphire chasings and clasps that glittered in the moonlight.

'Princess!' a honeyed voice called out, its speaker bowing politely over his horse's mane. Jet-black hair fell to his shoulders and framed his clean-shaven face. His laughing indigo eyes, which she knew only too well, matched the peacock feather he wore in his hair. 'How lovely you look tonight.'

IV

Krishna's retinue sat their mounts like wraiths behind him. Twenty armoured guardsmen rode escort. Thankfully, there was no Bheem, which meant these men were not here for her. *Blessed be Prakioni!*

Krishna smiled. 'Where are you bound at this time of night, Princess Draupadi?'

'Just for an evening stroll,' she replied, curtly.

'How charmingly reckless of you. Brother,' Krishna turned to Balram, 'why don't you ride up ahead while I share a private word with our honoured guest?'

Balram nodded and the entire retinue rode on, draping Draupadi in a shower of dust.

'And might I enquire who your lovely companion on this night stroll is?' Krishna's eyes swung to Kalavati, who stood behind Draupadi, her face shadowed by the deep hood of her cloak, barely visible.

'She is Kalavati, handmaiden to Lady Jambavati.'

Krishna hesitated. 'Charmed. I heard of your woe in the market today, Mistress Kalavati. How fares your hand?'

'Just a scratch, My Lord,' Kalavati answered in a strange new accent, surprising Draupadi.

'I do not know what Lady Jambavati was thinking to send you to man her stall in the festival. I thank Prakioni for sending a priest to rescue you.'

'And two brave hedge knights, My Lord,' Kalavati added softly, again in a voice that did not sound like hers. Maybe the wine was infecting her too.

'Aye,' Krishna nodded. 'Good to know chivalry still exists… even in hedge knights.'

Draupadi felt out of place, having no idea what the pair were talking about.

Krishna turned to her. 'Apologies, Princess, for our prattle. But I must confess I am rather annoyed with your husband for what he did to my poor wife's handmaiden in the market today. He may be a giant in body, but a dwarf when it comes to manners.'

Draupadi was shocked. Looking at Kalavati's maimed fingers, she asked, aghast, 'Bheem did this! I apologize—'

'The Princess need not apologize. Prince Bheem has already done so.'

'Bheem apologized?' Now that was more shocking.

'A tale for another time,' Kalavati murmured. 'My Lord, I must hurry back to Lady Jambavati.'

'Yes, that would be wise. I will ensure the Princess is safely escorted home.'

Kalavati bowed deep, and headed into the shadows.

'Come, Draupadi, ride with me. Let's talk.'

V

As they rode back, Draupadi saw the Keep was astir. Turning back, she noticed the guardsmen had been doubled on the walls of the Iron Curfew. 'What is going on?' she asked, surprised by this activity.

'Eh,' he said dismissively, 'some scout eager to climb the ranks has brought news of army regiments a league from the Walls. No, no, there is no cause for worry. We just have the one enemy. Fortunately for us, the Emperor is too honourable to breach his own terms.'

'Meaning?'

'The Armistice does not end for another four months. So, there will be peace till then.'

'Then why all this running around?'

'You can never be too safe, eh? But it's nothing. Balram is riding to the redoubts to ascertain if we are to face any imminent discomforts. A colleague of ours was murdered in a tavern this afternoon, and… But that is not why I stopped you. I wished to speak to you about the grudge you apparently hold against me.'

'I hold no grudge,' Draupadi said flatly.

'I confess,' Krishna continued as if Draupadi had not spoken, 'that I have been remiss in my duty to you. Matters of great import have occupied my mind, and the tribulations of your husband has done little to ease my hours.'

'Husbands,' she corrected him.

Krishna's shoulders stiffened. 'I know you are annoyed—'

'Annoyed doesn't even begin to cut it,' Draupadi said, glad Krishna could not see her face. 'You ruined my life.'

'That's unfair,' Krishna said. 'I never anticipated Kunti would command Yudhistir to marry you! And I underestimated your… prowess. With your father agreeing, the alternative would have been far worse, Draupadi.'

'Are you trying to flatter or insult me?' Draupadi fumed. 'Yudhistir told me it was you who rescued them from the fire in Varnavrat; you who sheltered them. How did you even know there would be a fire? Why did you not tell me Arjun was alive? Why did he not reveal himself before? Had I wed him then, at the swayamvar, Mother Kunti would never have dared command all the brothers to share me as a common wife. You held the strings and you are telling me you did not *anticipate*…' Draupadi shut her mouth, her lips clipped together, twisting her fingers in her fury.

An awkward silence prevailed for the next painfully long moments as the horse trotted on. Then Krishna said, 'I accept I was wrong, Draupadi. At the cost of humility, I admit I have a tendency to think further than most men, dig deeper, see wider, and consequently, when I make a mistake, it tends to be more calamitous. Draupadi, you may not see me as honourable, but I had only honourable intentions.'

'Had you even remained and lent me your support—'

'Shush!' Krishna hissed.

Draupadi did not like being interrupted, but then even she heard it. Like a sword cutting through ice, the sound of shouts jolted them both. A rider thundered to where they were and slid from his horse. 'Krishna!' he shouted. 'We are fucked!'

'What is it, Satyaki?' Krishna asked.

Satyaki yanked off his winged helm. His young eyes blinked away the sweat rolling down his face. He spoke so fast that Draupadi could barely comprehend what he said. 'Under attack—Satyabhama defies them at Dreamstone. Everything on fire—our water jets helpless against the flames—Sorcery!'

'Calm down, Satyaki,' Krishna said, jumping down from his mount. 'Now tell me. Slowly. What is it?'

'We are under siege, Krishna!' Satyaki half-shrieked.

'What are you talking about?' Krishna seized Satyaki's coat. 'I would have known it if Jarasandh had left Magadh to march towards Mathura—'

'These are no Magadhans,' Satyaki stuttered, panting. 'At least we spied no Lion banners.' He took a jagged breath, trying to calm his racing heart. 'The *Greeks* are at our gates!'

'Blazebane…' Krishna uttered in a whisper that chilled Draupadi, though she had no idea what he meant. 'Satyaki, head to Jambavan! He has something—'

Satyaki interrupted him. 'There is more.'

'Out with it, dammit!' Krishna hissed.

'The Greeks have Bhagadatt's airavats with them.'

SHAKUNI

I

'My King... My Lords!' shouted Sahadev over the disbelieving chatter that steadily gained in volume with every heartbeat.

There had always been dissension about who was the elder of the Kaurava scions, Duryodhan or Yudhistir. The birth of Duryodhan, in the Hastinapur Palace, had been witnessed in royal tradition and documented in the archives. The problem had arisen when former Queen Kunti appeared, to claim *her* son was the elder. Having been born in the forest, with none to witness, the date of Yudhistir's birth had so far hinged upon Kunti's word alone, muttered only in kitchen and tavern gossip. But Sahadev's declaration in open court had finally staked Yudhistir's claim, and unfortunately, due to Shakuni's manoeuvres, Duryodhan was not present to defend his.

'Some of you look shocked by my declaration,' Sahadev said gravely. 'It is perhaps a difficult fact to accept, considering you have been misled for years that Prince Duryodhan is the eldest Kaurava Prince. But Mother Kunti is a woman of impeccable virtue and integrity. She accompanied my father on his self-imposed exile, as a dutiful wife should. She suffered in silence. Indeed, there are no records, no parchments, in the forest, but Mother kept track of the passage of time by the markings she made on an ancient banyan tree near the hermitage we were born in. We have sworn testimonies by five Namins of note, who visited the said tree, and carried out their own readings. According to these testimonials, which have been filed with the clerks, there is no doubt that Prince Yudhistir is a summer older than Prince Duryodhan.' Suddenly, Sahadev tugged at his collar and signalled to the guards at the entrance. 'It is stifling in here. Open the doors and let us breathe!'

The doors parted and a cooling breeze washed over the gathering, along with a rising roar, like that of a crowd at a tournament. Shakuni heard the ominous, repetitive chanting: '*Yudhistir! Yudhistir! Yudhistir!*' The name, passing through a thousand throats, echoed off the walls of the Halls of Justice. *Clever bastard!*

Sahadev turned back to the Tribunal. 'It would appear the people of Hastinapur have chosen their future King.'

'It is not their choice to make, boy!' roared Lord Purukutsa, a noted Black. 'Any more than it is yours! Prince Duryodhan has already been anointed as Crown Prince. Masking this as a property dispute was low, even for you, Madran.'

The King, whose face had turned pale as milk, nodded gravely. 'I am afraid Lord Purukutsa has the right of it, lad. Prince Duryodhan is already anointed Crown Prince.'

'Your Grace, the words of the Union are: *Law Above All*. Prince Duryodhan was anointed Crown Prince because my brother had supposedly died in the arson attack at Varnavrat. A rather hasty appointment, if I may say so. But my brother is back now, and the Law is clear – the Throne belongs to the eldest Kaurava scion of his generation *unless* abdicated by him. *Law Above All*, My Lords!' Sahadev repeated. 'And hear the sounds outside for a moment. They already know what we in this Hall are shy to admit. It would be unwise to ignore the opinion of the people, would it not?' He turned to the White Eagle. 'The support of the common folk can never be lightly dismissed, Grandsire, especially in these restless times.'

Vidur caught his cue. 'Indeed, if the wishes of the common folk were to be ignored, who can tell what tragedy might befall Hastina? Riots in the streets, or worse... With so many wealthy

Lords gathered here, it would be dangerous to upset the crowd, Your Grace. And after that turmoil in Panchal, I daresay we could do with some predictability.'

Shakuni winced. Vidur was in Yudhistir's pocket. That was why none of the clerks had warned Shakuni of Sahadev's plans when he had filed this suit. *Fuck*. Meanwhile, several nobles were shifting nervously on their benches, whispering to each other and looking cautiously towards the door. Shakuni signalled his Mists, who emerged from the shadows and carved a perimeter around the Hall and entrance, to maintain order. That would ensure their good behaviour, at least for now.

All the while, Sahadev stood smiling.

Vayu's beard! Shakuni knew this day would come, the day when Yudhistir would finally clash with Duryodhan, but he had not thought it would be so soon. He was not prepared. If Yudhistir was to be declared Crown Prince now, it would be a bloodless coup. Yes, Duryodhan might rant and seethe, but in his present lovesick despondence, he would not go against the Law. Shakuni's entire scheme would crumble to pieces. *A fighting chance is all I need.*

He beckoned to Bheeshma's aide, who hurried to him, bent low. Shakuni wrote a quick note on a scroll and asked him to hand it to Bheeshma. The man hurried back to the White Eagle. Upon reading the note, Bheeshma frowned, and then looked up at Shakuni, his eyes steady and piercing, his mind considering. Then he gave the faintest of nods.

'Lords of Hastinapur!' Bheeshma roared, effectively silencing the Hall. A commander needs a good battlefield voice, and Bheeshma had certainly proved the truth of that in many a battle. He used that voice now. 'I wholeheartedly believe Lady Kunti that Yudhistir, the natural child of my deceased nephew Pandu, is indeed the eldest Kaurava Prince.' There were shocked gasps, whistles, applause, curses, excited mutterings, and over it all, the rasping cough of the King. Bheeshma held up a hand and silence descended again in the great hall. 'And he is indeed fit to rule by virtue of his exemplary adherence to our Laws. But so is the present Crown Prince, Duryodhan, as demonstrated by his administrative reforms in the capital. The law on the matter is the eldest is chosen as Crown Prince, but the law also states that once a Prince is anointed under the eye of Vayu, only death relieves him of that duty. We are at a strange juncture in the history of our House, and a decision may indeed be required. But the law, as it stands, is that the King makes the decision, advised by the Imperial Council, the Council of Eight. Not the Council of Hundred. And not the people outside this Hall.'

Shakuni could have kissed the White Eagle! Bheeshma had chosen the perfect occasion to agree with him for the first time. He held his breath as Sahadev rose to protest, but a glare from the White Eagle silenced him. Shakuni knew what Sahadev would have said: Once a matter comes up before the Imperial Tribunal, it cannot be adjourned or dismissed without a ruling.

Bheeshma continued. 'That being said, I agree with young Sahadev here that it is time to put this uncertainty to rest. The Eight will now retire to the Private Hall of Deliberation, and shall not return here to the Halls of Justice till a decision has been reached on this contentious matter, which affects the very future of the Union.'

A weak throw, Shakuni told himself. *Yet a fighting chance.*

II

'Your Grace,' Yudhistir said, softly. 'You have been a father to us and the showering of your love has placed us in your eternal debt. As hard and painful as the subject under discussion is, the Grand Patriarch has always advised that one must keep head and heart separated in making judgements. Your Grace, pray believe that this was not a premeditated ambush by us, as it may perhaps appear. We have faced countless tribulations. Tragedy has made us impatient for peace. After the last assassination attempt, we thought it best to seek a declaration and acknowledgement of a truth that is already known.'

'And what truth be that, boy?' Kripa, the old Meru-assigned Acharya, a member of the Eight, asked. 'What you did today was not something you could have ever learned from me.'

'Not much of an education, I agree,' Sahadev said.

'Enough!' Yudhistir snapped at his brother. 'My apologies, Acharya. Sahadev is out of line.'

Sahadev returned his gaze to the book in his hand. It was the biggest book Shakuni had ever seen, a thick tome with cracked yellow pages of crabbed script, bound between faded leather covers. *The Codes: The Book of Dharma.* He resumed reading right where he had left off: 'Verse 81:110: *Since the days of the events that led to the Great Lanka War in the Age of Treta, the eldest living descendant of a King is presumed to be the Crown Prince, or in benighted circumstances, where there are no surviving male descendants, the eldest daughter of the King is chosen as Crown Princess, till such time she marries a person of suitable heritage, who then takes over as Regent of the kingdom in her stead till the coming of age of a male progeny. A prohibition on deviation from this rule, as confirmed by the Third Great Council of Kings, is not a product of frugality on part of men, but a conscious decision by the carpenters of kingscience, formed from the fires of the subtle failures of previous generations...* The ancients were rather verbose,' Sahadev complained. 'It is a two-page treatise on the subject of the eldest descendant as heir to the throne, Your Grace. I will desist from reading it out in full. Unless, of course, Acharya Kripa is of the opinion further excerpts are required to be read and heard.'

Shakuni looked at Kripa, who cast a glance of disdain at Sahadev. He was not one to surrender easily. 'But there is no legitimate evidence to confirm the age of Yudhistir, is there?' Kripa said. 'It has not been entered into the royal annals and archives. There are no witnesses to the actual pregnancy of Lady Kunti. Chaos must always give way to order. Prince Duryodhan's age is unchallenged and certifiable on every count.'

Shakuni shook his head in dismay. Kripa should have run this by him before he voiced it out loud.

Arjun turned from the window and threw Kripa a venomous look. 'Forgive me, Acharya, but you do not perhaps consider that my mother, once Queen of Hastinapur, was too busy collecting firewood, drawing water from wells, taking care of our ailing father, and being with child, in the most secluded forestlands, with jackals and hyenas as companions, to have had time to extract papyrus for scrolls, to make ink from charcoal and trim bird's feathers for quills, in order to note down the date and time of my brother's birth, and send it to Hastina for record-keeping.'

'But not, I think, beyond the ability of your father,' said Kripa in a cold voice.

'Do not let your heart get ahead of your mind, Prince,' Shakuni said, coming to Kripa's defence. 'It is a matter of pure law, and should be dealt with a dispassionate mind.'

'Is that what we are now?' Arjun's brilliant eyes looked around the chamber. 'Dispassionate?'

'Then let us come to pure law,' Sahadev swiftly intervened. 'Acharya Kripa, I understand your reservations. However, considering Mother Kunti is a former Queen of Hastinapur, she is entitled to the rights of the First Persons, is she not?'

Acharya Kripa nodded grudgingly.

'Ergo, questioning a First Person amounts to challenging a Royal Utterance. Under law, such a challenge, if it fails, is punishable by death. Death by... just a moment, Acharya...' Sahadev searched in the brittle yellowed pages of the book in theatrical fashion. 'Yes...' Sahadev began reading: '*A man who points an accusing finger at the divine sanctity of the King and his persons, if proven wrong, is guilty of sacrilege and shall be punished with contempt. A Namin's hands shall be broken. A Ksharja will be slain. A Drachma shall be quartered by horses. A Resht will be subject to—*'

'Yes, yes, I know what it bloody well says,' snorted Kripa. 'My ancestors were the one who wrote it, boy.'

'No one is questioning Lady Kunti's veracity,' Shakuni said placatingly. 'We are all aware she is a paragon of virtue.'

'Now that we are agreed on *that*,' Sahadev said, 'shall we continue?'

III

Hours passed discussing the Laws of the Union, old Tribunal decisions, and even teachings of the most highly renowned Acharyas of Meru, all to no avail. Subtle threats were made. Riots warned. A referendum proposed. Qualifications of voters debated. Neither side budged from its position. Time ran on like an onrushing river. Sahadev had been right. The people gathered outside would certainly grow restless. And if Panchal served any lesson, it was that restless crowds became violent mobs.

Shakuni's pleas to wait for Duryodhan, and for that matter, the rest of the members of the Council of Eight, were turned down by Bheeshma. He had promised the Hundred outside that the Tribunal members would not leave the room till a decision was made, and Bheeshma was known for adherence to his oaths. Yudhistir and Sahadev only too readily seconded his call.

Shakuni was just grasping that the situation had turned into a bar of soap he had no hold over any longer, when an idea hit him like a hiccup. *Thank you, my devious mind.* But he knew the idea could not seem to come from him. He snuggled up to Lord Mahamati, Master of Ships, a known Black, and whispered into his ear.

Mahamati looked at him as if he were mad. 'You cannot.'

'Do you see any other way around this?' Shakuni asked. Mahamati stroked his thin grey beard thoughtfully. 'Well?' Shakuni prodded.

'Fine! But you owe me for this, Shakuni!'

Moments later, Mahamati walked over to Bheeshma. Shakuni had not written the script from which Mahamati spoke, but whatever he said must have shocked the White Eagle, for he turned to look at Shakuni sharply. Then he let out a great sigh, as if defeated. After a moment's reflection, he nodded and cleared his throat.

'There seems to be no way to resolve this,' Bheeshma said at last in his rich, deep baritone voice, which he often used to drown out other voices. The chamber quieted. 'No way that does not involve fire and blood. It brings me no joy to suggest the grievous thing I contemplate, a terrible thing...' Bheeshma laid a hand on Yudhistir's shoulder. 'Yet, we who presume to rule must do terrible things for the good of the Union, however much it pains us.'

'What are you suggesting, Grandsire?' Sahadev asked.

'Partition.'

SHISHUPAL

I

Around the corner, a handsome boy was fingering a woodharp. Ahead, a woman was singing bawdy songs while pretty young girls pressed themselves against their lovers where the light of the lanterns could not reach them. The roads were crowded, local cityfolk mingling freely with all manner of people. A blacksmith, thick with muscle, laughed drunkenly at the japes of a wizened old Namin. Hardy sellswords and plump merchants swapped tales as their servants dismantled the stalls behind them. No one paid them any mind. Mathura seemed to be still celebrating, if the sound of distant fireworks was any indication. Celebrating what? He didn't know. Perhaps how they had managed to fool an entire Empire.

But they knew now. They had finally figured out that the Armistice was nothing but a mummer's farce, a fog behind which Mathura was planning to disappear. *And when the Lion comes to know of it, his roar will make mountains tremble.*

Turned out, though, Eklavvya already knew of Dvarka, long before Shishupal. He would have words with him about that, but for now they had to find a way out of Mathura. He had been shocked to find the path to the goat trail had been sealed shut. And while the hour was well past midnight, the revels were only now beginning to dwindle. It did not help that the alleys were full of prowling city guards, probably searching for the murderers of Gajraj.

By the maps he had studied, he knew they were in the First District. Somehow, they had to get to the Second, and bribe their way out of the city on a boat. Fortunately, escaping a city in the dark of night required stealth, and in matters of stealth, silence was imperative. This meant a world free of Eklavvya's monologues, something Shishupal had abandoned hope of.

They soon found themselves in a narrow alley that led to a residential colony. Shishupal still could not believe the sheer audacity of Krishna's gambit – to smuggle the entire population out right under Jarasandh's nose. Shishupal had to grudgingly admit Krishna had balls.

Too bad for Krishna, Jarasandh has Eklavvya.

Ironically, it was Eklavvya who brought a finger to his lips, instructing Shishupal to stay quiet. He made a few urgent hand signs which were probably code for army manoeuvres but resembled a classical dance. Shishupal glanced warily behind. Two women were standing at the mouth of an alley; their hooded cloaks hung to the ground.

'Draupadi!' a man's voice boomed into the silence of the patio, making one of the women jump. 'Why are you outside?'

Draupadi! One of the women pushed back her cowl, and it was indeed the Panchalan. Hate boiled inside Shishupal as Sudama's face flashed before him again.

'Bheem, I was just coming to rouse you. There is trouble at the Walls.'

'What do you mean? And what are those sounds? Are they still shooting fireworks at this hour? Come inside this moment!'

'Trouble at the walls?' Shishupal turned to Eklavvya. 'What do you reckon that means?'

Eklavvya did not respond. Instead, he set off at a run. *Xath's beard*, Shishupal grumbled. *What now?* But he followed nonetheless. They ran, jumping over railings, fences and rough-hewn compound walls of abandoned houses. He ran blindly behind Eklavvya till the boy stopped so suddenly that Shishupal almost crashed into him. He was staring at the door of what appeared to be a temple. It was secured with heavy chains.

'Climb up the belfry,' said Eklavvya solemnly.

Shishupal obliged. They ascended, ridge by ridge, till their feet touched the floor of the bell-house on the top. 'Why... are... we... here?' Shishupal panted.

But Eklavvya wasn't listening. He was staring into the horizon through his eyeglass, in the direction the sun was due to rise. The wind clawed at Eklavvya's messy hair. He pulled down his *shemagh* and turned to Shishupal, smiling wickedly.

'And what are you grinning about?'

Eklavvya handed him the eyeglass. 'Look over there at the Third Sister.'

Eyeing him suspiciously, Shishupal took the brass tube and stretched it towards the horizon. 'What in Xath's pits!' he cursed.

The Third Sister itself was veiled in a curtain of smoke, but Shishupal saw the windswept sky above it clearly enough. Arcing into the sky were hundreds of balls of fire, rippling through the air from huge siege towers. But the fire did not burn orange, red, yellow or any other hue of the sun. It was blue. Blue like the Yamuna.

Sixteen times the Magadhans had charged in the past and broken themselves against the Third Sister like waves against a cliff, while the Mathurans had merely hidden behind until the squall passed. And now the Third Sister was on fire! Shishupal saw the Eastern Gate explode as if it was nothing more than a bundle of firewood instead of an unbreachable barred and iron-studded gate. *Blazebane.* Shishupal whispered the name and felt dread crawl up his shoulder. *Kalyavan is here.*

He let the questions fly across his mind as quick as arrows, without pausing to answer them. Had Jarasandh ordered an attack on Mathura? Was it some other kingdom? Or had Jarasandh already uncovered the truth about Dvarka? Not bloody likely. Eklavvya and he would have been recalled if that had been so. And the Emperor would never violate the terms of the Armistice without notice.

But the truth was hard to deny when one could see it with their own eyes. The entire eastern stretch of the Third Sister was lit up like a dazzling blue comet by now. Portions of the Wall crumbled down as if it were made of sand. With yawning breaches in the Walls, the fireballs swept over the lower districts in a blanketing blaze. Seen from the belfry, it was as if a blue sun had erupted through the earth.

Sweat poured down Shishupal's face and trickled into his eyes. With the Third Sister breached, Mathura was suddenly wide open, he realized, and Eklavvya and he found themselves trapped in a city under siege; a city open to plunder, looting and rape. *Guess Dantavakra will now be heir to Chedi,* Shishupal thought as he handed back the eyeglass, almost in a trance, his mind elsewhere.

'What do you make of this?' he asked when they had climbed back down to ground level.

'Someone has been naughty.' Eklavvya sniggered. 'Let's find out more.'

Shishupal was aghast. *More?* If there was hell on earth, it was a city under siege. Mathura had saved its citizens from its horrors for ten summers, but it had all changed in one night. 'How can you laugh, Eklavvya? How are we to escape? If those Greeks find us, they will torture and burn us. And if the Mathurans find us, they will torture and hang us.'

'Shishupal worries too much. Agreed, the Third Sister is down, but those catapults cannot move through the messy alleys of the Lower Districts. Yes, there will be fire and fighting, but the attackers still have the two other Sisters to impregnate before they can be said to have a chance. Have faith in your adversary, friend.'

Shishupal followed Eklavvya blindly into the alleys, grumbling to himself. And it was then that he heard it – bestial cries. They sounded far away, but it was still a vicious, thunderous noise. He had heard the sound only once before in his life, before the Weighing Ceremony in Panchal, and had never wanted to hear it again. *Bhagadatt's airavats.*

'Ah, now *that* complicates things.' Eklavvya frowned.

Shishupal swore again, surprising Eklavvya with the profanities that slipped from his mouth. 'Yes, I too can swear. What do we do now?' Shishupal asked as they walked silently, without direction.

The winds had picked up, flapping their cloaks like living things. Torch flames fluttered like pennons along the street, and here and there the odd torch guttered out. Suddenly, Shishupal felt something whistle past his ear and a quarrel punctured a hole in the wall next to him. A hand muzzled his mouth and pulled him behind a cart. *Fuck, the Mathurans have found us!* The whistle of another quarrel confirmed his suspicion. He was going to die.

Eklavvya pulled out his dagger, its blade engraved with symbols of a long-lost language. Shishupal was all too aware of how defenceless he was. He had no shield, no sword. This was no time to risk heroics. He needed to hide. He squirmed out into the street, hands raised, glancing around warily as he rose to his feet.

'Don't come any closer!' a woman's voice warned in a surprisingly calm manner, a crossbow at the ready. It was the woman from the fountain, whom they had seen earlier with Draupadi.

'Don't shoot!' *That voice!* Shishupal felt his spine tingle. Catching his breath, Shishupal stepped forward, hands upheld in the universal gesture of surrender. 'It is I, Shishupal, My Lady,' he said cautiously, but with sure instinct. He felt her mismatched eyes focus on him, the blue shining deeper than the green. He took slow steps till he came into her crossbow's line of sight, then stopped.

'What happened to your face?' she asked.

'Disguise.'

'Not a very good one, is it?' Lady Rasha lowered the crossbow and stared at him. 'You're a long way from home, Commander.' Her icy voice still had the power of a concussion.

'Aren't we all, Lady Rasha?' Shishupal replied, slowly lowering his hands. He could not believe she was here, but thanked Xath for an ally, however nebulous the term.

'Rasha?' Eklavvya seemed confused. 'Her name is Kalavati. I heard her talking to—'

Lady Rasha looked at him and, miraculously, silenced Eklavvya. 'Shishupal, your friend is covered in blood.'

'A minor inconvenience, My Lady.' Eklavvya bowed. 'Be comforted the blood is none of Eklavvya's.'

Lady Rasha gave him a startled look. Eklavvya had that effect on people. She turned to Shishupal, who didn't fail to notice her fingers were still treading gingerly on the crossbow trigger. 'Shishupal and the Yaksha. As unlikely a pair as any I have seen. What brings *you* here… along with *him*? Has the Emperor finally decided to use assassins? You may be too late. Your lackeys on the Walls have got Krishna's attention.'

'It is not us. I am glad we ran into you. We have some questions, and seek a place to hide while we ask them.'

'Questions?'

'Too many questions, but for now one will do,' Shishupal said. 'Uhm… *who* has attacked Mathura?'

'Not *you*?' she asked. 'Now that's interesting.'

'What do you mean?'

'It's the Greek Warlord, Kalyavan. I reckoned the Emperor was working in tandem with him. You must have heard the airavats he has brought along?'

Shishupal nodded weakly. 'So Bhagadatt has come too?'

'I know very little so far. What I do know is that there is to be a parley on the morrow. That should clear things.' Lady Rasha looked up, her green eye squinting. 'I thought he was in bed with the Magadhans. So, either Kalyavan has decided to walk this path alone…'

If Kalyavan loses his gamble of single-handedly taking on Mathura, Jarasandh will lose his Northern army, and Bhagadatt's airavats in the bargain. Fuck! That's bad.

'… or the Emperor has left you to the dogs,' Lady Rasha added. 'Though from what I hear, there is no Lion amongst the banners.'

'Ah, the plot thickens…' Eklavvya chimed in as he pulled Gajraj's coin from his pocket. 'Kalyavan wants to hog all the glory for himself,' he grumbled.

'Never mind him, Lady Rasha.' Shishupal hesitated. 'Would it be possible for you to give us safe haven, at least till we find a way to escape from Mathura?'

'You can take my quarters.' Saying which, she drew out her keys and handed them to him. 'It is the third house on the left in the alley right beside the Keep. I don't know what you are doing in Mathura, and I don't really care, but my advice is to stay put. The city will be a mess by tomorrow.'

'Where are you off to, Lady Rasha? Should you not come with us? We have much to tell you, and to ask. For example, why *are* you here?' Shishupal suddenly remembered the talk about smuggling, between the Emperor and Lady Rasha, a year past. *They had been talking about smuggling her into Mathura*, he realized.

'Later.' Lady Rasha's tone brooked no argument. 'I have work to do. Blazebane isn't working for them as well as it should.'

Shishupal doubted that. If the holes in the Third Sister were any indication, it was working splendidly.

'Blazebane won't get them through the Second Sister,' Lady Rasha said, as if reading his mind. 'Krishna has dispatched some trickery to counter it.'

'We should come with you, My Lady.'

'No need. Alone, I can slip away unnoticed. Your southern skin, and his ungodly accent, will give us away. The last thing I want is to be caught by the Mathurans alongside the Yaksha himself. If that fool Kalyavan has decided to take Mathura on his own, he will need all the help he can get.'

Unbidden, the words of the Emperor to describe Kalyavan came to Shishupal's mind: *A green boy, more like to be brave than wise.* He could have laughed at how true Jarasandh's words had turned out to be, if he was not trapped in a city that was destined to soon be blood and ashes.

KRISHNA

I

Krishna felt he was gazing at a lurid painting, a ghastly piece on the horrors of war. Markets, statues, or anything else that had ever stood in the Third District, were gone. What was left behind were women and men, streaked in ash, struggling through the chaos, moving debris and trying to clear a path through the rubble. A few were frantically digging in the wreckage of their still-smoking houses, searching for any hint of life. In the avenue ahead, healers tended to a sorry group of people, all rendered homeless by the fire.

He passed sagging mounds of charred corpses, stacked beside the avenue like yesterday's leaves. Hundreds of them. Mostly poor refugees and farmers from the outskirts, who had fled to Mathura to escape the war but it seemed that, in the end, the war had caught up with them.

Krishna paused by a building that was still burning, felt the blue kiss of its heat on his cheeks. Nothing to be done but wait for the blazebane to die out. From where he stood, the hills of debris seemed to go on endlessly. Only three walls of the building that had once been the Temple of Yamuna still stood, its doorways gaping in an eternal moment of frozen terror. The arch of the city market, where dozens of merry stalls had once catered to the rich and the mighty, was now cracked and caked with slimy soot. It looked like a different place. It was difficult to believe this was where he had rallied the smallfolk in his rebellion against

Kans. And only a few strides away, near the smoking ruins of the fountain, was where he had met Satya. Even the tavern where he had tried to convince Balram to drink ale was now reduced to a blackened relic.

A man, clutching a baby wrapped in torn fragments from a fallen Mathuran flag, caught his attention. The man gazed at Krishna in silent desperation. Uncomfortable, Krishna gave his horse the slightest suggestion of a spur. The hooves of his mount clopped obediently into the black mud. Ahead, a boy on a crutch stood up hastily to salute him. Beside him in the street, a body lay hidden under rags, only a charred hand with long, painted nails visible.

Krishna felt exhausted. He had been overseeing the inflow of citizens from the Second District into the First, and the Third into the Second, but he had not been prepared for what he saw in the Third. He rode past the destroyed Dreamstone Spire, past the Third Sister, to where Balram stood, facing the red cloaks on the horizon. He was clad from head to foot in gilded scale armour, and looked like a gigantic fish standing on its tail.

Krishna swung down from the saddle and walked to his brother. 'The tempest has brought us luck,' he said, his voice reduced to a gravely croak from the onslaught of ash, smoke and death.

'Aye,' Balram responded. Resentment oozed from him like a cow that hasn't been milked. But he said nothing, letting the silence, the words unsaid, prickle at Krishna's conscience, as if it wasn't sufficiently armed to do the harm all by itself.

How could he have known Kalyavan would betray the Emperor? If he had, he would not have sent away half the Mathuran Army to secure Dvarka, now, would he? He was not stupid. This was… an aberration, a chance occurrence of monstrous proportions he could not have factored in, could he? *Could I have…?*

No, Krishna could not blame himself for the five patrolling squads who were ambushed outside the Walls by the Greeks, who had hidden in the dense forest cover on either side of the road. Or be blamed, for the stormy night had disguised their advance. They had taken the sentry columns in both the rear and the flanks.

After that, the dead Mathurans had been stripped bare of their uniforms.

And Krishna could hardly be responsible for the sentry's error on the Third Sister. The sentry must have squinted through the windy night to see moonlight flashing on Mathuran helmets. Those Mlecchás had even rubbed dirt on their exposed skin. He must have assumed it was the patrol squad returning from their shift, and would have lazily yelled at the duty sergeant to keep the gates open. By the time the Mathuran sentries realized the returning soldiers were of the wrong skin colour, it had been too late.

The Republican Army had repelled the Greeks in skirmishes along the Third Sister, but in the heat of battle had let the enormously high siege towers of the enemy creep too close for comfort. What followed was there for everyone to smell and see. But surely Krishna could not have predicted any of this! The safety of the Walls was Balram's responsibility. Yes, he had complained of lack of manpower. Yes, he had flagged countless times how vulnerable Mathura was to attack. But had there been any other solution? No. Soldiers were needed in Dvarka to safeguard it. And surely, the Sisters had been a beacon of safety for more than a decade? Could Krishna be really blamed for relying on them?

If Krishna was hoping for a voice in his mind to contradict him, telling him he could not possibly think of everything, that he already had so much else on his mind, that there was nothing anybody could have done, he did not hear it. The truth was that Krishna had not factored in Kalyavan's lust for glory. He thought back to the day of the Weighing Ceremony, when Niarkatt had insulted Kalyavan; the way his face had darkened. Krishna should have known then that the boy would do something hasty and stupid. Well, hasty at least, for so far Kalyavan's moves had been ingenious. *If only I could slay Niarkatt and hang his head on the ramparts!* But the fool had been one of the first on the carts to Dvarka.

But he could punish himself later for what he'd failed to predict. For now, Krishna was grateful the storm over the Yamuna had given him a chance. When, past midnight, the storm had struck and turned the blue flames back in the direction of the Greeks, Krishna could have kissed the page who had brought the news. It had not only bought him time, but a message of parley from the Mlecchá. *Time for talking.* Talking was something he was good at. He could do it for hours. There had to be something Kalyavan wanted which he could give him. All he had to do was figure out what it was. And so here he was, waiting beside Balram for Kalyavan to grace them with his presence.

On the horizon, between farms and villages, on the cart roads, in the patchwork of damp fields, Greek troops swarmed in their thousands. Not a huge army. Not a small one either, considering half the Mathuran troops were away. Mathura was, without doubt, vastly outnumbered.

Krishna saw no Pragjyotishan flags, however, which meant Bhagadatt was not present. *Bless Yami.* Another voice added: *He doesn't need to be, the bastard.* Though he could not count them, the airavats looked like hillocks. Great lumbering monsters with tusks that looked like they could gore through walls. The ones Bhagadatt had brought to Panchal had been scary enough, but the ones Kalyavan had here had legs like tree trunks. Blades were strapped to their long snouts. Mathurans possessed no war elephants, but it would not have mattered against these leviathans even if they had. Through his eyeglass, Krishna spotted many of the airavats dragging the siege towers which the Greeks had used to launch blazebane on the Third Sister. Others carried armoured placements on their backs, from where no doubt Eastern spearmen and archers would rain down steel and wood.

Since the land sloped down from the Third Sister, Krishna could not see beyond the immediate encampments, but he could swear there were no long lines of red tents, as he had seen on countless Magadhan sieges. A few pavilions, yes, but nothing to mark any preparations for a long stay. No smoke rose from cook-fires. No ditches had been dug to prevent supplies and reinforcements, meagre as they were, from reaching the beleaguered city. *Kalyavan does not intend to make this a long siege,* Krishna realized with dread.

Ahead, a score of horsemen detached themselves from the Greek lines and rode forward at a steady trot. A long flag streamed above their heads, an olive wreath on red silk, worked with Greek letters in golden thread. Under it was the white flag of parley, ominously small. There was no mistaking Kalyavan among the scores of straw-haired Greeks. He sat his destrier, a whip in his hand, wearing a leather jerkin over loose braccae. A crimson paludament was pinned to one shoulder with a great square-cut topaz.

'Krishna, my friend,' Kalyavan said cheerfully, his Greek accent pronounced.

'Archon,' Krishna returned politely. 'Welcome to Mathura. I see you have brought some warmth with you in this season of chill. I wish you had informed us of your intention so we could have prepared a more suitable welcome.'

'Well, you know what they say about surprise.' Kalyavan raised his palms like a child. 'It must jolt to work.'

'Why not come inside, Archon?' Krishna forced a smile. 'We could speak like civilized men.'

'Ah, soon enough, Krishna. I do intend to dine at the Senate House by nightfall. But as a conqueror, not a guest. Don't even try, Krishna,' he said, before Krishna could say anything. 'I am not interested in anything you have to offer. Immortality is the only thing that interests me, and that I will claim when I see my banners flying over the Iron Curfew. But let us play civil, for now. I suppose this giant at your side is your brother...'

Kalyavan was momentarily shaken from his play at the sight of the figure beside Balram. '... Forgive me Krishna, but my weakness has ever been for women in armour. This can only be Lady Satyabhama, the War Mistress?' He bowed in her direction. 'Your eyes, My Lady, are like onyx beyond price!'

Krishna had been so immersed in his own thoughts that he hadn't noticed Satyabhama come up. She shrugged now and said,

'If you had kissed Jarasandh's arse half as well, he might have lent you some soldiers.'

'And let him take credit for the victory? Nah, I do not share.' He winked at Satyabhama. 'Yes, the Emperor may be annoyed by my actions, but if I were to bring him Krishna's head, I reckon it would douse his anger.'

'Why have you called this parley?' Balram asked, unamused.

Kalyavan cleared his throat. One of his generals rode forward and unrolled a scroll. 'The terms offered are: if Mathura is surrendered peacefully to Archon Kalyavan, one of the Senators will be instated on the throne of Mathura, as a loyal subject of the Emperor, subject to payment of a monthly tribute.'

'How generous.' Balram's voice was hard as flint.

'Second, the citizens of the Republic will be permitted to live according to their own customs and laws. Third, the Usurper shall be delivered to the Greeks, bound in chains, that he may be conveyed to Rajgrih, for judgement by Emperor Jarasandh.' The man rolled up the scroll and looked up. 'Those are our terms. Refuse them and the Archon has decreed that Mathura be treated as any other conquered province. Many will be enslaved, many killed. Greek governors will be installed, and your Senate House turned into a Pantheon for our Gods.'

Before Krishna could spit at the general, Balram spoke, 'Your terms are unequivocally rejected. Mathurans are not in the habit of surrendering their own simply when asked. Particularly not to a flock of sheep in skirts. You might have razed one of our Walls with your trickery, but if you remember we have two more. You are just a little boy playing a man's game, Archon. Betraying your own Emperor! Your arrogance is worse than your absurd plumed helms. You disgusting little dirty-bottomed airavat fuckers!'

Kalyavan frowned and conferred quickly with the general, having lost the finer points of Balram's diatribe in translation. When he finally understood, Kalyavan laughed. 'I was hoping you would say that. But what to do? Heroes have to pretend at peace before they get down to battle. Farewell, friends.' He turned to Satyabhama and approached her. 'And you, My Lady, just come over to me. We will rule together, you as my *first* wife. Surely you can see Mathura stands no chance of winning? We have you surrounded and flanked.'

'Good. Now we can shoot at you from every direction.' Satyabhama smiled back at him. 'Motherfucker,' she added pleasantly.

Kalyavan stepped uncomfortably close to Satyabhama to respond, no doubt to say something cocky. There was a loud snap. The Greeks drew their swords, but Kalyavan bade them be still, smiling through his bruised lips. Satyabhama cracked her knuckles while Balram smiled, and Krishna sighed. Everyone has got something cocky to say till they get elbowed in the face.

SHISHUPAL

I

The Iron Curfew was crawling with people, some running barefoot, carrying sacks, and anything else they could salvage, children in tow. Every wagon that would move was stacked high with boxes, chests and mattresses, as well as all kinds of useless junk that would no doubt be the first to burn. Trying to save anything other than your own life was simply bad investment during a siege. Shishupal and Eklavvya passed many such hapless souls, huddled under blankets, on doorsteps of abandoned mills and houses, cramming the shadowy alleys that led to empty markets.

Going out of the Iron Curfew was not an option. But they were hungry. They walked to a nearby tavern that was still doing business. On the far wall of the tavern was a mural. Shishupal studied it with narrowed eyes. Krishna sat in the centre, with an assortment of Senators on either side. The citizens were drawn below the table, their hands flung in thankfulness to the sky, enjoying the benefits of the Republic's good governance. Under this mural, the words *For the People. By the People* were etched in golden letters. Some crusader for truth had managed to climb up and daub over *For* and *By* in streaky black to say: *Fuck the People. Loot the People.*

The tavern was filled with an echoing quiet made of absent sounds. No drunken brawls, no sizzling overcooked meat, no clanking of goblets, no chatter of voices. Men huddled together, drinking with quiet determination, in silence. The blackstone hearth in the corner held the heat of a long-dead fire. The barkeep stood behind a rickety table, ready to dive behind it at the first hint of trouble.

Into this desperate quiet walked Eklavvya, the God of Noise. 'Lads!' he shouted. 'Is this a tavern or a mourning house? You men act as if there was a siege going on outside.'

'Bugger off!' one of the men growled.

'Now they will not stare at us for the fear that we might walk to their tables and strike up a conversation,' Eklavvya whispered to Shishupal. 'And our cover will remain intact.'

Shishupal sat down wearily at the first empty table he found. They'd been holed up for two days in Lady Rasha's servants' quarters. Nothing came in. No messages, no food, no water, nothing. Eklavvya and Shishupal were down to their last coins, and the siege was just picking up. Shishupal raised a hand and called for two hot meals. He sat morose, pretending to listen to Eklavvya's monologue. So far, they'd managed to confirm that it was only the Greeks at the gates. No Lion or Airavat banners flew in their ranks. *Kalyavan had acted on his own. That idiot!* But he did hope Kalyavan won, for if he was defeated, it would weaken Jarasandh's unified front, and the Yamuna Wars would drag on for another ten years.

'Hoy!' Eklavvya knocked heavily on the table, startling Shishupal. 'You got some hungry men in here!'

The barkeep finally appeared with two bowls of stew and some flatbreads. 'Nine marks,' he said.

'What!' Shishupal was aghast. 'These cost no more than one mark.'

'War-time prices.' The man nudged him in the direction of the door. 'See the sign there?' There was indeed a sign that read: *Praices defferent in War Taime.*

'Quite the motivational quote,' said Eklavvya.

The barkeep was not amused. Grudgingly, Shishupal tossed him all the coins they had. Before the man could leave, however, Eklavvya caught him by the collar. 'Now that you've robbed the both of us, Eklavvya feels you owe us some generosities too.' He slid his knife up and down the man's thigh.

'Yes-yes,' the barkeep whimpered, 'what do you want? I can add spice to your stew.'

'Fuh! Information is what we seek, o purveyor of stale food and illicit brews. Many soldiers must come here. What's the grapevine telling you these days, my friend?'

'Eh, what?'

Shishupal interjected. 'He means, what news of the siege?'

'Not much by the looks of it. There is a lot of fighting out there. The Greeks are having to conquer every turn, every alley in the Third District. Their catapults can't find their way into this maze. Add to that the stormy winds, so their magic fire is out. Lord Krishna has also blanketed many portions of the Second Sister and the Curfew with blankets coated with, erm, something, erm, I can't remember what, but the thing is – covered under these blankets, the Walls won't catch that blue fire.'

'Why would they need catapults to manoeuvre the alleys? I heard they had enormous siege engines with dozens of catapults, and not to forget archers. Even the Magadhans cannot match the Greek siege towers. They could just rain blazebane arrows from a height at the Walls and beyond, no? Isn't that what they did to burn the Third District?'

'Aye. But didn't you hear what Lady Jambavati did?'

And so they heard of how Jambavati had single-handedly changed the rules of warfare. The thing was, catapults hurled huge slabs of rough-hewn asymmetrical rocks up into the air. Even with the perfect angle of a finely tuned catapult on the Third Sister, the rocks would peak, stall and dip to go to a maximum of two hundred yards, where they would wedge themselves deep into the earth. Which was why the Greeks had withdrawn their siege towers three hundred yards away from the Third Sister. This was standard practice in any battle. The Greeks had to wait to conquer the Third Sister, or whatever was left of it, and then bring the siege engines into the city to take the Second Sister.

Except, Krishna had reached out to his second wife, who was some kind of genius. She replaced the rocks with balls. Hundred-pound, perfectly round balls, easily produced by the local mason yards. When the first ball had arced into the air, the Greeks had laughed at how woefully short it had pitched. But they didn't laugh when it bounced the first time, and they certainly did not laugh when it bounced again and smashed into their ranks, rolling along the ground and picking up pace, thanks to the slope. The Greeks soon discovered that a rolling hundred-pound ball cannot be stopped by soldiers, wagons, tent poles, tethered mammoths, or siege engines. Only level ground can halt it, and by then...

'All the siege towers are gone?' Shishupal's eyes goggled in disbelief.

'Aye, our soldiers took advantage of the distraction, and were able to lead a quick sortie to throw *bellowers* from close quarters at the towers. They may have their magic fire, but we have Mathuran munitions. Now the plan is to just to sit this one out.'

'How does one sit a siege out?' Eklavvya asked.

'If I knew I would be a General, I reckon.'

'One can always aspire, my friend. Now off you go to fetch some more ale.' Once the man had scurried away like a hare chased by hounds, Eklavvya said, 'Have to give it to the industrious mind of the Mathuran masons, Shishupal. What an elegant solution. Eklavvya has much to learn from Krishna's wives.'

Shishupal ignored him. 'I, too, believe the Mathurans would do well to simply sit this out. If the Greeks are acting alone, they cannot possibly have a large enough army to conduct a long-drawn siege. They're relying on blazebane, but it doesn't work well in stormy weather, and needs a safe height from where it can be used.' He leaned his cheek on one curled fist.

'Eklavvya vacillates between the Mathurans and the Greeks, for the vicissitudes of fate and war are ever changing. But the point remains that Shishupal is assuming a status quo without considering two variables. The airavats...'

'Hmm yes...'

'And a far more dangerous variable than blazebane or airavats or griffins or walls – your friend, Lady Rasha.'

Shishupal did not smile. 'Aye, more dangerous alright.'

SHAKUNI

I

The table upon which the fate of the Union was being
deliberated had not always occupied the centre of the room.
The wear patterns on the vast rug covering the floor left little doubt
that it had been hastily pushed to its present position. The rug
itself was patterned with glorious scenes. Warriors, triumphant.
Kings, crowned. These were images from the Union's history the
current members of the Eight sat on, indifferent.

Shakuni's small mouth hinted at a smile as he stole deliberate
glances at Sahadev, ensuring the boy saw the flash of triumph on
his face. By now, the mystery of Shakuni's smug face had gnawed
away slowly at Sahadev's confidence. The way Shakuni constantly
interrupted Yudhistir with baseless requests, the way he reclined
in his chair with nonchalance, his whole manner of being spoke of
one who was least concerned by the outcome of the deliberations.
Sahadev's unease had begun to taint his sweat.

'I must interject,' Shakuni said lazily, for the hundredth time.

'Lord Shakuni!' Yudhistir hissed. 'Pray stop interrupting me.
Allow me to finish.'

'But Prince,' Shakuni intoned desultorily, 'it is my duty to
interject. Why are we…'

'No more, Lord Shakuni!' Yudhistir snapped. 'Not only the fate
of the Union, but also of the royal family, stands on a precipice.
I am confident His Grace will concur there should be no more

disruptions, and that no one outside the family be permitted to interrupt our discussions. No Acharyas. No Councilmen.'

Dhritarashtra waited for the others to object, waited for Acharya Kripa to seethe, for Lord Mahamati to swear. But they all stayed silent.

'Agreed, Prince.' Shakuni folded his hands in mock humility. 'I see the wisdom in your suggestion. But Prince Duryodhan is of Kaurava blood, and a member of the Eight, after all. Do you not feel it would be prudent to include him in this arrangement you propose?'

Yudhistir jumped to his feet. 'No, My Lord! Prince Duryodhan sits on the Council by virtue of being the Heir Apparent, which is the very thing under challenge now. The time for dallying is past. Passions are high. Hastinapur awaits. The King is present. The Imperial Tribunal is here. The Council of Hundred waits outside. We do not require anyone else.'

'But proceeding without him would ignore due process and can create complications,' Acharya Kripa warned. 'At least, not without a diktat to that effect.'

Yudhistir frowned, then nodded earnestly. 'Your Grace,' he said, the words coming out his mouth growing increasingly bitter, 'may I request the issuing of a diktat so that our peaceful talks can bear some fruit?'

'This is a disgrace!' Shakuni declared, half-heartedly. 'Since you are in so much of a rush to proceed, and seek to exclude members who are not Kaurava, perhaps you can word the diktat yourself, and submit it to His Grace for his consent. Are you able to do this yourself or do you need Sahadev to aid you in this as well?'

Yudhistir shoved Sahadev's warning hand away and said, his face as dark as the back of a stag beetle, 'Your Grace, may I be permitted to dictate the order in your stead? If you agree with the words, you may give it your stamp of approval.' Without waiting for the King to accede, Yudhistir turned to the scribe seated at the low table. Ignoring Sahadev's whispers of warning, he instructed in a clear voice: 'Add the necessary introductions, then inscribe, *Further to the ongoing negotiations before the Imperial Tribunal in*

*the matter of the succession to the throne of Hastinapur, instituted by
Sahadev Madrin, Third of His Name, let it be noted that interruptions
not pertaining to the contours of the issue of partition itself, either
physical or verbal, will not be floated, discussed, mentioned, argued
or voiced under any circumstances. And under no occurrence of event,
fortune, misfortune, deed, or misdeed, shall the ongoing proceedings be
interrupted by non-Kaurava parties. Nor shall the matter be left sub
judice or abandoned by the negotiating parties till such time a mutually
accepted conclusion is agreed upon by all attendant parties.'*

Yudhistir turned towards the White Eagle. 'Grandsire, I have
taken care to include your promise given in the Halls of Justice as
well. Is the Diktat acceptable to the King?'

'Is it not rather verbose, Prince?' Shakuni asked. 'We might be
here for a long time. I hope you know a King's Diktat can only be
overturned by the Council of Eight?'

Yudhistir ignored Shakuni as if he did not exist. 'Your Grace,
with your permission...'

A weary, impotent nod from the King followed. And just like
that, in half a minute of haste, Yudhistir unknowingly destroyed
what he had spent half his life trying to achieve.

KRISHNA

I

The sky was aswirl with shifting colours, reflecting the great fires that burned below. Blue nights had given way to orange dawns as the yellows and reds of common flame replaced the sapphires of blazebane in their war against mortar and stone in the Third District. The embers that had drifted through the night air like swarms of blue fireflies were gone, replaced now by sooty fingers that rose towards the heavens like thin, wispy giants on the horizon. The air itself tasted of ashes.

So far it was going according to plan. The Greeks were frustrated with the alley turns and cul-de-sacs littered across the Third District that did not allow their catapults to move to a position close to the Second Sister. So, for now, they could not throw blazebane and fire at or over it. This had given Krishna sufficient time to drape the Second Sister with alchemical blankets. Jambavan had been preparing them ever since Krishna had learned that Kalyavan had joined hands with the Emperor. So, while here and there some Greek soldiers managed to throw blazebane molotovs at the Wall, the blankets absorbed them as if they were no more than lighted matches flicked at it by the soldiers.

While the catapults and blazebane turned out to be of little help to the Greeks, ladder after ladder was propped up against the Second Sister as the Red Cloaks tried to climb up in strength. But Mathura had resisted every infiltration attempt by the Greeks so far, though one would not have thought so by looking upon the grim faces of the War Council in the Keep. Lord Akrur clutched his goblet like a drowning man clutching a floating branch. Balram frowned, wondering what advice of his had been ignored by the Senate so that he could justifiably sentence them all to death. Satyabhama, cold-eyed, sat with fists clenched. Old Ugrasen paced in the chamber with harsh determination.

'How fares Mathura, Lord Commander?' Ugrasen asked.

'Mathura is in chaos, My Lord,' Balram answered. 'Blazebane has been stopped. Curfews are in place. But some miscreants have seized this opportunity to riot, rape and rob since the City Guard has been called in to supplement the Republican Army. We also caught three soldiers and a farmer trying to sneak out of a postern.'

The opportunists have already begun their own sacking, Krishna thought. In a city under siege, there were always those who abandoned any pretence at civilization to profit from the crisis or settle old scores. Rape the wife of the landlord who evicted you. Rob the mistress' jewel which you always coveted. Escape over to the enemy with news in the hope you will get to share the spoils of war.

'And how are we dealing with these jackals?' Ugrasen asked.

'Spikes. Swords. Stones.'

'Good,' said Satyabhama. 'They are the first, but certainly not the last. Siege is perfect weather for treasons to bloom.'

Balram nodded and continued. 'As for the Greeks, we are doing all we can to frustrate them, but with half our fighting strength, we do not have enough soldiers to man the Walls for so long, even with rotation and rationing.'

'So, how many days?' Ugrasen asked.

'They may well scale the Second Sister within the fortnight,' Krishna replied. Shocked gasps came from around the table. 'But do not worry. We may not have soldiers to defend the entire city, but we have enough to defend the Second District if required.'

'We have a few regiments of the Republican Army,' Balram added, 'all of them stationed in the Second District. The Silver

Wolves are assisting the City Guard with the defence of the Iron Curfew. Their strength has been bolstered by some civilian volunteers, though I fear it is still not enough.'

'Volunteers?'

'Cooks, smiths, farmers, grooms... anyone who is able-bodied and can wield a weapon is being recruited.'

'What of the tunnels?' Kritavarman asked.

'The entrance to one of the tunnels in the Market Square is closed off,' Krishna said, 'for the Third District is prowling with Greeks. The other is inside the Curfew.'

'We should start the evacuation process,' Ugrasen said. 'Women and children first.'

'Honourable, My Lord,' Krishna said, 'but my spies report that a reserve force of Greeks is still encamped at the place where the tunnel exits. Fortunately, they do not suspect there is a trapdoor under the very ground on which they sit. But escape that way is not a viable option at the moment. I reckon it may open up in a day or two, for the Greeks are marching into Mathura in strength.'

'Can we not start sending them out in small batches?'

Krishna shook his head. 'Not yet. Yami forbid, should the Greeks smell that we are trying to escape, it won't take 'em long to block the tunnel and choke us all in there. It has to be a measure of last resort.'

'What of our boats in the Yamuna?' Akrur asked Kritavarman quietly, afraid of the answer.

'Due to the storm last night, the river is in flood, and the current too strong for the smaller boats. The rope-house in the Third District was completely burned down. Without the ropes, the bigger boats cannot be floated into the river.'

'Any support from allies?' Ugrasen asked.

'We have none... perhaps Hastina.' It was Krishna who spoke. 'And that is because, most fortunately, we have Draupadi. We have sent more than twenty ravens to Hastina. Perhaps half of them won through arrow and storm and hawks to make it to our friends there. I imagine they will need a few days to march,

but I am confident they will get here in seven days, well before
the Greeks scale the Second Sister. Mathura will hold out
till then.'

'What of Panchal?' Kritavarman asked.

'Our ravens to Panchal were killed by Greek scouts. And the
father bears no love for the daughter. I am not hopeful there. But
do not be overly concerned, My Lords. As I said, they need a
fortnight. We have all seen the Greek encampments. They don't
have the numbers to hold out for a long siege. Five days perhaps,'
Krishna said. 'I doubt they'll last even that long. We will do what
we have always done. Wait.'

'But the Third Sister...' began Akrur.

'The Third Sister is down, yes,' Krishna said in a strong voice
that silenced the murmurs, 'but blazebane cannot reach over
the Second Sister without the siege towers, which we have
destroyed. Their catapults will never make it through the Lower
Districts. Even if they do, the alchemical blankets are working.
The process of extracting carpets from every noble house to
supplement them is also underway. Without blazebane and
siege towers, the Greeks can do nothing to our Walls. They are,
of course, trying to climb up.' He laughed. 'But Mathura cannot
be easily impregnated. Remember, we have a fortnight. Help
will come. And if it doesn't, we will have ample time to use the
tunnels.'

The Senators nodded, as if in a trance, somewhat reassured by
Krishna's confident words. Krishna sighed. Hope was a strong
drug, especially when someone mixed it in your drink without
telling you. He sank back in his chair and folded his arms. His
eyes turned to Satyabhama. She was looking at him intently. Her
eyes were pretty, but they were unfortunately imprisoned in a
resting bitch face.

Deep breaths. There was nothing to worry about. Krishna knew
he had time. He would find a way out of this mess. If not, they
would escape through the tunnel under Syamantaka. He cursed
silently, wondering what had possessed him to let that dolt
Yudhistir take his griffin.

The door of the Senate Hall flung open. Akrur turned, frowning. 'What is the meaning of this? This is a closed War Council—'

'My Lords! Someone has opened a gate in the Second Sister! The Greeks have entered!' a page announced, half shrieking. Cold hands coiled around Krishna's throat.

Balram walked over to him with the charm of an evil glacier. 'There goes your fortnight.' Saying which, he left him in a gloom of silence.

II

Krishna had not closed his eyes all night. He had passed into a strange warlike wakefulness that lay in the realm beyond the jurisdiction of exhaustion.

'The Second Sister was first breached two days ago,' Balin, Captain of the Republican Army, explained in a monotonous tone, as if describing the weather. 'The first two assaults were driven back and we held the Burnished Gardens that night. But with our forces concentrated on that single breach, they were able to climb the eastern section of the Second Sister, and storm into the Plaza of Freedom. Ever since, the entire central section of the city has been one long marathon battle during the day,' the Captain reported. 'We mounted a few successful raids of our own under cover of darkness. Not a single step of Mathuran soil has been given without soaking it in Mlecchá blood.'

Perhaps Balin thought it would lift their spirits to know this, but it only made Krishna feel sick. This was not how it was supposed to go. He was meant to have more time.

'In a cruel irony of fate, since the Greeks have entered the Second Sister, they have stopped catapulting fire upon us as they would also torch their own soldiers,' Balin explained, as if Krishna hadn't understood.

Why hadn't the wretched Hastina forces turned up yet? What was holding them back? The Trial could not possibly have lasted this long. Was it possible Yudhistir had betrayed him having won the Hastina Throne? Krishna had not considered such an eventuality. Clearly, he hadn't considered many things.

'We have run out of space for the wounded in the Iron Curfew.' Lady Asmai had joined the War Council that day. 'I fear for what is to come. If they conquer the Second District, they will launch blazebane into the Iron Curfew, and we will be caught like mice in a trap.'

'I doubt that,' Satyabhama finally spoke. 'The twisting lanes of the Second District are way too many. We can make a stand. We can send the City Guard, every man, woman and child to the rooftops, to rain hell upon them. We can create ambushes at every turn, alley and roundabout. If we are mice, then let us show them the plague we can unleash.'

'Right you are, War Mistress.' Balin saluted.

'Now leave us, all of you. I will have a word with my husband.'

III

'When did you turn into a coward, Krishna?'

Krishna's dark skin flushed with outrage. 'Know who you speak to, Satyabhama! There is nothing to fear. If you remember, I have never been defeated.' The effect of his words was somewhat spoiled by the sound of an explosion in the distance.

Satyabhama made an obscene gesture with her fingers. 'You're feeling unsure, isn't that it?' she asked.

'And why would I feel that?'

'Because, for the first time, you do not have an escape plan. You do not have Garud. Your thoughts keep harking back to the secret third tunnel, the Syamantaka tunnel under the Senate House, and escaping from there, but you do not want to do that because then everyone will know the secret source of your power. Worse, they might think they don't need you any longer. You cannot escape alone with your family either, because you cannot leave Mathura to its fate. Behind those peacock feathers, there is a fragile conscience and a genuine love for this city and its people. Not to forget, it would interfere with your hero-image. That leaves the public tunnel inside the Curfew. Using the Curfew tunnel, however, is fraught with risk because then you must leave your chance of survival in the hand of destiny, and you have trust issues with fate.'

'Thank you, Satyabhama. I love hearing about my existential crisis while a battle is raging outside our doors. It is most restful.'

Satyabhama, however, was not finished. 'Somewhere inside, you are worried that this may be it. That you have finally taken a misstep and you will either lose, or die. And you don't know which is worse.'

Krishna groaned at being forced to look into the mirror of his soul.

'What are you the best at?' she asked.

'Livestock and manipulating minds,' Krishna said wearily. 'How does it matter?'

'Are you done feeling sorry?' Satyabhama took his hand and they walked to the window, looking out across the burning city that was theirs. 'You know why I fell in love with you?'

He gave a throaty chuckle. 'For my dashing good looks?'

'You didn't have the arms of a warrior. You were a lowborn cowherd, so there was no climbing up in station. Yes, you became rich, but so were many others. You wore the most bizarre clothes! Not to forget the small matter that you already had two wives.'

'I get it. I wasn't much of a catch.'

'It was your mind I loved, Krishna.' She held his face between her palms. 'You have a beautiful mind that can see a lighthouse through the densest fog. I try to stay two steps ahead of my enemy. You, on the hand, make the enemy take the steps *you* want. You can fool Yama if you put your mind to it. You are not Krishna because you have Garud or Syamantaka. You have Garud and Syamantaka because you are Krishna.'

He looked into her eyes, then leaned in for a kiss. She pushed him away. 'Are you serious?' she snapped.

'I thought we were having a moment...'

'If you were the Krishna I love, you would have known he wasn't getting any till he dazzles me. Maybe then...' she leaned close 'you will get what you want.'

'Ahem...' someone coughed.

Krishna turned to find Rain at the door. She saluted. 'Dire news. We were counting on the alleyways to slow down Kalyavan. Turns out he is using his airavats to raze the buildings on the way to the Iron Curfew. The alleys, turns and tiers won't matter as they are falling away like children's blocks. In a matter of hours, he will have cleared a straight path to the Curfew.'

Krishna straightened, willing the shivers away. His eyes had an odd glint. 'Come, Rain. Let's teach that boy some manners. But first, fetch me some livestock.'

IV

The sun was high but the duststorm kicked up by the crusading airavats effectively blocked it out, casting a pall over everything. The *mahouts* goaded the great beasts with their hooks till they rushed forward in maddened fury. There was little to distinguish their trumpeting from thunder. They smashed through the buildings of the Second District as if they were made of spider gauze instead of brick and mortar. There was no need for the Greek army to fight their way to the Iron Curfew. The layered and tiered defence Balram had spent months creating was levelled in moments. The archers, riding in towers atop the airavats, rained down arrows on any Republican Army soldier who tried to stop the beasts.

'He... just... cleared the city.' Akrur voiced the obvious as they stood on the Iron Curfew, watching the carnage of their city in disbelief.

'We have a moat around the Curfew,' Kritavarman said. 'The beasts may be tall but the Walls are still taller. Airavats don't wear armour. Our arrows will find them.'

'Can't take that chance,' Krishna said, his face grim. 'Rain, *now!*'

Orders went out. Wheels creaked and men groaned as they pushed the catapults up the sloping path to the parapets of the Iron Curfew.

'Krishna!' Kritavarman said, aghast. 'Are you planning to bomb your own city? Our army is still there.'

'And if you are,' Akrur remarked laconically, 'these catapults are too small.'

Krishna said nothing as he studied the small catapults carefully lined on top of the Curfew's ramparts. 'Kritavarman, get word out: let the evacuation through the tunnel in the Curfew begin. We cannot wait any longer. Divide them into groups, each group with an armed escort. Do not foolishly send out entire families. Each family leaves behind a man and a woman. Do not let any able-bodied man leave, especially masons, bricklayers, smiths, carpenters; retain them for repair work. If their families want to wait with them, put them to work as well. Use children to ransack the cupboards for any linen clothes they can find. Since we don't have any spare iron, get the women to glue linen into strips to make armour for the civilian volunteers. Get the men to strip down buildings and haul the nails they find in barrels to the smiths for arrowheads and spear blades. Understood?'

Kritavarman could only nod in awe, but the sound of grunting pigs distracted him. All the soldiers on the ramparts turned in surprise as a squad of Silver Wolves marched to take position before the catapults, holding the ropes that noosed the filthy oinking beasts. The pigs shone with oil and resin, the same substances Krishna had once smuggled to Yudhistir to coat the Mansion of lac at Varnavrat. The Wolves positioned themselves in a line and began hauling the pigs onto the spoons of the catapults. The pigs struggled, squealing in alarm, as if sensing danger but unable to do anything for their legs were tied. *Kalyavan has his pets. I have mine.*

'What is the meaning of this?' Akrur asked.

Krishna merely smiled. As the airavats came within shooting range of the catapults, he yelled, 'Release!'

The resin was lit. The pigs were set on fire. If the squealing had been loud before, it now reached a desperate crescendo. He could barely hear the slam of the catapult arm against the frame over their cries.

The airavats might as well have seen Yama swooping down on them. Their entire frontline was in disarray as flaming, squealing pigs descended from the sky. The airavats ran helter-skelter, trampling their own men. Their bladed tusks gored each other in their panic. Beasts bellowed; men screamed. The orderly march vanished in moments, replaced by a righteous run for survival.

Two Greek generals in the rear marshalled their men and the airavats of the second line and managed to charge towards the Iron Curfew amidst the rain of flying pigs. But once the discipline of an army falters, it takes a miracle to steady it again. The airavats, losing all sense of direction, rushed at the great walls of the Iron Curfew instead of its gates. One fell into the deep moat and others followed, one after the other, in some macabre brotherhood of death.

'Ready your bows!' roared Krishna.

All around bows creaked as they were drawn, aims taken, jaws clenched. The airavats struggled in the moat, tusks shining, tongues lolling, eyes filled with murderous hate.

'Now!'

Bowstrings twanged and arrows hissed down, followed by stones, javelins, sling shots and even nails. The archers took easy aim, picking off the Greeks below one by one. Krishna reckoned it took ten to fifteen arrows to bring an airavat down. The boilers dropped hot oil over the ones that still stood, enraging them. And it worked splendidly, for they turned on their own mahouts, spearing and trampling them with an ivory fury.

By the end of the day not a single airavat who had charged the Curfew remained. Emboldened by the feat on the Curfew, the Republican Army, hiding on the rooftops of the buildings in the

Second District, charged the Red Cloaks trailing the airavats who had been retreating. From above, and the rear, they attacked. They killed the mahouts of the surviving airavats with their arrows and, without a master, the beasts scattered away. Mathura had clearly won this round.

And Krishna had the best sex of his life that night.

SHAKUNI

I

'Partition on these terms is unacceptable.'

'Your terms are a pile of horseshit, is what he means to say!' Arjun had had enough. 'Are we beggars to be given alms? You give us Khandavprastha – a ruined fortress in the middle of an infested forest. And the fields of Kurukshetra. Nothing grows there. Not even hope. And Varnavrat – a village!' Arjun fumed. 'Do not forget the smallfolk are with us. Hastinapur remembers the Mansion of lac. They will rally to us, as will the Hundred.'

A threat backed by fact, Shakuni noted. It was true. If the matter went out of this chamber, partition would be forgotten and the King would not win even farmlands for his son.

'Arjun, this is not the way to address the King. You must beg pardon,' Yudhistir said sternly, but conveniently after Arjun was done outlining his discontent.

In the face of Arjun's ominous silence, Yudhistir turned to the others. 'I humbly apologize on my brother's behalf. Young blood often bubbles more than it actually boils. What he meant to say was that if there is to be Partition, it should be on equal terms. Equal as a whole; in terms of area, influence, and revenue. The areas that have been allotted to our share, generous as they are, are riddled with problems that cannot be compensated for even by your suggestion of monetary compensation for three years. It is not as if after three years Kurukshetra will start growing crops, or the Nagas who live there will become extinct.'

'You have Panchal, son,' Dhritarashtra pointed out.

And once again the discussions rambled on. Meanwhile, Shakuni twirled a scroll in his hands. Fidgeting with it. Unrolling it. Reading it. Sighing heavily. Sahadev finally caught the bait.

'What is it that you hold, Lord of Gandhar?' he asked.

'Oh this...' Shakuni said, apparently agitated. 'Most dreadful news, Prince, which I am unable to digest. But according to the Diktat, I must hold my tongue.' He dropped the scroll and it rolled over to Sahadev on the other side of the table. 'Ah, my stiff fingers. Prince, would you please be kind enough to return it. My back is not what it used to be.'

Sahadev narrowed his eyes. Sahadev picked up the scroll and stretched over the table to return it. As Shakuni had expected, he discreetly prised it open with thumb and index finger to take a peek at the scroll's contents. Before Shakuni could take the scroll back, Sahadev froze. He stood up with a start, hastily unrolling the scroll. 'Vayu save us! Brother, Mathura is under siege! Draupadi and Bheem are trapped! Forces numbering over six thousand have attacked the city with airavats!' He turned to Shakuni, whose mouth was turned down in grim pleasure. 'You knew!'

'We must leave for Mathura immediately!' The White Eagle was on his feet. For a man his age, he was both nimble and quick. 'It is a three-day ride even on the fastest horses.'

'We can take Garud. It will be faster,' said Arjun.

'Garud is not impervious to weapons,' Sahadev remarked. 'And only Yudhistir can ride him, and it will be too risky to put him in sight of their arrows. Can you teach Arjun how to fly Garud, brother?'

'Tarry a while longer, Lords and Lordlings,' Shakuni said, standing up with his hands spread before him, his voice clear as crystal. 'As dreadful as the news is, and as much as it pains my heart, it was upon Prince Yudhistir's request that His Grace passed a Diktat that nothing be permitted to interrupt these proceedings till a conclusion be reached. In fact...' He stretched a hand down to where Sahadev sat, and borrowed the Codes. Shakuni's hand shook under the weight of the heavy book but he lifted it and took it over to Acharya Kripa. 'The Diktat is now a matter of record, inked and sealed. It is the Will of the King,' said Shakuni. 'Acharya Kripa, would you please be so kind as to read out the relevant excerpt for the benefit of the attendant parties?'

Seeking the King's permission, Kripa stood and read: 'Verse 67:201. *A Monarch is Justice and Law forged into a sword, whose searing fury the Monarch himself is not immune from. The Diktat of a Monarch should be rarely exercised, and once uttered, cannot be unspoken, for the Monarch, as unmoving as the North Star, must be ever constant. Once the words of the Diktat are inscribed in ink, dye or blood, it becomes the Law. Even the King cannot undo it. Any change in such Law can only be brought about by the Will of the People so governed, exercised through each and all of the Eight, who possess the godgiven faculties to take decisions for the commonfolk.*

'Manu was rather verbose, Your Grace,' said Kripa. 'If I may be excused from reading on? Unless, of course, Prince Sahadev is of the opinion further excerpts require it?' He smiled at Sahadev, who stood slack-jawed. 'In short, Your Grace, unlike the decision on the Crown Prince, which was a referral from the Tribunal, amendment of a Diktat requires the entire Council of Eight. Not the Tribunal, not the Hundred, but the Eight; a process I can initiate right away.'

Kripa allowed Sahadev an agonizing moment to consider the implications, then said, 'Prince Duryodhan is a member of the Eight, as is Lord Shalya. We will send our fastest riders on Gandharan steeds to the Chorus, and pray they return to Hastina swiftly. With Mathura under siege by the Magadhan host, we can only hope the Emperor will spare Prince Bheem and Princess Draupadi from his wrath. Loath as I am to admit it, with Greek Fire and airavats, I am afraid Mathura's chances do not look promising.'

Sahadev stared at Shakuni. *All the books on earth cannot prepare you for what comes with experience, bastard,* Shakuni wanted to say, but for now he decided to let Sahadev imagine Shakuni's words. A few hours ago, it had been he chewing his nails, silently stewing and turning over various unlikely scenarios to get what he wanted. When the White Eagle had set them on the path of partition, Shakuni had to ensure Yudhistir got nothing out of it. That was why he had immediately drawn a line on the map of the Union. A clever line. Equal only in size. While Hastinapur itself was marked for Duryodhan, along with Gandhar and Anga, the enormous swathes of the Khandavprastha forest, along with Madra and Varnavrat, fell in Yudhistir's domain.

But Yudhistir would never have agreed to this. Madra was already Nakul and Sahadev's maternal legacy through their mother, Madri. And it was well known that Madra was a part of the Union only in name, for Shalya played his own games. Varnavrat barely passed for a town. And Khandavprastha was a ruin; worse, a dangerous place.

Shakuni could have forced it down their throats had he had the time to plant his seeds, or if he were alone with them. But with members of the Eight present in the chamber, and the Hundred outside... *no*. This was a different battlefield, with different rules. And that was when his prayers had been answered in the form of the scroll from the messenger. A messenger, who had ridden his horse to death to deliver a request. A request for urgent aid, it would seem, from a neighbour. How fortunate that he had run straight into one of Shakuni's Mists. All Shakuni had to do then was goad Yudhistir into digging a trap for himself, so the survival of his wife, brother and allies depended on how quickly he surrendered. And his plan had worked like a well-oiled rat trap.

Vidur, Master of Law, spoke, bringing Shakuni back to the present. 'Surely, the Codes provide for executive power in the King in times of war, when such formalities can be set aside,' he opined, looking at the White Eagle. 'There is precedent.'

'Indeed, Lord Vidur,' Acharya Kripa said calmy, 'there is. But *Hastina* is not at war. Mathura is. There is no such exemplary power granted to the King in another State's conflict.'

And just like that, the tables turned. Acharya Kripa did not even bother to suppress his sour smile.

But Shakuni held his breath. There was something in Yudhistir's eyes, something that glowed with the embers of ambition. He was too close to what he wanted to accept defeat. Even the White Eagle fixed his gaze upon Yudhistir, judging, appraising. Had it just been Bheem, Yudhistir might not have yielded. But Draupadi… she was the key to Panchal. Without her, he had no wheat to bargain with. The Reds would desert him. He had to think of the long game. He had to accept he had lost this hand.

'If only there was a way to resolve this contentious issue of Partition amicably, as soon as possible,' Acharya Kripa lamented. 'As Prince Sahadev has reminded us repeatedly, there are people waiting outside for this momentous decision. Alas, the rigours of dharma trample without bias king and commoner alike under its hooves.'

'I agree.'

A pall of silence fell. Everyone looked up.

'To what do you agree, son?' the King asked.

Yudhistir's voice held none of the wrath that shone in his eyes. 'I agree to your proposal, Your Grace.'

Arjun took a hasty step forward. 'This is ridicu—'

'*Arjun!* You forget yourself.' The King's voice was like a whiplash. *Finally, he shows some spine.* Arjun clenched his teeth so hard Shakuni thought his jaw must hurt.

'We will take Khandavprastha, Varnavrat and Madra,'Yudhistir said.

'Scribble that down, Scrollmaster,' Acharya Kripa ordered. 'In golden letters.'

'I have just one request, Your Grace,'Yudhistir said.

Request, hah! Another word for condition. Relief, however, sounded in Dhritarashtra's voice as he said in a flurry of words, 'I have always believed the Kauravas would eventually come together as a family and resolve our differences and heal any rifts, no matter how large the issue. Yudhistir, you have shown statesmanship today. Ask what you want, and it shall be yours.'

No, you idiot! Shakuni could not have hurried to him without making a fool of himself. *Fuck.*

Yudhistir took a deep breath. Any hint of anger had faded from his face. No complaint. 'I desire that the five of us brothers

– Bheem, Arjun, Nakul, Sahadev and I – and our descendants
and heirs be hereafter known as Pandavas, Sons of Pandu. Not
Kauravas.'

Dhritarashtra frowned, unsure what to make of the request.
Shakuni, on the other hand, could not believe his luck. He felt
like Fate had circled the place on the map where he now sat.
Pandavas versus Kauravas. Some people said there was little in a
name, but he knew better. A name is what defines, and names are
what divides. Lines were drawn between names. Hastily, Shakuni
chimed in, 'There is precedent for such a request, Your Grace. The
Balkhans are after all Kauravas in truth. A reasonable request,
Your Grace.'

Dhritarashtra, relying on Shakuni, nodded awkwardly. 'Very
well. Scribe, note my decision: *I, with the Royal power entrusted
in me as Head of the Imperial Council and King of the Union, grant
the Stronghold of Khandavprastha, with all its attendant lands and
earnings, to Yudhistir Kaurava Pandav, Son of Pandu, to make his
seat and rule henceforth as King of Khandavprastha, the Brother-
Kingdom of Hastinapur. King Yudhistir and his brothers and their
legitimate sons and descendants of the male line shall hold these lands
in perpetuity. The Lords of the Western Union will now be known
as the Lords of Khandavprastha, from Varnavrat to Vadeh, and shall
perform their duty to the House of Pandavas with Yudhistir as their
rightful liege.* The Eight consents?'

'Aye!'

'Case disposed,' Bheeshma said. 'Now bring the Queen of
Khandavprastha home.'

DRAUPADI

I

Draupadi warily approached one of the last remaining tents within the Iron Curfew. Most of the other tents were coming down. The noise was overwhelming: squadrons trading curses, captains bellowing commands, horses whickering and blowing, children crying. Mail shirts were tossed into barrels and rolled across the cobblestones of the streets to scour them clean. Women tossed pails of water over cook-fires. Stableboys shoed horses and pack-mules. Men-at-arms straightened swords at smithies and knocked the dents from breastplates. Civilians stood around mules, loading essentials for their journey through the tunnel.

None paid Draupadi any heed. A good thing considering she was sick of the Keep where she had been bunched with the other High Ladies of Mathura. A bard had played bawdy songs to liven the air, only to receive joyless laughter. Even at lunch, she had found every morsel to be flavoured with fear. She had needed to leave that room.

She did not know whether the Wolves would be assigned to her detail in the tunnels, and so she thought of going to meet them one last time. She pulled aside the tent flap and entered. Piety stood nearby, shield strapped to her right arm, sword in her gauntleted left hand, most of her face hidden by the side flaps of her helm. Bleed was flipping her knives, the blades slapping on the leather of her gloves. Calm was drinking ale from a jug. Storm was sprawled against a pile of bedrolls, picking her teeth with a fish bone.

'Princess!' Rain stood sharply to attention. 'How may we be of service?' The other Wolves stopped what they were doing and gathered round.

'I cannot be of any service; I am tired,' Storm moaned.

'Storm!' Rain hissed. 'Stand up! And where is your squad? Assemble those loafers. The Wolf Whistle has been blown.'

'I heard, I ain't deaf.' Storm looked at Rain sheepishly. 'My squad will be a little... delayed. They've all gotten the squats.'

'What! *All* of them? Did you cook again, Storm?' Vial asked.

Storm shrugged. 'If the War Mistress has decided to assemble an army of cowards with weak bellies, there is nothing I can do. The fish was fine.'

'Fish?' asked Piety, astonished. 'Where did you catch fish? The Yamuna is in spate.'

'I didn't catch it. I brought it with me... bought from a trader who paid it as a bribe to be allowed to take his chances on a boat.'

Rain stared at Storm, at a loss for words. Draupadi could not help but giggle. 'See, Rain, even the Princess agrees.'

'Pray do not let me be a hindrance,' Draupadi said quickly. 'I came merely to wish you safe travels.'

Rain nodded. 'My thanks, Princess. Some of us will be with you in the tunnel. The others you will see once they too are all out of the tunnel safely, Yama willing.'

'I can't believe we are running away from the battle!' Misery complained. 'Why were we put through all the phalanx training then?'

'It isn't running away,' Storm drawled. 'It's called withdrawing in good order. We are a patrol squad, for Yama's sake!'

Storm gestured to Draupadi to sit down. 'Don't mind Misery. She just thirsts for blood. They're all losing their minds with this waiting. But these are exciting times, eh? The Third Sister has been breached! The Second Sister opened! That hasn't happened in ten summers. And Lady Satyabhama is out there on a sortie, taking a stab at saving those poor fellows who could not run fast enough to the Curfew. Just between us, I don't understand why she has to be so heroic all the time. Heroic stands usually end with no one standing.'

'I'm sure she will be fine, Storm. Bheem told me the Greeks are losing most of their bouts with the Mathurans. A promising sign. Even Krishna is smiling.'

'A fat lot of good that will do him. He just misses his griffin, though I don't see why. It's useless anyway. Why can't he use a drakon?'

'Because drakons aren't found here, Storm,' Calm said in the voice of one talking to a child. 'And I've heard tell of that Greek Warlord. Has some prophecy around him that no Man can beat him. It gets him hard.'

Storm spat. 'Damn prophecies. They are nothing but conspiracies by Namins to stay relevant. I remember one around my birth as well. Sure got my mother riled enough to hang herself.'

Rain sighed. 'Calm, you might want to pass that ale around. We're about to go into a tunnel, and we will need our nerves about us. Especially if Storm keeps talking.'

'Aye, Captain, right you are. Listen, you ungrateful wenches, two mouthfuls each, then I get the rest. More than two swallows and I cut you down where you stand.'

'Aren't you such a doll, Calm.' Storm chuckled.

Draupadi was taking measure of the women around her. All strong. All worried. She was sure the sentiments inside the Hall were much the same as in all the tents along the Curfew. Some could not hold their bowels. Some could not stop drinking. Some prayed. War was an ugly business. But Draupadi was secure in the knowledge that she was too important a hostage to be harmed. While Satyabhama's words that flesh interested battle-drunk soldiers more than gold had worried her, she now knew she would be among the first to escape through the tunnel, guarded by these brave women. She felt safe.

'Rain! Storm took more than three sips!'

'Storm,' Rain said, 'one more sip and I promote you.'

Storm hastily gave the jug back to Calm. 'Apologies, Captain. I promise – no more!'

They heard a low whistle and a sudden stirring outside. 'War Mistress is back. It's time. Cutters, to me. My Lady, Piety will escort you to the Keep.'

'I will pray for you all.'

'Pray that Rain gets some stamina,' Storm quipped.

'Oh, shut up, Storm.'

KRISHNA

I

Krishna wiped the grime from his face as he walked away from the smithy where men were pouring metal into moulds for arrowheads. They would need thousands more if the Greeks came calling in full strength. He passed the makeshift cages and pens by the Walls, where goats and hens huddled together, their numbers severely depleted. Sighing, he craned his neck up to see the archers resting on the Walls, untroubled by the commotion below.

While they had lost many of their airavats, the Greeks had not lost their spirit. Last he looked, they were squatting in houses, the ones not levelled by the airavats, making themselves comfortable. He did not know what they were waiting for, nightfall, beasts or something new. In any event, Mathura seemed to have earned a respite.

Last night, they had tried storming the Walls, but the Iron Curfew was too high. Their catapults, re-assembled again, did manage to throw blazebane-rocks, but the ones that did smash against the lower stone walls just bounced off, doing some damage but nothing meaningful, partly thanks to Jambavan's carpets, and partly thanks to the stone of its build. Only the ones that actually hit the ramparts would have had any significant effect, as the rampart was built of wood, easy to catch fire, and only supported from below, therefore susceptible to shatter. But without their siege towers, the Greeks could not achieve the height they needed to inflict real harm.

The Mathurans did not fail to entertain their guests with their hospitality either. They conducted sharp sorties outside the Curfew to inflict losses and lower Greek morale. Twice, they managed to burn the catapults the Greeks had re-built. Krishna spotted Satyabhama returning from one such raid. *Even bloodied and dirty, she looks bewitching,* he thought. Satya barked a command to her squad to go freshen up. Krishna surveyed her. Her armour was unclasped. Her long dagger had snapped a finger's length from the tip, but her sword seemed intact, though rimmed scarlet and brown.

Satyabhama saw his eyes upon her and called, 'Like what you see, My Lord?'

We must leave. Satya will not stop going to the frontlines, and I cannot risk her life. The Iron Curfew still held strong but the week had been full of surprises. 'I need to buy you Assyrian steel, Satya. You always manage to make a mess of your sword,' he said, walking up to her.

'If it ain't messy, you aren't doing it right.'

'I see that philosophy has now extended from bed to other aspects of your life. What happened there?' he asked, seeing that her trouser had been ripped from under her greaves, revealing a generous amount of leg.

'The Greeks, you know. Quite handsy.'

A flash of rage sparked through Krishna but he held himself in control. He thought of asking her to head the evacuation party through the tunnels. But asking Satyabhama to walk away from danger was like convincing a stag to try meat.

'I need my soldiers focused, Satya,' Krishna joked. 'Change into something more conservative, would you?'

'Aye, husband.'

'Feels like Pragjyotisha all over again, does it not?'

'The weather was better there.'

He would have kissed her deep for all Mathura to see, but a clout on the head from his wife in front of his soldiers would not have helped his image as a leader.

'How are things inside the Walls?' she asked.

'Bad. Balram had to sentence an entire family to death for spying for the Greeks. Likely they had been promised safe passage if they opened the gates.'

'Or they were hungry. Food is growing scarce.'

'How did the people take it?' Satyabhama asked.

'Disturbingly well. I am glad it is the Greeks outside there instead of the Magadhans. Given those pale-skinned foreigners, the cityfolk would rather die than be enslaved by the likes of them. However, some have taken it upon themselves to exact vigilante justice upon anyone suspicious. I had spread a rumour that the Greeks poisoned the water supply to stop them from ransacking the public tanks, and now I have bands of men stopping and searching individuals at random. A man delivering powder for the munitions was torn apart by a crowd.'

'The price of peace,' Satyabhama said, just as Draupadi was escorted in by a Silver Wolf. 'Princess, why aren't you with the High Ladies?'

'Lady Satyabhama.' Draupadi bowed, a sheepish look in her eyes. 'The room is filled with endless sobbing. Everyone's face is puffy from crying.'

'Shush, child.' Satyabhama bit back the hint of a smile. 'Say no more. There is strength in those tears, you know. But if you will not have them, come, join us. We were just heading to the Council Chamber. Be forewarned, Bheem will be there.'

'Wouldn't you like to clean up first?' Krishna called from behind her.

'My bloodied clothes always help you make your point, Krishna.'

II

Ugrasen stood by the window which gave a clear view of the ramparts as well as the Second District, for the Keep's eastern side was connected to the inner walls of the Iron Curfew. In fact, there were catwalks on the lower levels for ease of communication of instructions from the Council to the Curfew. Krishna joined him by the window and followed his gaze to the battlements, where five Red Cloaks dangled from a rope by their wrists, burning. He had no affinity for such torture. The drawn-out agony, the stink, the shrieks, it was all inhumane. But there were no trophies for good behaviour in battle. Maybe those Mlecchás would think again before they tried to creep in under cover of darkness and disturb the well-earned sleep of his people.

Beyond the Curfew, another flock of Red Cloaks could be seen streaming through the Second District in bloodied confusion. Ever since the gates of the Second Sister had been opened to the Greeks by a traitor, plunder had been the word of the day. The soldiers had managed to escort many of the citizens inside the Iron Curfew, especially those who carried gold. The ones who did not, hid in houses, hovels or holes in the ground in the Second District, hoping the Greeks would simply ignore them and move to shinier houses. Here and there, the remnants of the Republican Army and City Guard held on, but they could do little to compromise the Red Cloaks' advance.

'We have nothing to worry about,' Ugrasen rumbled. 'The Iron Curfew is impregnable.' Nonetheless, his voice shook. Till a few days ago, the Second and Third Sisters had been impregnable too.

'The evacuation has begun. Some soldiers have gone ahead to clear the way. But now with the Red Cloaks streaming into the city, I doubt we will find any foes when we emerge. I suggest the Council start moving with the first batches—'

'NO!' Kritavarman and Balram cried in unison.

'We will exit last. Guerrilla tactics is one thing,' Kritavarman said. 'Running away and abandoning your people is against the creed of war and honour.'

So is dying, Krishna thought. 'Against the creed of *Ksharjas*,' he corrected, 'which we, incidentally, are not.'

'What are the words *we* live by, Krishna?' Balram interjected. '*Deeds, not Birth.*'

I could just leave them here to die, Krishna reflected, knowing he never would. *Why do they have to be such fools?*

'Where is Satyaki?' Kritavarman asked suddenly. 'Taken a headstart into the tunnel, has he?'

'I have sent him on a mission,' Krishna said.

'Of course you have.'

'I, for one, stand with Krishna,' Akrur said. 'We should leave when the going is good.'

'I won't die a craven!' Kritavarman hissed through clenched teeth.

'Or a fool!' retorted Balram. 'Why are we sending soldiers with the people when we are desperate for defenders? If we were at full strength here, even without the Walls, they could never have taken us down.'

'So much talk,' Bheem complained, massaging his temples. 'Let us go out and kill them. Without their blue fire, they are nothing.'

'You stay out of it!' Akrur bristled. 'You're no Mathuran. You shouldn't even be here.'

'Make me leave then.' Bheem twirled his mace.

'Boys,' Satyabhama said in a voice that wasn't really loud but hurt their ears as much it hurt their egos. She walked to one of the other windows and squinted out before saying, 'Be Men.'

'My apologies, Senators,' Krishna sighed. 'The stress of a siege gets to the best of us. But we cannot bicker amongst ourselves. Look at our Walls! The Greeks can fling themselves at the Iron Curfew all day for all the good it will do them. We have enough time to evacuate and escape, *all* of us. No one will be left behind.'

'I have one doubt,' Satyabhama said, squinting into the distance. Krishna was annoyed at being interrupted but her voice was uncharacteristically low. 'I am sure Kalyavan knows all this. Not about the tunnels, but he must know that he cannot climb the Curfew for it is a lot taller than the Second Sister, and has a smaller circumference, making it easier to guard. So why the half-hearted attempts? It must be a distraction...' She murmured this more to herself than to the others. 'Any reports on movement in Magadh?'

'Not that we know of,' replied Balram. 'And if the Emperor comes, it will be for Kalyavan, not us.'

'I don't understand,' said Satyabhama. 'That means Kalyavan is not stalling for help. They have made only one attempt to scale the Curfew. They are just crowding inside those houses—' Satyabhama froze. 'Krishna, pass me the eyeglass!' He handed it to her but could not see what had snared her attention.

'Why question blessings, War Mistress?' Akrur asked, pouring himself another glass of wine.

'Misfortunes often don the mask of blessings, Senator,' Satyabhama said without turning. 'Why are they carrying shovels into the houses?' She pressed the eyeglass closer to her eye, as if that would make things clearer. 'See there, and even there. Is a shovel needed in any way to create their catapults or siege towers?'

'Axes, perhaps,' Krishna said. 'Can't think why they would need shovels. And our sorties will never let them build a siege tower.'

'What if he is not trying to climb *over* our walls?' She turned so quickly towards Krishna that for a moment his head spun. He met her eyes, and like lovers in a dance they read each other's mind. *Under the walls.*

Krishna's jaw dropped. '*Yami's mercy!* They are digging! They are mining under the Iron Curfew! Everyone, leave the Keep now!'

As he turned to leave, he saw Ugrasen, still standing by the window. 'Lord Ugrasen! We must leave now!' he called urgently.

Ugrasen turned, a weak old man, a tired smile on his lined face as he nodded. That was the last thing Krishna remembered before the world plummeted around him.

SHISHUPAL

I

The wind on the terrace was blessedly cool, and only faintly reeked of smoke. A stool and a cot were the only furniture on the roof in Lady Rasha's quarters. Shishupal fidgeted nervously, watching the monkey-like clambering of the soldiers on the Iron Curfew. He was grateful for this exquisite, albeit accidental, unobstructed view of the Iron Curfew, as well as the Keep.

'The fighting seems to have stopped,' Shishupal said. 'Should we go out to check if we can smuggle into the tunnels? Are you listening?'

Eklavvya exhaled a sigh, wiggling his toes beneath a threadbare sheet. 'Thanks to your unkind prodding, blissful dreams have indeed released Eklavvya from their ample bosoms into the frigid arms of undisturbed reality.'

'What do you mean *undisturbed*?' Shishupal frowned.

'There may not be any fighting but we still cannot escape.' Eklavvya rose wearily and stretched his back. 'Not until the tunnel's entrance is choked with cityfolk. Only then will we be able to slip in unnoticed. Though now that you have woken Eklavvya, he does wonder: why do all sturdy things have to be so ugly. For all its strength, the Curfew is fucking hideous.'

As if offended, the Iron Curfew exploded. Flame-wreathed rocks scattered as a section of the Iron Curfew broke apart with thunderous reverberations. Then came another explosion and a blinding flash. The cracked section of the Wall now lay flattened in a wave. Stone and earth rattled down like unseasonal hail over the ash-layered rubble of the Curfew

Shishupal threw himself down on the floor, his desire to look tough beside the Yaksha greatly outweighed by his desire to stay alive. He didn't hear the thunderous sounds of the double detonations until some time later, because for some reason sound is slower than seeing. A vast crater now yawned between the jagged edges where the impregnable Iron Curfew had been breached. On either side of the vast crater the Curfew stretched, apparently oblivious it had been violated. Ash rode the breeze in playful abandon.

And then sounds of cracking filled the air. Shishupal turned in a trance towards the Keep that was connected to the Curfew. Cracks spread out on its walls like the greedy tentacles of a kraken. And then, before his disbelieving eyes, the Keep slowly toppled and slid onto the ground. Stones rained down from the tilting Keep, pinging onto the roofs of houses and into the street below.

'The beautiful taste of blood, the fragrance of charred flesh, the song of swords and the fruity stink of death,' Eklavvya chanted, utterly unmoved. 'Ah battle! And we have prime seats to view it unfold,' he said as he wiped the seat of the stool and languidly sat down.

'I may be wrong,' Shishupal said, rubbing the dust from his face as he rose warily to his feet, 'but I think the Yamuna Wars are at an end.'

DRAUPADI

I

The rain of stones had ceased, finally, and now only dust commanded the sky. The ruined side of the Keep behind them was burning, belching heavy black smoke that was no doubt visible from the farthest point of the Walls. Or so Draupadi hoped as she fervently prayed to Prakioni for Hastina to rescue them before it was too late.

She had been one of the first to be rescued from the wreckage of the Keep. Even now, soldiers were escorting members of the War Council to safety, though she could barely see them through the thick veil of dust around her. She could hear little above the cracking and felling of the stone that still seemed to ring in her ears. All she felt was Bheem's cruel grip on her wrist.

How did we survive? She dared to look up, and saw the faint outline of the Iron Curfew. The gates were still obstinately shut, but beside them a section of the Wall had vanished. Instead, a massive hole gaped like the maw of some monster.

'Time to leave, Draupadi,' Bheem grumbled.

'But shouldn't we wait for Krishna?' she asked. 'I do not see him anywhere. It's only a small gap in the Wall. It will be repaired soon.'

'It was Krishna who commanded me to take you through the tunnel to safety if something like this happened. And that's what I'm doing,' Bheem said gloomily, as if escorting his wife to safety featured low on his list of things to do. 'I should be out there killing some Greeks. Now I will have to rub shoulders with all the poor filth scampering in there, who are no doubt squeaking like mice in the dark. I hate that sound. It makes my head hurt. Come now.'

As she felt herself dragged away, Draupadi saw Satyabhama emerge from a side door of the sinking Keep, dust roiling up behind her like a wind-tossed shroud. Overcome by a giddy rush of courage, she resisted Bheem's tugging and called out Satyabhama's name. The War Mistress looked over at her and briefly nodded before returning to her soldiers. *I wish I could have thanked you better for your lessons,* Draupadi thought. *Prakioni look after you.*

'No time to waste, woman.' Bheem suddenly bent and hoisted her up on his shoulder like a sack of grain. Draupadi glanced back at Mathura one last time before she entered the tunnel. A sudden splash of crimson caught her eye like a scarlet shadow. *The Red Cloaks are here!* A cold dread swept through her as she saw a Greek emerge through the hole in the Iron Curfew. He had a horn in his hand. A moment later, a long gallant note echoed out over the First District.

The Battle of Mathura had begun.

BATTLE OF MATHURA

PART I

 KRISHNA's breath snagged as he was escorted out of the sinking Keep. A coughing fit clutched his throat, as sudden as a punch in the gut. He doubled up, his chest buzzing with each choking gasp. He felt a hand on his shoulder, a voice asking urgently: 'Sir, your orders?' Krishna stared back dumbly at the man who spoke, then up the bailey towards the Wall. A sea of scarlet flooded in through what seemed to be a hole in the Curfew.

Greeks in their dozens. Hundreds. Arrows flitted from the Curfew down into them. Bodies fell on each other. But they kept coming. The Red Cloaks were everywhere now, slamming at shield-walls, charging at the soldiers, and hacking down any wounded that limped away from them. Krishna's body shivered; he could not think. Ugrasen was dead. He had seen him die. No, he could not mope over that now. He needed silence to think, but his ears were full of the mad din.

Get out of Mathura! a voice within him roared. Too late to run now. He'd had his chance, and now the Greeks were everywhere. 'Not without Satyabhama,' he whispered.

The man who had asked him for orders must have heard him, for he answered that she was already out of the building and had engaged the Greeks. Krishna looked at the man again and realized he was one of the soldiers Balram had assigned to him. 'Your orders, Sir?' the man asked again, his squad behind him waiting earnestly for Krishna's instructions, as if he had all the answers.

Krishna shook off the shock. 'Ask Balram to reserve the best of our soldiers, and send them only when Kalyavan enters. The Archon is too naïve to leave the fighting to his men. Kill the head, the body will die. The rest of you follow me. We will join up with the War Mistress' forces. Do you know where she is?'

The soldier nodded and pointed. All Krishna could see was a Wolf standard in the distance. That was good enough. His squad formed a protective circle around him, and one of them handed him a shield and a helm.

As he donned the helm, Krishna saw that despite his low opinion of the City Guard, it had rallied swiftly, and now marched with pointed lances to the hole in the Iron Curfew, turning it into a barbed jaw. Not that it would matter. Mathura was lost. It would not be long before the Greeks overwhelmed the meagre Mathuran forces, or found the tunnels. It would be a massacre then. Good thing the rest of his family had followed orders and had been among the first to head into the tunnel. All he needed now was enough time to fetch Satya and escape. *Provided I manage to survive that long.*

But if he died today, he would at least die with the satisfaction of having lost to an extremely well-played manoeuvre. Students would study this battle for ages to come. And they would remember him. No one forgot Ravan because he lost. *History is not a plate reserved for victors alone.* Krishna sighed at the futility of his hopes, at his own narcissism. If only he could get Kalyavan to agree to a trial by battle, Balram could take care of him. He should have proposed it earlier, but had not imagined it would come to this.

The squad with Krishna in their midst soon charged into the broiling mess of Red Cloaks and Blue Robes. The ground was slippery and sodden with mud and blood. Krishna stumbled over a corpse, but somehow managed to retain his balance. Instinctively, he raised his shield, and a spear thudded into it, numbing his arm with its force. A sudden rage filled Krishna's mind. A ravenous rage. How did a Mlecchá dare to attack him? He snarled. The battle shrank to the size of the eye-slits in his helm. 'For Mathura!' he growled, spit flying from between his bared teeth.

His squad bellowed, 'For Krishna!'

Swords screamed, spears jabbed, flesh burst apart; Krishna's circle of guards was doing a good job as they marched through the press like a spiked ball. Men roared. Krishna roared with them. His squad did not let many Greeks breach their circle, but the unlucky ones who did, Krishna took care of with zest. All the training Balram had put him through in the last two decades kicked in. Krishna opened a swordsman from shoulder to armpit, caught the shoulder of another and rammed the rim of his shield through the man's throat so hard that he choked to death on the spot.

For a while Krishna thought of nothing. Not Mathura. Not Kalyavan. Not Garud. Nothing. All thought had fled his mind, along with fear. He no longer felt the ache in his back or the weight of his armour. Death danced around him, but time blurred, and even stopped, as his body went into a frenzy of pure instinct. There was only the fight, the enemy, the next man who wanted him dead. So, the only thing to do was kill him before he killed you. Satyabhama had called it blood song. Balram called it battle fever. Whatever its name, Krishna was now sick with it.

Krishna forced himself on. There was no politics here. No mind games. No waiting. 'Satya!' he shouted. Feral and barbaric, he grunted and pushed, kneed and heaved, chopping and slashing. Men and women were fighting everywhere, shouting, swinging blades and shooting arrows. He heard Balram's voice over the madness: 'Push them out of the hole! Beyond the hole!'

But Krishna had other worries. By now the circle around him had broken. Some were dead. Some scattered into different pockets of fighting. The crowd had grown too thick. Less fighting and shouting, more shoving and grunting. He dodged just in time to save himself from a Mathuran rider who was flailing his morning star wildly among Mathurans and Greeks alike. It was only after he had ridden past that Krishna saw that the man's skull was split open like a watermelon. *Yama will be busy today.*

Krishna gasped as he took a hard blow across his shield, stumbling back, his shield almost dropping from his arm. Before the Red Cloak could skewer him, a Mathuran rammed bodily into the Greek. They fell to the ground, grappling in the mud in murderous fury. Krishna was stunned and on his knees, blood trickling into his eyes and over his face. The rim of his own shield had cracked against his forehead. The battle fever in him began to ebb now. His head hurt. His armour felt heavy. The idea of a charge suddenly seemed ludicrous. What had possessed him? He was a General, not a foolish calf. He should have been on the roof of a house, giving instructions, *commanding*, not fighting in the thick of things, putting his own life on the line.

He rose, picking up his sword slowly. He remembered Kans saying: *Never try taming a bull by its horns when you can tame it with its tail.* It was good counsel, even from an enemy. Krishna lazily stabbed the Greek still struggling with the Mathuran on the ground through the back, uncaring about things like honour and code. He pulled up the Mathuran. 'My gratitude, soldier. Now run to Satyabhama and tell her—'

'Die!'

A man buried his axe into the skull of the soldier Krishna had been talking to, then slammed Krishna with his shield so hard that Krishna's head rang. *Not the head again.* Krishna turned from the blow like a temple dancer, arm circling, his sword accidentally slicing through the Greek's neck, laying it bare to the bone. 'You die!' Krishna managed to say before he fell to the ground, bleeding from the two injuries to his head, blackness closing in on him.

A waft of cold wind softly caressed his cheek. Krishna turned his fading attention towards the Iron Curfew. The last thing he saw was Kalyavan stroll through the hole, long hair tied back with a string, a sword across his shoulders like a milkmaid's yoke, arms slung casually over the blade. Over the screams of dying men and the cries of the wounded, his voice rose: 'I am here, my friends!' Red Cloaks circled him, their shields interlocking to intercept any stray arrow. From their throats rose the chilling war cry: *Hauuu!*

 SHISHUPAL felt his skin tingle when the Greek war cries floated out over the bailey, echoing through the buildings like ghostly voices. He finally saw the boy who had betrayed the Emperor, who had decided to take on Mathura on his own. And who, rather than wait for his army to decimate the Mathurans, had entered the battlefield. Like every hero, he had quite a sense of theatre. *Kalyavan does not lack guts, that's for sure. Or skill, apparently.*

Within moments, he was in the midst of the Mathurans, his sword making blurred circles around him, scattering men

as if they were nothing but clouds. Light reflected strangely on
the gemmed crosspiece of his sword as he whirled it around in
blinding arcs.

Eklavvya crouched beside Shishupal, enjoying the view of the
battle that raged in the distance. They were safe in the house for
now. Shishupal had considered following the Mathurans into the
tunnel, but knew he would be trampled by the crowd or cut down
by the guards. And once the Greeks won, the tunnel would become
a graveyard. Or so he told himself. It probably had nothing to do
with the fact that he had spied Lady Rukmini, the woman who
had left him at the altar for Krishna, enter the tunnel. Most men
would deny such a hard truth, but Shishupal knew two truths
could peacefully coexist. But there was another problem. Eklavvya
was growing jealous.

'You know, if watching Kalyavan show off is so difficult for you
to digest, you can leave from the tunnel.'

'And leave poor Shishupal to the hounds of war? Eklavvya
might be envious of that dolt showing off, but it is going to take
a whole lot more than spite to suppress Eklavvya's chivalry. Ah, I
know that large man!' he exclaimed, pointing towards the running
figure of a giant. 'He moves fast for a man with such large thighs!'

Kalyavan's eyes burned bright as he saw Balram charge towards
him, smashing Greeks left and right with his elephantine mace,
leaving a trail of burst heads in his wake.

'You had charming things to say at the parley, didn't you?'
Kalyavan shouted to Balram over the furore around them. 'Tell
me, do giants die the same way as men?' Balram lifted his bloodied
mace onto his shoulder and stared in deadly defiance. 'Silent type?'
Kalyavan grinned.

Shishupal could see Balram's monstrous chest swell, and
wondered what fighting the bastard would feel like. How in
Xath's name would you stop him once he started to move?
It would be like trying to stop a chariot. The gargantuan mace
notwithstanding, the sheer mass on the man's body was enough
for Shishupal to thank Xath it was Kalyavan, and not he, who
faced Balram.

'The man is mad to face Balram alone! The tougher his foe, the happier he seems to be!' Shishupal whispered, staring at Kalyavan smiling at Balram like a mother playing peekaboo with her toddler.

'Don't tempt Eklavvya, Shishupal!' Eklavvya fumed like an envious mistress. 'It is all he can do to not go down there, and claim his share of blood and bodies.'

Shishupal shook his head. *Another madman.* 'This could be the duel of the year and it is happening right under our noses and it...' And it was over before Shishupal's words were out of his mouth.

Balram's mace went up quickly, but Kalyavan was quicker as he rammed the pommel of his sword into Balram's mouth, snapping his head back. Kalyavan turned his sword in a circle above his head and leaned back as he slashed. The blade sliced through Balram's right cheek and went out the left. Balram bellowed in pain as he took a step back, stumbled on a discarded pile of sacks, and fell on his arse. He tried to rise, using his mace as a crutch, but Kalyavan lazily kicked it away. Balram fell flat on the ground.

Kalyavan beat Balram in single combat in a goddamn heartbeat! Shishupal stared in amazement. *Unbelievable!*

'Disappointing,' Kalyavan said, placing his sword lightly on Balram's neck. 'But perhaps this will serve an important lesson for you in your next birth – the mountain can never hurt the mist.' Kalyavan was about to slit Balram's throat when he was pushed away by someone crashing into his side, shield first. Kalyavan's legs wobbled but he managed to stay afoot. He looked offended, as if someone had cheated in a game. 'Spoilsport,' he grumbled. 'Then again it would be a waste of good steel upon *his* neck. But *your* neck on the other hand, My Lady... no number of rubies would be enough.'

Balram remained spread-eagled on the ground, unable to believe what had happened. He gasped for breath, one muscled hand in the mud, the other on his bleeding face.

'Healers, to me!' Satyabhama shouted.

Healers rushed to Balram and dragged him away, even as what was left of his squad guarded their retreat.

Kalyavan did not even glance their way. 'War Mistress, we finally meet without your husband to interfere. It is my rotten luck that it is on a battlefield instead of on a bed. I have not been able to push you out of my mind ever since you elbowed me in the face.' He dragged in a long breath and blew it out through thin lips as he lifted his sword. 'Is this really how it must begin between us?'

'No,' said Satyabhama. 'But this is how it will end.'

 RAIN whacked a shield with her sword, got hers whacked in response. But she was a large woman. She swiftly pulled the shield to herself; bringing the Greek upon her, she shoved him over her back and then tossed him behind her. With a mighty crunch, she smashed her boot into his face. *Crunch. Crunch. Die.* She needed to get the Silver Wolves to safety. They were a goddamn rescue squad, not trained for skirmishes like these. Another Greek charged at her, sword raised high. Rain lifted her shield but the sword never landed. Warily, she looked over the rim of her shield and saw the man looking in the direction where soldiers of either side had ceased fighting.

Did someone surrender? Rain wondered. And then, as if an unsung truce had been struck amongst the soldiers, friend and foe gathered silently in a circle. It was a circle of death. *A duel,* she thought. Rain knew she could use the break. Her shield arm hurt, and she was not growing any younger. She lowered her shield and walked to the haphazard circle of fighters growing around the two contestants in the middle, eager for the best view of the death that was doubtless on the cards. Rain spied sullen faces in the crowd, faces eager to get on with the killing rather than wait, sick with the blood song, but doing nothing. It was if they were spectators to a play, and it would be rude to disturb by killing other spectators.

By the time Rain wedged herself between the soldiers to see, the duel had already peaked. *Yama's balls!* she gasped. *It's the War*

Mistress. She saw Satyabhama slash at Kalyavan's head, but the Greek snaked under her blade. He hefted his sword up with furious speed as Satyabhama's steel swept down. The blades rang together with a finger-jarring clang.

They parted, but Kalyavan was grinning as he thrust forward his sword like a spear. Satyabhama wrenched herself sideways, and his sword hissed past. It caught her elbow greave, ripping it off. But Satyabhama was already thrusting her own sword at him. But the point of her steel only caught air as Kalyavan slid away again.

What the... She knew Kalyavan could have easily severed her unprotected elbow; instead, he brandished the bloody scarlet edge of his sword at the Greeks, earning their cheers, as he circled her like a predator.

Rain scoffed. Skill and showing off often went hand in hand in accomplished swordsmen. Clearly, Kalyavan had not become what he was by forfeiting chances to strike a pose.

'My sword is Assyrian steel, War Mistress,' Kalyavan said. 'No armour can stop it.' He smiled at Satyabhama's set face, blowing her a kiss and waving his two-handed sword in a fool's flourish. 'You know the prophecy I carry on my shoulders,' he said. 'I cannot be beaten, love. So why fight? Look around. Mathura is doomed. Soon it will be sacked, its false idols torn down.'

'Perhaps...' Satyabhama said calmly, taking furious but controlled breaths. Holding her shield to her breast she darted forward, her one-handed sword at the ready. 'But you won't live to see it.'

Kalyavan struck back like a viper in heat, darting in to thrust, his legs moving too fast for Rain to see. Her own arm twitched as she thought how she would have blocked his thrust, only to realize she would have been dead. It had been a feint. However, Satyabhama managed to parry him, but only just. Rain realized the boy might have been a prancing fool, but his swordwork was not. The balance, the stance, the angle of his blade, gave him all manner of options to attack her. Yet he did not. He just mocked feints, and forced Satyabhama to frantically change her guard. *Kalyavan is teasing Satyabhama.* Rain had never seen anyone handle a sword better than Satyabhama, yet here this boy was playing with her as if he were an arrogant instructor, and Satyabhama a petulant student. Rain's mouth began to taste fear. The tension made her feel sick to her stomach.

By now, Kalyavan was all over the circle, nimble as a squirrel. Satyabhama, on the other hand, was grounded. But if Rain was honest, Satyabhama seemed on the back foot now. She was no longer attacking. Rain gasped as Kalyavan's sword hissed at Satyabhama, who dodged it narrowly, forcing away his backhanded swing and reeling back.

'Gaia smiles on you, War Mistress,' Kalyavan said as he stepped over a discarded pile of jute sacks packed with grains. 'You are swift, I will grant you that. I wait with great anticipation to see how smoothly you move in bed when you surrender.'

The Greeks cheered while the Mathurans rumbled angrily.

'Oh, you have *no* idea, Greek.' Satyabhama winked, distracting him just enough to thrust her shield at him.

He jumped back with a laugh. 'Cheeky.'

 STORM was shocked to see Kalyavan flirting with Satyabhama as if she was nothing more than a pest he would swat in his own time. 'Arsehole, fucking arsehole!' she hissed through tight lips. Her ears throbbed with the diabolical rage of battle, the clashing of blades. Soldiers shoved her and she was borne back and forward in the press of avid-eyed, blood-thirsty spectators.

Storm told herself that she hated this; that it was too risky for Satyabhama to wager her life; that she wanted to break the circle and descend on Kalyavan and save the woman who had saved her. But the truth was she loved it. Loved the violence. Loved the delight it brought. She felt her heart thump as Kalyavan feinted and attacked from the right; felt her throat go hoarse from screaming when Satyabhama parried and dodged.

Kalyavan's blade crashed into her shield again. This time, however, the wood seemed to explode inward under the force of his blow. He pushed his blade against the battered shield on Satyabhama's forearm. She went back, sliding in the muddy ground. Kalyavan's sword was held just short of Satyabhama's nose, but she did not panic. The War Mistress' eyes were fixed on the scarlet edge of his steel. *The bastard was right, his blade is Assyrian steel.* It would cut through the shield if she did not move. Satyabhama finally got purchase as her heels hit a corpse and brought the two of them into a tangled halt. With his free hand, Kalyavan drove his fist into her mouth. But Satyabhama kept her feet, blood trickling from her nose down her lips. They spat in each other's faces, blades scraping as they twisted their grips, shifted their balance, jerking their aching legs like a pair of drunken dancers unable to decide who should take the lead. Kalyavan punched again, but this time Satyabhama moved her head to dodge it, and bit the side of his palm. She wrenched her head back, gouging out a piece of flesh. Kalyavan's blood felt like warm rain as it sprayed across Storm's face.

'I told you,' Satyabhama said, spitting the bitten flesh from her mouth. 'You have no idea.' She grinned, her teeth pink with blood as she shook the ruined shield from her arm into the mud.

Kalyavan's mouth opened wide in surprise as he stepped back, clutching his injured hand to his chest. And then he grinned. 'Now we got us a fight!'

Storm cursed. Kalyavan seemed determined not only to win this but to make a show of it. To show everyone who had called him a Mlecchá that he was a warrior to be feared. He spread his arms wide, urging the crowd to cheer louder. Applause could be addictive, Storm knew.

She had bitten her nails bloody with the tension. Helplessness made her want to rip someone's innards out. Satyabhama spun with savage speed, sword sweeping in a low cut. But Kalyavan jumped, bringing his Assyrian steel sword on the War Mistress' neck. The ruby crowning the crosspiece glowed red, like the eye of a maddened bull. Satyabhama ducked and stepped around the blade. She kicked dirt into Kalyavan's face. He staggered back, almost stumbling. Before he had a chance to regain his balance, she thrust at him. Kalyavan instinctively parried. *Thrust, thrust, parry, slash, parry, block, block.* They moved back, only to descend upon each other like vultures battling over the last piece of dead meat. And not once did the grin leave Kalyavan's face.

 MISERY hated the way Kalyavan grinned. Hated this charade. This wasn't some comedy play. A battle was going on, for fuck's sake! Was she the only one who remembered that the Greeks had breached the Iron Curfew? The Mathurans should have used this distraction to plug the hole. Instead, everyone had joined the Greeks to gawp at the fight, as if they had sauntered in for a feast. They were all bellowing like animals in a slaughterhouse.

Meanwhile, the two warriors circled each other again, eyeing an opening, weapons thrust high, feet pawing the mud. Misery had to admit the two were good. Really good. Kalyavan was wielding a longsword, but handled it like a rapier. He laughed as he picked up his left leg to deftly dodge a low cut of Satyabhama's sword. Misery found nothing funny about any of it.

But then she saw something. A parry from Kalyavan that was just a wee bit late. She could see Kalyavan had grown sluggish. He was still attacking, but no longer feinting. Yet he still grinned, expertly blocking Satyabhama's thrusts. *How is he so fucking confident even when he is lumbering and panting?*

In that moment it hit her. The prophecy Calm had told them about in the tent. It was the source of his strength. Not in some divine-cosmic-power way, but because it made him *feel* invincible. She looked at the stump where her arm should have been, and then at the axe she held in the other. Satyabhama had told her once that sometimes when you believe something strongly enough, you can will it to be true. That was how Misery had become a soldier. Kalyavan was the same. His strength lay in his overconfidence.

His power lay in the belief his soldiers had in him. *Time to fucking shatter it.*

WO-MAN! WO-MAN! she began to chant at the top of her voice as she tapped her shield rhythmically. She saw Rain look at her, her face as hard as stone. Misery met her eyes, and nodded. Rain understood.

WOMAN! WOMAN! WOMAN! Rain repeated it, louder. The chant spread like a plague amongst the Wolves. Kalyavan paused momentarily to listen, then his eyes widened only the slightest bit as he understood the implication. His grin vanished, and he raced towards Satyabhama, as if to outrun his doubts. *I knew it.* Misery flinched at the flash of steel, but clung to her cheers as if her life depended on it. For Kalyavan's prophecy boasted that no *man* could kill him.

But Satyabhama was no man.

 CALM inched closer as Kalyavan's sword arm flashed up. She screamed '*Woman!*' with all her might at every swing Satyabhama made. She could see the chanting was getting to Kalyavan, for he threw her a glance that no doubt conveyed his wish to throttle her. Doubt began to creep over his face. Perhaps because he felt exhausted. Perhaps because no man had lasted this long against him in a duel. Whatever it was, the invincible Greek was tiring. The Red Cloaks too had grown ominously silent, their shoulders drooping, their faces crestfallen. The constant, rhythmic chants of the Wolves seemed to have eroded their enthusiasm.

There was a movement in the watching circle as Krishna appeared, a blood-soaked bandage wrapped around his head. Trembling, he watched as his wife and his foe conversed with swords. Even he joined in the *Woman!* chant. Satyabhama lifted her chin briefly when she caught sight of him from the corner of her eye. Calm could see Krishna barely managed to suppress the urge to call off the duel. He knew he could not insult Satyabhama.

Kalyavan had grown dark and deadly now, his arrogance having abandoned him. He had taken off most of his armour to gain speed. Satyabhama followed suit. Calm understood it would be madness for them to duel on in full armour. They did not have strength on their side, but they had skill and speed aplenty. This was the duel that mattered, and the tide was turning. Satyabhama's legwork had looked sluggish before, but that had been a feint. Calm had always known it. She had been preserving her strength. Kalyavan's speed had made him look godlike before. But that's the thing about being fast. The gazelle eventually runs out of air. Stamina matters more than speed in the hunt, as in swordplay.

 LIST could see Kalyavan's sword growing heavier every time he swung it. He was barely hitting back. They were both bleeding. Kalyavan's breeches were soaked from the wound on his leg, and the hand Satyabhama had bitten was raw. Blood streaked Satyabhama's arms and cheek. But Kalyavan was the one panting more, which at the moment seemed more important than who was bleeding more. List was sure Kalyavan had reached the same conclusion: he was the better swordsman but Satyabhama had somehow outlasted and outwitted him. She had taken her share of cuts to let Kalyavan get ahead of himself, and now the Greek was in trouble.

Kalyavan let out a low chuckle. Stripped of vanity, his boyish face looked innocent. 'My only regret is…' He took a deep breath and flew at her so fast that List barely saw his legs. Satyabhama ran to confront him, throwing her shield in his face. Surprised, Kalyavan ducked and found Satyabhama's ready sword aimed at his neck. He barely managed to dodge left. The sword ripped his thin mailed shirt, and the skin below his ribs, watering the earth with his blood.

He fell to his knees, longsword slipping from his hand. Panting, he folded over. Satyabhama was behind him, turning slowly, surely... The Mathurans were screaming themselves hoarse. The Greeks were cursing, urging Kalyavan to get up. He dragged himself to his knees, bloody, dazed. He clawed for his longsword and rose. If he was to die this day, he sure as hell was not going to do it on his knees.

Satyabhama wasted no time with final words. She bought a purchase on the pile of jute sacks, and leaped high at Kalyavan. Time slowed. The jump lasted an age, her arm descending in a smooth arc, its every movement standing out like a flame in darkness. Kalyavan turned a moment too late, but with a defiant cry nonetheless. He turned his blade in his hand to parry the onslaught. It was far from his best swing, his grip loose in his sticky trembling fingers. The ruby on the crosspiece of Kalyavan's sword caught the light, and glowed like a living thing. List shielded her eyes.

List heard Kalyavan before she saw him. His scream filled her head. Satyabhama's sword had missed his skull but had stolen an ear. Kalyavan had a hand pressed to his head, face contorted in pain, blood bubbling from the wound between his fingers and running down his neck. He had, by some miracle, managed to twist a hair away from Satyabhama's finisher. Having carved off Kalyavan's ear, Satyabhama's sword had plunged into the earth with a dull thud, the ear still stuck to the blade.

Satyabhama stood frozen in her stance, as still as a statue. Then her left hand reached up and gently touched the sword stuck in her chest, the blood running down the length of the blade.

RAIN felt her mouth go dry. Kalyavan's sword had plunged through Satyabhama's chest to the hilt, with the blade silhouetted against the setting sun behind her. They stood in silence a moment longer. Wind stirred the leaves of the trees lining the Wall, making them rustle, shaking a few dry bits of green down onto the shoulders of the soldiers. Strangely, now that it was quiet, Rain could hear the chirping of birds. And while she knew it was in her head, she could hear the silent scream from Krishna's lips.

Satyabhama sputtered blood and frowned at the ruby-embedded crossguard sticking out from her ribs, and then upwards at the sun which had betrayed her. But the guilty sun was behind her, setting swiftly in its shame. Her eyes turned to Krishna. 'Rotten luck...' Satyabhama said, smiling. And just like that, she fell like a stone.

Krishna rushed forward even as Kalyavan caught Satyabhama, breaking her fall, pulling his sword free. Her blood welled out like a crimson tide. Her knotted hair opened then, cascading to reach below her waist. Satyabhama and Kalyavan formed a ghastly silhouette against the setting sun, looking like forlorn lovers joined in death. Kalyavan lowered her gently to the ground and ordered a Greek soldier, who stood lost in a trance, to bring her fallen shield. Kalyavan handed it to Krishna, who placed it over her.

And so, the War Mistress of Mathura slept with her shield for a blanket, covering the bloody hole in her chest.

Rain held back her tears and walked to where Kalyavan and Krishna knelt beside Satyabhama's body. 'An honourable death is its own reward,' she said, her voice as dead as dreams. Bending on one knee, she closed Satyabhama's eyes that still held an expression of surprise.

Rising, Rain gave the terse command: 'Wolves!'

The shocked Silver Wolves responded instantly. The ones who were close by marched in to form a circle around Satyabhama's body. Mathuran and Greek soldiers alike parted, giving them a wide berth. They stood to attention, their right hands over their hearts. Silent. Waiting.

Rain clicked her boots together and placed her fist on her chest. Dozens of swords were unsheathed at the same time by the Silver Wolves, all along the long stretch of the Iron Curfew, across the field of battle, and around their fallen leader.

 SHISHUPAL shuddered as the sound of the synchronized unsheathing of swords rolled like a wave across the Iron Curfew. *A steel salute for the War Mistress.* The terrifying sound raised prickles up and down his arms.

'That gesture is far more frightening than any war cry Eklavvya has ever heard.'

Shishupal nodded. He saw Kalyavan glance at Krishna through bloodied eyes, his face a wretched mixture of remorse and relief. Turning to his soldiers he said, 'The sun has set. Break battle!'

Shishupal was shocked. How naïve could Kalyavan be! One did not take chances in battle. A twist of fate and the victor could find a sword through her heart. But then, Kalyavan himself was grievously wounded. Perhaps he was just buying time to retreat to a healer.

The initial shock having faded, Kalyavan limped to where his squire stood, holding his horse, a faint hint of his old swagger returning, somewhat elevated by a face that was missing an ear. In this realm, where scars were as popular as swords, Kalyavan had finally proven his mettle to all. But there was something different this time. As if, in the span of one duel, Kalyavan had aged a decade.

'If you surrender by dawn,' Kalyavan said as he turned at the hole in the Iron Curfew, 'I will spare the common folk. One night. That is what the War Mistress bought you with her life.'

BATTLE OF MATHURA

PART II

Control thy passions lest they take vengeance on thee.
—**Epictetus**

 KRISHNA tried to keep his eyes on the road, such as it was, chewing his tongue, trembling fingers fumbling with the clasps of his plate, smeared with her blood. He tried to ignore the sounds of weeping that floated through the air behind him. The Wolves had built her a pyre. Many had sobbed even before the flames had begun to consume her. But Krishna could not have stayed to watch her body turn to ash. Rain had told him that it had been her will that her ashes be preserved, to be mixed with his own, and dispersed in the Yamuna together. Krishna had asked Rain to fuck off.

His teeth were chattering by the time he reached the steps of the Senate. His eyes were dry even though it felt like he hadn't stopped crying. *You dumb stupid—!* he cursed silently as he collapsed. *You selfish egoistical—* He could not even utter the profanities in his mind, as if she was suddenly going to appear behind him with a strict reprimand. Would she? Please... would she? Krishna's eyes watched the sky till the last embers from her pyre went out. Anger at her found fertile soil in his heart. He forced her picture from his mind. Her grim nods in public. Her laughter at home. Her cold eyes that only danced for him. The beads of sweat that trickled down her back when she rode him. Her glance of support in the Senate. His part in every dream of hers. Her part in every dream of his. How they had dreamed of ruling a world together. How they had fought for it... And how she had let it all go in a stupid fucking duel! Her selfishness gripped his gut in spasms of anguish. How he wished he could wound her to make her betrayal stop hurting.

He closed his eyes. He did not know why, but for the first time in his life, he prayed. To all the Gods. She had always said the Gods were indifferent to Man's fate. But he had to try. He just wanted it to be undone. *Take it all away. Take Mathura away. Resurrect Kans. Just give me Satya back. Please...*

His mind desperately clung to every detail that had led to her death, searching for anything that could have happened differently so she would still be alive. If Niarkatt had not insulted

Kalyavan in Panchal. If he himself had evacuated Mathura earlier. If Balram had been faster. *Anything, Yami! Anything!* Helplessness rose within him in a flood, burning his throat like acid. He could not breathe. The demons of his mind, meanwhile, gorged on a feast of remorse and regret. He opened his eyes, his face quivering into a spasm. His chin trembled as he screamed soundlessly. Hot breath was all that left his quaking lungs. He screamed again and again but no one heard him.

It doesn't take much time for guilt to turn into anger. Krishna longed to face Kalyavan, to pour scalding oil down his throat. To stab him again and again. A hundred deaths would not be enough. Her voice rose in his head: *You are Krishna. No one has ever beaten you.* He nodded grimly. *And no one ever will.* The battle fever that had coursed through his body earlier paled in comparison to the rage he felt now. He felt reckless, mad. A faint voice of caution struggled to be heard. But he was past caring, past all consequences. There are few things more dangerous than a man who has nothing to lose.

He rose to return to the Curfew. By the time he reached there, the sky above Mathura was alive with the sound of vultures. The fire beyond the breached walls was in its twilight. The distant trumpeting of an airavat filled the night sky. *Some still live. We shall see for how long.*

With Balram injured, and… her gone, command had fallen to Krishna. Before he had escaped from her funeral, he had asked Kritavarman to ensure every citizen in the First District was inside the tunnel before dawn. Kritavarman had hesitated, then finally voiced his concerns. Wise concerns. Of how little time there was to get everyone in. How they could not outrun Kalyavan. How easily the Greeks could find the tunnel if they arrived to find the First District empty. In reply, Krishna had called for a few heroes.

Heroes. A fancy name for foolish volunteers. But it worked, as it always did. When he reached the Curfew, Kritavarman and his men stood ready, armed. So did the City Guard, and whatever remained of the Republican Army. But he was surprised to also find the Silver Wolves. All of them. The Wolves were not an army regiment. They were just a search-and-rescue operation. *Well, they will rescue this city tonight,* Krishna thought coldly, for a city was not defined by its boundaries but by its people. *If they survive, Mathura survives. If they survive, I win.*

He issued terse commands to the leaders of the platoons, and they relayed these to their contingents. Grim nods followed as Mathura began to prepare. Meanwhile, Krishna climbed to the ramparts to take the measure of the Greek army beyond. The Greeks had left only a motley squad in front of the Curfew. If their lanterns were any indication, most of the Red Cloaks seemed scattered in the Second District. The Greeks might have taken a break from battle, but the sacking of his city continued. Clearly, Kalyavan seemed confident about having won the battle already. Krishna could not wait to cure him of the notion.

He turned back to look at the preparations below. On what had turned into a killing field, soldiers were collecting armour and weapons from the bodies of the fallen. Krishna watched with impassive eyes as a city guard picked up a severed hand and extracted the cutlass by prising open the fingers before throwing the limb away like yesterday's trash. Krishna nodded, as if in approval. They needed all the weapons they could get. For the only way to save Mathura was for the surviving soldiers to charge their way past thousands of Greeks to the second tunnel. This would divert their attention and buy the citizens enough time to escape through the first tunnel. It was a suicide charge. But as long as Greeks died, Krishna had no complaints.

'You've a plan, I assume?' Rain walked up to join him on the battlements. 'That is, besides fleeing.'

'Just buy me time.' Krishna saw how her eyes had turned into a graveyard of unshed tears. The Silver Wolves had been Satyabhama's girls and, like her, they were infamous for their practice of brutal pragmatism. 'Satyabhama will be avenged.'

'That is all we need to hear.'

They heard the urgent sound of boots. They turned towards the hulking mass of Balram, hobbling towards them, assisted by Storm, of all people. Not that Balram had ever been a pretty sight to behold, but the deep gash on either side of his mouth gave him the look of a ghoul.

'I know what you inten*th* to do, you sly bas*th*ard,' he said, his speech garbled due to the wound. 'We will make a sor*th*ie through the assembled Greeks ou*th*side, keep them away from the Curfew, while *th*rying to run for the ou*th*er walls when Kri*th*avarman floods Mathura. I doub*th* we will survive, though. The *th*wisting alleys will be our undoing. Bu*th* I'm glad you do no*th* mean *th*o le*th* Kalyavan win, even if i*th* means drowning your own men.'

A grave look passed between Rain and Krishna, before they burst out laughing. A hollow laugh but a laugh nonetheless. Balram fumed. 'No*th* funny.'

And they laughed again.

Storm left them to approach Rain. 'So, a suicide charge I hear.'

Rain nodded, still grinning. 'The only way we can make it to that tunnel in the Market Square.'

'You don't have to sell me on it. Nothing like the imminent loss of life to let you know you are truly alive.' Storm gave a hacking laugh and slapped Rain's shoulder as they all turned to look at their city, while the stars swam above them in unseen currents.

 SHISHUPAL and Eklavvya had used the chaos following Satyabhama's death to change into Mathuran uniforms and slip into their ranks. It was hardly a safe choice considering the Greeks were intent on blowing Mathura to bits. But it was the best of the bad options available. The tunnel seemed like a death trap. Staying put in the house made no sense. Once the sacking started, death would be the least of their worries. Hiding amidst the Mathuran soldiers was their only choice. Once out of the Curfew, they would change back to their clothes and find a Greek soldier to take them to Kalyavan. When Kalyavan recognized Shishupal, he would arrange safe escort to Magadh. Shishupal was aware that his plan depended on a lot of *ifs*.

'Mathurans!' Balram's voice rang in the ears of the wretched few assembled in the rubble of the Iron Curfew. It seemed Kalyavan's dagger had not found his tongue. 'We are here *th*o buy enough *th*ime for our people to escape through the *th*unnel.' *I stand corrected.*

Eklavvya turned quizzical eyes on Shishupal. *Thunnel?*

'Our army con*th*inues to figh*th* the Mlecchás in the Second! We will help them. *Th*urn every alley in*th*o a ba*th*leground.' He thumped his fist against his chest. A dramatic sight, if somewhat marred by the snickering of the soldiers. 'So, here I am, asking you—' Balram fell to the ground with a thud.

A group of soldiers arrived with a pallet onto which they hoisted the unconscious Balram and, with wordless salutes to the rest, carried him towards the mouth of the tunnel.

Hoofbeats sounded. Shishupal peered from under his cowl to see Senator Akrur riding up to Krishna, who appeared to be taking his brother's collapse with stoic calm.

'I thought the potion would never work, and we would have to sit through his entire speech!' Akrur said with a twisted smile.

'Poor sod. He finally got his chance to die heroically and I robbed him of it. But Dvarka needs him. I am rather surprised to find you still here, Lord Akrur,' Krishna said. 'I would have thought you would be the first to leave.'

'Aye...' Akrur scratched his bulging stomach under his customized breastplate. 'I did not fit in the tunnel.'

Shishupal saw Krishna look at Akrur for a long moment, then nod.

'Don't give me that *now-I-respect-you* look. As your wife always said, one can justify anything with the phrase *for the greater good.*' Akrur bowed slightly. 'Farewell, Lord Krishna.'

Krishna smiled. 'Lord Akrur, there is still that other tunnel in the Market Square... just in case.'

Akrur smiled as he rode off. *Bravery comes in the most unexpected shapes.*

Shishupal heard a soldier shout: 'Inform the archers and catapult engineers on the Wall that we are beginning our assault now. It's the pincer manoeuvre. They are to provide cover with their arrows and rocks on the centre and the east, where the Greeks are the thickest. Assemble the gate companies. Silver Wolves, take the west. Regiment soldiers, with a few Wolves and cavalry soldiers, to the centre. Everyone else, to the east. All three shock troop units will slice through the Mlecchás and converge on the Market Square. Mathura will be flooded soon. We have to find our way out before that, and force the Greeks to chase us. Sapper Captains, prepare your munitions.'

'We march behind the Silver Wolves to the west,' Shishupal whispered to Eklavvya. 'They will face the least resistance. The moment opportunity presents...' Eklavvya nodded and took off before Shishupal could finish. Shishupal loped after him. 'Are you alright?'

'Yes. It just saddens Eklavvya's heart to see these brave soldiers...'

Shishupal clicked his tongue against his teeth sympathetically. 'You heard that big woman... a good death is its own reward.'

'And what of a good kill?' Eklavvya turned, his eyes blazing with lust for blood. 'Just look at them! Such warriors! Eklavvya could have got a chance to kill them all had not that wretched fool taken away his chance! Do you call that a fair reward?'

RAIN clasped Storm's hand before she unsheathed her sword. It was the signal. No drums. No war cries. They slipped out of a postern gate of the Curfew, quiet as whispers. Errant thoughts smuggled themselves into her mind when she really needed it to be silent: Should they have volunteered for this charge? Why did she feel like taking a shit now? Why did the Greeks wear red cloaks which made them easy targets? *Oh just clear your mind!*

And then she saw the Greeks fifty strides away. The thought that one of them might be Kalyavan cleared the mists in her mind. The image of Satyabhama on the pyre burned into her eyes as if someone had branded it with a hot iron. Rain felt the thrill of battle burn in her breast. Her hand hurt with the force with which she gripped her sword. *Break!* She gave the sign, her fist flashing up, fingers outspread.

Rain's squad went west; Akrur, Satwadhan and the City Guard proceeded on horseback straight ahead, along with Misery, Calm and a regiment of the army; and the remainder of the army went east. *Pincer.*

Her Wolves had now broken from the shadows and were scurrying forward, bent double. Her sword gleamed faintly as the moon slipped from the clouds. The Greeks closest to them were struggling to hoist a banner, the pole slipping in the mud. Rain chewed at her lip, unable to believe they still hadn't been spotted as they crept across the picket lines. *Not for long.* A Red Cloak frowned in their direction, a look of puzzlement on his face as he squinted into the darkness. Everyone held their breath. 'What the—' and then he had an arrow in his neck.

Rain barely heard the bowstring snap. So much for surprise. More Greeks spilled into the light with torches, trying to arrange themselves into a semblance of order.

Storm raced past Rain. 'Surprise, motherfuckers!'

Rain shook her head. As the Leader of the Wolves, it fell upon her to come up with a better opening line. '*For Satyabhama!*' she cried into the night. It was echoed behind her. *For Satyabhama!*

Wood cracked, metal screeched, and flesh burst open as they crashed into the Greeks. The shouts were deafening. Rain's own the fiercest among them. She twisted sideways, missing a fumbling spear thrust by a lad young enough to be her son. She rammed her shield into his mouth, snapping his head back and sending him crashing into a Greek bowman. There was barely space to swing. She turned to slay the man she had rammed, but found him already dead with an arrow in his neck. *No matter.* She saw a frozen bowman stare at her with fear. *Good. Fear is good.*

TELLIS could barely move. Hadn't they won the battle? That is what they had been told. Then why had the Mathurans attacked them? All those armoured legs had charged towards them like some vengeful beast. Not the wild charge of a mob, but a purposeful jog. Most were young women. One had a short pixie cut. One was fat. Tellis wasn't afraid of any woman but there was something wrong with these Mathurans. He had seen the one the Archon had fought. It had been by Gaia's luck that he had survived, no matter what he claimed afterwards.

Shit, shit! They should have run. Why the hell did Cilix and the rest stay? He had wanted to nudge Cilix and urge him to get out. Why should they give a shit whether Kalyavan got to win a city he did not even plan to rule? Kalyavan was a runt, for fuck's sake.

The Mathurans had suddenly advanced in their direction. Fumbling, he'd tried to draw an arrow from his quiver. Just then, Cilix was rammed against him by a tall woman's shield. Tellis had faltered and the arrow loosed from his fingers had flown up into the air, and returned to dig itself deep into Cilix's neck. Tellis now stared blankly at the tall woman, barely realizing that he had murdered his friend, even as she crashed into him with her shoulder, dropping him to the ground. She stomped on his neck with her boot and charged ahead. Tellis coughed out blood, happy not to have been hacked by her sword. Someone screamed near him: '*Die! Die!*' He tried to turn towards the voice but realized he could not. His neck was broken. *Oh fuck.*

RAIN heard Storm roar '*Die! Die!*' behind her as she stabbed a boy on the ground. Onward. The Greek formation had finally broken, making it easier for her to slash with her blade. She cleaved another man like meat, opening great blood-spitting wounds. She dodged an arrow and broke a bow as a Greek tried to defend himself. There were more Greeks ahead, forming a shield-wall. She crashed into them before they could, her swing slicing open the neck of the shield bearer closest to her. Other Wolves crashed into the shield line, howling. The line finally faltered as they lurched back and fell.

Rain snarled as she swung and hacked. The fire of battle had faded, her arm was feeling sore from having held the shield for so long. Her legs shook. The Greeks retreated, turned and ran. Rain decided against chasing them.

'You, alright?' Storm leaned over, grinning. Rain saw she was gripping her arm, blood oozing from between her fingers.

'Why're you grinning like a fool?'

'Because you're obviously too old for a suicide charge, my love,' retorted Storm.

Rain grunted, forcing herself to stand erect. She knew Storm was right. She was too old for this shit. She picked up her shield again. Her stubbly hair was matted with blood. Greek war cries sounded in the distance. 'You, okay?' she asked.

'Ah, this... a scratch.'

'Bleeding a lot for a scratch, no?'

'You call this a lot? Look, they've started raining arrows on the centre.' Storm grinned. 'Come, we got to move. Try and keep up this time!'

SHISHUPAL ran after the Silver Wolves in a daze. The Wolves had blazed through the first line of Greeks. Turned out that most of the Greeks had retreated to their camps beyond the First District, with Kalyavan, as Krishna had said. Shishupal wasn't complaining. *The fewer Greeks we encounter, the less likely we die here.*

He turned left just in time to see a hail of arrows descend on the Greeks facing the central Mathuran detachment. The Greeks were numerous there but none had bothered to form a shield roof. At the first sight of arrows, they ran. *Guess none of them wanted to just squat and get peppered with shafts.*

Suddenly, detonations cracked through the night. Shishupal was jolted, as if one had burst next to him. But the Wolves hadn't used theirs yet. *That ought to wake the Greeks,* he thought glumly as he heard more of the damn cursers explode in the distance. *Too soon,* he reckoned. Some Mathuran in the central detachment had probably got too jumpy. Nerves can do that to you in battle and shit on the best laid plans. *Best I focus on my own road ahead.* Just as he thought he had regained his balance, he stumbled over a corpse.

'Wonderful,' said Eklavvya.

'Everything feels wonderful when the men you have to kill are just corpses on the road.'

'Not true,' Eklavvya said as he slowed his jog. Shishupal followed his gaze to one of Kalyavan's lot, who was crawling away, dragging his bloody legs behind him. Eklavvya smashed the Greek's skull in passing, with the back of his borrowed axe. He turned to Shishupal. 'Can Shishupal hasten his feet? The tunes of combat tug at Eklavvya's heart like a lost lover.'

More like opium to an addict. But Shishupal did not chastise him. He had no clue whether the Greeks were now the Empire's enemies or not. *Only time will tell, I suppose.* For now, he had to stay alive. Why had he not escaped through the tunnel when he had the chance? Or better, why the hell had he even entered Mathura? He shook his head like the answer might drop out of his ears. Just made his headache worse.

The grass beneath his feet soon levelled off, then began to slope down, giving way to cobbled streets. Between the shoulders of the soldiers ahead, he caught glimpses of the fighting. The colony through which he was running had escaped the wrath of the airavats. Here and there, evidence of the last stand that a faction of the Mathuran Army had made was visible. The dead lay carelessly strewn about. As Balram had said, not one cobblestone had gone uncontested. However, Shishupal knew the Red Cloaks would be assembling their own lines by now, mean, crude faces all, and they would face the onslaught of Mathura with their own fury.

 PRAXIS spurred his highbred horse between the tents set up in an open park in the Second District, sending idling soldiers scattering. He slid from the saddle, nearly fell, then stormed into the tent of his incompetent superior, but not before twitching his scarlet cloak into place. He had no idea how this wretched man had been promoted to *Matarchis* above him. *Oh but I do...* The Archon and this fool were both half-bloods.

'Sir! The Mathurans have attacked! I have a message from the Marshal of the reserve force.'

The Matarchis did not even raise his head to look at him. 'Do not enter till I say you may, Pox,' he said.

By Gaia, he hated the name! Praxis had been only seven when he had scratched his blisters. He had been cured but the illness had left a constellation of marks behind. Not that anyone sympathised with him. This was the army. A nickname was like a scar, to be carried till your last breath, or till you were promoted.

'What attack? We won.'

'They have used their remaining forces to launch an all-out attack.' Praxis thrust the scroll at him as if he were thrusting a spear in the Matarchis' face. 'The men we left at the Curfew have been decimated. Even now they are hacking through our sentry points in three lines! I cannot find the Archon. I must insist that we hurry, else we will be routed.'

'Must you?' The Matarchis gave a small smile. 'The Archon is resting. He will not rise till dawn. And do remember the hierarchy, Pox.'

It was all Praxis could do not to slap him.

The Matarchis rose lazily and stepped out of the tent. 'Alright, gather up!' Whatever his inadequacies, he knew how to issue commands. 'It seems some folks don't know when they are beaten.' He sighed. He looked at Praxis. 'Let's teach these cow-fuckers some manners.'

Men slapped down visors, strapped on helmets and shook their shields. The soldiers were excited. There had been little to plunder, and this had angered the far-from-home Greeks. They had been promised rich pickings. But they found most of the houses stripped and abandoned. There had been even fewer Mathurans to kill. It was as if Mathura was a ghost-city.

This will give them a channel for their pent-up fury, Praxis thought grimly. *It will be good for their morale.*

'Pox.' The Matarchis turned to him. 'Since you brought this important news to me on time, it is only fitting I reward you. Why don't you lead the charge? Take three airavats. I will give the other two to Helios.'

Praxis gave a kind of stuttering wheeze, suddenly too scared to speak. He was a commanding officer, not a lowly pleb to go into the frontlines. But Praxis would die before giving the Matarchis the satisfaction of seeing his fear. Moreover, there were three airavats with his division. Yes, he would use this opportunity to inspire awe and loyalty amongst his men. None would call him Pox again.

'Honoured to, Sir.'

 SHISHUPAL tried not to panic when he heard the distant trumpeting of the airavats. The Silver Wolves had done exceptionally well. In fact, they were actually winning! He jogged behind the Wolves through the narrow alleys, avoiding the trail of bloodied bodies they left in their wake. The Wolves may have been few, but blood lust was always a good substitute for numbers. The Market Square was so close now. Just two alleys away. He just had to trust his chances that they would not run into an airavat.

Chances that disappeared when the cobbles beneath Shishupal's boots began to tremble. The Wolves huddled in alleyways leading from a roundabout. Soon, the first of the Greeks arrived, wearing leather armour and plumed helmets, wielding spears, swords, and their round shields. The Greeks were better armed and more numerous, but the narrow alleyways reduced their advantage.

Not that it would matter in a while. Three giant-tusked leviathans marched ahead of the Greeks, shaking their huge heads left and right, brick walls on either side falling apart like stacks of cards.

'Archers, ready!' Rain called. 'Aim for the eye when I give the order!'

'Should've brought some pigs with us,' Storm quipped.

'Shut up, Storm. Here they come.'

The airavats entered the alley where Shishupal was being slowly pushed back by the fearful soldiers ahead. 'We are going to die,' he whispered.

'How exciting!' Eklavvya squeaked, eyes riveted.

Suddenly, soldiers and citizens who had been hiding in the houses on either side boiled into the alleyway. Some burst out from the doors, some emerged from dark niches. From the rooftops, some poured burning gravel on the third airavat in the line below. The beast roared in pain. The mahout tried to halt the beast, but agony had a way of eroding loyalty. The beast grabbed the mahout's poking rod and tossed it along with the mahout into the air. Trumpeting, the airavat turned and shambled back the way it had come, trampling three Greek soldiers who had not been nimble enough to dodge out of the way.

Shouts erupted as rag-tag crews of farmers and labourers ran out of their houses with burning torches, cudgels, pitchforks and clubs, stabbing, smashing and poking the belly of the second airavat from down under. Shishupal was sure they did not have a plan or even know what had suddenly inspired them, but he for one did not begrudge their patriotism. The more bodies between Shishupal and certain death, the more comfortably he breathed.

Meanwhile, the Silver Wolves looked at each other, then Storm uttered one word that captured the essence of the moment: '*Yay!*' The Wolves charged, joining in the fray. They dodged the bladed tusks of the airavat in the front and ran to charge at the Greek soldiers behind, who had rallied against the citizens. Once the Wolves had run past, the line of crossbow-women left behind peppered the mahout of the first airavat with their bolts. The confused airavat, anchorless, just stopped and looked around, confused, like a bride's father whom no one paid attention to after the dowry had been given away.

'Let's go!' said Eklavvya cheerfully.

Shishupal was only glad to be on the other side of the airavat. Worming against the wall, he finally slipped behind the beast. Eklavvya's maniacal laughter snatched his attention. He saw Eklavvya holding a Greek, impeccably dressed, against the wall by his neck.

'By the Spirits, you are one ugly bastard, aren't you?' he said as he stabbed the eyes of the soldier with his fingers. He turned to Shishupal, smiling hard as the man screamed. 'Look at the pox marks on his face. He looks like a diseased leaf!'

 STORM smiled grimly as a Red Cloak charged her. His spear raked her shield. She threw her shield aside and chopped down with her steel. Blood sprayed over her gauntlet as she carved the man open from neck to navel. On the other side of the street, Bleed and Rain brought down a cavalry archer between them. While Bleed ran to finish him off, Rain spun around and threw a spear she had picked up from a Greek at another cavalry archer, throwing him off his horse onto the cobbled stones. Storm laughed. Ever since she had seen that boy laugh like a madman as he stabbed a poxed Greek in the eye, she was filled with the blood song. It was infectious. She was so drunk with slaughter now that she felt she could have taken on an airavat one on one.

Seemed like someone heard her wish. There was one airavat left, the one bathed in hot gravel and oil. The mahouts with their drums had managed to turn the retreating beast towards the Mathurans again. Storm went for his hind legs while Whistler and Bleed, flanked by three city guards, ducked around the mighty tusks, slashing at the snake-like nose. But that only drove the bastard mad. The airavat tore through the ranks of

Mathurans. Limbs flew. Blood sprayed. Storm saw none of this. 'Out of my fucking way!' she screeched, shoving a Mathuran aside and using the body of another as a platform to jump. The way Satyabhama had. Metal flashed. And like a plough through soft soil, her steel dug into the meaty part of the beast's tail, cutting it off. The airavat lost its balance and collapsed against a wall head first, crushing Bleed.

Storm ran to Whistler and helped her drag Bleed out. Only then did she notice Bleed's legs had been left behind. Whistler let the legless body drop and ran past Storm, screaming like a maniac at the Greeks, sword in the air.

 MATHIOS had heard the Mathurans consumed drugs that drove them into a frenzy. The woman who charged at him did indeed look half-mad, swinging her sword even after he had chopped her down. His Captain had commanded them to retreat to a parallel alley after the last airavat collapsed into a wall. *The coward wanted to hide.* Not Mathios. He wanted to attack from the front, and win his olive branch, and finally scram enough for his daughter's dowry. But he followed the Captain, for if there were none to witness his actions, who would reward him?

Explosions rocked the alley into which they had retreated, sending clouds of dust that momentarily lifted the entire place from darkness. *Ah, my moment of glory!* Mathios left his Captain and charged towards the Mathurans, who were engaged with a squadron of Greeks ahead, two airavats amidst them. He raced past an airavat and slid his dagger into the neck of the first woman he saw. She fell to her knees, one hand clutched to her throat. Mathios did not wait. He moved to the next woman, thrusting his dagger into her spine and dragging it upwards. The woman turned, clawing weakly at his breastplate, bubbles forming on her lips. He pulled out the blade, wiped it on the woman's sleeve and shoved her aside. *What kind of men sent women to do their fighting?*

Quarrels whistled around him, and he instinctively hid behind the second airavat. He peeked to see a squad of Mathurans battling Greeks up the sloping alley. Curiously, a circle of archers had surrounded a one-armed woman who had a satchel slung across her chest. Mathios realized that the airavat he was behind was not marching ahead. And then he saw the mahout's body, a bolt stuck in his head. *I have to do everything here.* Mathios took his dagger and pricked the beast's leg. It screamed and charged up the street. Mathios ran behind, grinning.

 MISERY felt in her satchel. She had only two cursers and one bellower left. Her squad, the central detachment, engaged the Greeks while she advanced cautiously down the slope with a score of archers encircling her, so that she could throw her munitions at the two airavats below. Calm had volunteered, but Misery was the best at rock-throwing. A bellower was, however, not something you threw into a crowded alley. She would have to find a way to make sure she hit the beasts spot on with the two cursers she had left. Considering the airavat in the lead was not moving, it might be the easier target. As if it had divined her thoughts, the hitherto unmoving airavat rampaged up the slope. It crashed into Greeks and Mathurans alike, crushing many underfoot, slicing open others with its four tusk-blades.

Misery turned to wink at Calm and shouted, 'Run!' even as she felt the trunk coil around her. She took out the bellower and looked into the eyes of the airavat. 'Eat this, bitch!' she yelled as she threw the bellower straight into the airavat's open mouth with an underhand throw. *Finally, a hero's death.*

 MENAS wondered why he was here amongst the Greeks when he was an Easterner. He had grown up loving airavats. He loved the cold of the East. The abundance of forest. His mother had told him to join the army even if it was under a Rakshasa King. There was honour in defending your borders, she had said. So, he had done so, as a mahout. But here he was, in a foreign land, fighting men and women who had nothing to do with him. His King had sent him to Mathura, and he had obeyed. It had been madness. Burning pigs in the air! His airavat, Mavant, had been terrified. The Greeks called airavats *behemoths*. So unimaginative. Yet here he was, fighting amidst them, a long way from home, and not for anything he understood or stood to gain from.

The city had been a maze of inclined alleys, turns and barricades, terrible to navigate. Ahead, the head mahout, Mandar, had run into a squadron of women-warriors, clad in grey, and been killed by a bolt. Menas was surprised to see the women make a stand. No one stood against an airavat. And then, the riderless airavat *Imanyan*, had charged ahead screeching when a Greek had pricked her with his dagger. Imanyan had been Mavant's mate. So, without warning, Mavant had charged right behind her. From his seat, Menas had spied a one-armed woman in the guarded circle reach into her satchel and cry out.

All he remembered later was seeing the man who had pricked Imanyan be blown to smithereens before he himself was punched in the chest. He had fallen off Mavant and lain sprawled on the ground. Ahead, the explosion had taken apart buildings on either side of the alley. Menas had tried to rise, but realized he had broken his leg. A sad trumpet snatched his attention. *No... no...* he cried as he saw Mavant stumble. 'Mavant!' The sound of hooves answered him; he saw a posse of Mathuran cavalry charging down the alley. His last thought before a horseman beheaded him was: who would take care of Mavant when he was gone?

 CALM rolled over to one side and pulled herself up against a wall. Her lungs burned. But her heart burned worse. Diving into a gulley with armour on was no mean feat. She had lost the other members of her squad in the explosion. Misery had been a fool to use the bellower. Brave, but a fool nonetheless. Calm found herself wishing she was back in Panchal. Those annoying women trying to get her to don jewels seemed suddenly bearable in comparison to soldiering.

Focus. She leaned sideways to peer into the alley. She could see no Greeks advancing up the sloping street. The first airavat had blown apart. The second airavat had crumbled against a wall, the explosion having torn its trunk off. She smiled. *Good.* Suddenly, Calm thought she saw a shadow move in the window of the brothel opposite, third floor. Probably another Mathuran in hiding. There were hundreds of them, holed up in their houses in the Second District. *But one could never be too careful.* Eyes fixed on the window, she raised her crossbow.

She heard the scrape of horseshoes on stone and turned to see the meagre Mathuran cavalry race past her down the slope. She took a deep breath and started to rise, hoping to hitch a lift. She glanced one last time at the opposite window. A flash of black. A gasp of surprise. A cracking sound. Calm's head was thrown back, crunching against the wall behind. Something wet trickled down her nose, tickling her. She heard her bow clatter to the ground, then felt a stab of pain as she fell sideways, hitting her head on the open sewer.

She'd done that once before as a child. Playing in the alley was forbidden during trading hours, but she had not heeded that injunction. Her mother had pushed her into the sewer to save her from a passing chariot, getting knocked over by the horses herself. The local healer had demanded coin, coin urchins did not possess. Her mother had died after hours of suffering.

Oh... forgive me, Mother. I promise I will never play on the streets again...

AKRUR had never seen so many dead Mathurans in one place, not even during the Coup. *Wonder who had the fine idea of setting off a bellower in a crowded place?* But it seemed not all had died by being blown apart. Reining in his horse, he saw the Wolf, Composed or Calm, whatever her name was, fallen on her side, a bolt in her forehead. Akrur had signalled two of his soldiers into the building in front of the dead soldier. Moments later, munitions went off. A flare of flame burst through the second-floor windows. Shrieks. Two Greek soldiers, wreathed in flames, tumbled out of the window into the street below.

'C'mon!' Satwadhan shouted after him. 'We will fall behind!'

Akrur had half a mind to plead a twisted ankle and turn tail, but that would have opened him up to more disgruntled Mathurans hiding in the houses. One had already thrown nightsoil at him. Yes, he had been an aggressive moneylender before, but could they not see he was being heroic for them now? Some people just did not know how to be grateful. 'Alright, alright, I'm coming,' he shouted as he spurred his mount ahead. He had made it so far. Just a little longer.

The Market Square was almost upon them. The suicide charge no longer seemed such a bad idea. And the tunnel there would be completely empty, and Akrur could walk into it like a king. Ahead, Satwadhan returned to his sword with a child's delight. Turned out he was rather good at killing people. A tanner's boy grown into a knight. Who would have guessed? Akrur saw him lean down from his saddle and decapitate a man crawling on the street towards a fallen airavat. Easterner by the look of his garb. *To die so far from home, so young...* Akrur sighed. *At least you saved costs on your funeral, boy.*

 RAIN heard the reports. Piety and Brinda's companies, along with the rest of the eastern detachment, had reached the Market Square. *They will be making their way to the tunnel.* The central detachment was nowhere to be seen. She could only hope that Misery, Calm, and the others were fine. The meagre force left by Rain at the breach in the Iron Curfew was manned by Vial, List, and some new recruits, but Rain had not heard from them either.

'Wolves! To the Square!' she roared, and set off. She could not worry about things she could no longer control. Just one more turn, and over the barricade, was the street leading to the Market Square. That was all she cared about.

Storm was running right on her heels, so when Rain suddenly stopped, Storm bounced off her back and stumbled backwards. 'Ow, you bloody bull!'

But Rain did not hear her. Right by the barricade, blood-smeared Mathurans were hobbling back, dragging their wounded friends. Rain stopped a city guard with a hand on his shoulder. 'What happened?'

'Blood bath!' he shrieked, shaking her off. 'Where were you, you bastard? You should have helped us!' he yelled, lifting an accusing finger at her.

Another soldier dragged him away, calling over his shoulder, 'Don't mind him, Rain. Red Cloaks have flooded the Market Square. Many of our soldiers are still fighting, but we are out of munitions. And they still have an airavat with them. We have no choice but to retreat.'

Rain gulped as she stared across the darkened square beyond the barricade. *So close... they had been so close.* But no, it was no time to dwell on spilled milk, as Krishna would have said. 'Alright ladies, we turn!' she called out. 'We cut through the Meat Farms and try another angle.'

But they seemed not to be listening, for she was pushed forward, carried to the barricade on an irresistible momentum, like a boat on the crest of a wave. *What is happening?* Someone shouted a reply but Rain could not hear over the din. The message, however, spread like a roaring tide. 'It's the Greeks!' someone close by finally said. 'Their horsemen have cut off our retreat. They are charging at us! We can't stay here; we'll be cut down like dogs! Have to push ahead!'

'Now wait...' Rain tried to shoulder her way through the breathless press to reach her Wolves, but there was no getting through. By now, even she could see red banners in the distance. Greeks behind them, and Greeks in front of them. There was nowhere to run. She found Storm's grinning face when a shove from behind squashed her up against Storm, their noses almost touching.

'Not how I imagined this.' Storm smiled. 'But I'm up for it if you are.' Rain looked at her, confused. 'Making love while stuck between the hammer and the anvil,' explained Storm.

'Shut up, Storm,' Rain said, hoping her heart would not burst through her ribs. Bodies squeezed tighter around her. The eastern detachment from the Market Square wanted to turn back, while her soldiers and the western squad were pushing forward. *I am going to die, trampled under my own people.* Suddenly, she tottered into empty space. The soldiers around her stopped pushing as they saw a squad of Mathuran cavalry emerge from a side lane beyond the barricade. *The central detachment!* The Mathuran horsemen charged forward, swords swinging. *Yes!*

'Misery and Calm will be with them!' Storm screeched. 'They have a bellower!'

'I suppose we have nowhere to go now but forward.' Rain grinned.

 SHISHUPAL knew he would never make it to the Square. But he could not stay here. The Greek cavalry had somehow flanked them from behind, and were now in hot pursuit. *So much for staying behind everyone.* 'Move!' he screamed, shoving the soldiers ahead. He could not see Eklavvya. The Valka was short, and must have squeezed through the bodies

ahead. He was about to give up when, like a gift, the press of
soldiers relented, and everyone began to run.

But it was too late.

Shishupal stumbled forward. Around him, desperate faces ran
for their lives. A Greek rider passed him, trampling a Silver Wolf
under the hooves of his horse. Shishupal snatched a fearful look
behind and saw another rider bearing down on him. He tried
to run faster, but he knew a man could not outrun a horse. The
thunder of hooves behind him grew louder. *Fuck it!* He might
as well face Yama with a sword in hand. He stopped running,
unsheathed his blade and turned. He could see the grin on the
bastard's face as the horse galloped closer. Abruptly, he was pushed
to one side, the breath driven out of his body in a whoosh as the
tip of the rider's sword whispered past his ear. He looked up to see
a blood-smeared face smiling at him.

'Not yet, Shishupal,' Eklavvya said, as he dragged him up the
stairs to a charred building, kicked open its axe-scarred door and
pushed him inside. Shishupal stumbled over a corpse and fell on
his knees. A torch still burned weakly beside the body, bathing the
dead face in a dim glow, the expression one of pure pain. *Poor chap.*

'Bloody Greek Fire!' Eklavvya cursed as he picked up the torch,
waving it around.

Shishupal winced at the smell of death inside the fetid room.
'What do we do now?'

'The Greeks and Mathurans will die by the hundreds at the
Square. No point in serving up our bodies for the slaughter.
Eklavvya doesn't reckon any of the Greeks would be interested in
looting a burned house, so he suggests patience and prayer on the
menu for the night.'

'I cannot seem to get rid of you two.' The woman's voice had
been reduced to a gravelly croak.

Shishupal swung around sharply. *Xath preserve my soul!* Runnels
of blood crept down from her temple. A clump of hair was matted
with clots on the left side, the rest a bedraggled mess of grime
and blood. 'Lady Rasha! What happened to you?' Shishupal's jolt

of happiness at seeing a familiar face disappeared in concern for her state.

'I managed to open the Second Sister,' she said, smiling proudly. 'What that blazebane could not do, I did.' A fierce light came into those eyes. 'But the Greeks boiled over the gates faster than I had anticipated.' She shivered at the memory. 'Ashes, it hurts!' She held on the wall for support. 'But I'm alive, ain't I?' she said drunkenly as she stepped closer to the glow of the torch Eklavvya held.

It was then that Shishupal saw a bruise at the corner of her mouth, saw that her clothes were in tatters. A slash had caught the padded blouse she wore, revealing part of a bruised breast. Her feet were stained brown with dry blood. Her body shivered as she drew breath in pained gasps. 'At least the bastard left me alive.'

It took a moment for Shishupal to understand what she meant. *By Xath's own blood, no!* Rage and grief filled him, jostling each other for space in his soul. *Lady Rasha...* But he did not dare reach out and touch her.

'Do not pity me,' Lady Rasha said sternly. 'The moment he turned, I took a dagger to his balls. He begged. But if it didn't work for me, it shouldn't have worked for him, right?'

Before Shishupal could say anything, Eklavvya stepped forward. He looked suddenly different, all buffoonery gone. 'My Lady, Eklavvya promises we will get out of here to somewhere with warm water and a comfortable bed. Time enough for other thoughts when the sun rises. Till then let the moon lull you to sleep.'

'That sounds like a good idea.' She nodded, taking Eklavvya's outstretched hands. He lifted her up easily.

'You are safe now, Lady Rasha,' he said, and set off up the stairs of the house, the woman curled in his arms, face pressed to his chest.

Seeing the most psychotic man and the most dangerous woman thus, so wounded, so vulnerable, struck Shishupal dumb. Silently, fiercely, he prayed. Prayed that the Wolves would deliver dread slaughter to every Greek left alive.

 AKRUR was saddle-sore by the time they killed the poor beast. The horse had done all Akrur could have asked of him – bitten, stamped and kicked at the Red Cloaks. But then someone had climbed up the horse's rump and thrown Akrur from the saddle and stabbed the horse in the neck.

He felt the sudden tug of a hand and saw Satwadhan helping him up. Akrur rose wearily, feeling the tender birth of bruises under his torn armour, but his bones were somehow still intact. All that flesh had finally been of some use. He looked at Satwadhan, covered in cuts and bruises, horseless. To think they had thought they would sweep down on the enemy on horseback; such arrogance could only come from atop a saddle. The Greeks were too many. The ones in the Second District, the ones outside the Third Sister, had all converged to this one point of life and death.

Behind him, he saw Rain appear with her weary soldiers. How on earth she had managed to get the Silver Wolves this far on foot was beyond Akrur's understanding in that moment. All that mattered was that they had.

'Perhaps we should retreat behind those brave women, eh, Satwadhan?'

A spear flashed past Akrur's face and took Satwadhan in the face, dropping him dead. Akrur turned. The spear had been thrown from atop an airavat that was calmly strolling towards him, behind seven Red Cloaks. *No point in running.* It would be embarrassing if the airavat caught up with him. He raised his sword, thought of a joke, and laughed to himself as he strolled towards the enemy. As he imagined Satyabhama would have done.

 RAIN charged into the Greeks with what remained of the Silver Wolves. *So many of them, so few of us...* The Mathuran cavalry had failed against the Greek infantry and their airavat.

A laugh caught her attention. She saw Akrur up ahead. Surrounded by the Greeks, Akrur fought on, his body slashed in more than a dozen places. His sword was cut in half, but he was laughing. It was that maniacal laugh that chilled the Greeks who heard it. Blood sprayed on his laughing face as he cut two more Greeks with a single swipe of his broken longsword. His humour lasted but a moment longer. Then the airavat's trunk coiled around him, crushing his hips before throwing him to the ground like a broken branch. Akrur met his end when his stomach was trampled underfoot, his innards spilling out of him like overflowing milk from a pot.

Behind him, the battle raged on. No quarter was given, no mercy shown. The Mathurans kept fighting. Civilian and soldier fought the Red Cloaks side by side. Horses and men moved in a dance of death around the remaining Mathurans, till at last they fell.

Cold horror swept through Rain. *We can't win. We must surrender.* A helm, the head still in it, rolled wildly across her feet, probably kicked by one of the horses. It was a Silver Wolf. *Piety.* And then Rain saw the rest of her naked body. Knots tightened in her gut as she comprehended the brutal way she had been raped. Ahead, she saw similar red-limbed, stripped corpses of Silver Wolves. *The eastern squad that had reached first...* Her very soul twisted with pain. *Yama protect us!*

'I don't think surrender is an option,' Storm said. 'The bastards aren't taking any prisoners.'

Rain turned to her soldiers. She did all she could to ignore the quiet grief in their eyes. They were trapped between enemies that would rape, devour and obliterate them from the earth. The least they could do was make their lives miserable while they were at it. Her soldiers seemed to read her mind, for they nodded and tapped their shields. Rain discarded her shield for a mace, and strapped the broken standard of the Silver Wolves to her back.

'*For Satyabhama!*' they roared. The echo of their war cry rolled through her being, along with sadness, regret, and the long sigh of a final breath.

 STORM needed to be drunk. Since ale was in short supply, blood would have to do. She burst into the fountain in the middle of the Square. The rough flagstones below were framed with blackening blood. Tears stung her eyes but refused to fall. Her friends were dead or dying, but Mathura still had to be saved. Satyabhama's death could not be in vain.

Beside her, Rain had become someone else. She almost looked like Satyabhama reincarnate as she finished Greek soldiers with a borrowed mace in one hand and a short sword in the other. Pikes drove into her abdomen, lifting her into the air. Her sword arm cut through the shafts of the pikes, and she landed amongst the Greek bodies, cutting and smashing even as she fell. Storm saw an axe sever her mace arm, blood spraying from the stump of her arm onto the attacker's face. Rain used her sword arm to stab his throat. He fell, gurgling on his own blood and bile. Two more pikes jabbed through the gaps in her breastplate, finding muscle and bone. Rain went down, and with her the broken standard of the Silver Wolves that she had strapped to her back.

The Market Square had become a hell of stomping hooves, clashing metal and blood. Shields were pulled down, helms ripped from heads. Weapons were snagged, and everywhere Storm looked, there was blood. She could not see a single familiar face. But she did not have time to dawdle. Another Greek came within range. Storm swung her sword with the last of her strength, watching his head spin away from his body. She felt a knife stab the underside of her right knee, searing up into the joint. Storm slashed weakly down with her shield, barely enough to push the Greek away. The knife snapped, leaving behind a few inches of blade in her knee that scratched and sliced the tendons within.

Someone shouted a warning as bows twanged. Storm raised her shield instinctively but ran right on, leg burning, voice hoarse from screaming. She chopped an archer down and then swung at a big Easterner carrying the Mlecchá standard. He dodged and she ended up chopping the standard in half. The standard fell on

Storm, the flag tangling her sword. She tore a hole through the flag to see a group of Greeks plunge at her. The world narrowed to a strip of red, black and grey before her eyes as the Greeks wrapped the flag around her. She thrashed and struggled like a fish caught in a snare, felt alien hands tear her armour, rip apart her clothes. In the midst of this, she heard a distant explosion, and almost felt the air tear around her. She could hear the sound of waves like the faintest whisper of a fabric being torn apart. *The dams*, she realized even as her sword whirled in blind but deadly arcs. Her defiance lasted only a moment longer before the enemy overpowered her, stripped her naked and swallowed her in the mindless frenzy of war.

 KRISHNA stood in the last remaining tower of the Senate. He had turned his eyeglass to the Hakkus, perhaps too dazed to notice, or too numb to care, about the fateful end of the Wolves. For a moment he had almost begun to *hope*. How his soldiers had managed to blitz through the Second District for hours, and how their heroic efforts had vanished in the wink of an eye in the Market Square, he would never know. But he had no time to ponder on dreams, hopes and tragic ends.

He lit the torch. The signal given, an explosion erupted on the northern end that faced the mighty Yamuna River. The Hakkus that held back the waters collapsed in a heap of debris, and the river rushed in, steering its way through the bazaar. To think that just a few days before a celebration had taken place amidst those very stalls. *How the winds of destiny shifted in the turn of a moon.*

But then Krishna saw the waters did not rush further in the way he had thought they would. They did not ram down the stalls and the houses. The river was supposed to charge in like a bull, not creep through the alleys like an anxious tourist. Something was wrong. And then the river began to turn, as if disappointed, back to its original course. *Fuck!* Instead of entering his city like a flood, the river spread like spilled milk, and then... just stopped. *The river was supposed to be in spate!*

Krishna turned away stony-faced, refusing to believe that his godsluck had abandoned him altogether. He strode towards the stairs that led to the Senate Hall. He knew the last of the Mathurans would clash with the Greeks inside the Iron Curfew soon, but they would not be able to hold the Red Cloaks back. Soldiers, failed. Flood, failed. It was down to his last gambit.

A while later, a smoky breeze wafted in through the door of the Senate Hall as Krishna walked in, making the flames of the wall sconces flicker and sway. Ornate carvings crowded the ceiling; painted figures holding hands. He had given some of his greatest speeches here. A place of majesty; a place where Mankind's greatest invention was born by toppling a monarchy – the Republic. Curiously, born right over the Daevas' greatest secret in this world.

None but he knew that the second entrance to the Syamantaka lay right under the speaker's podium, standing at which Krishna had deflected countless questions from the Senators about the location of the so-called Syamantaka Jewel. Life was full of these little ironies. The Syamantaka was connected to another tunnel that led to the alternative entrance, the tunnel through which the priceless artefacts of the Syamantaka were even now being transported under the watchful eye of Satyaki and Jambavan. The tunnel Krishna had meant to use with Satyabhama to escape Mathura. The tunnel that would be Kalyavan's doom.

 LIST stood gloomily outside the Iron Curfew, surveying the smouldering hole in it. The charge by the soldiers had bought time for the masons to effect repairs. It was not a fine job, but it would keep the Greeks out. The last of the citizens of Mathura had headed into the tunnel, its entrance well disguised beneath cedar branches and piles of moss. She watched the line of wounded soldiers being helped back to the

healers behind the Curfew. Vial was there, supervising. The little girl had a knack for herbs. List, on the other hand, yearned to head into battle to help her sisters. If the explosions were any indication, the fighting seemed to have taken all over the Second District. But that had been a while ago.

Still there was no news from Rain or Calm's squads. *They will be fine,* she told herself as she paused to wipe ash-smeared sweat from her brow. *They will be safely inside the tunnel, and the Greeks won't know what hit them when they drown under the river. The water must have submerged the northern districts by now.* Though she had to grudgingly admit that if Mathura was flooding right now, the Greeks did not quite create the racket she had imagined.

From the corner of her eye, she caught sight of movement around the dead beasts in the moat. Crossbow poised, she marched to where she thought she saw something move. A boy darted out from behind an airavat's corpse, holding a torch in one hand and a thread in another. He was lighting a taper that ran along the moat. *Like it would help. That is not how you mine under a wall, boy.* She saw the lit taper dart between the bodies of the beasts. It was then that she saw where the taper was headed – the saddles on the airavats. Urns. Scores of urns, some broken, filled with a blue burning liquid. *Blazebane!* With a piercing scream she jumped into the moat to extinguish the taper.

But it was too late.

 KRISHNA passed through the underground tunnel to the wooden door that led to the Syamantaka. Two dour-faced soldiers, spears polished to a murderous glint, stood guarding the portal. 'Lord Krishna!' one saluted. 'What news from above? Have the Greeks been defeated?'

Krishna did not respond as he hurried through the door. He emerged from the tunnel into another, that was more of a long winding cavern than a tunnel. Water splattered from broken gutters onto the rough-hewn stones. A wet procession of mules and carts tramped along, carrying the treasures of the Syamantaka to safety.

'Krishna!' Satyaki rushed to him. '*What happened? Have the Greeks gone?*' He was almost hysterical in his anxiety. 'Most of the Syamantaka has been transported! Just the people left. You have injured your head. *What happened?*'

Krishna grasped Satyaki's collar and pulled his face close to his own. Satyaki quieted. 'Has everything been transported? *Everything?*'

'Yes! I mean most... The alchemy contraption is well on its way to safe harbour. The Garden of Is has been carefully split into a hundred pots and that's what I was just loading into the carts. Thirty more pots to go. And...' Satyaki shuddered as if uttering the name brought forth a nightmare 'the sarcophagus... as decided, we are leaving it behind. Once everyone is out, Jambavan will burn the place down.'

'Bring it out.'

'Uh... what?'

'Mathura has fallen. Ugrasen is dead. The Silver Wolves are gone. The City Guard and the army decimated...' Talking hurt, as if stinging nettles had been stuffed down his throat. 'Satyabhama is dead.'

Satyaki mouth gaped open, his eyes frozen. 'Krishna...'

'BRING IT OUT!'

 VIAL was inside the Iron Curfew, tending to the wounded, when she heard the explosions. She was glad List had left her alone. She could not face her patriotic drivel just then. Satyabhama was dead. They should have honoured her memory by living, not sacrificing themselves for a city that had discarded them. But her thoughts abandoned her when the cobbles shook under her. And then she saw blue, luminous cracks spread across huge sections of the Iron Curfew,

until the Wall itself exploded, swallowing all the archers atop it in a blue storm.

Horror rising within her, she saw blue flames rush into the streets, spreading like a flood unleashed. Her legs seemed to weigh a ton as she forced herself to flee. Heat beat upon Vial as she ran. But that demonic fire was faster. Vial dived into a pile of jute sacks and pulled them over her as she trapped her eyes shut, even as she felt the kiss of blazebane on her cheeks.

After what seemed an eternity, she opened her eyes again. She heard horse hooves pounding the cobbles. *I survived!* She pushed herself from the pile of scorched sacks to see that most of the Iron Curfew was nothing but a heap of rubble and ash now. Blue-tongued fires still burned in isolated patches around her. And riding into this glare of burning buildings was the man who had killed Satyabhama.

He spotted Vial, slowed his canter, and swung his warhorse round to approach her. 'Where is Krishna?' he asked with a smile that might have been charming if not for his earless face. 'Tell me now, and I might just let your friend die a painless death.'

One of his soldiers threw a naked woman down near Vial. The woman's face was hidden by her upflung arms. Kalyavan shouted something in Greek. Vial did not understand what he said, but he saw the soldier drape a cloak over the woman. There were bruise marks all over her body. And her hair seemed to have been cut off by shears. *By the Gods.* Vial started crying when she recognized her.

KRISHNA noticed that not much had changed in his good-father's appearance in the last three decades. He looked ageless, as did the three other Rikshas who had stayed back with him to help with the evacuation. Jambavan had always credited the Syamantaka with keeping him young. He believed the ship was somehow unanchored in time. Yet, despite his youthful looks, Jambavan possessed a grandfatherly ambience.

'Fuck off!' Krishna hissed.

'*No*, Krishna! I know the grief you suffer.' Jambavan was almost holding him in the air, his paws curled around his shoulders, his tufted ears twitching irritably. 'But you cannot let the world burn!'

'If you haven't noticed, it's already burning, Jambavan. Out of my way or I'll have you arrested.'

'Son, you are not using your wits,' he said slowly, his voice rumbling in the cavern. 'You don't even have any soldiers with you. Now, take a deep breath. Do not force me to stop you. You know I can. I can't... oh...'

Jambavan was startled when Krishna embraced him. His voice was gentle, low, when he said, 'I understand the pain of loss, Krishna.' He patted Krishna's back. Fatherly was probably his intention.

But Jambavan was right, Krishna realized. He was much stronger than him, and he did not have enough soldiers to overpower Jambavan, or the time to waste on such efforts.

'I myself...' The rest of Jambavan's words were lost in a gurgle of blood. His tufted ears drooped sadly. His eyes stared at Krishna in disappointment as Krishna stabbed him in the heart, again and again. Blood gushed hot over Krishna's hand, spattering the floor.

Krishna did not order the rest of the Rikshas killed, allowing them to leave with their riches. Relief gradually wiped the anger from their faces. And the last thoughts of retribution fled when they heard the sound of explosions above. For the next hour, they helped the two Mathuran guards to move the sarcophagus to where the stairs ascended to the Senate Hall above. Satyaki stayed with them, watching the pantomime with grim resignation.

A guard rushed in, heaving and panting. 'Sire, the Greeks are here! We heard their voices. Ten... twelve men.'

Hope they discover the trail I left them. 'Take positions,' Krishna said as he limped back through the fetid walkway back to the stairs. The light from his swinging lantern cast swaying shadows on the tunnel walls. Rotten slime and dark water dripped from above, while rats scampered in the slimy gutters.

'*Ow!*' Krishna's bare toe tore on a rusty nailhead. *Fate is a mean bully, that's a fact.* Even with Satyabhama dead, his city destroyed, his soldiers gone, Fate still found a way to drop another misfortune on his head.

There was a sudden sound of applause. Krishna stiffened. Scattered laughter. A whoop of hurrahs. Then Kalyavan's voice ran in the marbled hall above, echoing up and down the vaulted tunnel: 'Valiant Champions of the Yavanas! Let us just say Valiant Men of the Yavanas! Or just Yavanas!' A roar of laughter and claps. 'Let it never be said the Greeks are not conquerors! The Mathurans gave us a good fight; at least, their women did!' More cheering. 'Let no one dare to call us Mlecchá to our faces again! We are Glorious! We are Heroes!' Another swell of approval.

'The Old Lion was keen that we *assist* him and win his victory for him.' Silence. 'But I declined! He was ready to pay us a part of the Mathuran spoils. I told him, "Fuck off! We will take the spoils for ourselves!"' A rousing cheer. 'We have defeated the Mathurans, whom the armies of the Emperor could not touch. The Three Sisters, they boasted. Where, I ask?' Widespread laughter. 'But the battle isn't over, my friends. So, to your units. That girl said Krishna was here, inside. Find me Krishna! Find me where the rest of the goddamn Mathurans are hiding! Whoever finds one will get the choicest of women from my harem!'

Weapons and shields, plated arms and gauntleted fists shook in the air. '*Kalyavan! Kalyavan!*' Most of the men marched out hastily, eager to get first hand on the loot. Krishna heard the sound of their retreating boots.

'Archon, why did you let them go?' a voice asked. 'You saw the traces of the hole beneath that podium. There is a passageway right under us. The Mathurans are no doubt hiding here. We should storm in with strength.'

'Don't be foolish, Matarchis. Wave the torch over the floor and look at the boot impressions. Only one person seems to have walked across this space tonight. And I would wager my sword that it was Krishna. Scampering alone into a secret crypt... it has to be the vault where he has hidden the Syamantaka Jewel. Do you think these mercenaries would have remained loyal once they set their eyes on a wish-granting stone? You are the five men I trust with my life. Now, you two,' Krishna heard him command, 'stay here to guard our retreat. We do not want any surprises. The rest, down under we go. Carry swords as well as crowbars and pins.'

'What about the girl?' a voice asked.

'She looks half-dead anyway,' the one who was called Matarchis spoke.

'No, we will take her down. If Krishna is up to any tricks, we will remind him that we can play dirty as well.'

Hostage... Krishna thought. It didn't matter. After a hundred heartbeats, he saw four soldiers climb down the stairs, the two in front holding a girl between them. One held a lantern. Then he saw Kalyavan, the man he had been looking for, step down with a torch in one hand, his sword in the other. He wore an olive wreath around his head.

The Greeks searched the room to which the stairs led, cautiously, stopping short upon seeing the sarcophagus. 'What in the...!'

Krishna stood hidden in the shadows of the passageway on the other side of the room. The passageway that led to the Syamantaka was at one end, and the alternative exit at the other. He could see the men's eyes shimmer with greed in the dim light of the reflected lantern as they took in the ornate hieroglyphs meticulously carved on the box. Their glee, however, turned to shock and horror when they realized it was a tomb.

'Archon, we must leave at once!'

'Afraid of a corpse?' the Matarchis scoffed from behind. 'Must be some ancestor of Kans who was buried in this crypt.'

'The Vedans don't bury their dead, they burn them,' Kalyavan observed.

'Archon...' the man closest to the sarcophagus stuttered, 'he... seems alive. And the grains on the sarcophagus are swirling like magic.'

Kalyavan scoffed. 'To Mathurans, blazebane is magic. There is nothing called magic. Only mysteries to be unravelled. Open the tomb and get done with it. The Syamantaka might be inside it.'

'But...' the man said, 'it is ill to disturb the dead.'

'I thought you said he was not dead,' Kalyavan snapped. 'Now open it!'

The men nodded. The two carrying the woman put her down against the wall. Gabbling prayers, they used their swords and crowbars, grunting and wheezing in their effort. Finally, they prised open the lid. An angry hiss split the air. Krishna's eyes widened as he saw tendrils of crackling icy-blue smoke curl from the sarcophagus. It coiled around the Greeks, harmless but hateful.

And then something stirred in the open box. *Finally!* Krishna thought triumphantly. He could now only hope the Daevas had imprisoned the creature for a good reason, or he would be forced to turn to a measure of last resort. He stared impassively at the bellower in his hand.

 CHASTHANA was a Matarchis, and a runt like Kalyavan. Half-breed, the Vedans called them. Fear was something unknown to runts. Yet, in that moment, he did not feel like the brave man he used to be, if it was indeed bravery and not stupidity. For the man who rose from the coffin sent ripples of fear through him. It was not as if the man, if he could be called that, had done something to earn his shivers. It was instinctive, as if the very air around him was somehow tainted.

The man turned to look at them. He was large, as if born of a race of Titans long dead. His eyes were jet black, his pupils almost invisible. They peered out of his eyes as if from the end of tunnels. His long hair writhed in a wind that touched no one else. His skin was almost white, stretched taut like parchment drawn tight over a skull. Water pooled around his feet as ice fell from his skin. Chasthana spied a missing wrist, though the slash was rimmed with a reddish-brown icy ring. Chain marks showed around his neck, as if he had been throttled. The Titan turned a strange-looking dagger in his other hand. Reflected torchlight glimmered on the ice shards scattered over the man's midnight armour.

Aeneas edged closer, as if in a trance. 'What are you?' he whispered in a trembling voice. 'Are you a demon?'

'I doubt he knows Greek,' Kalyavan said, no trace of fear in his voice. Chasthana didn't like that. He had wanted Kalyavan to cower, as he did. 'Krishna!' Kalyavan shouted into the empty black air, 'If you think a giant can scare me, stow that thought deep away, cowherd.'

The Titan slowly lifted his head. His withered wide mouth stretched into a condescending grin, revealing teeth encrusted with ice. Muscles tautened along his neck, his shoulders and arms in twisting, shaking lines. 'Savitre?' he whispered in a hoarse voice that sounded like a knife softly drawn across bone. Chasthana knew the Titan spoke in the tongue of the First Empire, but he did not understand the words.

'What did he say?' Aeneas asked.

'Sounded like *Seetre*.' Chasthana trembled. 'Archon, we should leave.'

'Thorin! Where is he?' Muchuk Und asked, looking at his wrist. 'Asha…' The last word was an icy whisper that misted out of his mouth.

'Enough! I don't care for this nonsense. Kill him!' commanded Kalyavan.

Kill him? Can he even be killed?

Chasthana's eyes flickered from Aeneas to the Titan, unsure. But a command was a command. He nodded at Aeneas and the other soldier whose name he did not remember, wishing they had more men. The two cranked the crossbows they had picked up from the corpses of Mathuran soldiers. The machines rattled but the bolts glanced off the Titan's armour. Any other man would have dropped dead from hits at such close range. The Titan merely looked at his assailants, his eyes filled with rage. There was a brief motion and the flash of the old dagger. The soldiers fell on either side of him, as if in a coordinated dance, their throats cut.

What just happened? Chasthana stepped back, afraid, stepping on the lantern. Suddenly, an unspeakable pain burned between his lungs. He managed to move his head to look down and saw something glinting there. But only for a moment. The dagger slipped out of him as fast as it had slipped in. 'Oh, c'mon! We had just won,' he wheezed. But the words barely came out. It had all happened so fast.

 KRISHNA saw Muchuk Und kill three men in the span of a thought. Kalyavan set down his torch. He neither grunted nor roared as he unsheathed his sword and darted forward, feinting left, then swinging to the right. Muchuk Und parried with his dagger, but Kalyavan was fast too. And a sword had a longer reach than a dagger. He turned at blinding speed and scratched Muchuk Und's exposed arm. A strange-coloured blood dripped from the wound.

Before Kalyavan could deliver another blow, Muchuk Und's hand dropped the dagger and darted out to seize Kalyavan's neck, fingers sinking into it, driving the blood out. Muchuk Und gripped Kalyavan's throat and lifted him up, bringing him up to his face. The Greek's body spasmed as a convulsion wracked him, his feet thrashing a foot above the ground. Leaves rained down from his olive crown. Muchuk Und looked at his arm. His thin, bloodless lips curved into a cruel smile. 'Thank you for this gift… It feels good to be human again.' He spoke in the First Tongue even as he tossed Kalyavan away. Kalyavan flew through the air. With a dull thud, he struck the stairs.

'What did you do to me?' Kalyavan gasped, groaning in pain. 'How…. did you do that?'

'So much darkness here…' Muchuk Und sighed in pleasure. 'Darkness is my ally, Mortal. Witness.'

What little Krishna could see was from the swirling blue light coming from the open sarcophagus. Muchuk Und lifted his dagger and scratched on its blade, then began moving his hand as if he was painting on air. Krishna almost gasped loudly when he saw a white circle emerge in the air. Muchuk Und then *drew* a few glyphs in it.

'Those things don't work, friend,' Kalyavan said, echoing Krishna's own thoughts.

Muchuk Und was old, probably a thousand years old. He wouldn't know that Mortals could not conjure Mandalas anymore. *Fuck*. Krishna took out the bellower. *Best be done with it.*

And then, the air about Muchuk Und twisted and danced, as though his reflection had suddenly been disturbed in the waters of a lake. Darkness swirled around Kalyavan in jade-rimmed outlines, like a tornado, ever expanding with the sounds of the storm. The air behind Muchuk Und began to warp, shimmering with a light darker than night.

'What the...' Kalyavan grunted in Greek, rising slowly to his feet. 'That's impossible! Mandalas don't work!'

'Ah... the release. Witness, Mortal!'

A mighty blast of wind swept through the cavern and sent Krishna tumbling. The bellower fell from his hand. He tried to rise but the wind whipped at his eyes. An armoured gauntlet tore from his arm, then a greave from his leg. His cloak tore and flapped about him like a living thing. Krishna turned to see Kalyavan had fallen to his knees and was clawing at his chest. The very ground began to tremble and quake. It was as if Krishna could almost taste the ancient misery, the unyielding hate in Muchuk Und.

'They will pay for what they did to me,' Muchuk Und rasped. Krishna saw his dagger flame, as if its blade was afire. 'Too long have we been cheated, duped, and betrayed by our masters. Vengeance shall be mine! And you will be my death offering to Yama. Oh.' Muchuk Und suddenly squinted at the girl's figure lying unconscious to one side, as if felled by a blow. 'You... you are special, are you not? It seems our destinies are intertwined.' Muchuk Und walked towards her, the black storm still billowing around the room. He pulled back the cloak from the girl's face, and the agony in Krishna's gut rose like a fist of fire. *Oh, no...*

At that moment, Kalyavan rose, grunting and cursing. Then three things happened at once. Kalyavan swung his sword, a defiant scream on his lips. Muchuk Und touched the girl's cheek with his dagger. And the Silver Wolf opened her eyes with a jolt, her pupils enlarging as if they were exploding in her eyes.

Kalyavan stopped short as if hit by an invisible wall. His hands still raised, his body began to glow from inside like a burning ember, a glowing coal about to explode. Light poured out through his eyes and luminous cracks began to appear in his arms, his cheeks, his legs. Kalyavan screamed.

Krishna smiled. Satyaki tugged at his arm in horror, distracting him from the delights of seeing his revenge fulfilled. 'We must leave! It is all falling apart. Shit, is that a bellower there? I'll get it before it explodes.'

'No,' Krishna said. 'Leave it.'

 SHISHUPAL unsheathed his sword. Men were shouting right outside the broken door that dangled from twisted hinges. *Cravens die many deaths, but the valiant tastes of it but once*, he had heard a bard once tell. A lot of shit, if anyone asked him. He knew he was brave, and knew he would die swinging his sword. That did not mean he was not close to shitting his trousers. He used the anger over what had been done to Lady Rasha to steel his nerves.

'I can't believe this is the place we were tasked to bring our blades to,' a voice said, curiously speaking Sanskrit. Heavy footsteps came closer.

'Aye, the city looks like a rubbish yard. The Emperor could not conquer *this*?' another man asked in genuine surprise. 'Now that we are up in arms, maybe we should head down South. I hear southern women are freer in their ways. I could do with a victory parade, and a grateful lass.'

'The South can sink in the gutter for all I care,' the first voice spoke. 'This is no fucking fun! It's as if these Mlecchás were too tired to even raise their swords. And where are the ones we were sent to save?'

Shishupal froze. *Save?*

'We'll find them. Still a long way to go.'

The voices grew distant as they left. Once the footsteps receded, Shishupal ran up the stairs. *What did he mean by save?* Eklavvya was sitting on the floor by the bed on which Lady Rasha slept. He paid them no heed as he stormed to the terrace. The moon came and went as the clouds tore across the sky. And in the flickering moonlight, he could see the banners, the red eagle flying high on the standards. He could not believe it.

Hastina has finally come!

He raised Eklavvya's eyeglass and stretched it towards the Third Sister, or what remained of it, anyway. The Hastina army had attacked the rear of the Greeks, charging the exhausted, battle-worn Red Cloaks with full force. Armoured men on armoured steeds stabbed and slashed at snarling Greeks. The last of the Mathurans, hope renewed, fought afoot, their horses down.

It was not a battle, it was a rout. The Greeks did not stand a chance. Many Red Cloaks readily surrendered. The Mathurans cheered wearily, embracing their Hastina allies as if they had saved the day.

Too late. Much too late.

As he scanned the horizon, Shishupal could see Mathura was finished, half drowned and half burnt. Whatever remained had been smashed underfoot by airavats.

Eklavvya came to stand beside him. 'Somehow, we have survived the night, friend. It's all over, eh?'

The answer came in a way Shishupal least expected. The earth tolled like a gong. A rumbling quake shook the ground. They turned as one in the direction of the First District. On the horizon, a jade pillar of fire rose skyward with an earth-shattering explosion, ferociously reshaping the dark sky. Their eyes followed the column upwards, higher and higher. The pillar seemed to rise from the ruins of the Iron Curfew. Swirls of green swayed away from the pillar of fire in the sky in great bands, as if Prakioni herself had unfurled her green locks. It continued to claw upwards with a sizzling roar in an explosive struggle.

And then the jade column slowly softened in the night. A large mass of darkened dust floated in the air. The night sky looked like an open wound.

'What... was... that?' whispered Shishupal, his feet rooted to the ground. He heard Eklavvya turn to leave. 'Where are you going! Do you know what that was!'

'Eklavvya's eyes have had their fill of watching rainbow fires. He is leaving.' He walked off, shaking his head, still muttering under his breath. 'First blue, then green... is this a joke? No, World, do not answer!'

 KRISHNA turned back to see the jade flames lick out in every direction, chasing them like a living hair of a Goddess bent on devouring them. Krishna was tired. It felt like he had run for miles through a burning furnace. Felt like red-hot needles were piercing his lungs. But he did not stop running. He could not. Fear and desperation lent his legs strength.

'Yes, there's the door!' gasped Satyaki. Molten cracks spread like veins across the stone walls on either side of the door. Satyaki froze, but Krishna yanked the door open. A wave of heat hit Krishna in the back like a mighty punch. There was the sound of a landslide as flames erupted in a loud breath through the open door, bursting out in an explosion. They were both thrown into the air. The two guards running behind them were incinerated. Krishna crashed against a wall on the opposite side of the street, and then dropped in a flaccid heap, all his meticulous plans flung away with his sword. That's the trouble with plans. They rarely survive being chased through a tunnel by a resurrected Elemental.

SHAKUNI walked alone over the bloodied earth into the Iron Curfew. After what they had seen of the jade pillar, most of the Hastina soldiers had refused to enter the First District till a Namin priest had sanctified the place.

Shakuni cared nothing for such superstitions, but he was saddened by the fall of Mathura. It was not an ancient civilization like Ayodhya or Hastinapur, or a large city like Rajgrih. But Mathura had been the leader of a brave new world in Aryavrat; a trader city, in contrast to the military cities of the past. It was said Mathura had ushered in a change, an industrial and moral revolution. It was a city of commerce and industry, where Men decided their own fates, not caste. Shakuni felt no sympathy for the Mathurans, but seeing the hope of an entire Age crumble into the dust did little to lift his spirits.

Signs of war were everywhere. Burning ox-carts, broken chariot wheels, ransacked houses, remnants of horses, mules, airavats, men, women and children lay scattered like seeds in a field at the start of the sowing season. Flies danced clumsily over the bodies. Some trampled, some slain, most burnt. Here and there, clusters of bodies in blue lay in mounds, evidencing the brave and desperate last stand by the Mathuran soldiers.

Sahadev rode up alongside Shakuni. 'What do you think of all this, My Lord?'

Shakuni raised his brows at the lack of hostility in Sahadev's voice. *A graceful loser.* That was rare indeed. *Or is the game still on?*

Sahadev read his thoughts. 'Civility is the only route to coexistence, Lord Shakuni. Unless you have a better way to deal with the fallout of your actions?'

'I do.' Shakuni flashed his broken smile. 'But I am too pretty for prison. Any luck finding Krishna's body?'

'No, My Lord. But the body count is high… and most of them burnt beyond recognition. I am headed to the source of that jade pillar of flame. Coming?'

Shakuni was impressed. No signs of hesitation. No fear. A worthy adversary. 'Certainly,' Shakuni replied. 'Try and keep up with my pace.'

They walked past the ruins of the Keep to where the Senate House used to be. Where the grand building of democracy had once stood in white magnificence, there was an enormous, gaping hole, lined with shredded plaster, broken beams and dangling frames. Dust still showered into the yawning maw below. The earth itself shuddered with remembered terror. Neither spoke a word.

The only spot not smoking into strings of green-black ghosts was fifty paces down. It glistened like a lake of water. *Is that a crater?* Shakuni wondered as Sahadev helped him navigate the slope. A hollowed mound stood in a green circle, a strange blackened tree at its centre. Shakuni had never witnessed such a conflagration, not from any Mathuran munition. If Krishna had found a way to create a munition of such power, Shakuni dreaded the implication of such an invention. But if he had, why had he not used it on the Greeks, when they were still outside the gates?

He squinted at the blackened mass in the centre, so deformed it could scarcely be called a tree. Then his eyes narrowed. *The Daevas take me!* Hastily, he stepped back, his weak leg protesting. It wasn't a tree! It was a man, a tall man! The body was an incinerated ruin, burned beyond recognition. It was still steaming. The hands were outstretched, holding a sword with a ruby-studded crosspiece, the steel still glinting.

Sahadev joined Shakuni, studying the body as they inched closer. Stray green waves of fire, like candle flames, were still alight on parts of his body. The corpse's hands were stretched in a pose of attack. Whatever had happened had not allowed him to complete his swing.

Shakuni felt numb. He withdrew a kerchief and mopped the sweat from his face. 'I know him...' No one forgot an Assyrian blade, and he'd seen the fool brandish it more times at the swayamvar than he wished to remember. 'Kalyavan.'

'There are tracks here...' Sahadev murmured, unfazed by Shakuni's revelation.

What! Someone walked out of this alive? Shakuni turned to observe the hardened footprints on the soft earth left by the eruption. *Was it an animal? No... only two legs. But such enormous prints.* Sudden fear flooded his soul as he saw the trail lead in an unmistakable north-eastern direction.

'Whatever it was,' Shakuni said, his face pale, 'it is long gone. No point attempting to find it.'

'Unless, of course, it has stopped to find us,' Sahadev remarked. Reaching down, he snatched the sword from the burnt body, but dropped it with a jolt as the hot blade singed his hand. In a whiff of dust and smoke, the ruin of Kalyavan's body crumbled to ash before their eyes, leaving no trace on earth of the warrior who it was said no man born in this Age could kill.

'Guess the prophecy was false after all,' Sahadev said, inspecting his raw palm, but Shakuni wasn't listening. He was confused. If Kalyavan was dead and Mathura destroyed, who won?

 KRISHNA dreamed of Mathura. A bygone dream. A city of fantasy scarcely touched by the past. A city of dreamers and alchemists. A city where even the wind carried the memory of revolution, magic and flutes, and cobbled lanes meandered like creeks. Of a city where women wielded swords, coin-counters ruled, where griffins flew in the air, and every month saw a new carnival, making the whole place seem like a theatre. A theatre he ran as the unseen puppeteer behind the screen.

His head throbbed as he woke with an aching jolt. One knee was drawn up awkwardly towards his chest, the other trapped under something hard. After groaning attempts to move, he gave up. Where was he?

'Krish... Krishna...'

Krishna twisted around as best he could and managed to open his eyes in narrow slits. *Nothingness.*

'Krishna...'

That voice... Satyaki. What is he doing here? I must call to him... assuage his fears. Where is everyone? Where is Balram? Satyabhama... where is Satya?

He opened his eyes. Finding himself buried under a pile of rubble, he pushed at it with weary hands, cursing breathlessly at no one in particular. Light seeped in. Frantically, he enlarged the opening. He dragged himself out and collapsed on the street, drained by the effort. His ears listened for enemy sounds through his laboured breathing. There were none.

He remembered Satyaki and turned back to pull him out. Krishna put his head against Satyaki's chest, and then pumped it. Satyaki gasped and coughed out dirt. He lay curled in the way of an unborn babe, drawing gulps of fresh air into his lungs. He would live.

Krishna fell back on the ground, coughing hard. He just lay there, staring up at the sky, which was a pale shade of blue, almost white. Clean and pure. No trailing fireballs. No smoke. No falling ash. Just pristine blue.

Krishna laughed. *Kalyavan. Greeks. Blazebane. Airavats. Muchuk Und. All dead.*

'What happened?' Satyaki croaked painfully, raising his head and squinting through bloodshot eyes, his throat raspy from dust and smoke.

'Why, Satyaki, didn't you hear the news?' Krishna smiled weakly, half-blinded by tears. 'I won the War.'

EPILOGUE

JUSTICE

He had been a loyal friend. He had done the honourable thing, hadn't he? Yet this was where honour and loyalty had brought him. Imprisoned and chained like a rabid dog.

Karna squinted, then stared, seeing nothing but dust-hued blackness. He could not see his own hand in front of his face. Not that he could move it anyway. They had chained his wrists to the ceiling. His ankles had not been spared either, for chains tethered him to the ground. He was grateful for the thin breastplate he had been born with. It soothed the pain in his ribs. But it did nothing for his exposed arms. If he stretched his toes, his feet just touched the clammy stones, giving his wrists momentary relief from the throbbing agony of bearing the weight of his suspended body. But the respite was short-lived, for his calves protested, burning fiercely till he had to let go and swing by his chafed wrists once again.

The cell felt thick with fear, the looming threat so heavy it made the hairs on his neck prickle. *Without his horse, had Duryodhan been able to escape? Or even survive?* The jump had been a deep one. But, with Karna holding up an army at the only exit, the Prince had not had the luxury of options.

Her freckled face under red hair swam before Karna's swollen eyes. *I should never have brought her into this.* Did the Emperor think she was connected to their foolhardy plan? If he did, would he be content to exile her, or would he be more direct in his punishment? *She would live.* She was the most resourceful woman he knew.

Perhaps I should think about saving myself for a change. He would have laughed if he could. But there was little to ponder on the subject. His mind had already flipped around like a frog in hot water, seeking any desperate way out of the trap they had so stupidly walked into. Would he have to negotiate with his captors? After all, the guards had called him a 'political prisoner'. He grunted. He had been done with talking after Prakar Mardin, yet here he was again, in an even more disadvantageous position than he had been on the *Fat Mistress.*

A strange certainty haunted him. The certainty of death. Political prisoner or not, one look at the Resht mark on his neck and he was sure his 'protection' would melt away like mist on the hills. *How should I go?* Kill as many of these southern mongrels with his bare hands as he could? No. He should go with dignity. Like the Highmaster he was. Or ought he to wait to be taken to his captor, and take his chances with him? Or with Mati, if she was there. Surely, it was she who had planned this trap? *The bitch.*

Karna had lost track of time. He had tried to measure it by the changing of the guards, but he had not heard a sound from without for hours, or had it been days? By now, in the madness of blindness, Karna's mind refused to stay still, like a doe caught in a net, tormenting him as much as his manacles.

He hung his head. He had thrown his life away, all for nothing. *Arjun.* He still wondered whether it had been an accident that the Prince of Bows had pierced a hole in Sudama's head. Or had it been Shishupal's fault? Or his own? He doubted the upcoming trial would yield any result other than the obvious one, though Duryodhan had seemed optimistic. Did it even matter? He could not blame Arjun for something he had caused. *The Abyss take me!*

A distant rattling made him jerk up his head. He felt a weight in the air, the weight of the sky before a ravaging storm. Keys turned in a lock. He squinted in the direction of the sound, only to be stabbed by light as the door slammed open. Through slitted eyes he saw an enormous silhouette come down the steps, lit by the flickering light of torches held by those behind him. Heavy boots scraped the moist floor, creating a menacing sound.

'I trust our hospitality has made you feel welcome, Highmaster,' a smooth voice said.

It did not come from the giant silhouette, but from behind him. The man stepped forward. He looked like the Goddess of Life had boiled every ounce of fat from his flesh to render him just bone, skin and hair. His eyes were like chipped stone, black and sharp. His black robes had enormous sleeves and a golden lion brooch was fastened on his chest. Around his throat he wore an enormous *rudrakash*; around his waist a belt of bleached crocodile leather. Karna had seen him at the ball. *Narag Jhestal*. The one who had caught them. Head Priest of the Unni Ehtral.

'Dimvak, if you will,' Jhestal said softly.

Dimvak gave a silent command. Soon enough, the torches were lit, the light from the flames creeping across the moss-encrusted walls, slick with moisture. Every sconce now boasted a torch, making the cell as painfully bright as it had once been dark. Habit more than hope made Karna look around to assess his chances. The plaster was flaking, speckled with green mould. The half-hearted attempt at scrubbing clean a long bloodstain on the wall opposite remained in mute testimony for all to see. A stone slab, crowded with unsubtle tools of the prison craft, was illuminated as well.

Jhestal approached the slab, tracing a finger along its cold edge. He produced a water clock from his sleeve and placed it upside down on the only available space. 'So... who are you?'

Karna saw no point in not answering the man. 'I have told your men a hundred times. I am Karna, Highmaster of Anga, of the Hastina Union!'

'And your friend whom we caught is Prince Duryodhan, Heir Apparent of the Union?' Jhestal smirked. 'Yes, we've heard that tale.'

Caught! Karna did not know whether to be glad Duryodhan had survived the fall or horrified that he was in another cell like this one. 'He is a Prince. He has immunity from…'

Jhestal raised a hand. 'Spare me your protestations. Let us try another question. Why are you here?'

'I have told you already.'

'So, you are saying that a Prince of the Union, a Highmaster, and a whore decided to smuggle themselves into our city?'

Karna froze. *They have her too.*

'And smuggled yourself in for what purpose you will not tell. Let us assume there is a noble motive behind your entry. Yet you entered the Empire without even an armed escort to safeguard you.' Jhestal raised his brows at Dimvak, who shrugged.

'It is either what you say, or you are spies working for the Mathurans, here to assassinate the Emperor and pin the blame on the Union, while your masters continue their dirty work. Now, which of these seems more likely?'

Karna sighed, twisting his wrists in the rings despite the shooting agony that shot down his arms into his torso.

'Young man, I have been a priest of the Ehtral for decades, and I have seen people grovel, lie, cheat, and confess. What I have gleaned in all that time is that the most likely answer is usually the right answer.'

'I speak the truth!'

'And how do you explain your… magical armour?' He uttered the word 'magical' with evident disgust. 'A most fascinating object. Strange that a Highmaster wears gold on his chest while a Prince dons a servant's garb.'

'I was born with it.'

Dimvak grunted as he went over to the brazier and squatted beside it. He blew impatiently on the coals, a scarlet glow flaring across his face.

Jhestal, on the other hand, shook his head sadly, as if disappointed with a promising student. 'A Resht cur, born with golden armour? My, my, are you a miracle! Maybe, after we are done, the Saptarishis might want to look at you, eh? Or are you perhaps another invention of what the Usurper calls "science"? An aberration. A mutilation of our very nature? Which do you think more likely, Dimvak?'

Karna hissed through gritted teeth. The truth clearly seemed implausible to Jhestal. 'Have someone from Hastina brought here,' he said in a calm voice. 'They can identify Prince Duryodhan. Or summon the Emperor himself; he saw us at the Panchalan swayamvar. Or Lord Shishupal...' Karna remembered the image of his dead nephew atop Shishupal's shoulders and quickly shook it off. 'Ask him! He knows us!'

'How convenient that Lord Shishupal is away in the North on a diplomatic mission. You already knew that, didn't you? And you think the Emperor has time to visit prison cells to personally talk to vermin like you? He is the God-King, blessed by Xath and Yama. He leaves the sanitization of the Empire to us, his servants. But then again....' Jhestal scratched his gaunt chin, 'I suppose he is right, Dimvak. We cannot hang them before we have verified his claims. If he is who he says he is, then he is entitled to immunity from criminal prosecution. Is that not what you Northerners call it?

It worked! Karna was shocked. 'Aye...'

'But not civil remedies, correct?'

Karna had no idea what that meant. Jhestal seemed to read his mind. 'Ah yes, law isn't the strong suit of spies, is it? The law, as it stands, allows me to take possession of your wealth till the truth is revealed, as surety for good behaviour. Your Union invented the concept. A bail bond, they call it.'

'What do you think I possess that you can take? Duryodhan had some rings...' Karna stopped, cursing himself for being so naïve.

Jhestal's eyes glinted with a malice Karna was all too familiar with. The priest turned to Dimvak, who dropped a few gold rings onto the brazier, where they slid down among the coals. Karna's breath caught in his throat. He gave a strangled gasp.

'You did confess to illegally entering the Empire.' As Jhestal spoke, Dimvak walked towards Karna. 'You are new to this, are you not?' Jhestal gave a sad smile. 'Anyway, till we verify your claims, we will need something from you. It is a time of war. The Empire needs all the gold it can lay its hands on, and confessed spies can hardly expect to keep their possessions in such times.'

Dimvak held Karna's face and stuffed a rag between his teeth, then returned to the brazier.

'That should make it easier,' Jhestal said. 'Begin.'

The squeal of metal snapped Karna's attention back. He saw Dimvak drag a sharp, pointed rod from the brazier amidst a shower of white sparks. Karna's guts churned. Dimvak stepped forward and pressed the orange-hot metal end onto Karna shoulder, and dug inside his skin-breastplate. Blood poured copiously. Karna's muffled screams echoed off the walls.

'He wasn't lying. It *is* part of his skin,' Dimvak said.

'I don't care about the details of what an abomination he is. Strip him the way he was made before Xath.'

Dimvak nodded and dug deeper. It sounded like ice being dropped into a pan of hot oil. Combined with Karna's agonized cries, it was a heart-wrenching sound. Karna's body thrashed and shuddered like a fish on a hook; his back arched hideously, the manacles on his hands threatening to give way. But Dimvak kept a firm grip, all the while working grim-faced.

Foul steam shot up from where the iron had finally found a way inside the armour. Karna's screams were garbled now, mindless. With pursed lips, Dimvak blew at the steam rising from where he had skinned Karna, and continued to dig in the iron. He sliced downwards to the armpit. Blood splattered Dimvak's face. But Dimvak might as well have been cutting open a stag for dinner the way he laboured on, unfazed.

Karna could not breathe. He would have lost consciousness had the pain not been relentless in its embrace. Sparks flew before his eyes like a swarm of bees as Dimvak began to pierce his skin to create a space between his breastplate and his bare flesh. All the while, Jhestal stood mute, an eye on the water clock.

Suddenly, the sizzling and shrieking grew quiet. Spit frothed around the rag between Karna's bared teeth. He was whimpering like a beaten dog.

'What is it?' Jhestal asked, annoyed.

Dimvak grunted and yanked out the iron. Karna was dragged back from semi-consciousness to another scream; a short one, that faded into a groan. Dimvak pointed to the end of the rod that had cooled to a dark red, smeared with blood and charred flesh. The cell stank of burnt flesh. He tossed the rod onto the coals, waiting for it to heat again.

Jhestal crossed to Karna and grabbed the drooping head, yanking it back. He tapped Karna's chest, one, two, three times, then pulled at the singed edges of the breastplate, wrinkling his nose. All Jhestal saw was blackened, raw, skinless flesh under the breastplate. 'It does look like part of his skin,' he murmured.

'Like I said,' Dimvak grunted, returning with the rod.

Jhestal stepped back. Karna's eye did not leave the looming orange top of the rod as it fizzed in the air towards him, anticipating the scorching pain.

Dimvak leaned forward. 'Sorry, kid. It's just business.'

But before Dimvak could move, there was a flutter of cloaks and the sound of feet moving quickly.

'Your Worship!'

From the corner of a bloodshot eye, Karna saw three blurry figures in the doorway, dressed in identical grey robes, a black patch over each left eye.

'I trust you have good reason to disturb me thus.'

His acolytes shrank under his searing gaze. 'Your Worship, we have just received news from our spies in the North. It appears the Greek Kalyavan has marched on Mathura, alone. Hastina has sent soldiers to aid Mathura. There are rumours of airavats from the East...'

'Fuck!' Dimvak remarked eloquently.

'Does the Emperor know?'

'Not yet, Your Worship.'

'Dimvak, with me.' Jhestal sprang out of the cell without a word, leaving Karna bleeding and burnt.

His men left after dousing the torches. Karna noticed they had forgotten to shut the door tight, leaving a faint trickle of light to mar the cell's gloom. The crack in the door funnelled in cold air and Karna soon grew cold as ice. Every painful breath sent a fresh stab of pain through him.

He heard a soft scuffling of feet on stone. His head jerked up, fearing Jhestal had returned. But the sound did not come from outside. He glimpsed movement from the corner of his eye and tried to look behind him, but all he could see was a spray of ice particles glittering in the door-light. And then a girl emerged from the pool of darkness, dressed in a ragged robe. She was no more than eleven or twelve, but her face was a web of scars. Another figure rose behind her. A dark-skinned boy... or a girl, he could not tell. The scarred girl quickly walked up to him and removed the rag from his mouth.

It was then that Karna saw him.

The towering figure walked towards him, still shrouded in shadow, clutching a battleaxe in his wrinkled hands. Karna would have known him anywhere. He closed his eyes. Opened them again. 'Acharya Parshuram.' The words were a white mist.

The Namin set his axe down.

'There are thousands of Magadhans outside.'

'But none in this cell. And… does it matter?'

The scarred girl approached with a jug. He would have liked to warn her to run away, leave the monster she was apprenticed to, but this was no time for selfless advice. He was thirsty. He opened his mouth. She stood on her toes, struggling to get the spout to his mouth. He swallowed greedily, coughed, and drank more, most of the water trickling down his neck onto his chest, where they had attempted to slice the breastplate off.

'I've read so much about you,' she said, gazing at him like a long-lost friend. 'You are even more handsome than the Matron said.'

'Masha!' Parshuram's voice was a whiplash. In silence, the girl retraced her steps to his side.

'Come to kill me finally, Acharya?' Karna asked softly.

'Maybe. Last I heard, you were at a wedding and got an innocent boy killed. How did you end up here?'

'Long story.'

'Should have killed yourself when I told you to, boy.'

'Just do it, Acharya. I am ready.' Karna lifted his chin, baring his throat. 'I've been ready a long time.'

Parshuram's eyes narrowed to furious slits in their pink sockets. His dried lips slid back in a vicious smile. The sinews in his neck grew taut as he picked up his axe, preparing to slash through the outstretched neck with one mighty blow. Karna's breath hissed out of his throat, his neck tingling in anticipation of the much-awaited release. *At last.* But Acharya Parshuram's arm did not move.

'I stand for justice, Karna. Something I could never teach you. And now I see why. You *will* die by my hand, but when the *true* you rises to threaten the realm. Not before. It will be Justice,' he uttered ominously as if his words made sense to Karna.

The Acharya scratched his matted beard and looked at Karna's half-plucked skin-armour. 'I see I trained you well to keep your true nature hidden. I thought skinning you alive would bring it out, yet it remains caged.'

The memory of it pierced Karna as painfully as Dimvak's rod had done. 'I am no longer that beast.'

'Prophecy does not lie, Highmaster. Sooner or later, you will let go and lay your hand upon the World of Man, to darken it. But I will be there, waiting. For I am the Champion of Dawn. I stand in your way. It has been so foretold. But rest for now. I promise to make your death as painless as possible. It is the least I can do for a former apprentice. Come, children.'

Masha and the other girl retreated into the shadows.

'Until we meet again... *Son of Darkness.*'

And then he was gone, like the last trails of mist on a gust of wind. Dying embers were all that remained on the brazier. And in the rising blackness of night, a chained animal growled.

TO BE CONTINUED IN ...

DANCE OF SHADOWS

In the aftermath of a colossal battle, the splitting of the Union, and the resurrection of an ancient foe, the future of the realm hangs perilously in the balance. From the ancient fortress of Hastinapur to the forbidding shores of Kalinga, chaos reigns. But questions blow in the wind, unanswered.

Did Parshuram and his apprentice fail in the task cast upon them by the Seven? Why is Karna imprisoned by Jhestal in Magadh? And why is Mati risking her life to help the Princess of Balkh uncover age-old secrets? While fires rage in Mathura, these questions plunge the Magadhan Empire into a maelstrom of blood and ruin.

Against this backdrop of turmoil, bitter enemies become friends and old allies stab each other in the back. Savage Nagas and enigmatic Rakshasas return to the fold. And the sun of humanity begins to set even as the shadows gather to dance.

ACKNOWLEDGEMENTS

Iwould like to begin by thanking George R. R. Martin for *A Song of Ice and Fire*. I might not have met him in person (yet) but he inspired a lawyer to steal a few hours every night for half a decade; to turn the stardust of his dreams into paragraphs on paper.

I have already dedicated this book to them, but it is simply not enough – my First Readers, Mahwash and Astha: thank you for your unfailing patience.

Continuing my Oscar Award-esque Acceptance Speech, I thank my family: my mother, for her unwavering faith in me, and for buying me history comics when I was a boy; my father, for being this book's foremost marketer, and my little brother, for inspiring everyone around him to follow their dreams. I also want to thank my friends: Milli, Shravya and Ritika. Thank you so much everyone for believing in me.

On to the book world, where the number of people I owe could fill the *USS Enterprise*. First and foremost, my agent Oliver Cheetham, whose enthusiasm for the book is rivalled only by my mother's, and who continues to guide me to lofty heights. I will follow him blindly into Mordor if he so advises.

I will also be forever indebted to Matt from The Broken Binding, who deserves more chocolate pie than I can possibly provide.

To the modern-day Michelangelo, Micaela Alcaino: I bow humbly for the ethereal cover of this book that none can pass by without a third glance.

I raise a glass to the royalty of book bloggers, Mihir and Petrik: you are generous, wonderful people, and I would not be here without you. And to all the writers and reviewers whose paths have crossed mine on the internet, who've provided help and advice, who waved to my book from your Twitter towers: you helped carry *Sons of Darkness* on a magical carpet from my little home town to all corners of the realm. You know who you are. My heartfelt thanks to you all.

To the dream team at Head of Zeus, including but by no means limited to Nic, Sophie (my pen pal) and Polly, the excitement shown by you folks for *Sons of Darkness* is all the validation an aspiring author with borderline narcissism needs.

And lastly, yet firstly, I thank Chandralekha for helping me squeeze the fullest potential out of this manuscript. Without her masterful editorial vision, you would be holding a very different book.